To Paul,
with all best wishes,
Karen Thornber

Empire
of Texts
in Motion

Chinese, Korean,
and Taiwanese
Transculturations
of Japanese
Literature

Harvard-Yenching Institute Monographs 67

Japanese writers welcome Zhou Zuoren, 1931. Second from left: Shimazaki Tōson, then Zhou Zuoren, Mushakōji Saneatsu, Satō Haruo, and Kikuchi Kan. Reproduced by permission of Mainichi Shinbunsha.

Empire
of Texts
in Motion

Chinese, Korean,
and Taiwanese
Transculturations
of Japanese
Literature

Karen Laura Thornber

Published by the Harvard University Asia Center
and distributed by Harvard University Press
Cambridge (Massachusetts) and London, 2009

Printed in the United States of America

The Harvard-Yenching Institute, founded in 1928 and headquartered at Harvard University, is a foundation dedicated to the advancement of higher education in the humanities and social sciences in East and Southeast Asia. The Institute supports advanced research at Harvard by faculty members of certain Asian universities and doctoral studies at Harvard and other universities by junior faculty at the same universities. It also supports East Asian studies at Harvard through contributions to the Harvard-Yenching Library and publication of the *Harvard Journal of Asiatic Studies* and books on premodern East Asian history and literature.

Portions of the Introduction, Chapter 4, and Chapter 7 previously appeared in condensed form in Karen L. Thornber, "Early Twentieth-Century Intra-East Asian Literary Contact Nebulae: Transculturating Censored Japanese Literature in Chinese and Korean," *Journal of Asian Studies* 68:3 (August 2009). © 2009 Cambridge University Press. Reprinted with permission.

Library of Congress Cataloging-in-Publication Data

Thornber, Karen Laura.
  Empire of texts in motion : Chinese, Korean, and Taiwanese transculturations of Japanese literature / Karen Laura Thornber.
    p. cm. -- (Harvard-Yenching Institute monographs ; 67)
  Includes bibliographical references and index.
  ISBN 978-0-674-03625-3 (cloth : acid-free paper)
    1. Japanese literature--History and criticism. 2. Japanese literature--China--History and criticism. 3. Japanese literature--Korea--History and criticism. 4. Japanese literature--Taiwan--History and criticism. 5. Translating and interpreting. 6. Intertextuality. I. Title.
  PL720.T47 2009
  895.6'0995--dc22

                                                                          2009017179

Index by the author

⊗ Printed on acid-free paper

Last figure below indicates year of this printing

19 18 17 16 15 14 13 12 11 10 09

For Tom,
for love and happiness
beyond measure or description

Acknowledgments

One of the many pleasures of doing this project has been the opportunity to live extensively and travel widely in East Asia: throughout Manchuria, across the border of North Korea on the Yalu River, to Beijing, Shanghai, and Nanjing, throughout Japan, South Korea, and Taiwan, and to Hong Kong. I have come to see that there is much to be said for leaving physical and intellectual comfort zones in order to comb archives, libraries, and bookstores in diverse places, to spend days and nights on dusty floors surrounded by piles of vernacular materials, to ask the difficult questions of these sources and of ourselves. Present throughout has been the powerful desire to understand how peoples and cultural products interact with and transform one another within and across neighborhoods, cities, cultures, nations, regions, and the globe—particularly when economic, political, and social relationships are significantly unbalanced. I have sought to learn how with this knowledge we might change our own ways of thinking not only about individual artistic media, countries, and regions, but also about the particularities and commonalities of human experience and cultural production across time and space. Extensive interaction and transformation take place within ethnic, linguistic, national, and other divides. But even a brief visit to the archives also reveals tremendous multidirectional activity across such boundaries, activity that embodies and creates vast networks of fluid transculturating spaces, spaces I call contact nebulae. I had little idea when I began research for this book just how expansive these nebulae and networks would be and just how complex their dynamics. Hundreds of cartons of books and photocopies and a full basement later, I still believe that I have uncovered only the crest of the tsunami.

Timely completion of a project of this breadth and depth would have been impossible without the support of numerous individuals and institutions, for which I am grateful. Research for this book took me to dozens of libraries, universities, and bookstores in China, Japan, Korea, Taiwan, and the United States, as well as Canada, Europe, and South America. I am indebted to the financial support of the American Association of University Women (Dissertation Fellowship), Blakemore Foundation (two Blakemore Freeman Fellowships for language study in Japan and Taiwan), GARIOA/Fulbright Alumni Association, Japan Foundation, Japan-United States Educational Commission, Korea Society (Peter Ohm Fellowship for language study in Korea), Northeast Asia Council of the Association for Asian Studies, Satoh Artcraft Research Foundation and the Tsuchida Foundation, United States Department of Education (Fulbright-Hays Doctoral Dissertation Research Abroad Fellowship [research in Korea and Taiwan] and two Foreign Language and Area Studies Academic Year Fellowships), United States Department of State (Institute of International Exchange Fulbright Fellowship [research in Japan]), and the Woodrow Wilson National Fellowship Foundation (Andrew W. Mellon Fellowship in Humanistic Studies), as well as, at Harvard University, the Achilles Fang Prize, Asia Center, Clark Fund for Faculty Research, Department of East Asian Languages and Civilizations, Department of Literature and Comparative Literature, Fairbank Center for Chinese Studies, Graduate Society, Korea Institute, and Reischauer Institute of Japanese Studies.

I would like to thank my professors, colleagues, and friends at Princeton, Harvard, and around the world for their advice, encouragement, and inspiration: Ryūichi Abé, Jon Abel, Barbara Akiba, Sonja Arntzen, Ed Baker, Doris Bargen, Kevin Bell, Sandra Bermann, Ted Bestor, Homi Bhabha, Steven Biel, Peter Bol, Hal Bolitho, Marjan Boogert, Dani Botsman, Michael Bourdaghs, Svetlana Boym, Mary Brinton, Victor Brombert, Larry Buell, Richard Calichman, Deirdre Chetham, Leo Ching, Kyo Cho, Eileen Chow, Joaquim Coelho, Martin Collcutt, Verena Conley, Ruiko Connor, Edwin Cranston, Fumiko Cranston, David Damrosch, Wiebke Denecke, Alexander Des Forges, Theodor D'Haen, Wanda Di Bernardo, Carter Eckert, Mark Elliott, Jacob Emery, Jim Engell, Gus Espada, Melissa Feuerstein, Laura

Frader, Matthew Fraleigh, Sarah Frederick, Poshek Fu, Fujii Shōzō, Ken George, Ted Gilman, Christina Gilmartin, Luis Girón-Negrón, Carol Gluck, Michael Goldman, Andrew Gordon, Bill Granara, Alison Grinthal, Keven Halliday, John Hamilton, Christopher Hanscom, Helen Hardacre, Tom Hare, Henrietta Harrison, Chris Hill, Hosea Hirata, Frankie Hoff, Bob Hollander, David Howell, Huang Yingzhe, Wilt Idema, Charles Inouye, Wesley Jacobsen, Marius Jansen, Biodun Jeyifo, Barbara Johnson, Christopher Johnson, Ed Kamens, Susan Kashiwa, Sari Kawana, Fujio Kawashima, Peter Kelley, Adam Kern, Robert Khan, Bill Kirby, John Kim, Sun Joo Kim, Richard King, Faye Kleeman, Philip Kuhn, Shigehisa Kuriyama, Shiamin Kwa, Nayoung Aimee Kwon, Susan Laurence, Leo Ou-fan Lee, Indra Levy, Lital Levy, Wai-yee Li, Liao Ping-hui, E. Perry Link, Yukio Lippit, Susan Lively, Luo Liang, Chris Lupke, Richard Lynn, Edward Mack, Seiichi Makino, Doug Mao, Satomi Matsumura, Stacie Matsumoto, Senko Maynard, David McCann, Melissa McCormick, Christie McDonald, Ian Miller, Earl Miner, Mike Molasky, Sandy Naddaff, Greg Nagy, Izumi Nakayama, Susan Napier, Abé Markus Nornes, Richard Okada, Steve Owen, Elizabeth Perry, Sam Perry, Susan Pharr, Andy Plaks, Janet Poole, Cody Poulton, Michael Puett, Sindhu Revuluri, Panagiotis Roilos, Paul Rouzer, Gilbert Rozman, Jay Rubin, Judith Ryan, Peter Sacks, Kazuko Sakaguchi, Naoki Sakai, Atsuko Sakaki, Jordan Sand, Miryam Sas, Paul Schalow, Sekine Ken, Jayanthi Selinger, Marc Shell, Yoshiaki Shimizu, Emi Shimokawa, Haruo Shirane, Joanna Handlin Smith, Werner Sollors, Diana Sorensen, David Stahl, Jackie Stone, Susan Suleiman, Ronald Suleski, Rebecca Suter, Tomi Suzuki, Michael Szonyi, Mitsuru Tajima, Alan Tansman, Tarumi Chie, Xiaofei Tian, Bill Todd, John Treat, Jing Tsu, Jun Uchida, Atsuko Ueda, Keith Vincent, Ezra Vogel, Janet Walker, David Wang, Dennis Washburn, Jeff Wasserstrom, Jason Webb, Melissa Wender, Ellen Widmer, Mark Williams, Ruth Wisse, Michelle Yeh, Steven Yao, Tomiko Yoda, Eve Zimmerman, and Jonathan Zwicker. For assisting with research affiliations in East Asia, and for many helpful conversations, special thanks to Komori Yōichi, Hiwatari Nobuhiro, and Greg Noble at the University of Tokyo, Kwŏn Yŏngmin at Seoul National University and Kim Uchang at Korea University, and Peng Hsiao-yen at Academia Sinica (Taiwan). I'm also grateful to my editor William M. Hammell, two anonymous referees, and the staff of the Harvard University Asia Center Publications Program for expert editorial and production care.

For the many laughs and for your unconditional love and understanding, thank you to my family — Anne Havens Fuller; Bill Havens, and Julie Hunt; Carolyn Havens Niemann and Michael, Adam, Jake, and Matthew; Kathy Havens Whitten and Emily and Nate; Evan Preisser and Juliette Thornber; my grandparents Lois and Chalmers Thornber, my sister Carol Thornber, and my parents Karvel and Nora Thornber. And finally, to my spouse Tom Havens, thank you for the endless proofreading and stimulating discussions, and for a decade of love and happiness beyond measure or description.

Contents

Conventions

Chinese words are transcribed in *pinyin*, Japanese words in the modified Hepburn system used by *Kenkyūsha's New Japanese-English Dictionary*, and Korean words in a modified McCune-Reischauer system. Transcriptions of Korean generally are based on how syllables are written, not on how they are pronounced. Thank you to Bruce Fulton for help with Korean romanization.

In cases where persons with East Asian names writing in East Asian languages list alternative transcriptions of their names, I give both the standard and the alternative transcriptions. In cases where titles of East Asian language sources incorporate words from other East Asian languages, I give these words first as they are pronounced in the other East Asian language, then in brackets provide their standard transcription.

East Asian names are given in the customary East Asian order, with family name preceding personal name, except for cases of Western-language publications in which the name order is usually reversed. Macrons are omitted over long vowels in the most familiar Japanese place names; breves are omitted over vowels in the most familiar Korean place names.

Unless otherwise indicated, translations from Chinese, French, German, Japanese, Korean, Portuguese, and Spanish are my own.

Empire
of Texts
in Motion

Chinese, Korean,
and Taiwanese
Transculturations
of Japanese
Literature

INTRODUCTION

Empire, Transculturation, and Literary Contact Nebulae

Cultures and cultural products are constantly in motion, grappling with and interpenetrating one another within and across artistic, ethnic, geographic, linguistic, political, ideological, and temporal frontiers. In so doing, they create and embody fluid spaces of transculturation, where transculturation is understood as the "many different processes of [their] assimilation, adaptation, rejection, parody, resistance, loss, and ultimately transformation."[1] Simultaneously affirming and undermining cultural capital and authority at the same time that it creates identities, transculturating almost always entails negotiating power dynamics.[2] It thus can be particularly vibrant in empires and postimperial spaces. In the nineteenth- and twentieth-century British, French, Ottoman, American, Portuguese, Russian, Soviet, Spanish, and Japanese empires and their aftermaths, (post)colonial, (post)semicolonial, and other subjugated peoples and their (former) imperial counterparts engaged with and transformed one another's cultures and cultural products. Often defying binaries and borders, they produced fascinating amalgams of resistance, collaboration, and acquiescence.[3]

Mary Louise Pratt identifies transculturation in empire as a phenomenon of the "contact zone," a term she coined to describe "social spaces where disparate cultures meet, clash, and grapple with each other, often in highly asymmetrical relations of domination and subordination."[4] More specifically, the contact zone as Pratt understands it is the space of imperial encounters, the space in which peoples geographically and historically separated come into contact with each other and establish on-going relations, usually involving conditions of coercion, radical inequality, and intractable conflict . . . the term "contact" [borrowed from linguistics, where the phrase "contact language" indicates an improvised language that develops among speakers of different tongues] foregrounds the interactive, improvisational dimensions of imperial encounters so easily ignored or suppressed.[5]

Among the most intriguing of these spaces are artistic contact zones, or more precisely, considering their rapidly changing and frequently ambiguous borders, *artistic contact nebulae* (nebulas). The term *artistic contact nebulae* designates the physical and creative spaces where dancers, dramatists, musicians, painters, sculptors, writers, and other artists from cultures/nations in unequal power relationships grapple with and transculturate one another's creative output.[6] Among the most vibrant subsets of artistic contact nebulae are *literary contact nebulae*, active sites both physical and creative of readerly contact, writerly contact, and textual contact, intertwined modes of transculturation that depend to some degree on linguistic contact and often involve travel. In this context, "readerly contact" refers to reading creative texts (texts with aesthetic ambitions, imaginative writing) from cultures/nations in asymmetrical power relationships with one's own; "writerly contact" to interactions among creative writers from conflicting societies; "textual contact" to transculturating creative texts in this environment (appropriating genres, styles, and themes, as well as transculturating individual literary works via the related and at times concomitant strategies of interpreting, adapting, translating, and intertextualizing); and "linguistic contact" to engaging with the language of the society oppressing or oppressed by one's own.[7]

This book explores the dynamics of intra–East Asian literary contact nebulae in the Japanese empire between 1895 and 1945. It is the first in any language to unearth the complex relationships among the imperial Japanese, semicolonial Chinese, colonial Korean and Taiwanese, and informally colonial (i.e., occupied) Manchurian literary worlds.[8] Drawing largely on sources in Chinese, Japanese, and Korean, as well as English, French, German, Spanish, and Portuguese, it is based on extensive research in vernacular archives in China, Japan, Korea, and Taiwan. Chapter 1 highlights key aspects of early twentieth-century intra–East Asian travel and linguistic, readerly, and writerly contact. But the book's principal concern is textual contact, particularly the transculturating of individual creative works. I argue that while actively transculturating so-called "Western" literatures—the subject of most comparative scholarship on twentieth-century East Asian literatures—Chinese, Japanese, Korean, and Taiwanese writers also engaged a great deal with one another's creative output.[9] In so doing, they formed vibrant nebulae of intra–East Asian textual contact that intermingled with other literary and artistic contacts.

Early twentieth-century intra–East Asian literary contact nebulae diverge in two principal ways from the contact zones discussed by Pratt and others.[10] Not unique to artistic contact spaces in the Japanese empire, these differences reveal underexamined facets of transculturation in sites of unequal power relationships, particularly empires and postimperial spaces. First, imperial encounters in early twentieth-century East Asia, far from occurring solely among peoples geographically, historically, and culturally distant (i.e., China, Japan, Korea, and Taiwan vis-à-vis America and Europe), instead were dominated by exchanges among regional neighbors with long-standing relationships. As is well known, China was the cultural center of East Asia until the late nineteenth century, and Korea an active transmitter of Chinese as well as Korean culture to Japan. Internal chaos and American and European oppression in China, paired with Japan's emergence as a colonial power at the end of the nineteenth century, radically transformed rather than introduced contacts among East Asian peoples and cultures. To be sure, early twentieth-century intra–East Asian contact nebulae intermingled with contact nebulae that more closely fit Pratt's definition, namely those where East Asian and European/American peoples and cultures engaged with one another and established ongoing if ambivalent relations. But scholarship that posits imperial encounters, let alone power imbalances, as necessarily occurring between the West and the Rest risks becoming ensnared in some of the same biases it deconstructs.[11] Second, as in other empires and postimperial spaces, transcultural encounters in intra–East Asian artistic contact nebulae rarely replicated either the steep hierarchies presupposed by (post)colonial and (post)semicolonial peoples, or those promoted by imperial discourse, hierarchies that at times reached the extreme of "exploitation unto death."[12] Instead, artistic contact nebulae are characterized by atmospheres of greater reciprocity and diminished claims of authority than those of many other (post)imperial spaces.

The fluidity of textual contact is particularly striking. Most writers are avid readers. Unable or unwilling to let the texts they consume have the final word, they often reconfigure and frequently transculturate (reconfigure across borders, however understood) genres, languages, styles, and themes, as well as individual creative works. They reconfigure *interpretively*—in the form of literary criticism (understood in its broadest sense as discourse on literature regardless of approach), *interlingually*—by translating and adapting (rewriting loosely into another language), and *intertextually*, weaving transposed fragments from predecessors into their own creative works. Many texts are interpretively, interlingually, and intertextually reconfigured; interpretive, interlingual, and intertextual reconfigurations themselves often intermingle within a single text. Through their reconfigurations writers not only demonstrate their grasp of literatures, languages, and aesthetics of composition, but they also both affirm and deny one another's cultural capital and authority: the former by permanently incorporating literary predecessors into their own artistic fabrics and in so doing contributing to the survival of these texts, and the latter by picking them apart, if not dismembering them entirely. Naturally, much textual transculturation occurs among creative work from peoples not in current or recent conflict with one another. Literary engagement and struggle also frequently take place within borders. Far from uncritically endorsing discourse from their immediate cultural, geographic, and linguistic spaces, writers often contest this production and assert the validity and at times superiority of their individual beliefs and methods. Likewise, reconfiguration within the oeuvre of a single writer if not a single text is not unusual: artists rework their own narratives in later creations, with varied motives and ramifications.

The simultaneous affirming and denying of cultural capital and authority inherent in textual transculturation have particular significance when they involve groups that are in notably uneven power relationships; teasing out intra-(post)imperial networks of literary transformation enhances our understanding of local, regional, and global cultural dynamics.[13] What are the implications of interweaving hundreds if not thousands of texts into different cultural fabrics under the conditions of empire and its aftermaths, whether interpretively, interlingually, or intertextually? Is so doing denying the validity of the host culture, and, in the case of the subjugated, granting the subjugator the final word? Transculturations, whatever their form, permanently alter and often significantly violate the landscapes of their host cultures. They also reconstruct existing cultural products: at the same time that they integrate foreign bodies, they also dislocate if not shatter them. As in many imperial spaces, literary transculturation in early twentieth-century East Asia appeared in a highly charged political milieu in which cultural production almost inevitably involved both collaboration with and criticism of the colonial enterprise. Concentrating on artistic contacts in the Japanese imperium while interweaving discussion of related phenomena from a variety of other literary contact nebulae, this book probes the dynamics of these complex and paradoxical negotiations; it analyzes the significance of how the literary works of one space are transculturated in/by another when political relations are unequal, even openly hostile, and when one people is or recently has been under the domineering hand of another.

I am most concerned with (post)colonial and (post)semicolonial transculturation of literature from (former) metropoles, especially colonial Korean and Taiwanese, occupied Manchurian, and semicolonial Chinese writings on and adaptations, translations, and intertextualizations of Japanese literature within the Japanese empire.[14] There is no question that imperialism deeply impacts the cultures and cultural products, including the languages and literary production, of both (post)colonial spaces and (former) metropoles. As Simon Gikandi has argued, "colonial cultures [were] central in the transformation of English identities . . . the writing of English and colonial identities becomes more complicated the greater the interaction between the two entities."[15] The hybridity of peoples and cultural products in empires and postimperial spaces is undeniable, and distinctions between colonized and colonizer and between their cultural products are often constructed.[16] To be sure, in many empires and postimperial spaces, key facets of travel, linguistic contact, and writerly contact are apt to be asymmetric. Colonial and postcolonial writers tend to be proficient if not fluent in the language of the (former) imperial power, often publishing in it themselves, and many receive at least part of their education in the (former) metropole. In contrast, although a significant number of metropolitan writers make at least brief trips to their nation's (former) colonies, they often go as tourists or, during the imperial period, as short-term promoters of empire; they rarely learn the local language(s) of these spaces, much less receive their educations there.[17] Likewise, the desire of (post)colonial writers to be respected by, if not join the literary establishment of the (former) metropole generally exceeds that of writers from the (former) metropole eager to become part of (post)colonial literary circles. On the other hand, readerly and textual contacts tend to be more balanced, with (post)colonial writers and those from the (former) metropole reading and transculturating one another's creative work in diverse ways not as dependent on standing in the official imperial hierarchy.[18]

Writers across early twentieth-century East Asia discussed, translated, adapted, and intertextualized Chinese and, to a lesser extent, Korean and Taiwanese literatures. But Japanese literature, enjoying more cultural capital and authority than ever before in part because of Japan's new imperial status, was the most frequently reworked East Asian textual corpus. Moreover, in contrast with their counterparts in many other colonial sites, where the most active transculturation of imperial texts took place after decolonization,[19] Chinese, Korean, and Taiwanese writers—inheritors of two of the world's longest, richest, and most voluminous literary traditions (Chinese and Korean)—transculturated thousands of Japanese novels, plays, poems, and short stories during the colonial period itself. While probing the intricate web of transcultural interactions that characterized early twentieth-century East Asian literatures, that is, the blurred boundaries and complicated relationships among the Chinese, occupied Manchurian, Japanese, Korean, and Taiwanese literary worlds, I am not implying that we replace sinocentrism and Eurocentrism with Japancentrism. Rather, I analyze semicolonial Chinese, occupied Manchurian, and colonial Korean and Taiwanese transculturations of Japanese literature as the most active, but by no means the only, vectors of intra–East Asian cultural negotiation.

Part of what makes the cultural flows of the Japanese empire unusually fascinating and separates them from those of most European empires is Japan's long engagement with and oftentimes adulation of Chinese and Korean creative products. Unlike Egypt and the Arab world, which had lost significant cultural currency with Europe and the United States long before colonization, and other (post)colonial spaces in Africa, the Americas, and South and Southeast Asia, which before colonization had enjoyed only minimal cultural prestige with Western nations, China was the intellectual center of East Asia from the beginning of the Common Era until the late nineteenth century; literary Chinese remained the lingua franca for Chinese, Japanese, and Korean scholars through the end of the Qing dynasty (1644–1911).[20] For a millennium or more, Chinese cultural products, including literature, circulated widely in the region, and across the centuries Japanese and Korean writers transculturated many volumes of Chinese texts. During the Tokugawa period (1600–1868) some Japanese elites began to assert superiority over Manchu China, attempting "to create the illusion of an East Asian world order that was Japanese in design and Japanese in focus."[21] But sinology continued to dominate Japanese intellectual life. The Tokugawa nobility eagerly purchased Chinese paintings, books from China, and Japanese reprints of Chinese works; books from China, for instance, enjoyed a large presence in the libraries of Tokugawa rulers.[22] Between the Opium War in China (1839–42) and the first treaties between Japan and Western nations (1854), Tokugawa elites also devoured Chinese books on Europe. But the most widely circulated Chinese texts at this time were the principal works of Ming (1368–1644) and Qing vernacular fiction, most of which were translated into Japanese multiple times. In addition, Japanese literati used the Chinese vernacular in their own writing, composing dozens of popular narratives in Chinese.[23]

The Korean cultural impact on premodern Japan also was immense. Early Korea not only was an active transmitter of Chinese culture to Japan but also was greatly admired in its own right. Japanese leaders coveted the talents of Korean intellectuals and artisans: in the seventh century, they welcomed Korean literati refugees; during the fourteenth and fifteenth centuries, they requested that Korean specialists in ink painting and calligraphy accompany official Korean embassies to Japan; and during military operations against Korea between 1592 and 1598, they kidnapped Korean artists and plundered Korean libraries. In the seventeenth and eighteenth centuries, the Tokugawa government went to great lengths to impress visiting Koreans with Japanese greatness, but Japanese artists, eager to learn from their Korean colleagues, are reported to have sought the advice of Korean envoys at all hours of the day and night. Respect for Korean judgment was so high that Korean endorsement of a work of Japanese art virtually guaranteed its success.[24]

Circumstances changed significantly in the nineteenth century. China's loss to Great Britain in the Opium War and the subsequent establishment of numerous foreign treaty ports on its soil, combined with Japan's emergence as a unified state after the Meiji Restoration of 1868, dealt a large blow to China's leverage in East Asian political and cultural affairs. Sinology, to be sure, remained an important discipline in Japan and Korea well into the twentieth century. But the Japanese turned increasingly to the United States and Europe and strengthened their nation in part by transculturating Western economic, political, social, and cultural institutions. Impressed by Japan's success at thwarting Western imperialist ventures, Chinese and Koreans wrote volumes on their East Asian neighbor.[25] As the Korean reformer Yun Ch'iho (1865–1945) ecstatically proclaimed on his brief visit to Tokyo in 1893:

Japan is perhaps the most delightful country in the world at least to me. The politeness of the people, their cleanliness, their obliging disposition, their hospitality, their high mindedness, their pretty women, their clean streets . . . their bath-houses . . . all this and other innumerable agreeable little ways and things just made me intoxicated with perfect delight. . . . If I had the means to choose my home at my pleasure, Japan would be the country. I don't want to live in China with its abominable smells or in America where racial prejudice and discrimination hold their horrid sway, or in Korea as long as its infernal government lasts. O blessed Japan! The Paradise of the East! The Garden of the World![26]

Far from universal, Yun Ch'iho's impressions nevertheless were emblematic of a notable shift in East Asian cultural authority from China, and secondarily Korea, to Japan.

Japan's decisive victory over China in the Sino-Japanese War (1894–95) cemented its position as the flourishing prototype of a new Asian modernity; this acclaim was reinforced by its defeat of Russia in the Russo-Japanese War (1904–5).[27] Intra–East Asian travel, as well as linguistic, writerly, readerly, and textual contact, however uneven and ambiguous because of Japan's dual position as imperial power and gateway to coveted Western science and culture, were hallmarks of early twentieth-century intra–East Asian literary contact nebulae. Just as (post)colonial African, Caribbean, East-Central European, Latin American, Middle Eastern, and South and Southeast Asian writers often were educated in imperial metropoles, so too did the majority of East Asia's prominent colonial and semicolonial literary figures study in or at least visit Japan. The preeminent Chinese writer Guo Moruo (1892–1978) once asserted: "The modern Chinese literary world has been constructed for the most part by writers who studied in Japan. . . . We can even say that China's new literature was baptized by Japan."[28] Experience in Japan was also important for writers hailing from occupied Manchuria,[29] and was even more decisive for

Korean and Taiwanese literatures; it is generally understood that three-quarters of Korea's and Taiwan's major early twentieth-century writers received at least part of their educations in Japan or spent significant time there.[30] In addition, just as European writers frequently traveled to colonial sites, nearly all of Japan's principal early twentieth-century writers visited China, however briefly, and many also traveled to Korea, occupied Manchuria, and Taiwan.[31]

Linguistic contact involved even more writers than did travel. To be sure, although generally trained in classical Chinese, few early twentieth-century Japanese intellectuals were proficient in vernacular Chinese, much less Korean, and still fewer Chinese and Taiwanese intellectuals knew Korean. But imperial Japanese language policies, like those of other metropoles, mandated Japanese language instruction in schools in Korea, Taiwan, and occupied Manchuria.[32] This ensured that most writers from these regions had at least a rudimentary knowledge of Japanese. Chinese institutions began offering Japanese language instruction in the late 1890s, and Japanese engaged in a number of cultural enterprises in China, but the early twentieth-century Chinese writers who learned Japanese often obtained most of their training in Japan.[33] The large numbers of early twentieth-century Chinese, Korean, and Taiwanese writers who attended Japanese institutions both at home and in Japan, as well as those who, whether or not they spent time in Japan, read and translated Japanese literature and published creative work in Japanese, in many cases long before they were prohibited from publishing in Chinese and Korean, together demonstrate significant intra–East Asian linguistic contact throughout the (semi)colonial period. Linguistic contact was particularly complex in Taiwan, where writers negotiated among modern Japanese, literary Chinese, vernacular Mandarin, and vernacular Taiwanese dialects,[34] but throughout the empire it resulted in the production of intriguingly hybridized translingual and transnational creative work.

Travel and linguistic contact open wider doors to readerly, writerly, and textual contact.[35] Japanese, Korean, and Taiwanese readers alike voraciously consumed creative works by preeminent contemporary Chinese writers, particularly Lu Xun (1881–1936). Even more striking was how eagerly Chinese, Koreans, and Taiwanese devoured Japanese literature: by most estimates, they read more Japanese drama, poetry, and prose during the first decades of the twentieth century than their predecessors had in the previous thousand years combined.[36] Such readerly experiences prompted many colonial/semi-colonial East Asians who had been focusing on engineering, medicine, and other more practical professions themselves to become writers. Intra–East Asian readerly contact frequently intertwined with writerly contact as budding writers and established literary figures alike sought out their East Asian counterparts at home and abroad. From early in the imperial period, Chinese, Japanese, Korean, and Taiwanese writers regularly socialized with one another, joined one another's literary societies, published in one another's periodicals, and forged deep friendships. But imperial discourse and embedded biases exacted their toll, complicating these artistic relationships.

For much of the (semi)colonial period intra–East Asian writerly contact consisted of unstable amalgams of supporting and undermining one another's creative output. So too did textual contact, the most striking aspect of intra–East Asian literary contact nebulae. Japanese, Korean, and Taiwanese writings on and adaptations, translations, and intertextualizations of Chinese literature were significant at this time, as were Chinese and Japanese transculturations of Korean literature, but Chinese, Korean, and Taiwanese transculturations of Japanese creative works numerically overshadowed other intra–East Asian textual contacts. Relatively few studies that discuss East Asian cultures in a comparative context have explored this dynamic literary engagement. Rather, the principal concerns have been 1) Japanese, Korean, and Taiwanese fascination, if not obsession, with classical Chinese literature and culture until the early twentieth century; 2) twentieth-century Chinese, Japanese, Korean, and Taiwanese frenetic consumption of Western literatures and cultures; 3) late twentieth- and early twenty-first century intra–East Asian popular culture flows; and 4) American and European enthrallment with the "Orient."[37] Western-language studies that explore modern intra–East Asian literary relationships tend not to focus on the transculturation of specific literary works. They analyze parallels, reveal how Japanese creative texts served as windows on the West, and examine the appropriation of literary genres, styles, and themes. Certainly modern Chinese, Koreans, and Taiwanese involved themselves profoundly with American and European literatures, this engagement regularly surpassing their engagement with Japanese literature. Just as occasional nineteenth-century colonial Bengali writers longed to be labeled the "clones" of certain English writers, so too some early twentieth-century Chinese writers became involved in what Leo Lee has dubbed a "fetish of personal identification" with their Western counterparts.[38] It is also true that Japan and its literature facilitated Chinese, Korean, and Taiwanese encounters with American and European literatures. Colonial and semicolonial writers likewise frequently emulated Japanese language reforms and appropriated prominent Japanese literary genres—including the political novel, free-verse poetry, the I-novel, proletarian fiction, modernist poetry and prose, and even battlefront literature. But, just as important, they also transculturated individual texts. Examining these transculturations can shed new insight into the dynamic cultural struggles and negotiations that take place in spaces of dramatically unbalanced power relationships, and in the Japanese empire specifically.

Scholars in East Asia today are focusing increasingly on the intertextualizing of modern Japanese literature in Chinese, Korean, and Taiwanese creative works, yet they usually speak of the resulting relationships as manifesting "influence." The influence paradigm allows critics to establish writers' interactions with literary predecessors, but it also frequently assumes a relatively straightforward transfer of commodities from a "creator" to a "receiver," implying simple (post)colonial and (post)semicolonial appropriation or absorption of Japanese cultural products. In reality, far from demonstrating subaltern indebtedness, Chinese, Korean, and Taiwanese engagements with Japanese texts often expose fundamental ambivalence toward Japan and its cultural products. The modern literature of the imperial overlord was simultaneously embraced and rejected and its cultural capital and authority both acknowledged and severely challenged as colonial and semicolonial East Asians constructed and deconstructed identities. The weaving of metropolitan creative works into (post)colonial and (post)semicolonial artistic fabrics ripples with meaning in many directions and is a central—yet often, in the case of East Asia, overlooked—component of empire.

Situating Literary Contact Nebulae in the Japanese Empire

Our understanding of empire, and the Japanese empire in particular, derives in good part from accounts that focus on the doctrines and methods of imperial state formation as absorbed voluntarily or under duress by colonial and semicolonial peoples. This absorption has been presented as occurring in two principal forms. Imperial powers, often with the support of local collaborators, impose policies that enable them to increase political and economic penetration; these policies generally exploit colonial and semicolonial resources and frequently attempt to assimilate colonial and semicolonial peoples. In contrast, colonial and semicolonial peoples, as part of national self-strengthening, enthusiastically seek out from imperial powers what they regard as superior ideas and institutions. Both these modalities of foreign system integration posit a clear hierarchy, whether of oppressor/oppressed or benefactor/supplicant. Yet more fluid forms of transculturation also proliferate in empire, particularly in artistic contact nebulae. In these ambiguous social spaces, which include both physical sites and creative products, people from societies in unequal power relationships grapple with one another's cultural output in atmospheres of increased reciprocity and diminished hierarchies of authority. Recent scholarship on settler colonialism has exposed complex interactions among authorities based in imperial capitals, local administrators, metropolitan settlers, and colonial/semicolonial peoples of all ranks, yet its focus on ideology, law and representation, and struggles over land and labor obscures the massive transcultural negotiations that also occur in empire.[39]

Japanese Encroachments and Impositions

At its most bloated in 1942, the Japanese empire stretched from the borders of Burma and India to the Solomon Islands in the South Pacific, and from Attu and Kiska in the Aleutians to the rainforests of New Guinea.[40] Japan's territorial encroachment on East Asia accelerated in 1895, with its military victory over China and acquisition of Taiwan as its first colony. After defeating Russia in 1905, the Japanese colonized southern Sakhalin and established Korea as their protectorate; in 1910 they annexed Korea outright. Japan also continued to gnaw away at China geographically and economically. The Japanese obtained the South Manchurian leasehold (Liaodong Peninsula) in 1905 under the terms of the Treaty of Portsmouth and in 1914 took over the German concession in Shandong and German islands in the Pacific. Japan seized Manchuria (northeast China) in 1931, establishing the puppet state (informal colony) of Manchukuo in 1932. Full-scale war with China erupted at Marco Polo Bridge outside Beijing in July 1937, and by 1938 Japan controlled the eastern coast of China (including Beijing, Nanjing, and Shanghai), part of Inner Mongolia, and all of Manchuria. During the early twentieth century, the Japanese also enjoyed substantial economic control over additional areas of China. The Boxer Protocol of 1901, four follow-up agreements with the United States building on the Treaty of Portsmouth of 1905, the Twenty-One Demands imposed on the weak government of Yuan Shikai (1859–1916) in 1915, the Versailles Peace Treaty of 1919, and especially the Nine-Power Commercial Treaty of 1922 solidified Japan's commercial position in large swaths of China.

In addition to imposing political, military, and economic demands on the region, the Japanese also pursued their vision of becoming the cultural leader of East Asia. Colonial authorities advocated regimes of *dōka* (assimilation into Japanese culture and loss of ethnic and national identity) and *kōminka* (conversion into dutiful imperial subjects), attempting to strip Koreans and Taiwanese of their identities. In Korea, the governor-general and his ruthless police force, composed of both Japanese and Korean officers, encroached on every area of colonial life, including urban planning, commerce, education, health and public welfare, language, morals, politics, public services, publishing, and religion.[41] Efforts to integrate Koreans more fully into the empire increased after Japan seized Manchuria in 1931. The strategy of *naisen ittai* (unification of the homeland and Korea), a radical social experiment introduced after the beginning of all-out war with China in 1937, called for the Korean people's total Japanization in "form, mind, blood, and flesh."[42] Koreans were ordered to take Japanese names, worship at Shinto shrines, and speak and write only in Japanese. By the end of the colonial period, approximately one-quarter of the Korean population and most of the Korean elite knew Japanese, compared with less than 1 percent in 1913.[43]

The Japanese invested considerably fewer resources in managing Taiwan than Korea, but on the whole they pursued similar policies of oppression. The colonial police controlled nearly all civil affairs, imposing agriculture, hygiene, tax, and security regulations and intruding into a wide variety of personal matters. Japanese exploitation of the Qing *baojia* (Jpn. *hokō*) structure of mutual household surveillance enforced tight control over the Taiwanese population. For its part, Japanese-language training worked to alienate Taiwanese from China and integrate them into the Japanese cultural sphere. In the late 1930s, striving to integrate the island into Japan culturally as well as economically, militarily, and politically, the Japanese also expected Taiwanese to adopt Japanese names, publish only in Japanese, and pay homage to the Japanese sun goddess Amaterasu. When Taiwan was returned to China in 1945, more than half the population knew at least some spoken Japanese, up from less than 1 percent in 1905.[44]

Unlike its colonization of Korea and Taiwan, Japanese encroachment on the Chinese mainland was primarily economic and military. Japan engaged in a number of cultural enterprises in China, but these paled against its economic and military weight. The principal exception was in the puppet state of Manchuria. Although authorities there described the informal colony as a space of *gozoku kyōwa* (five races in harmony), the Japanese imposed their way of life on the existing population: they designated Shinto the national religion and declared Japanese the first national language to be learned throughout the territory.[45] In many respects occupied Manchuria was no more sovereign than Japan's formal colonies.[46]

Compliance and Collaboration

Early in the colonial period, local resistance movements successfully tempered some of the most oppressive Japanese policies. Their effectiveness quickly waned, however, and compliance and collaboration — often present well before formal colonization and almost always necessary for the success of colonial enterprises — soon became virtually unavoidable.[47] Starting early in the colonial period, nearly all channels of upward mobility in Korea and Taiwan were located in Japanese-dominated institutions and required knowledge of the Japanese language.[48] The mobilization campaigns of the late 1930s and early 1940s ensured that much of the colonial population was involved in the Japanese war effort — from elites, including writers such as the Korean poet Im Haksu (1911–82), propagandizing for Japan both at home and on foreign battlefields, to laborers working in Japan, to comfort women serving and soldiers fighting in the Japanese army, to uneducated farmers spying on their neighbors, to children taken out of school to toil in factories and fields.

Colonial authorities promoted the genres of *shinnichi bungaku* (pro-Japanese literature) and *kōmin bungaku* (imperial-subject literature), which endorsed the Japanese imperialist agenda and often were written in Japanese. A variety of factors motivated Koreans, Taiwanese, and Chinese, particularly those in occupied areas, to write texts in this vein: like collaborators in other arenas, some believed their actions ultimately would benefit their homelands, some feared the repercussions of not supporting the colonial power, and some were swept away by colonial propaganda.[49] On the other hand, pro-Japanese and imperial-subject literature represented only a fraction of most writers' total creative output, and despite its enthusiastic rhetoric it often revealed ambivalence vis-à-vis Japan.

The volumes of Japanese-language works by Koreans, Taiwanese, and to a lesser extent Chinese that do not explicitly promote Japanese designs on East Asia are even more ambiguous. Writing in the language of the (former) imperial power is a common phenomenon in empire and postimperial spaces, and no small number of Koreans and Taiwanese composed at least some of their texts in Japanese.[50] Significantly, many did so long before the Japanese government officially banned publication in Chinese and Korean late in the colonial period. Written by colonial peoples for both Japanese and transcolonial audiences, creating what Gilles Deleuze and Félix Guattari have somewhat condescendingly termed "minor literatures" (literatures in "major" languages by "minority" groups),[51] these Japanese-language texts embody the contradictions of cultural production in empire. But so do those by Taiwanese and Koreans written in Chinese and Korean, especially after these languages were officially prohibited. Choice of language, often tied deeply to questions of national, cultural, and personal identity, can be a simple artistic prerogative but frequently is also a political statement and at times a revolutionary act.[52] Yet, as is often true of texts by multilingual writers, the rhetoric of Korean and Taiwanese Japanese-language literary works is frequently even more significant than the language in which they are crafted.[53] The translingual nature of creative texts by Koreans and Taiwanese—their incorporating Japanese vocabulary and syntax into Korean—and Chinese-language works and Chinese, Korean, and Hokkien (Taiwanese) vocabulary and syntax into Japanese-language works—expands the perimeters and obfuscates the boundaries of individual languages.[54] And regardless of the language in which they are written, these works often negotiate intensely with the cultural products of the imperial power.

Chinese resisted Japanese expansion on the mainland as early as the Twenty-One Demands (1915) and May Fourth Movement (1919), and anti-Japanese boycotts broke out in major cities after the Japanese takeover of Manchuria (1931). Yet compliance and collaboration with the Japanese imperialist agenda also were common, particularly in Japanese-occupied regions.[55] Shortly after all-out war erupted in 1937, the Japanese attempted to coerce local Chinese talent into creating literary works and staging theatrical productions that supported the Japanese occupation of China. Chinese writers ultimately produced very few creative texts that explicitly advocated Japanese imperialism, but some participated in Sino-Japanese cultural functions and wrote testimonials and editorials supporting the Japanese.[56] Chinese wrote in Japanese in much smaller numbers than their Korean and Taiwanese counterparts, but their Japanese-language literature raises many of the same questions. Imperialism in occupied Manchuria was more collaborative than in other areas of China. In the early 1940s, the Japanese easily mobilized writers there to assist with war propaganda, yet, as in China proper, state-sponsored organizations had little impact on the literature created.[57] On the other hand, despite the ardent patriotism of the Manchurian warlord Zhang Xueliang (1901–2001), the nationalist protest against Japan was not nearly as vocal as the myth of widespread resistance in Manchuria suggests.[58]

Self-Strengthening Initiatives

As in many colonial spaces, the lines distinguishing collaboration, acquiescence, and resistance were blurred throughout East Asia for much of the early twentieth century. Some of what the Japanese foisted on China, occupied Manchuria, Korea, and Taiwan was never accepted, some was embraced, and much was simply endured. At the same time, colonial and semicolonial peoples actively sought out and enthusiastically incorporated what they considered more advanced knowledge from Japan. Chinese, Koreans, and Taiwanese became deeply involved with national self-strengthening as Japan tightened its grip on East Asia. They hoped to stem the increasing tide of Japanese (and, in the case of China, Western) imperialism, establish independent legitimacy, and be recognized regionally and globally. Believing educational opportunities in their homelands insufficient, whether because of Japanese-imposed quotas in Korea, Taiwan, and occupied Manchuria (where the Japanese reserved most seats at the best schools for Japanese) or an outdated system in the rest of China, hundreds of thousands of colonial and semicolonial elites chose to study in Japan. While there, they became deeply engrossed in the social and political currents swirling in the metropole, including socialism, anarchism, communism, and feminism, which they believed could bolster their societies. Language reform was another pressing concern of colonial and semicolonial intellectuals, no small number of whom were inspired by Japan's recent *genbun itchi* (unity of speech and writing) movement. For instance, the many versions of *baihua* (the new written vernacular) that proliferated in

China in the 1920s were hybrids not only of classical Chinese, the premodern vernacular, and contemporary colloquial speech but also of Japanese and Western syntactical structures.[59] Similarly, in the late nineteenth and early twentieth centuries, Chinese, Koreans, and Taiwanese transplanted into their languages hundreds of Japanese verbal compounds, many of which paradoxically had their origins in China, with altered meanings.[60] In these and other ways, colonial and semicolonial peoples actively followed Japanese blueprints in the hopes of building up, if not liberating, their homelands.

Literary Contact Nebulae

In addition to impositions by imperial fiat and self-strengthening by the (semi)colonized, a third and frequently overlooked modality of foreign system integration in empire is the transnational cultural negotiation that takes place in artistic contact nebulae, spaces of greater reciprocity and diminished claims of authority. Throughout the early twentieth century, Chinese, Japanese, Koreans, and Taiwanese grappled with and transculturated one another's films, music, nonverbal arts, folk arts, comedy, popular culture, and a variety of media phenomena, including the *moga* (modern girl).[61] For instance, both Japanese and Koreans reconfigured the folk ballad "Arirang," making this song of lost love and homesickness one of the most widely known pieces of music in the empire. As E. Taylor Atkins notes:

Although a song of Korean origin . . . its flexible lyrical and melodic structure made it possible for Koreans and Japanese to adapt it for different expressive purposes. It proved malleable enough to articulate Korean indignation toward Japanese colonial domination, Japanese fantasies of a primordial Korean wonderland, and the ambivalence of both peoples toward the transformative effects of modernity.[62]

But East Asian literatures were also dominant vehicles of intra-empire cultural negotiation. Although seldom enjoying the cachet of Western literatures, Chinese, Japanese, Korean, and Taiwanese literatures were dynamically consumed and transculturated throughout the empire, and their active circulation resulted in a surprisingly integrated East Asian print culture decades before Japanese authorities and colonial/semicolonial collaborators called for the creation of such an entity. The reciprocal flow and transculturation of texts between China and both Korea and Taiwan was more sizable than it had ever been; the early twentieth century also marked the first significant literary exchanges between Korea and Taiwan. Not surprisingly, Chinese readers in occupied Manchuria, many of whom had embraced China's contemporary literature before Japanese occupation, remained avid consumers of it. At the same time, Japanese gradually began reading and transculturating contemporary Korean, Taiwanese, and particularly Chinese literatures. Still, the flows of Japanese literature to Chinese, Korean, and Taiwanese readers, not to mention the streams of adaptations, translations, critical studies, and intertextualizations of Japanese literature by colonial and semicolonial writers, were the largest.

To be sure, a handful of Chinese, Korean, and Taiwanese writers—including the prominent Chinese reformer Liang Qichao (1873–1929)—believed Japanese literature (in Liang's case the Japanese political novel) a superior product that had contributed directly to Japan's economic and military success and thought that if it were disseminated and reproduced in their societies it would have a similar effect. Others found that Japanese literature provided a welcome window into Western literatures; they believed that if they emulated Japanese literature, they would elevate the status of their homelands. In addition, the dichotomy of (semi)colonizer/(semi)colonized, although mediated, often persisted in literary negotiations; Japanese writers welcomed Chinese, Korean, and Taiwanese writers into their homes and literary coteries and published large quantities of their creative work, yet seldom treated them as true equals. But relegating early twentieth-century intra–East Asian cultural negotiation to submissive Chinese, Korean, and Taiwanese imitation of a more advanced culture or to dominant Japanese control over colonial and semicolonial cultural production obscures the complex and ambiguous dynamics of these interplays and ignores a major component of empire, its "web of mutually constitutive discursive networks."[63]

For most of the colonial period, cross-cultural currents were created willingly by enthusiastic Chinese, Korean, and Taiwanese readers and writers; before the outbreak of total war with China in 1937, the Japanese government did little to impose Japan's literature on other Asians. The one exception was students, who encountered it in required textbooks. Beginning early in the colonial period, the Japanese established numerous libraries in Korea and Taiwan, making hundreds of thousands of Japanese books, including tens of thousands of creative texts, available to colonial and semicolonial peoples.[64] But the Japanese did not force them to read these literary works. In Manchuria, Japanese authorities destroyed hundreds of thousands of Chinese books immediately after taking over the region in 1931; they stocked the newly emptied shelves with Japanese books and severely restricted textual inflows from China proper. The Japanese believed it imperative to sever cultural ties between Manchuria and the remainder of China. Literature was a principal target of these endeavors because the Manchurian literary field was closely integrated with that of Beijing, Shanghai, and other Chinese literary centers.[65] But even in occupied Manchuria, the Japanese authorities did not require residents to read Japanese literary works, much less transculturate them. Expatriate Japanese communities, often with the cooperation of local leaders, occasionally used Japanese plays and other creative works to attempt to inculcate colonial and semicolonial peoples with "Japanese values." Yet these projects, including the March 1919 Kabuki initiative in Korea, were market-driven, not compulsory.[66] Even the Japanese government's official cultural agency—the Kokusai Bunka Shinkōkai (K.B.S. or Society for International Cultural Relations, est. 1934)—which actively promoted Japanese culture outside Asia, put very low priority on distributing Japanese literature in China and the colonies.[67]

Most exports of Japanese literature to China, occupied Manchuria, Korea, and Taiwan depended on the initiative of private citizens. In the late 1920s and early 1930s, Japanese publishers, bookstores, and entrepreneurs looked to these areas, where the numbers of both Japanese settlers and local people able to read Japanese were steadily increasing, as attractive markets for the mountains of unsold *enpon* (one-yen books) and other books that overflowed warehouses in Japan. Private companies such as the Teikoku Tosho Fukyūkai (Society for the Popularization of Imperial Books) sold Japanese remainders in Korea, Taiwan, and occupied Manchuria, while organizations close to the state, including the South Manchuria Railway Company, facilitated the distribution of literary works to China, occupied Manchuria, Korea, and Taiwan, where both Japanese settlers and local peoples welcomed them.[68] Also, it is important to remember that throughout the Japanese empire there was no shortage of Western literature in translation for those eager to read foreign texts. For most of the imperial period, reading Japanese literature outside of school, much less transculturating it, was almost always a deliberate choice.

It has long been understood that regulating cultural production and consumption is one of the most effective means of controlling societies, and scholars increasingly are examining the relationship between culture and imperialism, including writing as an instrument or enabler of empire.[69] But only after the outbreak of total war with China in 1937, following decades of voluntary consumption and transculturation, did the Japanese state actively promote Japanese literature in China, Korea, and Taiwan in any systematic way.[70] Beginning in the late 1930s it dispatched Japanese writers across East Asia, where they were joined by film experts, painters, publishers, reporters, and theater figures. Artists were sent "to bear witness to Japan's superior culture" and to use their creative products as propaganda tools.[71] The Japanese also encouraged translation of their literature in occupied areas of China, where comprehension of the Japanese language was not as widespread as in Korea and Taiwan. In addition, they began employing the rubric of *Dai Tōa bungaku* (Greater East Asian literature), arguing that literature could bring disparate regions together "under the unifying code of the Japanese language."[72] The diffusion of haiku and *waka* (short, fixed-syllable Japanese poems) throughout the empire was an important part of this process. As Faye Kleeman has noted, "the colonial poetic cartography closely parallels the outline of political and military conquest, spanning an area from the Kurile Islands to Manchuria, Korea, Taiwan, and the South Pacific."[73]

Culminating Japan's efforts to use literature to unite the empire were the Dai Tōa Bungakusha Taikai (Greater East Asian Writers Conferences) of the early 1940s, which assembled first in Tokyo (1942, 1943) and then in Nanjing (1944) and brought together leading writers, editors, and critics from Japan, Korea, Taiwan, China, occupied Manchuria, Mongolia, and other parts of Asia. These meetings generally are believed to mark the formation of an East Asian literary sphere centered on the Japanese cultural tradition and coterminous with the Japanese empire.[74] In fact, by the time they were convened, twentieth-century Chinese, Japanese, Koreans, and Taiwanese had been engaging in travel and linguistic, readerly, writerly, and textual contact for decades, creating literary contact nebulae oddly suggestive of, but in the end very different from, the imperial cultural ambit trumpeted by the Japanese state.[75] The willing and enthusiastic engagement of colonial and semicolonial East Asians with Japanese literature is significant, not only in light of their historical spurning of Japanese culture, but also considering the oppressive political, cultural, economic, and military policies Japan foisted on the region after 1895.

Boundaries among East Asian authors and literatures were fogged during the colonial period as Chinese, Japanese, Korean, and Taiwanese writers worked with one another and with one another's creative products. Writers published in lands in which they had not been born or raised or with which they did not identify most closely, in forms and styles not habitual to the languages used, and in languages that were not their ostensible "mother tongues" or did not "match" their cultures. The Palestinian Arab writer Anton Shammas (1950–), who publishes in both Hebrew and Arabic, has commented on the insecurity this situation can provoke: "I feel an exile in Arabic, the language of my blood. I feel an exile in Hebrew, my stepmother tongue."[76] Similarly, the contemporary English-language writer Ha Jin (1956–) captures well the problems inherent in associating language with nation/culture, and, more generally, in dividing peoples and cultural products along national lines. Born and raised in China but having lived in the United States since the mid-1980s, he once remarked, "without question, I am a Chinese writer, not an American-Chinese poet, though I write in English. If this sounds absurd, the absurdity is historical rather than personal . . . since I can hardly publish anything in Chinese now."[77]

Recent discussions concerning the "borders" of "national" literatures have focused on the relationships among languages and individual, cultural, and national identities. We have questioned how to categorize exophonic writing, that is to say texts an author writes in languages other than his/her "native" tongue.[78] Likewise, we have interrogated how to classify translocal writing, that is, texts a writer publishes outside his/her homeland or adopted home (however loosely defined); we also have probed how to think about translingual writing, in this case texts published in a language not usually associated with or not "native" to the place of publication (the latter includes a substantial subset of the Francophone, Lusophone, sinophone, etc.). More controversially, we have questioned how to categorize texts where writer and language "belong" to different nations or cultures (e.g., Japanese-language texts by so-called "non-Japanese").[79] Although texts such as these have often fallen through the cracks, marginalized on account of an ultimately constructed homelessness (the work of readers, writers, and scholars alike), they are best understood as inherently transcultural, as contact nebulae belonging to several heterogeneous literary worlds.[80]

This is even more true of textual transculturations. Interpretive, interlingual, and intertextual transculturations long have been understood as facilitating the cross-pollination of literary worlds. Nevertheless, adaptations and translations tend to be marginalized, dismissed as derivatives of the same literature (often national/cultural) as the texts they transculturate, and they are rarely talked about as components of the literatures associated with the languages they employ; for their part, interpretive and intertextual transculturations are often discussed as belonging solely to literary spheres distinct from the texts they transculturate. In fact, like their sources (which also transculturate predecessors), they also belong to and bring together multiple heterogeneous literary corpuses.[81]

But for clarity, and to highlight the interplays among what conventionally have been discussed as the relatively separate spheres of twentieth-century Chinese, Japanese, Korean, and Taiwanese literatures, in this book the modifiers Chinese, Japanese, Korean, and Taiwanese that precede such terms as "literary work," "criticism," and "intertextualization" refer to the primary identity of the writer/transculturator, regardless of the language or place of publication of the text. Modifiers preceding "adaptation" and "translation" refer both to the target language and to the primary identity of the adapter/translator (e.g., "Chinese translation" = translation into the Chinese language by someone generally considered or considering him/herself to be Chinese). Exceptions and ambiguities are discussed on a case-by-case basis. Nationality, culture, and national and cultural identities can be notoriously arbitrary and are often multiple, particularly in cases of people who have spent substantial time in and identify with multiple places, who are born to parents with different cultural identities, whose homelands have been overtaken by peoples of other identities, or who have not spent much if any time in their ostensible "homelands." Moreover, the constructed and often manipulated categories "Chinese," "Japanese," "Korean," and "Taiwanese," not to mention "Western" —whether they refer to individuals, societies, languages, or literatures—are far from discrete homogenous entities.[82] These designations naturally obscure major differences, differences that require continued scholarly attention. But separation along these lines also obscures distinctive transcultural interfaces and contact nebulae. Both the Japanese language and the many divisions within Chinese, Japanese, Korean, and Taiwanese literatures helped to promote links with like-minded writers elsewhere in the empire, creating a hybrid transnational early twentieth-century East Asian literary field.

Empire of Texts in Motion

This book concentrates on literary contact nebulae in early twentieth-century East Asia in order to help transform our understanding of the Chinese, Japanese, Korean, and Taiwanese cultural landscapes, as well as of the Japanese empire more broadly. But it also posits a research agenda for the study of texts consumed and created in other nineteenth- and twentieth-century empires and their aftermaths. More broadly, it opens pathways for examining literary works produced in the context of unequal power relationships, whether we approach these texts from the standpoint of comparative literature, world literature, area studies, cultural studies, history, or some combination of these and other methodologies. Even cultural products never consumed outside narrow communities of origin do not stand alone, untouched by predecessors, indifferent to contemporaries, unnoticed by successors; how much more deeply intertwined with other cultural products are the countless texts that traverse cultural and political lines? The many unexplored interactions among the literatures and literary worlds of colonial, semicolonial, and otherwise subjugated African, Caribbean, East-Central European, Latin American, Middle Eastern, and South and Southeast Asian spaces on the one hand, and American and European literatures of all eras on the other, are vitally important areas of further study. Also important are the literary dialogues emerging from religious, regional, and internal struggles and colonialisms as well as inter-(semi)colonial networks and rivalries, the regularly overlooked yet strikingly complex relationships among postcolonial and postsemicolonial literatures and those of former imperial but often still hegemonic powers, the frequent overhauls of "canonical" works that appear in texts by women, minorities, immigrants, and other disenfranchised groups, and the engagement of "canonical" texts with marginalized literatures. Regardless of specialization, in the future we need to do more to contextualize peoples, texts, and phenomena beyond their immediate cultural and geographical surroundings. This book replaces comfort zones with contact nebulae by unraveling tangled transcultural webs of consumption and production. It hypothesizes that for understanding most literatures and cultures, particularly those of nineteenth- and twentieth-century empires and their aftermaths, it is essential to analyze how creative texts are transspatialized and how spaces are transtextualized. That is to say, how writers throughout metropoles, colonies, semicolonies, postimperial spaces, and other regions, by negotiating with and ultimately transforming one another's creative products, cracked apart textual bodies, incorporating intra-empire literary fragments large and small into their own cultural spaces, and in so doing further hybridizing these spaces and those of their predecessors.

As we proceed, it is worthwhile to bear in mind the approach of the French literature scholar Victor Brombert:

No single theoretical formulation, however ingenious, can possibly accommodate the specific thrust and quality of a given work. Wary of preformatted definitions, I have preferred to be an attentive reader and interpreter of the works under discussion, to remain flexible in my approach. . . . What mattered to me in all cases was to respect the texture and inner coherence of the works in question.[83]

Drawing from a diverse array of primary and critical sources, I aim to reveal the interactions among writers and texts as multifaceted and in many cases resisting classification.

Chapter 1 probes the scale and complexity of both travel and readerly and writerly contact in the Japanese empire, allowing fuller appreciation of the textual contact that took place in late nineteenth- and early twentieth-century East Asia. As in most imperial spaces, texts by metropolitan writers had a greater immediacy to colonial and semicolonial literary figures than products of unfamiliar hands from alien lands. Japanese creative works were more than discrete artifacts to be at once emulated and despised because of their production in a more modernized society with oppressive colonial/semicolonial policies. Instead, as the output of writers whom they sometimes knew personally, and the output of a metropole with which they often were intimately familiar, Japanese literary works embodied some of the greatest ambiguities confronting colonial and semicolonial intellectuals.

After Chapter 1, the narrative focuses on textual contact and divides into two parts, the first dealing with interpretive and interlingual transculturations (critical studies, adaptations, and translations) and the second with intertextual transculturations of Japanese literature. All three are explored as taking place within a context of polyvectoral intra–East Asian and inter-regional (primarily East Asian and Western) transculturation. Chinese, Korean, and Taiwanese critical studies, adaptations, translations, and intertextualizations of Japanese literature, of which only a handful existed before the twentieth century, formed the dominant but not the only current of intra–East Asian textual contact in Japan's colonial and semicolonial imperium. Numbering in the thousands, these transculturations are a vital but little-known part of the swirling vortex of peoples, ideas, and texts that characterized cultural contact in early twentieth-century East Asia. They also embody a fundamental characteristic of the colonial and semicolonial landscape: the blending of resistance, acquiescence, and collaboration. Their presence grants importance, if not narrative and cultural capital and authority, to the Japanese texts they transculturate. On the other hand, whether interpretive, interlingual, or intertextual, these transculturations offer novel interpretations that frequently challenge the validity of prior textual assumptions and often overturn established works. Moreover, in selecting which Japanese texts to transculturate, Chinese, Korean, and Taiwanese writers often deviated from the Japanese *bundan* (literary establishment), creating alternative Japanese canons.

Part I examines intra–East Asian critical studies, adaptations, and translations of early twentieth-century Japanese literature in the context of interpretive and interlingual transculturation in empire. Chinese, Korean, and Taiwanese writers interpretively and interlingually interwove hundreds of Japanese novels, plays, poems, and short stories into their own cultural fabrics, reversing the sinocentric cultural flow that had dominated East Asia for centuries. Chapter 2, focusing on Chinese, Korean, and Taiwanese critical writings about Japanese literature, is concerned both with the anxiety of colonial and semicolonial intellectuals vis-à-vis the creative products of the imperial hegemon and with explicit challenges to imperial cultural capital and authority. Chapters 3 and 4 concentrate on colonial and semicolonial adaptations and translations of Japanese literature, from exceptionally free to nearly literal transpositions. These chapters, bisected by the Chinese, Korean, and Taiwanese new culture and literature movements of the late 1910s and early 1920s, emphasize the conflicting functions of adapting/translating in the East Asian colonial and semicolonial sphere. Throughout, I highlight the inherent paradox of interpreting, adapting, and translating: the concurrent validating and denying of cultural capital and authority through the selection of texts and the manner of transculturation, key issues in empire and other spaces of unbalanced power relationships.

Part II brings out the ambivalence of intertextual transculturation and the implications of simultaneously pulling apart Japanese literature and interweaving—often relatively silently—its fragments into colonial and semicolonial creative work. It relates this phenomenon to intertextualizing in empire more generally. Chapter 5 highlights the critical significance of intertextuality as a literary strategy employed by politically and socially subordinated writers and summarizes how early twentieth-century Chinese, Korean, and Taiwanese writers incorporated transposed allusions to Japanese literature into their creative texts. Subsequent chapters address three of the most pressing problems confronting early twentieth-century East Asians in a context of international strife and imperialist pressure on each of the societies involved. Chapter 6 looks at how Chinese, Korean, and Taiwanese literary works intertextually transculturate Japanese literary works to give new perspectives on suffering. Chapter 7 demonstrates how colonial and semicolonial writers use intertexts from Japanese literature to interrogate the construction and dynamics of relationships, whether interpersonal—among lovers, relatives, friends, comrades, enemies, or strangers—or intrasocietal, between people and their communities or homelands more generally. Chapter 8 explores how Chinese, Korean, and Taiwanese intertextualizations problematize Japanese constructions of agency. The book concludes with a brief epilogue addressing postwar intra–East Asian cultural negotiation. Analyzing literature and other artistic genres that quickly rebounded from wartime and resumed their roles as key transcultural conduits allows us to move beyond studying postwar Chinese, Japanese, Korean, and Taiwanese cultural products in isolation, focusing primarily on the nature of their encounters with the contemporary West, and discussing only popular culture as transcending frontiers.

In light of the massive transspatializing of texts and transtextualizing of spaces that took place in early twentieth-century East Asia, how separate are what have been designated modern "Chinese," "Japanese," "Korean," and "Taiwanese" literatures? More generally, to what extent should we refine our understanding of national literatures—looking more closely at transculturation and contact nebulae within national cubbyholes—and to what extent should the paradigm of national literatures be displaced, with the focus shifted to spatial and textual contact nebulae themselves? Political borders are rarely stable, cultural and linguistic boundaries even less so, but cross-border contacts often are precisely what stimulate assertions of difference; flows and interactions of peoples and cultural products consistently obfuscate boundaries, but by triggering identity anxieties they frequently reinforce them as well. Divisions along national and linguistic lines provide the substrate of much humanistic discourse. But increasingly, scholarship on the networks that inspire and reject such divisions is projecting a tantalizing vision of diverse contact nebulae made up of churning and intermingling cultural vectors.

The future of comparative literature lies partly in exploring more fully the dynamics of literary contact nebulae, understood broadly; the future of humanistic area studies requires examining cultural products in regional and global perspective. The current spotlight on habitually disregarded peoples and cultural phenomena—such as resident Koreans and their literatures (in Japan), the Japanese-language compositions of colonial and even postcolonial Korean and Taiwanese writers, the Chinese-language compositions of Japanese writers in both the premodern and modern periods, and the heteroglossia of the Japanophone and sinophone more generally—is welcome and long overdue. But we also should look more closely at the rapid circulation, dislocation, and reconfiguration—particularly transculturation—of cultural products. Teasing out local, national, regional, and global networks of transculturation yields a clearer picture of the world's artistic landscape and a sharper image of each of its deeply intertwined literatures. The chapters that follow take up this project for a key moment in the history of modern empires, Japan's overseas imperium between 1895 and 1945.

ONE

Travel, Readerly Contact, and Writerly Contact in the Japanese Empire

The Japanese imperium, like most empires of the nineteenth and twentieth centuries, was characterized by multiple imbricated artistic contact nebulae. Differences were simultaneously undermined and reinforced: frequent transcultural interactions destabilized frontiers, yet colonial policies, not to mention anxieties intensified by increased transcultural encounters, often resulted in powerful rhetoric of separateness. Closely integrated with one another, travel, readerly contact, and writerly contact flourished in this environment, creating numerous literary contact nebulae that illuminate the ambiguities of cultural negotiation in empires and their aftermaths.

(Former) metropoles often pull powerfully on colonial and postcolonial intellectuals, who travel in large numbers to their cities, enroll in their schools and universities, learn their languages, and forge friendships with professional counterparts. In the nineteenth and twentieth centuries, seeking opportunities not available at home, hundreds of thousands of students from Africa, the Caribbean, East-Central Europe, Latin America, the Middle East, and South and Southeast Asia went to Europe (including Russia/the Soviet Union) and the United States for their educations, at the same time that comparable numbers of semicolonial Chinese and colonial Korean and Taiwanese intellectuals studied in Japan. Their experiences in metropoles were decidedly mixed: many were welcomed professionally but also endured prejudice and harassment because of their origins. Japan's conflicting rhetoric of superiority and affinity, not to mention its long history of cultural subservience to China and Korea, made conditions particularly ambivalent for colonial and semicolonial East Asians. But intellectuals who visited Japan, like those who traveled to Europe and the United States, persisted in obtaining the knowledge and skills that allowed them to play important roles in transforming their homelands. After returning, many of these men and women occupied influential positions in business, education, industry, medicine, the military, and politics, not to mention the literary, performing, and nonverbal arts.

The colonies and semicolonies also were alluring. Hundreds of thousands of intellectuals from imperial powers, including many major artists, visited the lands under their nations' dominion. Some stayed for years, joining large settler populations. But their journeys, frequently driven by curiosity, conceit, political fiat, or economic opportunity, were usually more brief than their colonial and semicolonial counterparts' sojourns in the metropole. In general, they interacted minimally with local peoples and rarely learned colonial and semicolonial languages or studied at local institutions. Intercolonial/semicolonial travel also was not unknown and in some cases quite significant. But as in many other parts of the world, in East Asia the vectors of travel by colonial and semicolonial intellectuals to the imperial metropolis outstripped others in depth and duration.

Metropolitan cultural products, consumed by colonial and semicolonial peoples both abroad and at home, often proved even more irresistible than the imperial metropolis itself. Books were especially addictive, forming nebulae of sustained readerly contact. As Homi Bhabha reminds us, "There is a scene in the cultural writings of English colonialism which repeats so insistently after the early nineteenth century—and, through that repetition, so triumphantly *inaugurates* a literature of empire. . . . It is the scenario, played out in the wild and wordless wastes of colonial India, Africa, the Caribbean, of the sudden, fortuitous discovery of the English book." Of course, as Bhabha also notes, books were seldom left untouched: "The discovery of the book is, at once, a moment of originality and authority, as well as a process of displacement that, paradoxically, makes the presence of the book wondrous to the extent to which it is repeated, translated, misread, displaced."[1]

Literary education was an important part of many colonial projects. Beginning in 1835, the British used it in India to strengthen the authority and legitimacy of their government, institutions, and laws, as well as ostensibly to build character.[2] But even under such conditions, readerly contact often was voluntary, and devotion frequently flowed from initial encounters. Traders introduced Shakespeare to India in the eighteenth century, building theaters and performing a range of plays in the hope of simultaneously entertaining and enlightening, but English theater, and Shakespeare in particular, quickly acquired a local following that has endured to this day.[3] Not surprisingly, writers were among the most passionate readers of literature from the metropole. The Indian author Anita Desai (1937–) recalls that as a child, after playing outside until dark, "we came home and read for the hundredth time our treasured copies of the works of Dickens, the Brontë sisters, Wordsworth and Milton."[4] The Trinidadian writer C. L. R. James (1901–89) similarly makes no secret of his early passion for English literature:

> I had read [Thackeray's *Vanity Fair*] when I was about eight, and of all the books that passed through that house this one became my Homer and my bible. I read it through from the first page to the last, then started again, read to the end and started again. Whenever I finished a new book I turned to my *Vanity Fair*. For years I had no notion that it was a classical novel. I read it because I wanted to. . . . When I discovered in the college library that besides *Vanity Fair* Thackeray had written thirty-six other volumes . . . I read them through straight, two volumes at a time, and read them for twenty years after. . . . After Thackeray there was Dickens, George Eliot and the whole bunch of English novelists. Followed the poets in Matthew Arnold's selections, Shelley, Keats and Byron; Milton and Spenser. But in the public library in town there was everything, Fielding, Byron, with all of *Don Juan*. I discovered criticism: Hazlitt, Lamb and Coleridge, Saintsbury and Gosse, *The Encyclopaedia Britannica, Chambers' Encyclopaedia* . . . I cannot possibly remember all I read then, and every now and then I still look up an essay or a passage and find that I had read it before I was eighteen . . . for cricket and English literature I fed an inexhaustible passion.[5]

The Taiwanese writer Ye Shitao (1925–) likewise describes devouring Japanese literature as a young man, noting in his memoirs:

> I read day and night. I read just about every Chinese and foreign novel that one could buy at that time in colonial Taiwan. Of course, Japanese literature was my main focus. . . . I read texts by Izumi Kyōka [1873–1939], Ozaki Kōyō [1867–1903], Kunikida Doppo [1871–1908], Futabatei Shimei [1864–1909], and other great Meiji [1868–1912] works. I particularly liked Higuchi Ichiyō [1872–96]. . . . Reading Japanese literature already was my addiction. From the Meiji writers, I moved directly into the world of Taishō [1912–26] texts. I read everything from Natsume Sōseki [1867–1916], Akutagawa Ryūnosuke [1892–1927], the Shirakabaha [White Birch Society], and the Shinkankakuha [neo-

sensationalists], to some left-wing authors of the Rōnōha [Labor-Farmer Faction]; there wasn't anything I didn't read. Before my second year of middle school I had read just about all of the major Japanese writers.[6]

   To be sure, a number of metropolitan readers were avid consumers of colonial and semicolonial literature, snapping up books (primarily translations) as quickly as they became available. A sizable market for Chinese literature developed in Japan after the Japanese seizure of Manchuria in 1931; even Japanese textbooks included selections of contemporary Chinese creative writing.[7] The Japanese outpouring of grief following Lu Xun's death in 1936—in the form of essays, special journal issues in his memory, and eventually monographic studies—reveals clearly the strong feelings intellectuals in Japan harbored for their Chinese counterpart. As David Pollack believes regarding the Japanese embrace of Lu Xun's thought, "the powerful writings of the modern Chinese writer Lu Xun concerning the perils of tradition and the desperate need for modernization were widely read in Japan and taken to heart there possibly even more than they were in China."[8] Japanese also were impressed with Chinese theater. A 1907 production in Tokyo of *Heinu yutian lu* (The Black Slave's Cry to Heaven), an adaptation of Harriet Beecher Stowe's (1811–1896) novel *Uncle Tom's Cabin* (1852) staged with the assistance of Japanese theater figures, received rave reviews; some Japanese critics declared the actors and their sets superior to Japanese counterparts.[9] Likewise, in 1937, after watching a performance of Cao Yu's (1910–96) *Richu* (Sunrise, 1935), staged by Chinese students in Tokyo, the eminent Japanese dramatist Akita Ujaku (1883–1962) exclaimed to his friend the Chinese writer Guo Moruo: "The Chinese truly are geniuses. Plays with the expansive scope of *Sunrise* seldom are seen in Japan."[10] Korean literature enjoyed less acclaim among Japanese, but a number of Japanese writers and editors were committed to making it available to Japanese readers. They had a variety of motives in so doing. In the mid-1930s the *Ōsaka mainichi Chōsenban* (Osaka Daily, Korea Edition) serialized a lineup of "Korean culture specials"—including collections of Korean literature—which it claimed together mapped out "a truly complete shrine of peninsular culture" for both Japanese and Korean readers.[11] Less hubristic, Kikuchi Kan (1888–1948) states in the editor's notes to the November 1939 issue of *Modan Nihon* (Modern Japan), "Diamond Mountain and *kisaeng* are all most people know about Korea. But Korea also has a literary establishment and many writers whose works we haven't seen. Fortunately in this supplement we are introducing many Korean texts, and that alone makes me happy."[12] Anthologies such as the *Manshū sakka shōsetsushū: Tanpopo* (Collection of Prose by Writers from Manchuria: Dandelion, 1940), and the two volumes of Kawabata Yasunari's (1899–1972) *Manshūkoku kakuminzoku sōsaku senshū* (Selected Works by Each of the Races of Manchuria, 1942, 1944) likewise were literary contact nebulae, making accessible writings by Chinese, Koreans, Japanese, and others from occupied Manchuria.[13] Some Chinese authors from this region, including Mei Niang (1920–), were celebrated throughout the empire.[14]

Inter-(semi)colonial readerly contact was also significant. The Korean writer Chang Hyŏkju's (1905–98) Japanese-language creative texts were available in Taiwan; the Taiwanese writer Lü Heruo (Lü Shidai, 1914–51), for instance, speaks in his diary of buying several copies of Chang Hyŏkju's works.[15] In fact, Lü Heruo was so excited about Chang Hyŏkju that he apparently changed his name in honor of his Korean counterpart: the first syllable of Lü Heruo's given name is the same Chinese character as the first syllable of Chang Hyŏkju's given name.[16] Taiwanese were eager to emulate Chang Hyŏkju's success and reprinted his output in Taiwanese journals including *Taiwan shinbungaku* (Taiwan New Literature) in part to provide examples for Taiwanese writers.[17]

Even more impressive was the consumption of modern Chinese literature by writers from occupied Manchuria, Korea, and Taiwan. In Taiwan, journals printed Chinese literature in both the original and Japanese translation. The Taiwanese writer Zhong Lihe (1915–60) recalled in a letter to the writer Liao Qingxiu (1927–) in 1957 that as a child in Taiwan, "we could buy collections of writings by Lu Xun, Ba Jin [1904–2005], Lao She [1899–1966], Mao Dun [1896–1981], Yu Dafu [1896–1945], and other greats of the dynamic new literature. I was so absorbed in these books that I almost forgot to eat and sleep."[18] May Fourth literature was also popular in Korea. As the writer and revolutionary Yu Su-in (1905–?) nostalgically remembered: "We read [Lu Xun's] 'Kuangren riji' [Diary of a Madman, 1918] many times and talked about it a lot, until we were so excited we too practically went mad."[19] May Fourth and other contemporary Chinese literature retained its appeal in Manchuria, despite Japanese prohibitions. Writers and publishers in northeast China had played an active role in China's new literature movements in the 1920s, and those who remained in the region after the Japanese takeover were not deterred by Japanese proscriptions against this corpus. They purchased Chinese literature in Japan and shipped it home, bypassing censors. For instance, while in Tokyo in the late 1930s and early 1940s, Mei Niang read large quantities of the "new literature" that had been banned in northeast China, including nearly all of Lu Xun's literary works and translations; she also read texts from areas in western China controlled by the Nationalist Party.[20]

Yet in contrast with colonial and semicolonial readers, who generally favored a broad spectrum of literature from the metropole, imperial interest in colonial and semicolonial creative work was comparatively subdued, centering on a small number of writers. It also was often biased. In East Asia, language barriers and a relative paucity of translations, both of which stemmed from Japanese belief in the superiority of their own cultural products, not to mention a strong readerly preference for Western creative works, impeded transcultural familiarity with contemporary Chinese, Korean, and Taiwanese literatures.

Not surprisingly, concomitant with intra-empire travel and readerly contact was significant writerly contact, as colonial, semicolonial, and metropolitan literary worlds entangled in myriad ways. Paris, London, Berlin, Tokyo, and other imperial cities were key nebulae of intra- and inter-empire literary interaction.[21] Beijing, Shanghai, Seoul, Taipei, Xinjing (Changchun), and urban centers in other colonies and semicolonies around the world also served as dynamic nebulae of intercultural artistic dialogue. Metropolitan and colonial/semicolonial writers regularly joined one another's literary societies, published in one another's periodicals, and forged deep friendships; intra- and inter-colonial/semicolonial literary dialogues also developed new and intriguing forms. These interactions in many cases resulted in intertwined literary cultures long before governments mandated the construction of such communities. But imperial discourse and embedded prejudices exacted their toll, complicating and often compromising artistic relationships. Many colonial and semicolonial dramatists, novelists, poets, and short story writers were troubled by the frequent failure of metropolitan literary establishments to regard them as true equals; their struggle for recognition resembled but ultimately was substantially greater than that of metropolitan writers based outside imperial metropolises. The shadow of collaboration also loomed large, even for colonial and semicolonial writers intent on strengthening if not liberating their homelands. Embracing literature from metropoles and working with their metropolitan counterparts, these writers often mixed complicity, acquiescence, and resistance. Analyzing intra–East Asian travel to and readerly and writerly contact in Tokyo and other urban nebulae helps set the stage for our examination of the region's textual contact, the main subject of this book.

Travel and Contact in the Metropole

Japan's victories over China in the Sino-Japanese War (1894–95) and Russia in the Russo-Japanese War (1904–5) and its consequent status as a world power were watersheds in the history of East Asian relations. As the strongest nation in the region, Japan quickly became the embodiment of a new Asian modernity. During the next four decades, several hundred thousand students and activists from across Asia traveled to its cities, making Japan a pulsating contact nebula. Korea began sending students to Japan several years after the Treaty of Kanghwa (1876), which opened the nation to Japanese trade; China sent students to Japan after its defeat in 1895. Taiwanese students started traveling to Japan in the mid-1910s, when demand for higher education exceeded opportunities at home. At the turn of the twentieth century, Taiwan was less developed than China and Korea, and its educated class smaller. In addition, the island was not subject to Western imperial pressure, having been excluded from the treaty-port system established by the Treaty of Nanjing (1842) that concluded the Opium War, and industrialization thus was not as urgent. Even so, more Taiwanese students eventually made it to Japan than those from occupied Manchuria, where Japanese authorities coerced most young adults into vocational studies.[22] The simultaneous traffic from China, occupied Manchuria, Korea, and Taiwan illuminates the widespread yet paradoxical attraction of Japan for colonial and semicolonial intellectuals.

Most colonial and semicolonial East Asians went to Japan to study the practical elements of Western civilization—engineering, fishery management, law, politics, medicine, military science, science, and technology—knowledge the Japanese recently had assimilated and reconfigured to their own advantage. While pursuing their studies, many visitors also became engrossed in the political ideas circulating in Japan and developed strong ties with Japanese reformers. In even larger numbers, Chinese, Koreans, and Taiwanese embraced Japan's many cultural opportunities, especially its vibrant publishing industry. Many of course were excited to find in Japan so many Chinese books, particularly classical texts, and they celebrated Japan's role as a storehouse of Chinese culture.[23] But they were also attracted to Japanese and Western offerings. The prolific Chinese essayist and translator Zhou Zuoren (1885-1967) enthusiastically described Tokyo's bookstore scene at the turn of the twentieth century: "[My brother] Lu Xun often went to used bookstores, and when he had a bit of money he also went to look at new books. We found Western-language books at Maruzen in Nihonbashi and at Nakanishiya in Kanda, and German books at Nankōdō in Hongō . . . Lu Xun also went to Tōkyōdō to read newly released Japanese books and magazines."[24]

Similarly, remarking on Tokyo book outlets in the 1930s, the Chinese writer and revolutionary Xie Bingying (1906-2000) noted: "The Tokyo publishing world moved at breakneck speed. Regardless of their fame, books were translated into Japanese within two weeks of their arrival in Tokyo. The books also were very cheap. So it's not at all surprising that so many foreigners—and particularly literary folks—came to Tokyo to study."[25] While in Japan, Chinese, Korean, and Taiwanese readers eagerly consumed Japanese and Western literatures (the latter initially in Japanese translation), translated Japanese and Western works (the latter initially from Japanese translations), and wrote creative texts in Chinese, Korean, and Japanese. They not only formed literary societies and founded literary journals with writers from their homelands but also developed close friendships with Japanese writers, participated in Japanese literary societies, and published in Japanese periodicals. Some metropolitan writers celebrated their work, but the Japanese literary establishment frequently slighted the output of their colonial and semicolonial counterparts.

The hybrid and ambivalent cultural, ethnic, and professional (including artistic) identities of colonial and semicolonial intellectuals who spent time in Japan further complicated the early twentieth-century East Asian cultural sphere.[26] Not particularly unusual, at least in terms of border blurring, were figures such as the internationally acclaimed composer, vocalist, and writer Jiang Wenye (1910-83), whose identification with multiple spaces (Taiwan, Japan, and China) segued into personal struggles over colonial modernity and his ethnic and artistic identities, and tussles among nationalism, modernism, and cosmopolitanism.[27] Born in Taiwan to a Hakka family that had emigrated from Fujian (southeast China), Jiang Wenye went to Japan as a young teenager, began a successful artistic career there under the tutelage of Japanese and European luminaries, then in the mid-1930s moved to China. He was based on the mainland for the remainder of his life despite political persecution and numerous invitations to relocate to Japan, Taiwan, Hong Kong, and Europe. Traveling frequently, Jiang Wenye maintained close ties with artistic circles worldwide. The products of sustained endeavors to capture the "spirit" of Taiwan and China, present and past, his compositions are fascinating tapestries of Chinese, Japanese, Taiwanese, and European artistic threads.

But they also point to the alienation and disorientation of the transnational artist. Japan, for instance, is an ambiguous presence in Jiang Wenye's anthology *Pekin mei* (Beijing Inscriptions, 1942), a collection published in Tokyo, framed by a prelude and coda, of 100 brief Japanese-language poems on Beijing. In "Jūsetsukai [Shichahai] no natsumatsuri" (Summer Festival at Jūsetsukai [Shichahai]), he writes, "I forgot where I came from / and where I was going. / When asked, Tokyo? / I lost my bearings."[28] Here Tokyo is neither a place of departure nor a destination. But the magnetism of the Japanese capital remains powerful; mere mention of the city confuses the poet. Beijing is also elusive. The poet writes eloquently about the Chinese city in *Beijing Inscriptions*, but indicates his inability to leave a mark. Declaring in the prelude, "I write indelibly on this flesh / what tries to write indelibly on / a hundred stone monuments / and a hundred bronze tripods," he suggests that he can write only on himself.[29] In the coda, he confirms this diagnosis, ambiguously urging his inscriptions to "relax, / and molder with this flesh."[30]

Several years after decolonization in 1945, the leading Korean short-story writer Kim Dong-in (1900–51) reminisced about his time at Tokyo's Meiji Gakuin (1915–16), the training ground of many eminent Koreans:

I rekindled my close relationship with [the poet] Chu Yohan [1900–79], and we discussed literature. My passion for literature gradually increased. Tokyo's Meiji Gakuin is a school with very deep ties to the Korean people. Individuals like [the reformers] Pak Yŏnghyo [1861–1939] and Kim Okgyun [1851–1894] head the academy's list of Korean alumni. Even when I was a student there, [the historian] Paek Namhun [1885–1967] was enrolled as a fifth-year student. [The historian and national-culture scholar] Mun Ilp'yŏng [1888–1939] and [the *p'ansori* master] Chŏng Kwangsu also were graduates of Meiji Gakuin. Paintings by the great artist Kim Kwanho [1890–1959] decorated the walls of the school even in my time. (Kim Kwanho was also a graduate of

Meiji Gakuin). Many of the stalwarts who now shoulder Korea's burdens entered society via this school.[31]

Kim Dong-in mentions Korean alumni from a variety of professions, but, with the exception of Chu Yohan, remains curiously silent concerning creative writers.[32] Later in the essay, Kim Dong-in makes it clear that, for better or worse, his literary companions at Meiji Gakuin were Japanese:

Beginning with Shimazaki Tōson [1872–1943], many Japanese writers were graduates of Meiji Gakuin. . . . [After I wrote a story in Japanese for the third-year journal] my classmates (Japanese kids) . . . wanted me to start a literary group with them. There were a number who felt this way. And there were many friends who said to me, grasping my hand tightly, "Your youthful passion and ambition eventually will make you a Korean fiction writer. I will become a Japanese fiction writer. Korea and Japan should interact with each other through literature. Let's maintain a literary friendship forever."

I've forgotten even the names of some of the friends I had in those days, but I wonder if they've fulfilled their early dreams of attaining distinction in life through their writing. Back then, even Arishima Takeo [1878–1923], Kikuchi Kan, and Akutagawa Ryūnosuke had yet to become famous. That was the era of Kikuchi Kan's teacher, Natsume Sōseki.

My time at Meiji Gakuin was one of overflowing youthful ambition. Added to this, when raising me, my father had pushed the idea of self-conceit so deep into my young mind that I looked down on many things, including Japanese literature. So strong was the conceit that even Victor Hugo was scorned as a vulgar writer. So while I participated in literary groups with my Japanese classmates, I always quietly wondered what kind of great students of literature could possibly emerge from your island country.[33]

Kim Dong-in's references to Japanese and not Korean writers to situate his years at Meiji Gakuin are a direct rejection of Yi Kwangsu (1892–1950), widely acknowledged as one of the founders of modern Korean literature and Korean literature's first prominent graduate of the institution (1910). Yi Kwangsu was beginning to emerge as a powerful force in the Korean literary world during the years to which Kim Dong-in refers. That Kim Dong-in made such remarks in 1949, when the wounds of the colonial period barely had begun to heal, doubtless stemmed less from his and Yi Kwangsu's contrasting approaches to literature than from his condemnation of Yi Kwangsu's collaboration with the Japanese; originally an outspoken Korean nationalist, Yi Kwangsu became one of Korea's most vocal promoters of Japanese imperialism. But Kim Dong-in's comments also curiously dismiss the many other eminent Korean writers who studied at Meiji Gakuin in the early twentieth century. Here he reveals his relationship with Korean writers and literature as no less ambiguous than that with Japanese writers and literature, the apparent disdain both spawn within him attributed to youthful conceit but likely stemming deeper.

The Allure of Japan

The large numbers of early twentieth-century Chinese, Koreans, and Taiwanese who received at least part of their training in Japan remind us that when examining early twentieth-century intra–East Asian relationships we need to look at more than trade agreements, treaties, and wars. Starting as a trickle, the current to Japan quickly became a flood. The first group of Chinese students arrived in Japan in 1896; taunted because of their long gowns and queues, some returned home within weeks. Most Chinese students, however, were undeterred. Estimates vary on the precise number who made the journey; many Chinese in Japan—particularly those attending school only part-time—did not formally register. Official figures show that there were only 13 Chinese students in Japan in 1896 and 18 in 1898. The numbers grew to several hundred in 1901 and in 1903 to more than 1,000.[34] Japan's victory over Russia in 1905 resulted in a tremendous influx of Chinese students, from 1,300 in 1904 to at least 8,000 and likely more than 10,000 in 1905 and 1906.[35] In contrast, in 1906 only several hundred Chinese students were studying in the United States.[36] The numbers of Chinese students in Japan declined after 1906 but recovered substantially several years after China's Republican Revolution (1911); by 1914 there were at least 5,000 Chinese students in Japan. The years 1914 to 1923 witnessed a fairly steady decrease (from 5,000 to 1,000), as other educational opportunities became more widely available, but then the figure rose to more than 3,000 in 1930. After another dip in 1932 and 1933 prompted by Japan's seizure of Manchuria, the number shot up to 6,500 in 1935 and remained fairly steady in 1936 and 1937. Chinese students began leaving Japan in large numbers after the outbreak of total war with China in July 1937, drawing the curtain on a remarkable chapter in Sino-Japanese interaction. The prolific Chinese writer Guo Moruo, who himself attended school in Japan, once declared that between 1896 and 1937 Japan hosted approximately 300,000 Chinese students. Guo Moruo's estimate is generous, but there is no denying Japan's overwhelming pull on Chinese longing for a better education than they believed could be obtained at home.

Japan's allure to Korean intellectuals was even greater. Many Koreans believed that Japan provided a compelling model of how to adapt to the modern world without losing national character.[37] Indeed, the ambivalence of many Korean intellectuals about Japanese encroachment and then colonization apparently was offset by their desire to study in the metropole. Japanese policies limiting the number of Korean students enrolled in higher schools in their homeland also impelled more and more young Koreans to seek educations in Japan. Small numbers of Korean students traveled to Japan as early as the 1880s, where they enrolled in institutions such as Keiō Gijuku, led by the prominent Meiji intellectual Fukuzawa Yukichi (1835–1901). During the early 1880s, Fukuzawa hosted a number of Korean students, welcoming them into his home and school; he was convinced that a weak Korea made Japan even more vulnerable to Western attack and believed it was Japan's responsibility to protect East Asia and lead its neighbors to civilization.[38] Korean interest in attending school in Japan increased substantially after the Sino-Japanese War. Roughly 200 Korean students resided in Japan in 1897; ten years later their numbers had increased to approximately 500 and by 1909 to nearly 800.[39] Before Japan annexed Korea in 1910, the Chinese student population in Japan dwarfed the number of Korean students there. But by 1912, more than 3,000 Koreans were pursuing their educations in Japan.[40] Three decades later, the count of Koreans enrolled at Japanese colleges and universities had ballooned to 13,000, and the total number of Korean students at all levels to 30,000.[41] During the 1910s, the population of Korean students in Japan varied greatly depending on political conditions, but between the Great Kantō Earthquake (1923) and the end of World War Two it increased steadily, resulting in a significantly greater percentage of Koreans than Chinese receiving their educations in Japan. Although impressive, these figures represent only a small proportion of the total number of Koreans who lived in Japan during the colonial period, particularly after Japan mobilized for war in 1938.[42] In fact, the colonial period stimulated a diaspora of Koreans on a scale never before seen in that nation's history. Between the Japanese takeover of the peninsula in 1905 and Japan's defeat in 1945, millions of Koreans moved to China (especially Manchuria), Japan, Sakhalin, and the Siberian maritime provinces; in 1944, more than 10 percent of Koreans lived outside Korea.[43]

Gradually drawn to self-strengthening, Taiwanese began studying in Japan several decades after the first large influxes of Chinese
and Korean students. As was true for Koreans, Taiwanese found it
easier to gain admission to higher schools in Japan than to win one
of the few slots Japanese authorities reserved for them in schools at
home. Thus, many of Taiwan's brightest and most ambitious youths
sailed northeast for their educations; nearly half studied medicine,
with law also well represented.[44] Official statistics show only 60 Taiwanese enrolled in Japanese schools in 1908 and fewer than 400 in
1915. But by the 1920s, Taiwanese demand for higher education
soared, and the Japanese government relaxed restrictions on the
number of Taiwanese students permitted to travel to the metropole.
According to police estimates, in 1922 at least 2,400 Taiwanese were
attending school in Japan. In the following decade, this number
increased to more than 4,000, and by 1942 the count of Taiwanese
students in Japan surpassed 7,000.[45] As was true for Koreans, a significantly greater percentage of Taiwanese than Chinese received
their educations in Japan, primarily because of Taiwan's status as
Japan's colony. Japan also was attractive to students from Manchuria; while only 116 were sent to Japan in 1933, the number jumped to
1,214 sent in 1935 and to 1,844 in 1937, then dipped back to about 1,200
sent in 1939 and 1940. Like their counterparts from China, Korea,
and Taiwan, the majority pursued studies in medicine, engineering,
and commerce.[46]

Chinese, Korean, and Taiwanese intellectuals in Japan generally
lived in Tokyo, where they attended a wide variety of secondary and
postsecondary schools, but some also pursued their educations as
far from the capital as Japan's southernmost island of Kyushu, which
for centuries had been the gateway between Japan and East Asia.[47]
Some were self-financed while others received money from the Japanese government, but the majority were sponsored by organizations
at home. East Asian leaders believed Japan provided an irresistible
example of how to repel Western threats and become an independent modern state. Its geographical proximity, common intellectual
heritage and orthography, and proliferation of short-term courses of
study tailored specifically for foreign students made Japan a favored
destination. To be sure, Japan was not always the first choice. The
Chinese writer Tian Han (1898–1968) was one of many who made
no secret of their original dreams of living in Europe or the United
States.[48] China, in turn, was the first choice of a significant number

of Taiwanese students who ended up in Japan. Yet once in Japan, most Chinese, Koreans, and Taiwanese took advantage of the opportunities available there; some stayed for years, even marrying Japanese. The Japanese government adopted stringent policies to control "troublesome" foreign visitors, but it generally embraced Japan's position as contact nebula, in this case as educator and bridge between East Asia and the West, and encouraged the flow of Chinese, Korean, and Taiwanese students into the country.

Chinese, Korean, and Taiwanese students in Japan frequently were drawn to the metropole's many activist currents. They were joined by East Asians who went to Japan primarily for political reasons. Colonial and semicolonial activists created their own organizations in Japan, of which Sun Yat-sen's (1866–1925) Tongmenghui (Revolutionary Alliance, est. 1905) was one of the earliest and most significant; the Revolutionary Alliance, which received assistance from sympathetic Japanese, was China's first national revolutionary organization and played a major role in overthrowing the Qing dynasty in 1911.[49] Activists from across Asia additionally forged strong ties with their Japanese counterparts after 1905, becoming involved in the Japanese anarchist, socialist, communist, and feminist movements. Beginning in the 1900s, Chinese in Japan attended meetings sponsored by the Japan Socialist Party and maintained contacts with its leaders, including Abe Isoo (1865–1949), Katayama Sen (1859–1933), and Kōtoku Shūsui (1871–1911). Chinese were particularly impressed by the Marxist economist Kawakami Hajime (1879–1946), and many who played important roles in the early Chinese Communist Party — including Ai Siqi (1910–66), Chen Wangdao (1891–1977), Dong Biwu (1886–1975), Li Dazhao (1888–1927), and Zhou Enlai (1898–1976) — spent time in Japan and had at least limited contact with Japanese Marxists.[50]

Sought out by other radical foreigners as well as by Japanese revolutionaries, Koreans also participated in the Japanese socialist and communist movements, and leading Japanese communists all seem to have had loyal Korean disciples.[51] By 1933, a large segment of Japan's underground communist labor movement was made up of resident Koreans, who had an indelible impact on its activities.[52] In addition, Koreans in Japan provided one of the brightest sparks for the March First Movement of 1919. Inspired by American President Woodrow Wilson's call for self-determination of peoples as a goal of World War One (part of his January 1918 Fourteen Points), they issued a declaration insisting on Korean independence and convinced Korean activists at home to join in the struggle. Although the massive demonstrations that followed in Seoul and throughout Korea failed to liberate Korea from Japanese control, the nationalist movement expanded via the exiled Taehan Min-guk Imsi Chŏngbu (Provisional Government of the Republic of Korea), established in Shanghai in April 1919. Taiwanese in Japan were similarly committed to political action, creating a number of nationalist, socialist, communist, and anarchist groups and forming friendships and alliances with prominent Japanese activists.[53] At times, Chinese, Koreans, and Taiwanese in Japan together protested Japanese injustices and collaborated with visiting activists from India, the Philippines, and Vietnam.

Women formed only a small percentage of the Chinese, Korean, and Taiwanese intellectuals in Japan, but most participated in the same activities as their male counterparts. For instance, Yun Simdŏk (1897–1926), the first woman to receive a scholarship from the Korean governor-general to study music in Japan, moved to Tokyo in 1915, spent three years at Aoyama Gakuin (Aoyama Academy) studying Japanese, and then in April 1918 transferred to Tōkyō Ongaku Gakkō (Tokyo Music School). For the next five years she flourished as a singer in Tokyo; returning to Japan in July 1926 after a tumultuous three years in Korea and Manchuria, she rejuvenated her career in the metropole only to commit double suicide with her lover, the dramatist Kim Ujin (1897–1926), in August of that year.[54] On the other hand, although many colonial and semicolonial women were encouraged by Japan's burgeoning feminist movement and found models in Japanese reforms, some, including Mei Niang and Dan Di (1916–92) from occupied Manchuria, were disturbed by Japanese attitudes toward women and protested the continued lack of opportunities available to women in the Japanese empire. As Norman Smith has noted, "Despite propaganda that dictated ideals of submissive, obedient good wives and wise mothers, the most prolific Chinese women writers in Manchukuo raised their pens to denounce the state's patriarchal foundations."[55] But even those who urged their countrywomen to heed the late Meiji Japanese model of "good wives and wise mothers" (ryōsai kenbo) to strengthen their own nations went on to play major roles in expanding opportunities for disenfranchised groups across East Asia.[56] In this way, Japan, and Tokyo in particular, was similar to other metropoles—both a nebula of transnational political ferment and a source of contagion for revolutionary ideas, many of them directed against the imperial government.

Readerly Contact in Japan

The political activities of Chinese, Koreans, and Taiwanese in Japan contributed importantly to nationalist and progressive movements in their homelands, but their engagement with the arts was even more significant in suturing together fresh constructs of modernity for their respective societies. Hundreds of Chinese, Koreans, and Taiwanese studied dance, film, music, painting, and sculpture in Japan. Many went to the metropole to receive advanced training in these arts, while others were drawn in after arriving.[57] Western literature, readily accessible in Japanese translation, also captivated visiting intellectuals, many of whom read European and American novels, plays, poems, and short stories as quickly as they became available; a small number were so inspired that they began studying English, French, German, or Russian at one of Tokyo's many foreign-language schools. Yet Chinese, Korean, and Taiwanese involvement with the world of Japanese letters was even more significant. Chinese and Korean intellectuals living in Japan in the 1870s and 1880s—including the Chinese poets and editors Huang Zunxian (1848–1905), Yao Wendong (1852–1927), and Yu Yue (Yu Quyuan, 1821–1906)—were among the first to engage seriously with Japanese creative texts, writing commentaries and publishing anthologies. They focused almost entirely on *kanshi* (Chinese-language poetry by Japanese), but their work with Japanese literature paved the way for the thousands of early twentieth-century colonial and semicolonial students and other visitors who engaged with modern Japanese literature not long after their arrival in Japan. Diaries and essays by Chinese, Koreans, and Taiwanese who lived in Japan, including men and women who went on to become major writers, reveal conspicuous consumption of both Japanese and Western literatures throughout the colonial period on a scale unprecedented in the history of East Asia.

Chinese and Korean intellectuals who went to Japan in the 1890s were captivated by the Japanese political novel. This genre, associated with the Jiyū Minken Undō (Freedom and Popular Rights Movement), had flourished in Japan in the 1880s; it lost popularity among Japanese with the promulgation of the Meiji Constitution in 1889 and the first meeting of the Diet in 1890.[58] But colonial and semicolonial intellectuals soon became engrossed in more contemporary fare. Lu Xun, who lived in Japan between 1902 and 1909, was only one of many East Asian visitors to Japan who read the daily installments of serialized literary works in newspapers and purchased the ensuing books. His brother Zhou Zuoren noted, "Lu Xun got a subscription to the *Asahi shinbun* [Asahi Newspaper] so he could read Sōseki's new work *Gubijinsō* [The Poppy, 1907]; he bought the book soon after it came out."[59]

The Meiji literary giant Sōseki also was a favorite of Yi Kwangsu, who in his diary entry for December 31, 1909 reports having read *The Poppy* within the past year, as well as texts by Tokutomi Roka (1868–1927), Kinoshita Naoe (1869–1937), Shimazaki Tōson, and other Japanese writers; Yi Kwangsu mixes references to Japanese literature with those to texts by Lord Byron, Aleksandr Pushkin, Maxim Gorky, Leo Tolstoy, and other European writers.[60] Yi Kwangsu continued reading Japanese and other literatures voraciously even as he was working on *Mujŏng* (Heartless, 1917), acclaimed as Korea's first "modern novel." He also portrayed some of his characters as readers of Japanese literature who consciously emulated Japanese characters. For instance, Kim Kyŏng, a teacher who attended school in Tokyo and the protagonist of the autobiographical short story "Kim Kyŏng" (1915), is a devoted fan of Japanese and European literature and philosophy. The narrator includes an explicit onomastic allusion, remarking that Kim Kyŏng read Kinoshita's *Hi no hashira* (Pillar of Fire, 1904) in a single night, his heart "transforming into an ocean of scorching flames," and that this young man longs to be like the characters in *Pillar of Fire*, filled with bravery, morality, and love.[61]

Chinese, Koreans, and Taiwanese in Japan in the 1910s and 1920s demonstrated similar enthusiasm for Japanese and other literatures. The Korean poet Chu Yohan, who lived in Japan from 1912 to 1919, embraced Japanese poetry and Japanese translations of European poetry. In the postwar essay "*Ch'angjo* sidae ŭi mundan" (The Literary World of *Creation* Days, 1956), he summarizes earlier literary encounters:

When I was a third-year student [at Meiji Gakuin in Tokyo] I read poetry anthologies like the collected works of Byron (in Japanese translation), *Omoide* [Remembrances, 1911] (an early work by Kitahara Hakushū [1885–1942]), and the selected works of Meiji's early Romantic poets (like Shimazaki Tōson, Kanbara Ariake [1875–1952], and Doi Bansui [1871–1952]). . . . In my fourth and fifth years I came across for the first time the Japanese translations of French fin-de-siècle poets [in anthologies edited by Nagai Kafū (1879–1959), Yosano Tekkan (1873–1935), and Ueda Bin (1874–1916)].[62]

Chu Yohan's comments echo those of the Korean novelist and pioneer of Korean naturalism Yŏm Sangsŏp (1897–1963), who lived in

Japan from 1912 to 1920 and returned in 1926, aiming to join the Japanese literary establishment. In his postwar essay "Munhak so-nyŏn sidae ŭi hoesang" (Reminiscences on a Literary Youth, 1955), Yŏm Sangsŏp notes that he read Tokutomi Roka's famous novel *Hototogisu* (The Cuckoo, 1899) even before studying the Korean classic *Ch'unhyang chŏn* (The Tale of Spring Fragrance); while in Japan he also read the bulk of Sōseki's and the critic Takayama Chogyū's (1871–1902) writings, as well as Japanese poetry and fiction by Japanese naturalists, who were then in their heyday.[63] A fiction enthusiast, the Chinese writer Yu Dafu, who lived in Japan at the same time as Chu Yohan and Yŏm Sangsŏp, claims that during his four years in high school he read approximately a thousand novels and short stories from Russia, Germany, England, Japan, and France.[64] Likewise, the Chinese playwright Tian Han, who lived in Japan from 1916 to 1922, spent his free time browsing Tokyo bookstores, purchasing texts by the Japanese writers Akita Ujaku and Kunikida Doppo, the European playwrights Henrik Ibsen and William Shakespeare, and many others;[65] the Japanese novelist Muramatsu Shōfū (1889–1961) visited Tian Han in Shanghai shortly after the latter's return to China and noted that his bookshelves were "filled with English novels and Japanese literature."[66] Tian Han also enjoyed Tokyo's lively film culture, watching more than a hundred Japanese and Western movies during his stay. Japanese literature was no less appealing for Taiwanese like Zhang Shenqie (1904–65), a central figure in Taiwanese drama who lived in Japan from 1917 to 1923. As Zhang Shenqie reminisced in 1935, "the works of Japanese literature that most stimulated us back then were [Ozaki Kōyō's novel] *Konjiki yasha* [Gold Demon, 1897–1903] and [Tokutomi Roka's] *The Cuckoo*." He also indicated that he and other exchange students were excited by the oeuvre of Tokuda Shūsei (1871–1943), Arishima Takeo, and Natsume Sōseki.[67]

Colonial and semicolonial passion for Japanese and other literatures, particularly among creative writers living in the metropole, remained strong during the 1930s and 1940s. In his diary, the Taiwanese writer Lü Heruo, who lived in Japan from 1939 to 1942, includes dozens of references to reading foreign (non-Chinese/Taiwanese) novels and watching foreign plays and movies. In the first months of 1942 alone, he read texts and saw plays by Japanese writers and dramatists such as Hayashi Fumiko (1904–51), Kishida Kunio (1890–1954), Mafune Yutaka (1902–77), Muroo Saisei (1889–1962), and Tanizaki Jun'ichirō (1886–1965); he also watched Japanese films, read numerous

Japanese translations of European literature, and frequently attended Japanese productions of European dramas.[68] Like most colonial and semicolonial intellectuals who engaged with Japanese literature while in Japan, he continued reading this corpus after returning home.

Colonial and semicolonial readers embraced Japanese literature even during the final years of the colonial period, when Japanese oppression was at its most severe. Remarkably, some Koreans read Taishō Japan's preeminent short-story writer Akutagawa Ryūnosuke's stories by candlelight well into the 1940s,[69] while others found solace in the proletarian poetry of Nakano Shigeharu (1902–79) as American bombs rained down on Tokyo.[70] Some, including the Taiwanese writer Yang Kui (1905–85) in the short story "Zōsan no kage ni: nonki na jiisan no hanashi" (Behind Increased Production: The Tale of an Easygoing Old Man, 1944), also continued portraying characters who read Japanese literature. This voluntary, indeed eager colonial and semicolonial consumption of Japanese literature is remarkable, particularly considering East Asian peoples' historical spurning of Japanese creative products, and the stringent cultural, economic, military, and political policies Japan imposed on China and the colonies throughout the early twentieth century. Even more significant are the writerly contacts that intersected with this consumption, networks that provide further valuable insights into transcultural interaction in contact nebulae and more generally into the dynamics of empire.

Writerly Contact in Japan

Inspired in part by Japan's vibrant creative world, Chinese, Koreans, and Taiwanese in Japan not only eagerly consumed Japanese and other literatures but also formed a number of literary organizations, primarily along national lines. Among the most influential were the innovative Korean Ch'angjohoe (Creation Society, est. 1919) and Chinese Chuangzaoshe (Creation Society, est. 1921), whose members became dominant voices in modern Korean and Chinese literatures.[71] The latter group did not explicitly acknowledge the Korean Creation Society as its inspiration, but doubtless the choice of name was not coincidental. The founders of the Korean Creation Society, whose journal *Ch'angjo* (Creation) was Korea's first literary periodical, hoped to divert the course of their nation's literature away from the didacticism of writers such as Yi Kwangsu. Similarly, the leaders of the Chinese Creation Society called for "art for art's sake" and "literature for self-expression." Taiwanese in Japan also organized a number of arts societies, of which the Taiwan Yishu Yanjiuhui (Society for the Study of Taiwanese Art), reorganized by Taiwanese students in Tokyo in March 1933, was one of the most prominent. Members of this group, products of the colonial educational system and resentful of Japanese imperialism, called for a literature that would better serve the Taiwanese. The group's leaders—Wu Kunhuang (1909–89) and Zhang Wenhuan (1909–78)—writing in the first issue of their journal *Formosa* (July 1933), encouraged young Taiwanese to take responsibility for developing their own culture: "Taiwanese youth! To make our lives freer and richer we have to begin the Taiwanese literary movement with our own young hands."[72] The difficulties inherent in beginning a "Taiwanese" literature movement in Japan, not to mention in the Japanese language, were daunting. Yet launching such a movement in Taiwan under the close supervision of Japanese colonial authorities would have been even more challenging. Despite numerous hurdles, young colonial and semicolonial writers in Japan played a major role in laying the foundations for modern Chinese, Korean, and Taiwanese literatures.

Colonial and semicolonial writers living in Japan had many forums in which to circulate their work. They used not only periodicals based in their homelands but also those produced in Japan by Chinese, Korean, and Taiwanese cultural and political associations, smaller groups of friends, and enterprising individuals. These journals, whether devoted to literature or covering a wider range of topics, combined the creative output of Japan's East Asian visitors with work by their counterparts at home and frequently the works of Japanese and Western writers, often in translation. For instance, the inaugural issue of the Korean-language journal *Yesul undong* (Arts Movement, 1927), the mouthpiece of the Tokyo branch of the Korean Proletarian Arts League (abbreviated as KAPF, for the Esperanto name Korea Artista Proletaria Federacio), carried an essay by the Japanese proletarian writer Nakano Shigeharu, the leading poet and principal organizer of the Japanese prewar revolutionary literary movement. Many periodicals were short-lived, some disbanding within a few months or even after a single issue, yet they testify to the great energy and initiative of Chinese, Koreans, and Taiwanese in Japan. In fact, in the first years of the twentieth century, Chinese writers founded about as many journals in Japan as they did in China.[73] These journals and their successors helped launch the careers of some of early twentieth-century East Asia's literary giants.

Colonial and semicolonial literary organizations and journals based in Japan provided obvious forums for writers to socialize, discuss literature and politics, and publish their creative work. For the most part, Chinese, Koreans, and Taiwanese did so in isolation from one another; more inter-colonial/semicolonial literary relationships appear to have been forged outside Japan than blossomed inside its borders. But a good number of visiting East Asians enjoyed close ties with their Japanese counterparts, establishing friendships, participating in the activities of Japanese literary societies, and publishing in Japanese periodicals. On the surface, at least, this writerly contact (and the readerly contact with which it was closely related) allowed colonial and semicolonial writers to gain significant footing in the Japanese literary world. Large numbers of Chinese, Koreans, and Taiwanese in active dialogue with Japanese writers and the broad scope of their mutual interchanges mask dark undercurrents of Japanese prejudice, exclusivism, and the frequent refusal to believe colonial and semicolonial writers capable of holding their own on the world or even the imperial literary stage. On the other hand, it is important to remember that, like groups everywhere, most Japanese literary coteries were inherently selective and regularly rebuffed most homegrown talent as well. In this way, the experiences of colonial and semicolonial writers in Japan resembled those of many Japanese writers, particularly women, minorities, and those from outside the nation's power centers.

Theater formed an early locus of Sino-Japanese literary interchange. In 1907, Chinese students in Japan — including Li Shutong (1880–1942) and Ouyang Yuqian (1889–1962) — created the Chunliushe (Spring Willow Society), China's first modern drama troupe. Lu Jingruo (1885–1915), who joined the group the following year and served as its leader in Tokyo and then in Shanghai, was formally trained in both *shinpa* (new school drama) and *shingeki* (new drama). Some of Japan's most celebrated dramatists, including Fujisawa Asajirō (1866–1917), assisted Lu Jingruo and other members of this society from its earliest days. The Spring Willow Society and its successors performed a broad spectrum of Chinese, Japanese, and Western plays in both the Chinese and Japanese languages for audiences that included Chinese, Korean, Taiwanese, and Japanese aficionados. Chinese left-wing drama troupes in Tokyo also found many supporters among Japanese writers. In April 1935, the Zhonghua Huaju Tonghaohui (Chinese Drama Friendship Association) performed Chinese playwright Cao Yu's celebrated *Leiyu* (Thunderstorm, 1934) to rave reviews. Kageyama Saburō (1911–92), a member of the Teidai Engeki Kenkyūkai (Imperial University Drama Research Society), was particularly excited by the Chinese performance. He not only published an enthusiastic evaluation but also played the lead role in *Thunderstorm* the second time it was staged in Japan and helped translate this masterpiece into Japanese.[74] The eminent Japanese writer and theater figure Akita Ujaku was another great admirer and promoter of Chinese progressive theater. As the Chinese dramatist Du Xuan (1914–2004), who studied in Tokyo between 1933 and 1937, noted, "Akita actively helped and supported the activities of Chinese students in Japan and granted all our requests."[75]

Cao Yu's *Thunderstorm* and *Sunrise* were the most popular Chinese plays performed in Japan, but Tian Han was by far the best-connected Chinese theater figure there. He arrived in Japan in the fall of 1916 at the age of eighteen, began reading Japanese literature the following year, and attended lectures by the Japanese playwrights Okamoto Kidō (1872–1939) and Osanai Kaoru (1881–1928). His involvement with Japanese theater figures, including Akita Ujaku and Kikuchi Kan, only deepened with time. Tian Han also was one of the first Chinese to befriend a number of Japan's principal essayists, poets, and prose writers, including Satō Haruo (1892–1964), Satomi Ton (1888–1983), and Kume Masao (1891–1952). Describing his October 16, 1921 visit with Satō, he wrote: "We talked about Chinese legends, the Chinese translation and creative worlds, the big names in Japanese Meiji and Taishō literature, theater, and poetry, and introducing Japanese literature [to China]."[76] The two connected instantly. Tian Han returned to China the following year but kept in close contact with the friends he had made in Japan and got together with them when they visited his homeland.

Interactions between Chinese poets and prose writers living in Japan and their Japanese counterparts blossomed in the 1920s. Yu Dafu was particularly close to Satō Haruo, to whom he was introduced by Tian Han. The two remained friends until 1938, when Satō wrote the offensive story "Ajia no ko" (Child of Asia), which portrays Yu Dafu and Guo Moruo as cowardly and devious.[77] Despite growing hostilities between their two governments, many Chinese and Japanese writers in Japan — particularly those involved in revolutionary literary movements—increased their interactions throughout the 1920s and early 1930s. The Chinese revolutionary writer Xia Yan (1900–95) went to Japan in 1928 and became good friends with the progressive Japanese writer Fujimori Seikichi (1892–1977), some of whose works he translated into Chinese; the Chinese revolutionary writer Jiang Guangci (1901–31) went to Japan the following year and befriended the Japanese proletarian literary critic Kurahara Korehito (1902–91). Hu Feng (1903–85) also arrived in Japan in 1929 and took an almost immediate interest in the Japanese proletarian literary scene. His memoirs include numerous references to interactions with Japanese writers, some of whom were curious about the contemporary Chinese literary world. At one point, he comments that at a gathering at the home of the novelist and critic Eguchi Kan (1887–1975) he "was asked to introduce Chinese literary movements" to such Japanese cultural luminaries as Eguchi, Kobayashi Takiji (1903–33), and Ōya Sōichi (1900–70).[78] In the late 1930s and early 1940s, Chinese writers from occupied Manchuria established similar contacts with sympathetic Japanese peers in the metropole, some of whom even financed their activities,[79] but most interactions between Japanese writers and Chinese from occupied Manchuria took place in Japan's informal colony.

In addition to creating personal bonds with Japanese writers while in Japan, some Chinese writers published their creative works in Japanese literary journals, often in translation but occasionally— as in the case of the poets Huang Ying (1906–2005) and Lei Shiyu (1911–96)—in the original Japanese.[80] Huang Ying, son of a Chinese father and Japanese mother, began writing poetry while in middle school in Japan, and although he returned to China with his family after the 1923 Great Kantō Earthquake, he continued writing in Japanese and submitting his poetry to periodicals in China and Japan. He jumped from obscurity to fame in 1925, when his work caught the eye of the eminent Japanese poets Hagiwara Sakutarō (1886–1942) and Senge Motomaro (1888–1948); they honored him with first place in a contest sponsored by *Nihon shijin* (Japan Poet), a leading journal. Huang's poems appeared in *Japan Poet* and other Japanese periodicals, including the *Asahi shinbun*, and he wrote clandestinely in Japanese long after Japan's defeat.[81]

Lei Shiyu went to Japan in the early 1930s to study economics but soon began writing poetry in Japanese. His verse caught the attention of Arai Tetsu (1899–1944), editor of the Japanese proletarian literary magazine *Shi seishin* (Poetry Spirit), who printed some of his poems. Lei Shiyu's verse also appeared in the Japanese journals *Bunka shūdan* (Culture Group), *Shijin* (Poets), *Shijin taimuzu* (Poets' Times), *Bungaku annai* (Literary Guide), *Shijin jidai* (Poets' Age), and *Bungei* (Literary Arts), a remarkable array of publications.[82] In his essay "Wo zai Riben canjia zuoyi shige yundong de rizi" (My Days Participating in the Japanese Proletarian Poetry Movement, 1982), Lei Shiyu describes socializing and discussing the arts with myriad Japanese writers:

> After joining the Japanese left-wing proletarian poetry movement, I chatted with lots of folks over tea and participated in a bunch of informal discussions, and not just with poets. I talked with literary critics (like Moriyama Kei [1904–91]) . . . novelists (like Fujimori Seikichi and Tokunaga Sunao [1899–1958]), dramatists like Akita Ujaku . . . [and] the writer of fairy tales Makimoto Kusurō [1898–1956].[83]

Sabaku no uta (Song of the Desert, 1935), Lei Shiyu's first collection of poetry, was only the second Japanese-language poetry collection published by a Chinese writer, and it received high accolades from the Japanese literary establishment. In the preface to *Song of the Desert*, the Japanese writer Onchi Terutake (1901–67) calls Lei Shiyu a "promising progressive young poet"; he comments that Lei Shiyu's work has much to teach Japanese writers and that he looks forward to his Chinese colleague's continued participation in the Japanese poetry world.[84]

Japanese-language instruction was a staple of Korean education after annexation in 1910, so unlike their Chinese counterparts, many Korean intellectuals already were somewhat fluent in Japanese when they arrived in Japan. This facilitated communication between the Korean and Japanese literary worlds, which developed slowly in the 1910s, then snowballed in the 1920s and 1930s. The first major Korean writer to establish ties with Japanese counterparts and publish in Japanese journals was the poet Chu Yohan. In 1913, just a year after arriving in Japan, Chu Yohan began writing for Meiji Gakuin's journal *Hakkin gakuhō* (Platinum Bulletin), for which he also served as an editor. Like many colonial Korean writers, he composed his first published creative works in Japanese, not Korean.

Chu Yohan's work appeared in a number of Japanese literary journals in the 1910s, including *Bungei zasshi* (Literary Magazine), *Bungei sekai* (Literary World), *Bansō* (Accompaniment), and *Gendai shiika* (Modern Poetry); the inclusion of his writing in so many Japanese journals was truly impressive for a Korean writer at this time.[85]

Chu Yohan developed friendships with several Japanese writers and was particularly close to Kawaji Ryūkō (1888–1959), in whose group Shokō Shisha (Dawn Poetry Society) he participated. He once commented, "I grew close to Kawaji Ryūkō so was treated as a colleague in his journals, including *Modern Poetry* and *Akebono* [Dawn], and I continued to experiment with writing poems in Japanese."[86] Chu Yohan's experiments were fruitful; he was unquestionably the most successful Korean poet on the Japanese literary scene during the 1910s.

As was the case with Sino-Japanese literary friendships, Korean-Japanese literary relationships grew substantially in the following decades. The spread of Marxist-Leninist thought in the 1920s and 1930s greatly accelerated cross-cultural intellectual discourse. Although often critical of Korean revolutionary writers for being overly concerned with Korean independence, Japanese leftists encouraged many of them, including Kim Kijin (1903–85), who became one of the central figures of the Korean proletarian literary movement. Kim Kijin later wrote that he spent March 1920 to December 1921 living in Japan as the stereotypical literary youth, with Baudelaire in one hand and a drink in the other. But he supposedly was so moved by the Japanese critic Komaki Ōmi's (1894–1978) proletarian journal *Tane maku hito* (The Sower), which began its Tokyo run in October 1921, that he immediately abandoned his decadent lifestyle. At that point, Kim Kijin sought advice from Asō Hisashi (1891–1940) and Nakanishi Inosuke (1887–1958), both socialist writers affiliated with *The Sower*. He later recalled that his real hope in the 1920s had been "to make our journal *Paekjo* [White Tide] a Korean version of *The Sower*."[87] In fact, Asō Hisashi, Nakanishi Inosuke, and Yuasa Katsue (1910–82), who grew up in Korea and went to Japan in 1929 to attend Waseda University, helped numerous Koreans launch their careers. Few Japanese writers were as popular with Koreans in Japan as Nakano Shigeharu, who wrote extensively on Korea and like many Japanese proletarian figures generally was sympathetic to the plight of the colony. The Korean writers and activists Im Hwa (1908–53), Kim Duyong (1902–?), Kim Hoyŏng, Kim Namch'ŏn (1911–53), Kim Samgyu (1908–89), and Yi Pukman (1907–59) all developed close friendships with Nakano, as did a number of Korean theater figures who met Nakano through his actress wife.

Korean writers of all genres began publishing in Japanese journals in greater numbers in the 1920s, increasingly making these periodicals active contact nebulae. The modernist poet Chŏng Chiyong (1903–?), who lived in Japan from 1923 to 1929, received a degree in English from Dōshisha University in Kyoto and published his work in several Japanese journals, including *Fūkei* (Scenery), edited by the leading Japanese poet Kitahara Hakushū.[88] Korean proletarian writers enjoyed similar success. Chŏng Yŏn-gyu's story "Kessen no zen'ya" (Night before the Bloody Battle), which appeared in Aono Suekichi (1890–1961) and Nakanishi Inosuke's journal *Geijutsu sensen* (Arts Front) in 1922, was one of the first Japanese-language prose works published by a Korean in a mainstream Japanese journal. A trickle of Japanese-language creative texts by colonial Koreans followed, including a poem by Kim Hŭimyŏng in *Bungei sensen* (Literary Front) in 1925, a short story by Han Sik (1907–?) in *Puroretaria geijutsu* (Proletarian Arts) in 1927, and a poem by Kang Munsŏk in *Senki* (Battle Flag) two years later. These and other literary works by Koreans in Japan not only condemned Japanese colonial oppression but also expressed solidarity with the Japanese proletarian literary movement.[89] In addition to creative texts, Korean writers also published essays in Japanese proletarian literary journals. They introduced the Korean proletarian movement to Japanese readers, expressing solidarity with the Japanese proletarian movement while at the same time highlighting Japanese injustices against Korea. For instance, "Chōsen no geijutsu undō: Chōsen ni chūmoku seyo" (The Korean Arts Movement: Let's Focus on Korea, 1927), the first of Yi Pukman's five articles in Nakano's *Proletarian Arts*, discusses both the Korean proletarian literary movement and Japanese oppression.

The Korean and Japanese literary worlds became further intertwined during the 1930s and 1940s. Koreans published Japanese-language translations of American and European literature in a variety of Japanese periodicals.[90] Major Japanese journals such as *Kaizō* (Reconstruction), *Bungei shuto* (Literary Metropolis), *Bungei annai* (Literary Information), *Bungaku hyōron* (Literature Criticism), and *Bungei* (Literary Arts) all carried Japanese-language texts by Korean writers; several Japanese magazines published special issues devoted to Korea which included a sampling of Korean literary works.[91] Creative texts by Chang Hyŏkju and Kim Saryang (1914–50), two of Korea's most active Japanese-language writers, appeared in Japanese periodicals and on Japanese bookshelves with particular frequency at this time. The interactions of these figures with the Japanese literary world are a microcosm of the readerly and writerly contacts that flourished throughout the Japanese empire.

Chang Hyŏkju made his debut in the Japanese literary world in 1930 with the assistance of the Japanese poet and critic Katō Kazuo (1887–1951), editor of the journal *Daichi ni tatsu* (Standing on the Earth). Over the next few years, Chang Hyŏkju befriended numerous Japanese literary figures, including Eguchi Kan, Kikuchi Kan, Ōya Sōichi, and Hayashi Fusao (1903–75). In 1932, he joined the staff of *Literary Metropolis*, managed by the novelist Yasutaka Tokuzō (1889–1971), and in 1933, he won a prestigious *Reconstruction* prize for his story "Gakidō" (Hell of Hungry Spirits, 1932). "Hell of Hungry Spirits" exposes the exploitation of Korean workers and the upheaval of Korean society under Japanese colonial rule; the story captivated critics with its depictions of ethnic agony. In addition, its many *katakana* glosses, which provide Korean translations and pronunciations, introduce Japanese readers to the Korean language just as much as they assist Koreans reading Japanese.[92]

Throughout the 1930s, Chang Hyŏkju wrote in both Japanese and Korean, publishing in Japanese and Korean periodicals. He simultaneously serialized stories in the Korean newspapers *Tong-a ilbo* (East Asia Daily) and *Mae-il sinbo* (Daily News) and published in the Japanese journals *Reconstruction, Literary Metropolis, Literary Information, Bungei hyōron* (Literary Review), *Literary Arts, Shinchō* (New Tide), and *Chūō kōron* (Central Review) — an impressive lineup for a writer of any nationality, particularly a colonial Korean. Furthermore, during the 1930s and early 1940s, Japanese publishers including Kawade Shobō and Kaizōsha printed his Japanese-language works as individual volumes. Like Chang Hyŏkju, Kim Saryang also published widely in Japanese and Korean periodicals.[93] He arrived in Japan in 1932, majored in German literature at Tokyo Imperial University, and in 1936 formed the Japanese-language journal *Teibō* (Embankment) with some Korean and Japanese friends. Kim Saryang became the first Korean nominated for the esteemed Akutagawa Prize (the successor of the *Reconstruction* prize) for his story "Hikari no naka ni" (In the Light), which describes the brutality of Japanese assimilation policies and the grueling lives of Koreans in Japan and was published in the October 1939 issue of *Literary Metropolis*.

Japanese literary figures similarly encouraged the many Koreans who translated Korean-language texts into Japanese. Kim Soun (1907–81), one of the principal translators of Korean folklore and poetry, enjoyed particularly close ties with Japanese intellectuals, some of whom — including Shimazaki Tōson, Satō Haruo, Takamura Kōtarō

(1883–1956), Fujishima Takeji (1867–1943), and Munakata Shikō (1903–75) — wrote prefaces for his manuscripts. It is said that in 1928, at the age of 20, he brought a manuscript of translated Korean folksongs to the Japanese poet Kitahara Hakushū, who was so impressed that he threw a party in Kim Soun's honor. The following year, the Japanese publisher Taibunkan published Kim Soun's *Chōsen min'yōshū* (Collection of Korean Folksongs, 1929). This volume, and the many that followed, received strong endorsements not only from literary figures but also from intellectuals from a variety of disciplines such as the folklorist Yanagita Kunio (1875–1962), the lexicographer Shinmura Izuru (1876–1967), the composer Yamada Kōsaku (1886–1965), the painter Kishida Ryūsei (1891–1929), and the folklorist and scholar of Japanese literature Origuchi Shinobu (1887–1953).[94]

Like their Chinese counterparts, Korean and Taiwanese dramatists also quickly discovered a niche in Japan, creating troupes and working closely with Japanese theater figures. Yi Injik (1862–1916), Korea's first "new fiction writer" and "new playwright," frequently attended the theater while a student at Tōkyō Seiji Gakkō (Tokyo School of Politics) between 1900 and 1904; he studied Japanese *shinpa* in the Asakusa district of Tokyo on his return to Japan in 1908.[95] Yun Kyo-jung (1886–1954), a founder of the noted Korean drama group Munsu-sŏng, studied at the Japanese writer and critic Shimamura Hōgetsu's (1871–1918) Geijutsuza (Art Theater) while attending classes at the Tōkyō Shōka Gakkō (Tokyo Commercial School, now Hitotsubashi University). In 1923, Koreans in Tokyo including Pak Sŭnghoe (1901–64), Kim Pokjin (1901–41), and Kim Kijin formed the T'owŏlhoe (Earth-Moon Society), a group that performed original works and adaptations of foreign plays and until the mid-1930s was Korea's most prominent theater company. Similarly, while in Japan, Lin Boqiu (1920–98), Zhang Shenqie, Zhang Weixian (1905–77), and other pioneers of modern Taiwanese drama studied theater, formed troupes, and performed plays of many origins, including Japanese; the first theatrical performance by Taiwanese in Japan took place in 1919, more than a decade after the Spring Willow Society launched Chinese theater there.[96] Japan-based Taiwanese playwrights and performers were assisted by such prominent Japanese theater figures as Akita Ujaku and Murayama Tomoyoshi (1901–77) and established ties with Japanese and Chinese theater groups, with whom they frequently put on joint performances. For instance, in 1919, when Taiwanese students in Tokyo performed a dramatized version of Japanese editor and novelist Ozaki Kōyō's bestseller *Gold Demon*, the Chinese theater leaders Tian Han and Ouyang Yuqian helped with makeup and staging.

The close ties between Taiwanese and Japanese poets and prose writers were equally striking. The poet and composer Jiang Wenye went to Japan in 1923 to study electrical engineering but soon became engrossed in the arts and forged close ties with the writer Shimazaki Tōson (his Japanese-language teacher) and the leading conductor and composer Yamada Kōsaku. In addition to participating in Sasaki Takamaru's (1898–1968) revolutionary-drama study society, Yang Kui, who first went to Japan in the 1920s, became friends with Japanese proletarian writers such as Akita Ujaku, Hayama Yoshiki (1894–1945), and Nakano Shigeharu.[97] In addition, he enjoyed a warm relationship with Kishi Yamaji (1899–1973), the editor of *Literary Information*. Lü Heruo, in Japan in the late 1930s and early 1940s, similarly counted many Japanese writers and other artists, including musicians, among his companions. He studied vocal music at Shimoyagawa Keisuke's vocal music center and at Tokyo Seisen Ongaku Gakkō (Tokyo Vocal Music School) under Nagasaka Yoshiko (1891–1970), and also served as an editor for the publishing company Ōbunsha and then as part of a vocal group of the Tōhō Kokumingeki (Tōhō People's Theater).[98] For his part, Wu Yongfu (1913–2008), who lived in Japan from 1929 to 1935, studied with the modernist writer Yokomitsu Riichi (1898–1947) and the critic Kobayashi Hideo (1902–83) at Meiji Daigaku (Meiji University).[99] Even Taiwanese with limited Japan experience became close with leading Japanese cultural figures. On his brief visits to Japan, the Taiwanese writer and editor Zhang Wojun (1902–55), who was educated in China, became friends with the editors of *Central Review* and a number of Japanese proletarian artists; he also received advice and encouragement from several of the Japanese novelists and playwrights whose works he translated, including Mushakōji Saneatsu (1885–1976) and Shimazaki Tōson.

These and other networks led to the frequent appearance of Taiwanese writers in Japanese periodicals. The avant-garde writers Lin Yongxiu (1914–44) and Yang Chichang (1908–94), who lived in Japan in the late 1920s and early 1930s, published their work in Japanese poetry journals such as Momota Sōji's (1893–1955) *Shii no ki* (The Chinquapin Tree), *Shigaku* (Poetics), Kitasono Katsue's (1902–78) *Kōbe shijin* (The Kobe Poet), and literary magazines including *Mita bungaku* (Mita Literature).[100] Zhang Wenhuan and Wu Kunhuang also published some of their poetry in the Japanese proletarian journals *Shiika* (Poetry) and *Shi seishin* (Poetry Spirit); Zhang Wenhuan additionally developed ties with writers and editors of *Central Review*. Taiwanese prose writers — particularly Yang Kui and Long Yingzong (1911–99) — enjoyed even more publicity. Yang Kui was best known in Japan for "Shinbun haitatsufu" (The Paperboy, 1934), a short story on the trials of a young Taiwanese man trying to make his way in Japan, which won second place in a *Literature Criticism* competition. But he also published a variety of essays on Taiwanese literature and other subjects in *Literature Criticism*, fiction, essays, and translations in *Literary Guide*, and additional work in *Nihon gakugei shinbun* (Japan Arts Newspaper); in 1941, he joined the staff of *Literary Metropolis*. Long Yingzong's "Papaiya no aru machi" (Town of Papayas), a short story about the sharp disparities between the lives of Taiwanese and Japanese in Taiwan, found a home in *Reconstruction* in 1937 and won that journal's literary prize. Like Yang Kui, Long Yingzong continued to write for Japanese journals such as *Reconstruction, Literary Arts*, and *Literary Metropolis*, and his work soon appeared more frequently in Japanese periodicals than that of any other Taiwanese writer.

Friendships between colonial and semicolonial writers and their Japanese counterparts continued to blossom long after initial sojourns in Japan. Texts by Chinese, Korean, and Taiwanese literary artists who had returned home remained a staple of Japanese periodicals. Furthermore, many colonial and semicolonial writers made second and third trips to Japan, renewing friendships and forging new relationships. On a two-week visit to Japan in July 1927, five years after returning home from his first trip there, Tian Han not only saw old literary pals but also made the acquaintance of several more Japanese writers, including the poet Noguchi Yonejirō (1875–1947). Another important example of new ties in Japan is Zhou Zuoren's relationship with members of the elite White Birch Society (founded 1910), and particularly its leader, the writer Mushakōji Saneatsu. Zhou Zuoren returned to China in 1911 after six years in Japan, but he continued his subscription to *Shirakaba* (White Birch) and exchanged letters with Mushakōji. He was particularly intrigued by Mushakōji's depiction of his utopian socialist Atarashiki Mura (New Village) movement, established in 1918. Zhou Zuoren returned to Japan in 1919 to meet Mushakōji and examine the New Village for himself; he was well impressed with its emphasis on humanism and mutual assistance. Years after their initial encounter, Mushakōji commented simply: "I'm always impressed when I see him [Zhou Zuoren]. . . . The other day Shimazaki Tōson invited Zhou Zuoren, me, and a few others to dinner, and I had the same warm feelings as before."[101] Not surprisingly, Zhou Zuoren's subsequent anthologies of Japanese literature in translation included a disproportionate number of White Birch Society writers. Over the years, he wove ties with a number of other Japanese writers and intellectuals, and by his 1934 trip to Japan he was well known in Japanese cultural circles. In honor of his visit, the Japanese press publicized his accomplishments, as did such well-known Japanese literary figures as Mushakōji, Tanizaki Jun'ichirō, Horiguchi Daigaku (1892–1981), and Satō Haruo at various points in their careers.

Without question, the Chinese, Japanese, Korean, and Taiwanese literary worlds grew entangled to an unprecedented degree in early twentieth-century Japan. For the first time, large numbers of China's, Korea's, and Taiwan's leading playwrights, poets, and prose writers had significant experience in Japan, where they established friendships with their Japanese counterparts, joined their literary societies, and published in their journals. Clearly, the modern Chinese, Japanese, Korean, and Taiwanese literary worlds can no longer be regarded as separate spheres, distinct from one another; instead, their mutual interactions created unprecedented nebulae of readerly and writerly contacts driven largely by powerful appetites for one another's creative output. But at the same time that they obfuscated the lines among metropole, colony, and semicolony, literary collaborations also accentuated difference. Although seldom defined completely by the metropole/colonial or metropole/semicolonial divide, many intra–East Asian relationships in Japan were fraught with paradox, as visiting writers—like their counterparts in other fields—struggled to be respected simply as professionals, not as colonial/semicolonial professionals.

Ambivalent Moderns

The experiences of Chinese, Koreans, and Taiwanese in Japan were predictably varied. Japan was a stimulating place filled with exciting cultural and educational opportunities unavailable at home. The Taiwanese writer Wu Kunhuang, who studied at Nihon and Meiji Universities and worked closely with Japanese writers and theater figures, remarked in 1935: "Aren't we happy, those of us in Tokyo? Here we can study all sorts of things. So we absorb all kinds of knowledge. We make it our flesh, we make it our bones, and we have to take it back with us to Taiwan. I especially feel this responsibility."[102] The dedication and achievements of Chinese, Korean, and Taiwanese visitors often shattered ethnic stereotypes, at least among intellectuals.[103] Many colonial and semicolonial writers were treated with greater respect by Japanese in Japan than by the Japanese occupying their homelands.

Japanese writers and other artists frequently became supporters and even vocal cheerleaders for their colonial and semicolonial counterparts. In the essay "Nihon Puroretaria Geijutsu Renmei ni tsuite" (On the Japanese Proletarian Arts League, 1927), published in the first issue of the Korean revolutionary journal *Arts Movement*, Nakano Shigeharu speaks of the Japanese proletarian literary movement as welcoming Koreans with open arms.[104] Likewise, in his preface to Kim Soun's first anthology of modern Korean poetry in Japanese translation, *Nyūshoku no kumo* (Milkwhite Clouds, 1940), Satō Haruo applauds Korea's long tradition of cultural brilliance, even if this eminence stems from "elegantly digesting Chinese culture"; he speaks of preparing seats for Korean poets in the Japanese poetry world and of learning from his Korean colleagues.[105] So it is not surprising that some colonial and semicolonial writers spoke longingly of Japan and that Japanese writers lapped up such remarks. In his 1923 China travelogue "Fushigi na miyako 'Shanhai'" (The Strange City "Shanghai"), Muramatsu Shōfū reveals Tian Han's continuing warm feelings for the metropole, claiming that his Chinese friend told him, "I consider Tokyo my second home so [I] really miss it. . . . [My wife] also really misses Tokyo."[106] Asserting an even stronger attachment to the metropole, the Korean writer Chang Hyŏkju on several occasions claimed that he could not bear to be away from Tokyo. Many Koreans and other colonial/semicolonial intellectuals declared the metropolis a relative "heaven" compared with the "hell" of their homelands.[107]

Yet the reality is that many Japanese openly scorned their East Asian neighbors and ridiculed visitors and émigrés to Japan. Japanese feelings toward the Chinese following the Sino-Japanese War resembled their attitudes toward Koreans and Taiwanese. As Marius Jansen has noted:

The war precipitated an outburst of chauvinism and self-pride that was expressed as scorn for China . . . China and the Chinese were pilloried in popular press and song as the epitome of weakness, selfishness, inefficiency, disorganization, and cowardice. . . . The twentieth century thus opened with a dramatically new view of China in Meiji Japan. If the Meiji period began with governmental warnings that Westerners were worthy of being treated with the dignity accorded the Chinese, the twentieth century found the government even more hard pressed to assert the opposite side of the case.[108]

Even the name used by many Japanese to refer to China—Shina, as opposed to Chūgoku—proved offensive.

Circumstances only worsened as Japan continued its encroachment on Asia. In his May 31, 1917 diary entry, Yu Dafu mentions being taunted by Japanese for coming from a "weak country."[109] Xie Bingying describes Honma Hisao (1886–1981), a prominent Japanese scholar of English literature at Waseda University, as particularly courteous toward Chinese students. But she also paints life in Tokyo as torment. Describing an incident not long after the 1931 Japanese takeover of Mukden (Shenyang) in northeastern China, she remarks:

One morning, about a month after arriving in Tokyo, Wang and I were walking along a quiet lane lined with bamboo hedges when we saw three seven- or eight-year-old kids up ahead playing with marbles. When the boys saw us coming, they called, "Chinese, slaves of a dead country!" . . . As we neared the station we could still faintly hear the three little jerks calling in their high voices "Chinese, slaves of a dead country!" . . . Things daily grew more difficult. Subject to constant humiliation, all of us felt heavily oppressed. . . . Leaving Tokyo [that fall] was like leaving hell.[110]

Many Japanese showed similar disrespect toward Koreans and Taiwanese. Before and during the colonial period, Japanese disparaged Korea and Koreans in newspapers, magazines, and other media, their prejudice stemming from widespread feelings of superiority and negative impressions of supposed Korean backwardness. Japanese ethnographic fascination with Taiwanese aboriginal culture led to the frequent depiction of Taiwan as more barbaric than even Korea, and the portrayal of Taiwan as an island with little history and in desperate need of Japan's civilizing and ultimately assimilating hand. Taiwanese and Koreans in Japan hardly enjoyed equality, regardless of the degree of their "Japanization." Prejudice at times turned deadly: Japanese police and private citizens alike tortured and massacred thousands of Koreans and other foreigners in Japan after the Great Kantō Earthquake and fires of 1923. Both while in Japan and after returning home, many East Asians declared they would never forget being humiliated by the Japanese.[111]

Although a number of Chinese, Koreans, and Taiwanese wrote nostalgically about Tokyo and other Japanese cities,[112] most accounts of the experiences of colonial and semicolonial peoples in Japan underline the uncertainty of life in the metropole. Some eloquently depict the loneliness of foreign students in Japan — loneliness stemming as much from inherent melancholy and familial circumstance as from being in the metropole — despite initial exuberance at being offered the opportunity to study there. The narrator of the Korean writer Yi Kwangsu's short story "Ai ka" (Is It Love?, 1909) observes concerning Mun-gil (Jpn. Bunkichi), a Korean orphan who has come to Japan to pursue his education:

He feared that he might die not having accomplished anything. Then a ray of hope shone on him in the form of a high-ranking official who arranged for him to go to Tokyo to study. He was extraordinarily delighted and jumped for joy as though he'd found the gateway of his dreams. He went to Tokyo right away and entered the third year at a middle school in Shiba. He got good grades, and everyone thought he had promise. It was as though he had come out into the light after living in the dark. But truth be told, he wasn't happy. He gradually showed signs of loneliness. He met dozens, no, hundreds of people every day, but he couldn't call a single one his friend. He grieved and cried about this.[113]

Mun-gil spends an agonizingly lonely two years in Tokyo before meeting Misao, a young man, presumably Japanese, who returns his love. But the relationship between the two is awkward and lopsided at best and sends Mun-gil into even greater despair. "Is It Love?" concludes with a suicidal Mun-gil walking desolately along the tracks lamenting, "Oh, I'm lonely. . . . The stars are heartless. Where is the train? Why doesn't it come quickly and pulverize my head? His hot tears flowed endlessly."[114]

Other colonial and semicolonial writers, such as the Koreans Na Tohyang (1902–27) in the short story "Yŏ ilbalsa" (The Lady Barber, 1923) and Pak T'aewŏn (1909–86) in the short story "Ttakhan saramdŭl" (Pitiful People, 1934), emphasized the poverty experienced by exchange students in Japan, often by reappropriating motifs from modern Japanese literature.[115] But the majority of Chinese, Korean, and Taiwanese creative works on life in Japan also explored the ethnicity-based struggles experienced by foreign students there. Essays and short stories by the Chinese writers Lu Xun and Yu Dafu, the Taiwanese writers Wu Zhuoliu (1900–76) and Yang Kui, and many other colonial and semicolonial literary figures contrast the great generosity of some Japanese with the blatant hostility of others. More important, their tales reveal the conflicting sentiments many Chinese, Koreans, and Taiwanese harbored toward their homelands; they emphasize the difficulties of living in Japan while at the same time highlighting their lack of alternatives.[116]

One of the best-known Chinese accounts of life as an exchange student in Japan is Lu Xun's essay "Tengye xiansheng" (Mr. Fujino, 1926). Here Lu Xun describes his experiences as a young Chinese studying medicine in Sendai during the Russo-Japanese War. He depicts the staff at the medical college, his anatomy teacher Mr. Fujino, and some of his classmates as extremely helpful and compassionate: "In Sendai I received preferential treatment. Not only did the school cover my fees, several members of the staff made sure I had adequate housing and enough food to eat."[117] Mr. Fujino, concerned that Lu Xun does not understand his lectures, meticulously proofreads and corrects all his Chinese student's notes. But not everyone in Japan is so kind. Some of Lu Xun's classmates taunt him mercilessly and accuse him of cheating on the final exam. Significantly, however, it is Lu Xun, not his classmates, who criticizes China and the Chinese: "China is a weak country, so the Chinese of course are an inferior people. A Chinese would have to have help to get more than sixty points. No wonder they were suspicious of me." Lu Xun depicts his classmates as enthusiastically viewing slides of Japanese executing Chinese spies, yet he also reveals that "after I returned to China I saw bums watching criminals being shot, and they also cheered as though drunk."[118] In other words, Japanese bullies and Chinese bums both become excited by watching executions; the national identities of the spectator and the condemned are irrelevant. The narrator is harsher toward China than are his Japanese classmates; Japanese might believe Chinese inferior, but in this essay Chinese are their own greatest critics.

Like "Mr. Fujino," Yu Dafu's short story "Chenlun" (Sinking, 1921) depicts a young Chinese man attending school in Japan who is disturbed both by Japanese prejudice toward the Chinese and by China's own frailty. The nameless protagonist declares that the Japanese "despise Chinese the same way the Chinese despise pigs and dogs. The Japanese all call Chinese 'Shinajin.' In Japan, these three syllables are even more offensive than the Chinese expletive 'scoundrel.'"[119] Early twentieth-century Japanese frequently did call China "Shina" and Chinese "Shinajin." Yet the Chinese student in "Sinking" is not subjected to such abuse himself; in fact, most of the Japanese he encounters outside his school treat him with compassion. The protagonist has difficulties with his Japanese classmates, whom he assumes avoid him because he is Chinese, but the narrator depicts the student's isolation as self-imposed; after all, he rejects his Chinese peers and breaks off ties with his own family. Furthermore, the student ultimately blames all his problems on China, not Japan. Several times in "Sinking" the student chastises China for being so weak; the story concludes, like Yi Kwangsu's "Is It Love?," with the young protagonist threatening to commit suicide, this time by drowning.[120] Unlike Mun-gil, Yu Dafu's Chinese student blames his plight on his homeland: "Homeland, my homeland! You have killed me! . . . So many of your children continue to suffer."[121] But despite his concern for the future of his country, the student in "Sinking" does no more for China than Mun-gil does for Korea.

The first-person narrator of Yang Kui's "The Paperboy" (1934), a young Taiwanese man struggling to make a living in Japan, also despairs over the future of his homeland, but unlike Yu Dafu's protagonist he strives to make a difference. Deceived and left penniless by his boss at the Ozaki Newspaper Delivery Agency, he is rescued by his mentor Tanaka, who does not think twice about offering much-needed encouragement and helping him financially. Tanaka also introduces him to Itō, a Japanese worker who becomes a confidant and helps him obtain steady employment. The paperboy discovers that character does not depend on nationality: "At home in Taiwan I thought that all Japanese were evil, and I detested them. But after I came to Japan I realized that not all Japanese are bad people. . . . Just as there are good and bad Taiwanese, so too are there good and bad Japanese."[122] At the conclusion of "The Paperboy," the narrator returns to Taiwan, not to escape the difficulties of life in Japan as he originally had thought of doing but rather to work for his homeland, which is in desperate shape. More critical of Taiwan than the Japanese he encounters, he declares: "Full of conviction, I stared at the Taiwanese springtime from the deck of the ocean liner Hōraimaru. Were a single pin to prick its beautifully corpulent surface, putrid bloody pus would come gushing out."[123] His passion is admirable, but the possibility of restoring such a fragile ecosystem remains unclear.

Ethnicity-based conflicts come to the fore in Wu Zhuoliu's *Ajia no koji* (Orphan of Asia, 1945). The protagonist Hu Taiming is a young Taiwanese man who like many of his generation has been unable to find a satisfactory place within the Japanese colonial education system in Taiwan and, hoping to contribute something to his ailing homeland, travels to Japan to study physics. Immediately after his arrival, he contrasts the kindness of the Japanese he encounters in Tokyo with the contempt he often heard in the voices of Japanese in Taiwan: "Tokyo was an exhausting city. But the people were all kind. Everyone whom he asked for directions knowledgeably and politely showed him the way. They didn't sneer at him like the Japanese in Taiwan."[124] Taiming's Taiwanese friend Lan declares that the Japanese have treated him well because they are unaware he is from Taiwan, which they perceive as a hopelessly backward place. Lan advises Taiming, "It's better not to tell anyone you're from Taiwan. Our Japanese resembles the Kyushu dialect, so it's better to tell people that you're from Fukuoka or Kumamoto."[125] Yet Taiming is determined to be open about his ethnicity, and the next day he signs a lease on a room in the house of a Japanese army officer's widow. The woman and her daughter know he is from Taiwan, but they shower him with kindness. Similarly, Taiming is the first and only Taiwanese student in his physics school, but the narrator gives no indication that he is having difficulty being accepted by his Japanese peers.

Nationality becomes a real issue only during interactions with Chinese students in Japan. Not long after settling into a routine of long hours of study interrupted only by friendly communication with his Japanese landlady and her daughter, Taiming at Lan's urging attends a lecture sponsored by a Chinese association. The Chinese students with whom Taiming speaks assume from his accent that he is from Guangdong, and they welcome him warmly. Their attitudes change sharply when Taiming tells one of them that he actually is from Taiwan: "'What? Taiwan?'. . . In a fraction of a second their exchange spread around the room. Whispers of 'He's Taiwanese.' 'He might be a spy' spread like waves."[126] None of the Chinese at the meeting stop to think that were he a spy it is unlikely that he would be volunteering his origins. The narrator of *Orphan of Asia* accentuates the liminal position of many Taiwanese: fearful of being scorned by Japanese for being from a supposed backwater, they also are disliked by Chinese for their supposed collaboration with Japanese. And, as the narrator stresses later in *Orphan of Asia*, the only thing waiting for Taiwanese when they return to Taiwan is physical and psychological imprisonment.

Life in Japan was a challenge and source of internal conflict for visiting colonial and semicolonial intellectuals. Creative writers were welcomed into Japanese literary groups large and small, and their textual products appeared in mainstream Japanese publications as well as in minor periodicals. Japanese lauded some as powerful writers whose texts eloquently explored the human condition. For instance, the Japanese proletarian writer Hayama Yoshiki declared Long Yingzong's story "Town of Papayas" "not only the cry of the Taiwanese, but also the cries of all the oppressed classes. It is in the spirit of Pushkin, Gorky, and Lu Xun; it [has much] in common with Japanese proletarian work. It fully embodies the highest literary principles."[127] But just as the Nobel Prize committee hesitates to allow non-Western literatures to "shed their marginal status and be valued as 'universally human' like Western literatures,"[128] Japanese critics frequently praised Chinese, Korean, and Taiwanese writers for providing moving portraits of their homelands but remained silent on their contributions to world literature and thought. Other Japanese critics charged colonial and semicolonial writers with being "immature" and complained that they had inadequate command of Japanese or that they were simply copying Japanese and Western literatures. Literary contact nebulae in the Japanese empire, like those in other imperial spaces, frequently were ambiguous sites of adulation and rejection.

Kim Saryang, the nominee for the 1940 Akutagawa Prize, objected to Japanese prejudices. Frustrated with the Japanese reception of his creative output, he wrote his mother: "Under the title of my work were remarks by the author Satō Haruo: 'This I-novel ["In the Light"] fully incorporates the heart-rending fate of the [Korean] people.' But his comments pigeonholed my text."[129] The novelist Kawabata Yasunari, another member of the prize committee, also drew attention to the "Korean" origins of "In the Light," noting that he wanted to nominate Kim Saryang's work because "the author is Korean."[130] Some Japanese critics reviewed Kim Saryang's "In the Light" more favorably. Yet it was almost impossible for him, and for most Chinese, Korean, and Taiwanese writers, to escape peripheral status.

The case of Chang Hyŏkju is also notable. Criticized by some Korean intellectuals for writing in Japanese, Chang Hyŏkju enjoyed friendships with many in the Japanese literary establishment, and his work appeared in a range of Japanese periodicals, but Japanese critics insisted on emphasizing his colonial status. In a 1935 letter to the Japanese novelist Tokunaga Sunao he protested:

Why don't you see me as just another ordinary, individual writer? Isn't it an insult to look at me and think "Because he's Korean"? . . . I don't want to kill my identity as a writer. I have my own artistic sense. . . . [You, Murayama Tomoyoshi, and Kubokawa Ineko (Sata Ineko, 1904–98)] are trying to force me never to forget, not even for an instant, that I'm Korean and a colonial subject.[131]

But protest as they did, there was little colonial and semicolonial writers could do to change entrenched Japanese attitudes.

That Tokunaga and other Japanese intellectuals paid little attention to Chang Hyŏkju's objections is evident from the Japanese-literature scholar Kataoka Yoshikazu's discussion several years later of the Korean writer's short story "Ken [Kwŏn] to iu otoko" (A Man Named Kwŏn, 1933) in the Kokusai Bunka Shinkōkai's *Introduction to Modern Japanese Literature* (1939). Chang Hyŏkju was the only non-Japanese writer to appear in this anthology, which contains synopses and discussions of 84 literary works, and was distributed to the English-speaking world with the express purpose of enlightening foreigners "to some of the descriptive and literary beauty [of Japanese texts] which they cannot savour at first hand."[132] In some ways, the inclusion of Chang Hyŏkju's work in the *Introduction to Modern Japanese Literature* indicates the Korean writer's acceptance by the Japanese literary establishment. But Kataoka emphasizes the importance of Chang Hyŏkju's depictions of "local color" and undermines even this ambiguous praise, surrounding it with allegations concerning Chang Hyŏkju's dependence both on metropolitan predecessors and on Chinese writings tied to these predecessors:

The fact that this work . . . readily brings to mind such novels as [Sōseki's] *Botchan* [Little Master, 1906] and [Yokomitsu Riichi's] *Kikai* [Machine, 1930] goes to show that it does not measure up to the standards of a work which is convincingly original in design. . . . It can especially be said here, with due emphasis, that with Korea, a territory of a special significance to this country, as the setting of his story, he has depicted its local colour, its peculiar customs and manners . . . with a certain degree of success. And it is in such qualities that the special value of this work can be discerned. . . . The author . . . has both talent and ability of a fairly high order; [he] is an author whose subject-matter, because of his ties with the land of his birth, displays a great variety of colour and novelty. . . . He appears to have been particularly influenced, in no small degree, by the Chinese author Lu Hsin [Lu Xun]. . . . Lu Hsin was, essentially, an author who exhibited many points of resemblance to Sōseki's literary style and method of the earlier years of his career.[133]

Without question, colonial Korean writers, like writers the world over, discussed their homeland in their creative texts. But no less than their counterparts in other fields, they longed for recognition as artists who transcended the local and who could stand on their own in the East Asian regional and ultimately the global arenas. Furthermore, as will be discussed in Part II of this book, the strands of Japanese and Chinese texts woven into their creative works generally resulted much more from active negotiation with literary predecessors than from simple plagiarism or influence, as Kataoka implies. Also interesting here is how Kataoka contrasts colonial Korean and semicolonial Chinese engagement with Japanese cultural products, depicting the relationship between Lu Xun's and Sōseki's works as one of "resemblance," rather than indebtedness. In general, the Japanese literary establishment held contemporary Chinese creative production in higher esteem than that of Korea or Taiwan, despite (or because of) decades of colonial occupation.

One of the most revealing expressions of how ambivalent Chinese, Koreans, and Taiwanese felt vis-à-vis Japan comes from the Korean modernist Yi Sang (1910–37), who went to Tokyo in the fall of 1936, was arrested in February 1937, and died in Japan later that year. In his posthumous essay "Donggyŏng" (Tokyo, 1939), Yi Sang exaggerates the façades of Japanese modernity: "These days, the seven-story Mitsukoshi, Matsuzakaya, Itōya, Shirokiya, and Matsuya [all major department stores] don't sleep at night. However, we can't go inside. Why? The interiors are one story, not [as their façades suggest] seven stories."[134] But most of his critiques are more ambiguous. For instance, disappointed with the Japanese capital, he notes in the opening lines, "The Marunouchi Building I had imagined, better known as Marubiru, was at least four times the size of this 'Marubiru,' something magnificent. If I went to Broadway in New York, I might experience exactly the same disillusionment. At any rate, my first impression of Tokyo was, 'This city reeks of gasoline!' . . . The citizens of Tokyo smell like cars." Although downplaying emblems of the Japanese modern, Yi Sang freely admits that Tokyo is not the only city that would disappoint him. Moreover, he only somewhat tongue-in-cheek blames his inability to appreciate Tokyo's sights and smells on his own weak lungs and morality, the latter of which he claims "exudes a sour nineteenth-century odor." Similarly, later in the essay Yi Sang comments unfavorably on the Tsukiji Theater, Japan's first modern theater: "Covered with all sorts of posters, this center of the Japanese New Theater Movement looks to me like an awkwardly designed teahouse." Yet he also confesses to "occasionally attending this small theater."[135] In fact, he and thousands of other visiting Chinese, Koreans, and Taiwanese were enthusiastic theatergoers, attending performances and themselves performing at Tsukiji and many other theaters throughout the colonial period.

Tokyo provided literary artists from China, occupied Manchuria, Korea, and Taiwan with rich if often rocky soil for their creative activities and served as a fertile site of transculturation. The presence of hundreds of thousands of exchange students in Japan is an important component not only of early twentieth-century East Asian history, but also of early twentieth-century East Asian literatures. Japan was a crucial space of intra–East Asian literary interaction at formative moments in the careers of visiting artists. It was in Japan that many early twentieth-century Chinese, Korean, and Taiwanese writers first became engrossed in Japanese and Western literatures; it was there that many writerly contacts first blossomed. Colonial language policies and the proliferation of Japanese-language courses facilitated the integration of foreign writers into the Japanese literary community. Relationships between Chinese, Korean, and Taiwanese writers and their Japanese counterparts were seldom equal and occasionally strained, but regardless of Japanese hostility on the battlefront or the creative front, visiting East Asians found it difficult to resist the allure of making their mark in and on the Japanese literary landscape. This yearning to engage with the Japanese literary world, combined with Japanese interest in colonial and semicolonial textual production, resulted in decades of vibrant intra-empire literary entanglements.

Travel, Readerly Contact, and Writerly Contact in China, Occupied Manchuria, Korea, and Taiwan

Multiple spaces of intra-empire travel, readerly, and writerly contact dotted early twentieth-century East Asia. The largest nebulae generally swirled in Japan, but urban centers elsewhere in the empire also were active sites of transcultural contact. For much of the colonial period, Japanese creative texts in both the original and translation were available throughout the empire. This allowed for readerly contact independent of, although in many cases surrounding, travel to Japan. In his memoirs, Guo Moruo recalls that as a child in China he read the Chinese translation of the Japanese political novel *Keikoku bidan* (Inspiring Instances of Statesmanship, 1884) by Yano Ryūkei (1850–1931): "*Inspiring Instances of Statesmanship* [and other books and newspapers] arrived in a nearly steady stream, and we read them outside of class."[136] Huang Maocheng, the proprietor of one of colonial Taiwan's major bookstores—the Lanji Tushubu in Jiayi (est. 1916), later renamed the Lanji Shuju—took frequent book-buying trips to Japan and made Japanese texts available to customers throughout Taiwan via mail order.[137] These literary works fell into the hands of Taiwanese of all ages, but young people were particularly enthusiastic. Yang Kui, one of the founders of modern Taiwanese literature, later commented that as a teenager in Taiwan in the 1920s he "read everything that was available by Natsume Sōseki, Akutagawa Ryūnosuke, and the White Birch School," as well as English, French, and Russian literatures in Japanese translation.[138] Japanese literature also was readily accessible to diverse Korean audiences in the 1920s. The writer Kim Namch'ŏn reported becoming engrossed in texts by the Japanese poet Ishikawa Takuboku (1886–1912) and prose writers Akutagawa Ryūnosuke, Arishima Takeo, Kikuchi Kan, Kume Masao, and Yokomitsu Riichi while still in middle school in Korea.[139] Many children in the colonies were first exposed to Japanese literature in required textbooks, but no small number also avidly read Japanese novels, plays, poems, and short stories outside of class.

Japanese literature became even more accessible throughout the empire in the late 1920s, in large part because of the one-yen book boom, which made texts easily affordable and readily portable. Confronted with warehouses full of remaindered one-yen books, publishers took advantage of the large Japanese-literate populations outside the metropole, selling thousands of the one-yen books for a fraction of their original price. Uchiyama Kanzō (1885–1959), proprietor of the Uchiyama Shoten (Bookstore)—the largest Japanese bookstore in China proper between 1917 and 1947—speaks in his memoirs about being surrounded by mountains of one-yen books.[140] Taiwanese in China also were drawn to the Japanese literature that lined shelves there. The writer and translator Zhang Wojun, for instance, claimed to be delighted at obtaining recently published Japanese literary works in Beijing, including Kaizōsha's *Shinsen Hayama Yoshiki shū* (Newly Collected Works of Hayama Yoshiki, 1928), which he purchased in the spring of 1929.[141] Korean readers were no less enthusiastic. The Japanese businessman Bandō Kyōgo (1893–

1973), director of the Society for the Popularization of Imperial Books, peddled Japanese books in Seoul and numerous other colonial cities in the early 1930s. Korean demand for his books was apparently so high that for the two weeks he was in Seoul in 1932, business in the city's other bookstores supposedly came to a virtual standstill.[142]

Japanese periodicals carrying literary texts likewise found eager consumers in many parts of East Asia. The Chinese politician and adviser to the Chinese Association for International Understanding Zhang Xiangshan (1914–) commented: "In 1928, when I was fourteen, I [left home for Beijing] . . . was drawn into literature, and learned Japanese. I became familiar with proletarian literature by reading Japanese magazines."[143] The many Korean and particularly Chinese-language translations of Japanese literature further increased the availability of imperial cultural production in the colonies and China, as ultimately did the efforts of visiting Japanese writers during the mobilization campaigns of the late 1930s and early 1940s. Japanese literature was available in cities in Manchuria decades before Japanese occupation, but it was even more accessible after 1931, thanks to official Japanese intervention.

Readerly contact with Japanese literature in China, occupied Manchuria, Korea, and Taiwan overlapped with Japanese writerly travel to the colonies and China, which likewise played an important role in both clouding and accentuating divisions among East Asian literary worlds. Vectors of intra-empire literary travel were extensive and diverse, with Japanese writers journeying to China, occupied Manchuria, Korea, Taiwan, and numerous other sites as the Japanese expanded the boundaries of their empire. But they took place alongside significant inter-(semi)colonial travel, readerly contact, and writerly contact, China being a key destination for Korean and Taiwanese literary figures.[144] Reasons for travel to China varied. Some young intellectuals had family on the mainland, some had studied in Japan and found conditions there unsatisfactory, some simply refused to study in the metropole, and others were captivated by China's contemporary cultural movements.

China became a refuge for Koreans of all classes after Japan annexed Korea in 1910. Thanks to its geographical proximity and historical ties, Manchuria was a popular destination, but Koreans also looked to China's larger cities and treaty ports as safe havens. Shanghai became the base for Korean nationalists following Korea's March First Movement (1919), and for the next quarter century China remained the center of the Korean overseas independence movement.[145] As in Japan, Koreans in China engaged in a variety of literary activities and enjoyed close contact with local artists, forming multiple intra-East Asian literary contact nebulae; widespread exchange began in the late 1910s and reached its apex in the 1930s. The first major cooperative enterprise took place in 1917 when the Korean literary critic Hyŏn Ch'ŏl (1891–1965) went to Shanghai and together with the Chinese dramatist Ouyang Yuqian—who had been active with theater in Japan—opened a theater school, the Shanghai Xingqi Xiju Xuexiao.[146]

During the following decades, dozens of Korean writers visited or moved to China. While there they published creative texts in Chinese, Korean, and occasionally Japanese and established ties with Chinese, Japanese, and Russian writers. Not surprisingly, Lu Xun was a magnet for Korean intellectuals living in and traveling through Beijing and Shanghai. Some Koreans with whom he became close were the journalist Sin Ŏnjun (1904–38), the creative writer Yi Yuksa (1904–44), and the activist Yi Ugwan (1897–1984); Yi Yuksa first met Lu Xun at a memorial service in 1933 and later claimed this encounter established instant camaraderie: "Lu Xun grasped my hand firmly, and from that point on we were close friends."[147] Many Koreans found in Lu Xun a kindred soul, in part because of his sympathy toward Korea's plight, and they packed his lectures.[148] Although some Chinese writers dismissed as inferior the output of their Korean colleagues, and a few— reflecting contemporary Chinese attitudes toward Korea—had harsh words for Koreans in general, complaints of discrimination at the hands of the Chinese literary world do not seem to have been as common as those from contacts with Japanese writers.

Several of Taiwan's most prominent writers, including Zhang Shenqie and Zhang Wojun, actively participated in Chinese literary groups and published their work in Chinese periodicals; Taiwanese in China also formed their own associations and published their own journals.[149] Zhang Shenqie first went to China in 1923 after a brief stint at Aoyama Gakuin University in Japan; he spent time in Shanghai and Guangzhou and served as a professor in Beijing, where he taught a variety of subjects, including Japanese. While in China, he also organized a Taiwanese student association, founded literary journals, and translated Japanese literature. Zhang Wojun likewise first went to China in 1923, studied at some of China's premier institutions, started several periodicals, and became friends with Lu Xun and Zhou Zuoren. Other writers from Taiwan, including Liu Na'ou (1905–40) and Xu Dishan (1893–1941), spent many of their creative years on the mainland. Xu Dishan, a son of the famed Taiwanese poet Xu Nanying (1855–1917), was one of the founding members, along with Mao Dun and Zhou Zuoren, of the Wenxue Yanjiuhui (Literary Research Society), one of early twentieth-century China's principal literary organizations. Liu Na'ou left Taiwan at age sixteen, studied in Japan for six years, then moved to Shanghai, where he befriended Chinese modernists including Mu Shiying (1912–40) and Shi Zhecun (1905–2003) and became an important neosensationalist writer. Like other Korean and especially Taiwanese writers who integrated themselves into Chinese cultural circles, Liu Na'ou exemplified the growing links among the literary worlds of East Asia.

Even more significant for early twentieth-century intra–East Asian transculturation was Japanese intra-empire literary travel. As key destinations for Japanese writers, China, occupied Manchuria, Korea, and Taiwan were both scorned and embraced; as literary contact nebulae they witnessed their share of hostility among artists but also were characterized by cooperation and even, in the years before total war, festiveness. During the colonial period, hundreds of Japanese writers, ranging from those strongly opposed to Japanese expansion to ardent supporters of imperialism, joined the several million Japanese of various backgrounds who streamed to China, occupied Manchuria, Korea, and Taiwan and remained abroad for days, months, or years.[150] Many isolated themselves from local talent. These include Japanese avant-garde poets in Dalian, Manchuria in the 1920s, who often wrote about China and whose journal *A* (Asia), a precursor to the leading modernist journal *Shi to shiron* (Poetry and Poetics), featured work by Japanese and European writers, yet contained virtually nothing by Chinese. But a number of Japanese writers did engage in writerly contact. As in the metropole, the great volume and frequency of interactions among East Asian writers—whether voluntary or dispatched by Japanese authorities—often were complicated by unequal power relationships; Chinese, Korean, and Taiwanese often were frustrated at being pigeonholed by Japanese as "colonial" or "lesser" artists. Relationships were further undermined by the struggles of Japanese writers based outside Japan to be recognized themselves as peers by the Japanese literary establishment at home.

As in Japan, theater was an early nebula of intra–East Asian literary transculturation in China, Korea, and Taiwan. Unlike colonial sites in the Caribbean and elsewhere, where audiences consisted primarily of metropolitan expatriates, Japanese drama troupes entertained both locals and resident Japanese. In Korea, Japanese drama troupes performed to mixed audiences, and Japanese and Korean theater troupes put on joint productions even before Japanese colonization. In 1911, Kawakami Otojirō (1864–1911) became the first major Japanese theater figure to perform in Taiwan, and in following years Taiwanese and Japanese actors and theater groups put on joint productions.[151] Japanese theater troupes also traveled to China, where their performances were well attended. But as in the metropole, communication among poets and prose writers ultimately overshadowed that among dramatists.

The imperial and colonial/semicolonial literary worlds were more deeply intertwined in Taiwan than anywhere but the metropole itself. Much early creative collaboration was at the insistence of Japanese authorities who, faced with mounting Taiwanese resistance, sent famous Japanese poets to Taiwan to appease Taiwanese cultural figures. They strove for harmony via literary gatherings where writers from the two cultures traded poems in classical Chinese; Japanese feelings of superiority over their colonial subjects did not appear to infringe on their respect for classical Chinese language and literature.[152] In the following decades Japanese and Taiwanese composed poems together in both Chinese and Japanese at more spontaneous poetry gatherings.

Ties between Japanese and Taiwanese writers in Taiwan ebbed and flowed, but in the 1930s and early 1940s they grew particularly close; these years witnessed the formation of joint cultural societies that spanned the artistic spectrum. In 1931, Japanese and Taiwanese in Taiwan created what generally is acknowledged as the first Japanese-Taiwanese literary organization, the left-leaning Taiwan Bungei Sakka Kyōkai (Taiwan Literary Writers Association). Two years later, a small group of Taiwanese and Japanese poets in Tainan, Taiwan founded the Fengche Shishe (Le Moulin Poetry Society), whose journal *Fengche* (Le Moulin) published surrealist poetry and essays on surrealism.[153] Also in 1933, Japanese intellectuals in Taiwan joined with Taiwanese to form the Taiwan Bungeika Kyōkai (Taiwan Writers Association). The latter group was reorganized in April 1943 under National General Mobilization as the Taiwan Bungaku Hōkōkai (Taiwan Literature Patriotic Association), a group akin to the Chōsen Bunjin Hōkokukai (Korean Writers Patriotic Society).

Numerous periodicals by these and other Japanese-Taiwanese groups colored the Taiwanese landscape beginning in the first years of colonization. The *Taiwan nichinichi shinpō* (Taiwan Daily News), established by Japanese in Taiwan in 1898, included a Chinese-language section that published Chinese poems by both Japanese and Taiwanese. The trend of combining Japanese and Taiwanese writers under one cover continued for most of the colonial period but became more pronounced in the 1930s. Beginning with its first issue in July 1932, the biweekly Chinese-language literary journal *Nanyin* (Southern Accent) published texts by both Taiwanese and Japanese writers, the latter in Chinese translation. From its first issue in November 1934, the periodical *Taiwan bungei* (Taiwan Literature) carried works by both Taiwanese and Japanese, in the Chinese and Japanese languages, as did *Taiwan New Literature* from its first issue in October 1935. Similarly, the Japanese-language literary journal *Taiwan bungaku* (Taiwan Literature) featured both Taiwanese and Japanese writers, as did *Bungei Taiwan* (Literary Taiwan) and the second *Taiwan bungei* (Taiwan Literature). Only a fraction of the many Japanese who published in literary journals based in Taiwan actively participated in literary societies on the island, but the hybridity of the journals underscores the integration of the Taiwanese and Japanese literary fields in Taiwan in the early twentieth century.

Most discussions of early twentieth-century intra–East Asian travel and writerly contacts in China rightly highlight the Japanese expatriate Uchiyama Kanzō, who hosted grand parties and intimate gatherings at his bookstore in Shanghai that introduced visiting Japanese writers to local talent.[154] A lively meeting place, the Uchiyama Bookstore naturally played a crucial role in enabling Chinese, Japanese, and occasionally Korean writers to revitalize old friendships and develop new bonds.[155] But it was only one of many intra–East Asian literary contact nebulae in China. Coteries and periodicals there also became intriguing spaces of Sino-Japanese literary confluence, intermingling Chinese and Japanese management and literary output.

Journals managed by Chinese carried numerous translations of Japanese literature, while Japanese periodicals based in China introduced Chinese literature to the local Japanese population. One especially noteworthy Japanese publication in this regard is the *Pekin shūhō* (Peking Weekly Review), of which 400 issues were published between its launch in 1921 and folding in 1930; the journal's Japanese editors knew Lu Xun and his brother Zhou Zuoren personally and published numerous translations of Lu Xun's work.[156] In occupied Manchuria, Chinese and Japanese editors jointly managed several journals, including the prominent Japanese-owned *Xin Manzhou* (New Manchukuo) and *Qilin* (Unicorn). Japanese intellectuals also were involved to varying degrees with Manchuria-based Chinese literary coteries such as Yiwenzhi (Chronicle of the Arts), Wenxuan (Literary Selections), and Wencong (Literary Collective), all founded in 1939.[157] For its part, the *Daban Huawen meiri* (Chinese Osaka Daily), established by Japanese leftist writers and pro-China sympathizers, many of whom sought refuge in occupied Manchuria in the mid- to late 1930s, served as a forum for the controversial work of prominent writers from occupied Manchuria. Tightening controls on literary production in the early 1940s, Japanese authorities in Manchuria and other occupied regions of China issued increased artistic guidelines and promoted membership in official literary associations such as the Wenhuahui (Culture Association, est. 1937) and Manzhou Wenyijia Xuehui (Manchukuo Writers and Artists Association, est. 1941). In contrast to the voluntary associations of years past, these groups and the many that followed more forcefully brought together Japanese and Chinese writers.[158]

Some of the most noteworthy writerly contacts in China were between Chinese and pacifist Japanese. China provided a haven for Japanese pacifists in the late 1930s and early 1940s, and some antiwar writers developed especially close ties with Chinese. Principal among them was Kaji Wataru (1903–82), who sought refuge in China in 1936 after spending two years in a Japanese prison for violating the Peace Preservation Law and did not return to Japan until after the war.[159] He arrived in Shanghai knowing little Chinese but quickly became close with the ailing Lu Xun. In 1937, frustrated with having to dodge both the Japanese military police and a hostile Chinese public, Kaji fled to Hong Kong, but he went to Wuhan (capital of Hubei province, central China) in March 1938 at the invitation of Chen Cheng (1897–1965), a political and military leader who learned about him from the writer Guo Moruo and the politician Zhou Enlai. In Wuhan, he worked to re-educate Japanese prisoners of war and in December 1939 formed the Nihonjin Hansen Dōmei (Japanese People's Antiwar Alliance); the Nationalist government dissolved this group in 1941, believing its members too sympathetic to communism, but its supporters continued their antiwar operations against the Japanese military.

Like other pacifist Japanese writers living in China, Kaji published plays, poems, and essays that backed the Chinese cause; many of these, including his drama *San kyōdai* (Three Brothers, 1939), were translated quickly into Chinese and performed to enthusiastic audiences.[160] Kaji's antiwar activities in China brought him into close contact with a number of Chinese literary figures, some of whom became good friends, including Ah Long (1907–67), Guo Moruo, Hu Feng, Xia Yan, and Xiao Hong (1911–42). Furthermore, not only did his creations inspire Chinese writers—the success of *Three Brothers* led to a boom in Chinese antiwar plays—his discussions of Japanese literature also prompted renewed bursts of creative energy in his Chinese counterparts. Kaji and his partner Ikeda Sachiko (1913–76), a Japanese writer who lived in China from the age of thirteen, provided the poet, prose writer, and theorist Ah Long with detailed information on Japan's major wartime novels: Hino Ashihei's (1907–60) trilogy *Mugi to heitai* (Wheat and Soldiers, 1938), *Tsuchi to heitai* (Earth and Soldiers, 1938), and *Hana to heitai* (Flowers and Soldiers, 1938) and Ishikawa Tatsuzō's (1905–85) *Ikiteiru heitai* (Living Soldiers, 1938).[161] Frustrated that Japanese writers were discussing the Nanjing Massacre (1937) while their Chinese counterparts remained silent and dismayed that Japanese battlefront texts were being translated into Chinese multiple times within months of their release, Ah Long hurriedly wrote *Nanjing* (1939), the first and for 50 years one of very few Chinese fictional works dealing with the destruction of the city.[162] To be sure, whether in China or Japan, most Japanese writers supported, or at least pretended to support, Japan's war effort. But a vocal minority, many of whom lived and published on the mainland, refused to toe the line and instead became committed advocates for China.

Korea also became an active site of Japanese publication; by the end of the colonial period, Japanese in Korea were producing sixteen daily newspapers and numerous journals and magazines. Despite disparities in living conditions, Koreans and Japanese in Korea interacted frequently on the professional level, challenging distinctions between colonized and colonizer. Korean hosts warmly welcomed visiting Japanese literary artists such as the leading proletarian writer Nakanishi Inosuke, who visited Korea in 1925, and the poet Kawaji Ryūkō, who visited the colony in 1927, and published translations of their writings in Korean periodicals.

But it was not until the end of the 1930s that significant joint Korean-Japanese literary groups sprouted in Korea, largely a result of the April 1938 National General Mobilization. The first of these organizations, the Chōsen Bunjin Kyōkai (Korean Writers Association), was founded in October 1939 and consisted of approximately 250 Korean and Japanese figures; its declared purpose was to mobilize writers for "patriotic service to the state by pen." The second, the Chōsen Bunjin Hōkokukai (Korean Writers Patriotic Society, April 1943), was established nearly a year after its Japanese equivalent, the Nihon Bungaku Hōkokukai (Japan Literature Patriotic Association, May 1942). The Korean Writers Patriotic Society, a consolidation of all existing literary groups, was founded to promote "the culture of the imperial way."[163] In the late colonial period, some Japanese also assisted Korean writers in launching literary journals. For instance, Teramoto Kiichi and Sugimoto Nagao, editors of the *Chōsen shiden* (Korean Poetry World), helped the Korean critic Ch'oe Chaesŏ (1908–64), a fellow graduate of Keijō Imperial University and student of the Japanese poet Satō Kiyoshi (1914–40), establish the pro-Japanese journal *Kokumin bungaku* (People's Literature, 1941–45).[164] Ch'oe Chaesŏ in turn included the work of Japanese poets in his publication.

Intra–East Asian literary entanglements, particularly those among metropolitan and colonial/semicolonial writers and texts, proliferated in early twentieth-century China, occupied Manchuria, Korea, and Taiwan. Although most often created along national lines, coteries and periodicals in many cases embraced people and texts from across cultural and geographic divides. But as in the metropole, anxieties were high and the lines between integration and separation frequently were obscured. Takeuchi Yoshimi (1910–77), a founder of the Chūgoku Bungaku Kenkyūkai (Chinese Literary Research Association, est. 1934), the first society outside China devoted to the study and translation of modern Chinese literature, noted in 1948:

> Lu Xun was known in Japan quite early. Many Japanese writers traveled to Shanghai, met with him, and wrote about their experiences. . . . For the most part, the Japanese writers who met with Lu Xun hadn't read his works very carefully, and were attracted only by his reputation. In short, their meetings were political. They met with Lu Xun not as writers but as "China *rōnin*" [adventurers, exploiters, revolutionaries].[165]

Japanese ambivalence vis-à-vis the legitimacy of Chinese, Korean, and Taiwanese cultural production and the place of China, occupied Manchuria, Korea, and Taiwan in the Japanese empire, combined with colonial and semicolonial longing to be accepted by the Japanese without becoming their creative slaves, often resulted in bittersweet encounters. Declarations of association with Japanese counterparts were ubiquitous, as were important literary accolades, but they masked unequal patterns of authority. Japanese writers in China and the colonies—including those who had spent substantial time, if not most of their lives, outside Japan—frequently belittled local peoples. Attitudes toward colonial and semicolonial subjects are readily apparent in the many Japanese creative works that exoticize or otherwise demean Chinese, Koreans, and Taiwanese; in their essays as well, Japanese writers often declared colonial and semicolonial writers subpar or even childish.

This was especially true in Taiwan, where Japanese writers harped on the supposed immaturity of their Taiwanese counterparts. Patronizing remarks by Nishikawa Mitsuru (1908–99), one of the most active Japanese writers in Taiwan and a mentor to major Taiwanese writers such as Ye Shitao, incited the virulent *kuso riarizumu* (feces realism) debate. Nishikawa asserted that the graphic realism of much Taiwanese literature was but a "poor imitation of Western realism" and implied that its turdy truths also poorly imitated Japanese trends.[166] Whether residents or visitors, Japanese writers also often dehumanized the island's inhabitants, at times focusing on the "savagery" of Taiwanese aboriginies. Nakamura Chihei's (1908–63) short story "Kiri no bansha" (The Misty Barbarian Village, 1939) depicts the Musha Incident of 1930, in which Tayal tribespeople killed more than one hundred Japanese, as a battle between "savage" and "civilized." Other Japanese texts, including Satō Haruo's short story "Machō" (Devilbird, 1923), point out similarities between "barbaric" local peoples and supposedly civilized Japanese but still deny the former a voice. Told from an ethnographer's perspective, "Devilbird" ostensibly discusses the customs of a "barbaric" people in Taiwan but alludes to the recent murder of thousands of Koreans in Tokyo.[167] Japanese creative works focusing on Taiwanese of Chinese descent exhibit similar tendencies. The narrator of Satō Haruo's short story "Jokaisen kidan" (Strange Tale of the 'Precepts for Women' Fan, 1925), the most famous text on Taiwan by a Japanese writer, visits a decaying mansion in Taiwan, where he learns of the downfall of a prosperous Chinese family that lived on the island for several generations. The narrator is curious about Taiwanese history and has Taiwanese friends, but— in his quest to rival Edgar Allan Poe's (1809–49) famous short story "The Fall of the House of Usher" (1839)—ultimately gives distorted depictions of Taiwan and its people.[168]

Travel narratives by leading Japanese writers reveal mixed impressions of China and the colonies. Many express admiration for certain aspects of these sites but vocalize despair over their stench and squalor and show little confidence that these lands can escape from their misery. They also inevitably draw comparisons with Japan. While in London (1900–2), Sōseki had noted in his diary that the Chinese "are a far more glorious people than the Japanese" and urged Japanese to keep in mind "how much Japan has owed to China over the years"; just seven years later, in "Man-Kan tokoro dokoro" (Here and There in Manchuria and Korea, 1909), he adopted a disdainful attitude toward the Chinese, whom he called "cruel," "apathetic," and "filthy."[169] Easily romanticized from afar, the Chinese disappointed under closer examination. But Japan—while often depicted as superior—did not always come out on top. It was not unusual for Japanese writers to use their travelogues as forums, however subtle, to work through some of their unease vis-à-vis Japan. In "Shanhai yūki" (Shanghai Travelogue, 1921), Akutagawa Ryūnosuke comments that contemporary China is not the China of poetry and essays but rather that of fiction, "licentious, barbaric, and gluttonous." At one point, musing on the "romanticism" of beggars, he comments sarcastically: "Japanese beggars are not endowed with the supernatural filth of Chinese beggars."[170] On the other hand, he is not without praise for the Chinese, remarking, "traffic control in Japanese cities like Tokyo and Osaka . . . is nowhere near as effective as in Shanghai. I was somewhat scared by the bold rickshaw pullers and carriages, but looking at this fine scene [orderly traffic], I gradually cheered up."[171] More significant, he declares the orchestra at a dance hall in Shanghai superior to those in the Asakusa entertainment district of Tokyo.[172] Indeed, many Japanese recognized Shanghai as a formidable modern city, particularly after the Great Kantō Earthquake flattened large sections of the Tokyo metropolitan area. Other Japanese writers, such as Shimaki Kensaku (1903–45), focused on rural China, including Manchuria, and criticized Japanese authorities for not living up to their promises. Simon Gikandi's observations on the ambiguities of the colonizing gaze in nineteenth-century imperial European travel narratives hold true for the imperial Japanese gaze: "It is not enough to label colonial discourses as purely instruments of power, or, conversely, as discursive formations informed by some measure of colonial insurgency . . . [this discourse] functions as a critique of its conditions of possibility but affirms those conditions in the process."[173]

Some Japanese creative writers and critics were as ill-disposed to legitimize Chinese, Korean, and Taiwanese literary contributions as they were to cast aside prejudices toward China and the colonies. In 1940, the prolific scholar of classical Japanese literature Takagi Ichinosuke (1888–1974), summarily dismissing centuries of Korean cultural achievement, brazenly asserted, "Frankly speaking, what Korea lacks more than anything is a classical literature. But luckily, the literature of the Nara and Heian courts can serve, just as they are, as the classics of Korea."[174] Other reactions were more subtle, including Tanizaki Jun'ichirō's description of his encounters with Chinese writers in Shanghai in 1926. Uchiyama Kanzō threw him a party at his bookstore where Tanizaki ate and drank with a number of Chinese literary luminaries, including Guo Moruo, Ouyang Yuqian, Tian Han, and Xie Liuli (1898–1945). Tian Han and Ouyang Yuqian then organized a second gathering in Tanizaki's honor, to which they invited 90 writers, artists, and other creative types from as far away as Beijing. Tanizaki was amazed by the kindness of the Chinese literary community and their interest in Japanese literature. In "Shanhai kōyūki" (Record of Shanghai Friends, 1926), an eloquent discussion of his time in Shanghai, he reveals that he cares much less about Chinese creative production than about Chinese engagement with Japanese literature:

I'd seen Zhou Zuoren's translations of modern Japanese prose but hadn't expected that in the eight years [since my first trip to Shanghai in 1918] Japanese literature would have been introduced [in China in such large quantities]. . . . Members of the Chinese literary world are much more familiar with conditions in the Japanese literary world than we had imagined. In fact, there are six or seven Chinese students who earned degrees in literature from Japanese imperial universities who now work at the Commercial Press, and they tirelessly keep up with what's being published in Tokyo. . . . [At the party hosted by Uchiyama] everyone spoke Japanese as much as possible. . . . Since I moved to Kansai, it's been a long time since I've heard such a pure Tokyo accent at a party. . . . We began talking about the conditions of the Chinese literary and theatrical worlds. More than anything, I wanted to learn about the range and types of Japanese literature that had been translated into Chinese. . . . I told the Chinese at the party that I wanted to collect as many translations of Japanese literature as I could, and take them back as souvenirs to the Japanese literary world. . . . [Another evening I was chatting with Guo Moruo and Tian Han, and] Tian Han criticized Japanese writers. His observations were right on the mark. I was completely taken aback by how much of our literature the Chinese have read, and how much inside knowledge they have of our literary world.[175]

Tanizaki indicates his enthusiasm for contemporary Chinese writers as based largely on their familiarity with Japanese literature, their translations of this corpus, and their command of the Japanese language; he expresses no real interest in their creative work. Japanese writers were eager to socialize with their colonial and semicolonial counterparts, but Chinese, Korean, and Taiwanese literary output often fell by the wayside.

In a pessimistic letter to the Japanese sinologist Masuda Wataru (1903–77) written shortly before his death, Lu Xun accused the poet Noguchi Yonejirō and novelist Nagayo Yoshirō (1888–1961) of completely misrepresenting their conversations with him. Despite having interacted with dozens of Japanese writers while living in Shanghai, a dismayed Lu Xun was upset enough to conclude from his disagreement with Noguchi and Nagayo that vast gulfs in the backgrounds and lifestyles of Chinese and Japanese writers made mutual understanding nearly impossible.[176] Lu Xun was overstating the case, but relationships among Japanese writers and their Chinese, Korean, and Taiwanese counterparts often were strained, and lively intra–East Asian cultural relations were shadowed, and at length beclouded, by the specter of ever-tightening colonial rule as Japan mobilized its imperium for total war. Much interaction was from the outset hostage, and eventually prisoner, to Japan's colonial policies.

By the time some 1,500 writers from across Asia gathered in Tokyo's Imperial Hotel for the first Greater East Asia Writers Conference (1942), Chinese, Japanese, Korean, and Taiwanese writers had been engaging in intra–East Asian travel, interacting in person, and reading one another's literatures for decades. An infrared satellite photograph of early twentieth-century intra–East Asian literary activity likely would depict Japan as a roiling hotspot, China as a simmering swirl, and Korea and Taiwan as lukewarm pools ringed with active nodes. The continuous interaction of peoples, ideas, and texts that characterized early twentieth-century intra–East Asian cultural relations created literary contact nebulae that transformed the artistic landscape of East Asia. Many of these nebulae, particularly those based in Tokyo, helped promote the rapid transmission of Western literatures, but they also facilitated intra–East Asian literary transculturation on an unprecedented scale. Multidirectional culture-crossing literary caravans carved out new pathways on the East Asian textual field — a landscape long dominated by sinocentric exports.[177] But the flows of texts from Japan to China, Korea, and Taiwan generally were the heaviest trans–East Asian cultural vectors during this era; the flows of Chinese, Korean, and Taiwanese students to Japan's shores likewise exceeded other components of intra–East Asian travel. Japanese cities offered numerous opportunities for colonial and semicolonial writers, whether they were just embarking on their careers, already had begun to publish in their homelands, or were long since established. Other contact nebulae in China, occupied Manchuria, Korea, and Taiwan provided further opportunities for intra–East Asian transculturation. Whether in the metropole or at home, Chinese, Korean, and Taiwanese literary artists seldom received the recognition from Japanese writers for which they hoped, but neither did metropolitan editors and critics completely disregard their colonial and semicolonial counterparts.

Dialogues among readers and writers were awkward but significant. Even more so were those among creative texts. The high level of Chinese, Japanese, Korean, and Taiwanese engagement with one another's literary worlds is illuminated even further when we consider the textual contact, and particularly the interpretive, interlingual, and intertextual transculturation taking place in literary contact nebulae throughout East Asia, examined in the following chapters.

PART I

Interpretive and Interlingual Transculturation

Often appearing together, interpretive and interlingual transculturations of creative texts (i.e., literary criticism, adaptations, and translations) lend valuable insights into how individuals and societies
negotiate with literary output across frontiers.[1] Import, bookseller,
and library records illuminate patterns of availability, sales, browsing, and circulation, but they tell little about how texts are actually
read. In contrast, by integrating literary works into different cultural
spheres, interpretive and interlingual transculturations reveal not
only the scale and scope but also the intricacies and ethics of cross-
cultural engagement on many levels, from the local, to the national,
to the global.[2] They generally do so more openly than intertextual
transculturations, examined in Part II. Probing how and to what
effect literatures are discussed, adapted, and translated allows us to
appreciate better the many paradoxes of literary contact nebulae.

Regardless of how they transform their sources, literary criticism,
adaptations, and translations involve texts from one space penetrating the textual and conceptual webs of other spaces.[3] But engaging
"foreign" texts via literary criticism, adaptation, and translation is
rarely a neutral exercise; cultural legitimacy and authority are at
once affirmed, challenged, and denied as individual texts and entire
literary landscapes are altered and sometimes significantly violated.
Lawrence Venuti's remarks about translation also ring true for adaptation and literary criticism: "The ethnocentric violence of translation
is inevitable: in the translating process, foreign languages, texts, and

cultures will always undergo some degree and form of reduction, exclusion, inscription. Yet the domestic work on foreign cultures can be a foreignizing intervention, pitched to question existing canons at home."[4] The implications of interpretation, adaptation, and translation are powerful when these processes take place in a setting — such as empires and often their aftermaths — of radically asymmetrical power relationships. In such spaces, interpretive and interlingual transculturation, when performed by the (former) imperial power (or at least by those sympathetic to it), often becomes a manipulative apparatus: metropolitan texts, of which the Bible is the most frequently cited example, are twisted to seduce (post)colonial peoples; for their part, (post)colonial texts are distorted to justify and enable (post)imperial agendas. When performed by the (post)colony (or at least those sympathetic to it), interpretive and interlingual transculturation frequently becomes a negotiating device: local texts are promoted as evidence, often directly rebutting imperial rhetoric, of (post)colonial cultural achievement either by hegemonic or local norms, while literature from the metropole is both celebrated and vilified, if not, as the *antropofagistas* of Brazil have claimed, cannibalized.[5] Reconfigurations of texts from (former) colonized spaces into the language/literary sphere of the (former) imperial power have received greater scholarly attention than recastings of literature from the (former) metropole. Yet the latter often highlight even more than the former the paradoxes of translation, adaptation, and interpretation and give fresh insights into these fundamental and frequently explicit forms of transculturation.

By now, translation has been abundantly exposed as a potential form of exploitation. Yunte Huang has argued that it is a process whereby "multiple readings of the 'original' are reduced to a version that foregrounds the translator's own agenda."[6] Similarly, as the South African writer and translator J. M. Coetzee has noted:

There is never enough closeness of fit between languages for formal features of a work to be mapped across from one language to another without shifts of value. Thus the work continually presents its translator with moments of choice. Something must be 'lost' [and something must be 'gained']; that is, features embodying certain complexes of values must be replaced with features embodying different complexes of values in the target language. At such moments the translator chooses in accordance with his [/her] conception of the whole — there is no way of simply translating the words. These choices are based, literally, on preconceptions, pre-judgment, prejudice.[7]

It also has become commonplace to speak of translation as a political if not revolutionary act. Lawrence Venuti both echoes and prefigures the findings of numerous other scholars:

> The greatest scandal of translation [is that] asymmetries, inequities, relations of domination and dependence exist in every act of translating, of putting the translated in the service of the translating culture. Translators are complicit in the institutional exploitation of foreign texts and cultures. But there have also been translators who acted just as dubiously on their own, not in the employ of any bureaucracy.[8]

Translation is not the only form of transculturation with such characteristics—adaptations and literary criticism, although frequently overlooked, are equally revealing of transcultural struggle, negotiation, and manipulation.

Recent research has brought to light the power that translations wield in colonial and postcolonial spaces when penned by writers from the (former) metropole sympathetic to imperial discourse, evident in their ability both to rationalize domination and to increase the attraction of empire. Examining translations of Indian texts into English by British writers from the eighteenth century to the present, Tejaswini Niranjana focuses on the construction of the colonial and postcolonial subject, arguing that translation is a "significant technology of colonial domination," one that "reinforces hegemonic versions of the colonized."[9] Although erroneously conflating "non-Western" and "Third World" literatures, Anuradha Dingwaney takes this notion one step farther and argues not only that Western translators determine what non-Western literature is read and "what counts in terms of representations of the 'Third World' in the West" but also that their power "moves out in ever-widening circles to affect what various 'Third World' readers themselves come to see as apt representations of their own and other non-Western cultures."[10] In her study of translation as underwriting both French and British efforts to colonize Egypt and Egyptian responses to the colonial enterprise, Shaden Tageldin brings this argument to a bold conclusion: "the translated word—by calling on the self to forget itself (if not its language) in the memory of another—annexes a colonized people to its colonizer far more effectively than arms."[11]

To be sure, edifices of domination constructed by translation and other forms of textual contact are easily damaged. In his controversial novel *Noli Me Tángere* (Touch Me Not, 1887) the Filipino writer and nationalist José Rizal (1861–96) reveals how quickly hierarchies can be compromised when translation breaks down. Midway through the text, the narrator depicts Father Damasco's Filipino congregation sitting patiently through the Latin and Spanish sections of his sermon; although understanding very little, the local people play with his words, piecing together sometimes humorous variations of his discourse. In contrast, the part of the sermon he delivers in Tagalog is so incomprehensible, and shows such disregard for the local language, that his audience quickly grows bored and the congregation descends into chaos. But here, as in other parts of *Touch Me Not* where translation is compromised, order quickly is re-established and the complicity of translation with imperial encroachment and colonization confirmed.[12]

Imperial abuse and misuse of its own and colonial/postcolonial languages and cultures through criticism, adaptation, and translation are well documented. But what happens when subjugated peoples perform these types of transculturations? The critical focus on American and European reconfigurations of their own and colonial/postcolonial literary works has illuminated processes of domination and exploitation inherent in much transculturation. Yet it also has glossed over the many studies, translations, and adaptations of literature from (former) metropoles by colonial and postcolonial writers, which in some arenas significantly outnumbered efforts of writers from the (former) metropole to reconfigure both their own and colonial/postcolonial texts. In the Japanese empire, for instance, Chinese, Korean, and Taiwanese writers transculturated greater quantities of Japanese literature than Japanese writers did literature from China, occupied Manchuria, Korea, and Taiwan; in fact, Koreans themselves wrote a number of the Japanese-language commentaries, adaptations, and translations of Korean literature that were published in both Japan and Korea. Not surprisingly, interpretive and interlingual transculturations of Japanese literature likewise greatly outnumbered inter-(semi)colonial commentaries, adaptations, and translations.[13] The next three chapters discuss the polyvalence of different forms of early twentieth-century intra–East Asian interpretive and interlingual transculturation; the principal focus is Chinese, Korean, and Taiwanese criticism, adaptation, and translation of Japanese literary works.

Interpretive and interlingual transculturations of metropolitan literatures by colonial and postcolonial writers often stemmed from their desire to increase the consumption of metropolitan literary works they or others deemed important. In many cases, colonial and postcolonial critics, adapters, and translators hoped that their transculturations not only would inform and enlighten local readers but also would inspire creative trends that would refresh ethnic, regional, and national literatures and make them more widely recognized. Believing American and European literatures in many cases superior to what was being produced in their homelands, late-nineteenth and early twentieth-century semicolonial Chinese and colonial Koreans and Taiwanese adapted, translated, and wrote widely about Western novels, plays, poems, and short stories. At the same time, they also adapted, translated, and wrote about Japanese literature, both for the indirect access recent Japanese works afforded to coveted Western literary trends and because of the pleasures and frustrations of Japanese literature itself.

Chinese, Korean, and Taiwanese critical studies, adaptations, and translations — whether of Japanese or Western literatures — challenged their respective local canons and encouraged new trends in the arts, transforming colonial and semicolonial literatures in myriad ways. But they did not stop there. Often openly weaving foreign literatures into Chinese, Korean, and Taiwanese creative fabrics, these many adaptations, translations, and commentaries both affirmed and denied Japanese and Western cultural capital and authority. The implications of adapting, translating, and writing about Japanese literature were even more significant than those of transculturating Western literatures: in Korea, Taiwan, and occupied Manchuria, Western imperialist threats paled in comparison with Japanese dominion. In China, the cumulative economic, political, and psychological weight of Japanese encroachment in the twentieth century was greater than that of any single Western power.

Rarely can transculturations deter or even delay imperial cultural conquest. Discussing translation and Christian conversion in Tagalog society under early Spanish rule, Vicente L. Rafael argues that Spaniards and Tagalogs "read into the other's language and behavior possibilities that the original speakers had not intended or foreseen"; he emphasizes the ongoing reciprocity of Spanish-Tagalog interactions but concedes that the Tagalogs ultimately yielded to Spanish rhetoric:

For the Spaniards, translation was always a matter of reducing the native language and culture to accessible objects for and subjects of divine and imperial intervention. For the Tagalogs, translation was a process less of internalizing colonial-Christian conventions than of evading their totalizing grip by repeatedly marking the differences between their language and interests and those of the Spaniards. [But by the early eighteenth century, Tagalog conversion] coincided with rather than simply circumvented Spanish intentions. The consolidation of the colonial hierarchy over time made this sort of conversion conceivable.[14]

The Mexican writer Carlos Fuentes's (1928–) short story "Las dos orillas" (The Two Shores, 1992) concedes even less power to translation. A recasting of Bernal Díaz del Castillo's sixteenth-century account of Hernán Cortés's conquest of Mexico, *Historia verdadera de la conquista de la Nueva España* (The True History of the Conquest of New Spain), this text exposes mistranslation—even when done consciously and in good faith—as incapable of thwarting the sweeping tide of imperialism. Speaking from his grave, the narrator Jerónimo Aguilar, one of Cortés's translators, reveals that he twisted Cortés's rhetoric in an attempt to forestall Spanish conquest of the Aztecs. But his mistranslations, the truths he tells the Aztecs while pretending to remain faithful to Cortés, serve as little more than prophesies of Mexico's demise:

> I translated, I betrayed, I invented. . . . But since what I said would happen actually did happen, converting my false words into reality, wasn't I right to translate the commander backwards and with my lies to tell the Aztecs the truth? Or were my words, perhaps, a mere exchange, and I just an intermediary (the translator), the wellspring of a fatal destiny that transformed deceit into truth?[15]

Aguilar's "mistranslations" of *The True History of the Conquest of New Spain*, on the other hand, create not a prophecy but a fantasy. Concluding his account of the Spanish conquest of Mexico with a depiction of the Mayan conquest of Spain, the narrator asks, "What would have happened if what happened didn't? What would have happened if what didn't happen did?"[16] But this fantasy is undermined; Aguilar warns the reader not to think of the discovery of Spain by the Mayas as an "ideal" and suggests that the oppression of "bloody popes and Indian chiefs" has simply replaced that of Catholic kings.[17] Critical studies, adaptations, and translations by colonial and postcolonial peoples and their sympathizers seldom can prevent or even significantly postpone imperial thrusts, but they do undermine them. As Michael Cronin has noted, sources can be "manipulated, invented or substituted, or the status of the original subverted."[18]

Chinese, Korean, and Taiwanese writers interlaced hundreds of Japanese novels, plays, poems, and short stories into their own cultural fabrics via critical studies, adaptations, and translations, reversing the textual flows from China that had dominated East Asia for centuries and helping make Japanese literature the most frequently transculturated, at least within the region, of the four modern East Asian literatures. To be sure, for most of the colonial period Chinese, Korean, and Taiwanese interpretive and interlingual transculturations of Western works outnumbered those from Japan, but adaptations, translations, and critical studies of Japanese literature occupied a vital position in early twentieth-century East Asia. Chinese, Korean, and Taiwanese writers at once asserted the validity of and resisted Japanese discourse even more strongly than they did Western works. The differences stemmed primarily from Japan's paradoxical position as cultural beacon, colonial/semicolonial overlord, and (beginning in the 1930s) wartime opponent, after centuries of East Asian sinocentrism and disregard of Japanese cultural products.

Published in newspapers and journals, as separate volumes, and in collections, interpretive and interlingual transculturations of Japanese literature reconfigured texts ranging from Japanese bestsellers to obscure works that have been all but forgotten. An excellent manifestation of the "long tail" marketplace phenomenon decades before the coining of the term, colonial and semicolonial adaptations, translations, and critical studies together provide evidence that Chinese, Koreans, and Taiwanese engaged seriously with a wide swath of Japanese literature.[19] These forms of textual contact demonstrate that colonial and semicolonial intellectuals, regardless of their opinions about Japan and the legitimacy of its cultural products, strived to make Japanese literature available to a wider segment of the colonial and semicolonial population at the same time that they were unwilling to accept imperial texts without modification. Intertwining Japanese works into their own languages and cultural edifices, Chinese, Koreans, and Taiwanese asserted control over this literature while affirming its cultural capital and authority. Creating an alternative Japanese "canon" on colonial and semicolonial terms, writers from across East Asia placed their stamp on the cultural products of the imperial hegemon at the same time that they altered their own literary landscapes. Maria Tymoczko and Edwin Gentzler's remarks likening translators to double agents also capture the situation of those who adapt and write about creative texts:

[Translators] often find themselves simultaneously caught in both camps, representing both the institutions in power and those seeking empowerment. Indeed, often a certain ethics of translation limits the amount of advocating a translator can do on behalf of either party, which puts the translator in a nearly impossible situation—similar to a lawyer having to represent both the plaintiff and the defendant in the same case. Often with divided allegiances, representing the status quo while simultaneously introducing new forms of representation, the translator acts as a kind of double agent in the process of cultural negotiation.[20]

As Lawrence Venuti likewise has commented, "the translator is an agent of linguistic and cultural alienation, the one who establishes the monumentality of the foreign text, its worthiness of translation, but only by showing that it is not a monument, that it needs translation to locate and foreground the self-difference that decides its worthiness."[21] These insights apply *a fortiori* to interpretive and interlingual transculturation in the Japanese empire.

The early twentieth-century East Asian literary landscape was a terrain of remarkably nuanced, sometimes subtle, sometimes trenchant transcultural negotiation and struggle as Chinese, Japanese, Koreans, and Taiwanese reshaped the textual creations of their East Asian neighbors. Although at times articulating in their adaptations, translations, and discussions of literature what would have been next to impossible in most political or economic venues, those who performed these transculturations might not have had an obvious impact on the course of the Japanese empire. But their intellectual and artistic defiance and embrace of Japanese culture daubed strong and distinctive colorations on the outcome of empire in each of their respective homelands.

TWO

Transcultural Literary Criticism
in the Japanese Empire

Intra-empire and intra-postimperial literary criticism, understood in the broadest sense as writings of all sorts about creative texts from other cultures in the empire/postimperium, are vital forms of textual contact and interpretive transculturation. Whether advertising blurbs, explanatory notes, reviews, articles, chapters (including those accompanying translations and anthologies), or separate volumes, writings on literature often provide first contacts with creative texts. Frequently bold and trenchant, they impact patterns of literary consumption and production. Both colonial and postcolonial writings on literature from the (former) metropole and writings from the (former) metropole on colonial and postcolonial literatures expose readers to creative texts from societies in hierarchical relationships with their own; literary criticism by colonial or postcolonial subjects of one another's writings likewise is a key gateway to diverse cultural production. In nineteenth- and twentieth-century empires and subsequent postimperial spaces, critics wrote about literatures from around the world, in many cases hoping to introduce new discourses that could enliven or revolutionize local literatures, or perhaps even reform their homelands. Yet intra-empire and intra-postimperial literary criticism is particularly charged because of the often inescapable verticalities of cultural capital and authority in the (post)colonial setting.

Intra-empire literary criticism opens important windows on negotiations with the culture subjugating or subjugated by one's own, and with other cultures dominated by the same imperial power; intra-postimperial literary criticism does the same with the society that dominated or was dominated by one's own, or with others that experienced similar domination. These negotiations by literary critics generally are more explicit than other forms of literary transculturation such as adaptations, translations, and intertextualizations. Intra-empire and intra-postimperial evaluations of literature range from unabashed praise to unmitigated critique, from the intellectually rigorous to the impressionistic, and from relative objectivity to overwhelming subjectivity. They sometimes draw heavily from earlier literary and cultural commentary, providing multilayered rewritings of both creative and critical texts. Critics also compare local creative works with literature from elsewhere in the empire/postimperium and variously urge writers to eschew, to be wary of, or to follow intra-empire and intra-postimperial templates. More significantly, intra-empire/postimperial examinations of novels, plays, poems, and short stories, even when appraisals are ostensibly quite narrow in focus, often are seemingly concerned more with questions of cultural production and the nature of culture itself than with individual writers or creative works. More so than via many other media, transculturation via literary criticism provides impetus for sweeping assessments of the (former) metropole, colony, and similarly colonized spaces, toward which critics often reveal great ambivalence.

Whatever their evaluations, intra-empire and intra-postimperial literary critics leave marks on disparate cultural landscapes; regardless of how virulent the attack or effervescent the applause, they openly interweave the discourse of the (former) imperial power, colony, or similarly colonized space into their own cultural fabric. Stephen Owen has rightly argued that interpretation offers "essential insight into broad areas of concern, desires, and repressed possibilities that lie behind both the writing and reading of literature."[1] These concerns, desires, and repressed possibilities frequently are magnified in empires and postimperial locales. In such spaces, transcultural literary criticism, seldom a neutral act, and one that constructs and deconstructs identities, often explicitly affirms and challenges cultural capital and authority and involves some degree of collaboration with as well as criticism of the imperial enterprise. Writings about literature readily reveal the complex dynamics of transnational cultural struggles. They take on particular significance if other transculturations are in short supply.

Intra–East Asian literary criticism was an important part of cultural output in the Japanese empire. Writings on Japanese literature dominated this criticism, but these writings are best understood in the context of other vectors of intra-empire textual commentary. To begin with, Japanese writings on Korean, Taiwanese, and occupied Manchurian literatures often were dismissive of colonial cultural production. Reviews of the Taiwanese writer Yang Kui's prizewinning story "The Paperboy" (1934) are revealing in this regard. The prize committee did not speak of the "The Paperboy" as a great work of art. Instead, some praised Yang Kui's "sincerity" and applauded his ability to convey "true feelings" and to "draw the reader in," while others called "The Paperboy" childish and substandard. After summarizing the strengths and weaknesses of this story, the Japanese proletarian writer Fujimori Seikichi declared, "we must be lenient when judging texts by farmers and workers, and particularly so when working with texts from the colonies."[2] That is, colonial production is so inherently inferior that it must be judged by separate standards. These comments are significant coming from Fujimori, who was close friends with Chinese writers such as Xia Yan and Lei Shiyu. On the other hand, Chinese writers enjoyed significantly more cultural capital with the Japanese than did their Korean and Taiwanese counterparts. Korean dismissal of Taiwanese literature is also noteworthy, feelings of inter-colonial rivalry and superiority often overshadowing those of solidarity. For instance, in 1940 the Korean journal *Inmun p'yŏngnon* (Humanities Criticism) published a special issue on East Asian literature that included Japanese, Chinese, and Korean literatures, but had nothing on literature from Taiwan.

Taiwanese writers, on the other hand, frequently looked up to their Korean counterparts. The minutes for the February 5, 1935 meeting of the Taiwan Bungei Renmei Tōkyō Shibu (Taiwan Literature Association, Tokyo Branch) declare that because Taiwanese writers have been working extremely hard, "we are confident that in the near future the Taiwanese literary world will yield a writer like the Korean Chang Hyŏkju."[3] But this emulation was intertwined with deep anxiety. Hearing that the Taiwanese writer Yang Kui had won an award for "The Paperboy," Lai Minghong (1915–58), one of the founding members of the Taiwan Literature Association, wrote plaintively: "After much arduous labor, one of our own Taiwanese writers advanced into the Japanese literary establishment, a year after a Korean. . . . The creative style [of "The Paperboy"] is childish and certainly not up to the level of Chō Kakuchū [Chang Hyŏkju]. But Chō's work does not treat the historical reality of the colonies as vividly as Yang's."[4] Here Lai Minghong begrudgingly praises his Korean counterpart while asserting Taiwanese validity, revealing the competitive nature of inter-colonial literary production.

Writings on colonial literatures also were didactic, with Japanese critics in particular expressing strong opinions about the directions these textual corpuses should take. The first issue of the journal *Taiwan New Literature* (1936) carries comments from fifteen Japanese writers under the heading "Taiwan no shinbungaku ni shomō suru koto" (Our Hopes for Taiwan's New Literature). The Japanese proletarian writer Kishi Yamaji echoes some of his colleagues when he declares that the most important task of colonial literature is to give a concrete picture of life in the colonies; not permitted to stand on its own, Taiwanese literature is to teach the Japanese about Taiwan.[5] Similarly, creative writers in Manchuria were urged to "promote positive depictions of Manchukuo."[6] Needless to say, such directives were not regularly heeded.

In contrast with Korean and Taiwanese literatures, contemporary Chinese literature attracted substantial critical attention throughout the empire. In Taiwan, critics discussed the writings of a number of prominent Chinese literary figures, including Bing Xin (1900–99), Guo Moruo, Jiang Guangci, Yu Dafu, Zhang Ziping (1893–1959), Zhou Zuoren, and particularly Lu Xun. In 1934 the Taiwanese writer and critic Huang Shide (1909–99) summed up Taiwanese admiration for Lu Xun when he quoted extensively from the latter's famed "A Q zhengzhuan" (The True Story of Ah Q, 1921) in an essay on character description and claimed Lu Xun a master of this technique.[7] Many articles on Chinese writers stemmed from personal encounters in China, Japan, and occasionally Taiwan.[8] Other essays on Chinese literature by Taiwanese spoke more generally of Chinese language and literature reforms, sparking a series of debates on the direction Taiwanese literature itself should take.

Colonial Korean scholars wrote widely on both classical and modern Chinese literature.[9] The critic Yang Paekhwa (Yang Kŏnsik, 1889–1938) concurrently published articles as varied as "Munhak hyŏkmyŏng e sŏ hyŏkmyŏng munhak: Chungguk munhak" (From Literary Revolution to Revolutionary Literature: Chinese Literature, 1930) and "Chungguk ŭi myŏngjak sosŏl *Hongrumong* [Hongloumeng] ŭi kojung" (A Historical Study of China's Masterpiece, the

Novel *Dream of the Red Chamber* [by Cao Xueqin (1715–1763)], 1930).[10] Although at times expressing their distaste for contemporary Chinese literary production, occasionally even urging a return to the Chinese classics, Korean literary figures often looked to Chinese creative works for inspiration. They valued texts by Liang Qichao, Hu Shi (1891–1962), Lu Xun, and their contemporaries as the cultural products of a society that although fallen from glory still had much to offer its even more deeply compromised colonial neighbors. Koreans continued to write on Chinese literature into the 1940s. Significant in this context is the article "China hangjŏn chakga ŭi haeng-bang" (The Whereabouts of Chinese Resistance Writers), included in the Korean journal *Munjang*'s (Writing) "Chŏnsŏn munhak sŏn" (Selections of Battlefront Literature, 1940) series, which ran intermittently between March 1939 and February 1941.[11] As its title suggests, this essay talks about the comings and goings of Chinese writers such as Ding Ling (1904–86), Lao She, Mao Dun, and Yu Dafu. Placed below Korean-language translations of the work of the leading Japanese battlefront writer Ozaki Shirō (1898–1964), and revealing familiarity with the literary world of Japan's wartime opponent, "The Whereabouts of Chinese Resistance Writers" provides an important foil to the prominent position of Japanese literature in "Selections of Battlefront Literature."[12]

Also interesting is how some Korean publications on Chinese literature transculturate Japanese criticism. Early twentieth-century Japanese published extensively on both modern and classical Chinese literature, and, considering the close ties between the Korean and Japanese literary worlds and their mutual — if unbalanced — fascination with one another's writing, it is not at all surprising that Korean critics kept abreast of Japanese scholarship on Chinese literature. But sometimes their dependence is striking. For instance, rather than engaging directly with Chinese sources, Yang Paekhwa's article "Ho Chŏk [Hu Shi] ssi rŭl chungsim ŭ ro han Chungguk ŭi munhak hyŏkmyŏng" (Hu Shi and China's Literary Revolution, November 1920–February 1921) is an unacknowledged translation of the prolific Japanese scholar of Chinese literature Aoki Masaru's (1887–1964) article "Ko Teki [Hu Shi] o chūshin ni uzumaite iru bungaku kaku-mei" (The Literary Revolution Swirling around Hu Shi, September–November 1920). To be sure, the subtitle of Yang Paekhwa's first installment points to a predecessor: "Ch'oegŭn palhaeng doen *China-hak* chapji e sŏ" (From a Recent Issue of the Journal *Shinagaku* [China

Studies]), but Yang Paekhwa stops short of mentioning a specific article, much less that his essay is a translation; later installments do not mention a predecessor.[13]

We can only speculate why Yang Paekhwa did not reference Aoki's article. Perhaps he wanted to appear more familiar with contemporary Chinese literature than he was. Perhaps he did not want to advertise his reliance on Japanese scholarship so soon after the March First Movement (Korea, 1919). More important are the implications of his silence, a silence that exculpates the critic from acknowledging Japanese cultural capital. This silence encapsulates early twentieth-century Korean anxiety vis-à-vis both Chinese creative and Japanese critical authority, and it emblematizes the concurrent affirmations and dismissals of this authority that characterized much discourse throughout various intra–East Asian literary contact nebulae.

To be sure, Japanese critics devoted most of their attention to Western creative production; their scholarship on literature from China often focused on premodern classics. But they also wrote on more contemporary fare, particularly in the 1930s, as Japanese sought to "know China." Takeuchi Yoshimi, a founder of the Chinese Literary Research Association in 1934 and one of Japan's foremost scholars of contemporary Chinese literature later remarked:

Why weren't we aware that there are people in China like us? When we study history or Asian geography at school, we're not taught that there are people there. That's certainly how I remember it. So I was shocked [when I arrived in China in 1932]. I saw with my own eyes that there indeed were many people living very vivaciously [in China]. I wanted to know what these people were thinking, but unfortunately I didn't know their language. . . . I felt that my inability to enter into the hearts of the many people living lives similar to mine in the country next to mine was a fatal problem. I decided then to study. . . . I slowly learned to read, chewing away at their modern literature. At that time there weren't many translations or introductions of modern Chinese literature in Japan. . . . In the [Japanese] universities they did no modern literature. . . . In the past we had *kangaku* and *shinagaku*, but I didn't do this dead scholarship. Instead, I worked to change our scholarship, searching the hearts of the living people who were our neighbors.[14]

Between 1937 and 1945, Japanese published a variety of secondary scholarship on Chinese literature, including general studies, more focused examinations on such topics as the May Fourth Movement (China, 1919), literature of the period of Chinese reunification (1926–27), resistance literature, the Chinese novel, Chinese theater, literature from occupied Manchuria, and a plethora of articles on individual writers.[15]

Evaluations of contemporary Chinese literature diverged widely. A number of critics underlined China's debt to other literatures. The Japanese poet Kaneko Mitsuharu (1895–1945) comments in "Nanshi no geijutsukai" (The Arts World of South China, 1926):

Originally, China's new literary world consisted of writers with French training, American training, German training, and so forth, but the people at the center of the movement to create the so-called future literary world all have Japanese training. Even Hu Shi of Peking University has been greatly influenced by the humanism of Mushakōji's White Birch Society. . . . In the past two or three years, the number of Chinese reading Japanese books has grown substantially. Even American and European books are freely read in Japanese translation. . . . In short, it's not an exaggeration to say that China's contemporary literary world has been directly influenced by the Japanese literary world of the White Birch Society era. In a word, China's literary world is still in its infancy. It's importing blood and meat from abroad and chewing on it.[16]

Kaneko dismisses modern Chinese writers as relying heavily on Japanese books, both translations and creative texts. His patronizing comments ironically resemble those of the many scholars who dismissed modern Japanese literature as overly dependent on foreign trends.

Writings on Lu Xun, the most commonly discussed Chinese literary figure in Japan, also varied. In the second part of his essay "The Literary Revolution Swirling around Hu Shi" (October 1920), Aoki Masaru labels Lu Xun's poetry "mediocre" as compared with the work of his contemporaries, but in the third part (November 1920) he applauds the freshness of Lu Xun's prose, especially his recent "Diary of a Madman" (1918).[17] In the 1920s and 1930s, Japanese proletarian critics tended to dismiss Lu Xun as a "petit bourgeois writer," but others were moved by his discussions of the master-slave relationship: Takeuchi Yoshimi, for instance, "argued persuasively *against* the tendency to identify Asia's position [vis-à-vis the West] as simply that of the slave. This was the lesson he learned from . . . Lu Xun, who wrote that the slave's overriding desire was to become the master and so arrogate power to himself."[18] Other Japanese, such as Satō Haruo, were fascinated by Lu Xun's relationship with classical Chinese culture and tended to pay less attention to his political and social agenda. But the majority of early twentieth-century Japanese scholars of Lu Xun—including his biographer and translator

Masuda Wataru—appreciated his skills as a writer and his dedication to scholarship.[19]

Japanese, Koreans, and Taiwanese wrote prolifically on modern Chinese literature, but the most extensive vectors of intra–East Asian literary criticism were writings on Japanese literature. Like many colonial and postcolonial intellectuals, early twentieth-century Chinese, Korean, and Taiwanese scholars and literary artists wrote energetically about a vast compass of foreign literature, striving not only to introduce literatures from abroad but also to establish a modern literary criticism in their homelands. Their critical techniques—important tools in their struggles to extricate their societies from cultural conventions and construct local modernities without succumbing to foreign models—reveal complicated relationships with both Japanese and Western creative texts. Kirk Denton's comments on early twentieth-century Chinese writings about literature apply as well to those from Korea and to a limited extent Taiwan:

They are the product of the historical crisis that developed as China's long cultural heritage, faced with the technological and military superiority of the West and Japan, appeared increasingly obsolete and incapable of self-regeneration. Intellectuals, the stewards of this elite cultural tradition, were compelled to confront fundamental questions about the origins of this cultural collapse and the sources of [their society's] future rejuvenation. This process of intellectual exploration and the move toward modernity was embodied in, among other things, writings about literature. . . . Writings about literature . . . give voice to a difficult and complex experience with modernity.[20]

Chinese, Korean, and Taiwanese commentaries on Japanese literature, although not as voluminous as their writings on Western literatures, reveal intense negotiations with foreign cultural products. Anxieties toward Japanese creative forms are readily visible in their general discussions of literature, but critical studies devoted to Japanese literature expose interactions with texts from the imperial center as especially entangled. These essays, articles, and books range from comparatively straightforward summaries or literary histories, the latter a relatively new genre in early twentieth-century East Asia, to impassioned diatribes.[21] Semicolonial Chinese and colonial Korean and Taiwanese discussions of Japanese literature, regardless of when or where they were written, did everything from passionately endorse to stridently condemn metropolitan texts. Impressionistic, oscillating between adulating and castigating specific literary works, they were sometimes broad-brushed and relatively shallow. Many who wrote about literature were themselves accomplished creative writers, translators, and scholars, but their literary criticism was not always as sophisticated as their other textual output.

What they sometimes lacked in erudition, colonial and semicolonial writings about Japanese literature more than made up for by exposing both the breadth of intra–East Asian textual consumption throughout the colonial period and the simultaneous attraction and repulsion of things Japanese. Although they rarely addressed Japanese imperial policy per se, writings about Japanese literature often went beyond probing individual texts, writers, or even larger movements in the arts. Instead, raising questions about Japanese creativity, authenticity, and ultimately cultural legitimacy — questions that echoed concerns the Japanese had about their own culture as they struggled to emulate the West without losing Japanese identity — Chinese, Korean, and Taiwanese critiques of Japanese creative works provided a ripe forum, and one often quite explicit, for querying Japanese cultural capital and authority.

Colonial and semicolonial literary critics exploited Japan's alleged Achilles' heel: its extensive integration of classical Chinese and more recently Western cultural forms. These critics argued that despite its economic and military successes, despite foisting its customs and language on the people under its dominion, Japan was not a cultural leader. In fact, some scoffed, its entire premodern culture was a mere replica of China's and its modern culture a mere simulacrum of the West's. Such writers thereby debunked Japanese claims to cultural superiority and implied that Japan's grip over Asia was tight on the sword but superficial on the pen.

These misgivings were not unique to colonial and semicolonial critics. Increasingly concerned with being "original," many Japanese intellectuals of the mid-Meiji period (1868-1912) challenged the validity of imitating creative predecessors — a regimen once considered de rigueur for building artistic reputations. As Dennis Washburn puts it:

The difference between the modern anxiety of cultural borrowing and eighteenth- and early nineteenth-century attitudes about originality and adaptation is striking. [The Japanese writer Ueda] Akinari's [1734-1809] method of composition . . . made no effort to hide his literary debts. In contrast the conflicted position of those Meiji writers who wanted to emulate Western practices while maintaining or reestablishing a connection to their native literary traditions left no space for Akinari's more openhearted position. The strong nationalist positions of some *kokugakusha* [National Learning scholars] gained in influence during the second half of the nineteenth century in part because of the perception that the flood of outside influences would overwhelm Japanese culture.[22]

In short, Meiji-era culture was "defined by its preoccupation with the paradox of how to translate . . . Western modernity into Japan without losing the essence of cultural identity."[23] Ironically, the more they condemned Japanese literature for mimicking Chinese and Western literatures, the more colonial and semicolonial critics themselves adhered to Japanese and ultimately Western discourse on creativity. In their discussions of Japanese literature, Chinese, Korean, and Taiwanese critics adapted standards derived largely from their readings of Japanese and Western literary criticism, particularly the emphasis on originality.

Interweaving Japanese creative and critical texts ever more deeply into their own cultural tapestries, Chinese, Korean, and Taiwanese condensations of Japanese literature—published in general studies of literature, as introductions and conclusions to adaptations and translations of Japanese literature, as separate articles, notes, or advertisements, and as monographs—afford remarkable insights into how colonial and semicolonial East Asian intellectuals negotiated with Japanese culture. Because relatively few adaptations and translations of Japanese literature were published in Taiwan, examining Taiwanese critical studies is particularly important for understanding the transculturation of Japanese literature in that corner of Japan's imperium. By the time large numbers of Taiwanese went to Japan to study—the 1920s, more than two decades after Chinese began arriving in Japan en masse—not only were Chinese-language translations produced on the mainland already available in Taiwan, but also a large segment of the island's educated population could read Japanese works in the original. Thus, Taiwanese transculturation of Japanese literature primarily involved critical studies, publication of Japanese texts (in the original Japanese) in Taiwanese journals, and intertextualizing Japanese creative works.

Trajectories of Discourse on Japanese Literature

Intra-East Asian literary commentary has a long history in the form of Japanese and Korean discussions of Chinese literature, but there are few records of scholars from China, Korea, or Taiwan writing on Japanese discourse of any kind before modern times.[24] Not until Japan's emergence as the prototype of a new Asian modernity in the late nineteenth century did other East Asians begin writing about Japanese literature. Their examinations had an auspicious beginning in the work of Huang Zunxian, a prolific poet who became China's pioneering Japanologist. Huang Zunxian was one of the first non-Japanese East Asians to write about Japanese literature, and although his scope was limited to *kanshi* and *kanbun* (Chinese-language poetry and prose composed by Japanese), he possessed encyclopedic knowledge of these genres. He was unstinting in his appreciation of Japanese literature, including the verses of his contemporaries, but his discussions of Japanese cultural products in comparative perspective prefigured debates that swirled passionately throughout the Japanese empire concerning Japanese innovation, authenticity, and superiority.

As counselor to the imperial Chinese legation (embassy) to Tokyo beginning in 1877, Huang Zunxian lived in Japan until 1882 and published two major works on his experiences: *Riben zashi shi* (Poems on Miscellaneous Subjects from Japan, 1879) and *Ribenguo zhi* (Treatises on Japan, 1890).[25] Huang went to great lengths to research Chinese precedents for Japanese court ritual, literary forms, music, philosophy, and religion, but he did not assert Chinese cultural superiority. Instead, his writings reveal deep respect for Japanese elite culture. He spoke of it as equivalent to Chinese elite culture, frequently using the term *siwen*, "this shared culture of ours."[26] In comments appended to a poem in *Poems on Miscellaneous Subjects from Japan*, he declared: "At literati drinking parties [Japanese] poets picked up their brushes and chanted their verses at length. The best compositions often threatened to overtake works of Tang [618-907] and Song [960-1279] China."[27] Elsewhere in the same work, Huang asserted: "Japanese naturally excel at writing . . . if we read something by Ogyū Sorai [1666-1728] using Chinese pronunciation, it very easily becomes on par with texts from China. How could we say the same about writers from Annam or Korea?"[28] Here, Huang both establishes Japanese poetry as worth studying and reverses the positions of Korea and Japan in the historical East Asian hierarchy. But like most critics, his concerns were not solely literary. As Richard Lynn has noted, Huang believed that Japan "had charted exactly the right course . . . preservation of culture, especially high culture, 'this culture of ours' (*siwen* 斯文) while at the same time successfully modernizing—and he was convinced that this was the course China too should take."[29] But his words fell on deaf ears and were not taken seriously until after China's defeat in the Sino-Japanese War (1895).

Late Qing intellectuals such as Huang Zunxian laid impressive groundwork for early twentieth-century colonial and semicolonial writings on Japanese literature, which were a small but significant part of the newly inaugurated modern literary criticism that took off in China, Korea, and Taiwan in the late 1910s and early 1920s, but had its origins, at least in China, at the turn of the century. Although dedicated examinations of Japanese literature initially were a low priority—between 1904 and 1917 Chinese published only a handful of articles,[30] and Koreans and Taiwanese virtually nothing at all—in the 1900s and 1910s, Chinese and Korean adapters and translators of Japanese literature often appended critical remarks, and comments on Japanese literature found their ways into essays on a variety of topics. These interpretations were followed in the late 1910s and early 1920s by essays and then monographs devoted to Japanese literature. Zhou Zuoren's April 1918 article "Riben jin sanshinian xiaoshuo zhi fada" (The Development of Japanese Fiction over the Last Thirty Years) broke new ground as the first substantial colonial/semicolonial critical examination of Japanese literature. It begins with comments on Japanese creativity, summarizes literature ranging from the eleventh-century *Genji monogatari* (The Tale of Genji) to Meiji political novels, and discusses recent Japanese writers and literary trends.[31]

Interest in foreign literatures swelled in China, Korea, and Taiwan in the late 1910s and early 1920s, propelled in part by the explosion in publishing that followed the March First Movement and May Fourth Movement. But studies devoted to Japanese literature did not take off until after the one-yen book boom of the late 1920s.[32] This boom also coincided with the inauguration of intra–East Asian books devoted to Japanese literature, the first of which was the Chinese writer Xie Liuyi's hefty *Riben wenxueshi* (History of Japanese Literature, 1929). The *History of Japanese Literature* follows the course of some literary histories written by Japanese, covering Japanese literature from ancient times to the present, with additional material on Japanese society, language, literary groups, and journals.[33] Although they did not publish full-dress monographs on Japanese literature until after liberation, Koreans and Taiwanese wrote numerous articles on this corpus during the latter half of the colonial period (1920–45), introducing it to local audiences and raising various interpretive questions. Even the outbreak of World War Two did little to dampen the study of Japanese literature, particularly in China: in the early 1940s, Ouyang Zichuan, Wang Xilu, You Bingyin, Zhang Shifang, and others published interpretive articles and monographs on the subject.[34]

Early twentieth-century Chinese, Korean, and Taiwanese critical studies of Japanese literature cover most genres and periods. In the 1930s, for instance, the Taiwanese poet Xie Xueyu surveyed Japanese prose and poetry written in classical Chinese. Xie Liuyi's monograph discusses early Japanese genres and texts as varied as eighth-century *fudoki* (local gazetteers), the *Kojiki* (Record of Ancient Matters, 712), the *Man'yōshū* (Collection of Ten Thousand Leaves, eighth c.), and *jidaimono* (period pieces popular during the Tokugawa period, 1600–1868). Even the Korean critic Sŏ Dusu's short essay "Ilbon munhak ŭi t'ŭkjil" (Characteristics of Japanese Literature, 1940) brings up everything from Japan's earliest histories—the *Record of Ancient Matters* and *Nihon shoki* (Chronicles of Japan, 720), to early poetry anthologies such as the *Collection of Ten Thousand Leaves* and *Shin Kokinshū* (New Collection of Poems Ancient and Modern, 1205), to the narratives *Taketori monogatari* (Tale of the Bamboo Cutter, ninth c.), *Ise monogatari* (Tales of Ise, tenth c.), and *The Tale of Genji*, to *nō* drama (fl. Muromachi period, 1336–1573), kabuki plays (fl. Tokugawa period), and the twentieth-century writer Tanizaki Jun'ichirō.[35] The wide variety of materials discussed in these and other critical studies reveals colonial and semicolonial familiarity with a broad spectrum of Japanese literature.

But as with other forms of literary transculturation, modern Japanese literature—produced by a society that had successfully resisted foreign takeover—drew the most attention. In fact, in 1942, the China-based Taiwanese writer Zhang Wojun lamented what he perceived as an overemphasis on contemporary Japanese fare. He believed this prejudice prevented Chinese and Taiwanese from knowing as much about early Japanese literature as they did about Western literatures:

Those who research literature all know [about English, French, German, Russian, etc. writers] but very few know that Japan has the *Collection of Ten Thousand Leaves*, *The Tale of Genji*, the *Heike monogatari* [Tale of the Heike, thirteenth c.], Matsuo Bashō's [1644–1694] haiku, and [Ihara] Saikaku's [1642–1693] novels. All that people know about Japanese literature are modern texts, such as the works of Natsume Sōseki, Mushakōji Saneatsu, Shiga Naoya [1883–1971], Akutagawa Ryūnosuke, and the like. But these authors do not represent all of Japanese literature; they only represent modern Japanese literature.[36]

Shunned outside Japan for centuries as the cultural products of an inferior nation and in many cases as little more than extensions of classical Chinese literature, early Japanese texts—which also presented substantial linguistic challenges to foreign readers—did not become a significant part of Chinese, Korean, and Taiwanese critical discourse on Japanese literature until well after liberation in 1945.

Japan as Launching Pad

Japanese literature was not the only literature Chinese, Koreans, and Taiwanese transculturated via critical analyses. Prompted in part by Japanese studies of foreign texts as well as the desire to introduce a broad spectrum of foreign literatures, inaugurate new literatures and critical styles, and encourage reform in their homelands, they also wrote extensively about European and American literatures and transnational literary phenomena. Colonial and semicolonial discussions of the latter provide some of the most fascinating transculturations of Japanese texts; they reveal deep misgivings about the metropolitan literary world, particularly the authority and authenticity of its writers when compared with their Western counterparts. Although general examinations of literature cited and frequently extolled Japanese literature, they ultimately presented it as the launching pad of colonial and semicolonial creative endeavors, not as something to be emulated in and of itself.

The Chinese dramatist Tian Han's lengthy essay "Shiren yu laodong wenti" (Poets and the Labor Problem, 1920) is an excellent example of this development. Exploring the relationship between literature and social movements, in addition to setting forth his vision for Chinese poetry, Tian Han invokes several Japanese literary figures, including Kuriyagawa Hakuson (1880–1923), Tsubouchi Shōyō, the poets Ikuta Shungetsu (1892–1930), Shimamura Hōgetsu, and Shiratori Seigo (1890–1973), and the Christian socialist Kagawa Toyohiko (1888–1960), as well as numerous Western writers.[37] The essay strongly implies that Japanese writers have much to offer but are not at the pinnacle of their profession and do not rank among the world's literary elite. Separating the West from the Rest, Tian Han sets the tone early in the essay: "Every time I read a book [for my study of social problems] I find many Western poems that I've read; these poems have numerous connections with today's labor problems."[38] Tian Han does not reveal whether the books he is reading are Chinese, Japanese, or from outside East Asia, but he states explicitly that the poetry cited in them comes from the West.

Throughout "Poets and the Labor Problem," Tian Han depicts the work of Japanese writers—both their creative texts and critical studies—primarily as guides to Western literature and thought, not as achievements in their own right. In so doing, he assigns Japanese literature a subordinate position. His treatment of Japanese literature is particularly striking in the final pages of the essay, where he cites Ikuta Shungetsu's remarks on the importance of personal integrity in writing poetry and the poet's need to work on strength of character before cultivating craft. Tian Han notes that Shungetsu believed "training to be a poet is training to be a human being" and then comments, "I really love reading this 'poetic' essay by Ikuta Shungetsu and am itching to translate the entire thing for the youths of the Young China Association."[39] His excitement is palpable and continues to strengthen. Including several additional citations from Shungetsu's work on European poetry, Tian Han declares, "If there is truth to the notion that 'training to be a poet is training to be a human being,'" then this is where China's new poets need to start.[40] The procedural advice of the Japanese poet, based on his study of European poetry, is a beginning. But the world's great literary figures—those whose creative texts have the most to give—are from the West. Tian Han concludes the body of "Poets and the Labor Problem" by proclaiming: "Please read Homer, Virgil, Dante, Goethe, and Shakespeare. How much food have they given us?"[41] In his estimation, based more on impressions than empirical data, no Japanese literary figure could match the contributions of the Western greats.

Japanese exposés on literature also provide a bouncing-off point in the Taiwanese writer Qiu Gengguang's essay "Chuangzuo dongji yu biaoxian wenti" (Motivation to Create and Problems with Expression, 1942), although here Japanese discussions are directly challenged rather than subtly undermined, and their authenticity rather than their authority questioned. "Motivation to Create and Problems with Expression"—the opening article of the first issue of the journal *Taiwan Literature*—begins with a quotation from the Japanese writer Mushakōji Saneatsu: "Mushakōji Saneatsu says, 'I can't discuss literature with people who don't really know loneliness.'"[42] *Taiwan Literature*, the flagship publication of the Taiwan Literature Association (a group of primarily Taiwanese writers), thus paradoxically opens with a quotation from a Japanese writer, drawing immediate attention to the metropolitan literary world. But Qiu Gengguang quickly challenges Mushakōji's blanket dismissal of people who do not "know loneliness" and even calls into question the integrity of his Japanese counterpart, declaring, "People are vapid. People aren't honest. . . . Wherever you go there is only hypocrisy. There are only nasty people. So those who aren't lonely cannot truly love litera-ture."[43] Implying that the hypocritical Mushakōji will discuss his craft only with those already capable of "loving literature," Qiu Geng-guang hints at the limitations of the Japanese writer's commitment. On the other hand, since loneliness is after all a common human experience, Mushakōji's audience is not particularly exclusive. Qiu Gengguang's comments on this Japanese predecessor are shrouded in ambiguity.

References to other Japanese writers in "Motivation to Create and Problems in Expression" are equally problematic. Qiu Gengguang begins his final paragraph by citing Kuriyagawa, to whose "symbol of suffering" he already has referred several times.[44] " 'Literature is pure life expression. Literature is completely separated from the op-pression and coercion of the outside world. It needs to be based on an absolutely free mind and express a person's individual world.' This is what Mr. Kuriyagawa Hakuson has said, but except for dar-ing writers very few can expose themselves completely faithfully."[45] Not only does Qiu Gengguang critique Kuriyagawa's statements more openly than he does Mushakōji's, but he also implies that Kuriyagawa, perhaps like Mushakōji, cannot be "completely faith-ful." Even more important, in taking on one of China's most beloved Japanese literary critics—Kuriyagawa's lectures at Kyoto University attracted scores of Chinese students, and he was popular among Chinese literary luminaries including Lu Xun, Guo Moruo, Yu Dafu, Tian Han, and Hu Feng, who translated many of his texts—the Tai-wanese Qiu Gengguang questions Chinese adoration of metropolitan criticism.

Whether they depicted Japanese writers as stellar guides to West-ern literary thought but not world-class authors, or as untrust-worthy guides who nevertheless had much worth listening to, Chinese, Korean, and Taiwanese explorations of general literary phe-nomena exposed reservations about Japanese texts and writers. Even more revealing negotiations and struggles with the metropolitan lit-erary establishment were in studies devoted primarily to Japanese literature.

Leaping among Texts and Cultures

At times more emotional than analytical despite calls for a rigorous overhaul of conventional commentary, early twentieth-century East Asian writings about literature, particularly discussions of Japanese literature, articulated visceral reactions to creative works from the metropole. Some East Asian writings condemned these texts outright, while others endorsed them wholeheartedly; whether discussing a single text or summarizing Japanese creative output, most interpretations fell somewhere in between. What united colonial and semicolonial writings about Japanese literature were not their evaluations of this body of texts but rather their sweeping assessments of Japanese culture: some accused the Japanese of cultural incompetence if not shortcomings in national character, based on perceived deficiencies in literary output, whereas others lauded Japanese texts not only as fine examples of literary craftsmanship but also for their potential ability to enlighten entire societies.

Ba Jin's and Han Shiheng's sharp critiques and Lu Xun's and Zhang Wojun's strong endorsements of Japanese literature are particularly noteworthy in this regard. While in Japan in the mid-1930s, Ba Jin, one of twentieth-century China's most towering writers, studied Japanese, read Japanese and other literatures, and purchased anthologies such as the massive *Gendai Nihon bungaku zenshū* (Complete Collection of Modern Japanese Literature, 1926–31). He also wrote fiction and essays, including "Ji duan bu gongjing de hua" (Some Irreverent Words, 1935), a scathing attack on Japanese literature and culture that also rebuts Japanese critiques of Chinese culture.[46] Ba Jin asks: "It is said that literature in Japan already has developed to a surprising degree, [particularly the *tsūzoku shōsetsu* (popular novel)] . . . which is all about love and chivalrous swordsmen. Doesn't the popularity of this kind of novel . . . show that Japanese literature already has fallen to an astonishingly low level?"[47] He also calls dramas by Nagayo Yoshirō "childish" and argues that they compare unfavorably with their Chinese counterparts; he claims that it is only because the Japanese have such low standards that they applaud Nagayo. Similarly, Ba Jin argues that when reading literary works by Akutagawa Ryūnosuke he feels only disgust; he declares that only one or two stories in the hefty *Akutagawa Ryūnosuke shū* (Collection of Writings by Akutagawa Ryūnosuke, 1928) are worth rereading. In truth, although several of Akutagawa's Chinese translators, including Feng Zitao, claimed that his texts were not as popular in

China as might be expected, Akutagawa was one of the most frequently consumed and transculturated Japanese writers in China. Many Chinese were stunned at his suicide, and several Chinese periodicals published special issues in his memory. Thus, in "Some Irreverent Words" Ba Jin attacks not only Akutagawa but also Chinese adoration of this Japanese luminary.

But Ba Jin reserves his harshest criticism for Japanese naturalism, homing in on two of its most prominent writers, Tayama Katai (1871–1930) and Shimazaki Tōson; he chastises Katai and Tōson for straying from the relative detachment of French naturalism as exhibited by Émile Zola (1840–1902), and instead exposing dirty secrets for personal gain. He argues that Katai depicts "unnecessary tragedy" in *Futon* (The Quilt, 1907), a novel Ba Jin terms "cowardly" (*qienuo*). And then Ba Jin turns to Tōson, claiming that although many Japanese writers—such as Mushakōji Saneatsu, Kume Masao, and Matsuoka Yuzuru (1891–1969)—discuss their personal relationships in their creative texts, Tōson is the infamous "master" of this craft: "in his works one can find the worst examples [of exploiting other people]."[48] Referring to Tōson's controversial novel *Shinsei* (New Life, 1919), which discusses the Japanese writer's scandalous relationship with his niece, Ba Jin criticizes him for sacrificing the young girl for his own literary glory:[49] "The hero of *New Life* is such a selfish, such a cowardly person! But Tōson wasted how many words scheming to depict himself as a mighty, very bold, and very sincere character? Naturally, these schemes failed."[50]

In truth, whatever schemes existed had not failed. By the time Ba Jin wrote "Some Irreverent Words," two Chinese translations of *New Life* already had been published, one in 1927 and another abridged version in 1934. The following decade, the Taiwanese writer Zhang Wojun, who translated Tōson's lengthy historical novel *Yoakemae* (Before the Dawn, 1935) during the war, encouraged Chinese to take a closer look at this Japanese literary giant, arguing that translating and introducing Tōson's works "would certainly enliven the Chinese literary world."[51] When Tōson died in August 1943, some Chinese and Taiwanese literary figures published essays in his memory, including Zhou Zuoren, who noted that his interest in Tōson stemmed from his days as a student in Japan four decades before.[52] But Ba Jin could not forgive Tōson for sacrificing life for art. Nor could he make peace with the broader corpus of Japanese literature. Ba Jin concludes "Some Irreverent Words" by asserting, "Japanese literature is not worth looking at . . . it's a shame I can't let Akutagawa hear these irreverent words."[53] In this essay, he launches a strident attack against Japanese literature, yet, like those of so many colonial and semicolonial literary critics, his diatribe is paradoxically vitiated by his admission to having read large quantities of this corpus.[54]

Noteworthy as well is how Ba Jin's attitudes toward Japanese literature changed after the war. For instance, in the essay "Wenxue shenghuo wushi nian" (Fifty Years of the Literary Life, 1980) he reveals that he considers among his teachers such leading early twentieth-century Japanese writers as Natsume Sōseki, Tayama Katai, Akutagawa, Mushakōji, and especially Arishima Takeo, one of whose essays he "sometimes recites."[55] In a conversation with the Japanese writer Kinoshita Junji (1914–2006) during his visit to Japan in April 1980, Ba Jin declared:

Chinese writers have two things to learn from their Japanese counterparts. The first is that Japanese writers are very hardworking. They do a lot of research and make sure that they understand things deeply. The other is that they write a lot. They're very diligent. . . . Japanese writers have written a lot and the quality is high. On those points we can't match them.[56]

It is possible that, just as Ba Jin's comments on Japanese literature in "Some Irreverent Words" likely are colored by anger toward Japan's imperialist program, these remarks stem more from his frustration with contemporary Chinese literary production than from his admiration of Japanese writers per se. But even so, they serve as a reminder of the deep imbrication of literary contact nebulae with more rigidly hierarchical spaces.[57]

Colonial and semicolonial critiques of Japanese literature frequently ventured beyond creative texts and became convenient forums for broader condemnations. Discussing Japanese literature not in isolation but instead as a central component of the imperial body, writings on Japanese textual production tied it to numerous other art forms and even national character. In this way, Japanese artistic deficiencies were portrayed as signs of broader cultural if not national decay. The scope of literary criticism increased as Chinese, Korean, and Taiwanese intellectuals sought effective means of negotiating with multiple facets of imperial culture. Condemning much more than metropolitan creative texts, Ba Jin's "Some Irreverent Words" begins:

It's been eight years since I read [Akutagawa's] "Chōkō yūki" [(Travel Along the Yangtze, 1924). In this text, Akutagawa asked] "What is there in contemporary China? Politics, scholarship, the economy, art, aren't they all crashing? Particularly art—since the mid-nineteenth century, has there been a single work the Chinese could be proud of?" This is what Akutagawa said ten years ago to his friend Nishimura [while in China]. . . . But I don't know whether the extremely intelligent Akutagawa, after returning home, also replaced the word "China" in his question with the word "Japan" and asked the Japanese [whether they had anything of which to be proud].[58]

Ba Jin's answer, not surprisingly, is a resounding "no," and to strengthen his position he cites Japanese scholars who have commented on shortcomings in Japanese culture; their critiques are presumably more authentic than those from outsiders. Discussing deficiencies in Japanese music, painting, and literature, "Some Irreverent Words" attacks a multitude of Japanese creative forms.

Han Shiheng went one step farther and linked perceived deficiencies in literature and the literary establishment with those in national character. In the preface of *Xiandai Riben xiaoshuo* (Modern Japanese Fiction, 1929), his collection of ten Japanese creative works in Chinese translation, he disparages Japanese literature and argues that its weaknesses stem from the Japanese people's inherent inferiority:

Regretfully, we must say that Japanese literature truly has no great works. Now there certainly are those who will ask, "What constitutes great literature?" What I mean is that the success of a text does not depend entirely on its artistry but rather lies in its deep investigation of life. Thus the joy and the sadness that a work expresses cannot be the private affairs of a single individual. Rather, these emotions belong to a people, or even the entire human race. . . . Now we must ask why modern Japanese literature does not reach this profound and lasting condition. . . . The primary cause lies in the character of the Japanese.[59]

Yet like many Chinese, Korean, and Taiwanese commentators on Japanese literature, Han Shiheng's essentialist misapprehensions about the metropole and its cultural productions did not prevent him from consuming the latter in great quantities and disseminating Japanese literature to his compatriots via commentary and translation.

Across the spectrum from critics like Ba Jin and Han Shiheng were Chinese, Koreans, and Taiwanese who lauded Japanese literature and argued that it had much to teach them about both the Japanese and themselves. In an essay published in 1942, the Taiwanese writer and critic Zhang Wojun linked literary output and national character, as had Han Shiheng, but Zhang depicted Japanese literature as worth studying: "If we read Japanese literature, then we can know the Japanese national character and Japanese customs and sensibilities."[60] In "Guanyu Daoqi Tengcun [Shimazaki Tōson]" (On Shimazaki Tōson,

1942) he went even farther and contended that Japanese literature, particularly Tōson's "Arashi" (Storm, 1927)—a short story where Tōson revealed his devotion to his four children—could teach readers how to behave toward their families: this text "will show fathers and mothers how to love their children dearly and will show children how to love and respect their parents."[61] This statement echoes those of the Korean translators of Arishima Takeo's essay "Chiisaki mono e" (To My Little Ones, 1918), translated into Korean in 1921, and Fukuda Masao's (1893–1952) dramatic poem "Airakuko" (Child of Grief and Pleasure, 1919), translated into Korean in 1924, who believed these texts expressed ideals of loyalty and love that could greatly assist the Korean people.

In "Riben wenhua de zai renshi" (Becoming Reacquainted with Japanese Culture, 1943), Zhang Wojun offered an even more comprehensive reason for studying Japanese literature and culture: "Because Japanese once received Chinese culture . . . [researching Japan] not only will allow us to understand Japanese culture but also will help us understand our own culture. . . . The amount of learning that has been lost in China and can be recaptured from studying Japanese culture is not small."[62] He complains that while most Japanese tend to know something about Chinese culture, few Chinese know anything about Japan; he urges Chinese intellectuals to introduce to China "Japanese history, geography, religion, philosophy, literature, art, law, and economics, even sensibilities and customs."[63]

Even more portentous was the outlook of Lu Xun. In his discussion of Mushakōji Saneatsu's antiwar play *Aru seinen no yume* (The Dream of a Certain Young Man, 1916), Lu Xun argued that studying this text would have a bearing on nothing less than the future of China itself. The first preface to his translation of *The Dream of a Certain Young Man*, written in 1919, describes his admiration for Mushakōji's work: "I was very moved upon finishing it. I thought the ideas expressed were penetrating, the confidence exhibited firm, and the voice also very profound."[64] Lu Xun's second preface, written three months later, outlines the importance of making this play available to the Chinese:

I already mentioned that the aim of this play is to protest war. There's no need for the translator to repeat himself. But I think there'll be some readers who believe that because Japan is a nation that goes to war easily the Japanese should become familiar with this play, but that the Chinese have no such need. I personally believe that this couldn't be farther from the truth: indeed, the Chinese people themselves aren't skilled fighters but they by no means curse war. . . . In discussions of Japan's recent annexation of Korea we always say, "Korea is really our vassal state." As long as we hear this kind of talk we should be afraid.

I believe this play also can cure many of the chronic illnesses in traditional Chinese thought. Thus, translating this play into Chinese is a matter of great significance.[65]

Here and in other essays, Lu Xun urged Chinese to take a closer look at Japanese literature; he believed that learning about this corpus could help Chinese further strengthen their nation.

Discussions of the heuristic value of Japanese literature, however hyperbolic, frequently broached its connections with foreign audiences and literatures. Colonial and semicolonial intellectuals paid particularly close attention to the spread of Japanese literature in Europe and the United States, often using its success with Western readers and impact on Western literatures to justify their own engagement with it. For instance, in the preface to the three-volume *Xiandai Riben xiaoshuoji* (Collection of Modern Japanese Stories, 1923), the first anthology of Japanese literature in Chinese translation, Zhou Zuoren comments that twentieth-century Japanese literature has made remarkable strides and that many Japanese creative texts have "world value" and "can be compared with modern European literatures."[66] Likewise, in the opening lines of *History of Japanese Literature* (1929), the first intra-empire monograph on Japanese literature, Xie Liuyi cites Japanese success on the world creative stage:

Japanese literature of the last twenty years already has won an important position in world literature. . . . In recent years our own literature also has been influenced to some degree by Japanese literature. With each passing day the number of Chinese translations of works by Japanese writers is increasing tremendously. Some German and Russian universities have Japanese literature departments where students research Japanese language and literature; the French poetry world has been influenced by Japanese *haikai* [comic poems]. This shows without a doubt that Japanese literature already has attracted the world's attention.[67]

On the other hand, Chinese, Koreans, and Taiwanese did not blindly follow trends in Western engagement with Japanese literature. To begin with, they ignored the American and European fascination with premodern Japanese culture, generally believing it inferior to Chinese and Korean production. In addition, having fewer preconceived notions concerning modern Japanese literature than their Western counterparts, they wrote about, adapted, and translated a greater variety of late-nineteenth and early twentieth-century Japanese texts.

Yet critics also advocated studying Japanese literature precisely because of its close ties with Western literatures. At the beginning of *History of Japanese Literature*, Xie Liuyi declares, "the current of modern European literature surged to the East and was completely accepted by Japanese literature. If we want to study what kind of influence the European literary current is sure to have on the literatures of each East Asian country . . . it is only in Japanese literature that we can find the answer."[68] The Korean revolutionary writer Im Hwa continued this argument in the essay "Chosŏn munhak yŏngu ŭi il kwaje: sin munhaksa ŭi pangbŏpnon" (A Thesis on the Study of Korean Literature: Methodology for a History of New Literature, 1940), where he declares that modern Korean writing owes much to Japanese literature and that to understand their own literature better, Koreans need to look closely at Japanese works:

A detailed study of Japanese literature, or Meiji and Taishō literary history, is even more important than a direct study of Western literature. This is because our new literature received Western literature through Japanese literature. Moreover, Japanese literature did not so much transfer itself to Korean literature as it gave Western literature to Korean literature. It did so via translations, creation, and criticism.[69]

On the other hand, Im Hwa continues, Korean literature is closer to Japanese literature than to European literature. Even more important, he claims it essential that Koreans recognize that the new literature of Korea benefited greatly from the late nineteenth-century Japanese movement to unite written and spoken languages (*genbun itchi*). He states flatly that Korean literature "transplanted the style of Meiji literature."[70] Like Xie Liuyi and numerous other colonial and semi-colonial critics, Im Hwa emphasized Japanese literature's role as transmitter of Western literature while recognizing the important part played by Japanese literature itself in developing other East Asian literatures. Although Im Hwa divided literature into "new [Korean] literature" (*sin munhak*), "Japanese literature" (*Ilbon munhak*), and "Western literature" (*sŏgu munhak*), his comments on literary transfer expose the amorphousness of the boundaries among Japanese, Korean, and Western literatures in the early twentieth century.

Writing in the same vein, in "Ping Juchi Kuan [Kikuchi Kan] jin zhu *Riben wenxue annei* [Nihon bungaku annai]" (Comments on Kikuchi Kan's Recent *Guide to Japanese Literature*, 1939) the Taiwanese critic Zhang Wojun evaluates Japan's impact on contemporary Chinese literature and notes what Chinese can learn from Japanese texts.

But, as he also indicates in this essay, prejudices toward Japanese literature and culture run deep. He critiques the common perception that classical Japanese literature derives from Chinese literature and that modern Japanese writing replicates Western literature:

People think of Japanese literature just as they think of Japanese culture: before the Meiji period it was transplanted from China, and after the Meiji period it was transplanted from the West. What was transplanted from China the Chinese already had had for a long time; what was transplanted from the West could be directly sought in the West. Thus the tendency for considerable disdain. Thanks to recent introductions and translations of Japanese literature, people already are gradually recognizing the inaccuracies of these ideas. There is no doubt that the Japanese have transplanted Chinese and Western literatures. But things particular to the Japanese, like their lives, feelings, and character, must be sought in Japanese literary works. These are things we must know.[71]

Several years later, in "Becoming Reacquainted with Japanese Culture," he additionally lamented: "All along we Chinese have been excessively indifferent to Japanese culture. . . . Even since the late Qing, when the Chinese began studying foreign cultures, very few have eagerly studied Japanese culture. . . . [our] superficial conception of Japanese culture makes our people dismiss it."[72] This dour view echoes what Xie Liuyi had said in the preface of his 1929 *History of Japanese Literature*: "There are many Chinese who still look down on Japanese literature and language, wrongly thinking they're the same as their Chinese counterparts. . . . These mistakes need to be corrected."[73] Despite their attempts to change the status quo, Xie Liuyi and Zhang Wojun were outnumbered by colonial and semicolonial critics who thought little of writing dismissive evaluations of Japanese literature, revealing more about their own anxieties than the texts they nominally were discussing.

To rectify sweeping preconceptions both positive and negative was a particular challenge in the colonial and semicolonial environment, where critiques of Japanese literature easily became occasions for assessments—however veiled—of colonial and semicolonial policies. Negotiating with imperial texts was a loaded act with multiple ramifications. Whatever they sometimes lacked in penetrating insights into individual writers and creative works, Chinese, Korean, and Taiwanese discussions of Japanese literature were vitally concerned with the place of this literature in their own and other societies. A large part of this concern stemmed from doubts about Japan's cultural authority, based on its sustained emulation of the foreign.

Calculating Debt

The question of Japan's obsession with foreign cultures—Chinese in the past and Western in the present—and related debates on Japanese creativity, legitimacy, and authority—reverberated throughout the Japanese empire, including Japan itself, where intellectuals queried the authenticity of their nation's "translation culture": "Almost all of the [Meiji] oligarchy's policies were dependent to some degree on the translation of Western political, legal, and technological knowledge. . . . the growing volume of translations drew attention to the issue of the long-term effects of cultural borrowing on the true character of Japan." [74] But while Japanese spoke of maintaining the "true character" of Japanese culture, colonial and semicolonial intellectuals such as Xie Liuyi and Zhang Wojun raised the stakes and, by emphasizing Japan's "debt" to other cultures, questioned the very existence of a distinct Japanese culture.

One subset of colonial and semicolonial essays on Japanese literature takes indebtedness for granted. Texts by Chu Yohan, Hwang Sŏk-u (1895–1960), Ham Ildon (1899–?), and Yang Chichang state matter-of-factly that Japanese writings have been "influenced" by other literatures but do not elaborate on this point. The Korean poet Chu Yohan's two-part essay "Ilbon kŭndae si ch'o" (Summary of Modern Japanese Poetry, 1919), often cited as the first Korean study of Japanese literature, begins, "for the past fifty years new Japanese literature has been influenced by Western civilization." Under this influence Japan's new poetry "resembles Western poetry."[75] But rather than develop this claim, Chu Yohan turns to the Japanese movements themselves and translates selections from ten major Japanese symbolist, romantic, and aesthetic poets.

Others, such as the Korean writer Hwang Sŏk-u, paid even less heed to the putatively foreign origins of Japanese literature. Hwang opens his essay "Ilbon sidan ŭi idae kyŏnghyang" (The Two Major Trends of the Japanese Poetic World, 1920) with comments not on Japanese indebtedness to Western culture but instead on Japanese artistic movements, listing a multitude of names:

If we were to summarize the largest trend in Japanese poetry we of course would have to say the colloquial free verse movement, but within this trend there is the symbolist poetry movement, begun by Miki Rofū [1889–1964] and Hinatsu Kōnosuke [1890–1971] and led by the young poets Yanagisawa Ken [1889–1953], Saijō Yaso [1892–1970], and Kitamura Hatsuo [1897–1922]. There is also the popular poetry movement, which struggles against the symbolist movement and is led by Fukuda Masao [1893–1952], Tomita Saika [1890–1984], Katō Kazuo [1887–1951], and Shiratori Seigo [1890–1973].[76]

When he addresses the Western connection, Hwang Sŏk-u discusses not influence on Japanese literature but instead Japanese translations of European literature, including Ueda Bin's landmark *Kaichōon* (Sound of the Tide, 1905), an anthology of primarily French and Belgian symbolist poems. Hwang summarizes the diffusion of symbolism throughout Europe but does not depict Japanese symbolism as derivative or secondary to European versions. Similarly, in "Myŏngch'i munhak sajŏk koch'al" (Historical Study of Meiji Literature, 1927), which outlines Japanese literature from the eighth-century *Record of Ancient Matters* through the early twentieth century, the Korean critic Ham Ildon refers to the Chinese and Western impact on Japanese literature but also speaks of Japanese literature as worthy of study in its own right.[77] And in "Esupuri nūbō to shi seishin" (Esprit Nouveau and the Poetic Spirit, 1936), the Taiwanese avant-garde poet Yang Chichang (1908–94) depicts new trends in Japanese literature as closely related to European modernism, but hardly their obedient offspring.[78] Elsewhere, in fact, Yang Chichang applauds the Japanese surrealist poet and literature scholar Nishiwaki Junzaburō (1894–1982) for opening a new phase of literary criticism.[79]

But for many critics, including Zhang Shenqie, Lu Xun, Xie Liuyi, and Zhou Zuoren, understandings of Japan's "debt" to other literatures were complex and deeply ramified. Zhang Shenqie's verbose 1935 denunciation of Japanese literature as derivative of other literatures openly condemns metropolitan creative products, although it at the same time paradoxically reveals the Taiwanese critic's familiarity with them. Even more remarkable is that most Chinese, Korean, and Taiwanese scholars who discussed Japanese creativity, or the lack thereof, did not propose that their societies cast Japanese literature aside in favor of more "authentic" texts (namely, those created in the West or in early China). Instead, they focused on how much their respective societies had to learn from the Japanese example. So Japan's material success strongly mitigated challenges to Japanese cultural capital and authority; if anything, geopolitical legitimacy in the world arena enhanced its artistic clout.

Zhang Shenqie depicts early Japanese writing as a spinoff of Chinese literature and post-1868 literature as a subsidiary of Western letters in "Dui Taiwan xinwenxue luxian de yi ti'an" (One Proposal for the Course of Taiwanese New Literature, 1935). He writes:

From ancient times, the course of Japanese literature was to accept the course of Chinese literature. . . . motives and methods for creating [and this is true even of *waka* and haiku] were just about all from Chinese literary forms. There were no exclusive inventions. . . . As for modern Japanese literature, we can say that it is entirely a copy of European and American modern literature. . . . Everyone knows that all of modern Japanese literature was influenced by Western literature. The so-called pioneers of modern Japanese literature also all were directly or indirectly influenced by Western literature . . . Futabatei Shimei, Kuroiwa Ruikō, Tsubouchi Shōyō, Mori Ōgai, and Tokutomi Sohō [1863–1957] imported Western literature. And Ozaki Kōyō, Natsume Sōseki, Ishikawa Takuboku, Kunikida Doppo, Arishima Takeo, Tokutomi Roka, Tokuda Shūsei, and many others followed on their heels and created the so-called Japanese literary world. After them, Nakamura Murao [1886–1949], Masamune Hakuchō [1879–1962], Mushakōji Saneatsu, Kikuchi Kan, Hasegawa Nyozekan, Kume Masao, Akutagawa Ryūnosuke, Tanizaki Jun'ichirō, and others used the flavors of European and American literary schools to expand the Japanese literary world.[80]

Here Zhang Shenqie dismisses Japanese literature as merely copying other literatures, a common accusation at the time, but suggests that this shortcoming has not stopped him from reading the corpus extensively, or at least pretending to do so. In this sense, Japanese literature remained something of a guilty pleasure throughout the empire. The Chinese, Korean, and Taiwanese love-hate relationship with Japanese literature is particularly clear in critiques like Zhang Shenqie's that inundate the reader with inventories of writers and titles, indicating the breadth and at times fascination of even the harshest critic.

For other colonial and semicolonial literary critics, Japan's alleged lack of an innate civilization was a positive attribute; these intellectuals argued that because it was not weighed down by its past, Japan could adapt readily to changing world circumstances. As Lu Xun remarked in 1925:

[Kuriyagawa Hakuson] berates his country [Japan] for not having an original civilization or any exceptional figures. This is right on target. Japan's culture first was modeled after China, and then after Europe. Not only does Japan have no one like Confucius or [other Chinese luminaries]. Since the sciences took off, there's been [no one who can compare with the European geniuses]. . . . All in all, Japan has no innate civilization or great world figures . . . but I think that it is only because of this that Japan could become what it is today. Because the country has very few antiquities, the grip of the past isn't powerful. As things change, Japan too can very easily change and always be fit for survival. It's not like an ancient country that merrily continues on, relying on an innate and obsolete civilization that has made it utterly inflexible, and ends up on the road to destruction. If China doesn't reform completely, Japan will outlive it.[81]

Some critics were even bolder and made a case for both studying and imitating Japanese writing. In "The Development of Japanese Fiction over the Last Thirty Years" (1918), Zhou Zuoren denies persistent claims that Japanese literature is unworthy of separate examination because its premodern forms are carbon copies of Chinese literature and its modern forms are mere derivatives of Western antecedents. From the outset, he argues that Japanese culture is not mimetic but instead stems from "creative imitation," with the emphasis on "creative":

Many presume that Japanese culture is a result of "imitation." There also are people in the West who assert, "Japanese civilization is the daughter of Chinese civilization." This kind of talk tells only part of the story. We can say that in general Japanese culture is one of "creative imitation." . . . [The English art critic Laurence Binyon (1869–1943) has argued that] "believing Japanese art is nothing but an imitation of Chinese art shows a superficial understanding." This is also true when talking about Japanese literature.[82]

Zhou Zuoren adds that if the Chinese wish to "cure" their fiction and create their own modern literature, they must "imitate" foreign works, including those from Japan. He calls on the Chinese literary establishment to "start from the very beginning" by creating a Chinese *Shōsetsu shinzui* (Essence of the Novel, 1886), a critical work by the Japanese novelist Tsubouchi Shōyō (1859–1935) that called for a new Japanese literature and for many years was regarded as the origin of modern Japanese literature.[83] According to Zhou Zuoren, the Chinese should not only acknowledge but also imitate the ingenuity of an East Asian neighbor once deemed culturally inferior.

Regardless of how Chinese, Korean, and Taiwanese literary critics spun the connections between Japanese and Western literatures, their attention to these ties both subverted and solidified Japanese cultural capital and authority, revealing the intense ambiguity of cultural struggle in the colonial/semicolonial realm. Premodern Japan's diminutive cultural capital in East Asia, followed by its rapid development into the prototype of East Asian modernity and a colonial/ semicolonial power, made these negotiations particularly volatile. Discourse on cultural superiority did not play as large a role in the Japanese empire as in some other nineteenth- and twentieth-century empires, but imperial Japanese increasingly portrayed themselves as the cultural as well as political and economic pacesetters of Asia.

Critical studies of Japanese literature by colonized and semicolonized subjects explicitly challenged but also in many ways succumbed to this imperial cultural hegemony.

Negotiating with Japanese Literary Criticism

Colonial and semicolonial engagement with metropolitan cultural dominance is particularly complex in critical studies that draw significantly, and often explicitly, from Japanese counterparts. Chinese, Korean, and Taiwanese writers made no secret of consuming Japanese writings about literature, and in their work they frequently ended up taking material from Japanese critical writings on Japanese literature. Neither complaints that the Japanese lacked originality nor the perception that Japanese criticism was biased stopped them from drawing on Japanese interpretations. The studies that resulted are intriguing multilayered confections that transculturate both critical and creative Japanese texts. On the surface, colonial and semicolonial studies generally accede more readily to Japanese creative authority than those which do not reference Japanese secondary sources, but they also pose intricate challenges to both creative and critical legitimacy.

Chinese and Korean intellectuals began paying serious attention to Japanese literary criticism in the late nineteenth century and Taiwanese intellectuals several decades later. Predictably, the earliest intra–East Asian negotiations with Japanese critical studies recast Japanese discussions not of Japanese but of Chinese literature. In 1897, the Japanese scholar Kojō Tandō (Teikichi, 1866–1949) published a 700-page history of Chinese literature, the *Shina bungakushi* (History of Chinese Literature), and the following year Sasakawa Rinpū (Sasakawa Taneo, 1870–1949) — then Japan's leading specialist on Chinese literature — produced a text with the identical title. The circulation of these monographs was not limited to Japanese audiences; Sasakawa's *History of Chinese Literature* was translated into Chinese in 1903 and, as the Chinese scholar Lin Quanjia (1877–1921) later revealed, this text inspired him to write his own history of Chinese literature the following year, the very different *Zhongguo wenxueshi* (History of Chinese Literature, 1904).[84] Chinese, Korean, and eventually Taiwanese intellectuals became fascinated by Japanese writings on classical Chinese literature, as well as by Japanese criticism of American and European literary works, the latter of which they translated in large quantities. Yet they also began looking more closely at Japanese discussions of Japanese literature. Occasionally they reprinted these appraisals in their own periodicals—both in translation and the original—and at times added commentaries, but most often they let the Japanese critical studies speak for themselves.

Even more significant than reprintings of Japanese discussions of Japanese literature were colonial and semicolonial efforts to incorporate them into their own essays on literature from the metropole. By greatly condensing Japanese sources, scholars in China, Korea, and Taiwan transformed metropolitan discourse. Some of their narratives, including Ch'oe Chaesŏ's "Tangmok Sunsam [Karaki Junzō, 1904–80] chŏ, *Kŭndae Ilbon munhak ŭi chŏn-gae* [Kindai Nihon bungaku no tenkai]" (Karaki Junzō's *The Development of Modern Japanese Literature*, October 1939), claim to summarize a single Japanese study of Japanese literature, while others, like Sŏ Dusu's "Characteristics of Japanese Literature" (1940), use multiple Japanese sources to frame their discussions of Japanese literature.

The title of Ch'oe Chaesŏ's essay explicitly links his study to a prolific Japanese critic's hefty volume. The essay's subtitle, "Cha-a ŭi paljŏn kwa munjang ŭi pyŏnch'ŏn" (Development of the Self and Changes in Writing), suggests that this is the focus of both Karaki's work and Ch'oe Chaesŏ's discussion, while the opening line—"This is a précis of Karaki Junzō's *The Development of Modern Japanese Literature* (published June 1939)"—reinforces that Ch'oe Chaesŏ's essay, instead of engaging directly with Japanese literature, will summarize a recent Japanese volume on Japanese literature.[85] The clear implication is that the essay will allow Korean readers access to both creative and critical Japanese writing while submitting to Japanese interpretations.

But such strategies are deceptive. The "development of the self" is not the principal concern of Karaki's volume; instead, the "development of the self" relates to the subject of Karaki's opening chapter, "Meiji bungaku ni okeru jiga no hattenshi" (History of the Development of the Self in Meiji Literature). The scope of the Japanese critic's work is broader than Ch'oe Chaesŏ suggests. Even more important, Ch'oe Chaesŏ counters Karaki's claims concerning the origins of modern Japanese literature. Karaki identifies Futabatei Shimei, the author of Japan's so-called "first modern novel," and Kitamura Tōkoku (1868–94), a parent of Japanese romanticism, as the "sources of modern Japanese literature." Ch'oe, on the other hand, concludes his essay by declaring, "It is safe to say that the headwaters of modern Japanese literature are literary sketching (*sasaengmun/shaseibun*) and naturalism."[86] Proposing a different understanding of something as fundamental as the sources of modern Japanese literature, the Korean critic launches a subtle yet important subversion of a metropolitan critical authority.

Sŏ Dusu's "The Characteristics of Japanese Literature" takes a different approach, drawing from multiple Japanese sources. The second section of the essay opens with a lengthy quotation, in Korean translation, from the first chapter of the Japanese journalist and social critic Hasegawa Nyozekan's (1875–1969) popular volume *Nihonteki seikaku* (The Japanese Character, 1938).[87] Unusual for East Asian literary criticism at this time, this quotation is followed by a bibliographic citation that gives not only Nyozekan's full name and the title of his monograph, but also the page in *The Japanese Character* where the quotation can be found. Sŏ Dusu's references to outside criticism here and throughout "The Characteristics of Japanese Literature" as much demonstrate his knowledge of and reliance on Japanese critical writings as they facilitate his readers' own forays into the genre. A list of thirteen sources, eleven by Japanese critics, concludes "The Characteristics of Japanese Literature"; this bibliography most obviously reinforces Sŏ Dusu's dependence on outside scholarship, particularly recent Japanese writings, but it also provides his Korean audience — many of whom in 1940 would have been able to read Japanese criticism in the original Japanese — with a handy outline of supplementary reading.[88]

Yet the significance of these references involves more than their presence and positioning within the Korean essay. As his title suggests, Sŏ Dusu talks about Japanese literature, tossing around insights and stereotypes, while introducing a range of Japanese creative texts and literary movements. But like many purported examinations of Japanese literature by Chinese, Korean, and Taiwanese critics, "The Characteristics of Japanese Literature" uses literature as a launching pad for discussions of Japanese culture. Sŏ Dusu's references to Nyozekan are particularly fascinating in this regard. Long a vocal critic of Japanese militarism but intimidated in the mid-1930s by increasing government repression, Nyozekan used his deliberations on Japanese character to counter ultra-nationalist ideology more subtly.[89] *The Japanese Character* brims with discussions of Japan's alleged historical tolerance and, indeed, embrace of the foreign. In the second section of "The Characteristics of Japanese Literature," Sŏ Dusu translates into Korean one of Nyozekan's early remarks on this topic: "Although there have been interruptions, it's safe to say that the Japanese have welcomed the intrusion of outside peoples and faiths more than nearly any other society on earth. . . . What defines our national character is much more our tendency to assimilate [Jpn. *dōka*; Kr. *donghwa*], something that has been cultivated over our long history, than our tendency to exclude, which arises in response to particular conditions."[90] Here Nyozekan (and Sŏ Dusu) cleverly twist *dōka*, a buzzword of Japanese imperial rhetoric that referred to the forced assimilation of colonial peoples into Japanese culture, instead to denote Japan's embrace and transculturation of the foreign.

In the final section of his essay, Sŏ Dusu again cites Nyozekan's observations on how Japan preserves and develops its culture while incorporating the foreign; he additionally notes the consequences of so doing. Questions of assimilation silently loom. Is there a way to reclaim agency, a way for Koreans likewise to twist being assimilated into Japanese culture into assimilating Japanese culture? Like Japan, Korea had a long history of actively engaging with foreign cultural products; Sŏ Dusu's essay — with its references and lengthy bibliography — was only the latest, and not so subtle, example of this phenomenon. Appearing in Korean after publication in that language was banned, "The Characteristics of Japanese Literature" alludes to Korean possibilities and potentials in the face of increasing Japanese infringement on the freedom of expression of colonial subjects.

But often acquiescence to Japanese critical authority overshadowed these potentials and possibilities. A number of colonial and semicolonial writers justified their engagement with particular Japanese texts based on their popularity in Japan. The Taiwanese critic Zhang Wojun's essay "*Aiyu* [Aiyoku] yizhe yinyan" (Notes from the Translator of *Aiyoku* [Lust], 1926) is a patchwork of Japanese celebrations of Mushakōji's *Aiyoku* (Lust, 1926) framed by Zhang's own endorsement of this play. Direct quotations from enthusiastic Japanese evaluations of *Lust* by the well-known Japanese writers Masamune Hakuchō, Fujimori Junzō (1897–?), Uno Kōji (1891–1961), and Hirotsu Kazuo (1891–1968) occupy nearly half of the essay.[91] Zhang's reliance on Japanese interpretations to justify his translation of Mushakōji stands out in light of Mushakōji's great popularity in China and the abundance of positive assessments already penned by major Chinese critics including Lu Xun and Zhou Zuoren, assessments with which — having arrived in China from Taiwan in 1923 and quickly becoming deeply involved in the literary world there —

Zhang Wojun almost certainly was familiar. Inundating his essay with extracts from Japanese critics, Zhang implies that Japanese evaluations of their own work are to be taken more seriously than those by their Chinese counterparts.

Zhang Wojun's exclusion of Chinese evaluations of Japanese literature in favor of Japanese critical studies is even more evident in "Comments on Kikuchi Kan's Recent *Guide to Japanese Literature*" (1939), written more than a decade after "Notes from the Translator of *Lust*." In this introduction to his translation of Kikuchi Kan's 1938 study of Japanese literature, Zhang laments that even after years of writing about modern Japanese literature, the Chinese have yet to compose an appropriate introduction to this corpus. He asserts that Kikuchi Kan's study is "the best introduction to Japanese literature — at least for those in our country who aspire to research Japanese literature." He explains that what makes *Guide to Japanese Literature* particularly appealing are its concise expression and broad content; Kikuchi Kan introduces not only Japanese literature from earliest times to the modern period, but also "European and American masterpieces."[92]

The latter remark is especially ironic considering that Zhang Wojun begins his comments by complaining that few see Japanese literature as anything other than a copy of Chinese or Western texts. In fact, Zhang's choice of Kikuchi's work as an introduction to Japanese literature is even more incongruous. In this book, Kikuchi not only discusses Western influences on Japanese literature, as did most of his contemporaries; more important, he devotes nearly a quarter of the volume to examining American and European writers and texts. Although Kikuchi explains that to understand modern Japanese literature one must "know foreign [Western] literature," devoting so much space to foreign literature in a section titled "Required Reading" in a book titled *Guide to Japanese Literature* — at a time when Japanese were publishing any number of books explicitly devoted to foreign literatures — suggests that he has run out of things to say concerning Japanese literature, and ultimately that he believes this literature cannot stand on its own. Later in *Guide to Japanese Literature*, Kikuchi laments: "No people devours foreign literature more ravenously than the Japanese, but it's sad that Japanese literary works are not introduced [outside Japan]. This is because of the extreme difficulty of the Japanese language."[93] He conveniently ignored, or perhaps was unaware, that by the late 1930s the Chinese — deterred by neither language barriers nor cultural misgivings — had published hundreds of volumes of Japanese literature in Chinese translation, including at least twenty volumes of Kikuchi's work. But even Kikuchi, devoting so much space to summaries of Western literature in *Guide to Japanese Literature*, did not explore Japanese literature as fully as he might have. That Zhang Wojun celebrated such an introduction to Japanese literature reveals more than anything his dismay with Chinese discussion of this body of texts. It also underhandedly points to the Taiwanese critic's misgivings concerning the authenticity of Japanese literature and its separateness from Western models.

Chinese, Korean, and Taiwanese enthusiasm for Japanese literary criticism raises an interesting question: what are the implications of introducing Japanese literature via summaries or translations of Japanese literary criticism, rather than in studies ostensibly or actually based primarily on colonial/semicolonial readings of Japanese creative works? On the one hand, summaries and translations of metropolitan literary criticism allow the colonial/semicolonial audience greater insight not only into Japanese literature but also into how Japanese evaluated their own writings. They also afford the colonial/semicolonial critic further opportunities to negotiate with Japanese texts. Yet openly relying on Japanese interpretations and dismissing local discourse also suggests intellectual subordination to metropolitan rhetoric, or simple laziness.

In the case of Zhang Wojun, what are the implications of choosing a Japanese critical study as concerned with Western literature, and as silent on connections between Japanese and Chinese/Korean literatures, as Kikuchi Kan's *Guide to Japanese Literature*? Western literature enjoyed significant cultural capital throughout the Japanese empire, and underlining the similarities between Japanese and Western literature was an excellent strategy for at once promoting and debasing Japanese literature. That a Japanese critic voices the similarities, rather than a colonial/semicolonial critic, in some sense makes the claims harder to dismiss. Yet at the same time that they increase Japanese literature's appeal, imputed parallels with Western literature also challenge Japanese creativity and often authority.

Most Chinese, Koreans, and Taiwanese who wrote about Japanese literature were at least somewhat familiar with Japanese literary criticism. In the reference matter of *History of Japanese Literature* (1929), Xie Liuyi included a bibliography of several hundred Japanese sources that he claimed was "for those who aspire to study Japanese literature in depth."[94] In addition to revealing the broad scope of Xie Liuyi's research, this list also proved useful to subsequent Chinese, Korean, and Taiwanese critics of Japanese literature. Some colonial and semicolonial observers chastised the Japanese literary establishment for producing a bulky yet biased body of scholarship. For instance, in 1934, the Chinese critic and translator Han Shiheng asserted that Japanese writers were concerned solely with enhancing their social position and reaping material benefits and claimed that they blindly promoted whatever their friends had written, regardless of merit: "Today's Japanese literary establishment is severely lacking in critics; there have been almost no rigorous critics . . . most of the critics just praise one another."[95] The Japanese literary establishment at times was as ripe a target for literary critics as Japanese texts themselves. Echoing Han Shiheng, the Chinese critic Zhang Shifang concludes his 1942 study of Japanese wartime literature by commenting that the Japanese literary establishment is still "filled with weary, weak, hollow, and declining phenomena."[96] But regardless of their irritation with the perceived biases of Japanese literary criticism, Chinese, Korean, and Taiwanese writers frequently used Japanese studies as the bases for their own interpretations, or occasionally—through translation—as their virtual replacements.

Calls by Im Hwa, Lu Xun, Xie Liuyi, Zhang Wojun, Zhou Zuoren, and numerous other Chinese, Korean, and Taiwanese literary critics to look closely at, if not emulate, Japanese techniques, did not go unheeded. Nor did the many harsh critiques of the Japanese literary establishment and its textual products, and by extension Japanese culture—including those by Ba Jin, Han Shiheng, and Zhang Shenqie—go unnoticed. Intra-empire discourse on metropolitan literature, some of which also transculturated literary criticism from Japan, not only introduced colonial and semicolonial readers to a broad spectrum of Japanese writing but also added vital perspectives to larger early twentieth-century East Asian dialogues on cultural production. By interweaving Japanese texts into Chinese, Korean, and Taiwanese rhetorical fabrics, discussions of Japanese literature—whatever their stance—impelled colonial and semicolonial peoples to look more closely at the trajectories of their own creative outputs and to replot their positions on East Asian and ultimately global cultural tapestries.

Significantly, this negotiation was just as urgent after liberation. Zhang Shenqie, who in "One Proposal for the Course of Taiwanese New Literature" (1935) had stressed the derivativeness of Japanese literature, two decades later in *Tan Riben, shuo Zhongguo* (Discussing Japan, Speaking about China, 1954) portrayed it as a formidable rival of Chinese literature, one that he claimed the Chinese had to overtake in all due haste lest they forever lose the opportunity. He declared that Japanese culture was neck and neck with the West, which "clearly proves the Japanese people's ability and excellence." In his opinion, if the Chinese did not do their utmost to overtake the Japanese they would forever lose the opportunity to catch up.[97] This and many other examples serve as solemn reminders that the perceived threats Japanese culture posed to East Asian sovereignty did not disappear with surrender and decolonization.

The Chinese writer Lei Shiyu, an active participant in the early twentieth-century Japanese literary sphere and one of the few Chinese creative figures to publish extensively in Japanese, maintained a lifelong interest in Japanese literature. Four years before his death he published *Riben wenxue jianshi* (A Brief History of Japanese Literature, 1992), a survey of everything from Japan's earliest myths to contemporary texts. In the opening lines, Lei Shiyu underlined the significance of the Japanese literary tradition in East Asian history and painted a picture of unremitting cultural exchange with China:

> Japanese literature constitutes an important part of East Asian literature, and its connections with Chinese literature are the most intimate. China and Japan have been in contact for more than a thousand years, and not only because of their geographical proximity. The Chinese and Japanese also use the same characters for writing, which facilitates cultural communication. Uninterrupted cultural exchange between the two countries has gone on for a very long time.[98]

Cultural exchange was long and uninterrupted, but it also was chaotic, plagued with snarls. The impassioned rhetoric that characterizes much Chinese, Korean, and Taiwanese discourse on Japanese writings is matched if not exceeded by the emotionalism and bias found in Japanese assessments of colonial and semicolonial literature. Regardless of their origins or subject matter, critical studies result from intense engagement with texts and generally reveal cultural attitudes more openly than other forms of textual contact. Although largely neglected in studies of transculturation, contact nebulae of literary criticism provide sharp insights into intra-empire cultural negotiation. Yet interpretive transculturations cannot be studied in isolation, so it is to interlingual transculturations—namely, adaptations and translations—that I now turn.

THREE

Multiple Vectors and Early Interlingual Transculturations of Japanese Literature

Interpretive and interlingual transculturations of creative texts engage in multiple layers of negotiation. In empires and postimperial sites, these forms of textual contact often embody the ambivalence of (post)colonial writers toward the cultural output of the (former) metropole, of writers from the (former) metropole toward the cultural products of their (post)colonial counterparts, as well as of inter-(post)colonial relations. Interpretive and intertextual transculturations also obscure and at times deeply compromise dichotomies. Critical studies, regardless of tenor, often reduce creative works to fragments of their former selves and frequently serve as springboards for discourse on broader political, social, and cultural concerns. For instance, Japanese discussions of Chinese, Korean, and Taiwanese literary works often alleged colonial and semicolonial inferiority, while in colonial and semicolonial East Asia, commentaries on metropolitan novels, plays, poems, and short stories tended to segue into challenges against imperial cultural legitimacy and authority. In contrast, by transculturating creative works into local languages, adaptations and translations create tangible alternative literary corpuses. Whether veering sharply from nominal sources to create the loosest of adaptations, or translating texts as faithfully as possible, (former) metropolitan and (post)colonial adaptations and translations become new versions of literary texts from elsewhere in the (former) empire, competing with their sources for physical and figurative shelf space. Their rewritings of literary predecessors form another subset of contact nebulae that provides further insights into the dynamics of literary transculturation.

Printed texts are relatively inexpensive, quickly reproducible, and require no special packaging; whether smuggled or declared they readily traverse political frontiers. But crossing linguistic borders is another matter. While most cultural products can be consumed, if only in part, almost immediately after arriving in new environments, the printed text frequently requires significant intervention in the form of interlingual transposition if it is to be accessible to readers in its new home. Richard Jacquemond's comments on nineteenth- and early twentieth-century Egyptian rewritings of French literature describe many early encounters:

> [Interlingual transculturation] consisted most frequently in a very free transposition of the French narrative and actually was not called a "translation" (*tarjama*), but "adaptation" (*iqtibas*), "arabization" (*tar'ib*), or even "egyptianization" (*tamsir*). The French text was not treated as a whole which ought to be respected and fully rendered; rather, it was completely transformed into something familiar to the Arab readership in its style, form and content.[1]

As Jacquemond suggests, in many cases mediation initially takes the form of adapting or naturalizing source texts: rewriting them in local languages, moving settings from more distant places to closer to home, changing names to those familiar to the intended audience, and manipulating content (deleting or adding passages, making ideological, practical, or factual revisions to existing discourse) to reflect the concerns of the adapter in addition to the mores of new sites.

In general, this form of transculturation remains popular even after decades of contact. Some writers adapt canonical texts in ways that accentuate the commonalities of human experience. For instance, South Africa's renowned playwright Welcome Msomi reworked *Macbeth* in the Zulu-language play *uMabatha* (1969), "using Shakespeare's play about the power-hungry thane Macbeth to retell the story of Shaka, the greatest, if most feared, king of the Zulus."[2] Regicide is condemned in *Macbeth* and exalted in *uMabatha*, pointing—like many disparities between the two plays—to large cultural gaps between England and Africa. But together the remarkably parallel scripts highlight the universality of despotism and violence. Other writers adapt canonical works to address more current concerns. Shortly before his death, the Ghanaian playwright Joe de Graft (1924–78), who had engaged with Shakespeare's oeuvre since secondary school, rewrote *Macbeth* as *Mambo, or Let's Play Games My Husband* (1978). Unlike *uMabatha*, de Graft's play, by connecting with the atrocities taking place in Idi Amin's Uganda, exposes more recent horrors unleashed on the African continent.[3] Similarly, as the South African director Janet Suzman has commented concerning the motivation behind her staging of *Othello* in the late 1980s:

The wind prevailing in South Africa in the year 1987 was still as foul as ever. . . . The status quo looked as if it might continue to the crack of doom. . . . [Thinking of *Othello* we were] fired up after ten frustrating years of keeping a constant vigil for the play that might speak not just to [us] as actors but to our anguished country. The story of a mixed marriage systematically destroyed . . . seemed to embrace the larger context of South Africa just perfectly.[4]

Adaptations continue to flourish as writers not only contribute to the survival of literary predecessors, including those from societies in distinctly unequal power relationships with their own, but also — by greatly transforming these predecessors — declare a mitigated form of cultural independence.[5]

But as familiarity with and desire for the foreign increase, loose renderings are joined by translations. Rather than a tool with which to naturalize the unfamiliar, this more faithful form of textual contact often is embraced as an expedient way to learn about different peoples and places. It also is lauded as something that will allow readers and writers more readily to transform themselves, their society's literature, and in some cases even their society itself. This is as evident in Vishnu Khare's *Maru-Pradesh aur anya kavitayen* (1960), the Indian writer's collection of close Hindi translations of T. S. Eliot, as it is in early twentieth-century Chinese, Japanese, Korean, and Taiwanese debates on translation and translations of literature from around the world.[6]

Adapters, translators, and their publishers have varied motives — everything from making money and increasing circulation of texts they find personally compelling, to providing themselves and other local talent with foreign models that will help them develop new writing styles and in some cases even impel them to jump-start their nation's cultural production, to exposing readers to new ideas that will lead them to reevaluate their societies and ultimately allow them to embrace or even instigate reform if not revolution. Irene Eber writes concerning the attitudes of early twentieth-century Chinese intellectuals toward translation: "Above all, [literature] was to establish new values that would contribute toward changing China from a backward to a modern state. . . . Translating . . . was part of these writers' agenda."[7] Indeed, Lu Xun, Zhou Zuoren, and many of their contemporaries, "saw literary translation as a means of altering China's subordinate position in geopolitical relations."[8] Creative writers likewise looked to translations for new literary styles. As Ohsawa Yoshihiro notes concerning translation in late nineteenth- and early twentieth-century Japan, "In their attempts to create a 'new' written Japanese based on the vernacular language, writers in the Meiji period turned to translations of Western works for inspiration."[9]

But regardless of aim, the fundamental results are analogous: adaptations and translations are contact nebulae of transcultural intervention and often struggle. Although a number are silent or misleading concerning their origins, many advertise themselves as transpositions of textual predecessors, listing both "writer" and "adapter/translator." This grants authority to sources at the same time it points to their malleability.[10] In some cases, adaptations and translations taunt their textual predecessors and even the societies with which these predecessors are associated. For instance, in his late nineteenth-century adaptation of Shakespeare's *The Comedy of Errors*, the Indian writer Munshi Ratna Chand replaces Dromio's description of Nell as "spherical, like a globe," a site where he could "find out countries" including England "in her chin," with the lines: "This [England] was such a tiny country that exceedingly hard as I looked, I could nowhere find it." Hindustan (India), on the other hand, is the first country located: "Hindustan was in her face, for just as Hindustan is the best of all countries, so was her face the best part of her person."[11] But adaptations and translations generally are more subtle. Far from marginal, they stand at the heart of transcultural negotiation.

Adaptations and translations can rigorously exploit their sources, enhancing the linguistic and aesthetic dimensions of receiving cultures.[12] Those in early twentieth-century East Asia were no exception: they considerably enriched Chinese, Japanese, Korean, and Taiwanese languages and literatures. Yet even more significant than their more measurable cultural impact—introducing not only knowledge and ideas but also words, grammar patterns, styles of writing, genres, and themes—are the insights these adaptations and translations offer into writers' mingled revulsion and veneration of predecessors.[13] As inherently ambiguous processes, adaptation and translation are especially fraught in environments of significantly uneven power relationships, where clashes among cultures can be acute and have important implications. By manipulating creative texts, adapters and translators in this environment often dismantle existing rhetoric while at the same time giving it greater prominence.

For most of the colonial period, East Asian adaptations and translations of Western literatures outnumbered those of creative texts from elsewhere in the empire. But what they sometimes lacked in bulk, inter-(semi)colonial adaptations and translations, Japanese adaptations and translations of (semi)colonial literatures, and particularly (semi)colonial adaptations and translations of Japanese literature more than made up for in significance. As in many empires and post-imperial spaces, these dynamic intra-empire literary contact nebulae were key sites of cultural negotiation that offer new light on the morphemics of empire and on processes of textual contact more generally.

Adapting and Translating Chinese, Korean, and Taiwanese Literatures in the Japanese Empire

As was true of literary criticism, adaptations and translations of Japanese literature outnumbered other forms of intra-empire interlingual transculturation. But examining briefly these other forms is important for a more comprehensive understanding of textual contact in early twentieth-century East Asia. Particularly significant are Japanese adaptations/translations of Korean literature and Japanese and Korean adaptations/translations of Chinese literature. Adaptations and translations of Taiwanese literature by other East Asians, adaptations and translations of Korean literature by Chinese and Taiwanese, and Taiwanese adaptations/translations of Chinese literature played smaller roles.[14] As the cultural products of lands colonized by Japan, Korean and particularly Taiwanese literatures were not regarded in particularly high esteem by other East Asians; in addition, the increasing body of Japanese-language Korean and Taiwanese literatures also decreased the impetus for translation.

Early twentieth-century Japanese-language adaptations and translations of Korean-language literature embody many of the paradoxes of textual contact in empire. A wide variety of Korean-language creative writing was adapted and translated into Japanese during the colonial period: folksongs, classical novels, and contemporary poetry, prose, and drama.[15] The years surrounding colonization saw the adaptation and translation of a number of classical Korean texts thanks to the efforts of such groups as the Chōsen Kenkyūkai (Society for the Study of Korea, est. 1908) and the Chōsen Kosho Kankōkai (Society for the Publication of Old Korean Books, est. 1909). The *Chō-sen bungaku kessakushū* (Collection of Korean Masterpieces), the first anthology of classical Korean novels in the Japanese language and the result of Korean and Japanese collaboration, appeared in 1924. Transculturation of early Korean works and their contemporary adaptations continued intermittently through much of the colonial period. For instance, the first Japanese-language rewriting of a Korean play was of *Ch'unhyang chŏn* (The Tale of Spring Fragrance), one of Korea's most popular folktales; the Japanese-language version of this Korean classic was first performed in 1938.

Focus shifted to contemporary material during the latter half of the 1920s. The 1925 translation of Hyŏn Chin-gŏn's short story "Pul" (Fire, 1925), eight months after its appearance in Korean, is said to have marked the first translation of twentieth-century Korean literature into Japanese. This was followed by translations of five prose works in 1926 and four in 1927 and 1928, one of which was of Yi Kwangsu's famed *Mujŏng* (Heartless, 1917); Yi Kwangsu was the most frequently translated modern Korean writer during the colonial period. During the early 1930s, translation activities dropped off considerably, then rebounded in 1936. Between April and June of that year, translations of the work of six Korean women writers were serialized in the *Ōsaka Mainichi, Korea Edition*. In July 1936 Hosoi Hajime (1886–1934) put out the three-volume *Chōsen sōsho* (Korean Library), which contained translations of fourteen classical Korean works. During the so-called Korea boom of the late 1930s and early 1940s, when journals such as *Modern Japan* devoted special issues to the colony, a handful of Korean prose works were translated annually; in 1940, Japanese published the first three anthologies of translated modern Korean prose, including the *Chōsen bungaku senshū* (Selected Works of Korean Literature, a three-volume anthology of Korean stories) and a collection of Yi Kwangsu's prose in translation.[16] Japanese published several additional translations of Korean literature during the final years of the colonial period.[17]

But as the case of Kim Soun (discussed in Chapter 1) suggests, much of this material was translated by Koreans, not by Japanese. Learning Korean was never a high priority for Japanese writers, and in truth, few Japanese had the opportunity to learn Korean, especially in the 1930s and 1940s. Despite devoting considerable effort to distributing Korean writings, many Japanese scholars of Korea openly disparaged Korean culture and history and throughout the colonial period used adaptations and translations to reinforce stereotypes. Shakuo Shunjō (Tōhō, 1875–?), whose Society for the Publication of Old Korean Books was then the largest publisher of Korean historical materials, declared that Korea "has no great art [and] no great literature"; he urged Koreans to "forget Korean history" and "abandon the Korean language and customs." Similarly, the journalist Aoyagi Tsunatarō (1877–1932), one of Japan's most productive adapters/translators of early Korean texts, condemned Korean culture and history as characterized by decay and corruption.[18] Not surprisingly, many adaptations and translations by the Society for the Study of Korea "highlight the issue of factionalism as a leitmotif in Korean dynastic history. . . . their aim was to 'satirize and dramatize' these incidents which witnessed fierce factional struggles. . . . By depicting Korean history as fraught with internecine conflict and devoid of unity, the settler pundits tried to use literature for the purpose of legitimizing Japanese colonial rule as providing a political stability unknown in the history of Korea."[19] Also reinforcing stereotypes were the wildly popular (among Japanese) kabuki performances of the Japanese-language version, penned by Chang Hyŏkju, of *The Tale of Spring Fragrance*, performances embraced in part for their trendy colonial kitsch.[20] As Susan Bassnett and Harish Trivedi have noted, textual contact of this sort is "a means both of containing the artistic achievements of writers in other languages and of asserting the supremacy of the dominant . . . culture."[21]

Chinese literature fared somewhat better than its Korean counterpart in intra-empire adaptation and translation. East Asia maintained its attachment to classical Chinese literature well after China's defeat in the Sino-Japanese War. During the first half of the colonial period (1895–1920), Taiwanese intellectuals established private schools to teach the classics, founded poetry groups to promote the classics, and did what they could throughout Taiwan to ensure that classical Chinese studies thrived on the island.[22] Japanese and Koreans adapted and translated volumes of classical Chinese drama, poetry, and essays on aesthetics, as well as anthologies of classical Chinese literature; Japanese reconfigured the great sixteenth-century novel *Shui hu zhuan* (Water Margin) at least six times between 1896 and 1937.[23] Eventually, however, classical Chinese creative texts had to share shelf space with their contemporary counterparts. The first Japanese-language translations of modern Chinese literature were done by Chinese including

Zhou Zuoren, but Japanese translators soon emerged.[24] On the other hand, except for Satō Haruo and a few other prominent Japanese creative writers, most Japanese who translated modern Chinese literature were lesser known individuals. This contrasts with intra-empire adapting and translating of Japanese literature, which involved China's, occupied Manchuria's, Korea's, and Taiwan's most prominent literary figures.[25] Intra-empire translations of modern Chinese literature reveal that if China no longer was the cultural center of East Asia, and in fact often was derided as woefully behind the times, nonetheless its modern textual products contributed significantly to regional creative exchange. They did so even as China suffered from imperialism and war.

Japanese published a number of translations of contemporary Chinese literature beginning in the 1920s.[26] In July 1926, the journal *Reconstruction* issued a summer supplement on Chinese literature, with translations of short stories and plays by Guo Moruo, Tian Han, and Zhang Ziping; poetry by Xu Zhimo (1897–1931); and an essay by Hu Shi. Between 1935 and 1943, the Chinese Literary Research Association published dozens of Japanese-language translations of such Chinese writers as Guo Moruo, Huang Zunxian, Lao She, Lu Xun, Mao Dun, Xie Bingying, Yu Dafu, Zhang Ziping, and Zhou Zuoren in its periodicals *Chūgoku bungaku geppō* (Chinese Literature Monthly) and *Chūgoku bungaku* (Chinese Literature). Japanese also published collections of Chinese literature in translation, including the eight-volume *Gendai Shina bungaku zenshū* (Complete Works of Modern Chinese Literature, 1940) and several anthologies of Lu Xun's writing. Among these is the seven-volume *Dai Ro Jin* [Lu Xun] *zenshū* (The Complete Works of the Great Lu Xun, 1937), which ironically preceded by a year the first major Chinese collection of Lu Xun's works, the *Lu Xun quanji* (The Complete Works of Lu Xun, 1938). Japanese also published translations of literature by writers (mostly Chinese) from occupied Manchuria, at times juxtaposing these translations with creative texts by Japanese writers.[27]

In short, whatever their stance on Japanese imperial pressures in China, Japanese writers were drawn to the contemporary literary output of their continental neighbor after the mid-1920s, a time of deepening national involvement with the Asian mainland and gradual disenchantment with liberal internationalism as voiced by the West. It is not surprising that Japanese readers felt especially congenial with contemporary Chinese works that queried that country's progress with establishing national unity and social transformation, as well as literary reforms that consciously or unconsciously resembled Japan's example of an alternative Asian modernity. Japanese translations of Chinese literature were consumed not only by Japanese but also by Taiwanese and Koreans, and they at times were celebrated in colonial fiction. The Taiwanese writer Long Yingzong's prizewinning story "Town of Papayas" includes a character who is "deeply impressed by Satō Haruo's [translation of] Lu Xun's 'Guxiang' [Hometown, 1921]" even though he believes the artistic level of Chinese literature rather low because of that nation's internal turmoil.[28]

In general, Chinese writers, many of whom had close ties with their Japanese counterparts, welcomed the increased readership translations made possible. But they also had harsh words for some of their translators. Lu Xun, for one, was displeased with Inoue Kōbai's *Ro Jin* [Lu Xun] *zenshū* (Complete Works of Lu Xun, 1932) and complained about his translator in letters to Japanese friends.[29] Also noteworthy is the case of Ōuchi Takao (Yamaguchi Shin'ichi, 1907–80), who while living in Shanghai in the mid-1920s became friends with left-wing Chinese writers such as Tian Han, Yu Dafu, and Ouyang Yuqian.[30] The following decade, after a stint with the South Manchuria Railway, Ōuchi became Japan's principal translator of literature from Manchuria and rendered into Japanese more than a hundred works by Chinese writers who lived in Japan's informal colony. Ōuchi was one of the few Japanese scholars of Manchurian literature who took Chinese contributions seriously, but his attitudes toward Chinese writers in Manchuria shifted noticeably during the 1940s, when he turned to promoting literature advocated by Japanese authorities. This, combined with his failure to alert Chinese writers that he was translating their texts, perhaps explains Chinese ambivalence toward his projects: several writers Ōuchi translated remained suspicious of his motives decades later and even confessed to having altered plots so that texts would appeal to Japanese readers. Of course, even then, writers could not assume that their texts were being translated without substantial revisions.

Korean intellectuals admired a number of Chinese reformers, particularly Liang Qichao, whose thought they embraced. Dozens of Liang's essays on civilization, education, enlightenment, literature, patriotism, women's rights, and Western political and social theories were introduced, adapted, and translated into Korean in the late nineteenth and early twentieth centuries, as were his biographies and stories of heroes and patriots. Koreans also continued adapting and translating classical Chinese literature, even as they sharply criticized their ancestors' fascination with things Chinese.[31] But like their Japanese counterparts, Koreans did not begin translating contemporary Chinese literature until the 1920s, a preference for modern texts now challenging earlier interest in the classics. Yang Paekhwa, a scholar of both modern and premodern Chinese literature, was the first Korean translator of modern Chinese literature, and his nine-installment translation of "new poetry" by Chinese writers such as Guo Moruo, Hu Shi, and Tian Han, published in *Dongmyŏng* (Eastern Light) between 1922 and 1923, cleared the track for other Korean adaptations and translations.[32] Koreans published *Chungguk tanp'yŏn sosŏljip* (Collection of Chinese Short Stories), their first anthology of contemporary Chinese literature, in 1929. Highlighting the significance of China as a potential role model, one advertisement for this collection read, "Learn about newly awakened China! Read this volume to learn about China!" Another declared, "Young Koreans must read the sentiments of young Chinese in their time of trial."[33] Early twentieth-century Korean intellectuals perceived translation of Chinese literature as a vital activity, one with significant implications and possibly sweeping consequences.

Translations increased in the 1930s. Lu Xun's prose was a favorite, but theater also was popular, particularly plays that spoke of resistance and women's rights. Interestingly, colonial Korean translations of contemporary Chinese theater significantly outnumber those from Japan—even though more Koreans could read Japanese than Chinese originals—suggesting a stronger interest in the social and political questions addressed by many Chinese plays than in the more psychological issues probed in Japanese theater.[34] The war years were unfavorable to Korean translations of Chinese literature. Not only was publishing in Korean technically prohibited, but the Japanese also banned many works of modern Chinese literature, including Lu Xun's writings.[35] Even so, Koreans continued to translate texts from the mainland into the 1940s. The Korean journal *Writing*, for instance, included samples of battlefront literature by Xie Bingying and Zhou Wen (1907–52) in its "Selections of Battlefront Literature" series, which was devoted primarily to translations of Japanese war literature. The Chinese extracts give varying perspectives on war, highlighting uncertainties such as the inscrutability of the "traitor," the questionable validity of the "all-clear" following the air-raid siren, and women's roles in wartime. Contemporary China offered numerous philosophical, ideological, and cultural positions that appealed to colonial Koreans, who had much in common with their continental neighbors. It is only natural that Koreans, who for centuries had looked to China for cultural guidance, should — after some initial hesitation — again turn their attention there. With the exception of Manchuria and pockets under foreign control, China had remained a sovereign state and thus was attractive to Korean intellectuals.

Intra-Empire Adaptations and Translations of Japanese Literature

Chinese and Koreans published scores of adaptations and translations of Japanese and Western literatures in the 1900s and 1910s. Like many nineteenth-century Japanese writers in their negotiations with premodern Chinese and then European and American literatures, most early twentieth-century Chinese and Korean writers initially were more concerned with naturalizing foreign texts than with providing accurate replicas.[36] In Korea and China, fewer than 20 percent of interlingual rewritings published before the new culture movements of the late 1910s and early 1920s can be considered translations, that is to say, relatively faithful to their sources.

Although not embraced by the Taiwanese — by the time Taiwanese writers became engrossed in foreign literatures in the 1920s, close translations into Chinese had mainly replaced adaptations — adapted works enjoyed phenomenal success for nearly two decades in China and Korea. In contrast, translations at first struggled commercially. An example is Lu Xun and Zhou Zuoren's two-volume *Yuwai xiaoshuoji* (Short Stories from Abroad, 1909), a collection of sixteen European stories in relatively faithful Chinese translation, which initially sold a very disappointing twenty copies.[37] As Lawrence Venuti has noted,

In opposition to the comforting Confucian familiarity offered by many late Qing translations, [in *Short Stories from Abroad*] Lu Xun and Zhou Zuoren's strategies were designed to convey the unsettling strangeness of modern ideas and forms. . . . instead of the domestication favored by a British theorist like Tytler, Lu Xun and Zhou Zuoren followed the foreignizing strategies favored by German theorists like Goethe and Schleiermacher, whose writings they encountered while studying in Japan . . . [Lu Xun] made his aim explicit: "instead of translating to give people 'pleasure,' . . . I often try to make them uncomfortable, or even exasperated, furious and bitter."[38]

Lu Xun was ahead of his time, but not by much: what once exasperated and angered soon became all the rage. Spurred by the March First Movement, May Fourth Movement, and increasing popular demand for literature from abroad, Chinese, Koreans, and Taiwanese in the late 1910s and 1920s displayed greater fidelity to sources.[39] Even so, they continued to alter Japanese and Western texts significantly. The boundary between adaptations and translations is diaphanous; just what distance a literary work can stray from its source before crossing the line is often unclear. How adapters, translators, and their critics label these products can shed light on processes of transcultural understanding. But beyond labels, even greater insights into these struggles can be found through probing the ceaseless interactions among adaptations/translations and their source texts, especially by exploring translinguistic recastings of creative works.

Chinese, Koreans, and Taiwanese adapted and translated a broad palette of Japanese creative products during the first half of the twentieth century—from ancient texts to those written only days or hours before, from classical poetry to contemporary drama—but they particularly favored late-nineteenth and early twentieth-century Japanese prose fiction. Adaptations and translations of Japanese literature testified to Japanese cultural achievement and legitimacy, yet they also showed how easily these could be manipulated. Colonial and semicolonial adaptations and translations of Japanese novels, plays, poems, and short stories recast Japanese texts in complex ways that resist easy generalization. Even so, several major trends emerged that trace partly to historical circumstances and illuminate modes of colonial and semicolonial engagement: struggle, challenge, resistance, acquiescence, solidarity, and the ultimate blurring of these dynamics. The most significant negotiations with source texts generally occurred within storylines, but their extratextual/paratextual components—including covers, introductions, commentaries, conclusions, and illustrations—also frequently were sites of active engagement.[40]

In the decades surrounding Japanese colonization of Taiwan (1895) and Korea (1910) and increasing pressure on China, some adapters and translators of Japanese literature highlighted contrasts between Japanese and Chinese/Koreans, as well as Japan and China/Korea, without denying countervailing cultural connections. Other more autoethnographic adaptations and translations amended Japanese depictions of China/Korea and Chinese/Koreans.[41] Some did both. On the whole, Korean adaptations and translations were more concerned than their Chinese counterparts with negotiating difference, in part because of Japan's patronizing attitude toward Korea, manifested in multiple arenas and grounded in the belief that Koreans needed to be "rescued" by Japanese.[42] Korean writers keenly sensed this contradiction of Japanese colonialism: Tokyo trumpeted the sameness of Koreans and Japanese and called for assimilation yet never let Koreans become equals. At times, Korean adapters and translators contrasted the gloom in store for colonial and semicolonial peoples with Japan's glorious prospects as portrayed in late nineteenth-century Japanese novels called *miraiki* (records of the future). More frequently, they rebutted extratextual and intratextual Japanese rhetoric on Korean inferiority by portraying Koreans as stronger or at least as having more potential than Japanese. Yet they simultaneously pointed to indissoluble connections with the metropole, placing their characters in similar situations as Japanese predecessors, not to mention underscoring textual ties with Japanese literary works.

For their part, Chinese adaptations and translations published at the time tended to grapple with Japanese depictions of China/ Chinese more than their Korean counterparts tackled the colonial power's portrayals of Korea/Koreans, in part because of Japan's particularly vocal contempt of China. Chinese adaptations and translations occasionally replaced Japanese discourse on Chinese feebleness and inferiority—discourse often voiced by the Chinese themselves—with talk of Chinese endurance, if not strength. But many Chinese transculturations of Japanese literature published between the late 1890s and 1910s were more ambiguous. They revealed the great challenge facing adapters and translators confronted by foreign attacks, both textual and military, on their homelands. On the one hand, repeating these attacks in adaptations and translations reaffirms stereotypes, the consequences of which are magnified in the colonial/semicolonial context. Yet repeating negative portrayals also provides adapters and translators with excellent angles from which to critique their own societies, in addition to alerting readers to outside perceptions. On the other hand, muting criticism allows adapters and translators to paint rosier pictures of their homelands than those found in foreign texts, although doing so gives readers false impressions of foreign attitudes and ultimately portrays literary predecessors as more open-minded than they actually are.

Adaptations and translations published after World War One likewise negotiated with Japanese portrayals of Chinese and Koreans, as well as with depictions of Japanese aggression and military might, but were less concerned with negotiating difference. Both adaptations and intertextualizations tend to move settings closer to home, thereby distinguishing among sites more easily than do translations.[43] Generally exhibiting more fidelity to their Japanese sources than earlier attempts, translations in the final decades of the Japanese empire nevertheless remained tenacious negotiators. Particularly striking are translations of battlefront literature (texts by Japanese writers sent as correspondents to battlefields across Asia in the 1930s and early 1940s), which bargained with Japanese creative works that at once reveal the brutality of imperial soldiers but also make a case for their humanity. These translations, as well as those of Japanese proletarian literature, also occasionally transculturated censored Japanese literature; replacing censorship marks with words, in many ways they were more complete or even "authentic" than their imperial predecessors. But they also were targets of further textual contact.[44]

To be sure, for most of the colonial period, Chinese, Korean, and Taiwanese adaptations and translations of Western literatures outnumbered those of Japanese creative texts. Enthrallment with the West largely because of its imperialist designs and global power, combined with increasing ambivalence toward Japan, boosted lopsided literary publication statistics, with English-language titles leading the list. But Japanese-language literature was the fifth most frequently adapted and translated body of creative texts in late Qing China (1644–1911), and between 1912 and 1940, it occupied second place behind English-language literatures.[45] Between 1895 and liberation in 1945, Japanese literature stood in sixth place in Korea, where many readers could consume it in the original Japanese.[46] The ratio of Taiwanese adaptations and translations of Japanese literature to those of literatures from America and Europe is unclear, absent comprehensive data on Taiwanese adaptation and translation, but the proportions are likely similar. What Chinese, Korean, and Taiwanese adaptations and translations of Japanese literature lacked in numbers, they more than made up for in importance. They nailed shut the coffin of East Asian sinocentrism, overturning centuries of neglect of Japanese cultural products. They ensured Japanese literature a permanent place in the twentieth-century Chinese, Korean, and Taiwanese textual fabrics. They gave Japanese creative works tremendous visibility outside the archipelago. As remains true today, early twentieth-century Chinese, Korean, and Taiwanese adaptations and translations of Japanese literature outnumbered those available to American and European readers. But they also challenged the newly constructed modern Japanese canon. Not only did adapters and translators transform the many hundreds of texts they rewrote, they also intermittently ignored freshly minted Japanese bestsellers while heavily promoting literary works barely known in Japan. Thus, although reconfiguring numerous Japanese hits, they did not blindly follow the dictates of the Japanese literary establishment or the tastes of the Japanese reading public. Chinese, Korean, and Taiwanese adaptations and translations, like transculturations of literatures from many metropoles, demonstrated how quickly cultural constructions and cultures themselves can be at once subverted and reinforced.

Among the most intriguing early twentieth-century Chinese, Korean, and Taiwanese adaptations and translations of Japanese literature are those based on texts written around the first and second Sino-Japanese Wars (1894–95 and 1937–45), including creative works by such bestselling and/or highly censored Japanese authors as Suehiro Tetchō, Tōkai Sanshi, Ozaki Kōyō, Tokutomi Roka, Ishikawa Tatsuzō, Hino Ashihei, and Hayashi Fumiko. Also fascinating are interlingual transculturations of Japanese proletarian writers such as Nakano Shigeharu. These adaptations and translations grapple with imperial rhetoric in ways that highlight the poignant ambiguities of textual consumption and production in empire. But they are best appreciated in the broader context of adaptation and translation of Japanese literature. The number of these reconfigurations was so large, and the range of texts involved so vast, that it is productive to divide the colonial period at the end of World War One, which coincides with the Chinese, Korean, and Taiwanese new-culture movements of the late 1910s and early 1920s.

Early Trajectories of (Semi)colonial Adaptation and Translation, 1895–1919

Late nineteenth-century Chinese anthologies of Japanese literature, including the multiple collections edited by Yu Yue and Yao Wendong, were among the first of their kind and paved the way for East Asia's early twentieth-century boom in adapting and translating Japanese literature.[47] Yao Wendong explained his motives for anthologizing Japanese literature for Chinese consumption: "Although Japan and my nation are neighbors, the exchange of literature by famous authors of both countries is rare. This is such a deplorable thing in Sino-Japanese relations and in literary circles."[48] Scarcely could Yao Wendong have predicted the massive human and textual cross-cultural flows that spread out across East Asia during the next half century.

The transformation of Japanese literature from a body of texts largely ignored by its Asian neighbors to the principal source of intra–East Asian textual transculturation began after 1895 with Chinese and Korean adaptations and translations of Japanese novels and plays. Principally responsible for these recastings were Chinese and Koreans who had spent time in Japan or admired the recent achievements of their East Asian neighbor. As the first significant transculturation of Japanese cultural products outside Japan, adaptations of Japanese literature were popular in China and Korea; increasing literacy rates, more advanced production methods, and greater curiosity about the foreign all boosted sales. Although the first Chinese adaptations and translations date at least to the Western Zhou (1045–771 BCE), when the court established a bureau to facilitate communication with non-Han peoples, writers began systematically adapting and translating Japanese books of all kinds only after China's defeat in the first Sino-Japanese War (1895). During the next ten years, the Chinese adapted and translated more Japanese-language books (321) than they did books in all other foreign languages combined (212).[49] As the great Qing intellectual Liang Qichao noted: "there were dozens of regular journals [for publishing translations and adaptations from the Japanese]. Every time a new book appeared in Japan, there were several translators. The infusion of new thought was like a spreading fire."[50] The Chinese formed a number of organizations in both China and Japan dedicated to rewriting Japanese books into Chinese, and Japanese also played an important role in recasting their titles into Chinese, joining the staffs of several late Qing periodicals.[51]

Along with this burgeoning interest in Japanese scholarship came a new appreciation for foreign literatures, particularly novels, as appropriate objects of adaptation and occasionally translation. This was a first in China, where foreign literary works, regardless of their origins, were not embraced until the turn of the twentieth century.[52] But now prominent intellectuals, enticed in part by late nineteenth-century Japanese dedication to adapting and translating Western literature and shaken by Japan's decisive victory in the Sino-Japanese War, began advocating foreign fiction as a powerful agent of socio-political change and strongly promoted its adaptation/translation into Chinese. In addition, believing that aspects of their own literary heritage had done them more harm than good, particularly in light of China's startling defeat, reform-minded Chinese also hoped that making available fiction from abroad would provide local authors with new models and expedite the development of modern Chinese literature. The latter, they believed, was essential to China's maturity into a modern nation.

Adaptations and translations of creative texts took off quickly. Before 1911, they accounted for nearly half of all the literary works published in China, and between 1902 and 1907 the number of adapted and translated titles slightly surpassed that of texts originally written in Chinese. In the following decade, they retained a strong presence but dropped noticeably, comprising approximately one-fifth of the titles published in China.[53] Not surprisingly, many adaptations transculturated not purported Western "originals" but Japanese adaptations and translations of Western texts. In so doing, they created complex literary entanglements. For instance, Jules Verne's *Deux ans de vacances* (Two Years of Vacation, 1888), only the second full-length foreign novel adapted into vernacular Chinese, first was re-done in English as *Two Years Vacation* (1889) by an anonymous writer, then in Japanese by Morita Shiken as *Jūgo shōnen* (A Fifteen-year-old Boy, 1896), and later in Chinese (in Japan) by Liang Qichao and Luo Pu as *Shiwu xiao haojie* (A Fifteen-year-old Hero, 1902).[54] Once adapted or translated into Chinese, creative texts continued to have numerous afterlives. One of the most famous examples is Wu Woyao's (1866–1910) *Dianshu qitan* (Strange Tales of Electricity, 1905), which, relying heavily on an earlier Chinese adaptation by Fan Qingzhou, paraphrases a text by the Japanese writer Kikuchi Yūhō (1870–1947), which itself is an abridgement of an English story.[55] Textual permutations were seemingly infinite, as Chinese writers rewrote and readers hungrily devoured multiple versions of literary works from around the world. Moreover, creative texts from Japan and elsewhere did not find in China their final resting place; Chinese adaptations of Japanese fiction facilitated its dispersion to other parts of Asia, including Vietnam and Indonesia.[56]

As transculturations of texts from a semicolonizer with which cultural ties were particularly ambiguous, adaptations and translations of Japanese literature occupied an important place in the Chinese literary sphere. Chinese-language transculturations of Japanese novels thrived in the early days of Chinese transculturation of foreign literatures. In fact, between 1898 (the failed Hundred Days Reform) and 1911 (the end of the Qing), the Chinese adapted and translated close to 60 Japanese novels—compared with only 41 adaptations/ translations of Japanese adaptations/translations of Western literature.[57] Adaptations and translations fell off between the overthrow of the Qing and the May Fourth Movement (1919); more than half of the volumes of adapted/translated Japanese literature published during this period actually were readaptations/retranslations of Japanese novels that already had been recast into Chinese during the first decade of the twentieth century. But they nevertheless remained in demand.[58]

The first Chinese to adapt and translate Japanese literature focused on Japanese political novels, which by 1900 had long since lost their popularity in Japan but were extolled by leading Chinese intellectuals as powerful vehicles of social change. Political novels were explicit propaganda that flourished in Japan in the 1880s, inspired by the nineteenth-century English political novel and closely tied to the Freedom and Popular Rights Movement (see Chapter 1). This genre's three most celebrated texts all were adapted/translated into Chinese. Liang Qichao serialized an adaptation of much of Shiba Shirō's (Tōkai Sanshi, 1852–1922) *Kajin no kigū* (Chance Meetings with Beautiful Women, 1885–97) in his journal *Qing yi bao* (China Discussion) from November 1898 to January 1900. He went as far as Chapter 12 and then replaced this novel in *China Discussion* with an adaptation of Yano Ryūkei's (1850–1931) *Keikoku bidan* (Inspiring Instances of Statesmanship, 1884), which ran from January to December 1900. Suehiro Tetchō's (1849–96) *Setchūbai* (Plum Blossoms in the Snow, 1886) was transposed into Chinese in 1903 by Xiong Gai.[59] Arguing that political novels had played an important role in transforming countries around the world, including Japan, Liang Qichao endorsed their adaptation/translation as vital to China's future.[60] He showed great respect for Japanese creative output, no small gesture at the turn of the twentieth century when Japanese literature was only beginning to emerge as a worthy commodity in the eyes of other East Asians.

The Japanese domestic novel was another genre transculturated frequently during the 1900s and 1910s; translated into Chinese in 1908 by Lin Shu (1852–1924) and Wei Yi, Tokutomi Roka's bestselling *The Cuckoo* (1899) was especially popular.[61] Japanese detective stories, science fiction, and adventure novels also were adapted and translated frequently in the years leading up to the May Fourth period, as was Japanese drama.[62] Chinese audiences were particularly drawn to adaptations of plays by Satō Kōroku (1874–1949), which provided strikingly realistic portrayals of social problems. Beginning with the Chinese writer and editor Li Boyuan's (1867–1906) adaptation of Yano's *Inspiring Instances of Statesmanship* into a play, many Japanese novels were also adapted for the Chinese theater, which resulted in even more complex webs of transculturation. One Japanese novel conspicuously absent in print and on stage in China was Ozaki Kōyō's *The Gold Demon* (1903), a Japanese bestseller also popular in Korea and Taiwan. Why this novel was not translated in China until 1983, whereas Chinese rewrote three of Kōyō's less popular works in 1906, remains unclear. But the Chinese *Gold Demon*'s delayed publication is an excellent example of the alterations textual contact imposes on foreign cultural corpuses. Not interested in simply reproducing the Japanese modern canon in Chinese, early twentieth-century Chinese adapters and translators of Japanese literature instead creatively transculturated both bodies of individual texts and the body of Japanese literature itself.

Adaptations and translations enjoy a long history in Korea. Korean adaptation and translation of Chinese books date back over a millennium, but until the late nineteenth century Koreans essentially ignored books from Japan and the West. This changed in the early 1880s, when several groups of Christian missionaries and their Korean assistants loosely translated selected biblical texts, as well as hymns and other religious songs.[63] Literary works from Japan and the West became popular objects of adaptation and translation in the early 1900s as Korean intellectuals came to believe that making these texts available in Korean would help discredit antiquated ideas and accelerate the growth of modern Korean literature, which as in China was seen as a central ingredient in the development of a modern nation that would be respected on the world stage.

Korean adaptations and translations of Western literature relied heavily on Japanese, and occasionally Chinese, adaptations and translations. For instance, the Korean *Ŭnsegye* (Silver World, 1908), reworks the Japanese novel *Gin sekai* (Silver World), which is an adaptation of W. H. G. Kingston's *The Begum's Fortune* (1879), itself an adaptation of Jules Verne's *Les cinq cents millions de la Bégum* (The Begum's Millions, 1879). Similarly, Yi Sanghyŏp's (1893–1957) novel *Chŏnbuwŏn* (Jealousy of the Faithful Wife, 1914–15) is a readaptation of the Japanese novelist Kuroiwa Ruikō's *Suteobune* (Small Drifting Boat,

1895), itself an adaptation of the British writer Mary Elizabeth Braddon's (1837-1915) *Diavola, or, Nobody's Daughter* (1866-67).[64] As much as these adaptations underline the porousness of textual boundaries and the frequency of textual border-crossings, they are not as significant as Korean transculturations of Japanese literary works, texts from the nation that was at once a cultural beacon and colonial oppressor.

Korean adaptations and translations of Japanese literature accounted for approximately 20 percent of all interlingual transculturations of foreign literature in the years surrounding colonization in 1910.[65] As in China, Japanese political and domestic novels were particularly popular objects of adaptation and translation, and some Korean rewritings of Japanese literature—including *Inspiring Instances of Statesmanship*—appear to have relied on Chinese adaptations and translations. Other Korean adaptations and translations were based on earlier Korean rewritings of Japanese literature. For instance, the Korean writer Ch'oe Ch'ansik (1881-1951) rewrote Japanese and Korean versions of *Plum Blossoms in the Snow* in his novel *Kŭmgangmun* (Kŭmgang Gate, 1914).[66] In addition to *Plum Blossoms in the Snow*, *The Gold Demon*, and *The Cuckoo*, Koreans also adapted Kikuchi Yūhō's *Ono ga tsumi* (My Sin, 1900), Oguri Fūyō's (1875-1926) *Konjiki yasha shūhen* (Conclusion of *Konjiki yasha*, 1903), and Watanabe Katei's (1864-1926) *Sōfuren* (Longing for His Compassion, 1904).[67] These and other adaptations and translations of Japanese literature were instantly popular and played an important part not only in increasing newspaper circulation but also in the rise of the Korean *sin sosŏl* (new fiction). Japanese and Koreans also reworked "original" texts and (re)adaptations/translations for the stage, and Korean plays based on novels—including many from Japan—occupied a growing position in the repertory after 1913.[68] Moreover, Japanese and to a lesser extent Korean drama troupes crossed borders frequently, planting further seeds of transculturation.[69]

The years between Japan's decisive victory in the first Sino-Japanese War and the Korean March First Movement and the Chinese May Fourth Movement were a time of unprecedented Japanese encroachment on China and Korea. But Japanese literature, far from repelling Chinese and Koreans, proved irresistible, even though newly colonized and semicolonized peoples might well have ignored it without repercussion. On the one hand, Japanese creative works were easy targets for adaptation and translation. With Japanese authorities generally remaining silent on questions of textual transculturation, Chinese and Korean adapters and translators were free to do with Japanese literary works what they liked and what local markets could support. They took advantage of these opportunities, creating texts that addressed top concerns of audiences at home while at the same time undermining Japanese sources, if not attacking the Japanese themselves. But the deeper they eroded metropolitan literary authority, the more their texts became aligned, if not allied, with metropolitan cultural production: they asserted cultural independence by transforming the Japanese literary corpus, but in so doing revealed partial dependence on this body of texts, and ultimately on Japanese cultural capital and authority, for creative expression. These early adaptations and translations thus embody many of the ambiguities of cultural production and negotiation in the literary contact nebulae of Japan's colonial/semicolonial imperium.

Confronting Contempt and Probing Difference

Adapting and translating creative texts can give writers new perspectives with which to address the challenges facing their societies. But the significance of much textual contact transcends its ability to inspire discourse that works through contemporary quagmires. Adapting and translating dozens of Japanese literary works in the 1900s and 1910s, early colonial/semicolonial East Asians repeatedly challenged Japanese narrative, and ultimately cultural, authority in two principal ways. Adaptations and translations of Japanese literature frequently amended Japanese depictions of their East Asian neighbors, at times muting and at times reinforcing Japanese prejudices and stereotypes. Other Korean and Chinese adaptations naturalized source texts, moving settings to Korea/China and depicting Korean/Chinese characters in ways that underlined contrasts but also pointed to connections between their societies and the metropole. Together negotiating contempt and difference, probing the resilience of their peoples and the future of their societies, early intra–East Asian adaptations and translations of Japanese literature made powerful statements about Japanese colonialism, semicolonialism, and imperialism.

Amending Japanese Discourse on East Asia

The first Sino-Japanese War dislodged China from its semicolonial position in Korea and opened the door for Japan to expand its interests on the peninsula, marking the rise of Japan to prominence in East

Asia. Japanese elites applauded the war: the Christian leader Uchimura Kanzō (1861–1930) called it "righteous," and the renowned intellectual Fukuzawa Yukichi labeled it a struggle "between a country which is trying to develop civilization and a country which disturbs the development of civilization." Respect for Koreans also plunged rapidly during the war, as Japanese believed their East Asian neighbors increasingly needed Japanese "rescue." Japan's triumph on the battlefield unleashed even more arrogance, showered in a typhoon of anti-Korean and anti-Chinese rhetoric in print and on stage.[70] Chinese and Koreans living in Japan in ever-greater numbers in the decade after the war were directly exposed to this jingoism.

An important cluster of East Asia's earliest adaptations and translations of Japanese literary works, following closely on Japan's decisive military victory, amended Japanese discourse on East Asia. When adapting or translating Japanese creative texts, many Chinese and Koreans not surprisingly deleted or at least heavily edited passages that slandered China/Korea, and they added segments more congenial to local audiences. In so doing, they paradoxically created a group of texts that advertised themselves as transculturations of Japanese creative works but gave altered impressions of Japanese attitudes toward other parts of Asia. Yet negotiations with Japanese cultural products were even more intricate in transculturations that were more faithful to their source texts, that is, translations that repeated rhetoric demeaning Chinese/Koreans but also added challenges to Japanese arrogance and contempt. To be sure, Chinese and Korean adapters and translators often were highly critical of their own societies, making it difficult for them to dismiss Japanese condemnations. At the same time, they refused to accept Japanese rhetoric tout court, so they created amalgams of censure and endorsement.

With Japanese discourse of the late nineteenth and early twentieth centuries generally expressing more condescension toward China than Korea, it is not surprising that Chinese adaptations and translations amending Japanese depictions of their country outnumber their Korean counterparts. Two principal embodiments of these complex negotiations are Liang Qichao's adaptation of Shiba Shirō's best-selling political novel *Chance Meetings with Beautiful Women* (1885–97), serialized between 1898 and 1900 as *Jiaren qiyu* (Chance Meetings with Beautiful Women), and Lin Shu and Wei Yi's translation of Tokutomi Roka's bestselling *The Cuckoo* (1899), published in China in 1908 as *Burugui* (The Cuckoo). Both Japanese novels glorify Japan's rise to power at the expense of East Asia, but their Chinese transculturations reveal the contradictions inherent in amending Japanese discourse on the region.

Beautiful Women, Tarnished Countries

Chance Meetings with Beautiful Women is likely the first Japanese literary work adapted or translated in East Asia in the modern period, and one of the first ever. Convention has it that Liang Qichao read the novel as he was fleeing to Japan after the failed Hundred Days Reform of 1898. Greatly impressed, and believing that novels of this sort would help push China to reform as they apparently had other societies, he began serializing a Chinese translation of *Chance Meetings with Beautiful Women* two months after arriving in Tokyo. Liang Qichao used *xinwen*, a new style that combined colloquial speech with Japanese compounds.[71]

Shiba Shirō's novel is the story of Tōkai Sanshi (lit. Wanderer of the Eastern Seas), a young Japanese man visiting Philadelphia and its environs who strikes up friendships with two women, the Irish Kōren (likely Colleen) and Spanish Yūran (likely Yolanda). Kōren tells her new Japanese friend about English oppression of Ireland, while Yūran discusses her family's ordeals with corruption at the Spanish court and among Spanish reformers. Soon thereafter, attention turns to China, and Yūran's servant Fanqing (a homonym of "anti-Qing") reveals that he came to the United States to escape Manchu (Qing) oppression only to find that Americans discriminate heavily against Chinese. The novel describes the struggles of numerous nations against foreign oppression. Its exposés are frequently one-dimensional; together they divide the world into oppressed and oppressors, leaving little room for more ambiguous dynamics. On the other hand, the novel gives a panorama of contemporary world affairs and underlines the traumas the powerful are wont to inflict on places and peoples they deem inferior. Yet the political climate in Japan changed considerably between 1885, when Shiba Shirō began serializing *Chance Meetings with Beautiful Women*, and 1897, when he completed the novel. The second half (Chapters 10–16), which dates from 1891, turns its back on concern for oppressed peoples and advocates Japanese imperialism in East Asia. *Chance Meetings with Beautiful Women*, the political novel that at first appeared to provide foundation stones for Chinese reform, soon became its Sisyphean nemesis.

A text that begins as a translation and concludes as an adaptation, Liang Qichao's Chinese *Chance Meetings with Beautiful Women* for the most part adheres to the first ten chapters of Shiba Shirō's novel but radically reworks the final sections. Notably, the Chinese translation reproduces Yolanda's celebration in Chapter 2 of Japan as the hope of Asia:

Your country has reformed its government and, taking from America what is useful and tossing aside what isn't, now is steadily increasing its wealth and power. . . . Those who look at you are surprised and wipe their eyes. Those who hear of you are surprised and incline toward you. Just as the sun climbs in the eastern skies, so too is your country soaring in Asia. Your revered leader has given his people political freedom, and the people have sworn to follow him. . . . All people will be happy. Korea will send envoys. The Ryukyu Islands will submit to your rule. The time then will come for you to do great things in East Asia. Your nation will take control and preside over an Asian alliance. In the East, people will no longer be in such danger. In the West, you will suppress the domination of England and France. In the South, you will tear up China's evil customs. In the North, you will foil Russia's schemes. You will oppose the policy of European countries to look contemptuously at East Asian peoples, interfering in their domestic affairs and making them subservient. Only your country can provide the flavor of self-government and independence and spread the light of civilization.[72]

In both the Japanese and the Chinese *Chance Meetings with Beautiful Women*, this passage opens the door for Japanese involvement in East Asian and world affairs. To be sure, the Chinese version of the novel — while retaining Yolanda's comments concerning the East, West (England, France), and North (Russia) — omits Yolanda's explicit reference to China's corruption and Japan's assuming responsibility for Chinese affairs. But the translation does preserve the Japanese text's rhetoric advocating Japanese guidance of the peoples of the East and the nations of East Asia, implicitly including Chinese and China. The attempt to remove China/Chinese from discussions of Japan's rise to power leaves numerous loopholes.

Elsewhere, the Chinese translation repeats, if not escalates, attacks on the Qing. It is true that under pressure from leading Chinese intellectuals such as Kang Youwei (1858–1927), who believed Shiba Shirō's diatribes against the Qing compromised reform efforts, Liang Qichao omitted much of the controversial material contained in the first part of *Chance Meetings with Beautiful Women*.[73] But he closely reproduced Chapter 10, where the Japanese novel not only chastises Koreans for being ungrateful for Japanese help but also harshly criticizes Chinese for meddling in Korean politics, exposes Chinese crimes in Korea, and urges Japan to be uncompromising in its dealings with China.[74] Overall, the first part of Liang Qichao's text dampens the Chinese criticism of China voiced in his Japanese predecessor, but retains Japanese censure. The manipulation of the Japanese *Chance Meetings with Beautiful Women* implies that criticism is less dangerous when voiced by an exterior source than when voiced by a Chinese. It takes the position that outside censure must be censored only when it becomes overwhelming, but that there is no easy way to determine just when this becomes the case. In truth, outside censure in many cases enhances reform efforts.

The paradoxes inherent in amending Japanese discourse on China are brought to the forefront in the final six chapters of the Chinese *Chance Meetings with Beautiful Women*, where the Chinese translator reconstructs Japanese attacks on Chinese policy toward Korea and Japan. Here he erases arguments both for China's exit from Korea and for Japanese control of the peninsula, as well as the Japanese narrator's critiques of the Qing. Significantly, such discourse is not replaced with pro-Chinese and anti-Japanese rhetoric, suggesting the Chinese writer's own ambivalence. The second half of the Chinese *Chance Meetings with Beautiful Women*, much of which did not make it into *China Discussion*, thus ironically depicts a less arrogant and antagonistic Japan than its Japanese predecessor. But it also portrays a China badly in need of reform. The challenge to the translator becomes particularly acute in the novel's final chapter (Chapter 16), where the deletions pile up until the narrator finally abandons his text.[75] Breaking from the Japanese novel, Liang Qichao wraps up the Chinese *Chance Meetings with Beautiful Women*:

Originally, Korea was China's vassal state. It is the duty of the great power to restore order to the vassal state when things are chaotic. At that time, Korea was plagued by domestic trouble and foreign invasion. It sent a petition to China, asking for help. So it was only right for China to send troops to Korea. But Japan then was in the process of reinventing itself and was incredibly arrogant. Trying to test its strength, it was causing problems in East Asia. It saw that it could take advantage of the Qing court and mislead Koreans. It therefore supported Korea and launched hostilities against China. The Qing had no idea what was going on and thought that Japan was the same as before. . . . After three hundred years of peace, the generals did not know anything about troops, and the officers did not use commands. How could this corrupt and rotten, sick and old country compete against reborn Japan, a Japan cruel and savage but one with civilization and thought? Such differences in strength and knowledge. So China was first defeated in Korea, and then at Liaodong. It had to cede Taiwan and pay a huge indemnity. But we Japanese are much more ambitious than that. We still think that's not sufficient. The triumvirate of Russia, Germany, and France suddenly intervened . . . [and the Japanese quickly retroceded Liaodong]. Many idealistic young men in the countryside censured their leaders for acting this way. They don't yet know the pains of government.[76]

This finale reveals many of the conflicts facing early twentieth-century Chinese writers and other intellectuals as they struggled to reform their country without surrendering to Japanese propaganda, not to mention its military and economic might. The narrator first poses a simple dichotomy: China is right and Japan is wrong. China did the right thing by helping Korea, while arrogant Japan, like a street bully, needlessly incited war. But then things become more complex. The narrator reveals that China's leaders have no idea what is going on next door in Japan, much less in the world, and that this ignorance has dire consequences. Frustration with the Manchu court bubbles over: "How could this corrupt and rotten, sick and old country compete against reborn Japan?" Not that Japan is particularly admirable: it has "civilization and thought," but far from taming the country, these elements of modernity have made Japan even more brutal. Substantiating this claim and echoing many of the sentiments in the Japanese *Chance Meetings with Beautiful Women*, the Japanese narrator in this Chinese version of the novel announces, "We Japanese are much more ambitious than that. We still think that's not sufficient." Here the Chinese novel depicts the Japanese as a menacing force, one longing to take on the world. The novel refers to Western intervention after the ceasefire, reminding the reader that the only forces holding Japan back are the very ones preying on China. The Japanese received China's Liaodong Peninsula as part of the Treaty of Shimonoseki (April 17, 1895) that concluded the Sino-Japanese War. But Japan was forced to give the peninsula back to China six days later under pressure from France, Russia, and Germany.

The Chinese adaptation/translation makes clear the need for internal reform if China is to survive. Confronting a conundrum characteristic of colonial/semicolonial struggles with literature from the metropole that discusses the colony/semicolony, the concluding passage of the Chinese *Chance Meetings with Beautiful Women* makes it clear that Japan and the West remain dangerous foes whose designs on the mainland cannot be ignored.

The Cackling Cuckoo

The Japanese political novel provided an excellent window into imperial Japanese desire and served as an inspiration for Chinese reform, but its rhetoric could be sustained only up to a point. China's
engagement with this genre was short-lived; interest in more contemporary fare increased as larger numbers of Chinese studied in
Tokyo and other Japanese cities. The first tsunami of Chinese students arrived in Japan in the aftermath of the Russo-Japanese War
(1904–5), not long after the publication of Tokutomi Roka's bestseller
The Cuckoo in 1899. Chinese readers quickly were sucked into *Cuckoo-
mania*, which by that point was spreading across the globe; in the
years after its publication, *The Cuckoo* was adapted/translated into
eleven languages, including Chinese and Korean, and was reworked
multiple times for stage and screen. *The Cuckoo* coincides with the
Sino-Japanese War and is at once a celebration of Japan's military
prowess and a love story about the naval officer Takeo and his wife
Namiko, a young woman dying of tuberculosis whose mother-in-
law forces her out of the marital home. Takeo, who has been fighting
with Japanese forces in China, returns to Japan to discover that his
mother has divorced him from his wife. His further attempts to see
Namiko are thwarted, with the exception of a momentary glimpse
at a railway station. Namiko dies soon after this sighting, and Takeo
does not make it to her deathbed in time, which adds even greater
melodrama and pathos to her passing.[77]

Early Chinese theatrical adaptations of *The Cuckoo* took great lib-
erties with Roka's novel. In his version, Ma Jiangshi, who had studied
in Tokyo and was a member of China's first modern drama troupe,
transferred the action to Beijing, gave his characters Chinese names,
and changed the dramatis personae. Most important, he omitted the
novel's battle scenes. The text that in Japanese intertwines threads
of tragic romance with those of maritime warfare became a play focusing on domestic traumas.[78] As such, it spoke directly to increasing
Chinese frustration with their own social structure, which left little
room for individual choice. Lacking naval battle scenes, it was, of
course, much easier to stage. But there are deeper implications. Ma
Jiangshi's play and others like it, underlining the damage Chinese
convention inflicted on marital relationships and on women in particular, were far from celebrations of China. On the other hand, sparing Chinese from having to watch their nation's defeat, this play
also masked the impact of these conventions not only on individual

families but also on China's ability to thwart foreign aggression and compete in the world arena.

The translation of *The Cuckoo* by Lin Shu and his interpreter Wei Yi, published in 1908, offered no such protections. Unlike most Chinese and Korean translations and adaptations of Japanese literature, Lin Shu and Wei Yi's text is based not on the Japanese version of the novel but on its first English translation, a relatively close rendering by Sakae Shioya and E. F. Edgett published in 1904. Further complicating matters was Lin Shu's inability to read Japanese, English, or any foreign language; with the exception of several places where the text states explicitly "Lin Shu says . . ." the Chinese translation does not specify which alterations to the Japanese novel via its English version were at Lin Shu's instigation and which were the work of Wei Yi, although the distinction is not particularly important. What is notable is that for transposing this novel into Chinese — the only Japanese text out of more than one hundred creative works from eleven countries that he adapted/translated with the help of an interpreter — Lin Shu did not enlist (or at least did not admit to enlisting) the assistance of someone who could read the text in its original language.[79] Considering the ever-increasing numbers of Chinese able to read Japanese after the Sino-Japanese War, and the fervor with which Chinese studying in Japan read *The Cuckoo* and adapted it for the theater, Lin Shu's choice is noteworthy. It perhaps stemmed from assumptions that the translation would be taken more seriously if it were associated with a Western configuration. But explicitly announcing on its first page that it is a retranslation of an English translation, albeit one penned in part by a Japanese (Shioya Sakae), rather than a direct translation from Japanese, pulls the Chinese *Cuckoo* even farther out of Japanese hands. This undermining of Japanese narrative authority is no small move in transculturating a text that, while primarily a novel about the plight of young lovers separated by family and war, also highlights Japanese martial glory and Chinese defeat. For a late Qing transculturation, Lin Shu and Wei Yi's *Cuckoo* is surprisingly faithful to its textual predecessors in spite of its multilayered sources. This novel reproduces not only their moving descriptions of Japanese losses and Chinese endurance, as would be expected, but also their portrayals of Japanese valor and Chinese weakness. Its struggles with how to address Chinese failures as well as Japanese attitudes toward China reveal the dilemmas facing many early twentieth-century colonial and semicolonial East Asian writers.

Toning down some of its predecessors' military fanfare, the Chinese *Cuckoo* portrays Chinese and Japanese in a different light from the English and Japanese versions of the novel. For instance, in the first part of both Roka's *Cuckoo* and its English translation, Japanese troops arrive in Hong Kong "to great cheers" from a crowd of presumably mixed ethnicity, but the Chinese *Cuckoo* makes no mention of cheers, noting only that the local Japanese population "surged down to the sea to welcome them."[80] The crowd has lost its diversity, suggesting that only Japanese would be excited to see Japanese troops. Moreover, their greeting is not vocalized; the cheers have been muted. Soon thereafter, the novel addresses the so-called Korea Incident, the 1894 Tonghak uprising that served as a welcome excuse for Chinese and Japanese troops to descend on Korea, triggering the Sino-Japanese War. The Japanese and English *Cuckoo*s open the final chapter of Part 2 with, " 'Extra! Extra! Extra on the Korea problem!' So shouted a newsboy." In contrast, the chapter in the Chinese *Cuckoo* mediates the palpable and retrospective excitement in the Japanese and English versions by repositioning physical markers: "Outside the Kawashimas' gate there was a child selling newspapers. He shook the bell and shouted, 'An extraordinary event.' "[81]

At times, the Chinese translation excises Roka's militaristic flourishes. Describing a decisive battle between Chinese and Japanese forces on the Yellow Sea, the Japanese narrator and his English translator exuberantly speak of the waves boiling and foaming around the ships like huge serpents coiling around a giant whale. The Chinese narrator declines the opportunity to translate this flowery phrase and instead jumps to a straightforward description of troop movement.[82] Similarly, whereas the Japanese *Cuckoo* depicts the war as ending "just like a great bird settling its wings," and the English *Cuckoo* gleefully announces, "the war ended with the impressiveness of an eagle gathering its wings for flight," the Chinese *Cuckoo* states simply, "the fighting ended."[83]

The translators' additions are also important. In regular type but indented, or squeezed between sentences in smaller print than the main narrative, they stand out in a novel without paragraph breaks. The added material variously explains, contradicts, and editorializes, allowing the Chinese *Cuckoo* to draw attention to what it perceives as the strengths and shortcomings of its source. For instance, the translator interrupts the novel's discussion of the final days of the war, when Chinese positions were falling rapidly, to let readers know that "China's stalwarts [*zhuangshi*] remember" this or that event.[84] The Chinese *Cuckoo* does not deny the Japanese account, but it does depict Chinese as more than shadows engulfed by what the Japanese and English *Cuckoo*s refer to as the "tide of the Japanese Imperial Army."[85] More significant is how the added remarks rewrite both intratextual and extratexual discourse. For instance, the translators comment that the return of the Liaodong Peninsula to China after the 1895 Triple Intervention is "China's shame."[86] Especially telling is the way this remark offsets contemporary Japanese claims to shame at "losing" the peninsula. As Marius Jansen has noted, "The indemnity [3 million yen to Japan to defray its war costs, which ultimately broke the Qing treasury] was increased in partial compensation, but no amount of payment could make up for the sense of outrage and humiliation that was left by the 'Triple Intervention.' An imperial rescript exhorted Japanese to remain calm and diligent in adversity."[87] Contradicting Japanese claims of chagrin, the Chinese *Cuckoo* asserts that the shame rests solely on China's shoulders; Western nations were meddling in Japanese affairs, but the Chinese were even more at the mercy of foreign powers. In fact, China's shame was less the return of the peninsula than its having been ceded in the first place, that is to say, the ease with which the Liaodong Peninsula was tossed among countries at the Shimonoseki peace conference earlier that year. This is only one of several instances where the Chinese translators' comments spin both intratextual and contemporary phenomena.[88]

Rather than quietly transform the Japanese novel to address better the needs of its Chinese audience as did many of their contemporaries, the Chinese translators of *The Cuckoo* reminded their readers that theirs was a Chinese reconfiguration of a Japanese novel.[89] In so doing, the Chinese *Cuckoo* not only aroused sympathy for a young Japanese couple, tugging on the heartstrings of empathic readers who themselves likely had experienced the traumas of an oppressive family system. It also provided Chinese with an explicitly mediated window on a bestselling Japanese version of Japanese victory and Chinese defeat in the Sino-Japanese War. In the opening lines of his preface, Lin Shu remarks that *The Cuckoo* — depicting the tragedies of young lovers preyed on by cruel elders — is the most heartwrenching of the dozens of texts he has so far translated. This comment rightly has been construed as signifying Lin Shu's great appreciation for the book he was translating. Frequently overlooked has been Lin Shu's quick segue to war, advising readers that passages in *The Cuckoo* also discuss it "in great detail" and then spending the next pages, not merely lines, detailing the war and its implications. Lin Shu calls on Chinese to learn from what has happened and reveals great concern with the nation's future. He laments that he is already old, that there is little time for him to "dedicate my life to the country." But this novel is a beginning: may its sincere shouts, he pleads, rouse his compatriots.[90] Lin Shu and Wei Yi's recasting of Roka's *Cuckoo* highlights the paradoxical problems of adapting and translating in contexts of significantly uneven power relationships.

Imperial China's decline, precipitated by domestic turmoil and pressures from abroad, began decades before the outbreak of the Sino-Japanese War. Although Huang Zunxian and other Chinese intellectuals in the nineteenth century, well aware of Japan's increasing strength, had urged Chinese to look more closely at their neighbors to the east, it was not until its military victory that Chinese leaders believed it fundamentally important to take Japan seriously. This monumental change in intra–East Asian cultural, political, and social dynamics, manifested most vividly by the arrival of Chinese students on Japan's shores, resulted in increased Japanese arrogance and Chinese feelings of inferiority. Chinese transculturations of Shiba Shirō's *Chance Meetings with Beautiful Women* and Tokutomi Roka's *The Cuckoo*, by revising, excising, and adding words and passages, interrogated but did not dismiss Japanese rhetoric, particularly on China. Certainly, most transculturations of Japanese literature, whether intra–East Asian or from further afield, had an agenda. But the implications of these revisions were particularly powerful in a nation of failed reforms and increasing submission to powers around the world, and in a region still shaking from Japan's unexpected victories over regional and global powers.

Negotiating Difference

Like their Chinese counterparts, Korean adaptations and translations of Japanese literature often amended Japanese portrayals of Korea/Koreans,[91] but they even more frequently contrasted Korea/Koreans with Japan/Japanese both intratextually (juxtaposing the two in the same literary work) and intertextually (replacing Japan/Japanese with Korea/Koreans in a manner that negotiated difference). Yet by tying themselves, often explicitly, to particular Japanese literary works, they also highlighted the inevitable links, for better or worse, between the two lands and societies. Some Chinese adaptations and translations of Japanese literature similarly emphasized difference while acknowledging Japanese cultural or at least narrative legitimacy, but this tendency is more apparent in Korean transculturations. Questions of difference were more urgent in Korea, where forced assimilation was tinged with discrimination.[92]

Running the gamut from depicting Koreans as having a bleaker future than Japanese, to underlining Koreans' superior potential, to portraying them as stronger and more intelligent than Japanese, these transculturations often reveal somewhat deeper anxieties than Chinese rectifications of Japanese portrayals of Chinese. Not satisfied with amending Japanese texts, Korean-language rewritings of the 1900s and 1910s highlighted divides between the metropole and its colony, differences that shamed both spaces: colonial adaptations undermined Japanese projections of a rosy (Japanese) future by revealing the high price others would have to pay for its realization, while also chastising Koreans for not exploring and taking greater advantage of their latent promise.

Rewriting the Future: Plum Blossoms in Korean Snow

In his 1908 adaptation of Suehiro Tetchō's political novel *Plum Blossoms in the Snow* (1886), also entitled *Plum Blossoms in the Snow* (*Sŏljungmae*), the Korean writer Gu Yŏnhak replaced Tetchō's vision of a glorious future for Japan with a gloomy forecast for Korea. In so doing, he underlined the discrepancies between the metropole and its protectorate — the Japanese declared Korea their protectorate in 1905 and by 1908 it was well on its way to becoming a colony — and anticipated the broad aftershocks of colonization. The Korean *Plum Blossoms in the Snow* undercuts Japan's projection of its own greatness by highlighting Japanese duplicity, as well as Korean respect for Western models.

Tetchō's *Plum Blossoms in the Snow* opens in Japan in 2040. Two men speak glowingly of the strength of the Japanese nation, which they attribute to the foresight of the Meiji emperor; their conversation quickly turns to the recent discovery of a memorial celebrating Kunino Motoi (lit. foundation of the nation), a man whose career is the focus of two novels: *Plum Blossoms in the Snow* and its sequel *Kakan'ō* (Song Thrushes among the Flowers, 1887). The body of Tetchō's *Plum Blossoms in the Snow*, presented as the first of the two recently discovered manuscripts, describes Kunino's adventures. An impoverished young politician who after extensive travels assumes the helm of the political club Seigisha (Justice), he is pulled from the brink of eviction from his residence by an anonymous benefactress who admires his activism. He soon lands in jail for allegedly participating in revolutionary activities, but after his release, he travels to Hakone, where he encounters Tominaga Haru (lit. spring of everlasting fortune), who turns out to be his benefactress; the two become engaged despite the attempts of Tominaga's uncle to marry her off to one of his friends. Like most political novels, *Plum Blossoms in the Snow* includes impassioned political speeches and debates on reform strategies. Kunino's story continues in *Song Thrushes among the Flowers*, published the following year but not adapted into Korean; this popular sequel finds Kunino battling opposing political forces yet ultimately coming out on top: a representative assembly is established and his political party wins a sweeping victory in the general election.

The Korean adaptation of *Plum Blossoms in the Snow* deflates its Japanese predecessor. Gu Yŏnhak does away with the Japanese novel's futurist prologue, where the narrator extols the wonders of Japan in the twenty-first century and the nation's rise to world dominance: not only do merchant ships from around the world fill Tokyo's harbor, "there is not a single spot on earth where the Japanese flag does not fly."[93] In his prologue, the Japanese narrator also celebrates the high ethical standards of his nation's well-regulated government, declaring, "There is freedom of speech and assembly, and the absence of abuse is unlike anything in history."[94] Not surprisingly, the Korean adaptation leaves out these assertions.

Koreans do not have the luxury of imagining a splendid future. Replacing the fanfare of trumpets with human cries, Gu Yŏnhak's adaptation begins with the wails of a dying woman: "Exhausted from her lengthy illness, her entire body emaciated, her strength so depleted that she could not sit, the 50-something woman lay on the ground and called for her daughter Maesŏn with a hacking cough."[95] The sense of being deprived of a future does not end here; instead, it pervades the Korean adaptation. Whereas Kunino's name suggests that he is a "founder of the nation," the name of the protagonist of the Korean adaptation, Yi T'aesun, insinuates that he is literally "following the peace of the Yi dynasty" (1392–1910), in other words, that he is stuck in a past, and one that was hardly peaceful: the Yi (Chosŏn) dynasty was scarred by a war with Japan, Manchu invasions, literati purges, factional strife that led many intellectuals to flee politics, and eventually dynastic chaos, national crisis, imperial aggression, and Japanese colonization.[96]

But what makes the Korean protagonist's story especially poignant is that, far from passively adhering to the old, as his name suggests, he struggles unsuccessfully to improve his nation. The Korean *Plum Blossoms in the Snow* swaps the Japanese political world of the 1880s, including its Freedom and Popular Rights Movement and demand for a national assembly, with Korea at the turn of the twentieth century. The novel takes place between 1896 and 1908 and gives considerable attention to the activities of the Dokrip Hyŏphoe (Independence Club, est. 1896), the first and most influential of the many Korean organizations seeking national independence and the "rights of the people."[97] Yi T'aesun repeatedly calls for political and social reform and relentlessly pushes for more enlightened policies, which in his view generally come from the West. Although both the Japanese and the Korean versions of *Plum Blossoms in the Snow* extol freedom and "popular rights," the Korean text—taking place in an era when loss of sovereignty was imminent—ultimately portrays a society desperate for Western lifejackets before being washed overboard, rather than one sailing into the sunset, as the Japanese novelist Natsume Sōseki put it in the seventh episode of *Yume jūya* (Ten Nights of Dreams, 1908).[98] Yi T'aesun's insistence on the importance of following Western models stands out in a novel that reconfigures the declarations of Japanese dominance in Tetchō's *Plum Blossoms in the Snow*. Moreover, adapting a Japanese predecessor ostensibly concerned with freedom and "popular rights," Gu Yŏnhak's text exposes the hypocrisy of a nation that deems its slogans applicable only to Japanese.

While replacing depictions of a triumphant nation with those of a declining one, drawing attention to the gulf between Japan and other parts of East Asia, particularly Korea, the Korean adaptation of *Plum Blossoms in the Snow* also highlights what has allowed the Japanese to dream such dreams in the first place. In so doing, it suggests that the future Japan anticipates is not without splendor, but its actualization will come at too high a price. By transculturating one of Meiji Japan's most prominent political novels, the Korean adaptation of *Plum Blossoms in the Snow* provides an alternate vision of East Asian cultural dynamics, one that draws attention to the hardships of life for non-Japanese, hardships for which Japan was at least partly responsible. The Korean version nevertheless depicts the (nearly) colonized as refusing to capitulate without a struggle, and in fact fighting many of the same battles in their country as the Japanese had at home.

Questions of strength and resilience, of secondary importance in the Korean *Plum Blossoms in the Snow*, come to the fore in other Chinese and Korean adaptations of Japanese creative texts. But whereas Chinese adaptations tend to amend Japanese depictions of China by attacking Japanese literary creations, Korean adaptations contrast Japan unfavorably with Korea, thereby attacking Japan itself.

Making the Case for Korean Strength

Many early twentieth-century Korean and especially Chinese adaptations and translations of Japanese literature vacillated—often within the same text—between portraying their homelands and compatriots favorably and being openly critical in the hopes of inciting change. But others went one step further and asserted strength if not supremacy, whether in terms of professional expertise, physical resilience, narrative prowess, moral courage, or some combination of these and other traits. This was particularly true in Korea. With the peninsula rapidly being taken over by Japan, a nation whose previous invasions Korea had successfully thwarted, some reconfigurations of Japanese literature argued the case for inherent Korean superiority. That Korean transpositions of Japanese literature display such faith in Korean potential illustrates the powerful ambivalence of cultural production in the colonial context. On the one hand, these texts suggest subservience to a Japanese model and assumption of its legitimacy. Yet on the other they indicate Korean writers' determination to assert agency, to produce Korean creative texts that, although based on Japanese creative texts, not only are unquestionably Korean in focus but also give Korean writers and performers the last word: while Japanese authorities worked to "Japanize" Korea, Korean writers worked to "Koreanize" Japanese literary products. Even more ironically, their adaptations/translations of Japanese literature often were published in the only Korean-language newspaper in Korea during the 1910s, the *Daily News*, which was managed and censored by the Japanese governor-general. Like its two contemporaries, the English-language *Seoul Press* and Japanese-language *Keijō nippō* (Seoul Daily), the *Daily News* regularly supported the policies of the Japanese administration, spoke of the merits of Korean-Japanese assimilation, and discussed the shortcomings of Korean society.[99] In this way, Korean adaptations of Japanese literature sabotaged not only their Japanese sources but also their Japanized publication venue.

Adapting and translating Japanese texts in part to emphasize Korean strength had roots in the Korean reformer Yu Kilchun's popular *Sŏyu kyŏnmun* (Observations from a Journey to the West, 1895), which draws heavily from the leading Japanese intellectual Fukuzawa Yukichi's *Seiyō jijō* (Conditions in the West, 1870), nineteenth-century Japan's best-known book on the West.[100] Although not an adaptation of a literary work, *Observations from a Journey to the West* exemplifies important processes of textual negotiation that helped pave the way for further transculturations of Japanese writings. Yu Kilchun first traveled to Japan as part of the 62-member Sinsa Yuramdan (Gentlemen's Observation Mission, 1881), which spent more than two months touring Japanese institutions and learning how Japanese had assimilated Western education, science, and technology. He stayed on in Japan, becoming one of the first Korean students to attend school there when he enrolled in Fukuzawa's Keiō Gijuku (now Keiō University). Several years later, he joined Korea's inaugural diplomatic mission to the West, where he again stayed behind, becoming the first Korean student in the United States. Yu Kilchun's observations from his time in America and Europe—he returned to Korea via Europe in 1885—provided the inspiration for *Observations from a Journey to the West*, which he wrote between 1887 and 1892 and published in Japan several years later with Fukuzawa's help. As the first widely distributed work in Korea concerning the West, *Observations from a Journey to the West* had a substantial impact on Korean thought and was cited frequently in the years following its publication.[101]

Unlike Fukuzawa, Yu Kilchun opens his narrative with a long description of world geography, but otherwise his book relies heavily on Fukuzawa's *Conditions in the West*. Although Yu Kilchun does not say so explicitly, the title *Observations from a Journey to the West* refers to both his and Fukuzawa's observations. Yu Kilchun also transplanted nearly 300 Japanese neologisms from Fukuzawa's volume into his own, and thus into the Korean language, most of which are still used today.[102] In addition, again following Fukuzawa's lead, he created one of the earliest major Korean nonfiction texts written in *gukhanmun*, a mixture of hangul and Chinese graphs; Yu Kilchun states in his preface that this format makes his text available to a wider audience than one written entirely in Chinese.[103]

What are the intercultural implications of Yu Kilchun's depending so heavily on Fukuzawa's text, despite his own wide travels? In some respects, allowing the Japanese text to help determine the shape of his own work shows Yu Kilchun's deference to a Japanese model, rather like centuries of East Asian writers who retraced the routes of their predecessors and incorporated earlier observations into their travel writings. But more significant is how Yu Kilchun adapts Fukuzawa's narrative. By providing a text that resembles *Conditions in the West* in many places but diverges from it significantly in others, Yu Kilchun ends up contradicting Fukuzawa—and the Japanese—more blatantly than he would have had he published a text with fewer obvious ties to a Japanese predecessor. For instance, in the section "Kaehwa ŭi tŭnggŭp" (Levels of Civilization), Yu Kilchun makes several assertions of Korean equality, if not superiority, that are enhanced by their position in an adaptation of a Japanese text. Yu Kilchun declares that there is nothing inherently remarkable about the modern Japanese and Western inventions that people hold in such high esteem; they simply are outgrowths of earlier discoveries, many of which have their roots in China and Korea. Korea, he implies, has the potential to speed far ahead of Japan and the West; if Koreans only were more committed to advancing their culture, their accomplishments easily would outstrip those of other nations:

Novel and wondrous principles were not lacking in former times, nor are they newly created today. . . . It might seem as though the talents and knowledge of the present generation surpass those of our ancestors. But the truth is that people elaborate on the things made by their forefathers. The steamship is novel, but it is built along the lines of earlier ships. The steam-driven vehicle is novel, but it never could have come about without the benefit of earlier models of vehicle manufacture. The same is true in every field: new methods could not have developed without the accomplishments of past generations. Our country also has famous products: Koryŏ [935–1392] ceramics are known around the globe, the "turtle boat" invented by Yi Ch'ungmu [Yi Sunsin, 1545–98] was the world's first armored warship, the iron type invented by our government printing office was also the first in the world. Had the people of our country studied tirelessly and implemented useful ways and principles, our nation now would be world famous for millions of things. Sadly, younger generations have not elaborated on the models provided by the past.[104]

Yu Kilchun thus affirms Korean preeminence in a text devoted to the wonders of the West that is based heavily on a Japanese bestseller, printed in a nation that scorned his own, and published with the assistance of the writer of this bestseller, who by the late 1880s had abandoned his project of "enlightening" East Asia and instead was calling for Japanese hegemony in the region.[105] In so doing, Yu Kilchun determinedly asserts Korean potential at a time when so doing was becoming increasingly difficult.

Confident about their national cultural potential, some Korean-language rewriters of Japanese literature in the early twentieth century made additional arguments for Korean strength and superiority. Their texts occupied a crucial position on the Korean literary menu during the years surrounding annexation in 1910, and how they transculturated Japanese creative works offers insights into some of the concerns weighing on early twentieth-century Korean intellectuals. Principal targets of the first years of adapting and translating, Japanese political novels like *Plum Blossoms in the Snow* soon were replaced by domestic novels, as Koreans became more engaged with contemporary Japanese literary production.

Cho Iljae (1887–1944), a reporter for the *Daily News*, was one of the busiest Korean adapters of Japanese novels in the 1910s, reworking Kikuchi Yūhō's *My Sin*, Tokutomi Roka's *The Cuckoo*, Ozaki Kōyō's *The Gold Demon*, and several other Japanese bestsellers as both plays and novels.[106] He began serializing an adaptation of *My Sin* in the *Daily News* on July 17, 1912 under the title *Ssang-oknu* (A Pair of Jeweled Tears). This adaptation, which ran until February 4, 1913, at times on the front page of the paper, was one of a number of transculturations that added "tears" to Japanese titles, marking at once increased melodrama and the sorrow of colonial Korea. Kikuchi's *My Sin* was already well known in Korea. A Japanese drama troupe first performed a theatrical adaptation of this novel there in January 1908; more than a dozen performances followed between 1908 and 1911, making *My Sin* one of the most frequently staged plays by Japanese drama troupes in Korea during the early colonial period. Theatrical adaptations of Kikuchi's texts also were presented by Korean theater companies like the Hyŏksindan, which took many of its plays from the Japanese *shinpa* (new school) theater. But Cho Iljae's prose adaptation *A Pair of Jeweled Tears* was even more popular in Korea than its Japanese source.

The advertisement for this adaptation, appearing in the July 17, 1912 issue of the *Daily News*, labels it a "translation of the novel *My Sin*, the most famous novel in Japan." It also notes that *A Pair of Jeweled Tears* has been revised to reflect Korean customs.[107] Interestingly, however, the actual installments of *A Pair of Jeweled Tears* list Cho Iljae as the author (*chŏ*), not the adapter or translator, suggesting at once creative independence and colonial anxiety. Although the plot of *A Pair of Jeweled Tears* is similar to that of *My Sin*, Cho Iljae not only changes place and personal names from Japanese to Korean but also revises, adds to, and omits segments of the Japanese text. One of the most significant transformations involves highlighting Korean medical expertise, a field supposedly dominated in East Asia by the Japanese.

Kikuchi's *My Sin* features Tamaki, a woman plagued with guilt for having a son out of wedlock. When she eventually marries, she does not tell her husband Takahiro about this child, whom she mistakenly thought had died shortly after birth. Takahiro learns of the boy only after the boy and the son he had had with Tamaki drown together. Upset at Tamaki's deception, Takahiro demands a separation. Tamaki and Takahiro are reconciled three years later, after Takahiro contracts typhoid fever in Saigon and Tamaki, having become a successful nurse in Taiwan, rushes to his bedside to take over his care. The two have an emotional reconciliation, and Takahiro recovers; the novel concludes with the couple back in Japan expecting a child and looking forward to a meaningful life together. Similarly, Cho Iljae's *A Pair of Jeweled Tears* tells the story of Kyŏngja, a woman who does not inform her husband Chŏng Ukjo about her previous marriage to Sŏ Pyŏngsam and the child they had together. Burdened with guilt, Kyŏngja rapidly loses strength and Ukjo takes her to a doctor, who turns out to be none other than her former husband Pyŏngsam. As in the Japanese novel, the female protagonist's first and second sons meet, become friends, and drown together; only after their deaths does she reveal her secret. Deeply disturbed by what he has learned, Ukjo leaves Kyŏngja and moves to China; Kyŏngja becomes a successful nurse in Pyongyang. A year and a half later, learning that Ukjo, now in Nagasaki, is gravely ill, Kyŏngja rushes to Japan and takes over his treatment. Ukjo heals quickly, and on the way home to Korea the two reconcile; several months later Kyŏngja becomes pregnant, and the two vow to raise a child who will contribute to society.

Kikuchi's *My Sin* underlines Tamaki's pivotal position in the Red Cross Hospital in colonial Taiwan, referring to her as "the flower of the Taipei Red Cross Hospital" and commenting that "as the head nurse at the Taipei Red Cross Hospital, as the Eastern [Florence]

Nightingale [1820–1910], her name wasn't known just in Taiwan. She was the subject of much discussion even on the main island [Japan]."[108] Tamaki also heals Chinese, who have heard great things about her and travel to her hospital from China. But even more noteworthy is her success at the Red Cross Hospital in colonial Saigon, which is run by the French and employs Japanese as assistants. *My Sin* boldly depicts the Japanese nurse as holding her own with the European medical establishment; the French hospital director, aware of Tamaki's success in Taiwan, puts her in charge of her husband's care.

In contrast, highlighting colonial Korean medical expertise, and, even more important, the accomplishments of colonial Korean medical personnel in Japan, Cho Iljae's Korean adaptation *A Pair of Jeweled Tears* at once repeats and reverses this framework. When Kyŏngja arrives at the Red Cross Hospital in Nagasaki she talks not with a Japanese doctor but with a Korean doctor who graduated from Nagasaki Medical College and now is working at the hospital. Aware of Kyŏngja's professional expertise, the Japanese director of the hospital puts her in charge of Ukjo's care. *A Pair of Jeweled Tears* concludes not simply with the impending birth of a child whose parents vow will contribute to society, but with an implicit reminder to the thousands of Koreans then streaming to Japan for a modern education—many of whom went specifically to study medicine—that the Japanese were not inherently superior.[109] Locating the hospital scene in Nagasaki, long the entryway into Japan of Chinese, Korean, and Western knowledge, reinforces this sentiment. Nagasaki Medical College itself, founded in 1857, was Japan's first Western-style medical school, and doctors there enjoyed ties with Dutch medical professionals; beginning in the 1900s, a number of Chinese and Koreans also trained at this institution, with the first Chinese student graduating in 1909.[110] *A Pair of Jeweled Tears* suggests that Koreans, like Japanese, are capable of and should take responsibility for repairing their own ills, that they have much to learn from the Japanese (both scientific knowledge and how to assimilate the foreign) but should not depend on a Japanese or other outside cure. In so doing, this adaptation counters what some Korean modernizers, including Yun Ch'iho, had urged in the years leading up to colonization, namely that Koreans and Chinese "march together to the beat of modernization with Japan in the lead."[111]

My Sin was very popular in Japan, particularly among women, as was its adaptation *A Pair of Jeweled Tears* in Korea, but readers in both countries were even more excited about Roka's *The Cuckoo*. Cho Iljae was one of three Koreans who rewrote *The Cuckoo* in 1912; his version, a Korean-language translation entitled *Pulyŏgwi* (*The Cuckoo*), was published in Japan on August 20, 1912. Kim Ujin's Korean adaptation, *Yuhwau* (Pomegranate Blossoms in the Rain) came out on September 15, 1912, and Sŏn-u Il's (1881–1936) edition, titled *Tugyŏnsŏng* (Song of the Cuckoo), appeared in two parts, the first on February 20, 1912, and the second on September 20.[112] These three works rewrite Roka's text, one another, and Japanese and Korean dramatic adaptations of *The Cuckoo*. It is likely that Cho Iljae, Kim Ujin, and Sŏn-u Il all had watched *The Cuckoo* on stage, performed by both Japanese and Korean drama troupes, inasmuch as Japanese plays based on *The Cuckoo* were staged in Tokyo beginning in 1901 and within several years were presented in Korea by Japanese companies. *The Cuckoo* was the most popular Japanese play in Korea, and it later became an important part of the Korean repertory; it was first performed by a Korean drama company in Korean in March 1912, only one month after the appearance of the first part of Sŏn-u Il's adaptation and several months before the publication of both Kim Ujin's version and the second part of Cho Iljae's.[113]

Korean adaptations of *The Cuckoo* retained much of the novel's unapologetic nationalism but also posed defiant challenges to their Japanese predecessor.[114] Advertised as a translation of Tokutomi Roka's text and published in Japan, Cho Iljae's Korean-language *Cuckoo* resembles its Japanese-language source more closely than the reconfigurations that preceded it or followed closely on its heels. Divided into 27 chapters like the Japanese and Chinese *Cuckoo*s, it retains Japanese character and place names, underlining them and spelling them out phonetically. Like his Chinese counterpart, the narrator of the Korean *Cuckoo* tones down some of the military rhetoric in the Japanese *Cuckoo*—tellingly, none of the illustrations included in the Korean *Cuckoo* show battle scenes; the narrator also replaces "our country" with "Japan." But in general, Cho Iljae follows the Japanese novel, creating for Korean readers a view of both Japanese family life and perceptions of the Sino-Japanese War.[115]

In contrast, Kim Ujin's *Pomegranate Blossoms in the Rain* and Sŏn-u Il's *Song of the Cuckoo*—perhaps partially in reaction to Cho Iljae's relatively faithful version—abridge the Japanese *Cuckoo* and move the setting from the Sino-Japanese to the Russo-Japanese War. The male protagonists of these Korean adaptations voluntarily join the

Japanese military. Names, nationalities, and settings have changed, but the excitement over battle that resounds in the pages of Roka's text echoes in Kim Ujin's and Sŏn-u Il's versions. As *Pomegranate Blossoms in the Rain* declares, "War is the foundation of peace and peace is the beginning of war. The Sino-Japanese War took place in 1894 and 1895. Japan won at last, and there was peace, [but then Russia started causing problems]."[116] Coming on the heels of Japan's colonization of Korea, these outbursts of pro-Japanese sentiment are noteworthy, yet there is more to them than meets the eye. Undoubtedly they vocalized the sentiments of some Koreans. They likewise were an effective means of appeasing Japanese authorities and warding off Japanese censorship. But these expressions do not stand unchallenged.

Kim Ujin's *Pomegranate Blossoms in the Rain* features Kim Sŏljŏng, a Korean exchange student in Kyoto engaged to Ch'oe Yŏnghyŏn, an alumnus of a Japanese naval academy and currently a student at London Naval College. After graduating, Sŏljŏng returns to Seoul and waits for Yŏnghyŏn, who has become a lieutenant in the Japanese navy; they marry when he returns home on a brief leave. With Yŏnghyŏn soon back at the front, Sŏljŏng is driven from her new home by her abusive mother-in-law, falls ill, and later is told that Yŏnghyŏn has been killed in battle; similarly, after he is discharged, Yŏnghyŏn hears that Sŏljŏng has died. Later, returning home from a trip to Korea's Diamond Mountain, Yŏnghyŏn stops at a friend's house, where he discovers that Sŏljŏng in fact is still alive; the two are happily reunited.

Kim Ujin transculturates many elements of Roka's tale in *Pomegranate Blossoms in the Rain*, but one of his more significant changes is the rewriting of Takeo and Namiko's tragic separation as a joyful reunion. The ending of *Pomegranate Blossoms in the Rain* is formulaic and echoes many classical Korean and other East Asian tales. Yet omitting some of the more provocative and evocative segments of Roka's text, the very ones that contributed to its success in Japan, Kim Ujin in one sense partly denies the legitimacy of *The Cuckoo*'s premise. The triumph of love and truth, *Pomegranate Blossoms in the Rain* suggests, liberates people from the need to romanticize suffering and obsess over illness, death, and dying. Paradoxically, in so doing, the reader—including the colonial subject—is liberated from *The Cuckoo* itself. Where *A Pair of Jeweled Tears* (Cho Iljae's adaptation of the Japanese novel *My Sin*) depicts a Korean female nurse as more adept than Japanese male doctors, Kim Ujin's *Pomegranate Blossoms in the Rain* portrays Koreans as more physically resilient than their Japanese textual predecessors.

Sŏn-u Il's *Song of the Cuckoo*, on the other hand, strives to outshine its Japanese predecessor not in depicting characters with greater skills despite lesser status (as does Cho Iljae's *A Pair of Jeweled Tears*) nor in presenting characters with greater endurance (as does Kim Ujin's *Pomegranate Blossoms in the Rain*), but rather in offering a text with an ending even more emotional than the heightened sentimentality of the Japanese *Cuckoo*'s final paragraphs. The story of Yi Pungnam and his wife, Sŏn-u Il's *Song of the Cuckoo* follows the original plot of Roka's novel more closely than does Kim Ujin's version. Discovering that his mother has divorced him from his wife because she fears the latter's pulmonary tuberculosis will infect him and bring an end to the family line, Yi Pungnam is distraught. He joins the Japanese navy in the Russo-Japanese War, believing he has nothing for which to live. But far from surrendering to his emotions and sacrificing himself on the battlefield, he fights bravely and ultimately saves his father-in-law's life. His wife dies soon thereafter, and *Song of the Cuckoo* concludes with Yi Pungnam and his father-in-law at her grave.

Sŏn-u Il's adaptation of Roka's *The Cuckoo* does not shy away from pro-Japanese rhetoric. It intertwines talk of embracing the "modern" (national enlightenment, education, women's rights, love as opposed to arranged marriage) and disregarding tradition with statements supporting the Japanese imperialist agenda in Asia: *Song of the Cuckoo* advocates loyalty to the Japanese emperor and promotes Japanese foreign policy, particularly Japan's objectives in the Russo-Japanese War.[117] But the pro-imperialist idiom is subtly undercut at the conclusion of the novel. While in *Pomegranate Blossoms in the Rain* Kim Ujin recasts the tearful ending of *The Cuckoo* as a joyful reunion, Sŏn-u Il's *Song of the Cuckoo* concludes with even more emotion than the Japanese version. The Japanese novel ends with Namiko's father urging the weeping Takeo to remain strong for the journey that lies ahead; Namiko's father attempts to divert Takeo's attention from his deceased wife's grave by asking him about his experiences in Taiwan. The Korean adaptation, while also featuring a fountain of tears, ends in the mountains, in the rain, the only sound a cuckoo's cries. Here, the nonhuman world swallows the tears of the lovelorn that saturated earlier pages of the text.[118]

The sentimental conclusion of the Japanese *Cuckoo* and the buoy-
ant conclusion of *Pomegranate Blossoms in the Rain*, the latter of which
indicates at least partial liberation from the Japanese text, in Sŏn-u
Il's version are both overcome by the landscape. The reversal in *Song
of the Cuckoo* of Kim Ujin's reversal of Roka's text is striking, but
more arresting still is its escalation of *The Cuckoo*'s sentimentality.
The Korean mountains, rains, and cuckoo appearing in the final lines
of the text silence the Japanese novel, and ultimately Japanese discourse. Featuring a singing cuckoo in title as in content, rather than
just a cuckoo, Kim Ujin's *Song of the Cuckoo* gestures to the power of
Korean voice.

Assertions of Korean strength and even superiority—whether
intratextual as in *A Pair of Jeweled Tears* (where the Korean female
nurse is able to do what Japanese male doctors cannot) or intertextual
as in both *Pomegranate Blossoms in the Rain* (where the characters are
more resilient than their Japanese predecessors) and *Song of the Cuckoo*
(where the conclusion exaggerates the already exaggerated emotions
of the Japanese novel)—are repeated in Cho Iljae's second major adaptation of a Japanese bestseller, that of Ozaki Kōyō's *The Gold Demon*
(1903). In 1913, Cho Iljae recast *The Gold Demon* as *Changhanmong* (Long
Teary Dream), a novel that trumpets Korean moral courage. *Long
Teary Dream* quickly became a favorite both on stage and in print, and
it was performed and reissued multiple times in the next few decades.
In 1926, it was made into a silent film, soon becoming one of Korea's
first cinematic sensations.[119] Cho Iljae's *Long Teary Dream* not only
moves the setting of Kōyō's *The Gold Demon* from flourishing Meiji
Tokyo to early colonial Seoul and its environs and changes the characters' names from Japanese to Korean, but it also portrays a female
protagonist (Sim Sun-ae) who is more stoic than her Japanese
counterpart. Surrendering her status but not her principles, Sun-ae
(lit. follow love) points to the possibilities for Koreans under colonial
oppression.

The plot of *Long Teary Dream* closely parallels that of *The Gold
Demon*.[120] Miya and Sun-ae, the Japanese and Korean female protagonists of these two novels, are shamed by their marriages to wealthy
men and yearn to return to their former heartthrobs, Kan'ichi and
Su-il. But the narrator of *Long Teary Dream* draws attention to Sun-ae's
chastity and faithfulness. Unlike Miya, Sun-ae refuses to consum-
mate her relationship with her wealthy husband.[121] Moreover, she
is courageous enough to leave him after he rapes her. Leaving one's

husband for love was almost unheard of in Korea in the 1910s; Korean women had won the right to remarry only a decade before. Yet the motif of sacrificing everything for love resonated deeply with Cho Iljae's Korean readers, many of whom no longer could endure conventional structures of marriage and family. Sun-ae's ultimate rejection of her husband served in part as an allegory for newly colonized Korea vis-à-vis Japan: the reluctant bride Korea—having failed to launch a sufficient defense—cohabited with Japan, but the novel *Long Teary Dream* suggests that complete surrender is not inevitable. Indeed, Sun-ae's escape indicates that liberation of some sort might just be possible. Written during the early years of colonial rule, Cho Iljae's *A Pair of Jeweled Tears* and *Long Teary Dream*, Kim Ujin's *Pomegranate Blossoms in the Rain*, Sŏn-u Il's *Song of the Cuckoo*, and other Korean adaptations and translations of Japanese creative texts manipulate Japanese discourse by pointing to Korean endurance and even superiority, whether manifested in ability to heal, physical stamina, literary strength, or moral courage.

Interlingual transculturations of Japanese creative works, many of them introducing vocabulary and creative styles that reappeared in Chinese and Korean literatures for decades, soared in the wake of *Chance Meetings with Beautiful Women*, *Plum Blossoms in the Snow*, *The Gold Demon*, *The Cuckoo*, *My Sin*, and other commercially and artistically successful Japanese novels. The mere existence of early twentieth-century Chinese and Korean adaptations and translations of Japanese literary works, particularly bestsellers, suggests a degree of submission to metropolitan prototypes. But transforming major components of Japanese artistic achievement, these interlingual transculturations also point to colonial and semicolonial agency. The negotiations involved in these transactions became even more intense in the second half of the Japanese colonial period between 1919 and 1945.

FOUR

From Cultural Innovation to Total War

The March First Movement in Korea (1919), the May Fourth Movement in China (1919), and the Taiwan New Literature movement of the late 1910s and early 1920s all stimulated a flood of new writing, including adaptations and translations of foreign literatures. Although it failed to liberate Korea, the March First Movement led to a publishing boom. As part of their new Cultural Policy (*bunka seiji*), Japanese authorities relaxed publication controls and granted permits for hundreds of Korean-language periodicals, many of which carried translations of foreign literatures. China's May Fourth Movement, politically an outgrowth of increasing concern over Chinese sovereignty and culturally an extension of recent calls to overhaul classical forms, was triggered by the transfer of Germany's rights in Shandong to Japan in the Treaty of Versailles (1919). This turn of events shocked Chinese, who like Koreans had been confident that Woodrow Wilson's call for self-determination of peoples also would apply to them, and it led to large demonstrations and national upheaval. Although they were unsuccessful in removing the Japanese from Shandong, the Chinese sought even more urgently "to redefine China's culture as a valid part of the modern world."[1] This resulted in a strengthened iconoclastic anticlassical movement to encourage writing in the vernacular and introduce foreign cultural products, both Western and Japanese. The Taiwan New Literature movement soon followed in the 1920s, likewise calling for writing in vernacular Chinese to spur social reform. Reading texts from China, Japan, and Western nations was an important part of this process, and Taiwanese translated more literature than ever before.

As in earlier decades, in the years following World War One Japanese literature was a contested space of transcultural negotiation throughout East Asia. But the stakes grew higher with the Japanese seizure of Manchuria in 1931, subsequent Japanese pressures on the mainland, the outbreak of total war with China in 1937, and increasingly stringent Japanese controls on its colonies Korea and Taiwan throughout the 1930s and early 1940s. In this charged environment, what was the relationship of Chinese, Korean, and Taiwanese interlingual transculturations of Japanese creative work with other vectors of intra-empire textual contact? What was the relationship between adaptation/translation and censorship, and how did adaptations/translations transculturate censored texts, particularly those that critiqued Japanese imperial ambitions even while promoting stereotypes of colonial/semicolonial peoples? How did adaptations/translations of battlefront literature, which described fighting in China and elsewhere in Asia in often gruesome detail, bargain with texts that exposed Japanese brutality but also drew attention to Chinese losses? What insights do interlingual transculturations of Japanese literature during these decades offer into literary contact nebulae more generally?

Trajectories of Adaptation and Translation, 1919–1945

Chinese and Koreans continued to adapt foreign literary works into the 1920s. The Korean writer Chin Hakmun's (1894–1974) *Am-yŏng* (Gloom, 1923), for instance, loosely reconfigures the Japanese writer Futabatei Shimei's novel *Sono omokage* (In His Image, 1906). As Chin Hakmun, who studied at Waseda University and Tokyo University of Foreign Studies (Tōkyō Gaikokugo Daigaku) in the 1910s, states explicitly in his preface: "this is neither a translation nor an original work."[2] But these projects were outnumbered by more faithful translations as Chinese and Korean writers grew more concerned with preserving the essence of sources, and readers became more receptive to texts that retained a foreign flavor, although with increased exposure this flavor was actually becoming less foreign. After World War One, Taiwanese, who began studying in Japan several decades after their Chinese and Korean counterparts, began transculturating literature from abroad in greater numbers; adhering relatively closely to source texts, most of their rewritings can be considered translations. Increased contact with other cultures made translations more enticing across China, Korea, and Taiwan, even among readers with strong anti-foreign sentiments.

To be sure, from the 1920s through liberation in 1945, Chinese, Korean, and Taiwanese interlingual transculturations of some Western literatures, particularly English-language texts, outnumbered those of Japanese literature. But as was true of earlier reconfiguration, what translations of Japanese literature may have lacked in volume they made up for in significance, particularly after the outbreak of total war in 1937. Chinese, Korean, and Taiwanese translations of Japanese literature not only provided East Asians with intellectual stimulation, entertainment, and multiple portholes into Japanese culture, they also introduced a wide range of styles and genres, many of which were incorporated into colonial and semicolonial writings. Yet colonial and semicolonial translations of texts from the metropole, particularly translations of battlefront literature, walked a fine line between discussing Japanese military might on the one hand and Chinese and Korean capitulation on the other. Using the words of Japanese writers to expose Japanese violence—at times circumventing strict censorship laws in China, Korea, Taiwan, and Japan itself—gave these translations particular maneuverability and credibility. But they also were notably concerned with how to rewrite the impact of Japanese oppression on its colonies and semicolony.

Chinese translations were the largest and most diverse group of early twentieth-century interlingual transculturations of Japanese literature. The market for these translations grew substantially in the 1920s and early 1930s. Books became more affordable and literacy and popular interest in Japan increased, buoyed in part by the desire to "know the enemy," even though the percentage of Chinese capable of reading the original Japanese texts remained low. Circumstances were different in Korea and Taiwan, where mounting restrictions on publishing in Korean and Chinese and greater Japanese-language proficiency—to the point where some, even in Taiwan, read Chinese literature not in the original Chinese but in Japanese translation—dampened incentives for translating Japanese literature.[3] Yet Korean and Taiwanese translators persisted, with some of the latter publishing Chinese-language translations of Japanese literature on the mainland.

Translators' motives and attitudes toward Japanese literature varied greatly. Many appended commentaries to their texts in which they enthusiastically promoted, harshly critiqued, or simply relayed factual information about their Japanese sources. There were those like the Chinese writer Guo Moruo, who in the preface to his 1930 translation of the Japanese novelist Natsume Sōseki's *Kusamakura* (Pillow of Grass, 1906) likened this work to a "richly fragrant, beautiful flower" that he "loved" and hoped would survive as he transplanted it into Chinese soil.[4] Shimazaki Tōson likewise received high praise from Zhang Wojun, the Taiwanese translator of his lengthy novel *Before the Dawn* (1935), who in 1943 declared, "I read this novel when it first came out in the *Central Review*. It is Tōson's masterpiece and a part of Japanese literary history that can be passed down for generations. I believe this without a shadow of a doubt."[5] Contrariwise, there were translators like the Chinese writer Han Shiheng, who in the preface to *Modern Japanese Fiction* (1929), his collection of Japanese short stories in Chinese translation, denounced the very texts for whose increased circulation he was responsible.[6]

Naturally, the reception of Japanese literature in translation also fluctuated. Library data, bookstore records, and personal diaries from early twentieth-century China, Korea, and Taiwan show how eagerly colonial and semicolonial readers consumed translations of metropolitan literature. But while a number of translations enjoyed nearly instant commercial success, others were purchased by only a handful of readers. Some in the Japanese literary establishment kept tabs on the translation of their texts in East Asia. Reactions were mixed. For every Akutagawa Ryūnosuke, who in 1925—commenting on Lu Xun and Zhou Zuoren's *Collection of Modern Japanese Stories* (1923), China's first anthology of Japanese literature in translation—somewhat grudgingly acknowledged, "There is no question that Chinese translations of Japanese literature compare rather favorably with the translations of Western literature currently coming out in Japan,"[7] there was someone like Eguchi Kan, who in 1934 enthusiastically proclaimed: "It is truly astonishing that Chinese translations and introductions of modern Japanese novels, plays, and criticism keep coming out, almost every month."[8]

Some Japanese offered to assist their East Asian translators. When Shimazaki Tōson learned that the Taiwanese writer Zhang Wojun was planning to translate *Before the Dawn* into Chinese, he pledged to help him any way he could. As Zhang Wojun later recalled, "[Tōson said to me sincerely], '*Before the Dawn* contains many old things that nowadays aren't well known, so if you have any questions please don't hesitate to contact me.' Hearing the esteemed writer say this moved me greatly."[9] Zhang Wojun promised Tōson that he would consult him when he had finished a draft of the translation, but Tōson died in August 1943, just days before the Taiwanese writer arrived in Tokyo for a follow-up visit. Other colonial and semicolonial writers were more fortunate and successfully collaborated with metropolitan counterparts, who occasionally provided their translations with prefaces or other commentaries. Several Japanese literary figures even seem to have written creative texts with consumption and possibly translation by Chinese or Koreans in mind. For instance, the Japanese proletarian writer Nakanishi Inosuke's lengthy novel *Neppū* (Hot Wind, 1928) contains notes for its Korean readers and translators; this novel exposes the difficulties encountered by the Indian independence movement, a topic with which frustrated colonial Koreans could easily relate. In some places, Nakanishi's notes illuminate the dangers of particular words and urge that they be omitted in translation, and in other places they append explanations for terms.[10] The Korean creative writer and journalist Yi Iksang (1895–1935) serialized a translation of *Hot Wind* in the Korean newspaper *Chosŏn ilbŏ* (Korea Daily News) in 311 installments between January and December 1926, well before this text was published as a book in Japan.[11]

Although encouraged by the Japanese literary establishment, most intra–East Asian translation of Japanese literature was voluntary. Exceptions are translations commissioned by Japanese authorities during the years of all-out war with China (1937–45), but these were only a small subset of the total. Chinese, Koreans, and Taiwanese not only made the cultural products of the metropole accessible to local readers but also undermined Japanese narrative and cultural capital and authority by creating their own Japanese canon, one that often diverged from the body of texts the Japanese literary establishment regarded as preeminent.

The Numbers

Increased fidelity to sources became an important concern among Chinese translators in the late 1910s and early 1920s, but the actual volume of translations of Japanese literature in China did not expand significantly until the Japanese one-yen book boom of the late 1920s. This marketing phenomenon, inaugurated in 1926 when the Japanese publishing house Kaizōsha released the multi-volume *Gendai Nihon bungaku zenshū* (Complete Works of Modern Japanese Literature), turned reading into a Japanese national obsession. One-yen books were popular as well with Chinese in Japan and at home, particularly those who frequented the Uchiyama Bookstore in Shanghai, the principal locus of Sino-Japanese literary exchange in semicolonial China. Uchiyama Kanzō, the shop's proprietor, noted with pride the connections between his store and the translation of hundreds of Japanese literary works into Chinese in the 1920s and 1930s: "Most of the books translated came from my store. . . . I knew all the [Chinese] translators very well, including Lu Xun, Guo Moruo, Tian Han, [and dozens of others] . . . and most who translated Japanese literature during those years were my customers."[12] Indeed, the publication of Chinese translations of Japanese literature was centered in Shanghai.[13]

Chinese publishers printed translations of Japanese literary works in journals and newspapers, as separate volumes, in the collected works of individual or multiple Japanese authors, and in anthologies of foreign literatures in translation. Between the May Fourth Movement and Japanese defeat in 1945, Chinese periodicals, including *Xiaoshuo yuebao* (Fiction Monthly), *Shijie ribao* (World Daily), *Wenxue zhoubao* (Literature Weekly), and *Wenxue* (Literature), carried the translations of well over 300 Japanese literary works.[14] In occupied China, including Manchuria, journals such as *Chronicle of the Arts* also published a number of Chinese-language translations of Japanese creative texts. Likewise, between the May Fourth Movement and Japan's seizure of Manchuria in 1931, Chinese published more than 120 titles of Japanese literature in translation: about two-thirds of these were titles containing work(s) by a single author and the rest were collections of Japanese works by multiple authors. Between 1919 and 1931, Chinese also translated more than 45 Japanese studies of foreign literature, including several examinations of Chinese literature. Despite the decline of Sino-Japanese political relations, between the Manchurian takeover and the outbreak of total war in 1937 Chinese published approximately 85 titles of Japanese literature in translation: 60 contained work(s) by a single author and 25 were collections of Japanese texts by multiple authors. During the same period, Chinese also published more than 30 translations of Japanese studies of foreign literature, including 10 on Chinese literature. Then between 1937 and 1945, the years of all-out war with Japan, Chinese published close to 50 titles of Japanese literature in translation containing the works of a single writer and approximately half that many with the works of multiple authors.[15] These numbers do not include Japanese texts that appeared in Chinese anthologies of translations from several literatures. Some of these books were published in occupied Manchuria, but many penned by writers from this region were published in China proper.

The large quantity of Chinese translations of Japanese literature contrasts with the situation in Korea. Approximately 50 titles of Japanese literature in Korean translation were published in the 1920s, out of the nearly 1,000 titles of literature in Korean translation produced during this decade. Translations of Japanese literature plummeted in the 1930s: only 4 of the more than 750 titles of literature in translation published between 1930 and 1936 were translations of Japanese works. Between 1937 and 1945, Koreans published only a single title of Japanese literature in Korean translation, as opposed to nearly 250 of Western literature. Translations of Japanese and other literatures also appeared in Korean periodicals throughout the colonial period. Although their precise numbers have yet to be determined, it is likely that the ratio of translations of Japanese texts to translations of Western texts in Korean periodicals is similar to the ratio of translations of Japanese texts to translations of Western texts published as individual books.[16]

This decline in Korean translations of Japanese literature does not point to decreased interest in metropolitan creative production. Rather, it reflects the fast-growing numbers of Koreans able to read Japanese literary works in the original and the increasing restrictions on the use of the Korean language. Moreover, just as Japanese literature was losing its appeal in Korea as an object of translation, it became an increasingly popular target of intertextualization, examined in Part II. Noteworthy, however, is that Koreans continued to publish Korean-language translations of Western texts well after Japan nominally prohibited publishing in Korean. This defiance of colonial decree reveals the dedication and cleverness of Korean writers in making foreign literatures available in Korean.[17]

Even more precarious was the situation in Taiwan. Taiwanese began translating foreign literatures in 1905, but unlike in Korea, few in Taiwan were interested in texts from abroad before the early 1920s.[18] Japanese literature was no exception. A few Japanese literary works were available in Taiwan at the end of the nineteenth century. Yet by the time significant numbers of Taiwanese traveled to Japan and became deeply engaged with Japanese literature during the late 1920s, several related factors deterred translation. First, colonial restrictions made publication in Chinese progressively more difficult.

Second and more important, increasing numbers of educated Taiwanese were able to read Japanese works in the original, and some
were even reading both classical and modern Chinese literature in
Japanese translation.[19] Finally, translations of Japanese literature were
booming in China, so Taiwanese had less motivation to translate
Japanese literature into Chinese. Some Taiwanese periodicals carried
Chinese-language translations of Japanese poetry and prose, include-
ing *Literary Taiwan, Di yi xian* (The First Line), *Taiwan bungei* (Taiwan
Literature), and *Taiwan minbao* (Taiwan People's News), but the increasing Japanese-language proficiency of educated Taiwanese resulted in an ever-shrinking interest in translating Japanese texts. In
fact, by the 1930s, Japanese literary works in the original Japanese
appeared more frequently in Taiwanese periodicals than did Chinese-
language translations of Japanese literature. It is true that Taiwanese
continued to adapt Japanese plays and prose works for their stage,
including the perennial favorites *The Cuckoo* and *The Gold Demon*,
as well as texts by Kikuchi Kan, particularly *Chichi kaeru* (Father Returns, 1920). In addition, some Taiwanese writers with strong ties
to both Japan and China, including Zhang Wojun and Zhang Shenqie, published translations of Japanese literature on the mainland.[20]
But despite their avid consumption of Japanese literature, proven by
their literary criticism and intertextualizing, Koreans and Taiwanese
made translation of Japanese literature a lower priority than did the
Chinese.

The Texts

More significant than numbers was the variety of texts translated.
In the first half of the twentieth century, Chinese, Koreans, and Taiwanese rewrote novels, plays, poems, and short stories by major
and minor Japanese figures alike. They translated many of early
twentieth-century Japan's literary bestsellers, hoping not only to
leave their mark on these celebrated works but also to capitalize on
their success. They also overlooked some of the metropole's most
renowned early twentieth-century creative texts, including Futabatei
Shimei's *Ukigumo* (Floating Clouds, 1889), often hailed as the first
modern Japanese novel, and Arishima Takeo's *Aru onna* (A Certain
Woman, 1919), which has been acclaimed as one of early twentieth-
century Japan's most "European novels." In the 1930s, Chinese published at least three anthologies of Arishima's work in Chinese translation, making the absence of *A Certain Woman* especially striking. At

the same time, Chinese, Korean, and Taiwanese translators together promoted a number of authors relatively neglected by audiences in Japan. Most obvious was the literary critic Kuriyagawa Hakuson, who was far more popular among early twentieth-century Chinese than he was at home. Negotiating with Japanese texts of all types, colonial and semicolonial East Asians broke away from the Japanese literary edifice and created alternative libraries of Japanese writing.

Prewar Translation

After the May Fourth Movement, twentieth-century Japanese fiction maintained its position as the most popular object of intra-empire translation in China, Korea, and Taiwan. Beginning in the 1920s, Chinese translated novels and short stories by the leading Japanese writers Akutagawa Ryūnosuke, Kunikida Doppo, Mori Ōgai, Natsume Sōseki, and Tanizaki Jun'ichirō, as well as prose by Japanese naturalist writers, members of the White Birch Society, and proletarian, modernist, and neosensationalist figures;[21] they additionally published collections of Japanese fiction in translation.[22] Koreans and Taiwanese also translated a number of Japanese prose works. Proletarian novels and short stories were particularly popular with Korean translators, while Taiwanese such as Zhang Shenqie and Zhang Wojun translated Japanese fiction from across the literary spectrum.[23] Censored texts had their own appeal, and translators at times published in their own languages literary works, or fragments from literary works, banned in Japan. Few stones were left unturned as colonial and semicolonial East Asians engaged deeply with Japanese novels and short stories, making the prose of their oppressor accessible to a wider audience.

Chinese, Koreans, and Taiwanese also translated a broad array of modern Japanese drama, poetry, and literary criticism, as well as premodern classics. During the 1920s and 1930s, Chinese published approximately 30 titles of Japanese drama in translation; translations of other plays appeared in collected works and periodicals.[24] Koreans and Taiwanese rewrote a smaller sampling of Japanese drama, including Akita Ujaku's "Kin Gyokkin [Kim Okgyun] no shi" (The Death of Kim Okgyun, 1920), which was rewritten in Korean only six months after it first appeared in Japanese. It is no surprise that Korean translators leapt at the opportunity to transform into Korean a play on Kim Okgyun, an eminent Korean reformer who had enjoyed close ties with Japan.[25]

Modern Japanese poetry likewise drew attention as an object of translation. Chinese, led by Zhou Zuoren, translated the work of several prominent Japanese poets, including Horiguchi Daigaku, Ikuta Shungetsu, Ishikawa Takuboku (1886–1912), and Senge Motomaro.[26] Japanese poetry had a profound impact on the creations of some of early twentieth-century Korea's leading poets, but with the exception of translations by Chu Yohan and Hwang Sŏk-u, the interlingual reconfiguration of Japanese poetry for the most part was limited to retranslations of Japanese translations of Western poetry. Literary figures such as Kim Ŏk (1896–?), often credited with introducing modern European poetry to Korea, at times based their translations on the work of such prominent Japanese translators as Horiguchi Daigaku, Nagai Kafū, and Ueda Bin.[27]

Their fascination with foreign literature also meant that Chinese, Korean, and Taiwanese intellectuals turned increasingly to Japanese writings both on Japanese literature and on literatures from around the world.[28] In fact, enjoying even more success than their creative counterparts, Japanese works of literary criticism accounted for more than one-third of the over 100 works of this genre the Chinese translated between 1900 and the mid-1940s.[29] Where Japanese literature failed to appeal, Japanese criticism filled the gap. Kuriyagawa Hakuson was particularly popular. Translated by top Chinese literary figures such as Lu Xun, Guo Moruo, Yu Dafu, Tian Han, and Hu Feng, his writings appeared in most of China's major literary magazines and were cited in essays on literature by many leading Chinese writers. Chinese were especially drawn to Kuriyagawa's *Symbol of Suffering*—published posthumously in 1924 and translated into Chinese later that year by Lu Xun and in 1925 by Feng Zikai (1898–1975)—which argues that all creative acts are born out of the struggle between repression and the forces of life.

Lafcadio Hearn (Koizumi Yakumo, 1850–1904), an Irishman born in Greece who after several decades in the United States moved permanently to Japan, was another frequently translated critic in early twentieth-century China. Hearn's voluminous writings on Japanese literature and culture were particularly popular in the 1930s. Chinese believed that Hearn, being a foreigner in Japan, had unique insights into Japanese character.[30] Koreans and Taiwanese also published works of Japanese literary criticism in translation. For instance, in 1930, Zhang Wojun translated Miyajima Shinzaburō's (1892–1934) *Gendai Nihon bungaku hyōron* (Commentary on Modern Japanese Literature), and in 1932 he translated Natsume Sōseki's *Bungakuron* (Literary Criticism, 1907). As eager consumers of foreign literatures and cultures, Chinese, Korean, and Taiwanese intellectuals turned to Japanese scholarship, often using it as a stepping stone to more extensive forays into Japanese and other creative corpuses.

Absorption with Japanese cultural production was not confined to contemporary fare. Chinese, Korean, and Taiwanese students in Japan were introduced to a broad range of early Japanese literature in required textbooks, some of which they embraced; a number of students and other foreign residents attended kabuki and other classical theater performances on their own time.[31] In their essays, colonial and semicolonial scholars of Japanese literature frequently referred to and occasionally celebrated prominent classical Japanese texts including *The Tale of Genji* as well as genres like haiku, *waka*, and *kanshi*. For instance, in "Kyubang munhak" (Literature of the Inner Room, 1917), the Korean critic Yi Pyŏngdo (1896–1989) applauds the Chinese poetry of both the Japanese poet Ema Saikō (1787–1861) and the Korean poet Hŏ Nansŏrhŏn (Hŏ Ch'ohŭi, 1563–89); he asserts at the beginning of his essay that "from earliest times women have been among our heroes and outstanding citizens, geniuses and scholars."[32] During the war years, some stressed the importance of making classical Japanese literature available in Chinese, but it was not until well after liberation in 1945 that Chinese, Koreans, and Taiwanese began translating substantial numbers of Japanese classical texts.[33] The linguistic challenges posed by classical Japanese literature partially deterred its translation, as did centuries of intra–East Asian apathy toward early Japanese texts and belief in the superiority of the Chinese classical canon. To be sure, had they wished to make a case for the derivativeness of classical Japanese literature, colonial and semicolonial East Asians could have translated examples from this corpus into local languages and attached explanatory notes to this effect. Yet the hearty engagement of early twentieth-century Chinese, Koreans, and Taiwanese with modern Japanese literature and their relative indifference toward premodern Japanese literature reflect a more urgent desire: to create a new literature inspired in part by Japan's recent creative output.

Censoring and Voicing the Unspeakable

Colonial and semicolonial East Asian intellectuals active between 1920 and 1945, like those in preceding decades, believed translation of foreign materials imperative to cultural progress and nation building. Like translations of most literatures, those of Japanese literature introduced themes, characters, and storylines—as well as words, styles, and genres—that enriched Chinese, Korean, and Taiwanese cultural production. Yet to focus exclusively on how translations affect local creative output is to gloss over their substantial manipulations of source texts and the powerful implications of these transformations, transformations made particularly ambiguous by colonialism, semicolonialism, war, and occupation. Among the most significant transculturations of this period, often launched within weeks or months of their Japanese sources, were translations of Japanese proletarian literature.

Because of their potentially subversive content, creative texts by writers affiliated with the proletarian literature movement were vulnerable targets of Japanese censors. Yet Chinese, Korean, and Taiwanese translators, with or without consulting the writers of their sources, occasionally reversed these official deletions. They did so by replacing blank spaces and *fuseji* (censorship marks) with both their own words and words from earlier versions of the Japanese texts. In so doing, they frequently took up taboo topics and created translations that at once echoed and renounced imperial rhetoric. Michael Holquist has likened translation to censorship, arguing "Are not all translations . . . acts of censorship in that they, too, are fated to readings performed between the lines? Both censorship and translation are strategies to control meaning that are unavoidably insufficient: the interlinearity characterizing both guarantees in each that something will—always—be left out."[34] In the case of some Chinese and Korean translations of censored Japanese literature, the most striking omissions were of the censorship marks themselves. Translators, in other words, censored the censors.

One of the most striking examples is the Korean translation of the Japanese proletarian writer Nakano Shigeharu's poem "Ame no furu Shinagawa eki" (Shinagawa Station in the Rain, February 1929). This poem, punctuated by three sets of censorship marks, depicts a Japanese revolutionary bidding farewell to and imagining the eventual glorious return to Japan of Korean revolutionaries who are being deported on the occasion of the enthronement of the Shōwa emperor (November 10, 1928); the revolutionaries include Yi Pukman, a Korean proletarian writer, and Kim Hoyŏng, a leader of the Korean labor movement in Japan, both of whom were friends with Nakano.[35]

"Shinagawa Station in the Rain" was quickly translated into Korean as "Pi nal-i nŭn P'umch'ŏn-yŏk" (Shinagawa Station in the Rain, May 1929); this anonymous translation was published in the Tokyo-based Korean-language proletarian periodical *Musanja* (Proletariat).

The Korean-language "Shinagawa Station in the Rain" presents itself as a more complete text than its Japanese predecessor, replacing most of the censorship marks in Nakano's poem with words. In fact, the editors of *Proletariat* published this poem as a Korean-language original, giving its title (in Korean) and Nakano's name, but not naming a translator.[36] By omitting reference to a translator, the editors suggest that what appears in the Korean journal are Nakano's unmediated words. The Japanese writer's close contacts with Korean literary figures — including Kim Duyong (the editor of *Proletariat*) and Yi Pukman (whom some have speculated was the Korean translator) — make it more than likely that he played a role in the Korean translation, but it is unclear which changes restore words from earlier Japanese-language drafts of Nakano's poem, which reflect Nakano's suggestions to the Korean translator, and which were at the instigation of the translator. Yet such distinctions are less important than how the Korean translation reworks the Japanese text.

Transculturating a Japanese poem that maligns colonial Koreans, the Korean-language "Shinagawa Station in the Rain" ambiguously smudges collaboration and resistance. It calls for a physical attack on the Japanese emperor yet repeats its predecessor's stereotypes of Koreans. The Korean "Shinagawa Station in the Rain" translates the Japanese poem's first extended set of censorship marks into lines that unflatteringly corporealize the emperor. Whereas in Nakano's poem the Japanese revolutionary notes that his drenched Korean friends "call to mind ```````` / call to mind ````` ````` ```` ``````," the Japanese revolutionary in the Korean translation urges, "You all, soaked with rain, think of the Japanese XX who is kicking you out / You all, soaked with rain, engrave before your eyes the hair on his head, his narrow forehead, his glasses, his mustache, his curved spine."[37] Undermining Japanese imperial authority, this depiction of the unnamed but clearly identifiable emperor corresponds closely with those in postwar Japanese-language versions of "Shinagawa Station in the Rain": "You all, soaked with rain, think of the Japanese emperor who pursues you / You all, soaked with rain, think of his mustache, glasses, and stooped shoulders."[38] These similarities reveal contact between Nakano and the Korean translator/translation, although it is unclear whether the May 1929 Korean translation was based on an earlier version of "Shinagawa Station in the Rain," whether Nakano came up with these phrases expressly for the Korean translation (perhaps together with his Korean translator), or whether Nakano in fact based his postwar revisions on a Korean translation in which he had not played an active part.

Even more dramatically, the prewar Japanese-language "Shinagawa Station in the Rain" concludes with the Japanese revolutionary urging his Korean friends to return to Japan and do the literally unspeakable:

Front and rear shield of the Japanese proletariat
Go and crush that hard thick slick ice
And make the long-dammed water gush forth
And then once again
Leap across the strait and dance right back
Pass through Kobe, Nagoya, enter Tokyo
Approach ````
Appear at ````
`````

Thrust up and hold `` jaw
`````````````

````````

Laugh between sobs in the ecstasy of warm ``[39]

The Korean translation converts these censorship marks into words, concluding with the body conjured becoming the body assaulted by Korean revolutionaries who have boldly returned to Tokyo:

Head and tail of the Japanese proletariat
Go and crush that hard thick slick ice
And make an unrestrained flood of the long-confined water
And then once again
Leap across the channel and come near
Pass through Kobe, Nagoya, enter Tokyo
Press on his person, appear before his face
CapXre X and seize his Xoat
Precisely at his veX aim the sickleX and
In the blood pulsating from head to foot,
In the ecstasy of burning reX,
Laugh! Cry![40]

This Korean translation retains a few censorship marks, referring to the emperor as X, and substituting X's for Korean syllables, including "capXre" for "capture," "Xoat" for "throat," "veX" for "veins,"
````````

"sickleX" for "sickles and other tools" or "sickle-tips," and "reX" for "revenge."[41] But by hiding so little, the X's mock rather than reinforce censorship. In another faux bow to the censors, the Korean translation is pointedly ambiguous about the fate of the emperor. The Japanese revolutionary urges his Korean friends to aim their weapons at the emperor's neck, but he does not actually tell them to push these curved tools against his throat, let alone cut him. Yet the verb *ddwida*, here translated as "pulsate," also can mean "spatter," giving the line after the reference to sickles an alternate reading: "In the blood [from the emperor's veins] spattering [you/him] from head to foot."[42] Either way, with vengeance "burning" inside revolutionaries aiming lethal weapons at the emperor's neck, regicide appears inevitable.[43]

Postwar Japanese renditions of "Shinagawa Station in the Rain" also replace the final stanza's censorship marks with words, but they greatly dilute the assertions of the colonial Korean translation:

> Goodbye Sin
> Goodbye Kim
> Goodbye Yi
> Goodbye Mrs. Yi
> Go and crush that hard thick slick ice
> Make the long-dammed water gush forth
> Front and rear shield of the Japanese proletariat
> Goodbye
> Until the day we laugh between sobs in the joy of revenge.[44]

This version of "Shinagawa Station in the Rain" alludes only vaguely to Koreans returning to Japan, and while the poem speaks of "revenge," it gives few specifics and omits any hint of lèse majesté.[45]

The Korean-language "Shinagawa Station in the Rain" challenges imperial authority more dramatically than both the prewar and postwar Japanese-language permutations. It is a key example of how colonial and semicolonial translations of metropolitan literary works, mocking the ham-handed efforts of metropolitan censors, became sites for voicing harsh condemnations of the imperial power and advocating attacks on its architects, including the emperor. By the late 1920s, Nakano had acquired notoriety as a leading proletarian figure, so it is noteworthy that the Korean-language translation was not officially censored, particularly considering how prominently it displays Nakano's name. Unlike Shakespeare in twentieth-century Malawi — where even controversial plays like *Julius Caesar* were given the green light for performance by despotic regimes while much tamer African drama was heavily censored—Nakano was not at all a "dead and apparently irrelevant [writer]."[46]

On the other hand, the Korean translation repeats and in some ways strengthens the poem's anti-Korean prejudices. It does the latter by deleting from the Japanese-language "Shinagawa Station in the Rain" wording that points to Korean humanity. The Korean-language "Shinagawa Station in the Rain" reproduces faithfully the Japanese revolutionary's assertion early in the poem that the hearts of the Koreans leaving Japan are frozen, and it repeats the Japanese version's description of departing Koreans as "black shadows." Yet by failing to translate the stanza that speaks of these revolutionaries' "boiling young cheeks on which water disappears," which in the Japanese poem mitigates the claim of icy hearts, the Korean-language translation leaves unchallenged the idea of Koreans as virtually frozen shadows until they attack the emperor.[47] The Korean translation suggests that attacking the emperor is what makes Koreans human. Also significant is how both the Japanese poem and its Korean translation declare Koreans the "front and rear shield of the Japanese proletariat," a comment that Nakano later confessed deeply bothered him and was motivated by "ethnocentric egoism."[48] Identifying Koreans as the head and tail of the Japanese proletariat reinforces segregation along national/ethnic lines, not unlike the imperial decree expelling Koreans from Japan. Furthermore, it urges Korean revolutionaries to protect their supposedly superior Japanese counterparts and likely sacrifice their lives for them. Repeating and in fact highlighting expectations of Korean subordination even while it advocates the murder of the figure who most readily epitomizes Japanese oppression of Koreans, the Korean translation of Nakano's poem "Shinagawa Station in the Rain" embodies the many paradoxes of literary contact nebulae in empire. Not surprisingly, both the Japanese poem and its Korean translation were quickly intertextualized, including in Im Hwa's poem "Usan pat-ŭn Yok'ohama ŭi pudu" (Yokohama Pier under the Umbrella, August 1929), examined in Chapter 7.

Translating the War

Wartime intra–East Asian literary contact nebulae entailed even more ambivalent readerly, writerly, and textual contact, as Chinese, Korean, and Taiwanese writers strived to integrate exposing Japanese aggression with preserving national dignity. After total war between

Japan and China broke out in 1937, military conscription and forced labor in Korea and Taiwan, combined with stringent restrictions on publishing in the Korean and Chinese languages, curtailed translation of Western literatures and nearly obliterated that of Japanese literature. Translation of Japanese literature fared better in China. To be sure, anti-Japanese sentiment narrowed the market for these texts; Japanese writers' increasing support of their country's war effort meant that some who had been translated in previous decades became less appealing to Chinese.[49] The turmoil of combat and unfavorable material circumstances, including the destruction of printing shops and publishing houses, also made translation difficult.

But Chinese continued to translate Japanese literature into the 1940s, including a variety of texts by Kimura Ki (1894–1979), Kunikida Doppo, Masamune Hakuchō, Nakagawa Yoichi (1897–1994), Satō Haruo, Natsume Sōseki, Shimazaki Tōson, Tanizaki Jun'ichirō, Tokuda Shūsei, Ueda Hiroshi (1905–66), and Yoshikawa Eiji (1892–1962).[50] In addition, classical Japanese literature, otherwise a low priority in early twentieth-century intra-East Asian transculturation, gained a small following among Chinese during the war years. Hoping to inculcate Chinese with the Japanese "spirit," Chinese and Japanese in occupied Manchuria and China proper translated several premodern texts, including abridged versions of the *Record of Ancient Matters* (712), *Collection of Ten Thousand Leaves* (eighth c.), *Tales of Ise* (ninth–tenth c.), and Kamo no Chōmei's (1155–1216) *Hōjōki* (Notes from a Ten Foot Square Hut, 1212).[51] Japanese pacifist literature, especially the oeuvre of Kaji Wataru, a leader of the Japanese antiwar movement in China, also attracted the attention of Chinese translators. Chinese published some translations of this literature in Japanese-occupied areas, especially Shanghai.[52]

One of the most significant subsets of Japanese literature translated into Chinese during the war years was Japanese battlefront literature—creative texts by Japanese writers who were sent as correspondents to front lines in China and elsewhere in Asia.[53] In general, these transculturations are more accurately referred to as translations than adaptations, but they often make substantial changes to their sources, sometimes by rendering into Chinese or Korean just a few pages of the Japanese-language text, and sometimes by replacing controversial passages with censorship marks; occasionally these translator-censored translations themselves censored Japanese censors, not unlike the Korean translation of Nakano's "Shinagawa

Station in the Rain," by replacing censorship marks with words. Chinese translated battlefront literature by Hino Ashihei, Ishikawa Tatsuzō, Kikuchi Kan, Mushakōji Saneatsu, Shishi Bunroku (1893–1969), and Tokutomi Sohō, among others. Several texts were translated multiple times, including Hino's *Wheat and Soldiers* (1938) and Ishikawa's *Living Soldiers* (1938). Hino was a prolific writer and Japanese army corporal who participated in the attack on Xuzhou (in eastern China, between Beijing and Shanghai) in the spring of 1938; written in diary form, *Wheat and Soldiers* covers May 4 to May 22 of that year. Hino followed with *Tsuchi to heitai* (Earth and Soldiers, 1938) and *Hana to heitai* (Flowers and Soldiers, 1938). Underlining the sacrifices made by courageous Japanese soldiers fighting in China and contrasting them with their Chinese counterparts, *Wheat and Soldiers* was an instant success in wartime Japan, selling more than a million copies. But after the war, Hino was vilified for supporting Japanese militarism in his writing and was castigated as one of Japan's worst "cultural war criminals" (*bunka senpan*).[54] Despite Hino's celebrations of Japanese military advances and portrayals of the Chinese as weak and cowardly, the Chinese produced two translations of *Wheat and Soldiers* in quick succession. The first, an abridged version by Wu Zhefei, was published by the anti-Japanese press Shanghai Zazhishe in December 1938.[55] The second, a more complete translation by Xue Li, was published by the collaborationist press Manzhouguo Tongxunshe Chubanbu in March 1939. *Earth and Soldiers* came out almost immediately in Chinese translation: Hino's novel was released in November 1938, both in the Japanese journal *Bungei shunjū* (Literary Spring and Autumn) and as a volume from the publisher Kaizōsha, while Jin Gu's Chinese translation was printed in December 1938 and published in January 1939 by Beijing's Dongfang Shudian.

Unlike Hino's novels, Ishikawa's *Living Soldiers* was little more than a title to readers in wartime Japan, or in the words of Gérard Genette, a "paratext without a text."[56] Based on Ishikawa's eyewitness observations and interviews with soldiers who participated in the Nanjing Massacre of 1937 — the six-week bloodbath in which Japanese brutally murdered tens or hundreds of thousands of Chinese civilians — *Living Soldiers* depicts a platoon of patriotic soldiers who, in addition to slaughtering Chinese on the battlefield, ruthlessly murder innocent civilians, rape Chinese women, and loot Chinese homes and shops. The novella also reveals Japanese anxieties about the war and the effects of war on individuals and peoples. It originally was included in the March 1938 issue of the journal *Central Review*, which was sent to distributors on February 17 and scheduled to be sold on February 19. But, on orders from the Toshoka (Book Section of the Keihōkyoku [Police Bureau]), the night of February 18 the staff of *Central Review* fanned out to police stations across Tokyo, where seized copies of the journal had been piled, and literally ripped Ishikawa's novella from individual copies.[57] This version of *Living Soldiers* contained numerous censorship marks, having been extensively censored both by the editors of the journal and by Ishikawa himself.[58] Far from placating the authorities, these marks only made the novella appear more subversive.[59] In the preface to the first postwar Japanese edition of *Living Soldiers*, which replaces most of the censorship marks in the 1938 *Central Review* version with words, Ishikawa refers to his novella as "a work I couldn't show anyone [before 1945]."[60] And it generally is discussed as such.[61]

But in fact, thanks to extensive intra–East Asian readerly, writerly, and textual contact, *Living Soldiers* circulated in multiple Chinese translations during the war.[62] The first of these translations—an abridged version by Bai Mu titled *Weisi de bing* (Soldiers Not Yet Deceased)—began serialization exactly a month after *Living Soldiers* was banned in Japan; it appeared between March 18 and April 8, 1938 in occupied Shanghai's *Damei wanbao* (Great American Evening News), a daily paper registered under United States sponsorship.[63] Bai Mu's version came out as a separate volume in occupied Shanghai in August 1938 from the publisher Zazhishe, which because of the text's popularity put out a reprint edition in 1939; this latter version of *Soldiers Not Yet Deceased* includes thirteen illustrations by Wang Zizheng. Zhang Shifang and the revolutionary writer Xia Yan, a prolific translator of Japanese literature, also published translations of *Living Soldiers* in 1938: Zhang Shifang in June in occupied Shanghai as *Huozhe de bingdui* (Living Soldiers) and Xia Yan in July in Guangzhou as *Weisi de bing* (Soldiers Not Yet Deceased). Xia Yan's translation was particularly popular, appearing in at least four editions within the next two years.[64] Both translations replicate many of the censorship marks present in the *Central Review* version of *Living Soldiers*.

Koreans also translated Japanese battlefront literature. Their rewritings are especially impressive in light of injunctions against publishing in Korean. Particularly notable is the "Selections of Battlefront Literature" series in the Korean literary journal *Writing* (1939–41). "Selections of Battlefront Literature" included partial translations of everything from Hino Ashihei's wartime trilogy, to Hayashi Fumiko's reportage *Sensen* (Battlefront, 1938), to fiction and reportage by the prolific wartime writers Niwa Fumio (1904–2005), Takemori Kazuo (1910–79), and Ueda Hiroshi. The one conspicuous omission from the roster of "Selections of Battlefront Literature" is Ishikawa's *Living Soldiers*, which likely was blocked by Japanese censors if not by the editors of *Writing*, who in their opening issue declared themselves loyal imperial subjects. *Writing* itself often is regarded as an organ of the Japanese colonial government, although its fealty to Japanese directives could not be taken for granted. By themselves, the passages in "Selections of Battlefront Literature" invariably give skewed impressions of the texts from which they are drawn. But together, they provide a representative sample of Japanese war literature, featuring campaigns on water, on land, and in the skies, as well as quieter moments of homesickness and grief over the loss of loved ones. The translations stand on their own: Japanese authors and titles (in Korean translation) are identified but nothing is said about the translators or where the translated passages fit into the schema of their Japanese sources. "Selections of Battlefront Literature" gave wartime Korean readers a glimpse of Japanese depictions of war with China, balanced somewhat on other pages of *Writing* by Chinese perceptions and by numerous translations of American and European literature, as well as a variety of essays on literature itself.

Japanese battlefront literature attracted Chinese and Koreans of varying ideologies. Both war enthusiasts and pacifists—the former who believed this genre testified to the righteousness of Japan's imperial mission, and the latter who welcomed its exposés of the high cost of warfare—ensured that it was translated into Chinese and Korean. Many, particularly in China, were drawn to its depictions of Chinese: some, hoping these texts would be wake-up calls for Chinese reform, celebrated how Japanese battlefront literature spread negative stereotypes of Chinese, while others, hoping to boost morale, focused on its profiles of Chinese courage. But regardless of their leanings, many who embraced this literature applauded its "truthful" depictions of life during wartime. Appearing primarily in introductions, afterwords, and other paratexts, many truth claims were explicit. In the preface to his translation of *Living Soldiers*, Bai Mu does not mince words, declaring, "The novel describes the real conditions of the battlefield in vivid detail. Moreover, the author did not do evil against his conscience and was not willing to cover up the cruel truths of war or the soldiers' disgust of war. So although this text is by a Japanese writer, its immortal value lies in its objectively portraying the facts of war."[65] These remarks counter Ishikawa's own opening note, appearing between the title and Chapter 1 of *Living Soldiers*: "There are many things about the Sino-Japanese War that are still prohibited to report. Therefore, this manuscript is not a faithful record of actual fighting. It is the author's attempt at a rather free creation. I want it to be recognized that everything—including the names of units, officers, and soldiers—is fiction."[66] Not prepared to relegate this novel's "cruel truths" to the work of a fertile imagination, Bai Mu argues that this text be read as depicting the "truth," or at least *a* truth, of the second Sino-Japanese War. Zhang Shifang similarly argued that the novella "exposes the truth, and isn't this 'truth' what the Japanese imperialists are most afraid of?"[67] As the Chinese writer Lin Lin (1910–) asserted, "We praise *Living Soldiers* highly because it gives the most truthful photographic record of the invasion and atrocities of the Japanese warlords."[68]

Chinese intellectuals also emphasized the truthfulness of Hino's *Wheat and Soldiers*. In his preface, Wu Zhefei admitted that the novel's exposé of Japanese brutality was not as illuminating as what was available in Ishikawa's *Living Soldiers*. Even so, he stated that he translated *Wheat and Soldiers* because it "objectively, albeit inadvertently, records the truth" and that, "as a living record, the diary of a march, it certainly will contribute a lot to our understanding of resistance."[69] His publishers also claimed that *Wheat and Soldiers* revealed the courage of the Chinese army and emphasized the novel's exposure of the truth. Inside the front cover, they announced: "Although the Japanese author does his utmost to exaggerate the supposed 'courage' of the 'imperial army,' *Wheat and Soldiers* in fact exposes the truth of the Japanese army, how they treat prisoners and ravage the people; on the other hand, it shows even more clearly the courage of the Chinese army. In this book we can see much of the 'truth of the enemy population.'"[70] In contrast, other translators found truth in this novel's depictions of the hardships faced by the Japanese army. In "*Mugi to heitai* o Chōsengo ni yakushite" (Translating *Wheat and Solders* into Korean, 1939), Nishimura Shintarō—one of the few Japanese to translate Japanese literature into other Asian languages during the colonial period—lamented that no writings adequately outlined Japanese sacrifices. He expressed hope that his translation would inspire gratitude toward the army and strengthen the readiness of Koreans on the homefront.[71] Nishimura's remarks are almost expected, considering that he translated Hino Ashihei's novel at the directive of the Japanese governor-general in Korea.[72] These conflicting comments show the diverse motivations for wartime translations of Japanese battlefront literature. But they also point to real anxiety over the implications of disseminating Japanese cultural products in China and Korea. Japanese literature appears to have been irresistible, but justifying its consumption—much less transculturation—was hardly straightforward. Even more significant, translations of this literature often significantly rewrote their Japanese source texts. Some openly omitted material; others, like those in the "Selections of Battlefront Literature," translated only several pages of their Japanese sources. The Japanese "truths" of the battlefield were not disseminated whole and indeed were transculturated extensively for colonial and semicolonial consumption.

Whether undertaken by Chinese, Koreans, or Japanese, some wartime translations were questionable in quality. Critics like Liu Yusheng, a Chinese cultural official and an associate of a collaborationist journal in Shanghai, complained: "Politically speaking, our relationship with Japan is unprecedentedly good today, yet our effort to introduce Japanese literature is appalling. . . . [Both in quantity and quality] our Japanese translations are much worse than in the late Qing period, not to mention the 1930s."[73] But the mere presence of these texts, not to mention their manipulation of Japanese sources, had important implications for (semi)colonial and post(semi)colonial East Asian negotiation with Japanese imperial as well as cultural authority. The reason is not far to find: if the first Sino-Japanese War (1894–95) sank a dagger in the heart of the Qing dynasty, the second Sino-Japanese War (1937–45) threatened China's future as an independent state with the specter of permanent subordination within Japan's ambitious New Order in East Asia, announced in November 1938, and its even more grandiose Greater East Asia Co-prosperity Sphere (Dai Tōa Kyōeiken), proclaimed in September 1940. There would be precious little room for the Chinese people, not to mention Koreans and Taiwanese, as autonomous subjects in such a regime of political and cultural domination emanating from Tokyo.

Censoring Violence, Educing the Ordinary

Much Japanese battlefront literature depicts the brutality of war while also making a case for the humanness and even humanity of Japanese soldiers. In general, this genre also professes to support Japan's war effort. These factors make it a particularly convoluted site of textual transculturation. Translators of Japanese battlefront literature, many of whom explicitly excluded material from their sources by translating only selected passages and/or including strings of periods or other censorship marks, were faced with the difficult dilemma of how best to rewrite Japanese depictions of Japanese military campaigns into the Chinese and Korean languages. They walked even finer lines than the previous generation of translators and adapters, such as Liang Qichao, Lin Shu and Wei Yi, Gu Yŏnhak, Cho Iljae, Kim Ujin, and Sŏn-u Il, in negotiating portrayals of Japanese power. What several decades ago was only feared had now become real: China was being invaded, its cities falling one by one, and Koreans and Taiwanese were being conscripted, sent to battle or factory labor for a land that was not their own.

Those rewriting Japanese battlefront literature into Chinese and Korean thus had several options. They could strive to follow their Japanese sources to the letter, depicting Japanese military might. So doing would give Chinese and Korean readers a better idea of Japanese perceptions and justifications of the war; it also would explain if not excuse Chinese losses and Korean and Taiwanese capitulation. But faithful translations also would point to Chinese and Korean weakness. Translators could play up Japanese aggression, adding to translations passages on Chinese suffering not present in their sources. Such a tactic would rectify some of the lacunae inherent in Japanese battlefront literature, but it also would call even greater attention to disparities in strength, as well as implying that Japanese literature was more vocal about Japanese atrocities than it actually was. Finally, translators could tone down their Japanese sources. So doing would point to Chinese strength, but it also would put the Japanese military in a more favorable light and gloss over the impact on Chinese of the Japanese invasion. Engaging with battlefront literature was thus fraught with choices, all of them likely to distort Japanese texts. Altering sources is an inevitable part of textual contact, but its implications are especially great when the source text depicts the deaths of one's compatriots and the destruction of one's homeland (in the case of Chinese) or highlights the military victories of the imperial power, fighting in which the colony has no choice but to play a part (in the case of Koreans and Taiwanese).

Interestingly, a number of Chinese and Korean translations of Japanese battlefront literature—including those of Hino Ashihei's *Wheat and Soldiers, Earth and Soldiers,* and *Flowers and Soldiers,* Ishikawa Tatsuzō's *Living Soldiers,* and Hayashi Fumiko's *Battlefront*—tone down their Japanese sources. On the whole, these texts give the impression of Japanese soldiers as more human, if not more humane, than do their Japanese sources. Often abridging and in fact censoring Japanese battlefront literature, they ignore or abbreviate sections that expose Japanese violence; some even focus on passages that highlight the humanness and humanity of Japanese soldiers. They thereby obscure Chinese weakness and suffering. On the other hand, these translations also tend to tone down if not omit paeans to imperial Japan, which makes them unlikely candidates for imperial propaganda. Just as the Korean translation of Nakano's poem "Shinagawa Station in the Rain," by calling for an attack on the Japanese emperor even while reinforcing ethnic stereotypes, embodies the many paradoxes of literary contact nebulae in empire, translations of Japanese battlefront literature reveal textual transculturation as a balancing act. They blur dichotomies of complicity and resistance and in so doing raise questions about the highly nuanced process of transculturation in wartime.

Converting Hurrahs to Silence: A More Ordinary Nation

Colonial and semicolonial translations of Japanese battlefront literature often delete Japanese depictions of Chinese allegiance to Japan. This is true of Wu Zhefei's Chinese translation of Hino Ashihei's *Wheat and Soldiers,* which does not reproduce the Japanese novel's portraits of Chinese celebrating the defeat of the Nationalists, assisting Japanese troops, and eagerly welcoming Japanese into their communities. The translation removes Hino's references to the "fetters of heavy taxation" imposed by the Nationalist regime, which the defeated Chinese, according to the Japanese novel, are all too happy to cast aside.[74] The Japanese narrator's musings that Chinese farmers could care less who controls China, just so long as their farming continues unimpeded, also are deleted.[75] Gone as well are the references to Chinese showering Japanese troops with Japanese flags and thanking them, of all things, for bringing peace to East Asia. The Japanese narrator writes, "Today [May 21] seemed like a Japanese national holiday. There were Japanese flags everywhere. . . . Some places had red paper stuck on them on which people had written 'Welcome

Great Japan,' 'Welcome Great Japan, Victorious Friends of China.' "[76] Japanese flags flutter furiously in this section of the Japanese *Wheat and Soldiers* but are absent in the Chinese translation.[77] On the other hand, although the translator removes Hino's portrait of Chinese enthusiasm for Japan, he does not replace it with tropes of resistance. Instead, Wu Zhefei swaps words with censorship marks, alerting readers of material that has quite literally been lost in translation.

But Wu Zhefei's Chinese translation of *Wheat and Soldiers* does more than remove Hino's depictions of Chinese eagerly welcoming Japanese troops. It also drops many of the novel's references to Japanese patriotism, including the narrator's remark that "when the day comes that I am killed by a bullet and my bones are buried in Chinese soil, more than anything I want to die thinking of my beloved homeland, crying 'Long live Japan' until I can breathe no more. Standing on that hill of pomegranates, I felt like just a bubble in majestic pounding waves."[78] The Chinese version even strips Japanese *wakō* (private traders and sometime pirates) of their glory, omitting the narrator's references to Japanese who centuries ago sailed up Chinese rivers and terrified the Chinese.[79] At the same time, the translation does not substitute Japanese pride with humility, instead supplanting words with censorship marks. Erasing but not replacing rhetoric of inherent Japanese superiority, it depicts Japan as a more ordinary nation than Hino's Japanese-language text while remaining silent about Chinese responses to invaders both historical and contemporary.

Food, Family, Friendship, Feeling: More Ordinary People

Chinese and Korean transpositions of battlefront literature frequently muted Japanese patriotic discourse. Likewise, rather than focusing on passages that discuss Japanese victories and the destruction of Chinese lives and property, many reproduced passages that point to the humanness and humaneness of Japanese soldiers. Portraying Japanese soldiers neither as monsters nor as larger than life figures, these passages highlight young men longing for food and family, their tenderness toward one another, and ultimately their empathy for Chinese civilians. In so doing, they paint a different portrait of wartime than their Japanese predecessors, a major consequence of which is to turn the spotlight away from Chinese suffering and frailty. So doing can preempt shame and low morale, but it also can minimize very real tragedies. This tendency is particularly striking in recastings, like those in the journal *Writing,* that reproduce only a fragment of their source texts.

A case in point is the Korean translation of Hino Ashihei's *Flowers and Soldiers.* In this novel, the third in Hino's trilogy, the narrator describes his experiences while guarding Hangzhou, the Southern Song capital south of Shanghai; *Flowers and Soldiers* also talks about the madness of war, Chinese nationalism (or the lack thereof), and the complexities of cross-cultural understanding.[80] Significantly, the passage from *Flowers and Soldiers* translated in the Korean journal *Writing* under the heading "Chŏnjang ŭi chŏngwŏl" (New Year's on the Battlefield) depicts Japanese soldiers as anxious not about their next military move but about how they will mark the New Year so far from home. *Flowers and Soldiers* and "New Year's on the Battlefield" both begin, "The seed of our headaches was wondering how we soldiers would celebrate the approaching New Year on this battlefield. We weren't worried about how we would fight off the attacking devils who got in the way of our festivities. What was troubling us on the dark battlefield desolated by the fires of war were doubts that we would really be able to eat [traditional New Year's treats] on New Year's."[81] The texts then veer from the availability of food to the movement of troops, with the narrators describing the Japanese arrival in snowy Hangzhou, but attention soon returns to the soldiers pondering how they will ring in the New Year. The Korean "New Year's on the Battlefield" wraps up with the soldiers realizing that because there has been no sign even of letters from home, they have virtually no chance of receiving packages of the desired treats.[82] By focusing on Japanese soldiers' strong ties to home — pointedly not to Japan as the imperial power but to their families, with whom they ordinarily would be enjoying New Year's delicacies — then ending immediately before the Japanese narrator details troop movements, the Korean translation of *Flowers and Soldiers* evokes sympathy for men away from home during the holidays.

Other intra-empire translations of Japanese battlefront literature, including the Chinese and Korean translations of Hino's *Wheat and Soldiers,* draw even more attention to strong familial bonds persisting in wartime. Wu Zhefei's Chinese translation of *Wheat and Soldiers* faithfully reproduces the Japanese version's depictions of Japanese troops longing for their families and of those at home waiting impatiently for their return.[83] But the Korean version of this novel is particularly striking. In 1941, the journal *Writing* included a partial translation of three diary entries from *Wheat and Soldiers*, which, the editors alerted their readers, were based on Nishimura Shintarō's 1939 Korean-language translation of the novel. In one of these entries, the narrator describes how while talking with colleagues he suddenly saw in one of them the face of his father. When asked why he was staring so intently, he pulled out some pictures of his family. The narrator then gushed to his companions that his father and mother "are the best in all of Japan," that his wife "is the most beautiful in the world," and that his children "are geniuses and prodigies."[84] Here the warrior is simply a proud son, husband, and father, a very human figure.

Translators did not stop with strong intrafamilial bonds; they also chose selections of Japanese battlefront literature that highlight friendships among Japanese soldiers and speak even of their compassion toward the Chinese. For instance, several issues of *Writing* contain excerpts from Hayashi Fumiko's reportage *Battlefront* (1938), an epistolary account of her time at the front. Hayashi worked for the *Asahi shinbun* and was one of the first Japanese women in Hankou (central China, southwest of Shanghai) after its fall to the Japanese in November 1938. The May 1939 issue of *Writing* includes a translation of part of the third letter of her text: "There are people who are afraid that when the war is over, all the ethics of the battlefield will return to Japan in a giant flood. But I cannot forget the simple friendships of soldiers that I witnessed on the battlefield."[85] She recounts a story a doctor told her about the grief with which soldiers faced the death of one of their own and declares that these are the morals that the troops will bring back to Japan. The Japanese-language version of *Battlefront* contains references to Japanese brutality. At one point the Japanese narrator writes, "The front has painful, barbaric aspects, but it also overflows with the truly magnificent, things that are so beautiful they're suffocating."[86] But beauty is relative. The narrator relates that she heard two Japanese soldiers discussing how best to kill a Chinese prisoner: one wanted to burn him at the stake, while the other—thinking of a Japanese prisoner who was killed this way—declares this too cruel and opts for a more expedient method. Observing the Japanese soldiers subsequently kill the prisoner "with a single, truly magnificent stroke of the sword," the narrator comments that he "died without a bit of agony . . . I don't think this method is the least bit brutal."[87] Brutality is as relative as beauty, and contrary to the narrator's claims this passage could be used as evidence of Japanese heartlessness in the guise of compassion—in other words, as a sign of just how far Japanese will go to justify killing. But the Korean translator avoids this murky ground and instead focuses on the kindness of Japanese soldiers toward one another.

If Chinese and Korean translations of Japanese battlefront literature are to be trusted, this empathy can be boundless, easily crossing political boundaries. Japanese sympathy for Chinese soldiers and civilians shines through in colonial and semicolonial translations of Japanese battlefront literature, particularly the Korean translations of *Wheat and Soldiers* and *Earth and Soldiers* included in the journal *Writing*. *Earth and Soldiers*, the second volume of Hino's best-selling trilogy but describing events that occurred before those in *Wheat and Soldiers*, takes the form of a collection of letters he wrote his younger brother Masao while fighting in China in the fall of 1937. The novel focuses on battles in China and how war transforms the psyche. But this would be difficult to discern simply from reading the passages translated in *Writing*.

Launching the "Selections of Battlefront Literature" series is the translation of the passage in Hino's *Earth and Soldiers* where the narrator and his men discover that Chinese troops have attacked Chinese civilians; those who survived the onslaught now are moaning painfully by the road, their children screaming inconsolably. The Japanese narrator twice leaves the trenches, risking his life to comfort a dying Chinese woman and her infant; he wraps the naked baby in one blanket and covers the mother with another, but the child continues to cry, making it impossible for anyone to sleep.[88] This passage, translated faithfully from the Japanese, establishes an ironic contrast between Chinese and Japanese soldiers: Chinese soldiers murder Chinese civilians, whereas Japanese soldiers are deeply moved by their plight and risk their lives to give them dignity in death. In Hino's novel, the depiction of Japanese kindness toward Chinese attacked by Chinese is balanced by references to Japanese murder of Chinese and Chinese murder of Japanese; in *Writing*, on the other hand, this scene stands apart, setting a compassionate tone for the journal's "Selections of Battlefront Literature."

What led to the choice of such episodes? Hino's wartime trilogy was hugely popular in Japan and embraced by Japanese authorities, so it is unlikely the anonymous translator(s) were concerned with censorship. If the goal was to propagandize for Japan, passages highlighting Japanese military glory and depicting Chinese as welcoming Japanese soldiers would have been more obvious choices. And if the translator(s) were critical of Japanese imperialism, Hino's novels include a number of episodes that likely would have been more appealing. Intentions are difficult to determine and ultimately tell us little about actual textual dynamics. But regardless of the motives of the translator(s), one thing the translations do accomplish is to make the Japanese appear less formidable.

In fact, Korean translators were at times quite obvious in this regard, choosing passages that depict Japanese soldiers as naïve and ineffective. The second installment of "Selections of Battlefront Literature" includes "Chŏkjŏn sangryuk" (Landing in the Face of the Enemy), a translation of Hino's description in *Earth and Soldiers* of Japanese troops stumbling onto Chinese soil.[89] Far from composed and primed for action, the troops—who have been traveling for weeks—slog blindly ashore; despite having gone through numerous drills, they are woefully ill-prepared for the realities of the battlefield: "The water was muddy. We couldn't see land anywhere. And the bullets didn't come. Someone behind me said that the enemy must not be around."[90] Ordered to jump off the boat, the troops find themselves in frigid water rising above their knees, their feet sinking deep into the mud. The narrator continues, "We had no idea where the shore was, and no idea where the enemy was. Conditions were completely different from what we'd been told on the boat and from what we'd imagined."[91] The Japanese troops hear bullets, but "none came our way, so for a moment we thought they weren't firing at us."[92] They are startled when seconds later embankments, trees, and steel towers suddenly appear in front of them, and bullets begin whizzing by. To be sure, this initial attack does not deter the Japanese, who almost immediately begin carving out a path of destruction. The Korean translation winds down with the narrator's remark that the Japanese set fire to every house in sight, correctly believing them repositories of Chinese troops and ammunition. But the final line of "Landing in the Face of the Enemy"—"it started to rain"—opens the possibility that these fires might be short-lived.[93] In the Japanese-language *Earth and Soldiers*, on the other hand, houses continue to burn, and the body count rises: "Here and there straw houses were ablaze, sending up fiery dark-red smoke. And in front of the burning houses were fallen Chinese soldiers."[94] Even more important, Japanese troops continue their advance. The translations of Hino's novels in *Writing* do not replace rhetoric on Japanese military might with that on Chinese, much less Korean strength, but by exposing Japanese compassion and incompetence, they nevertheless leave room for Chinese victory and Korean independence. After all, these texts suggest, Japanese soldiers are only human.

Playing Down Losses and Atrocities: More Ordinary Warfare

Chinese and Korean translations of Japanese battlefront literature, particularly Chinese translations of *Wheat and Soldiers* and *Living Soldiers*, reproduce relatively faithfully many of the segments from their source texts on the brutality of warfare. This includes everything from hints of executions, such as when Japanese soldiers in *Wheat and Soldiers* lead a Chinese prisoner across the field until "his figure vanished,"[95] to scenes featuring piles of corpses, both human and animal, as in *Living Soldiers*. At times, these translations replace the censorship marks in their Japanese sources with words that give a greater sense of the traumas of wartime. But the changes tend to be minor. For instance, the narrator of Ishikawa's *Living Soldiers* observes that "soldiers who went looking for • • • • • • were many but those who came home having come across any women were few. . . . That morning as well, small groups of three or four men with cigarettes in their mouths went off looking for • • • • • •." Xia Yan's translation reproduces these censorship marks and in fact removes Ishikawa's reference to "women" (which in the Japanese version actually undermines the Japanese writer's own censorship marks). But Bai Mu's translation swaps "• • • • • •" for "girls" (*guniang*).[96] Several pages later in their texts, Ishikawa, Bai Mu, and Xia Yan describe the abuse and murder of a Chinese woman the soldiers discover in a farmhouse, and not surprisingly their accounts all contain censorship marks. Yet here Bai Mu again replaces some of Ishikawa's censorship marks with words: "First Class Private Kondō looked down at her for awhile, and as he did so • • • • • • • • • again bubbled up," becomes "First Class Private Kondō looked down at her for awhile, and as he did so sexual desires again gushed up."[97]

But in general, intra-empire translations of Japanese battlefront literature delete more than they add, at times marking their changes with censorship marks, at others silently omitting text. Occasionally, these changes muffle suggestions of imminent violence. For instance, Ishikawa writes, "Before long, 'forage' became their pretext for going out. It next was used as a codeword. • • • • • • • • • • was used to mean looking for girls. The soldiers wanted to find young women." Zhang Shifang changes this to, "Before long • X X became their X X for going out. It then even was used as a codeword. The phrase X X X X X in particular meant to go looking for girls. It had been a long time since they'd seen young women."[98] Occasionally, changes are made that point to an attempt to save national face: Xia Yan's translation of *Living Soldiers* replaces the name of China's leader Chiang Kai-shek (1887–1975) and most of the name of his wife Soong Meiling (1897–2003) with censorship marks when translating the Japanese text's reference to Japanese troops occupying the couple's home.[99] But more frequently, deletions play down Chinese losses and Japanese atrocities, particularly actual Japanese abuse of Chinese women. In so doing, they depict China as less of a victim of Japanese attack than do their Japanese sources.[100]

For instance, the narrator of Hino's *Wheat and Soldiers* states that a Japanese battalion crushed the 3,000 Chinese they encountered near Zhaojiaji (in Hebei province, near Beijing); the survivors fled, leaving behind 500 corpses. Wu Zhefei's Chinese version mentions that there were 3,000 Chinese near Zhaojiaji but deletes the part about corpses lying in the fields.[101] Likewise, the Japanese narrator talks about how coming across a grape patch in the moonlight reminds him of childhood days gathering grapes. The Chinese translation breaks off here, omitting the subsequent reference in its Japanese source to the discovery of three putrid Chinese bodies.[102] The Chinese translation of *Wheat and Soldiers* even deletes Hino's references to Japanese thirst for Chinese blood: "I wanted to charge with my men. I was consumed with violent hatred toward the Chinese soldiers who so tormented my compatriots and threatened my life. I wanted to charge with my men, and with my hands attack the enemy soldiers, and kill them."[103] Likewise, Wu Zhefei's translation of the May 20 diary entry includes the Japanese narrator's finding trenches of corpses but downplays his desire to kill, omitting his remark that "On the field, how many times had I wanted to attack the Chinese soldiers with my own hands and kill them."[104] Furthermore, while Hino's novel refers to "Chinese corpses," the Chinese version speaks only of "corpses."

Translations of Ishikawa's *Living Soldiers*, as reconfigurations of a banned creative work, flout imperial authority by reviving censored words, especially words that expose Japanese aggression and atrocities in China. On the other hand, leaving crucial censored words unresuscitated, that is to say, further sanitizing Ishikawa's already diluted discourse on Japan's war with China, they also are in some ways complicit with the literary silence surrounding Japanese aggression. Sometimes, the changes are subtle. For instance, Ishikawa's text and Zhang Shifang's Chinese translation both include a passage in Chapter 7 that points to Corporal Kasahara's murder of Chinese prisoners at a brook on the outskirts of the airport. Both passages make liberal use of censorship marks, but whereas Ishikawa notes that "Kasahara, without wasting any time • • • • • • • • • • • • did away with the second and the third," Zhang Shifang writes, "Kasahara, without wasting time • the second, the third X X X."[105]

Bai Mu's *Soldiers Not Yet Deceased* distorts *Living Soldiers* more dramatically, converting Ishikawa's broad panoramas into a series of representative snapshots of wartime; although composed of thirteen chapters to Ishikawa's twelve and Xia Yan's ten, Bai Mu's text in fact is a collection of translations of brief passages from Ishikawa's novel. Many of these passages zero in on Japanese brutality, while others depict Japanese anxieties toward war and increased consciousness of life's fragility, in addition to Chinese responses to war. Furthermore, the volume *Soldiers Not Yet Deceased* precedes each passage with a line drawing by Wang Zizheng that embellishes Japanese written accounts of slaughter on and off the battlefield, accounts that generally mix description with censorship marks. Seven of the thirteen drawings depict Japanese having just murdered, murdering, or about to murder Chinese; three of these seven involve the abuse and murder of Chinese women, one of the subjects most prone to censorship among Chinese and Japanese alike.

The textual transformation of *Living Soldiers* is evident from the opening scene of Bai Mu's version. Whereas the first chapter of Ishikawa's novel discusses Japanese war dead, segues into the capture and murder of a Chinese man, and moves quickly to the endless travels of the Japanese army, the first chapter of Bai Mu's translation focuses entirely on the capture and murder of the Chinese man. It opens with a line drawing of a Japanese soldier, sword drawn, standing over a river containing the dead bodies of a man and a horse; the chapter concludes with the man falling into the river next to the horse, "just his muddy feet stretched to the sky."[106] In between, it describes how Japanese soldiers ruthlessly execute this man for burning his house, which has been commandeered by the invading army. Similarly, the fourth chapter of Bai Mu's *Soldiers Not Yet Deceased*, which translates the beginning of the third chapter of the Japanese version, opens with a line drawing of three Japanese soldiers staring at a woman's naked corpse; one of them is holding a knife in one hand and a gun in the other. The narrative then depicts Japanese soldiers on the prowl for Chinese women and their discovery and murder of a woman in a farmhouse: finding on her a gun and a piece of paper with unintelligible writing, the Japanese soldiers instantly assume she is a spy and stab her to death. Their corporal's response: "Aw, what a shame, what a shame."[107]

Yet whittling down discussion of war to a series of brutal but brief encounters comes at a high price. Unlike Xia Yan, who followed Ishikawa's discussion of the December 1937 attack on Nanjing and its environs relatively closely, Bai Mu leapfrogged almost entirely over these passages.[108] Chapter 10 of Bai Mu's *Soldiers Not Yet Deceased*, drawing from an early section of Chapter 7 of Ishikawa's *Living Soldiers*, describes the conditions of wounded Japanese soldiers in a makeshift hospital in Changzhou, near Nanjing; Chapter 11 of *Soldiers Not Yet Deceased*, drawing from Chapter 9 of *Living Soldiers*, finds Japanese soldiers looking for prostitutes in a defeated Nanjing. Chapter 11 of *Soldiers Not Yet Deceased* is titled "Nanjing," and its opening page in the August 1938 volume features a line drawing of burning buildings, but the narrative gives only a fleeting glimpse of the ruined city. Chapters 7 through 9 of *Living Soldiers* describe the havoc wreaked by Japanese troops as they marched to Nanjing and their destruction of the former Chinese capital, as well as atrocities committed against Chinese; these chapters are punctuated by censorship marks, but such marks ultimately reveal more than they hide, alerting the reader that controversial and very likely key passages have been deleted. In contrast, *Soldiers Not Yet Deceased* devotes only a few lines to the fires that continue to burn and to the corpses, both human and animal, that litter the streets of the city. Its omissions are particularly notable considering the ease with which Bai Mu translates other passages from Ishikawa's novel on the brutality of war.

To be sure, Bai Mu's self-censorship within the serialized *Soldiers Not Yet Deceased* is mediated by surrounding narrative. In remarks preceding the first installment, Bai Mu claims, "I selected some relatively interesting passages from *Living Soldiers* and translated them for your enjoyment."[109] He reveals instantly that his is an abridged translation. The phrase "relatively interesting," indicating that the reader is not to expect too much, betrays false humility, but it also suggests that the translator has omitted both the more lackluster and the potentially more interesting or even controversial passages. Several weeks later, the editors of the *Great American Evening News* complicated matters, encouraging their readers to compare Bai Mu's narrative on Nanjing with other reports. They published the first part of the article "Rijun zhanju hou zhi Nanjing" (Nanjing after the Occupation of the Japanese Army) two days before Bai Mu's chapter "Nanjing" (April 3, 1938). This article juxtaposes claims originally appearing in the *Xin shen bao* (a Shanghai-based Japanese-sponsored newspaper) that Japanese in Nanjing are treating Chinese benevolently, with reports that Chinese in Nanjing cannot begin to describe the horrors that descended on their city and dispatches from the *New York Times* on Japanese atrocities in Nanjing. Here "Nanjing after the Occupation of the Japanese Army" illuminates the multiplicity of narratives on Nanjing, cleverly undermining Japanese interpretations, both journalistic and novelistic. The second part of "Nanjing after the Occupation of the Japanese Army," which appeared on the same day as Bai Mu's chapter "Nanjing" (April 5, 1938), exposes additional Japanese atrocities in Nanjing. The editors of the *Great American Evening News* call attention to this article, referring readers of Bai Mu's "Nanjing" to "Nanjing after the Occupation of the Japanese Army," but not vice versa, thereby marginalizing the fictional account. In addition, Bai Mu reveals in the "Translator's Note" appended to the final installment of *Soldiers Not Yet Deceased* (April 18, 1938) that he omitted some sections of *Living Soldiers* concerning Japanese atrocities and that many of his friends have told him that his narrative gives a very distorted picture of what they personally witnessed in China. Here Bai Mu adopts a different attitude than in his preface, where he focused on inclusions, not exclusions.

Bai Mu's volume *Soldiers Not Yet Deceased,* published in book form four months after he finished serializing the translation, is even more ambiguous. In its preface, Bai Mu reveals that his is an abridged translation originally published in the *Great American Evening News*. He notes that, for the book, he had wanted to translate more of *Living Soldiers* than had been possible in the newspaper, but "some parts of the original had too many deletions."[110] It is probable that by "original" Bai Mu means the version ripped out of the March 1938 issue of *Central Review*, since this version did contain numerous censorship marks. In any case, we know that Chinese had access to this text: a month before the release of his book version of *Soldiers Not Yet Deceased*, Xia Yan published a translation with the same title that follows closely the version of Ishikawa's *Living Soldiers* appearing in the *Central Review*. The existence of Xia Yan's translation suggests that Bai Mu excluded material because it was controversial, not because it was unavailable. It also is possible that he was challenging Xia Yan's translation by reprinting his own "original," albeit this time one supplemented by graphic drawings.

Intriguing in this context are Bai Mu's claims, noted above, that *Living Soldiers* reveals the "truth" of war. Ironically, by translating only part of Ishikawa's novel, and by omitting most of the Japanese writer's discussion of Nanjing in particular, Bai Mu's *Soldiers Not Yet Deceased* covers up some of the "cruel truths" the Chinese translator applauds his Japanese predecessor for revealing. On the other hand, these cover-ups are themselves offset to greater or lesser extent by surrounding narratives. But just as the Korean writer Im Hwa challenged both Nakano's poem "Shinagawa Station in the Rain" and its Korean translation in his own poetry, Ishikawa's "facts" and "cruel truths," as well as their Chinese translations, were further disputed in the Chinese writer Ah Long's novel *Nanjing* (1939), examined in Chapter 6. Bai Mu's skimming over Nanjing reinforces his emphasis on total war with Japan as a chain of lethal events that take place over wide areas and involve diverse segments of the Chinese populace. But it also highlights the lengths to which some translators of battlefront literature went to modulate Japanese atrocities and Chinese losses.

Reporting losses is the more candid approach—and translators claimed the "truth" of their Japanese sources justified increasing their availability—but it also can be demoralizing and cause people to question the legitimacy of their leaders. Although the Nanjing Massacre is now a cause célèbre and has a small but important presence in contemporary Chinese literature and film,[111] for various reasons related to the stability of their own regimes, both the Nationalist Party and the Chinese Communist Party silenced creative writings about it until the 1980s: Ah Long's *Nanjing*, China's first creative work confronting the massacre, was not published until 1987, and then only after it had been considerably abridged and renamed *Nanjing xueji* (Nanjing Blood Sacrifice).[112]

Unlike survivors of the Holocaust, their families, and other concerned parties, who have published reams on the Nazis' slaughter of Jews and other so-called undesirables, Chinese creative writers were blocked from discussing Nanjing for nearly half a century. In the decades leading up to total war, some Chinese had used victimization and suffering as terms "enabling the articulation of a persistent identity."[113] But wartime suffering at the hands of the Japanese was a different story and called for new modalities of cultural identity.

Colonial and semicolonial writers, not indifferent to Japanese literature nor viewing it primarily as a conduit for European writings, as often has been argued, instead engaged vigorously with the creative output of the imperial hegemon. The trickle of early adaptations, the stream of translations, and the growing number of critical studies flowing through East Asia during the first half of the twentieth century indicate deep Chinese, Korean, and Taiwanese involvement with Japanese literature. Interweaving Japanese texts into their own literary terrain, colonial and semicolonial East Asian intellectuals at once gave these cultural products legitimacy and altered them significantly. Neither official cultural policy nor simple subaltern submission to the doctrines of Japanese modernity played a significant role in the rapid outpouring of Chinese, Korean, and Taiwanese interpretive and interlingual transculturations of Japanese literature between 1900 and 1945. Just as Japan was the principal site of intra–East Asian literary exchange during the colonial period, so too was Japanese literature its most fertile source. The large numbers of early twentieth-century critical studies, adaptations, and translations show that Japanese literature enjoyed broad circulation in the Chinese, Korean, and Taiwanese literary spheres, reversing centuries of apathy toward Japanese culture. They remind us that despite the darkening thundercloud of Japanese imperialism in East Asia and the outbreak of total war with China, and irrespective of colonial and semicolonial fascination with the West and its cultural products, Chinese, Koreans, and Taiwanese actively transculturated Japanese literature.

We are only beginning to understand the ramifications of intra-empire interpretive and interlingual transculturation. How significant are selections of texts and passages from texts? How significant are changes from and consistencies with sources? Which choices, changes, and consistencies, if any, result primarily from differences in language and culture, and which from more intricate negotiations? What do choices, changes, and consistencies reveal about literature, politics, and literary politics? And finally, what do they reveal about processes of transspatializing texts and transtextualizing spaces?

These complex questions point at many of the issues central to transculturation in artistic contact nebulae, literary and otherwise, and they invite further investigation in modern empires globally.

The critical studies, adaptations, and translations of Japanese literature that Chinese, Koreans, and Taiwanese produced in the early twentieth century form a major chapter in the history of East Asian cultural exchange. Forever blurring the simple dichotomy of complicity and resistance, they plot an index of the ups and downs, the tensions, and the ambivalences facing East Asians from many schools of thought as they negotiated with the cultural products of the nation that was at once a cultural beacon, an imperial power, and—in the case of China—a wartime enemy. Interpretively and interlingually integrating Japanese texts into their own literary landscapes, Chinese, Korean, and Taiwanese intellectuals refused to grant Japanese discourse the final word. But these transculturations tell only part of the story of intra–East Asian literary contact during the colonial and semicolonial period. Interpretive and interlingual transculturations were paralleled and intersected by intertextual transculturations, which provided a usually more tacit but equally powerful means of challenging and affirming the cultural capital and authority of imperial Japan, as well as of constructing and deconstructing identities. These dynamics are the subjects of Part II.

PART II

Intertextual Transculturation

The rapid movement of peoples, ideas, and texts throughout the Japanese empire created numerous literary contact nebulae, active sites of linguistic, readerly, writerly, and textual contact where intellectuals of different backgrounds forged relationships, consumed one another's literatures, read and published in multiple languages, and interpretively and interlingually transculturated one another's creative texts. The hybridity and multivalent discourse of the early twentieth-century East Asian cultural realm also yielded substantial numbers of intra-empire intertextual transculturations; Chinese, Japanese, Korean, and Taiwanese writers interlaced into their creative work manipulated fragments from and transposed allusions to literature from throughout the Japanese imperium. Many of the creative works that were interpretively and interlingually transculturated were also intertextualized, at times by the same literary figure, but intertextualization involved an even more substantial, albeit amorphous mass of East Asian drama, poetry, and prose.

Early twentieth-century intertextualization of classical East Asian literary predecessors is unmistakable, as is intracultural intertextualization of contemporary writings. Just as prominent and often appearing with the above are early twentieth-century East Asian intertextual reconfigurations of Western literatures, which have been the primary focus of comparative scholarship on modern East Asian literatures. Yet the intertextualization of contemporary creative works from other parts of the Japanese empire also is prevalent in early twentieth-century Chinese, Japanese, Korean, and Taiwanese literatures. Although at times explicit about their ties with predecessors, intertextual transculturations generally obscure their backgrounds more than do critical studies, adaptations, and translations. Modern intertextualizations also tend to be more elusive than their premodern counterparts, earlier literatures commonly making little secret of sources and editors and commentators taking up where creative writers leave off. But however concealed, intertextualizing is a key part of transculturating in empire and more generally of cultural negotiation in spaces with significant power asymmetries.

During the colonial period, East Asian transcultural intertextuality was generally translingual but also occurred frequently in Japanese-language literature written by Chinese, Koreans, and Taiwanese. Some intertextual transculturation was passive, a product of convention, shared predecessors or circumstances, or coincidence, but much was dynamic, the result of active, if cloaked, engagement with literary antecedents. In general, dynamic intertextuality appropriates, expresses solidarity with, and confronts source texts, enabling literary works both to rectify and to invite comparisons (often contrasts) with predecessors. Early twentieth-century intra–East Asian textual transculturation took place in a highly charged political milieu where cultural production almost inevitably involved some negotiated combination of collaboration with and criticism of the colonial/semicolonial enterprise. The incorporation of uncounted contemporary East Asian intertexts into literary works brims with meaning on many fronts and gives numerous insights into the region's cultural networks. East Asian intertextual transculturation of literary works from the Japanese empire involves a broad range of authors, genres, and themes and occupies a central place in the cultural struggles that took place among early twentieth-century East Asian intellectuals.

Intertextualization took place along all vectors, but as with interpretive and interlingual transculturation, Japanese literature was the most common target; Chinese, Korean, and Taiwanese writers transculturally intertextualized more Japanese literature than any other East Asian textual body at this time. Japan's ambiguous position in the first half of the twentieth century as gateway to coveted Western science and literature and as colonizing hegemon makes the interweaving of its texts into the creative work of semicolonized Chinese, occupied Manchurian, and formally colonized Korean and Taiwanese writers especially worth studying. Japan as an economic exploiter and military aggressor abroad was a very different kind of site and source by the mid-1930s from the neophyte imperialist it had been in the late nineteenth century, when the first Korean and Chinese students went to Tokyo. This difference is partially reflected in colonial and semicolonial intertextual transculturations of Japanese literature, which—like critical studies, adaptations, and translations—first were produced in the early 1900s with the influx of hundreds of thousands of East Asian students to Japan, and peaked in the late 1920s and early 1930s as the Chinese, Japanese, Korean, and Taiwanese literary worlds became more deeply entwined. But unlike adaptations and translations, intertextual transculturations of Japanese literature retained a strong presence in the late 1930s and early 1940s.

Like most creative works, those hailing from colonial/semicolonial East Asia are polyintertextual: they intertextualize multiple and often diverse predecessors. Here I am most concerned with creative texts that extensively intertextualize Japanese literature. This includes both texts that intertextualize primarily Japanese literary works and those that significantly intertextualize creative writing from several literatures, as long as one of these literatures is Japanese. As with other forms of textual contact, no subset of Japanese literature was off limits. Chinese, Korean, and Taiwanese writers intertextually recast Japanese creative works of all genres and schools, by writers ranging from Natsume Sōseki, Mori Ōgai, and other literary giants to minor figures who have been all but forgotten; it is humbling to recognize that many Japanese authors written out of contemporary histories occupy an important place, however silent, in the Chinese, Korean, and Taiwanese literary fabrics.

The implicit nature of much intertextual reconfiguration generally makes unearthing this literary dynamic more subjective than analyzing interpretations, adaptations, and translations. But the significance of intertextualizing lies less in how much is taken from literary predecessors than in how elements from these predecessors are transposed. Probing this form of transculturation allows for greater understanding of the literary contact nebulae that characterize many cultural spaces. Comprising four chapters, Part II focuses primarily on intertextual transculturations of Japanese literature throughout the empire. Placing the intra–East Asian intertextual transculturation of Japanese literature in broader context, Chapter 5 addresses the critical significance of intertextuality as a literary strategy employed by politically and socially subordinated writers around the world. Chapters 6 to 8 dissect the place of intertextualizing in some of East Asia's most tell-

ing literary perspectives on colonialism/semicolonialism and on co-
lonial-semicolonial-metropolitan cultural confrontations. Chapters 6
and 7 reveal how intertextualizations of Japanese literature reconceptualize suffering and human relationships, respectively. Chapter 8
shows how intertextualizations of Japanese literature frequently re-
draw cartographies of agency. Collectively, these were some of the
most pressing issues confronting early twentieth-century East Asians
at a time of internal discord, international strife, and imperialist pressures on each of the societies involved.

FIVE

Intertextuality, Empire, and East Asia

The term "intertextuality" generally refers to the presence of literary intertexts, understood as anything that links one creative work to another: explicit and implicit citations and transposed allusions, assimilations of substantive and structural features, and participation in literary conventions.[1] Literary intertexts, particularly allusions to creative predecessors, often are more difficult to identify within a given work than references to extratextual circumstances. But exploring the dynamics of this form of textual contact gives greater insights into literary contact nebulae than could emerge from focusing solely on a creative work's engagement with the experienced and imagined worlds. This is especially true in empire and its aftermaths, certainly in (former) metropolitan/(post)colonial and in inter-(post)colonial literary negotiations, but most of all in (post)colonial negotiations with writings from the (former) metropole. In straddling the hazy frontiers of resistance, acquiescence, and collaboration, the weaving of manipulated fragments of texts from the (former) metropole into their own creative output exemplifies the predicament of the (post)colonial writer. On the one hand, intertextualizing can signal refusal to succumb to the rhetoric of the (former) imperial power. On the other hand, massaging metropolitan creative works into bodies of colonial and postcolonial texts can legitimize metropolitan cultural capital and authority.[2]

No literary work stands alone, completely untouched by predecessors, indifferent to contemporaries, and unnoticed by successors. Gérard Genette calls attention to the palimpsestuous nature of texts, arguing, "there is no literary work that, to some degree and according to its readings, does not evoke some other literary work."[3] Literary creations are as inextricably tied to other textual products—both their contemporaries and those of earlier generations—as they are to the surrounding paratextual world with which they engage and frequently are presumed to reflect. Julia Kristeva coined the term intertextuality in 1966, but the phenomenon of intertextuality is as old as recorded human history; consciously or unconsciously, eagerly or reluctantly, writers have always woven fragments from textual predecessors into their own creations.[4] As the Egyptian scribe Khakheperresenb lamented in 2000 BCE: "Would I had phrases that are not known, utterances that are strange, in a new language that has not been used, free from repetition, not an utterance which has grown stale, which men of old have spoken."[5] Echoes of the *Epic of Gilgamesh* (third millennium BCE), the world's oldest known creative work and its "first true work of world literature," are readily apparent in Greek epics, the Bible, and the *Thousand and One Nights*, as well as contemporary novels.[6] In Latin literature, "almost every author, in almost everything he writes, acknowledges his antecedents, his predecessors—in a word, the [literary] tradition in which he was bred."[7] But the poet generally was not supposed to reduce creative production to slavish imitation of predecessors; as Horace (65–8 BCE) warned nascent writers: "Nor will you take pains to render word for word, like a scrupulous interpreter, or jump down, as you imitate, into some little hole from which shame or the rules of the work won't let you escape."[8]

Integrating "imitation" and "creativity" has been the source of no little anxiety for millennia of writers. Harold Bloom asserts that Western poetry, at least since the Renaissance, "is a history of anxiety and self-saving caricature, of distortion, of perverse, willful revisionism without which modern poetry as such could not exist." Claiming that distortion is the defining characteristic of the Western poetic tradition, he argues, "Poetic Influence . . . always proceeds by a misreading of the prior poet, an act of creative correction that is actually and necessarily a misinterpretation."[9] Bloom glosses over the many nuances of poetic intertextuality in Western literatures, not to mention those of other traditions, but there is no denying the apprehension with which creative writers the world over have faced literary antecedents.

Anxious as they might be vis-à-vis their predecessors, writers often have depended on them for validation. In premodern Japan, a work was deemed "literary" by virtue of its being indebted to earlier texts.[10] Generations of Japanese poets employed *honkadori* (allusive variation), echoing "the words, sometimes only the situation or conception, of a well-known earlier poem in such a way that recognizable elements are incorporated into a new meaning, but one in which the meaning of the earlier poem also enters, in a manner distinguished from mere borrowing and use of similar materials and expressions."[11] Likewise, for much of early Chinese literary history, intertextuality was a self-referential and self-preserving exercise; a creative work gained authority from citing, replicating, and revising predecessors.[12] During the Ming (1368–1644) and Qing (1644–1911) dynasties, nearly all major vernacular novels were reshaped and reincarnated in the form of *xushu* (sequels), which proved extremely popular.[13] Most early Korean writers wove strands from Chinese and Korean classics into their creative writing; intertexts from Chinese novels such as Wu Cheng'en's (1500–82) *Xiyouji* (Journey to the West, 1590s) and Cao Xueqin's (1715–63) *Hongloumeng* (The Dream of the Red Chamber, eighteenth c.) appear in a number of premodern Korean prose works, as do allusions to and direct citations of classical Chinese poetry.

Creative works intertextualize one another in myriad overlapping ways that seldom can be separated definitively. Although here I am most concerned with intertextualizing that actively confronts predecessors from spaces with greater cultural capital, it is important to have a broad understanding of how texts negotiate with one another, since many forms of intertextuality are at play in the literatures of Japan's empire, as in most literatures. Examining the various mechanisms by which intertextuality functions in East Asian and other literatures underscores the interactive nature of literary products. The most fundamental division of intertextualizations is between those that are passive and those that are dynamic. Passive intertextuality stems from similarities in circumstances and/or predecessors, from apparent coincidence, and from what often has been referred to as "influence," while dynamic intertextuality involves more active engagement with literary forebears.

Passive Intertextuality

Passive intertextuality generally materializes when a practice is so deeply engrained it becomes an anonymous convention (often referred to as "influence"), when two creative works possess a common antecedent, when they are temporally and culturally distant but are created under analogous conditions, or when they function as "simultaneous independent innovations, a confluence often symptomatic of new things happening in art."[14] In other words, passive intertextuality can stem from writers' employing (but not deeply engaging with) accepted literary practices, having read the same earlier work (but not one another's), having similar experiences (but no contact with one another's work), or otherwise seemingly coincidentally composing creative texts with numerous intersections.

Claudio Guillén points to the first of these conditions in distinguishing between intense, individual connections and more general conventions. He defines conventions as "common premises, usages, the collective air breathed by writers of an era. Conventions belong to the literary system of a moment in history. Was it necessary for a Renaissance poet to read Petrarch in order to write Petrarchan sonnets? How many people were petrarching without realizing it?"[15] Shared literary heritage similarly leads to the emergence in disparate spaces of texts that resemble one another. The Swiss writer Albert Cohen's (1895–1981) prose poem "Projections ou Après-Minuit à Genève" (Projections or After Midnight in Geneva, 1922) contains surprising parallels with James Joyce's (1882–1941) *Ulysses* (1922) and T. S. Eliot's (1888–1965) *The Waste Land* (1922), texts to which Cohen almost certainly did not have access. Cohen, Eliot, and Joyce drew from an almost identical array of earlier texts and put analogous themes—water, metamorphosis, and disguise—to strikingly similar use.[16] Examples of this type of passive relationship can be found throughout East Asian literatures as well. Most prominent are Japanese and Korean premodern literary works that draw heavily from the same Chinese texts and thus have much in common, even though premodern Japanese and Korean writers were not as familiar with one another's creative products as they were with those from China. Twentieth-century East Asian texts that allude to the same European literary work without engaging with one another also are quite common; likewise, some colonial Korean and Taiwanese and semicolonial Chinese texts resemble one another simply because writers are intertextualizing the same Japanese creative work.

In their comparative studies of East Asian and European literatures, Andrew Plaks and other scholars explore passive intertextuality that results from texts having been produced in environments that, although similar, were temporally and culturally separate.

Plaks outlines the remarkable correlations between East Asian and Western novels and dismisses notions that these connections stem from "mutual influence"; he demonstrates that the relationships between Western novels and their economic and social backgrounds are essentially replicated in the Chinese context.[17] Passive relationships can point to traits shared by diverse peoples, and understanding cultural specificity within a broader field of shared critical concerns allows for a deeper and more nuanced sense of commonality. Classifying similarities as "meaningful convergences between two equal traditions" and differences as indicative of "equal, mutually illuminating alternatives," critics such as Zong-qi Cai strive to remove cultural bias from comparative studies, allowing for a better understanding of our common humanity.[18]

Yet cultural bias is not so easily eradicated. Writing on the (mis)use of comparative literature to cast non-Western texts to fit the "Western paradigm," Takayuki Yokota-Murakami warns of the dangers inherent in focusing on perceived "commonalities": "categories, normally conceived to be so essential, universal, and abstract as to be applicable to non-Western cultures, are actually socioculturally and historically specific to the (modern) West. Consequently, an act of comparing Don Juan and an Eastern Don Juan, say, a Japanese *iro-otoko*, is that of subsuming the latter to the former in the name of common 'humanity.'"[19] Many have questioned the validity of comparing two literatures with no physical contact points, asking what purpose is served in juxtaposing, for instance, Greek epics and classical Chinese narratives. While this skepticism is not without foundation, and while the implicit concern that the study of non-Western literatures will be subsumed into that of Western literatures is well grounded, such comparative examinations have their place in their reminder that differences are not necessarily as great as sometimes is imagined.

In addition to similarities stemming from passive integration of conventions, shared predecessors, and analogous circumstances, artistic confluence—seemingly coincidental connections between contemporary texts—also abounds. For instance, Herman Melville's (1819–91) novel *Pierre* (1852) is an "unwitting recasting" of Honoré de Balzac's (1799–1850) *Illusions Perdus* (1843). Parallels proliferate in plot, characterization, self-reflexivity, and theme, but there is no indication that Melville actually read Balzac: "These novels parallel each other in such numerous, striking ways, both superficial and deeply theoretical, that what finally strikes us is their *not* influencing each other or deriving from a discrete earlier source." [20] Likewise, many similarities among twentieth-century East Asian and Western literatures are better ascribed to coincidence or global simultaneity than to "influence."[21] Numerous connections among early twentieth-century Chinese, Japanese, Korean, and Taiwanese creative works — particularly proletarian and modernist texts — also can be interpreted as instances of artistic confluence. Yet because so many writers actively engage with literary predecessors, a significant mass of intertextualizations are more accurately described as dynamic.

Dynamic Intertextuality

Passive intertextuality points to the continuing relevance of artistic conventions. It is a powerful marker of shared humanity and is a compelling reminder of the ubiquity of coincidence. Yet beyond all these is the more proactive form of dynamic intertextuality. Understanding the nature of dynamic intertextuality is particularly important when examining connections among literatures from groups and societies where relationships are tense, significantly unbalanced, or openly hostile. Construing intertextuality as passive happenstance saves time. Yet in cases of more dynamic interaction, such a merely coincidental construction ultimately strips writers, if not groups or societies, of agency. In its premise that there are few means of controlling networks with predecessors, that correlations just happen, an interpretation relying on passive coincidence reinforces the very assumptions of power and hierarchy it may be attempting to deconstruct. Interpretations allowing for dynamic engagement with previous works, on the other hand, reveal that intertextuality can be a very effective means of negotiation, enabling texts to intervene actively in and transform the legacy of their literary predecessors even as they affirm their authority.[22] Writers often toy with the words and phrases of their predecessors and manipulate them to striking effect. Christopher Ricks's definition of "allusion" captures best the mechanisms inherent in much dynamic intertextuality: "the calling into play — by poets — of the words and phrases of previous writers."[23]

Ricks also addresses the important question of authorial intent, which hovers in the background of much literary scholarship and particularly in discussions of intertextuality:

The question of intention bears upon allusion as it bears upon everything not only in literature but in every form of communication . . . it is not only proper but often obligatory to invoke authorial intention, while maintaining that there is (as Wittgenstein proposed) nothing self-contradictory or sly about positing the existence of unconscious or subconscious intentions.[24]

And the prefaces to the Japanese writer Nagai Kafū's "Yojōhan fusuma no shitabari" (Behind the Papering of the Four-and-a-half Mat Room, 1924) are a reminder that authorial declarations, when they do exist, are often unreliable.[25] Although it frequently is impossible to know how or if writers intend to negotiate with specific textual antecedents, twists on predecessors are so ubiquitous that they must be acknowledged — if not necessarily as something writers consciously plan, then as something that exists plainly in texts, often actively contributing to the structure and meaning of literary works.

It is not enough simply to call attention to the presence of intertexts. A mere list of actual or potential "origins" indicates only that the writer is well-read. Julia Kristeva and others have warned of the perils of a simple "study of sources" and wisely advocate focusing on how material is transposed as it moves from one format to another.[26] Such a strategy explains not only the "what" of writers' intertextual sources and "how" these materials are incorporated but also the "so what" of intertextual poetics, the "real implications of dialogues with literary predecessors."[27]

Until recently, scholars clustered many literary relationships under the rubric of influence. Using the influence paradigm allowed critics to demonstrate writers' fascination with or even outright emulation of textual antecedents, and it served as a gateway to understanding textual networking. But this paradigm tends to suppose an unproblematic transfer of commodities from a "creator" to a "receiver." Claudio Guillén persuasively argues against assuming that imaginative or mental events, like biological, chemical, and physical phenomena, necessarily obey the principle of the conservation of matter as they transmute into other forms: "the etymological image of flux, *flow — fluere* — would suggest that an influence represents an uninterrupted passage from one thing to another, and as a result that particular type of criticism tends to confuse influence with textual parallelism."[28] "Influence" also is entangled inexorably with notions of power; it suggests unilateral causality and the passivity of an "influenced" under the unchallenged dominance of an "influencer." Such an approach holds the writer and text hostage, denying them the possibility of creatively and actively intertextualizing literary predecessors.[29] This is not to suggest that texts never passively flow one into another or that those involved in the creative process are never held hostage by their predecessors, only that these phenomena occur less frequently than has been posited. The influence paradigm has troubling implications when used to discuss textual contact among antagonistic groups, particularly those in unequal power relationships. As Janet Ng has rightly argued, "The reception of a particular literary form from one polity that has aggressive designs on one's own culture requires tremendous reprocessing and filtering, a procedure so complex and so elusive that traditional comparative or influence studies cannot fully encompass it."[30]

Recent scholarship on twentieth-century intra–East Asian literary phenomena has provided valuable insights into cross-cultural trends and generic appropriations.[31] But we still need to probe more closely the intricacies of dynamic relationships among texts. Some scholars have addressed literary transfer as a question of cultural memory, focusing on displacement and aftershock as pathways to discovering the "constitutive disruptions, disjunctions, and displacements that occur in the negotiation of cultural exchange."[32] Although this methodology reveals important connections between the function of traumatic memory and the transference of cultural products, it does not leave sufficient room for discussing active engagement with literary predecessors. To be sure, similarities among creative texts cannot be indiscriminately assumed to be evidence of close intellectual connections, but they also frequently are much more than evidence of "families of minds."[33] The multiple webs of intertextual reconfiguration that characterize many literary fields cannot be attributed solely to aftershocks, however traumatic the cultural, economic, military, and political oppression to which writers were exposed. These intertextualizations call for further engagement via analyzing the dynamics of relationships among individual creative works.

Discussing ties among literary works in terms of dynamic intertextuality best captures the active wrestling with textual predecessors that characterizes much creative production. Dynamic intertextuality can be explicit, but it typically is implicit. Explicit intertextuality most often involves identical or nearly identical titles (intertitularity, title-intertextuality), characters with the same names or strikingly similar personalities (interfigurality, figures on loan), direct citations whether marked or unmarked (quotational allusions), and overt references to earlier texts (onomastic allusions).[34] The more texts travel, and the more diverse their backgrounds, the more explicit intertextuality goes undetected, making it in some sense implicit. But implicit intertextuality most often involves unattributed echoes, at once distinct and distorted, of literary works. Both explicit and implicit dynamic intertextual reconfigurations appropriate elements from, express solidarity with, and actively confront predecessors, among other strategies. Whether explicit or implicit, whether appropriative, solidaristic, confrontational, or a combination of these and other modes, some dynamic intertextual reconfigurations rectify literary antecedents, some invite comparisons, and some do both. They rectify predecessors by providing a different, occasionally satirical, but often more grounded portrayal of the characters and landscapes featured in their sources. In so doing they often assert the validity and identity of subjugated peoples and cultures. They invite comparisons with predecessors by replacing the characters and landscapes of their sources with new peoples and terrains (usually those of their homelands), frequently to establish contrasts among sites, but at times to emphasize affinities.

Dynamic intertextualizing can involve appropriating elements from earlier texts in part to increase artistic capital and narrative intensity without significantly challenging or undermining predecessors. Heightening artistic capital via dynamic intertextuality often is a feature of the textual contact that accompanies broader cultural encounters, both intra- and inter-regional. For instance, as Stephen Snyder has observed, "the authority European texts exercised over [the Japanese writer Nagai] Kafū [1879–1959] and others of his generation was extraordinary, approaching the mystical in an essay such as the panegyrical 'Mōpasan no sekizō o haisu' (Worshipping at the Statue of Maupassant)."[35] This authority encouraged literary innovation; Kafū's narratives draw heavily on the characterizations, moods, themes, and even plots of his "literary master" Guy de Maupassant (1850–93). Kafū and others of his generation also looked to European literatures for images of Japan, often repeating, not challenging, European stereotypes of Japan such as those in Pierre Loti's (1850–1923) racist and sexist novel *Madame Chrysanthème* (Madame Chrysanthemum, 1886).[36]

Dynamic intertextuality also is an effective strategy for heightening narrative intensity. China's modern classical poetry (*xinjiushi*), a deeply intertextual and increasingly popular genre, thanks in large part to the Internet, addresses contemporary concerns via conventional forms and a plethora of allusions—often quite humorous—to classical poets.[37] For its part, the Japanese writer Ōe Kenzaburō's (1935-) novel *Kojinteki na taiken* (A Personal Matter, 1964) appropriates elements of Jean-Paul Sartre's (1905-80) *La nausée* (Nausea, 1938) in ways that highlight the disgust with existence that permeates the Japanese text. Antoine and Bird (Bādo), the protagonists of Sartre's and Ōe's novels, both are sickly intellectuals prone to bouts of nausea and fixated on searching for their reflections in glass surfaces; believing a better life awaits far from home, they dream of travel. Images appropriated from Sartre's text accentuate the tenor of Ōe's novel.[38] So do those from Joseph Conrad's (1857-1924) *Heart of Darkness* (1902), particularly Marlow's description of his early encounter with a map of Africa: "It [Africa] had become a place of darkness . . . [with a river] resembling an immense snake uncoiled. . . . As I looked at the map of [Africa] in a shop window it fascinated me as a snake would a bird—a silly little bird." [39] Ōe's Bird is just as fascinated with Africa. *A Personal Matter* opens with him gazing down on a map in a showcase with several images of Africa. The largest image is said to resemble "the skull of a man who had drooped his head," the population distribution map is likened to a "dead head beginning to corrode," and the transportation map is said to be "a skinned painful head with capillary vessels completely exposed."[40] Similarly, the Japanese novel *Suna no onna* (The Woman in the Dunes, 1962) by Abe Kōbō (1924-93) reconfigures the French drawing room inside the vast hell depicted in Sartre's *Huis clos* (No Exit, 1944) as an inescapable sandpit in an isolated and surreal community of seaside dunes. *The Woman in the Dunes* uses this device partly to call attention to the imprisonment of modern individuals and their manipulation by the penetrating and voyeuristic "regard de l'Autre."[41] Indeed, writers throughout history have often used textual antecedents as storehouses from which to pick and choose material that will enhance their creative work as well as increase their artistic capital by the inevitable associations these plunderings evoke.

But many dynamic intertextual reconfigurations are more involved and come with additional strings attached. Some express solidarity with antecedents both textual and writerly. For instance, authors who identify or are identified with subjugated groups often look to predecessors in similar situations for inspiration and incorporate fragments of their texts into their own work. As Henry Louis Gates has argued, the African American writer Alice Walker (1944-), in her novel *The Color Purple* (1983), "turns to a black antecedent text [Zora

Neale Hurston's (1891–1960) *Their Eyes Were Watching God* (1937)] to claim literary ancestry, or motherhood, not only for content but for structure . . . after Walker . . . black authors could even more explicitly turn to black antecedent texts for both form and content."[42] Similarly, as Sandra M. Gilbert and Susan Gubar have revealed, "women of letters from Anne Bradstreet [1612–72] to Anne Brontë [1820–49] and on through Gertrude Stein [1874–1946] to Sylvia Plath [1932–63] [have] engaged in a complex, sometimes conspiratorial, sometimes convivial conversation that crossed national as well as temporal boundaries. And that conversation [has] been far more energetic, indeed far more rebellious, than we'd ever realized."[43]

Although often guided by gender, ethnic, linguistic, racial, national, and other divisions, solidaristic dynamic intertextuality easily transcends boundaries. Forging close ties in Europe, early twentieth-century African and African-American writers intertextualized one another's writing in ways that highlighted their solidarity.[44] Contemporary writers like the Mauritian playwright Dev Virahsawmy (1942–) have also engaged in trans(post)colonial solidarity in such texts as *Toufann: Enn fantezi antrwa ak* (Toufann: A Mauritian Fantasy, 1991), which intertextualizes both Shakespeare's *The Tempest* and the work of African writers like Chinua Achebe (1930–).[45] Likewise, early twentieth-century Chinese, Korean, and Taiwanese writers frequently lamented the fates of their East Asian neighbors and of subordinated groups the world over and paid homage to literatures from these sites in creations of their own. Empathic echoes of the Bengali writer Rabindranath Tagore's (1861–1941) poetry resound in the work of colonial and semicolonial East Asian writers like the Korean poet Han Yong-un (1879–1944), as do ripples of colonial and semicolonial literature from East Asia. The Irish poet William Butler Yeats (1865–1939) likewise openly admired Tagore, writing in his introduction to *Gitanjali (song offerings)*, Tagore's first collection in English, that these poems "stirred my blood as nothing has for years. . . . I have often had to close [the manuscript of these translations] lest some stranger would see how much it moved me. These lyrics . . . display in their thought a world I have dreamed of all my life long."[46] Not surprisingly, Yeats intertextually transculturated Tagore's poetry in his own. This phenomenon can be termed cross-border interdiscursivity, the "transformative transmission of different political vocabularies and cultural discourses between anticolonial spaces," and is manifested not only in literary expressions but also in political ideals, notions of national selfhood, equal-rights movements, and countless other arenas.[47]

Camaraderie among subordinated groups is not guaranteed. Chinese and Koreans harshly criticized Tagore for his grandiose visions of spiritual harmony and for advocating the revival of the so-called ancient ideals of the Orient. Postrealist African writers such as the Malian novelist Yambo Ouologuem (1940–) in *Le Devoir de violence* (Bound to Violence, 1968) likewise rejected the originary "African novel" of Achebe and the Guinean writer Camara Laye (1928–80).[48] Nor have women writers shied away from radically reworking the texts of female predecessors. The West Indian novelist Jean Rhys's (1890–1979) intertextualizing of Charlotte Brontë's (1816–55) *Jane Eyre* (1847) in *Wide Sargasso Sea* (1966) is only one of many examples of this phenomenon; *Wide Sargasso Sea* turns *Jane Eyre* inside out and reveals how it looks "to those characters who are traditionally denied speech, who are little more than pawns in a game controlled by others."[49]

As in Rhys's *Wide Sargasso Sea*, much dynamic intertextualizing is confrontational, actively negotiating with predecessors and jostling for literary terrain.[50] This intertextualizing frequently stems from successor anxiety, the seemingly inevitable feeling of inferiority when confronted with the writings of perceived literary masters whether ancient or contemporary: texts tackle elements of their predecessors and often struggle to surpass them, but rarely deny their cultural capital and narrative authority.[51] Confrontational intertextualizing can be urgent, engaging with the creative output of societies and literary circles that represent or recently represented a more immediate threat, whether political, military, or cultural. Or this intertextualizing can be engrossed, with writers transculturating literary predecessors from less menacing sites.

Such engrossed intertextual reconfiguration occurs throughout Boccaccio's (1313–75) texts, which incorporate hundreds of references to Dante's (1265–1321) oeuvre. Boccaccio's distant imitation of Dante challenges Dante's thought; had Boccaccio simply intended to record Dante's opinions, he likely would have been more open about his borrowing.[52] The defying of literary giants is more overt in the Japanese poet Matsuo Bashō's (1644–94) *Oku no hosomichi* (Narrow Road to the Deep North, 1689). There, stumbling on a stone monument that has provided fodder for a millennium of poets, Bashō takes up these popular lines from the Chinese poet Du Fu's (712–70) "Chun wang"

(Spring View): "The kingdom is destroyed, but the hills and rivers remain / In the city in spring, grass and trees grow deep." Bashō twists Du Fu's words: "Many places of yore have come down to us in poetry, but mountains crumble, rivers carve out new paths, covering roads and rocks with earth. Trees get old and are replaced."[53] Creating in his prose a mirror image of Du Fu's poem, Bashō at once emphasizes the instability of the nonhuman world and the resilience not only of the material fragments of human civilization but also of poetry itself. Yet nothing is static: moss gradually eats into monuments, while subsequent generations transform poetry. Later in *Narrow Road to the Deep North*, confronted with the ruins of Lord Yasuhira's house at Hiraizumi, Bashō cites Du Fu's poem and one by his companion Sora that is remarkably similar: "The words 'The kingdom is destroyed, but the hills and rivers remain / In the city in spring, grass and trees grow green' came to mind. . . . 'Summer grasses are all that remain of the dreams of ancient warriors.'"[54] But Bashō undercuts Du Fu and Sora almost immediately. Admiring two temple halls, he is relieved that former generations thought to build solid structures, thereby preventing nonhuman bodies from destroying buildings, breaking jeweled doors, and scattering treasures. Not as powerful as the Chinese poem suggested, the nonhuman here continues to be thwarted by the human. Bashō proposes that the relationship between the natural world and human creation/destruction, if not that between Chinese and Japanese poetry, is more complex than in Du Fu's imaginings.

Engrossed dynamic intertextuality is often playfully satiric, ridiculing contemporaries and antecedents through comic imitation or inversion. Intertextualizations of (post)colonial and (post)semicolonial creative texts by writers from (former) metropoles often take this form. For instance, in his intertextualization of Lu Xun's story "Shangshi: Juansheng de shouji" (Regret for the Past: Juansheng's Notes, 1925), the narrator of Akutagawa's story "Aru ahō no isshō" (A Fool's Life, 1927) implicitly mocks Juansheng's repeated references to healthy human wings by featuring a protagonist who lurches from dreams of floating flora to an obsession with airborne sparks, and who imagines himself flying to the sun only to come crashing to the ground. The pessimism of Akutagawa's protagonist *kare* (the Japanese pronoun "he") is as palpable as Juansheng's Pollyannaish optimism; while Juansheng hopes constantly for a better life, *kare* believes he has no choice but to wait for inevitable annihilation. Other examples of playfully satiric dynamic intertextuality include Vladimir Nabokov's (1899–1977) novel *Despair* (1936), which contains many parodic confrontations, or Bakhtinian microdialogues, with Fyodor Dostoevsky's (1821–81) novel *Crime and Punishment* (1866) and novella *The Double* (1846); *The Double* itself is an imitation (if not parody) of Nikolai Gogol's (1809–52) short story "The Overcoat" (1842).[55] *Despair* alludes repeatedly to Dostoevsky's writings; at one point the narrator, trying to find a title for his manuscript, lists "The Double" and "Crime and Punishment" as possibilities but quickly dismisses these as being "already used" and "a little crude," respectively: "By turning *The Double*'s anti-Gogolian technique of parody against its own inventor, [*Despair*] also succeeds in capturing Nabokov's complex attitude toward Dostoevsky, which mingles respect for that novella with general detestation."[56]

Satire of literary predecessors is even more intense, but no less playful, in the popular mid-Qing novel *Shuo Tang quanzhuan* (Complete Stories about the Tang [or, Telling Stories about the Tang], 1736), "an outrageous parody of seventeenth-century literati fiction, a literary game meant to amuse those readers who could appreciate [its] play."[57] Likewise, the protagonist of the Japanese writer Ihara Saikaku's (1642–93) *Kōshoku ichidai otoko* (The Man Who Loved Love, 1682) is a caricature of numerous Japanese romantic heroes, particularly Murasaki Shikibu's (973–1025?) amorist Prince Genji: "The entire novel is framed as a burlesque on *The Tale of Genji* and similarly divided into 54 chapters. Besides indulging in a wealth of incidental verbal parody, Saikaku often hints at comic parallels to the emotional adventures of the exquisitely sensitive Genji and his many ladies. Aristocratic love becomes farcical bourgeois lust in a parodic satire on the busy pleasure-seeking of his own time."[58] Not much separates Prince Genji from the amorous men and women who populate Saikaku's creative texts, nor them from him. By mockingly alluding to earlier literary works, Saikaku underlines the universality of human foolishness, if not absurdity. Like Chinese parodies of literati fiction, his burlesques contain dark undertones, but they are fundamentally playful in the sense that they mock predecessors that, whatever their cultural legacy, are not immediate threats.

Less mischievous is engrossed confrontational intertextualizing that chastises societies for building houses of cards that leave their successors only ruins. These include the Japanese novelist Hayashi Fumiko's (1904–51) *Ukigumo* (Floating Clouds, 1951). Attacking bravado that had dire consequences for following generations, Hayashi's novel overhauls both its landmark titular predecessor, Futabatei's *Ukigumo* (Floating Clouds, 1889), and much early twentieth-century Japanese travel writing. Hayashi's text replaces the overall giddiness and confidence of the Meiji period, when Japan was just embarking on its imperial project, with postwar hopelessness and despair. It also challenges many of the assumptions voiced in early twentieth-century Japanese travel literature, particularly the blanket declarations of difference between Japan and China, occupied Manchuria, Korea, and Taiwan. Redefining what it means to be a floating cloud, Hayashi's work confronts literary depictions of both late nineteenth-century modernizing brashness and early twentieth-century imperial arrogance.[59]

In contrast with engrossed confrontational intertextuality, urgent confrontational intertextuality generally challenges or overhauls the creative works of writers with greater cultural/social capital who represent, or in most cases whose societies represent (or at one time represented) more immediate threats. These confrontations appear throughout literature by (formerly) colonized and semicolonized peoples, trauma survivors, women, minorities, and other disenfranchised groups, and they both rectify and invite comparisons (most frequently contrasts) with the landscapes featured in earlier discourse. Elisa Martí-López's observations on the place of French literature in the formation of the nineteenth-century Spanish novel are equally applicable to literary reconfiguration wherever one culture threatens another, whether distantly or more urgently: "The struggle of mid-nineteenth-century literatos to emancipate Spanish literature from relations of cultural subordination was played out precisely in the intense quest for an autochthonous novel that appropriation made possible."[60] The creative output of subordinated groups cannot and should not be defined by negotiations with textual predecessors, particularly since this output often is itself intertextualized by literary successors, but there is no denying its passionate engagement with literary works from political and cultural power centers.[61]

Much literature of atrocity engages in urgent confrontational intertextuality, including Hiroshima survivor Hara Tamiki's (1905–51) trilogy *Natsu no hana* (Summer Flowers, 1949) and Auschwitz survivor Charlotte Delbo's (1913–85) trilogy *Auschwitz et après* (Auschwitz and After, 1970). Hara challenges both prewar discussions of trauma and his own prior writing on the atomic aftermath, while Delbo defies earlier French literature of atrocity — including André Schwartz-Bart's (1928-2006) *Le dernier des justes* (The Last of the Just, 1959), Piotr Rawicz's (1919-82) *Le sang du ciel* (Blood from the Sky, 1961), and Jorge Semprún's (1923-) *Le grand voyage* (The Long Journey, 1963) — as well as her own publications on the Holocaust such as *Le convoi du 24 janvier* (The Convoy of January 24), published five years before *Auschwitz and After*. Both *Summer Flowers* and *Auschwitz and After* call attention to the limitations of the written word and attempt to redefine literature's role in conveying the indescribable.[62]

Appearing frequently in writing by women, bitextuality — dialogue with both masculine and feminine voices — has been a central focus of gynocriticism, the feminist study of women's writing. One form of bitextuality uses confrontational intertextuality to rectify conventional rhetoric, toppling accepted ideas of womanhood. For instance, in *The Golden Apples* (1949), Eudora Welty (1909-2001) "gives us various female figures who not only stand for the female other as depicted in Yeats's poem ["Song of the Wandering Aengus," 1899] but who also, in having their own narratives and quests for identity, challenge the patriarchal discourse in which female figures are idealized 'others' by themselves taking up the questing role classically viewed as essentially male."[63]

Another form of bitextuality is male and female writers' disparate use of similar images, including those of enclosure and escape, to contrast the male and female experience: as Sandra Gilbert and Susan Gubar have noted, male writers generally have used imagery of enclosure and escape to explore the metaphysical and metaphorical nature of the male experience of institutional imprisonment, while female writers have used it to focus on the social imprisonment to which women are subjected. Cages, cellars, prisons, and tombs in Charles Dickens (1812-70) and Edgar Allen Poe, not to mention coffins in John Donne (1572-1631), have very different ramifications from analogous images in the work of Emily Dickinson (1830-86) and other female writers "who [were] actually living those constraints in the present. . . . Recording their own distinctively female experience, [female writers] are secretly [or not so secretly] working through and within the conventions of literary texts to define their own lives."[64] Turning to modern Japanese literature, Tsushima Yūko's (1947-) acclaimed novel *Chōji* (Child of Fortune, 1978) contains numerous distorted echoes of Ōe Kenzaburō's famed *A Personal Matter* (1964) and is in many ways an inversion or mirror image of its literary predecessor.

The isolated protagonists of both *Child of Fortune* and *A Personal Matter* are obsessed with glass, but Bird (the protagonist of *A Personal Matter*) successfully searches mirrors, shop windows, and other glass objects for reflections of himself, whereas the narrator of *Child of Fortune* repeatedly refers to the protagonist Kōko as looking through glass, at something or someone else, even in her dreams. Tsushima's text points to women's frequent inability to see themselves, the result of centuries of having been written off as creatures of darkness. It also draws attention to women's ability to see others, in contradistinction to Bird's solipsism.[65]

Literary works by racial and ethnic minorities likewise often intertextualize canonical texts, both challenging stereotypes and underlining difference. Challenges to stereotypes at times take the form of parody: Asian American writers like John Yao (1950–) countermock imagism's mimicry and American pop culture's pidginization of the Chinese language by incorporating even more extreme speech.[66] But, as in Toni Morrison's (1931–) intertextual recastings of William Faulkner's (1897–1962) oeuvre, rectifications more frequently shatter racial biases. Setting up contrasts is also common. In *Native Speaker* (1995), the Korean American writer Chang-Rae Lee (1965–) intertextualizes parts of F. Scott Fitzgerald's (1896–1940) *The Great Gatsby* (1925), focusing on problems of cultural assimilation amid discussions of social mobility. Japan's *zainichi bungaku*, literature by Japanese writers of Korean descent, likewise intertextually confronts canonical Japanese literature, drawing attention to the extra burdens facing ethnic minorities in Japan. For instance, the stuttering protagonist in Kin Kakuei's (Kim Hak-yŏng, 1938–85) novella *Kogoeru kuchi* (The Benumbed Mouth, 1966) recalls one of the most famous stutterers in modern Japanese literature, Mishima Yukio's (1925–70) character Mizoguchi in *Kinkakuji* (The Temple of the Golden Pavilion, 1956). The alienation of Kin Kakuei's protagonist, as both a Korean Japanese and a stutterer, surpasses even that of Mizoguchi. Likewise, Yū Miri's (1968–) play *Gurīn benchi* (Green Bench, 1992) intertextually confronts parts of the Japanese writer Takahashi Takako's (1932–) story "Sōjiki" (Congruent Figures, 1971). Both texts probe "extreme cases of a mother's sexual jealousy toward her daughter," but added to *Green Bench* are the intense struggles of Korean Japanese to find their place in mainstream Japanese society.[67]

Often even more dramatic are the thousands of intertextual transculturations of the literatures of (former) metropoles in (semi)colonial and post(semi)colonial creative texts. To be sure, some (semi)colonial and post(semi)colonial creative texts do not appear to go much beyond imitating metropolitan predecessors, "emulating in art whatever fashion [the] parent culture had recently regarded as acceptable."[68] Other intertextualizing, including that in the Cuban novelist Alejo Carpentier's (1904–80) *El arpa y la sombra* (The Harp and the Shadow, 1979), which claims to reconfigure parts of Christopher Columbus's diary, rewrites imperial heroes as villains.[69] Similarly, narratives such as the Brazilian writer Érico Lopes Veríssimo's (1905–75) short story "Metamorphosis," which features a cockroach that one day awakens as a woman, parody Eurocentric notions of the human and humane and depict the process of becoming human on European terms as wholly inhumane.[70] But much (semi)colonial and post(semi)colonial intertextual transculturating rectifies (post)imperial depictions of (post)colonial/(post)semicolonial peoples or invites comparisons (most often contrasts) between (post)colonial/(post)semicolonial and (post)imperial experiences.

Some (semi)colonial and post(semi)colonial writers employ "subversion by imitation": "Though ventriloquizing the colonizer's voice, though identifying themselves in the vocabulary of their oppression, they also mixed up and upturned dominant meanings. Their cleaving *to* colonial definitions of self was therefore *at the same time* a cleaving *from*."[71] Yet greater numbers challenge metropolitan portrayals of peoples (formerly) under their control as "subhuman, non-human, savage, and surreal," stereotypes that "acquired the status of conventional iconography" and saturated literary texts of all kinds.[72] As Gayatri Spivak has commented, "It should not be possible to read nineteenth-century British literature without remembering that imperialism, understood as England's social mission, was a crucial part of the cultural representation of England to the English. The role of literature in the production of cultural representation should not be ignored."[73] References and allusions to empire and depictions of imperial subjects appear particularly frequently in the nineteenth- and early twentieth-century British novel, but they also abound in French and American writing[74] and make their presence felt in early twentieth-century Japanese literature. And so it is not surprising that even when hegemony appeared unassailable, and long after decolonization, African, Caribbean, East-Central European, East Asian, Latin American, Middle Eastern, and South and Southeast Asian writers continued to rectify American, European, and Japanese literary works, creating often autoethnographic texts that undermined rhetoric that presumed to describe and categorize them.[75] In so doing, they constructed new identities and cultures.[76]

Joseph Conrad's *Heart of Darkness*, based on his experiences in the Congo and reinforcing European stereotypes of Africa as the "Dark Continent," was a frequent target, intertextualized by writers as diverse as the Nigerian novelist Chinua Achebe in *Things Fall Apart* (1958), the Trinidadian writer V. S. Naipaul (1932–) in *A Bend in the River* (1979), and the Sudanese novelist Tayeb Salih (1929–2009) in *Mawsim al-Hijra ilā al-Shamāl* (*Season of Migration to the North*, 1966).[77] (Semi)colonial and post(semi)colonial writers also regularly intertextually recast Shakespeare's plays, particularly *The Tempest*, largely because of its disturbing portrait of the semi-human "savage and deformed slave" Caliban.[78] For instance, the Martinican Francophone writer Aimé Césaire (1913–2008) reworks Shakespeare's *The Tempest* in *Une tempête; d'après "La tempête" de Shakespeare. Adaptation pour un théâtre nègre* (A Tempest; Based on Shakespeare's *The Tempest*. Adaptation for a Black Theater, 1969). *A Tempest* humanizes Shakespeare's Caliban and although not ridding him of Prospero gives him more verbal and physical freedom: he repeatedly stands up to Prospero, even demanding that Prospero call him X, "Like a man without a name. In fact, a man whose name has been stolen. . . . Each time you call me that, you'll be reminded of a fundamental truth, that you stole everything from me, even my identity! Uhuru [Freedom]!"[79]

Jean Rhys' novel *Wide Sargasso Sea* likewise autoethnographically intertextualizes Charlotte Brontë's *Jane Eyre*, particularly the character Bertha Antoinette Mason Rochester, Edward Rochester's lunatic Creole wife of ambiguous origin whom he keeps locked in the attic.[80] Denied a voice in Brontë's novel, Bertha is portrayed as a monster.[81] But in *Wide Sargasso Sea*, which is narrated in the first person, Antoinette tells her own story and comes across as a more human character: "In *Wide Sargasso Sea*, the madwoman silenced in *Jane Eyre* speaks, and her voice exposes and turns upside down the values, patriarchal and colonialist, upon which the plot and characters of Brontë's novel depend."[82] Likewise, in their dynamic intertextual transculturations of Japanese literature, Korean writers reclaimed Korean agency dangerously compromised by their Japanese counterparts. Although the Japanese proletarian poet Nakano Shigeharu was more sympathetic to the plight of colonial Koreans than many of his contemporaries, in poems like "Shinagawa Station in the Rain"

(1929), he oscillates between denigrating and romanticizing them. Korean writers were deeply troubled by this text and its Korean translation, and the revolutionary poet Im Hwa responded quickly to both with "Yokohama Pier under the Umbrella" (1929). Im Hwa's poem intertextualizes "Shinagawa Station in the Rain" in part to humanize Koreans; it additionally demands Japanese and Korean proletarian solidarity, something toward which Nakano's poem only feebly gestures.[83] (Semi)colonial and post(semi)colonial intellectuals did not hesitate to censure their own societies, and some—like the Chinese writer and politician Chen Duxiu (1872–1942)—even cited metropolitan critiques to support their arguments, but their creative works regularly debunked imperial stereotypes.[84]

In addition to rectifying metropolitan depictions of their peoples as subhuman savages ruled by passion or, in the case of Nakano, as disappearing shadows who are to serve as the "front and rear shields of the Japanese proletariat," (post)colonial and (post)semi-colonial writers grappled with metropolitan texts that wrote the traumas of besieged peoples out of history. For instance, the Chinese writer Ah Long openly rewrites Japanese (and Chinese) literary silence on atrocities in China by intertextually transculturating Ishikawa Tatsuzō's novella *Living Soldiers* (1938) and Hino Ashihei's trilogy of the same year *Wheat and Soldiers, Earth and Soldiers,* and *Flowers and Soldiers*—major Japanese wartime novels—in his own novel *Nanjing* (1939). *Nanjing* contains longer and more graphic accounts of the destruction wrought by Japanese troops in China than do either the Japanese battlefront novels or their Chinese translations. It also illuminates the atrocities Chinese troops committed against Chinese, a subject for the most part glossed over in literary accounts of this period.

Intertextually engaging with Albert Camus' (1913–60) *La peste* (The Plague, 1947), the Algerian Francophone novelist Mohammed Dib's (1920–2003) trilogy *La grande maison* (The Large House, 1952), *L'incendie* (The Fire, 1954), and *Le métier à tisser* (The Loom, 1957) similarly challenges the Camusian narrative's humanist rhetoric that transcends colonialism and skirts questions of colonial domination.[85] *The Plague,* typically read as an allegory of the spread of fascism across Europe, evokes sympathy for the French under German occupation (1940–44). But it also evades the thorny issue of France's colonization of Algeria. It takes place in Oran, Algeria's most "European" city, and although it features a journalist who came to study the city's Arab population, Arabs do not figure in the novel.[86] Dib corrects this absence in his trilogy, particularly in *The Loom*, where desperate beggars replace plague-infested rats.

Much intertextualizing that rectifies metropolitan portrayals of or silence concerning the (post)(semi)colonized gives speech to those denied a voice, even criminals.[87] But several texts take the opposite approach, drawing attention to the silence imposed on the subjugated. The South African writer J. M. Coetzee's (1940–) novel *Foe* (1986), a postmodern recasting of Daniel Defoe's (1660–1731) *Robinson Crusoe* (1719), reconfigures Robinson Crusoe's obedient servant Friday as a man whose tongue long ago was severed by African slave hunters. As Cruso speculates in *Foe*, "Perhaps they wanted to prevent him from ever telling his story: who he was, where his home lay, how it came about that he was taken. Perhaps they cut out the tongue of every cannibal they took, as a punishment. How will we ever know the truth?"[88] On the other hand, near the end of the novel, Friday takes the first steps at writing, a narrative move that tantalizingly suggests he might someday articulate his experiences.[89]

Other (semi)colonial and post(semi)colonial writers have been concerned less with rectifying metropolitan depictions of their societies than with highlighting differences between metropolitan and (semi)colonial/post(semi)colonial experiences. Common enough in intertextualizations of American and European literatures, including the Tibetan exile writer Jamyang Norbu's (1954–) *The Mandala of Sherlock Holmes* (2000), dynamic intertextuality that invites comparisons among different peoples abounds in early twentieth-century Chinese, Korean, and Taiwanese transculturations of Japanese literature. There is no shortage of early twentieth-century Japanese literary works that paint unflattering portraits of Chinese, Koreans, and Taiwanese.[90] As William Gardner has noted, "Japanese literati in the prewar and wartime periods [played an important role] in constructing an imaginative map or image of Japan's colonies and Asian neighbors in the eyes of the Japanese reading public."[91] But Japanese literature was not as central to Japan's imperial project as American and European literatures were to Western imperialism. More important to the proliferation of dynamic intertextuality that invites comparisons was Japanese pan-Asianism. During the Meiji period, pan-Asian writings romantically "emphasized Japanese commonalities with Asia and aimed at uniting Asian peoples and countries against Western encroachment" even as the Japanese colonized Korea and Taiwan and encroached on the Chinese mainland. As the Japanese state became more powerful, pan-Asianism metamorphosed into more intense claims of Japanese superiority over and leadership of Asia, even while stressing commonalities among cultures.[92] Countering this rhetoric in their confrontational intertextual recastings of Japanese literature, Chinese, Korean, and Taiwanese writers asserted their own selfhood and nationhood; they often did so while despairing for the future of their societies and in some cases supporting Japanese imperialism. Also at stake was Japan's insistence on "Japanizing" Koreans, Taiwanese, and Chinese residing in occupied Manchuria, an even more extreme form of mimicry than what emerged in European and American empires.[93] As explored in the following three chapters, much intra-Asian comparative dynamic intertextuality turns these efforts on their heads, most often negotiating Chinese, Korean, and Taiwanese separateness.

Not surprisingly, by engaging with a multiplicity of texts, numerous creative works both rewrite earlier depictions of characters and landscapes and distinguish (or liken) local circumstances from those portrayed in literary predecessors. Such works are abundant in early twentieth-century Chinese, Korean, and Taiwanese literatures. A prominent example from outside East Asia that helps put this intertextualizing into broader perspective is Chinua Achebe's novel *Things Fall Apart*. Achebe spoke of *Things Fall Apart* as a counter-discourse on Africa, an amending of the racism inherent in Joseph Conrad's *Heart of Darkness* and Joyce Cary's (1888–1957) *Mister Johnson* (1939):

> One of the things that probably finally [made me decide to write *Things Fall Apart*] was a novel set in Nigeria by Joyce Cary. I regard him as one of the outstanding British writers of the first part of this century . . . he wrote this novel called *Mister Johnson*, which is quite famous, and I feel that it's not—in spite of this man's ability, in spite of his sympathy and understanding, he could not get under the skin of his African. They just did not communicate. And I felt if a good writer could make this mess perhaps we ought to try our hand.[94]

In *Things Fall Apart*, Achebe portrays culture, philosophy, poetry, and especially dignity as inherent to African society, not as imported products. This rectifies Conrad's and Cary's narratives, which depict Africa as the antithesis of Europe and thus of civilization, a continent of irredeemable darkness and barbarity. The Africans Achebe presents are articulate; as the narrator of *Things Fall Apart* asserts early in the novel, "Among the Ibo the art of conversation is regarded very highly, and proverbs are the palm-oil with which words are eaten."[95]

But in addition to rectifying *Heart of Darkness,* Achebe's work also contrasts Africa's plight with the situation Yeats depicts in the poem "The Second Coming" (1920). Achebe took the title *Things Fall Apart* from the third line of Yeats's poem and appropriates the first four lines of "The Second Coming" as his epigraph: "Turning and turning in the widening gyre / The falcon cannot hear the falconer; / Things fall apart; the centre cannot hold; / Mere anarchy is loosed upon the world."[96] Yet even Yeats, who worked tirelessly for Irish independence and the dissolution of the British Empire—causes with which Achebe certainly could relate—does not remain unscathed. "Things" do in fact fall apart in *Things Fall Apart,* but Achebe, not speaking in terms as vague as Yeats's, does not depict a world bracing for the "Second Coming." Rather, he describes the "falling apart" of the Ibo civilization brought upon by a combination of internal decay and outside oppression, one that leaves little hope for the future.[97] Portraying the struggles of individual Ibo, Achebe not only codifies concrete historical moments but also, legitimizing these moments through their codification, implicitly calls for the addition of Africa to Yeats's cycle of history, articulated in *A Vision* (1925, 1937). Yeats's understanding of history, like that of most Europeans, overlooked the African continent.[98] Significant as well is Yeats's reference to a falcon that "cannot hear the falconer" and a center that "cannot hold." These images, when interpreted as foreshadowing liberation, allow Achebe's narrator to imbricate the colonial and postcolonial periods. After liberation, the falconer (the metropole) no longer will be able to communicate with its falcon (intermediary/collaborator), which it has trained to attack prey (the colony). When the center— namely, the colonial government—really does fall apart, it leaves behind mere anarchy.

Taking part of a single line of Yeats's "The Second Coming" for his title, Achebe risks subsuming his novel into Yeats's poem; the narrator of *Things Fall Apart* in some sense places his text as a footnote, albeit an elaborate one, to Yeats's allegedly more dominant work, describing what it means for "things" to "fall apart." Yet by including the first stanza of this poem as his epigraph, Achebe establishes the legitimacy of his own text. Even though Yeats's verse, as an epigraph, is used to set the tone of the story, the text of *Things Fall Apart* continues not with [Yeats's] "the blood-dimmed tide is loosed" but with "Okonkwo was well known throughout the nine villages and even beyond. His fame rested on solid personal achievements."[99] The story

continues in a very different vein from Yeats's poem. What might
have become an elaborate footnote, a mere example of things falling
apart, has radically intertextualized its predecessor.

The Chinese writer and painter Ji Xian's (1913–) wartime poem "Fei
yue de quan" (Dog Barking at the Moon, 1942) aptly expresses the
complex, ambiguous, and paradoxical relationships of (semi)colonial
and post(semi)colonial literatures with imperial and other antecedents.[100] The title echoes that of the Japanese surrealist poet Hagiwara
Sakutarō's celebrated anthology *Tsuki ni hoeru* (Howling at the Moon,
1917) and is identical to that of the surrealist Spanish artist Joan Miró's
(1893–1983) painting "Gos bordant a la lluna" (Dog Barking at the
Moon, 1926).[101] Ji Xian's "Dog Howling at the Moon" interlaces its
predecessors' principal features: a dog howling at the moon (present
in both Miró's painting and Hagiwara's poem "Kanashii tsukiyo"
[Sad Moonlit Night, 1914] in the anthology *Howling at the Moon*), singing girls (Hagiwara's poem), and railroad tracks (Miró's painting). It
begins with a train rolling by, then out of sight, carrying a dog that
howls at the moon. The tracks are said to "heave a sigh of relief" at
the train's, the dog's, and likely the artistic predecessors' (symbolic)
departure. The songs of naked girls astride cacti appear to replace
the dog's howls. But the final lines of the Chinese poem warn that
the dog's howls strike the moon and "shoot right back and gobble up
the girls' voices." [102] Having fallen off the track, the train does not
return, nor does the dog, but the Chinese "Dog Howling at the Moon"
emphasizes that there is no escaping the voice of the dog and, by extension, the voices of artistic predecessors. That the dog's howls first
appear to be replaced by and then ultimately consume the girls' ca-
cophonous voices, exchanging the polyvocality of Hagiwara's poem
for a single voice, points to the silencing of dissonant voices, including
those of colonial/semicolonial authors.

In most parts of the world, colonial and semicolonial legacies continue, and negotiations with the cultural products of former metropoles persist, even as writers from former metropoles become more
engaged with creative works from former (semi)colonial sites. To be
sure, when asked in a recent interview whether Nigerian writers of
her generation were freer to experiment than their predecessors,
Achebe's daughter Chimamanda Ngozi Adichie (1977–) remarked, "I
think so. I think there's a sense that we don't have to write back to
Empire the way Achebe and other writers have."[103] Some postcolonial
writers depict themselves as resting, albeit uneasily, under the eaves

of their metropolitan predecessors. In "Mingzhi [Meiji] cun Xiamu [Natsume] shuzhai qian" (In Front of Natsume's Study at Meiji Village, 1992) the Taiwanese poet Li Kuixian (1937–) claims that Natsume Sōseki "settled down in the cherry blooming season" but that he, who "has yet to find a settled place," sits under the eaves of Sōseki's study. The poet has not yet found his space, but for the moment Sōseki's study provides a welcome refuge.[104] Yet many literary voices continue to grapple with imperial antecedents. Sophomoric but telling is the Taiwanese writer Lin Huanzhang's (1939–) recent poem "Wo shi mao, bu!" (I Am a Cat, Not!, 2003), which calls to mind Sōseki's *Wagahai wa neko de aru* (I Am a Cat, 1906), a lengthy novel narrated by a cat who philosophizes on the absurdities of human behavior. In their opening lines, both the poet and the narrator of Sōseki's text assert "I'm a cat." But while Sōseki's cat continues with "I don't yet have a name," the Taiwanese poet declares "No! I'm a poet." In the following stanzas, the poet declares himself first a philosopher and then a "senseless person."[105] Lacking far more than a name, the Taiwanese cat/poet/philosopher/person struggles to define who he is, to negotiate his space and his place vis-à-vis weighty predecessors.

Striving to develop modern literatures they could call their own, yet that also would become part of world literature,[106] semicolonial Chinese and colonial Taiwanese and Korean writers intertextually reconfigured massive quantities of Japanese and European creative works, in addition to numerous predecessors from their own cultures, both classical and contemporary. They created intertwined literatures that were as concerned with providing foundations for productive artistic and national futures as they were with engaging actively with predecessors. Of course, much intertextualizing is not the result of conscious or meaningful engagement with textual antecedents. As Henri Peyre warns, "It is hard for [scholars] to concede that those authors whom we call imaginative have not spurred their imaginative creation through the perusal of everything that may have been published around them."[107] Yet not all intertextualizing can be dismissed as simple coincidence. The stakes are especially high when probing the relationships among the literatures of nations or peoples whose interactions are tense or openly hostile, particularly when one group is subjugating or has recently subjugated another. Unlike many of their Japanese counterparts, early twentieth-century Chinese, Korean, and Taiwanese writers generally were politically active and believed strongly in writers' responsibility to society. Examining how their creative work intertextualizes Japanese literature illuminates the place of literary production not only as a counter-discourse aimed directly at the cultural products of the imperial power, and often indirectly at the imperial power itself, but also as a means of constructing and deconstructing identities.

The Case of East Asia: An Overview

This chapter has explored various forms of intertextuality, first distinguishing between passive and dynamic intertextual contact, discussing various forms of both types of contact, and then examining urgent confrontational dynamic intertextuality in empire and post-imperial spaces in particular. Intertextualizing tends to rectify and invite comparisons with creative antecedents. But what concerns does it tackle as it amends and shifts the focus of literary predecessors? The next three chapters take up some of the most significant issues addressed by intertextual transculturations of Japanese literature in colonial and semicolonial East Asia: suffering, human relationships, and agency. Before addressing these dynamics, an overview of intra–East Asian intertextuality in the early twentieth century will reveal its great magnitude, comparable with that of intra-empire literary criticism and adaptation/translation, with which intertextual transculturations sometimes intertwined. Naturally, most of the Chinese, Japanese, Korean, and Taiwanese writers and texts discussed below also negotiate with Western literatures, as well as with those of their own cultures, both classical and contemporary. Since much less is known about vectors of early twentieth-century intra–East Asian intertextual transculturation than about other trajectories, I focus on literary works with significant intertextual transculturations of contemporary East Asian literatures, and Chinese, Korean, and Taiwanese intertextualizations of Japanese literature in particular (the most active vectors of early twentieth-century intra–East Asian intertextual transculturation) even when these intertextualizations cohabit with those of other literatures.[108]

The First Wave

The first wave of intra-empire intertextualizing occurred in the 1900s and early 1910s. The Japanese political novel was a ready target, particularly texts that described the future. Liang Qichao's recasting of Suehiro Tetchō's *Plum Blossoms in the Snow* (1886) in his unfinished

Xin Zhongguo weilaiji (The Future of New China, 1902) is the first prominent example of a Chinese intertextualization of a late nineteenth-century Japanese literary work. *The Future of New China* posits China as playing catch-up with Europe. Countering Tetchō's vision of a Japan with a glorious future, *The Future of New China* "solicits an ironic reading, as 'no future of new China.'"[109] Another early genre of interest was the late nineteenth-century Japanese allegorical novel. The Korean writer An Kuksŏn's (1878–1926) story "Kŭmsu hoe ŭi rok" (Record of the Conference of Birds and Beasts, 1908), which satirizes Korean society and politics, intertextualizes allegorical writings by Kanagaki Robun (1829–94) and Tajima Shōji (1852–1909).[110] Well into the 1910s, Japanese political and allegorical novels served as springboards for Chinese and Koreans to further their own political agendas and to differentiate circumstances in Japan from those elsewhere in East Asia.[111]

In their creative work, Chinese and Korean writers also intertextualized Japanese nonfiction and translations of texts deeply engaged with political concerns. Zeng Pu's (1872–1935) acclaimed novel *Niehaihua* (Flower in an Ocean of Sin, 1905) incorporates the Japanese anarchist Kemuyama Sentarō's (1877–1954) discussions of Russian nihilism.[112] Even more important, Ken'yūsha (The Society of Friends of the Inkstone) leader Yamada Bimyō's (1868–1910) translation of the Philippine writer and revolutionary José Rizal's *Touch Me Not* (1887) as *Chi no namida* (Tears of Blood, 1903), a title inspired by the Japanese writer Murai Gensai's (1863–1927) own *Chi no namida* (Tears of Blood, 1896), prompted the creation of texts of this title by Chinese and Korean writers. In 1903, the *Hubei xuesheng jie* (Hubei Students World), a nationalistic Chinese student journal in Tokyo, carried a text entitled *Xieleihen* (Traces of Bloody Tears). Ironically, the protagonist of *Traces of Bloody Tears* becomes engrossed in *Revenge of the Red and Black Peoples*, a book depicting the plight of oppressed races written by a Filipino (perhaps José Rizal) who is studying at the University of Spain.[113] Whereas the anonymous Chinese author of *Traces of Bloody Tears* broadens the focus of Rizal's novel by including the history of oppression in Africa and the Americas, the Korean writer Yi Injik turns the lens closer to home in *Hyŏl ŭi nu* (Tears of Blood, 1906). This novel features a Korean family torn apart by the Sino-Japanese War and is less critical of Chinese and Japanese treatment of Korea than of Korean apathy; the oppressed, the narrator implies, are not necessarily helpless victims. Although very different texts, both the Chinese and the Korean versions of *Tears of Blood* stoutly confront their Filipino and especially Japanese predecessors, highlighting the hardships facing Japan's East Asian neighbors.

Chinese and Korean writers also reworked fiction by members of the Ken'yūsha literary coterie, who promoted their creative texts as mere diversions. Intertextual recastings of these literary works frequently raised the political and literary stakes by underlining domestic suffering. The Chinese writer Su Manshu's (1884–1918) intertextualization of Ozaki Kōyō's *Ninin bikuni irozange* (Two Nuns' Confessions of Love, 1889) in *Duanhong lingyanji* (The Lone Swan, 1912) is only one example of this phenomenon; the narrators of both novels are obsessed with tears, yet *The Lone Swan*, like other Chinese recastings of Ken'yūsha writings, provides even more poignant expressions of grief.

Lu Xun and Yi Kwangsu

Lu Xun and Yi Kwangsu, often considered the founders of modern Chinese and Korean literatures, both grappled with Japanese literature during the 1910s and especially 1920s, intertextually recasting numerous Japanese works in their own fiction. Yi Kwangsu's short story "Kim Kyŏng" (1915) contains explicit references to Japanese texts such as the Christian socialist Kinoshita Naoe's *Pillar of Fire* (1904), while his "So-nyŏn ŭi piae" (The Sorrows of Youth, 1917) challenges Kunikida Doppo's text of the same title ("Shōnen no hiai," 1902), differentiating circumstances in Korea from those in Japan. Yi Kwangsu's *Heartless* (1917), often heralded as Korea's first modern novel, takes its title from Kuroiwa Ruikō's (1862–1920) Japanese translation (1902) of Victor Hugo's *Les Misérables* (1862); *Heartless* argues for an understanding of "unfeeling" beyond what is offered by the French novel in Japanese clothes. *Heartless* also confronts Futabatei Shimei's *Floating Clouds* (1889), Kinoshita Naoe's *Pillar of Fire*, and fiction by Natsume Sōseki.

Lu Xun likewise incorporated material from Sōseki's oeuvre. It is seldom remembered that his famed short story "The True Story of Ah Q" (1921) reconfigures not only numerous texts from Western literatures but also Natsume Sōseki's *I Am a Cat* (1906), highlighting the severity of China's decay vis-à-vis Japan. Several sections of Lu Xun's *Yecao* (Wild Grass, 1927) intertextualize segments of Sōseki's *Yume jūya* (Ten Nights of Dreams, 1908), transforming characters who abandon hope or are defeated into those who engage in endless rebellion. In contrast, Lu Xun's "Yijian xiaoshi" (A Small Incident, 1920) reworks Akutagawa Ryūnosuke's "Mikan" (Tangerines, 1919), posing deeper questions concerning the ties between individuals and society. Other fiction Lu Xun wrote in the 1910s and 1920s confronts texts by Arishima Takeo, Futabatei Shimei, Kikuchi Kan, Kunikida Doppo, Masaoka Shiki (1867–1902), Mori Ōgai, and Yokomitsu Riichi. Lu Xun intertextualized Japanese literature at most stages of his career; *Gushi xinbian* (Old Tales Retold, 1935), written shortly before his death, contains distinct reworkings not only of Chinese predecessors but also of the historical fiction of Akutagawa and Ōgai, further problematizing networks with textual predecessors near and far.[114]

The Twenties

Lu Xun and Yi Kwangsu were only two of the many East Asian writers who simultaneously flouted and confirmed the authority of Japanese creative production during the 1920s. Chinese, Koreans, and Taiwanese intertextualized a variety of Japanese writers and genres in their own creative work, forever scarring their Japanese sources at the same time that they perpetuated their legacy. Yu Dafu and Lao She (1899–1966) in China and Chang Hyŏkju, Hyŏn Chin-gŏn (1900–43), Kim Dong-in, and Kim Namch'ŏn in Korea grappled with fiction by Natsume Sōseki, Akutagawa Ryūnosuke, and others in their own creations. Chang Hyŏkju intertextuazlizes Sōseki's novella *Little Master* (1906) in "A Man Named Kwŏn" (1933), underlining the corruption pervading colonial Korean society and portraying it as more severe than the ills plaguing Japan; in "Hell of Hungry Spirits" (1932), he intertextualizes Sōseki's "Here and There in Manchuria and Korea" (1909) in part to highlight the suffering of Korean laborers.[115] Similarly, Lao She intertextually rewrites Akutagawa's novella *Kappa* (Kappa, 1927) in his novel *Maochengji* (City of Cats, 1933), questioning more searingly than his Japanese predecessor the value of diagnosing decay in a society seemingly beyond repair. Also intriguing is Kim Namch'ŏn's intertextual reconfiguration of Akutagawa's short story "Yabu no naka" (In a Grove, 1922) in "Si" (City, 1939), which the Korean writer dedicated to "the spirit of Akutagawa." Both stories consist of multiple versions of a murder, but "City" changes the focus from the identity of the murderer to the reason the murder took place,[116] pointing to the urgency of preventing future fatalities.

Kim Dong-in and the Chinese writers Mao Dun and Zhou Zuoren also intertextualized fiction and essays by Tanizaki Jun'ichirō, exposing shortcomings and arguing against assumptions made in the oeuvre of their Japanese predecessor. For instance, in "Chuangzao" (Creation, 1928), Mao Dun parodies the excessive focus on surface appearances in Tanizaki's novel *Chijin no ai* (A Fool's Love, 1925) by confining his story to a single room and the thoughts of a male protagonist. Zhou Zuoren's essay "Ruce dushu" (Reading on the Toilet, 1934) takes on the complaints of excess modernity articulated in Tanizaki's essay "In'ei raisan" (In Praise of Shadows, 1934). Similarly, Chinese writers such as Zhou Zuoren, Lu Xun, and Ye Shengtao (1894–1988) and Korean writers such as Kim Dong-in manipulated texts by members of the utopian Japanese White Birch Society, particularly those of its leader Mushakōji Saneatsu. While incorporating a Japanese framework, many addressed issues of more immediate concern to their respective societies. When Japanese and Chinese advocates of the New Village movement called for individualism and humanism, they similarly isolated themselves from a majority of their own people and felt guilty for their privileged statuses as intellectuals. But living in an industrial society, albeit one with considerable rural poverty, Mushakōji and other members of the White Birch Society could talk about the imagined "idyllic countryside" in a way that Chinese of the May Fourth era — a time when the majority of the population toiled in the countryside more desperately even than their impoverished Japanese counterparts — could not.[117]

Intertextual transculturations of creative works by Japanese naturalist writers also appeared frequently in the 1920s in China and Korea, intertwining the Japanese, Chinese, and Korean literary worlds ever more deeply.[118] Korean writers such as Chŏn Yŏngt'aek (1898–1968), Hyŏn Chin-gŏn, Kim Dong-in, and Yŏm Sangsŏp rewrote prose by the leading Japanese naturalists Kunikida Doppo, Iwano Hōmei (1873–1920), Tayama Katai, and Shimazaki Tōson. Hyŏn Chin-gŏn's story "Pul" (Fire, 1925) intertextually recasts Katai's novella *Jūemon no saigo* (The End of Jūemon, 1902) to privilege societal responsibility above fate.[119] Similarly, Yŏm Sangsŏp's *Samdae* (Three Generations, 1931) intertextualizes parts of Shimazaki Tōson's *Ie* (Family, 1911), as does Ba Jin's (1904–2005) *Jia* (Family, 1933); both *Three Generations* and the Chinese *Family* critique Tōson's relatively narrow focus and highlight the deep connections between the family and society. In fact, Ba Jin's three novels *Xinsheng* (New Life, 1932), *Family* (1933), and *Chun* (Spring, 1938) invert Tōson's *Haru* (Spring, 1908), *Family* (1911), and *Shinsei* (New Life, 1919).[120] Other dynamic intertextualizing of Japanese naturalist writings underlines colonial/semicolonial suffering. Chŏn Yŏngt'aek's short story "Ch'ŏnch'i? Ch'ŏnjae?" (Idiot? Genius?, 1919) reworks Kunikida Doppo's short story "Haru no tori" (Bird of Spring, 1904) in a way that deflates Doppo's Wordsworthian cele-bration of youth and nature, while Kim Dong-in's "Kamja" (Potatoes, 1925) recasts Doppo's short story "Gyūniku to bareisho" (Beef and Po-tatoes, 1901) to underline Korean poverty and apathy.[121]

Some Chinese, Korean, and Taiwanese writers also wrote intensely personal texts that closely resemble the Japanese I-novel, but they nearly always added an ironic twist. Confessional prose by Zhang Ziping (1893–1959) and Guo Moruo—called the "Mori Ōgai of Chi-na"[122]—and Yu Dafu's accounts of tormented sex and the isolated intellectual in short stories including "Sinking" (1921) closely resemble works by Kasai Zenzō (1887–1928), Satō Haruo, Shiga Naoya, and Ta-yama Katai, but emphasize the deep connections among the individ-ual, the family, and the nation. Some of Yu Dafu's other prose also in-tertextualizes fiction by Natsume Sōseki; Yu Dafu's short story "Chiguihua" (Late-Blooming Cassia, 1932) reworks the figure of the artist as depicted in Sōseki's novel *Pillow of Grass* (1906). In most cases, Chinese and Korean intertextualizations of these Japanese writings conjoin the political and the personal to a degree not seen in their predecessors.

Literature of the Vanguard, the Avant-Garde, and the Native Place

Chinese, Korean, and Taiwanese revolutionary writers, many of whom studied in Japan, intertextualized large quantities of Japanese literature in the 1920s and 1930s. The impact of Japanese proletarian fiction on the production of Chinese revolutionary literature was acknowledged as early as November 1925, when the Chinese journal *Yusi* (Threads of Talk) carried an essay that claimed Japanese litera-ture provided a model for Chinese revolutionary literature.[123] Chinese such as Mao Dun in "Chuncan" (Spring Silkworms, 1932), Xiao Hong (1911–42) in *Shengsi chang* (Field of Life and Death, 1934), Wu Zuxiang (1908–94) in "Yiqianbabai dan" (Eighteen Hundred Piculs, 1934), and Zhang Tianyi (1906–85) in "Chouhen" (Hatred, 1932) provided revolu-tionary criticisms of Japanese literary works on rural life from genres as diverse as agrarian, modernist, and proletarian fiction. These texts problematize Japanese depictions of rural dynamics and class rela-tions, often deconstructing assumptions concerning peasant life or visions of revolution as a relatively orderly process. Other Chinese revolutionary writers, including Jiang Guangci (1901-31), intertextualized Japanese portrayals of instant political or ideological conversion, providing a more complicated picture of the growth of revolutionary devotion. Some revolutionary writers also (re)incorporated the fragmented perspectives and narrative uncertainty found in Taishō stories such as Akutagawa's "In a Grove" (1922) and Shiga Naoya's "Han no hanzai" (Han's Crime, 1913). Chinese revolutionary playwrights such as Xia Yan intertextualized the work of Fujimori Seikichi (1892-1977) and other Japanese proletarian dramatists, frequently emphasizing Japanese oppression as well as class exploitation within China itself.[124]

In Korea, revolutionary writers such as Cho Myŏnghŭi (1894-1942) composed stories that query those of Japanese proletarian writers like Hayama Yoshiki, often by combining questions of class and colonial oppression. While Im Hwa amended Japanese literary depictions of Koreans, particularly those by Nakano Shigeharu, other Korean proletarian poets, including Kim Kijin, reworked Japanese poems on the proper role of the intellectual by Ishikawa Takuboku and others. Taiwanese writers involved with proletarian literature, including Yang Kui and Lü Heruo, likewise intertextualized progressive texts by Itō Einosuke (1903-59), Kobayashi Takiji, Moriyama Kei, Natsume Sōseki, Nishikawa Mitsuru, and Sasaki Toshirō (1900-33) in multiple ways that defy easy characterization.[125]

Japanese neosensationalist and modernist literatures were especially popular targets of intertextualizing by Chinese, Korean, and Taiwanese writers, who often cast a darker shadow on the glamour of urban life and depicted an intensity of struggle not present in their Japanese antecedents. Characters, images, and scenes in modernist texts by Iketani Shinzaburō (1900-33), Kataoka Teppei (1894-1944), Satō Haruo, Tanizaki Jun'ichirō, and Yokomitsu Riichi—particularly those of the modern girl and the modern city—frequently were reworked in literary creations by the Chinese writers Liu Na'ou, Shi Zhecun, and Mu Shiying, whom some called the Chinese Yokomitsu Riichi.[126] As the Chinese literary historian Xun Si described Mu Shiying several years after his death, stressing the polyintertextuality of his literary production: "A belly full of Horiguchi Daigaku–style witticisms, a Yokomitsu Riichi style of writing, a Hayashi Fusao style of creating new narrative forms, such is the content of Mr. Mu Shiying. Because of this, he made a great contribution to the second decade of new literature in China."[127] Intertextualizing novels and short stories by the Japanese writers Akutagawa Ryūnosuke and Yokomitsu Riichi, Korean modernists such as Yi Sang highlighted the ambiguities and the harsh realities of colonial modernity. One of the most poignant examples of this phenomenon is Yi Sang's intertextualizing of Akutagawa's "A Fool's Life" (1927) and "Haguruma" (Cogwheels, 1927) in his short story "Nalgae" (Wings, 1936). Taiwanese modernists likewise reappropriated numerous Japanese literary motifs, including depictions of Tokyo, Yokohama, and other major Japanese cities in their own creative work; they often drew attention to the disparity between urban life in the metropole and that in the colony, mainly Taipei.[128]

East Asians, particularly Koreans, likewise targeted Japanese modernist poetry.[129] Yi Sang's oeuvre contains much intertextualizing of verse by Hagiwara Sakutarō, Haruyama Yukio (1902–94), Kitasono Katsue, and Ueda Toshio (1900–82). His poems replicate distinctive punctuation, specialized vocabulary, and images that appear in the Japanese texts, but they frequently bring out the alienation and the ambivalent position of the colonial Korean artist. Like Haruyama, Yi Sang uses *katakana* (the Japanese phonetic alphabet for loan words) to transcribe Japanese speech that ordinarily would be written in *hiragana* (the Japanese phonetic alphabet for Japanese-derived speech). But whereas Haruyama writes out Western loan words and Japanese-derived parts of speech in *katakana*, Yi Sang reverses common usage, employing *hiragana* for Western loan words and *katakana* for Japanese-derived speech. As William Gardner has observed: "the 'abnormal reversibility' of Yi Sang's poetry is the uncanny mirror image of a Japanese modernism that is already embroiled in the twinned geopolitical situations of Western and Japanese imperialism."[130] Similarly, in his reworkings of poetry by Hagiwara Sakutarō, Kanbara Ariake, Kawaji Ryūkō, Miki Rofū, Shimazaki Tōson, and Ueda Bin, the Korean poet Chu Yohan repeats punctuation and vocabulary while accentuating depictions of grief, homesickness, loss, and alienation. One good example of this phenomenon is Chu Yohan's poem "Samidare no asa" (Morning of Early Summer Rain, 1916), which intertextualizes Miki Rofū's poem "Sariyuku gogatsu no shi" (Poem of Departing May, 1909). Both texts feature May scenes with blossoms scattering, but Chu Yohan intensifies the sorrow expressed in Miki Rofū's poem by transforming sunny skies into a rain-swept firmament, the overgrown, neglected garden into a graveyard, and nostalgia for the departing spring into a sinking soul and teary eyes; in the Japanese poem, it is memories that "secretly cry," not the poet himself.[131]

The poet Chŏng Chiyong's urban images, especially the cafés, and his depictions of the nonhuman contain distinct reminders of poems by Hagiwara Sakutarō, Kitagawa Fuyuhiko (1900–90), and Kitahara Hakushū, yet he often injects a greater sense of malaise. Poems by Kim Kirim (1908–?), another of Korea's leading modernist poets, share close ties with texts by Anzai Fuyue (1898–1965), Hagiwara Sakutarō, Haruyama Yukio, Kitahara Hakushū, Hirato Renkichi (1894–1922), and Kitagawa Fuyuhiko, but they separate themselves from their Japanese predecessors through an intensification of the empirical world. For its part, Hagiwara's blue cat was a particularly popular target of transcultural intertextualization. It reappears in poems by Hwang Sŏk-u—such as "Pyŏkmo ŭi myo" (Cat with Blue Hair, 1920)—in addition to those by Kim Hwasan (1905–70), Yi Changhŭi (1900–29), Yu Ch'ihwan (1908–67), and others, often as an even more sobering presence than in Hagiwara's collection *Aoneko* (The Blue Cat, 1923).[132]

Taiwanese poets also challenged aspects of Japanese modernist poetry. The oeuvre of the avant-garde writer Lin Yongxiu intertextually reconfigures poems by Maruyama Kaoru (1899–1974) and Tachihara Michizō (1914–39), while Yang Chichang intertextualized Japanese surrealist poetry by Hishiyama Shūzō (1909–67), Kitasono Katsue, Nishiwaki Junzaburō, and Sakamoto Etsurō (1906–69). In their intertextual transculturations, Lin Yongxiu and especially Yang Chichang intensified images of injury and resentment. Other Taiwanese poets wrote haiku and *tanka* that manipulate Japanese verse. Early twentieth-century Chinese poetry contains less intertextualizing of Japanese verse than do its Korean and Taiwanese counterparts, largely because of the secondary status of poetry in the early twentieth-century literary hierarchy. But among those that address Japanese texts, poems by Bing Xin and Guo Moruo rework Japanese *tanka*, haiku, and *shintaishi* (new poetry), particularly writings by Ishikawa Takuboku and Senge Motomaro (1888–1948). Complex intertextualizing of Senge Motomaro's oeuvre also appears in Zhou Zuoren's colloquial poems, including "Cangying" (Flies, 1920), as do hints from the work of Ikuta Shungetsu, but Zhou Zuoren often depicts a more unforgiving picture of human beings and their environments than do his Japanese predecessors.[133]

Postwar discussions of literature from occupied Manchuria have tended to focus on how this corpus counters extratextual Japanese discourse, including patriarchal rhetoric.[134] Contemporary declarations also diverted attention from intense intertextual relationships. In 1941, one official announcement asserted, "We use the Japanese literature that has been transplanted to this land as the warp, and the literature of the several original peoples [of Manchuria] as the woof. We assimilate the essence of world literature and create a completely independent literature."[135] By emphasizing the warp and woof of a group of texts as together weaving a hybrid and independent literature, rather than individual texts themselves as engaging closely with multiple predecessors, this understanding threatens to preclude dynamic intertextualizing. But in fact, writers in occupied Manchuria, like their counterparts in Korea, Taiwan, and China proper, also reworked Japanese creative texts. Some of the strongest connections appear to have been in the genre of "native place" literature, with Chinese writers such as Liang Shanding (1914–96) transculturating texts by key Japanese figures such as Kunikida Doppo, Shimazaki Tōson, and Satō Haruo in ways that underline the gap between conditions in Manchuria, Japanese imaginings of Manchuria, and Japanese depictions of their own *furusato* (native place).[136]

Further Intertextual Transculturation of Japanese Literature

As Ah Long's novel *Nanjing* demonstrates, Japanese battlefront literature was a particularly complex target not only of Chinese-language translation, but also of Chinese intertextualization. For their part, Taiwanese intertextually reconfigured Japanese wartime propaganda, including Murakami Genzō's (1910–2006) "Sayon no kane" (Bell of Sayon, 1941), reworked by Wu Mansha (1912–2005) as "Shayang de zhong: Aiguo xiaoshuo" (Bell of Sayon: A Tale of Patriotism, 1943); because he could not read Japanese, Wu Mansha based his story not on Murakami's script but on a performance in Taipei of the play based on Murakami's script. The Taiwanese version accentuates the sacrifices Taiwanese are making for the Japanese and exhibits even more patriotism than its Japanese predecessor.[137]

Chinese and Korean dramatists likewise frequently intertextualized plays, poems, and prose by their Japanese counterparts, offering further ripostes to Japanese cultural hegemony. The Chinese playwright Tian Han engaged actively in his own work with texts by Akita Ujaku, Ishikawa Takuboku, Kikuchi Kan, Tanizaki Jun'ichirō, and Yamamoto Yūzō (1887–1974). Tian Han's plays often provide harsher portraits of society and tend to be more sociopolitically engaged than the Japanese dramas he intertextualizes.[138] In Korea, the leading dramatist Kim Ujin published several plays that confront Arishima Takeo's writings by raising more insistent questions of agency.[139] Literature by Japanese women was not a major target of intertextualizing for colonial and semicolonial writers, but some Chinese and Koreans were particularly moved by the work of the Japanese feminist Yosano Akiko (1878–1942), citing her essays and creative output at the same time that they called attention to hardships facing colonial and Chinese women of which their Japanese counterparts were oblivious. Short stories by Higuchi Ichiyō also were a target of intertextualization, particularly by the Korean writer Kim Wŏnju (1896–1971), who changed her given name to Ilyŏp (the Korean rendering of Ichiyō) in honor of her Japanese predecessor; Kim Ilyŏp's oeuvre provides a more despairing vision than does Ichiyō's of the obstacles facing young East Asian women. Finally, we should keep in mind that Japanese studies of literature often provided the foundation for Chinese, Korean, and Taiwanese literary criticism.

Crossing Vectors

Chinese, Korean, and Taiwanese intertextualizations of Japanese literature formed the largest trajectories of early twentieth-century intra-East Asian intertextual transculturation. But like their interpretive and interlingual counterparts, they crisscrossed with numerous other intra-empire intertextual vectors. Just as British, French, and other writers from European metropoles frequently transculturated the literary production of their (post)colonial counterparts in their creative work, so did Japanese writers intertextualize colonial and semicolonial writings. Chinese, Korean, and Taiwanese myths and folktales provided fertile ground for some Japanese writers, including Nishikawa Mitsuru and Satō Haruo. Even larger numbers intertextualized contemporary Chinese, Korean, and Taiwanese drama, poetry, and prose in their creative work. To give just several examples: Nakano's poem "Shinagawa Station in the Rain" (1929), intertextualized by the Korean poet Im Hwa in "Yokohama Pier under the Umbrella" (1929), itself reworks the Korean revolutionary writer Yi Pukman's poem "Tsuihō" (Exile, September 1928).[140] Akutagawa's short stories "Juriano Kichisuke" (1919) and particularly "Konan no ōgi" (Fan of Hunan, 1926) intertextualize Lu Xun's story "Yao" (Medicine, 1919), while his stories "A Fool's Life" and "Cogwheels" intertextualize Lu Xun's story "Regret for the Past: Juansheng's Notes" (1925).[141] At times, Japanese intertextualization of Chinese, Korean, and Taiwanese literary works accentuated the naïveté and backwardness of colonial and semicolonial peoples, but in some cases it indicated respect for East Asian counterparts. Scholars are beginning to reveal the extent to which (post)imperial European literatures have engaged with (post)colonial literatures, and it is likely that further inquiries into Japanese intertextualization of other East Asian literatures will garner similar results.

Also important is inter-(semi)colonial intertextualization, particularly Korean and Taiwanese transculturations of Chinese literature.[142] The Taiwanese poet Yang Hua's (1906–36) seeming imitation of texts by Bing Xin and Guo Moruo deeply troubled contemporary critics, who complained that he was too subservient.[143] Other Taiwanese writers were subtler in their transculturations. Manipulated intertexts from Lu Xun's writings appear frequently in stories by Taiwanese writers such as Cai Qiutong (1900–84), Lai He (1894–1943), Yang Yunping (1906–2000), and Zhong Lihe (1915–60).[144] Taiwanese intertextualizations of Lu Xun at times provide even more explicit portrayals of helplessness and defeat, but also closer ties between the intellectual and his/her place of birth. Gu Ding (1916–64), referred to by some as the Manchurian Lu Xun, also intertextualized his Chinese predecessor, as did Korean writers such as Chang Hyŏkju and the poet Yi Yuksa.

Liang Qichao's output proved fertile for Korean writers as diverse as An Kuksŏn, Ch'oe Namsŏn, Han Yong-un (1879–1944), Pak Ŭnsik (1859–1926), Sin Ch'aeho (1880–1936), and Yi Haejo (1869–1927); these and other Korean intellectuals frequently intertextualized his arguments to promote reform in Korea.[145] Prose by Ch'ae Mansik (1902–50) and Hyŏn Chin-gŏn contains distinct ties with the work of Lao She: all three writers were concerned with the plight of women and the poor and the difficulties facing modern (semi)colonial intellectuals. Intertextualizing Chinese literature, some Korean writers, including Yi Sang, underlined the more desperate condition of colonial intellectuals when compared with their semicolonial Chinese counterparts as depicted by writers such as Yu Dafu. Chinese and Korean writers also wrote solidaristic portrayals of one another: Ba Jin, Guo Moruo, Jiang Guangci, and other Chinese addressed the dolor of colonial Koreans, while texts by Ch'oe Sŏhae (1901–32), Han Sŏlya

(1900–76), and other Korean writers express empathy for their Chinese counterparts.[146] Intertextualization of Korean literature in Taiwanese texts, and of Taiwanese literature in Korean texts, is relatively rare. Exceptions are the Korean writers Chang Hyŏkju and Kim Saryang and the Taiwanese writers Long Yingzong, Lü Heruo, Yang Kui, and Zhou Jinbo (1920–96)—all of whom wrote in Japanese—whose creative work is linked by a variety of intertexts that at times express solidarity with the dilemmas facing their East Asian neighbors and at times indicate more competitive relationships.[147]

These examples of intertextualization are suggestive, not comprehensive. They confirm that surprisingly large numbers of East Asian literary works were transculturated intertextually, as well as interpretively and interlingually. Exploring the multifaceted relationships among creative works allows us to appreciate more deeply processes of transspatializing texts and transtextualizing spaces, and the place of textual production, transculturation, and contact nebulae in empire and its aftermaths. We are only beginning to understand how East Asian writers grappled with one another's literary products and how the resulting ambivalent networks blur and accentuate boundaries among early twentieth-century Chinese, Japanese, Korean, and Taiwanese literatures and cultures.

SIX

Spotlight on Suffering

Suffering is a universal human experience and a central focus of literature. It is as difficult to imagine a literature that does not discuss suffering as it is to imagine a life without suffering. When attempting to translate seemingly untranslatable pain, literature in some sense compromises the unfathomable. But it also illuminates anguish in ways other discourses cannot. It offsets medical records that dehumanize the individual; it challenges scientific and historical accounts that focus primarily on facts and figures while remaining silent concerning personal experience. Notwithstanding his assertion that to write poetry after Auschwitz is barbaric, even Theodor W. Adorno conceded that art "may be the only remaining medium of truth in an age of incomprehensible terror and suffering."[1] Many, including the German artist Anselm Kiefer (1945-), have gone so far as to suggest that art can redeem humanity.[2]

Literary portrayals of suffering are a principal focus of dynamic intertextualizing, writers at once drawing inspiration from and engaging with creative predecessors. The frequent permutations of Dante's hell in literatures from around the world, the incarnations of the monster *taowu* in Chinese literature, the overturning of conventional depictions of violence in twentieth-century literature of atrocity, and the recasting of metaphorical prisons of male discourse in writing by women—these are some of the examples that spring immediately to mind. But their attention to local anguish against the backdrop of empire and its aftermath makes the reconfiguration of suffering especially intriguing in literary contact nebulae, and in (semi)colonial and post(semi)colonial dynamic intertextual transculturating of literary works from (former) metropoles in particular. Whether implicitly or explicitly rectifying imperial expressions of suffering, or inviting comparisons between the experiences of (semi)colonial and post(semi)colonial peoples and their metropolitan counterparts, (semi)colonial and post(semi)colonial writers have actively negotiated with thousands of novels, plays, poems, and short stories from (former) metropoles, intertextualizing them in ways that highlight personal and national anguish. Yet significantly, this urgent intertextualizing often is silent on sources of pain, or it depicts homegrown lethargy and internecine corruption as playing an equal or even greater role than foreign exploitation in the propagation of suffering. Often targeting metropolitan texts while allowing the metropole itself to escape relatively unscathed, intertextualizing embodies the dilemmas facing (semi)colonial and post(semi)colonial writers as they struggle with the diverse brushfires wreaking destruction across their lives and their lands. This was particularly true in early twentieth-century China, where Chinese critiques of their own national character outnumbered condemnations of Japan. But it was also true in colonial Korea and Taiwan, where concern with local corruption was deeply intertwined with anti-colonial rhetoric.

Narratives of suffering are a major part of early twentieth-century Chinese, Korean, and Taiwanese discourse, which is hardly surprising considering colonial and semicolonial East Asia's turbulent history and its clusters of socially and politically committed authors. Korean and Taiwanese intellectuals wrote extensively on the suffering of their peoples. Their Chinese contemporaries defined Chineseness in terms of suffering. As Jing Tsu has noted, "The experience of suffering encapsulated the political and aesthetic mood for an era of individual torment and social anguish. Wrestling torment from the privacy of individual psyches, the idea of suffering or depression (*kumen*) provided an expression for the modern epoch too powerful to be claimed by any individual."[3] Lamented, lampooned, and, particularly in China, often incorporated into a narrative of resilience, suffering appeared prominently in colonial and semicolonial East Asian literatures during the first half of the twentieth century.

Chinese, Korean, and Taiwanese creative texts from this period that spotlight suffering rarely show Japan as completely responsible for the anguish of its colonies and semicolony; in fact, they often do not mention the Japanese at all. Censorship, not to mention frustration with their own societies, led many writers to focus on closer wellsprings of pain. But the relative hesitancy of Chinese, Korean, and Taiwanese literary discourse on suffering to indict the metropole is overshadowed by its propensity for intertextualizing Japanese literature: a number of East Asian colonial and semicolonial novels, plays, poems, and short stories actively interweave transposed fragments from Japanese textual predecessors, some of which were also interpretively and interlingually transculturated, to give new perspectives on suffering. Naturally, intracultural intertextualizations, inter-(semi)colonial intertextualizations, and intertextualizations of Western literatures also reconfigure conceptions of suffering; creative works tend to be polyintertextual, significantly intertextualizing depictions of suffering from several literatures. But transposing Japanese discourse on suffering appears to have been a greater priority than rewriting Western discourse on the topic. This is understandable considering Japan's position as colonial/semicolonial power, invader, and wartime opponent.

Underlining the hardships faced by their own societies, Chinese, Korean, and Taiwanese writers frequently intertextualized Japanese creative works in ways that differentiated their homelands from Japan, implicitly or explicitly exposing them as more brutalized than the metropole, as spaces plagued by even greater burdens. Other colonial and semicolonial writers rectified Japanese portrayals of Chinese, Koreans, and Taiwanese, featuring characters subjected to greater hardships than those appearing in Japanese texts. But not all stopped there. More than simply depicting China, Korea, and Taiwan as worse off than Japan or contrasting Japan with its colonies and semicolony, some intertextualizations portrayed suffering as preventable in theory but nearly inevitable in practice, while others took suffering for granted, interweaving ambiguous silver linings of achievement that do little to diminish and in many cases simply accentuate anguish. By manipulating Japanese literature in this way, intertextualizations foregrounded the pervasiveness and profundity of suffering in colonial and semicolonial East Asia. Depictions of suffering—its causes, manifestations, and consequences, not to mention its exacerbaters, palliatives, and ameliorators—took multiple forms as early twentieth-century Chinese, Korean, and Taiwanese writers grappled at once with quotidian circumstances and literary predecessors, those from Japan in particular.

Colonial and semicolonial dynamic intertextualizations of Japanese literature address four imbricated types of suffering: suffering of unknown origin, suffering resulting from individual, familial, or national lethargy, suffering caused primarily by internecine corruption, and suffering attributable to both internecine corruption and foreign aggression. Generally, texts that redefine suffering of unknown origin depict more intense personal despair than their Japanese predecessors, while those that redefine suffering brought about by lethargy accentuate the poverty of colonial and semicolonial spaces. These two forms of intertextualization depict anguish and poverty as nearly impenetrable edifices, although they do not rule out their being alleviated and even in some cases being replaced by happiness.[4] In contrast, texts that redefine suffering which stems directly from internecine corruption or from a combination of internecine corruption and Japanese aggression tend to interweave colonial and semicolonial humanitarian, technological, and military achievements into their portrayals of Chinese, Korean, and Taiwanese agonies. These achievements are all the more remarkable for the counterpoint they provide with the hostile environment in which they occur, but they ultimately do little to ease suffering and in many cases simply exacerbate it. Together, these four types of dynamic intertextual reconfiguration of Japanese literature show personal suffering of unknown origin and suffering resulting from lethargy, whether personal or national, as more totalistic and difficult to offset than suffering caused by internecine corruption or Japanese aggression. Collectively, these transpositions of Japanese literature present suffering as sparing no one. Whether explicit or implicit, whether rectifying or contrasting, Chinese, Korean, and Taiwanese textual contact with Japanese literature that spotlights suffering negotiates with a wide range of narratives from the metropole, confronting everything from Japanese texts that grumble about excess wealth to those that discuss military advances in China.

Redefining Suffering of Unknown Origins: Spotlight on Despair

Depictions of psychological anguish abound in literature. As Elaine Scarry has commented: "*Psychological* suffering, though often difficult for any one person to express, *does* have referential content, *is* susceptible to verbal objectification, and is so habitually depicted in art that, as Thomas Mann's Settembrini reminds us, there is virtually no piece of literature that is *not* about suffering."[5]

While most plays and prose narratives that feature suffering give some indication as to its sources, poetry is not always so forthcoming. Their compact and fragmented bodies allow poems, should they so choose, easily to elide background information and to focus nearly exclusively on emotion. It is no surprise that a number of Chinese, Korean, and Taiwanese poetic intertextualizations of Japanese literature remain silent about the origins of this anguish. Poems by the Taiwanese modernist Yang Chichang and the Korean symbolist Hwang Sŏk-u are particularly striking in this regard. Yang Chichang in many ways plagiarizes Japanese poetry, lifting entire lines and even stanzas from Japanese poems while changing key words and phrases to accentuate the poet's suffering, but he does not indicate why the poet is in such pain.[6] Hwang Sŏk-u's intertextual reconfigurations likewise depict anguish of mysterious origin that is more intense than what is found in their Japanese predecessors. Denying suffering a source, Yang Chichang, Hwang Sŏk-u, and many other Chinese, Korean, and Taiwanese writers who intertextually transposed Japanese literature in ways that underlined colonial and semicolonial suffering, depicted it as elusive, and poignant, an intensely personal yet universal condition from which escape is unlikely but not impossible.

Transculturating Japanese Verse in Poetry by Yang Chichang

The Taiwanese writer Yang Chichang, who also went by the name Shui Yinping, was a knowledgeable reader of Western and Japanese literature, which he studied at Dai Tōa Bunka Gakuin (Greater East Asia Culture Academy) in Tokyo in the early 1930s. While in Japan, he also engaged in writerly contact, forging friendships with several Japanese creative figures including the neosensationalist Ryūtanji Yū (1901–92) and the leftist Iwafuji Yukio (1902–89), both of whom he met at the Colombin café in Ginza.[7] Not only is much of Yang Chichang's writing on poetry closely tied to essays by Japan's leading avant-garde poets, but his own creative work intertextualizes Japanese modernist poems by Hishiyama Shūzō, Kitasono Katsue, Nishiwaki Junzaburō, and Sakamoto Etsurō, doing so in ways that sometimes depict the Taiwanese poet as enduring greater suffering than his Japanese counterparts.

Beginning with its title, Yang Chichang's poem "Aki no umi" (Autumn Sea, 1935) closely follows Sakamoto's poem "Aki no umi" (Autumn Sea, 1934), save for a small modification of its Japanese predecessor's opening lines.[8] But this alteration makes all the difference. Sakamoto's poem begins: "Hopping–skipping–jumping / on the emerald liquid of the sea // The gull flew up to the distant second-story window / but the blue venetian blinds no longer try to open."[9] In contrast, Yang Chichang's "Autumn Sea" starts: "The whirring gull carried a poem / on the emerald liquid of the sea // and it flew up to my heart's window / but the blue venetian blinds no longer try to open."[10] Both poems feature a seagull that flies up to a window with blinds that appear to be permanently closed. But in the fourth line of Yang Chichang's poem the bird confronts not a blocked second-floor window but a closed heart, a heart that—for unknown reasons—has barricaded itself explicitly against poetry, and implicitly against hope. Futility infuses both poems, which conclude with their poets at sea, under a "bored sky," "catching pointless time" with their fishing gear, but the Taiwanese poem—with its closed heart—points to the presence of deeper anguish.

Other poems by Yang Chichang, including "Moeru hoo" (Burning Cheeks, 1935), engage in obvious polyintertextuality, incorporating lines from several Japanese poems in a way that underscores the immediacy of the colonial writer's anguish. But as is true of "Autumn Sea," "Burning Cheeks" does not explore why the poet is consumed by such feelings. "Burning Cheeks" opens with lines from Kitasono Katsue's "Kazarimado" (Show Window), continues with the Japanese poet's "Hodō" (Paved Road), and concludes with a line from his "Atsui monokuru 5" (Hot Monocle 5):[11]

Gloves of fallen leaves dance
In the flaxen sunset
On chests, on cheeks
The wind warms up in pockets

Autumn mist
Wraps streetlights in soft petals
In the flowing glimmer
of hatred and regret
Cheeks burn in high loneliness

Finely patterned arabesque the name of which I've forgotten
Ears, in the ringing of seashells,
The neighboring dunes
Desolate, by oneself, pity.[12]

The first stanza of Yang Chichang's "Burning Cheeks" reworks Kitasono Katsue's "Show Window," which paints a more accessible horizon:

In place of fallen leaves
The gloves of autumn line up
One on the chest and one on the cheeks
The wind is warming up inside my pockets
Clouds like mandarin oranges
go above glassy skyscrapers[13]

In Yang Chichang's "Burning Cheeks," the poet evokes a scene similar to that in Kitasono's poem but replaces clouds akin to tangerines moving above glassy skyscrapers with a flaxen sunset. Whereas the Japanese poem moves upward, taking the reader from the poet's body to the skyscraper and beyond, thereby overcoming the fallen leaves that he explicitly dismisses in his opening line, the Taiwanese poem begins beneath the setting sun, which although illuminating dancing leaves, restricts the poet's terrain.

Restricted movement results quickly in increased anguish. The second stanza of Yang Chichang's "Burning Cheeks" reworks this poem by Kitasono, "Paved Road":

Autumn mist
Wraps streetlights in soft petals
Closer than hatred, closer than regret
Between hand and hand
Fallen leaves stream
Cheeks of pedestrians shine like the crests of pampas grass[14]

The Taiwanese poem retains the first two lines of the Japanese poem, and both poems talk of hatred and regret. But whereas the Japanese poem depicts these two emotions as mitigated by fallen leaves, in the Taiwanese poem they are part of the flowing glimmer. Moreover, while in "Paved Road" the Japanese poet speaks of the pedestrians' cheeks as "shining," in the Taiwanese poem they are said to burn in great loneliness. In sum, the first stanza of the Taiwanese poem "Burning Cheeks" differentiates itself from its Japanese predecessor by creating a more enclosed environment, while the second stanza of "Burning Cheeks" underlines the proximity of hate and regret.

The third and final stanza of "Burning Cheeks" reworks part of this poem by Kitasono, "Hot Monocle 5":

Holding a broken beer bottle
On rocks at the seashore
I hear a horse
My hat is also torn
Desolate, by oneself, pity[15]

Both poets sit alone by the ocean, and both poems include the line "desolate, by oneself, pity," but Yang Chichang's narrator is more isolated from the world around him; unlike his Japanese counterpart, his memory is failing, and he hears the traces of sounds (the "ocean" ringing in seashells) rather than sounds themselves (the horse). Combining two complete Japanese poems and a line from a third, "Burning Cheeks" intensifies the expressions of psychological anguish—including anger, hatred, and isolation—voiced by its Japanese predecessors. Yang Chichang's textual foundations are readily apparent to those familiar with the work of Kitasono Katsue, the Taiwanese poet luring the reader into a familiar environment only to pull out the rug from underneath. But as in many intertextual transculturations of Japanese literature that highlight colonial and semicolonial suffering, the source of his emotional trauma remains enshrouded.[16]

Appropriating Hagiwara's *Blue Cat* in Korea

Hagiwara Sakutarō, generally acknowledged as one of twentieth-century Japan's greatest poets, burst onto the literary scene in 1917 with the publication of his first collection, *Howling at the Moon*, which not only was an immediate success domestically but quickly became a text in motion and a target of intra–East Asian textual contact. *Aoneko* (Blue Cat, 1923), his second anthology, attracted even greater attention both at home and abroad. This collection, which features a blue, melancholy cat, is punctuated by the frequent use of the word *yūutsu* (depression, melancholy).[17] The cat proved compelling to colonial and semicolonial writers, particularly Korean poets, and reappeared in verse by Hwang Sŏk-u, Kim Hwasan, Yi Changhǔi, and Yu Ch'ihwan.

Hwang Sŏk-u's recasting in "Cat with Blue Hair" (1920) of Hagiwara's "Aoneko" (Blue Cat) from the anthology *Blue Cat*, is particularly powerful. A pioneer of Korean symbolism, Hwang Sŏk-u earned a degree in politics and economics from Waseda University in Tokyo and after returning to Korea was an active contributor to *P'yehŏ* (Ruins) and other literary journals. Having published in Japanese poetry journals and struck up friendships with Japanese writers such as the poet Miki Rofū while in Japan, Hwang Sŏk-u was well versed in modern Japanese poetry, which he transculturated interpretively, interlingually, and intertextually.[18]

Just as in Yang Chichang's creations, the story behind the affliction articulated in Hwang Sŏk-u's "Cat with Blue Hair" remains unspoken. The move from "Blue Cat" to "Cat with Blue Hair" suggests the move from the true blue (native) Japanese to colonial Japanese subjects who are clothed, or clothe themselves in Japaneseness, but are not seen as blue to the core, and thus are forever regarded as inferior by Japanese and often by themselves. Ultimately, however, the Korean poem is silent on external causes, featuring instead a poet—perhaps the beggar who appears in the final lines of Hagiwara's poem—who claims that at the desolate place where his "soul takes a nap," a cat with blue hair, looking at his lonely heart, said:

> (Child, all your
> agony and all your fate
> I will make them boil
> in love similar to my burning life
> only if your heart
> becomes the sun
> of our world,
> only if it becomes Christ).[19]

"Cat with Blue Hair" alludes to a more desperate world than that which Hagiwara describes in "Blue Cat":

> Ah, able to sleep in the night of this large city
> is but the shadow of a single blue cat
> the shadow of a cat that tells the sad history of humankind
> the blue shadow of the happiness that I'm forever seeking.
> Whatever shadow I'm seeking
> Even on sleety days I long for Tokyo and think,
> Leaning there cold, against an alley wall
> What dreams is a beggar like this person dreaming?[20]

As often happens in colonial and semicolonial dynamic intertextualization of Japanese creative works, Hwang Sŏk-u's poem "Cat with Blue Hair" moves the setting from what Hagiwara describes as the "beautiful city" of Tokyo, with its fine architecture and lively streets, to the more barren landscape of an unspecified place we can assume is Korea or at least Japan as experienced by Koreans. Even more important, the narrator of "Cat with Blue Hair" plays off of Hagiwara's reference in the second stanza of the Japanese poem to "the shadow of a [blue] cat that tells the sad history of humankind." In the Japanese poem, this reference is followed by additional chatter about the poet's longing for Tokyo and the image of a beggar sitting on a rainy street, but the Korean poem talks about the blue cat itself, turning the shadow into a feline that points to the "sad history of mankind" and tantalizingly suggests how the poet's sorrow might be released.

In the Korean poem, the blue cat mysteriously tells the poet that he will "burn all [the poet's] agony and fate," but only if his heart "becomes the sun of our world" and only if it "becomes Christ." The poet's heart likely can no more become the sun than it can become Christ. Not only does the Korean poet suffer in a way the Japanese poet does not, the longing for Tokyo in "Blue Cat" having been transformed into "agony and fate"; suffering also is depicted as virtually impossible to overcome. As with much intra-empire intertextualizing of Japanese literature, the "sad history of humankind," mentioned in passing in the Japanese "Blue Cat," is accentuated in the words of the cat in the Korean "Cat with Blue Hair."[21] Like numerous counterparts, Yang Chichang's "Autumn Sea" and "Burning Cheeks" and Hwang Sŏk-u's "Cat with Blue Hair" headline the presence of anguish of unknown origin, either by inserting suffering where there was none or by carefully recrafting textual articulations of suffering to underline its potency, and in many cases near inevitability, in the colonial and semicolonial context.

Redefining Suffering Spawned by Lethargy: Spotlight on Poverty

Chinese, Korean, and Taiwanese dynamic intertextualization of Japanese literature that spotlights agonies of indeterminate origin constitutes only one row of the imbricated rooftiles of narratives on suffering that occupy a central position in the architecture of early twentieth-century colonial and semicolonial East Asian writing. Forming another key row is dynamic intertextualization that depicts suffering stemming primarily from lethargy, whether that of an individual, a family, or a society. More frequently than not, these texts focus on poverty, which although not a signal of lethargy, often is its result.

Rampant poverty afflicted much of early twentieth-century East Asia. To be sure, an influx of modernity patterned after the West inundated Japan in the late nineteenth and early twentieth centuries, making it the envy of Asia. Electricity, trains, the telegraph, and newspapers, soon followed by bicycles, sewing machines, magazines, pianos, records, radios, neon lights, café-bars, and elegant department stores, greatly enhanced life for the well-to-do in Japanese cities, especially Tokyo. But recent scholarship on the *moga* (modern girl) and *mobo* (modern boy) notwithstanding, only a small percentage of the population could take advantage of foreign imports and their domestic reconfigurations. Hundreds of thousands of impoverished Japanese city dwellers lived in unbearable slums, and in farm villages much of the population struggled for survival. In the northern prefectures, crop failures and famines occurred regularly. Until the end of World War Two, rural areas remained little touched by the changes occurring in urban milieus. Records left by destitute peasants, novels such as Nakatsuka Takashi's (1879–1915) *Tsuchi* (The Soil, 1910) and Arishima Takeo's *Kain no matsuei* (The Descendants of Cain, 1917), and prose works by Tokuda Shūsei capture well the acute misery many late nineteenth- and early twentieth-century Japanese experienced. Despite great increases in the nation's wealth and power, only a sliver of the population enjoyed a life cosseted by so-called modern amenities.[22]

Even so, the poverty in which much of the Japanese population was immured generally was not as pervasive as that experienced by semicolonial Chinese or colonial Koreans and Taiwanese, whether in Japan or at home. In certain industries, Chinese workers with elite jobs made a comfortable living, but China's economic growth—particularly in urban areas such as Shanghai—failed to reach not only the vast majority of city dwellers but also hundreds of millions of people in the countryside. Farmers and laborers throughout China endured terrible privation that was exacerbated by natural disasters such as the 1931 floods on the Yangzi River. For most, food was scarce and living conditions were primitive. As Jonathan Spence has noted, "In the absence of accurate data, all one can do is acknowledge that the variations of suffering were endless, and that as impoverished families died out, others emerged to take over . . . their struggle for survival."[23] Except for small pockets of urban wealth, Korea and Taiwan suffered similar fates; even Koreans and Taiwanese who worked in high positions in the colonial government did not enjoy the same material comforts as their Japanese colleagues.

Considering how poor and lacking in basic infrastructure much of East Asia was in the early twentieth century, it is not surprising that Chinese, Korean, and Taiwanese writers intertextualized Japanese literary works to underline the indigence of their people, both at home and abroad. Employing interfigurality (similar characters), intertitularity (similar titles), and other creative techniques, colonial and semicolonial writers implicitly and explicitly distinguished the experiences of Japanese from those of Chinese, Koreans, and Taiwanese. For instance, in the short story "Pitiful People" (1934), the Korean writer Pak T'aewŏn appropriates a familiar trope of the Japanese I-novel, the "impotent male intellectual inhabiting an upstairs room with his mental angst."[24] In remarkably similar scenes, Sun-gu, the protagonist of "Pitiful People," and Takenaka Tokio, the central character of Tayama Katai's prototypical I-novel *The Quilt* (1907), despondently huddle in dirty quilts. But while it is grief at losing his young protégé Yoshiko that drives Tokio into this corner, it is Sun-gu's despair at his abject poverty that drives him to seek refuge in one of the few things remaining in his room. Furthermore, whereas the dirt on the quilt in "Pitiful People" is an unmistakable mark of poverty, in the Japanese novel it is mediated by the familiar scent of Yoshiko, which awakens in Tokio a mixture of desire, sorrow, and despair.[25]

Even more powerful are Chinese, Korean, and Taiwanese literary works that intertextually confront Japanese texts expressing anxiety, however tongue-in-cheek, over what is perceived as overabundant food or modern conveniences for the urban well-to-do. In their acerbic yet sometimes subtle intertextualizations of these Japanese works, colonial and semicolonial writers accentuated the absence in their lands of the resources and amenities about which Japanese texts voice discontent. In so doing, they exposed — implicitly and explicitly — the differences between the lives of wealthy Japanese and those of Chinese, Koreans, and Taiwanese both at home and in Japan. What is more, dissatisfied with simply describing colonial and semicolonial poverty, they also addressed its causes, not the least of which was lethargy, whether individual, familial, or national in scale. Two prominent instances of this phenomenon are the Korean writer and devoted reader of Japanese literature Kim Dong-in's short story "Potatoes" (1925), which intertextualizes the Japanese writer Kunikida Doppo's short story "Beef and Potatoes" (1901), and the prolific Chinese translator of Japanese literature Zhou Zuoren's essay "Reading on the Toilet," which reworks the Japanese writer Tanizaki Jun'ichirō's essay "In Praise of Shadows."

Losing Sustenance, or Where's the Beef?

Kim Dong-in's short story "Potatoes" intertextually transposes Kunikida Doppo's short story "Beef and Potatoes" by contrasting the provisions available to wealthy Japanese and the malnutrition and near starvation of a Korean couple. But the Korean story also explores the origins of their poverty and suggests that the destitution experienced by the protagonist Poknyŏ and her husband is not inevitable. The confrontation with "Beef and Potatoes," which features a character who complains about the difficulties of farm life while lamenting a surfeit of potatoes, begins in the title "Potatoes": beef was a coveted luxury among the wealthy in Meiji Japan but was even more difficult to obtain in colonial Korea, where ordinary potatoes — as the story demonstrates — were precious commodities for many.[26] While the title of Doppo's short story points to a surplus, that of Kim Dong-in's points to an absence.

Doppo, whose texts frequently portray the individual's confrontation with an indifferent universe, was an important transitional figure in modern Japanese literature: Japanese naturalists and romanticists both pegged him as one of their own, but his texts appealed to a broad audience.[27] Korean and Chinese students in Japan in the early twentieth century first encountered Doppo's stories in textbooks, and many read his oeuvre outside of class. Intertexts from his stories appear in the creative products of numerous colonial and semicolonial writers.[28] Kim Dong-in, one of the founders of modern Korean fiction and a pioneer of Korean naturalism and realism, lived in Japan from 1914 to 1919; there he attended Meiji Gakuin and the Kawabata Bijutsu Gakkō (Kawabata Art School) and read Japanese and European literature in earnest.[29] Kim Dong-in's fiction intertextually transculturates modern Japanese literature from writers as diverse as Akutagawa Ryūnosuke, Arishima Takeo, Iwano Hōmei, Kunikida Doppo, Kikuchi Kan, Mushakōji Saneatsu, Tanizaki Jun'ichirō, Tayama Katai, and Tokuda Shūsei. But the challenge "Potatoes" launches against Doppo's "Beef and Potatoes" is one of the most significant, not only because of its powerful, albeit implicit contrast between living conditions in Japan and Korea, but also because of its exposure of apathy as partly responsible for this state of affairs.

Doppo's story records the conversation of a group of young men, members of the elite Meiji Club in Tokyo, on the relationship between "ideals" and "reality." The men speak in metaphors, ironically equating "ideals" with potatoes and "reality" with meat. Kamimura, the most vocal of the group, argues: "Ideals are a side dish to reality! It would be troubling not to have any potatoes at all, but completely annoying if there were only potatoes."[30] Discussing food in this manner, the members of this club immediately indicate their separation from the realities of the marketplace; in Meiji Japan, as in most societies, beef was more an "ideal" than were potatoes. Moreover, these wealthy young Japanese men take for granted the ready availability of food itself. Kamimura talks about the difficulties of being a potato farmer in Hokkaido, a vocation he had long idealized and briefly attempted; like many young urban Christians of his generation, Kamimura earlier had scoffed at his status-conscious and money-grubbing peers in Tokyo and had thought longingly of Japan's newest prefecture. But having experienced life in Hokkaido, he complains about the primitive living conditions on his farm and the reduction of his diet to little more than potatoes.

The removal of beef from Kim Dong-in's title begins the unraveling of "Beef and Potatoes" in the Korean story "Potatoes." Potatoes are presented as an "ideal" in both short stories, but in "Potatoes," unlike its Japanese predecessor, they are an "ideal" in the very real sense that they are almost impossible to obtain. Meat, incidentally, is completely absent in the Korean story. Unlike "Beef and Potatoes," which begins with a reference to the Western-style building that housed the Meiji Club, the Korean short story, which describes lives eked out in extreme poverty, opens grandly with: "Strife, adultery, murder, theft, begging, incarceration—the slums outside Ch'ilsŏng gate were the source of all the world's tragedies and stormy scenes."[31] Kamimura found life in Hokkaido difficult, but conditions there hardly compare to the life of the poor in Pyongyang, colonial Korea's leading industrial city. "Potatoes" focuses on the trials of Poknyŏ, a young woman sold to a slothful farmer. Kicked off their land, Poknyŏ and her husband become the poorest of the poor in Pyongyang and are reduced to stealing potatoes. The narrator outlines Poknyŏ's desperation and rapid fall into prostitution, painting a much grimmer portrait of existence than does "Beef and Potatoes." Whereas in the Japanese story Kamimura grows and then flees a surfeit of potatoes, many of the characters in "Potatoes" must steal just to obtain food. The wealthy young men of "Beef and Potatoes" jest that life would be "troublesome" without potatoes; "Potatoes" points to just how "troublesome" life has become without them. In fact, Poknyŏ and the other villagers steal from Chinese, not fellow Koreans, suggesting that, at least in this part of Korea, Koreans are more impoverished and thus perhaps lazier than Chinese.

Kim Dong-in's short story portrays Koreans as in more dire straits than both their Chinese neighbors and the Japanese characters in Doppo's story. On the other hand, "Potatoes" does not depict them as entirely the playthings of powers beyond their control. The ultimate demise of Poknyŏ and her husband stems from indolence, not outside circumstance. Early in the story, the narrator reveals that Poknyŏ's in-laws have been losing assets for some time and that her husband used his last 80 wŏn to purchase her. But the narrator then turns quickly to the role Poknyŏ's husband plays in the couple's unraveling: "He was an exceptionally lazy person. The village elders had used their influence to get him a sharecropper's plot, but he just scattered the seeds about, and ignored his plot. . . . He kept this up, and within a few years had so completely lost everyone's sympathy and trust that he no longer was able to obtain a plot in the village."[32] After Poknyŏ's family cuts off support, the couple moves to Pyongyang, where they become day laborers, then live-in servants. Once again, the laziness of Poknyŏ's husband is their Achilles' heel, and the couple eventually has no choice but to move to the slums outside Ch'ilsŏng Gate. Here Poknyŏ becomes a prostitute to support herself and her husband, but eventually her jealousy of her customer/lover Wang's new wife leads to her demise: she threatens to murder Wang's bride, and he in turn murders her. Although unfortunate, the fall of Poknyŏ and her husband is not inevitable; "Potatoes" depicts the couple as squandering numerous opportunities to extricate themselves from destitution and despair. The implication here is twofold. On the one hand, suffering—at least suffering caused by poverty— might be unbearable, but it theoretically is not inexorable. In practice, on the other hand, suffering is inevitable, at least for those, "Potatoes" suggests, who cannot escape from lethargy.

Okamoto, one of the young men conversing in "Beef and Potatoes," claims that his single wish is to be surprised: "I don't want to know the marvels of the universe. I want to be surprised by them."[33] Bored with existence, he longs for stimulation. Needless to say, the characters in "Potatoes," many of whom are fighting for survival, are not given the luxury of such ennui. Kim Dong-in's evocation of Doppo's "Beef and Potatoes" underlines the scarcity of food among the poor in colonial Korea, particularly when compared with what is available in the pantries of wealthy Japanese, and it ridicules the complaints of rich intellectuals such as Kamimura, whose definitions of hardship and poverty are far removed from those of Poknyŏ and her husband. Curiously contrasting Japanese elites not with their Korean counterparts but rather with Korean beggars leaves the story ample room to negotiate; suggesting but never asserting outright that Koreans in general have it much worse than Japanese, "Potatoes" highlights economic disparities both within and across borders. Moreover, depicting starvation as hardly a given, "Potatoes" precludes the shifting of accountability to forces over which the individual, regardless of nationality, has no control.

Overflowing Waste

The controversial Chinese intellectual Zhou Zuoren's essay "Reading on the Toilet" (1935) confronts Tanizaki's essay "In Praise of Shadows" (1934) even more directly than Kim Dong-in's "Potatoes" does Kunikida Doppo's "Beef and Potatoes." Rather than employing intertitularity to point in part to metropolitan and colonial/semicolonial difference, "Reading on the Toilet"—which includes references to a range of predecessors—not only explicitly compares conditions in China and Japan but also cites directly from "In Praise of Shadows." More important, it moves the focus from individual to national lethargy, paradoxically depicting poverty, or at least unclean sanitary facilities (indicators of poverty), as both inevitable and avoidable. Zhou Zuoren's essay, a humorous soliloquy on toilets as reading venues in East Asia from antiquity to the present, transforms the aesthetic lament of its Japanese predecessor on the surfeit of the modern into a commentary on China's and rural Japan's lack of modern infrastructure.

One of twentieth-century Japan's most prominent writers, fascinated with both ancient and contemporary China and best known for his powerful evocations of desire, Tanizaki acquired a distinct following among Chinese, Korean, and Taiwanese readers and writers. Intra-empire interpretive and interlingual transculturation of his prose took place on a broad scale. Intertextualization of his creative works appears most prominently in texts by the Korean writer Kim Dong-in and the Chinese writers and dramatists Ba Jin, Guo Moruo, Ouyang Yuqian, Tian Han, Yu Dafu, and Zhou Zuoren, all of whom studied in Japan. For his part, Zhou Zuoren wrote extensively on both modern and premodern Japanese culture, and he translated and intertextually reconfigured numerous Japanese creative works.[34] But despite Zhou Zuoren's deep engagement with Japanese culture and Tanizaki's enthrallment with China, the two did not meet until 1941.[35]

"Reading on the Toilet" initially likens sanitary facilities in China with those in Japan, but soon it distinguishes between them, combining discussion of Zhou Zuoren's own experiences in Chinese and

Japanese bathrooms with references to earlier musings on toilets, including Chinese and Indian Buddhist texts, Chinese essays, the Ming vernacular novel *Water Margin*, and Tanizaki's "In Praise of Shadows." Like many writers, although more openly than most, Zhou Zuoren engages a diverse array of antecedents, at times contradicting them to mark difference and at times using their comments to support his assertions. In fact, "Reading on the Toilet" opens with a lengthy citation from "Ruce dushu" (Reading on the Toilet), a section of the Qing commentator Hao Yixing's (1757–1825) *Shaishudang bilu* (Notes from the Studio of Airing Books in the Sun), that Zhou Zuoren immediately disputes: "Hao Yixing's comments are very interesting, but I disagree slightly, since I very much approve of reading on the toilet."[36] Employing intertitularity, Zhou Zuoren displaces a Chinese predecessor. But his negotiations with Tanizaki's "In Praise of Shadows" in "Reading on the Toilet" stand out, not only because they occupy more space than those with any other discourse, but also because "In Praise of Shadows," published just a year before, is the only contemporary text invoked. The struggle with Tanizaki thus is more urgent than that with the other texts brought into play in this brief essay.

"Reading on the Toilet" depicts toilets in rural Japan as similar to those in both urban and rural China; the essay describes facilities and practices in Zhejiang province, Nanjing, Kijō (in Miyazaki prefecture, Japan), Beijing, Dingzhou, and the Ryukyu Islands. Difficulties abound wherever Zhou Zuoren travels. Visiting toilets in Nanjing means walking down streets past piles of garbage; toilets in Beijing are exposed to the elements; toilets in Dingzhou are infested with pigs; and even though the latrine in rain-soaked Kijō is protected by a roof and door, it stands inconveniently in the middle of a field. Zhou Zuoren not only draws implicit parallels between the sanitary facilities in outlying and impoverished areas of Japan and those in China, but he also explicitly likens Chinese toilets to those in rural Japan, claiming the toilets in Dingzhou are "the type used in the Ryukyu Islands."[37] The Japanese did not gain undisputed control over the Ryukyus until the conclusion of the Sino-Japanese War (1895), but the islands long had been on the economic and conceptual outskirts of Japan.

Yet all is not equal. To be sure, Zhou Zuoren likens toilets in rural Japan to those in urban and rural China, as well as those in medieval Japanese Buddhist monasteries to those in their ancient Chinese and

Indian equivalents. But he also marks the stark difference between facilities in contemporary Japanese and Chinese monasteries. Furthermore, while remaining silent on conditions in Japan's cities, he implies that urban Japanese have it much better than their Chinese counterparts. In the second part of "Reading on the Toilet," Zhou Zuoren contrasts Tanizaki's idealized toilets both past and present with those available in contemporary China. Briefing the reader on the toilets featured in Tanizaki's "In Praise of Shadows," he comments: "In the temples of Kyoto and Nara, the toilets are all in the ancient style. They are dark, but spotless, and are placed in a grove where you can smell the leaves and moss. . . . Squatting in this dark place, with light filtering in through the paper screens, you can lose yourself in thought, or gaze out at the courtyard. The feelings you experience in such a place are truly beyond description."[38] Zhou Zuoren then quotes from "In Praise of Shadows" directly, translating Tanizaki's passage on the toilet as the perfect place to see the moon, listen to the sounds of nature, and enjoy the changing seasons; Zhou Zuoren also cites Tanizaki's claim that Japan's elegant toilets likely have inspired many a haiku poet and that the toilet is the most notable achievement of Japanese architecture.

Zhou Zuoren immediately reveals his unease with Tanizaki's comments, first launching a half-hearted attack: "Tanizaki is after all a poet, so in speaking so eloquently he's probably also dressing things up a bit," but retreating quickly, ambiguously adding: "Here I'm just referring to his [Tanizaki's] choice of words; as far as his meaning goes, there's no mistake."[39] The Chinese writer then discusses the important role monasteries played in the preservation and proliferation of arts in fifteenth- and sixteenth-century Japan and declares that the romantic transformation of toilets was an afterthought. In so doing, he implies that the Japanese are so talented that they were able to create splendid facilities with scarcely a thought. But they were not the only ones. In another twist, Zhou Zuoren praises the analogous concern of early Indian and Chinese Buddhists with sanitation.

Significantly, however, only the Japanese monks have been able to maintain their facilities; Zhou Zuoren distinguishes their supposedly splendid toilets with what is available in the temples of contemporary China. He complains that in 1921, when he was recuperating from an illness at a temple in the Western Hills near Beijing, "there was not a single decent toilet anywhere in the vicinity." And then he launches into a critique of sanitation in China more generally, quoting something he wrote at the time: "I am taken in by the beauty of the mountains and rivers. My only regret is that the area is not very clean, and the road smells something awful [from human waste] . . . I think that China is a very intriguing country. On the one hand, people have great difficulty finding nourishment, but they also have no means of disposing of their waste." Commenting on these earlier remarks, he notes: "Under these conditions, finding a Chinese temple with even basic toilet facilities would be a wonderful thing. . . . If Buddhist monks are so slovenly, how can we expect more from the common people?"[40] The second half of "Reading on the Toilet," based on Zhou Zuoren's personal experiences in China and readings of Japanese texts, proposes a vast gulf between sanitation in contemporary China and parts of Japan. But his ambiguous remarks on "In Praise of Shadows," not to mention the empirical evidence he provides in the first part of his essay, partially undermine such claims.

Particularly interesting here is Zhou Zuoren's reliance on "In Praise of Shadows," a move that complicates "Reading on the Toilet." Although he traveled widely during his many years in Japan and had first-hand experience with the allegedly spotless facilities at Japanese temples, Zhou Zuoren does not refer to these encounters; he instead mentions only his experiences with the accommodations available to Japanese on the margins, leaving it to Tanizaki to describe the facilities enjoyed by Buddhist monks and presumably wealthy urban Japanese. In so doing, he not only suggests that what Tanizaki describes might be nothing more than the products of an active imagination, or at least something off limits for Chinese visitors to Japan, but also points to Tanizaki's great remove from the realities of life for all but a tiny fraction of the Japanese population, a remove evident throughout "In Praise of Shadows." In this essay, Tanizaki repeatedly laments the loss of what he terms the "world of shadows" to the bright lights and sparkling fixtures of the West, but he ignores the poverty that continues to plague large swaths of Japan, not to mention the Japanese empire, and says little concerning the difficulties of life "in the shadows" for those without financial security.[41] Including descriptions of toilets in outlying areas of Japan in other parts of his essay, Zhou Zuoren undermines both Tanizaki's concerns that the porcelain and metal fixtures necessary for affordable indoor plumbing were not designed with Japanese tastes in mind and the Japanese writer's paeans to more "traditional" Japanese lavatories.

"Reading on the Toilet" exposes the vanity of Tanizaki's concern with the clash between "Western" fixtures and "Japanese" sensibility, suggesting that it overlooks the urgent need for hygienic modernity not only in China, a country with which Tanizaki enjoyed intimate ties and that appeared frequently in his creative output, but also in his (Tanizaki's) own backyard.[42] Improving sanitation in China, Korea, and Taiwan was an important part of the Japanese colonial and semi-colonial project, yet most facilities in these lands, and in Japan itself, left much to be desired.[43]

Zhou Zuoren challenges the premise of Tanizaki's "In Praise of Shadows," revealing that praising shadows was relatively easy for the handful whose lives were not confined to the shadows. Just as Kim Dong-in's short story "Potatoes" disputes the complaints of excess food and boredom voiced by the rich young men of Kunikida Doppo's short story "Beef and Potatoes," so too does "Reading on the Toilet" mock the criticism of excessive modernity articulated in "In Praise of Shadows." Both texts draw attention to economic disparities across and within national borders. But while Kim Dong-in's story strongly implies that severe indigence is preventable, that although beef and what it represents likely will remain out of reach for all but a privileged few, it is possible to live comfortably without it, Zhou Zuoren's essay leaves little room for negotiation. He implies that unsanitary living conditions are nearly a foregone conclusion, at least in China: if even the monks are slovenly, he asserts, what can be expected of people in general? Conditions in China are worse than in Japan, but the fault does not rest entirely or even largely with the Japanese, however snobbish their elite and however seemingly limited the vision of their writers. "Potatoes," "Reading on the Toilet," and numerous other Chinese, Korean, and Taiwanese creative works intertextually confront Japanese writings to contrast standards of living in Japan with those of other parts of East Asia. But while underlining the poverty of China and Japan's colonies, they also point to the squandering of agency at home, a more toxic form of human waste than what Zhou Zuoren describes wading through on the smelly streets of Beijing.

Redefining Suffering Brought on by Internecine Corruption

Chinese, Korean, and Taiwanese dynamic intertextualizations of Japanese literary works that redefine suffering of uncertain origin and suffering brought on by lethargy, whether individual or national, generally offer few hopeful prospects. Those that redefine suffering caused by internecine corruption, on the other hand, are somewhat more ambiguous. They tend to accentuate colonial and semicolonial achievement. But considering the suffering out of which they sprout, these achievements are in turn remarkable and unsettling. Three variations of this phenomenon are found in the Chinese revolutionary Zhang Tianyi's short story "Hatred" (1932), the Chinese modernist Mu Shiying's short story "Shanghai de hubuwu" (Shanghai Foxtrot, 1932), and the Korean naturalist Kim Dong-in's short story "Kwang-yŏm sonat'a" (Mad Flame Sonata, 1929). "Hatred," "Shanghai Foxtrot," and "Mad Flame Sonata" reconfigure prose by the Japanese modernist writers Yokomitsu Riichi and Akutagawa Ryūnosuke in ways that draw attention to national corruption as the principal source of suffering. Their emphasis on the greater suffering of Chinese and Koreans than Japanese ironically enables these stories to underscore and undermine Chinese and Korean humanitarian, technical, and artistic achievement.

Redefining Pain, Redefining Solidarity

The repulsiveness of rural life is a common theme in Chinese revolutionary texts, many of which intertextually reconfigure Japanese creative works to contrast conditions in Japan with those in China. But while showcasing abuse of impoverished Chinese, some literary works also offer expanded visions of human kindness. One example is Zhang Tianyi's short story "Hatred," which intertextualizes Yokomitsu Riichi's short story "Time" (1931) by spotlighting the greater hardships indigent Chinese suffer at the hands of their own people than do Japanese; yet at the same time "Hatred" also describes an arc of compassion much wider than what Yokomitsu depicts. "Hatred" implies that Chinese suffering and kindness alike exceed what can be found in Japan.

Yokomitsu was one of Japan's most prominent modernists and a leader of the Japanese neosensationalist school, which often clashed with the naturalist and proletarian literary movements that flourished in East Asia in the 1920s.[44] Peoples across the region consumed Yokomitsu's creations in the original Japanese as well as in Chinese and Korean translation; some readers were ardent fans, while others were highly critical. Yokomitsu's novels and short stories were intertextualized by Chinese modernist writers such as Liu Na'ou, Mu Shiying, and Shi Zhecun, as well as Chinese revolutionary writers such as Zhang Tianyi. Known especially for his socialist satires, Zhang Tianyi joined the Communist Party in 1925 and was one of China's most prolific revolutionary writers. Transposed intertexts from a variety of literatures are readily apparent in his creative work, including reconfigurations of Anton Chekov (1860–1904), Gogol, Maupassant, and Zola.[45] Zhang Tianyi's ties to Japanese literature were more tenuous, but he likely was familiar with this corpus through his mentor Lu Xun. As with most implicit intertextual reconfigurations, we cannot be certain of how consciously Zhang Tianyi was reworking Yokomitsu's short story "Time" in "Hatred." However, the many parallels between these two stories convincingly point to dynamic reconfiguration.

Both Yokomitsu's "Time" and Zhang Tianyi's "Hatred" follow a starving group on their journey through an unforgiving countryside, graphically describing the difficulties they endure. The suffering of the characters in "Hatred" is significantly greater than that of the characters in "Time," largely because of widespread national corruption: "Time" depicts several misanthropes as bringing the impoverished group to ruin, whereas "Hatred" blames China's military. Condemned to a world without sustenance, the characters populating "Hatred" are denied the relatively happy ending of "Time." Yet Zhang Tianyi's story expands not only notions of suffering but also ideas of human solidarity. "Time" paints a moving portrait of individuals with a long history who work together, however reluctantly, to ensure the survival of all group members. In contrast, "Hatred"—like other colonial and semicolonial intertextualizations that differentiate conditions in the Japanese metropole with those elsewhere in Asia—indicates as well the breakdown of barriers among and the potential unification of similarly subjugated groups.

"Time" reveals the plight of a drama troupe that has been abandoned by its manager. Unable to pay for their room and board thanks to unscrupulous colleagues who steal what money their vanished manager sends them, the remaining twelve members eventually decide to run off together. Reluctantly carrying Namiko, the weakest of the group, they break away one rainy night. The remainder of the story discusses their painful journey along a treacherous unfamiliar mountain road to nowhere. Similarly, "Hatred" centers on a tattered group of people forced from their homes who trudge along an endless road. The starving group in "Time" endures numerous hardships, but the narrator of "Hatred" intertextually rewrites key elements of

Yokomitsu's short story to underline the greater burden borne by his characters. Among other things, blood gushes more profusely and painfully in "Hatred" than in "Time." In the Japanese story, Namiko suffers from an unnamed illness but survives despite losing large amounts of blood. The private bleeding in "Time" becomes public and more severe in "Hatred," where the group encounters a civilian labor conscript bleeding profusely from gaping wounds infected by swarms of insects. Namiko's illness is a particularized, individual problem, whereas the conscript's mortal injuries apparently are a result of the endless internal fighting among warlords that plagued early twentieth-century China.

The narrator of "Hatred" also inverts the final scene of "Time." In the Japanese story, the thirsty troupe discovers a moonlit stream of water that magically rescues them from total dehydration. The characters of "Hatred," on the other hand, search unsuccessfully for water and are exposed not to soft moonlight but to a scorching and lethal sun. They depart the story as they entered—walking through the desert: "Yellow earth and yellow sky. The crimson sun. The edges of heaven and earth baked until they curled. Together they lifted up their blistered feet and moved forward on the burning sandy soil."[46] Tellingly, the only liquid here is trapped in blisters.

"Time" is narrated in the first person and "Hatred" in the third, suggesting that the characters in "Hatred" are too weak to tell their own story. But at the same time that he emphasizes Chinese suffering, the narrator of "Hatred" reconfigures the small-group consciousness depicted in "Time" as the consciousness of all exploited peoples, projecting a very different image of camaraderie and solidarity. In "Time," the twelve members of the drama troupe vow to work for one another. But relationships are strained even before departure, and circumstances deteriorate on the road: suspicions and accusations fly fast and furious, while fights abound and questions arise about obligations to Namiko, whose condition continues to deteriorate. Yet esprit de corps prevails, and the final scene offers a dramatic albeit saccharine picture of group cohesion:

I asked everyone to think of a way of getting water to Namiko. . . . Sasa suggested that it would be quickest if the remaining eleven of us lined up and passed the hat along in a relay. . . . We stood in the moonlight, at intervals of about twenty feet. . . . [After the hat came] I poured the few remaining drops into Namiko's mouth and for the first time she opened her eyes . . . another hat came and I poured the drops into her mouth. As I did this again and again I had a vision of my companions calling to one another as they toiled to scale the steep cliffs by the spring, their tired bodies illuminated by the moonlight. I poured the drops of water in the sick woman's mouth as though they were drops of moonlight.[47]

In contrast, the Chinese story "Hatred" argues both for group cohesiveness and for unity of the oppressed. While traveling across the landscape, a group of characters is confronted by a terrible smell and then a cry emanating from a bleeding Chinese civilian on the brink of death. Although themselves in pain, they stop to assist this stranger who was kidnapped, gashed, and tossed aside. They clearly recognize that the fate of this man, Wu Dalang, could have been their own, and they refuse to abandon him, instead watching over him until he dies. These individuals no sooner vow to retaliate against the violence done to Wu Dalang by attacking the first soldier who crosses their path than they spot three combatants straggling along. They easily capture these destitute men and, ignoring their pleas for mercy, vow to make them suffer. But the narrator indicates that, far from deserving such treatment, these soldiers instead are to be pitied. As the angry group pummels the hapless troops, the narrator informs the reader that these soldiers once were civilians "who likewise hated army slobs. They once were just like the people attacking them, but suffering from unbearable hunger, they ran off. . . . They are three solitary men in this baked and scorching world."[48] When one of the soldiers starts to cry, the group for the first time asks about their backgrounds. Learning that these three once were destitute men who joined the army only to ward off starvation and who quickly grew disillusioned with life on the battlefield, the group calls off their assault. The story ends with former soldiers and civilians together trudging across the desert. "Hatred" thus skillfully intertextualizes "Time," not only underlining the greater suffering Chinese experience at the hands of their own people but also portraying their compassion and solidarity as extending well beyond the immediate group, their kindness triumphing—at least temporarily—over brutality.

Randomness and the Modern City

Whereas Zhang Tianyi's "Hatred" implicitly contrasts conditions in China with those in Japan, Mu Shiying's short story "Shanghai Foxtrot" rectifies Japanese depictions of China, particularly those in Yokomitsu's novel *Shanhai* (Shanghai, 1931). As a matrix of Chinese modernity—a cosmopolitan metropolis, China's largest city (and the fifth largest in the world), the center of its publishing industry, and home to several foreign concessions[49] — early twentieth-century Shanghai captured the imaginations of writers the world over.[50] Yokomitsu Riichi's *Shanghai*, one of modern Japan's best-known creative works on China, narrates the experiences and conflicting emotions of Japanese expatriates living in Shanghai. Set amid the turbulence of 1925 — the May Thirtieth Incident, when Chinese workers in Shanghai, outraged by the murder of several compatriots at a Japanese textile mill, went on a massive strike; as well as increasing tensions over national sovereignty — the novel addresses many of the pressing political and social crises facing Shanghai, China, and East Asia in the mid-1920s. Differentiating itself from *Shanghai*, Mu Shiying's "Shanghai Foxtrot" removes nearly all discussion of these tumultuous events, replacing random politics with randomness and providing an even more troubling vision of the modern. It portrays the city as more brutal than does its Japanese predecessor, but also highlights the city's technological achievements. Just as the humanitarianism of the bedraggled travelers in the short story "Hatred" is magnified by their suffering, so too in "Shanghai Foxtrot" the flashing strobes of Shanghai seem all the more illuminating contrasted with the struggles for survival taking place in the darkness below.

Mu Shiying did not meet Yokomitsu until the late 1930s, but he was long an ardent reader of the Japanese neosensationalist.[51] He and other colonial and semicolonial modernists such as Liu Na'ou and Shi Zhecun actively reconfigured novels and short stories by Yokomitsu, Kataoka Teppei, and the gamut of Japanese neosensationalists. But the ties between Mu Shiying's and Yokomitsu's writings were particularly intricate, leading some to call him the "Chinese Yokomitsu." Korean, Taiwanese, and particularly Chinese neosensationalist writers were as fascinated with the "modern" — the modern girl, modern technology, modern entertainment — as their Japanese counterparts, but their intertextual transpositions of Japanese literature often cast an even darker shadow on the supposed glamour of city life. Some of their works, including Mu Shiying's "Shanghai Foxtrot," a fragmented short story that incorporates many of the experiments with language, space, and time that characterize Japanese and European modernist writings, additionally underscore technological advances and other material signs of modernity downplayed in many Japanese accounts of the Chinese city.[52]

"Shanghai Foxtrot" features a writer who, thinking of a possible novel on the city, implicitly dismisses Yokomitsu's portrayal of Shanghai:

Off to the side a long-haired unshaven writer looking at this absurdity. He thinks of a title: Chapter 2 pilgrimage—inspect the city's dark side SO-NATA . . . (The writer thinks:) chapter 1 pilgrimage gambling den chapter 2 pilgrimage street corner prostitutes chapter 3 pilgrimage dance hall chapter 4 pilgrimage what's more *The Eastern Miscellany, Fiction Monthly, Literature and Art Monthly* first sentence write the prostitution trade on Dama Road Beijing Street . . . . . . won't do.[53]

The first sections of this character's imagined work correspond loosely with the opening segments of Yokomitsu's novel, where prostitutes accost Sanki (the protagonist), the narrator reveals Sanki's apprehensions concerning shady monetary dealings at his firm, and Kōya (a childhood friend of Sanki who has come to Shanghai looking for a wife) and Yamaguchi (a longtime friend of Kōya) meet up in a dance hall. But the writer in "Shanghai Foxtrot" is not content with Yokomitsu's configuration and dismisses the narrative of his Japanese predecessor, declaring emphatically: "this won't do." The struggle with foreign texts is more difficult than imagined. Following a woman home, the writer in Mu Shiying's story reaffirms his desire to create but soon appears overwhelmed with foreign texts: "China's tragedy here is certainly material for a novel the year 1931 is my time *The Eastern Novel, North Star* every month a volume Japanese translations Russian translations translations from every country all publish Nobel prize and great and get rich."[54]

Appearing toward the conclusion of Mu Shiying's text, these passages cast "Shanghai Foxtrot" in a new light. The short story that initially presents itself as a fragment providing slivers of Shanghai street and dance hall life circa 1930 here reveals that it also is in direct competition with Japanese and other foreign texts, particularly those that offer a "foreign" view of Shanghai. The rivalry with Yokomitsu's *Shanghai* seems especially strong, in large part because of the Japanese writer's stature with Chinese modernist writers who generally emulated his creations with gusto, not to mention the recent Japanese seizure of Manchuria, alluded to but not discussed.

Yokomitsu's novel depicts Shanghai as a turbulent cesspool. As Gregory Golley has observed, "The confluence . . . of flesh and matter [in *Shanghai*] offers a grim parody on the sensory shock and material proliferation of modernity, unveiling the final ignominious phase of the chaotic process of production and consumption: the story of decay, of exhaustion, and, finally, of disposal."[55] But in "Shanghai Foxtrot," the city and its Chinese residents are truly desperate. The contrast between the opening scenes of *Shanghai* and "Shanghai Foxtrot" is notable: while the Japanese novel begins with talk of boats, cargo, and the busy river on which the city relies, "Shanghai Foxtrot"—which starts off "Shanghai. Paradise built on the surface of hell!"—speaks of "ashen wilds." Similarly, whereas Sanki, the first person appearing in Yokomitsu's novel, a man with the face of a "medieval hero," is confronted by prostitutes who pose no real threat, the first character introduced in "Shanghai Foxtrot" is accosted by men in black who murder him in cold blood.[56]

Sanki, who has been away from Japan for years, often feels as though his life is a series of jumbled episodes with no real purpose. Declaring, "I don't have a country, much less money," like many expatriates he never really feels as though he belongs.[57] The many lives Yokomitsu paints, caught up in the political and social turmoil of the era, brim with suffering and unanswered questions. But conditions in "Shanghai Foxtrot" are even worse. Here the city's rhythm is random, its beat arbitrary, its circular movements leaving no room for escape.[58] The Chinese short story provides a harsher assessment of the ills plaguing the modern city; its Shanghai is populated by a revolving series of paper figures who appear on deadly streets only to disappear quickly into sewers. The Chinese tale exposes the semicolonial city as an even more dangerous and senseless site than does its Japanese predecessor, a city where meaning is stripped from life and death.

Yet at the same time, "Shanghai Foxtrot" presents the city as more technologically advanced than does its Japanese predecessor, which begins in the fog and contains few evocations of the city as frequently depicted in early twentieth-century Chinese creative works, with new styles and technologies and illuminated by powerful flashing electric lights in a rainbow of colors.[59] In addition to the cars, electric trams, trains, and their accessories (horns, lights, rails, barriers) that crisscross the narrative, Mu Shiying's story refers repeatedly to high-speed elevators, endless rows of telephone poles, neon lights penetrating darkness, buildings popping up right and left, and elegant hotels. On the other hand, "Shanghai Foxtrot" makes no secret of the high price of these transformations, describing how new construction is nourished by the blood of workers killed on the job: "The corpse is removed. In the empty lot: ditches horizontal and vertical, steel bones, debris, still a pile of his blood. On the blood, spread cement, build up steel bones, a new restaurant rises up! A new dance hall rises up! A new hotel rises up! Take his strength, take his blood, take his life crushed beneath."[60] Bones and blood are mixed inextricably with construction materials, human beings the foundations on which buildings are erected.

Performing Violence in the Name of Art

Featuring a sadistic artist, Kim Dong-in's short story "Mad Flame Sonata" looks even more closely than "Shanghai Foxtrot" at the ramifications of condoning violence in the name of achievement. Violence is one of many sources of artistic inspiration. Most discussions of violence and art depict the artist as the chronicler of violence committed by others, not as the perpetrator of violence. However, a few of the world's most renowned artists—including Giotto di Bondone (c. 1267–1337), Michelangelo Buonarroti (1475–1564), Benvenuto Cellini (1500–71), Leone Leoni (1509–90), and Gianlorenzo Bernini (1598–1680) also were criminals, if not murderers.[61] Legends surrounding Michelangelo, in fact, declare that he "nailed some poor man to a board and pierced his heart with a spear, so as to paint a Crucifixion." Similarly, Giotto "bound a man to the cross . . . seized a dagger, and, shocking to tell, stabbed him to the heart! He then set about painting the dying agonies of the victim to his foul treachery."[62]

Not surprisingly, some creative texts portray artists who commit acts of physical or discursive violence at least in part to obtain inspiration for their art. Generally, these literary works are metaphors of the extreme measures that can be taken in the struggle to attain greatness. Among them are a handful of early twentieth-century Japanese texts, including the short stories "Shisei" (The Tattooer, 1910) by Tanizaki Jun'ichirō and "Jigokuhen" (Hell Screen, 1918) by Akutagawa Ryūnosuke; and the plays *Tōjūrō no koi* (Tōjūrō's Love, 1918) by Kikuchi Kan, and Mushakōji Saneatsu's *Lust* (1926) and *Aru gashitsu no nushi* (Master of a Certain Atelier, 1926).[63] These texts focus primarily on the psychology of the sadistic male artist and underline the brilliance of his artistic creations. They interrogate what it takes to create powerful works of art and propose that some individuals reach their maximum creative potential only after violating women; they portray women as expendable and suggest that the sacrifice of a woman is a small price to pay for a great work of art.[64] Largely evading discussion of the broader ramifications of sacrificing life for art, "The Tattooer," "Hell Screen," *Tōjūrō's Love*, *Lust*, and *Master of a Certain Atelier* depict society as reacting favorably toward work by an artist for whom violence is an integral part of the creative process.

The colonial Korean writer Kim Dong-in's short story "Mad Flame Sonata" (1929) intertextualizes these creative works, asking deeper questions about justifying violence and exploring which sacrifices—if any—should be made to create what are believed to be superior cultural products.[65] Reappropriating the figure of the violent artist, "Mad Flame Sonata" features a composer who repeatedly sets fires, defiles corpses, and commits murder to inspire his creation of artistic masterpieces. This story exposes the social consequences of continually condoning violence, issues only cursorily addressed in the Japanese texts "Mad Flame Sonata" reconfigures. In an immediate sense, "Mad Flame Sonata" is more critical both of artists who commit violence and of those who celebrate their work. In a more general sense, the Korean story expands on its Japanese predecessors by questioning forcefully when, if ever, violence can or should be excused. Transcultural intertextual analysis discloses the subtle and not so subtle ways the colonial writer transposes questions of the relationship between suffering and greatness posed by his counterparts from the imperial power.

"Mad Flame Sonata" contains a variety of intertexts from the Japanese creative works listed above, but the most significant literary confrontations occur between this story and "Hell Screen." Yoshihide and Sŏngsu—the protagonists of "Hell Screen" and "Mad Flame Sonata"—both depend on the fiery destruction of life and property for artistic inspiration. The narrator of "Mad Flame Sonata" replaces the painter Yoshihide, who sacrifices his daughter to create the painting of his dreams and then is so plagued with guilt that he commits suicide, with the composer Sŏngsu, who sets fires to countless buildings and murders untold numbers, all in the name of art. "Hell Screen" satirizes both the individual whose commitment to greatness makes him oblivious to the integrity of life beyond his person and a public so blinded by greatness that it condones violent actions. "Mad Flame Sonata" goes even farther: it brings out the consequences of condoning continued human sacrifice, namely, a landscape of terrible suffering, filled with charred bodies and buildings, garlanded with art of debatable value. It also questions the validity and necessity of trading human life for human creation. Ultimately, "Mad Flame Sonata" dismisses works born out of violence committed by the artist as possessing only fleeting value; exposing artistic greatness as a lethal fantasy, the story argues against violence in the name of greatness.

The narrator of "Mad Flame Sonata" presents individuals who, threatened with the loss of their culture, are even more desperate to obtain outstanding works of art than those in Akutagawa's story. Indeed, in Kim Dong-in's story, the renowned music critic Mr. K argues that artistic masterpieces do not simply embellish the edifices where they are displayed; they also elevate the culture of the land of their creator. K claims that Sŏngsu's compositions are "jewels that forever will brighten our culture," that they are "monuments of our [Korean] culture."[66] But K's desperate desire to advance "our culture," even at the expense of life and property, blinds him to contradictions in his own argument. Ironically, in his attempt to justify Sŏngsu's behavior, K also reveals that violence is not a prerequisite for greatness. K complains to his companion X, an "enlightenment specialist," that artists are slaves to imposed artistic guidelines and tells X that society needs artists who do not conform to the artistic "rules" handed down from above. Here K conflates breaking the rules of art (prescribed form and content) with violating the norms of social conduct (laws protecting life and property). In so doing, he implies that the absence of truly powerful art stems less from a dearth of burning buildings and dead bodies than from excessive compliance with pre-established artistic conventions and the failure of artists to experiment and take creative risks.

"Mad Flame Sonata" also challenges society's justification of violent acts by arguing that extreme measures are not the answer; the story not only depicts violence as unnecessary for greatness but also dismisses the "greatness" born out of violence as ephemeral. Near the end of their conversation, K tries to convince X that Sŏngsu's crimes are legitimate by arguing that Sŏngsu is a genius who appears "only once every thousand or ten thousand years" and that society has long been waiting for another Beethoven. Yet ironically, Sŏngsu is not the only artist whom K compares to Beethoven. Earlier in the story, K notes that Sŏngsu's father possessed a creative ferocity that "we haven't seen since Beethoven," one that "doesn't exist in modern composers."[67] K reveals that Sŏngsu's father never attained fame equal to his son's because his classmates did not think to transcribe his compositions, not because he was any less of a genius.

Similarly, although at the conclusion of "Mad Flame Sonata" K refers to Sŏngsu's creations as "monuments of our culture," earlier he reveals that Sŏngsu's notes actually lose considerable power after transcription and states that subsequent performances of his compositions, whether by Sŏngsu or another musician, are a disappointment. X suggests this is because the environment of the second performance is not as stimulating as that of the first. In other words, Sŏngsu not only depends on inspiration gleaned from criminal acts to create musical scores; the successful performance of these scores also requires circumstances of extreme destruction. K and X refer repeatedly to Sŏngsu's "great works," but the value of these compositions drops quickly, and they fail to inspire other artists. The hell screen of "Hell Screen," "a priceless treasure" even decades after Yoshihide's death,[68] is reappropriated in "Mad Flame Sonata" as musical compositions that—despite such fiery titles as "Mad Flame Sonata," "Angry Waves," and "Melody of Blood"—are surprisingly short-lived. Intertextualizing "Hell Screen," Kim Dong-in's short story makes the case that greatness does not depend on violence and that whatever greatness is born out of violence is fleeting. It demonstrates how, if violence goes unchecked, a charred landscape might be all that remains. On the other hand, the narrator's note at the beginning of "Mad Flame Sonata" that his protagonist Sŏngsu can also be thought of as "as an Albert, a Jim, a Mr. Hu [Chinese], or a Mr. Kimura [Japanese]" suggests that the talent of Koreans is no different from that of Chinese, Japanese, and Westerners; as the case of Sŏngsu's (nearly forgotten) father demonstrates, as a society, Koreans simply need to cultivate their talent more productively.

Intertextually transculturating works by the Japanese modernist writers Yokomitsu and Akutagawa, Zhang Tianyi's short story "Hatred," Mu Shiying's short story "Shanghai Foxtrot," and Kim Dong-in's short story "Mad Flame Sonata" portray Chinese and Korean suffering as greater than that experienced or imagined by Japanese. Yet spotlighting suffering also accentuates Chinese and Korean achievement. This phenomenon is a staple of those Chinese, Korean, and Taiwanese creative texts that rework Japanese writings so as to emphasize the local origins of colonial and semicolonial suffering. But it becomes even more striking in those intertextual reconfigurations that also evoke Japanese exploitation and aggression.

Redefining Suffering from Internecine Corruption and Foreign Aggression

Many early twentieth-century Chinese, Korean, and Taiwanese literary works that intertextualize Japanese creative texts in ways that highlight the physical and psychological pain experienced by colonial and semicolonial societies go one step farther by denouncing Japanese imperialism as at least partially to blame for the agony of their peoples. But as in the three stories discussed above, the emphasis on the greater suffering endured by subjugated societies does not preclude discussions of local achievement. Like "Hatred," the Taiwanese writer Yang Kui's short story "Behind Increased Production: The Tale of an Easygoing Old Man" (1944) emphasizes both Taiwanese suffering and humanity; like "Shanghai Foxtrot" and "Mad Painter," the Chinese writer Ah Long's novel *Nanjing* (1939) combines suffering and material successes, in this case military. Additionally, both "Behind Increased Production" and *Nanjing* refer explicitly to their Japanese predecessors, Natsume Sōseki's novel *Kōfu* (The Miner, 1908) and the wartime novels of Hino Ashihei and Ishikawa Tatsuzō, respectively. Directly tackling literary works by acclaimed Japanese writers, these Chinese texts are quintessential examples of transcultural literary struggle and negotiation in the hothouse of artistic contact nebulae in empire.

The Perils of Mining and Misreading

The prominent Taiwanese writer Yang Kui, who like many colonial and semicolonial East Asian writers was long an earnest reader of Sōseki,[69] intertextually reconfigured the latter's often forgotten novel *The Miner* in his short story "Behind Increased Production." Narrated in the first person, *The Miner* is the story of an educated young man who leaves Tokyo in despair after a relationship crumbles, is hired by a man procuring laborers, and determines to lose himself in the mines. The protagonist tells the reader something of the life of Japanese miners but dwells primarily on his own perceptions and experiences and spends pages analyzing himself, virtually ignoring his surroundings. "Behind Increased Production," also narrated in the first person, similarly describes an intellectual's visit to the mines, but under circumstances very different from those in *The Miner*: unlike his Japanese predecessor, he is dispatched by Japanese authorities. Hoping to encourage Taiwanese sacrifice and commitment to the

Japanese war effort, in 1944 the Information Section of the Taiwan governor-general's office commissioned "report literature" from Taiwanese writers; those selected were sent to various production sites to observe conditions and compose fictional accounts of their experiences. For various reasons, Yang Kui abandoned his tactic of nonparticipation and became involved in this project; "Behind Increased Production" is based loosely on his experiences visiting Taiwanese mines.[70] This short story draws attention to the suffering of colonial Taiwanese miners at the hands of Japanese imperialists and Taiwanese collaborators at the same time that it portrays Taiwanese miners as more intelligent and humane than their Japanese counterparts.

"Behind Increased Production" exposes the brutal working and living conditions of Taiwanese miners who have been forced to step up output to support Japan's war effort. To be sure, the narrator misleadingly claims that Sōseki depicts brutal mines and miners and falsely asserts that the Taiwanese are much better off than the Japanese workers in Sōseki's novel. Ultimately, this early reference to *The Miner* mocks Taiwanese misappropriations of Japanese discourse. Based on a blatant misreading of the Japanese novel, it calls into question the narrator's credibility and ultimately casts suspicion on the idyllic portrait that he—as a writer dispatched by the governor-general—attempts to paint of Taiwanese miners enthusiastically doing their part to assist Japan, and on the short story's tendency to idealize Japanese culture.

The narrator of "Behind Increased Production" studies Sōseki's *The Miner* to get an idea of what he will encounter when he visits mines in Taiwan. After seeing things for himself, he states that he is shocked at the disparity between Taiwanese mines and Sōseki's descriptions of Japanese mines: "I read Natsume Sōseki's *The Miner* to get some information [on mines in general] and got the strong impression that mines were gruesome and miners violent, so I was taken aback [by what I witnessed in Taiwan]."[71] This statement is paradoxical in several respects. To begin with, the narrator's mention of *The Miner* suggests that he is well versed in Japanese literature. Sōseki was one of early twentieth-century Japan's most esteemed writers, making an indelible mark on a broad range of genres, but *The Miner* was one of his least popular creations; 40 years after this novel's publication in Japan, only true Sōseki aficionados were likely to be aware of its existence. Yet the narrator's comment that he turned to *The Miner* as a resource on mines betrays his misreading of this text. *The Miner* is far from a reference work on Japanese mines: the novel refers to the dangerous working and filthy living conditions of Japanese miners, but this information is processed through the dense filter of the Japanese narrator's own subjective meanderings.

Second, the narrator's comment that in reading *The Miner* he "got the strong impression that mines were gruesome and miners violent" exposes additional gaps in his understanding of Sōseki's novel, at least as far as its depiction of "violent" miners is concerned. It is true that the narrator of *The Miner* initially likens the miners to savages, yet not only are these interpretations some of his most obviously biased, but also at the end of the novel he realizes the folly of his earlier opinions and rejects them outright. The narrator first declares the miners' faces inhuman, the visages of beasts:

[Their faces] were not ordinary human faces. They were pure miner faces. There's no other way to describe them . . . I couldn't find any trace of roundness, or warmth, or gentleness. In a word, they were savage. Strangely, the savage face seemed to be something shared by the entire group. When the black things beside the sunken hearth turned in my direction, in the blink of an eye there were fourteen or fifteen uniformly savage faces. The group around the sunken hearth on the other side of the room must have had the same faces. The faces that only a few moments ago had looked down on me from the window of the barracks as I climbed the hill were all like this. The faces of all ten thousand men living in the barracks were probably savage.[72]

Yet *The Miner* itself describes very little actual "savagery" and nothing worse than the narrator would have experienced daily in society outside the mines. In addition, although attacked by bedbugs at night and by the miners' glares and taunts during the day, the narrator discovers humanity in the mines in the form of Yasu, a young man who gives him valuable advice at this important juncture in his life. Moreover, at the conclusion of *The Miner* the narrator—having learned he is too ill to work in the mines—takes back his earlier comments on savage miners, concluding that their faces "weren't ugly, or frightening, or hateful. They were just faces. Just as the face of the most beautiful woman in Japan is only a face, so too were the miners' faces only faces. I too was just a human being made up of flesh and bone, completely without meaning."[73] Focusing only on the initial impressions of the narrator of *The Miner* and failing to recognize them as stereotypes the Japanese text itself debunks, the narrator of the Taiwanese short story reveals his study of this metropolitan "guide" as cursory at best. The text of "Behind

Increased Production" thus satirizes the colonial collaborator's misreading of metropolitan discourse.

"Behind Increased Production" also mocks the colonial collaborator's inability and perhaps refusal to acknowledge Taiwanese suffering. The narrator idealizes much of what he sees and hears, declaring that conditions in the Taiwanese mines are not nearly as bad as those portrayed in *The Miner*, but Yang Kui's text itself shows that in fact the Taiwanese mines are even more gruesome than those described in Sōseki's novel. The miners endure appalling living conditions: crowds of people are forced into tiny spaces plagued by leaking roofs and a shortage of materials for fixing them, in one of the wettest areas of the semitropical island. Furthermore, already fatigued and overworked, daily risking their lives in dangerous shafts, the miners of "Behind Increased Production" must accelerate their production to support the Japanese war effort. Satō, their Japanese boss, is surprisingly humane and sensitive to the needs of his charges, and the Japanese are not implicated directly, but there is little question that much of the suffering the Taiwanese miners endure, mitigated but hardly erased by their supposedly cheerful dedication to the metropole, stems from ever-increasing Japanese demands.[74] Japanese, as depicted in this short story, are all too eager to exploit Taiwanese resources and take advantage of Taiwanese labor, and Taiwanese bosses are all too willing to help them accomplish their objectives.

On the other hand, despite their living and working conditions, the miners in "Behind Increased Production" are more intelligent and compassionate than those who appear in *The Miner*, even considering the obvious biases of the narrators of both texts: for much of the novel, the narrator of *The Miner* sees only the workers' negative attributes, and for much of the story, the narrator of "Behind Increased Production" sees miners as little more than smiling workers for Japan. Whereas the miners in Sōseki's novel instantly reject the narrator, assuming that an educated city boy will not last a day in the mines, the Taiwanese miners warmly welcome the narrator of "Behind Increased Production." The latter reports that when his guide, the elderly Taiwanese miner Zhang, learns that his visit has been arranged by the Information Office of the Taiwan governorgeneral and that he will write a story on his experiences, he (Zhang) "clapped his hands happily like a child. He was a so-called ignorant illiterate man but was actually an enthusiastic reader of my writing as well as my teacher."[75] The narrator of "Behind Increased Production" reveals that Zhang is a day laborer who tended his fields and whose mental acumen and rich experiences provided the seeds of many of the narrator's creative works. As one critic of "Behind Increased Production" has noted, "Yang [Kui]'s praise for the miners, male and female, is nearly unqualified; their strengths are his narrator's weaknesses: they are good-natured and constantly aware of each other; they are his teachers—at both manual labor and the labor of the pen."[76] Indeed, unlike the workers in Sōseki's *The Miner*, who do little more than toil, sleep, eat, and taunt the narrator, the miners in "Behind Increased Production" are perceptive, politically aware, and artistically inclined. Not only is Zhang excited about helping the narrator with his latest creative project, but the miners also ask him to write a play for them and criticize the authorities for banning a drama about miners.

Transculturating *The Miner*, Yang Kui's story "Behind Increased Production" highlights at once the hardships Taiwanese must endure because of increasingly severe Japanese demands, and the astuteness and kindness of ordinary Taiwanese in spite of these harsh conditions. Moreover, by explicitly evoking *The Miner* in the opening pages of his story, and ultimately revealing that the Taiwanese intellectual uses this Japanese discourse not to expose the abuses of his people but rather to downplay them, "Behind Increased Production" brings out the ambiguity of the multilayered negotiations with imperial cultural products that take place in literary contact nebulae.

Intertextualizing Texts and Translations

Like "Behind Increased Production," the Chinese writer Ah Long's novel *Nanjing* (1939) intertextualizes Japanese war literature to highlight the abuse of Chinese civilians at the hands of both Japanese and Chinese troops. Yet rather than contrast conditions in colonial/semicolonial spaces with those in Japan, as does Yang Kui's story, *Nanjing* autoethnographically rectifies Japanese discourse on China; the novel, China's first literary account of the Nanjing Massacre, reveals many of the "truths" exposed in Japanese battlefront literature and its Chinese translations as "cover-ups." It at once depicts Chinese suffering as greater than what is acknowledged in Japanese textual predecessors and highlights Chinese military strength.

Nanjing explicitly transculturates four of Japan's major wartime novels: Ishikawa Tatsuzō's *Living Soldiers* and Hino Ashihei's *Soliders* trilogy. In a striking yet not unusual case of intra–East Asian writerly contact, Ah Long learned of Ishikawa's and Hino's novels from Kaji Wataru and Ikeda Sachiko, Japanese antiwar writers living in China. Deeply frustrated that Japanese writers were transforming the atrocities of Nanjing and destruction of other Chinese sites into "masterpieces" while their Chinese counterparts remained silent, and likely also disturbed by the speed with which Japanese war literature was being translated into Chinese, Ah Long argued in the postscript to *Nanjing* that creative texts on the Japanese invasion of China should come from China, not Japan:

> [The Japanese writer Ikeda Sachiko] told me that, in addition to Ishikawa Tatsuzō's *Living Soldiers*, the Japanese recently have published another lengthy report on the war. It [Hino Ashihei's trilogy] naturally extols invasion and war . . . I'm ashamed! For myself, and for the Chinese people. I'm ashamed! . . . And behind the shame, I'm angry! I can't believe these "masterpieces" weren't produced in China, but instead appeared in Japan, that they weren't produced by those resisting the war, but rather by the invaders. . . . This is a disgrace! . . . Does China have "masterpieces"? Of course it does! China has "masterpieces" written in blood! Moreover, if the "masterpieces" written in ink are carbon copies of the "masterpieces" written in blood, then the latter can soon come to light. These works will be greater than Hino Ashihei's *Wheat and Soldiers, Earth and Soldiers,* and *Flowers and Soldiers.* Otherwise, it's China's humiliation! And this is how I finally came to write *Nanjing.* But I don't have wild ambitions. It's just that my heart's angry.[77]

Particularly interesting here is Ah Long's assertion that Japan's "masterpieces" on the war are in fact carbon copies of Chinese texts, but copies that come to light before their sources. Scrambling the usual order of production, he simultaneously confirms and denies Japanese literary authority. Setting off the term "masterpiece" in quotation marks further highlights the ambivalence and the irony of both the Chinese and Japanese projects.

A mix of fiction and reportage, *Nanjing* focuses on the city between November and December 14, 1937; the novel contains longer and more graphic accounts of the destruction wrought by Japanese and Chinese troops in China than do either the Japanese battlefront novels it intertextualizes or the Chinese translations of these novels, examined in Chapter 4. The first chapter of *Nanjing* describes the damage Japanese air raids inflicted on the city and its people: "Yan Long witnessed a strong young man die an agonizing death, roaring like a mad dog, his neck pierced by the branch of a tree blown down by the bombs. He saw the peaceful restaurant where he had celebrated his wedding completely blown away by the bombs. And he also saw a severed bloodstained leg wearing silver high heels rolling down the street."[78]

Nanjing likewise speaks openly of the brutality of Japanese soldiers, particularly toward Chinese women:

> The occupation of Nanjing should have marked the end of the bloodshed, but in fact it marked the opposite. It was the beginning of the bloodshed.
>
> December 13 was a bloody day.
>
> The enemy ransacked the refugee zone and snatched all the money and young people.
>
> Smiling, the enemy held a "contest to behead 1,000 people" at the base of Zijin Mountain.
>
> The enemy invaded Jin Ling Women's University and captured the women.
>
> On the streets the enemy walked around shooting. Blood was flowing in the streets . . .
>
> The enemy stabbed one girl seven times: one gouging her large intestine, one severing her throat, one rendering her blind, one cutting her genitals, one cutting her from her left shoulder to her right buttock.[79]

Even the Japanese are depicted as recognizing the heinousness of their acts: the chapter ends with a Japanese soldier bursting into tears.

Further subverting Japanese war literature, as well as Chinese translations of this literature, *Nanjing* concludes with a Chinese battle victory. The version of Ishikawa's *Living Soldiers* that was to have appeared in the March 1938 issue of *Central Review*, as well as its Chinese translations, closes with Japanese troops leaving a defeated Nanjing and marching to new battlegrounds. In contrast, the epilogue of *Nanjing* depicts Chinese victory at Wuhu, the narrator declaring in the final lines: "Those responsible for the slaughter got their comeuppance. . . . December 20, Chinese troops took Wuhu."[80] Ishikawa's "living soldiers," transformed by the Chinese translators Bai Mu and Xia Yan into "soldiers not yet deceased," here perish.

But in truth, Japanese soldiers in Nanjing were anything but dead on December 20, just a week into the massacre. Moreover, when Ah Long made these remarks in October 1939, the Japanese held an even stronger position in China than at the time of their assault on Nanjing. Here we perceive clearly the struggle of Chinese writers to expose Japanese atrocities while preserving national dignity or perhaps simply their own sanity. The silence of Ah Long's novel concerning events in Nanjing on December 20 and surrounding weeks represents a lost opportunity to counter Japanese denials.

On the other hand, spotlighting the weeks immediately preceding the Nanjing Massacre allows *Nanjing* to expose the atrocities Chinese troops committed against Chinese, a subject for the most part glossed over in literary accounts of this period. The Chinese military not only torched Nanjing as part of its scorched earth policy of destruction of land and property in anticipation of invasion, it also killed and wounded Chinese civilians there.[81] By including graphic scenes of Chinese soldiers abusing Chinese civilians, *Nanjing* stresses more than *Living Soldiers* and especially its Chinese translations joint Chinese-Japanese responsibility. The Chinese troops that in many places are displayed sympathetically, and in the end give the nation hope, also terrorize their own people. Ah Long's novel ultimately reveals unconscious complicity between Chinese and Japanese forces in the destruction of Chinese civilians.[82]

What did Chinese, Korean, and Taiwanese writers hope to accomplish by transculturating Japanese literature in their own creative texts? How troubled were they by smudging the amorphous borders of complicity, acquiescence, and resistance—by incorporating the language of the oppressor into their own work while at the same time challenging and overturning many of its premises? There are no definitive answers to these questions. But we can be certain that Japanese creative output played an important role in Chinese, Korean, and Taiwanese literary discussions of the hardships faced by their societies, if only as an unstated but ominous antagonist.

Early twentieth-century Chinese, Korean, and Taiwanese literatures are suffused with narratives on the difficulties of colonial and semicolonial life, large numbers of which dynamically intertextualize Japanese novels, plays, poems, and short stories. By turning the spotlight on suffering from a variety of sources—everything from unknown origins to homegrown lethargy, internecine corruption, and foreign oppression—colonial and semicolonial intertextualizing of early twentieth-century Japanese literature actively differentiates circumstances at home from those in Japan while also rewriting Japanese portraits of the colonies and China. Works that depict suffering from unknown sources tend to emphasize its near inevitability, while those that describe suffering as resulting from internal corruption alone, or a combination of internecine corruption and foreign aggression, at times highlight colonial and semicolonial achievement, however fleeting. For the most part, these intertextual reconfigura-

tions portray colonial and semicolonial peoples as suffering more severely than do their Japanese source texts, implying that Japanese
have little conception of the misery that plagues surrounding lands.

At the conclusion of the essay "Sifa" (Ways of Dying, 1926), Zhou
Zuoren admits that he was inspired by the early twentieth-century
Japanese poet Masaoka Shiki: "While writing this essay I perhaps
got some hints from Masaoka Shiki's *haibun* [humorous prose piece]
'After Death' [1901]. But all words and ideas are my own."[83] Zhou
Zuoren acknowledges a debt to Shiki, but like many other colonial
and semicolonial writers, he is careful to distance himself from his
Japanese predecessor. And indeed, apart from their respective opening statements on the inevitability of death, "Ways of Dying" shares
very little with Shiki's "After Death" (1901).[84] Whereas Shiki's text
meditates on what happens to the body after death, including cre-
mation and burial, and discusses the writer's own feelings about
death, Zhou Zuoren's essay focuses on the abuses inflicted on the
living body and the great pain it suffers. He includes a disclaimer
that "some of the things I said here are jokes" but adds ominously,
"others are not."[85] Intensified physical and emotional anguish,
whether among human beings in general, as in "Ways of Dying,"
or subjugated peoples in particular, as in many of the texts examined
in this chapter, is one of the hallmarks of Chinese, Korean, and Taiwanese intertextualization of modern Japanese literature. Some of
these transculturations, including Zhou Zuoren's essays "Reading on
the Toilet" and "Ways of Dying," Ah Long's novel *Nanjing*, and
Yang Kui's short story "Behind Increased Production," explicitly cite
Japanese literary predecessors. Many more, such as Kim Dong-in's
"Potatoes," poems by Yang Chichang and Hwang Sŏk-u, Zhang
Tianyi's "Hatred," and Mu Shiying's "Shanghai Foxtrot," are less
open about their ties with Japanese creative works, relying on the
reader to uncover connections. But these literary works and many
others like them share a common rhetoric of textual contact, offering
novel perspectives on suffering. Other Chinese, Korean, and Taiwanese intertextualizations of early twentieth-century Japanese literature, while incorporating questions of colonial and semicolonial
suffering, negotiate even more aggressively with Japanese depictions
of human relationships and agency. It is these essential topics, and
their place in early twentieth-century intra–East Asian literary contact nebulae, that I examine in the next chapter.

SEVEN

Reconceptualizing Relationships:
Individuals, Families, Nations

Probing human relationships is as central to literature as delving into suffering. Even rarer than the creative text silent on suffering is the one unconcerned with human connections, whether inter-personal—among lovers, relatives, friends, comrades, enemies, or strangers—or intrasocietal, between people and their communities or nations. In many literary works, including most of those discussed in the previous chapter, suffering overshadows the relationships complicit in its perpetuation. But relationships themselves are key axes of creative texts, which scrutinize both the diverse networks that tie people together or keep them apart and the powerful roles gender, class, politics, ethnicity, race, language, and nationality play in these webs.

Literary depictions of relationships, like those of suffering, are a major focus of intertextual reconfiguration. We need only recall the frequent recasting of the bond between Odysseus and Penelope, most recently in Margaret Atwood's novel *The Penelopiad* (2005); the con-tinuing permutations of Rama and Sita's relationship (*Rāmāyana*) in literature, film, and other media across Asia; and, in Japan, East Asia, and beyond, the many incarnations of Genji's affairs in later *mono-gatari* (tales), *nō* drama, and a variety of other genres, including film and manga, to the present day. Much dynamic intertextualization of literary depictions of interpersonal and intrasocietal relationships is appropriative, solidaristic, or engrossed, involving the cultural products of relatively unthreatening groups or societies. But intertextualizations of relationships can be more urgent, particularly in (semi)colonial and post(semi)colonial transculturations of literary works from (former) metropoles, where rhetoric tends to be more personal and immediate. In addition to creating identities and cultures, writers actively negotiate with the cultural products of (former) oppressors at times to rectify the latter's depictions of interactions between (semi)colonial and post(semi)colonial peoples and their metropolitan counterparts. The Martinican Francophone writer Aimé Césaire's reconfiguration of Shakespeare's depictions of Prospero and Caliban's relationship in his *A Tempest* (1969) is among the most obvious examples of this phenomenon. Other (semi)colonial and post(semi)colonial intertextualizations of creative texts from (former) metropoles invite comparisons (most frequently contrasts) between the interpersonal and intrasocietal relationships experienced by (semi)colonial and post(semi)colonial peoples and those experienced by their counterparts in/from the (former) metropole. At times — such as in the Taiwanese writer Zhu Tianxin's (1958–) reconfiguration of familial relationships in Kawabata Yasunari's *Koto* (Ancient Capital, 1962) in her novella of the same title (*Gudu*, 1996) — these contrasts are explicit. At times contrasts are implicit, (semi)colonial and post(semi)colonial texts aligning themselves with but not referring directly to predecessors.

Just as they dynamically transculturated Japanese texts to give new perspectives on suffering, so too did early twentieth-century Chinese, Koreans, and Taiwanese transculturate this literature to provide new insights into human relationships, whether intra-(semi)colonial or between colonizer and (semi)colonized. Whether inviting comparison or rectifying, their works point to perceived lacunae in their predecessors. The most frequent focus was the tendency of Japanese creative texts — especially, but not solely, the I-novel — to depict characters relatively detached from society. In their discussions of Japanese literature, early twentieth-century Chinese, Korean, and Taiwanese writers at times chastised members of the metropolitan literary establishment for their personal apathy toward happenings outside their immediate social circles and for featuring characters who shared these attitudes. Dissatisfaction with Japanese creative trends is even more apparent in Chinese, Korean, and Taiwanese literary output, which on the whole depicts characters more deeply tangled in social and national webs.[1] A number of Chinese, Korean, and Taiwanese novels, plays, poems, and short stories go one step further to challenge specific texts from the metropole. They recast Japanese creative works in ways that depict even the most alienated (semi)colonial characters as deeply concerned with something beyond themselves: if not other individuals, then broader social issues or even the nation.

Colonial and semicolonial Chinese, Korean, and Taiwanese intertextualization embodies literary interdependence in subtly and not so subtly calling for an end to fantasies of isolation and urging greater acknowledgement of human sociability. These transpositions can be divided into four overlapping categories: those that highlight the connections between individual protagonists and the people they encounter, especially strangers; those that underscore the embedding of families within societies; those that conjoin the plight of the individual with that of the nation; and those that feature ties between individuals from different nations. Texts of the first three categories generally contrast the experiences of (semi)colonial peoples with those of their metropolitan counterparts, while those of the final category rectify Japanese depictions of relationships between Japanese and (semi)colonial peoples. Literary works by Chinese, Korean, and Taiwanese writers as varied in style, substance, and conviction as Lu Xun, Zhou Zuoren, Yu Dafu, Ba Jin, Yŏm Sangsŏp, Yang Kui, and Im Hwa—whose time in Japan together spanned much of the colonial period—undermine the social separations articulated in poems, short stories, and novels by Japanese writers ranging from Kobayashi Takiji and Nakano Shigeharu to Natsume Sōseki, Shimazaki Tōson, Akutagawa Ryūnosuke, Satō Haruo, and Senge Motomaro. Their texts and other colonial and semicolonial intertextualizations of Japanese literature rarely portray peaceful and integrated societies of politically active people concerned with national welfare and transnational harmony. Instead, they weave an intricate and often imprisoning tapestry that binds individuals inexorably to relatives and strangers, friends and enemies, and the nation. This web can best be likened to an all-encompassing net of chains that have varying degrees of slack: it is within the elasticity or tautness of these chains, not outside them, that characters in Chinese, Korean, and Taiwanese intertextual transculturations of Japanese literature cast different perspectives on the human relationships found in their Japanese literary antecedents and give new meanings to concepts of alienation, liberation, rebellion, and social integration.

Among Strangers

However fleeting, interactions with strangers can be revealing. Emotional baggage appears lighter, with so little time to probe personal histories. Liberty to query the unknown frequently increases, and with it the opportunity to learn more about not only the people one meets but also oneself, one's society, and humanity more generally. Like that of many literatures, early twentieth-century Japanese prose is suffused with characters who squander these opportunities, relegating strangers to part of the nonhuman landscape: they either do their best to ignore those who cross their paths or conversely turn them into imaginary figures over whom they obsess. Such texts were transculturated by Chinese, Korean, and Taiwanese creative works, which intertextually reconfigured them to depict more engaged interactions. But in some cases, colonial and semicolonial recastings in the end reveal such interactions as little more than beginnings, resolving very little if anything at all.

Principal examples of this phenomenon include the rewriting of Akutagawa Ryūnosuke's short story "Tangerines" (1919) in Lu Xun's short story "A Small Incident" (1920) and the reworking of Natsume Sōseki's novel *Pillow of Grass* (1906) in Yu Dafu's short story "Late-Blooming Cassia" (1932). Although neither "A Small Incident" nor "Late-Blooming Cassia" refers explicitly to these Japanese texts, the parallels are striking. There also is no question of Lu Xun's and Yu Dafu's familiarity with Akutagawa's and Sōseki's creative output. Arguably early twentieth-century Japan's most prolific writer of short stories and a favorite among colonial and semicolonial East Asian intellectuals, Akutagawa was one of the many Japanese whose prose Lu Xun translated into Chinese. Like Lu Xun, Yu Dafu was an enthusiastic reader and transculturator of Japanese literature, including texts by Sōseki, who was one of the most frequently reconfigured Japanese writers in colonial and semicolonial East Asia. It is likely that Yu Dafu's intertextualization of *Pillow of Grass* was motivated by his friend Guo Moruo's translation of this novel in 1930, its second translation into Chinese; *Pillow of Grass* was translated into Chinese a third time in 1941. Already present in the Chinese literary landscape in the early 1930s, in part because of its numerous references to classical Chinese literature, *Pillow of Grass* was further intertwined into twentieth-century Chinese literary networks via "Late-Blooming Cassia."

Collapsing Distances in the Short Short Story

The title "A Small Incident" is misleading. The three pages of Lu Xun's short story outline a short episode, and this text itself represents but a tiny part of Lu Xun's literary output. Yet "A Small Incident" also embodies an important trend in early twentieth-century Chinese literature: deconstructing the self-imposed isolation of many modern Japanese literary protagonists. The first-person narrators of "Tangerines" and "A Small Incident" both are travelers filled with ennui who describe how witnessing a stranger's unexpected act of kindness alters their perceptions of existence. Following closely the outline of "Tangerines," the Chinese narrator accentuates interpersonal and intrasocietal connections at four crucial junctures: early laments on life's futility, the disruption of his journey, witnessing a stranger's act of kindness, and transforming consciousness.[2] In so doing, "A Small Incident" exposes the narrator of "Tangerines" as being hopelessly trapped within himself. Yet Lu Xun's narrator is unable to act on his newfound knowledge, paradoxically making his impact on society no different from that of his Japanese predecessor.

"Tangerines" begins with a man traveling alone on a cloudy winter evening in an empty car of a Tokyo-Yokosuka train, wrapped in fatigue and boredom. The narrator of "A Small Incident" similarly begins by reflecting on the banality characterizing current affairs. But unlike his Japanese counterpart, the Chinese narrator does not attempt to escape. Plowing through the newspaper's reports on political affairs and bribery scandals, wedding announcements and obituaries, the narrator of "Tangerines" concludes that everything is absurd: "This train in the tunnel, this country girl, this evening paper drowning in mediocre reports, were nothing but symbols. Symbols of indecipherable, incongruous, and tedious human life."[3] He then tosses out his newspaper and retreats into himself: "I shut my eyes as though I were dead and began to doze off."[4] Oppressed by the banality of existence, which is only exacerbated by modern technology, the Japanese narrator withdraws from both the outside world and its mechanical and textual artifacts.

For his part, despite initial claims to the contrary, the narrator of "A Small Incident" reveals himself as more deeply affected by external events, incapable of drifting off to dreamland: "[Since moving to the capital six years ago] the number of so-called state affairs I have seen and heard is not at all small, but none really has made much of an impact on me . . . I would say only that they have increased my bad temper. Speaking truthfully, they teach me to despise people more each day. But there is one small incident that I thought significant and dragged me out of my funk, and I cannot forget it even now."[5] Remarking that political and other machinations only increase his irritability and exacerbate his disgust with humanity, exposing the persistence in memory of the "small incident," the Chinese narrator suggests that there can be no escape. The narrator of "Tangerines" finds solace in daydreams, but a similar haven is not offered his Chinese counterpart, likely because Chinese society is so imperiled.

A glance at how the voyages of both narrators are interrupted further reveals the elimination of distance that takes place in "A Small Incident." Soot and smoke billowing in from an open window (separating people) disrupts the Japanese traveler, while his rickshaw's collision with a pedestrian (eradicating space between people) cuts short the trip of the Chinese traveler. At first alone in his train car, the Japanese narrator suddenly finds a young girl sitting next to him. She opens the window just as the train is entering a tunnel, letting in smoke and soot that darken the car and cause him distress. In "A Small Incident," on the other hand, an elderly woman steps into the path of the rickshaw, her clothes catch on the vehicle, and she falls to the ground; the driver kindly stops to check on her condition. Neither young man understands why his journey should have been so inconvenienced; the narrator of "Tangerines" nearly scolds the girl, while the narrator of "A Small Incident," thinking the old woman is faking injury, urges his driver to continue on. But entanglements both literal and figurative bring the journey in "A Small Incident" to a close; the distance between bodies has been compressed and contact with strangers—for better or worse—is accentuated.

Comparing the acts of kindness both narrators witness after their journeys are disrupted further illuminates how "A Small Incident" bridges the distances articulated in "Tangerines." In the latter story, the girl's act of kindness involves motion through the window: she tosses bright tangerines to her brothers. In "A Small Incident," on the other hand, the rickshaw driver not only stops to check on the condition of the injured woman but also takes her arm, helps her up, and leads her to a nearby police station. Here, helping others involves physical contact with strangers and requires some personal sacrifice.

The fourth and final point of conjunction between "Tangerines" and "A Small Incident" is the narrators' seeming transformations of consciousness, and it is here that we find the most significant inter-textualization of the Japanese story. Both narrators are so affected by what they have seen that they begin to fantasize. But whereas the narrator of "Tangerines" claims to find new life by escaping inward into his own reveries, replicating to a certain extent his response to stimuli at the beginning of the story, the narrator of "A Small Incident" moves outward. The air in "Tangerines," saturated with soot, suddenly is filled with oranges. Breathless, the narrator declares that he "understands everything." He asserts: "I was conscious of a strange cheerful feeling welling up inside me . . . I gazed at the girl as though she were a different person."[6] He also claims that now he can forget some of his fatigue, some of indecipherable, incongruous, and tedious human life. But the story ends here, with every indication that forgetting leads not to understanding but to inertness.

Circumstances change in "A Small Incident," where the narrator's ominous fantasy leads to action. Believing himself threatened by the driver's retreating yet expanding body (a body that should shrink, not balloon, as the distance between the two men increases), the narrator reflexively — as though to defend his position and prove his superiority — pulls some money from his pocket and asks a policeman to give it to the driver. The narrator is not obliged to give the driver anything: at this time, riders paid only if they were taken to their desired destination. And indeed, pausing to think about what he has done, the narrator is even more baffled by his own behavior than he is by the driver's. What, he asks, was the meaning of his gesture? What right, he implies — turning the dissecting scalpel on himself — does he have to claim superiority via such a piddling act?[7] He questions the dynamics of interpersonal relationships in ways that do not occur to Akutagawa's protagonist.

In his final sentences, the narrator of "A Small Incident" admits that even though the events of years past have mostly faded from mind, he cannot stop thinking about the rickshaw incident: "I've forgotten the politics and the violence of those years just as completely as the classics I read as a child. There is just this small incident, frequently floating up before my eyes, from time to time even more distinct, teaching me shame, pressing me to turn over a new leaf, and increasing my courage and hope."[8] Here he intensifies the opening lines of "A Small Incident," reinforcing previously expressed sentiments. The concluding lines of "Tangerines" also echo comments made earlier in the story, yet to very different effect: the narrator moves even deeper into himself. His experience is an isolated incident that does not significantly impact his future, whereas his Chinese counterpart becomes more determined to change with each retelling.

Both "Tangerines" and "A Small Incident" demonstrate the potential impact of seemingly trivial incidents, but in the latter story, forgetfulness and oblivion are replaced first by action and thought, and then by memory, by the desire to do something and not just simply watch the world go by and complain about the incompetence or even downright dishonesty of the powerful. Yet the narrator of "A Small Incident" emphasizes that society still has much ground to cover: the political shenanigans continue, and even he, someone who has witnessed the gentler side of humanity, cannot stop himself from feeling increasingly antagonistic toward those around him. In addition, that the narrator of "A Small Incident" continues to return to this single incident, and that he apparently did not continue with his "charity," undermines his claim that he feels driven to reform and possesses new hope and courage. What, the story implicitly asks, is the point of undergoing such a "radical transformation" if one never moves beyond that one revelatory moment? When does hope become more of a liability than an asset? When must "courage" be acted on before it becomes cowardice? And finally, when does concentration on the self and the past, to the virtual exclusion of everything else, become just as detrimental as the isolation favored by the Japanese narrator? "A Small Incident" collapses distances articulated in "Tangerines" but offers no real answers to these and similar questions.

And so it is not surprising that Lu Xun's "small incident" itself became a target of reconfiguration by the Chinese writers Ba Jin and Zhang Tianyi, both of whom also wrote stories entitled "A Small Incident." Ba Jin's version, published in 1933, provides a particularly compelling point of comparison. Featuring a destitute peddler, Ba Jin's "small incident" mocks the account by Lu Xun's spoiled intellectual, who speaks so nobly of courage, hope, and change but does not translate language into action. And yet the peddler's desire for access to this privileged life is very much alive. Walking to the ocean, the famished father turns to his son: "My treasure, why weren't you born into a rich family? . . . My treasure, if you'd been born into another family you'd be going to school."[9] Walking into the waves to commit suicide in a manner eerily suggestive of Yu Dafu's protagonist in "Sinking" (1921), he repeats these sentiments: "If my child had been born into a rich family, now he certainly would be attending school."[10] The protagonist of Ba Jin's "A Small Incident" underlines the importance of birth over achievement in determining an individual's well-being; the narrative unravels the elastic networks connecting all humanity spun in Lu Xun's "A Small Incident" and recasts them as a more rigid and intricate amalgam of bonds that inhibit mobility, locking members of the same social class together and affording them little opportunity for meaningful interaction with those enchained by other fetters.

The Artist in/and the World

Like Lu Xun's "A Small Incident," Yu Dafu's short story "Late-Blooming Cassia" intertextually reworks Japanese prose—Natsume Sōseki's *Pillow of Grass*—to put forward very different human dynamics that nevertheless stop short of bringing about significant change. The first-person narrator of *Pillow of Grass*, a painter and poet, intersperses discussions of art, including numerous references to artistic predecessors and the role of the artist, with talk about his journey into the mountains, hearing about a young woman named Nami, conjuring up multiple visions of her, and finally meeting and talking with her. The novel concludes with his journey down the mountain to bid Kyūichi farewell as he departs for the Manchurian front to participate in the Russo-Japanese War; Nami stares after Kyūichi's train as it fades into the distance, and the narrator comments that he now is able to put the final touches on his mental portrait of her. Similarly, Mr. Yu, a writer and the first-person narrator of "Late-Blooming Cassia," opens his story with a letter from his friend Weng Zesheng that invites Yu to Weng's wedding at his mountain home. Yu then describes his journey into the mountains, where he meets Weng's sister Lian for the first time, forms a romantic image of her as a creature endowed with unearthly purity, and agrees to become her "brother." The story concludes with his journey down the mountain and departure on a train for Shanghai. We leave him watching well-wishers on the platform fade into the distance, excited that he soon will have the opportunity to complete the story he has been writing.

"Late-Blooming Cassia" appropriates the building blocks of Sōseki's *Pillow of Grass*: each text is narrated in the first-person by an artist who, tired of life and longing for renewal, goes into the mountains where he meets and is enchanted by a beautiful woman who is not available to him romantically but who inspires his art. Both texts conclude with journeys down mountains, trains fading into the distance, and the promise of artistic creation. But while in *Pillow of Grass* the narrator uses both creating and consuming art to justify isolating himself from humanity, the narrator of "Late-Blooming Cassia" depicts art as drawing him closer to others, allowing him to renew old ties and forge new ones. Most noteworthy in this respect is the transposition of Nami from a nonhuman apparition over whom the narrator obsesses into Lian, a woman in whose humanity he thrives.

The narrators of *Pillow of Grass* and "Late-Blooming Cassia" both are artists, but their views on art and human relationships diverge significantly: art removes the Japanese narrator from human companionship but brings the Chinese narrator closer. In the opening pages of *Pillow of Grass* the narrator lyrically expounds on how art can distract people from the offensiveness of daily life. He declares it the only medium capable of providing relief from existence and asserts that even latent poets and painters, those who never express themselves on paper, can be liberated:

This world is a difficult place in which to live. . . . Uproot the troubles and worries that make it a difficult place and see before you a welcoming world of poetry, painting, music, and sculpture. . . . Even the poet who has not written a verse and the painter who has not colored a bit of canvas . . . can create a universe without peer . . . and are happier than anyone.[11]

On the other hand, he also argues that art depends on detachment from others. At many junctures in *Pillow of Grass* the narrator emphasizes how important it is for artists to separate themselves from society and argues that poets only become poets when not involved with outside affairs. He declares that he embarked on his journey into the mountains "to distance myself from emotions" and asserts that even if he cannot escape all emotion, "my feelings will be just as pallid as if I were watching *nō* drama."[12] Sōseki's narrator goes to great lengths not to feel anything, or at least to pretend not to feel anything. He reveals that he chats with the local barber not because he cares about him as a person but because he believes the barber could be the subject of a painting or poem. Similarly, he tells Nami that he will fall in love with her — if this is what she wants. Nami comments on the "inhumanity" of his vision of love, but he protests that his attitude is nonhuman (*hininjō*), not inhuman (*funinjō*).[13] Summarizing the events of the last few days, the narrator declares that it is essential for him, the "pure artist," to view the mountains, the sea, and the people he encounters as nothing but pieces of scenery.

Throughout the novel, the narrator explains his actions in the context of his "nonhuman" trip. The irony is that while he scribbles out some poetry and frequently cites the creations of others, his efforts to separate himself from the world do not enable him to create a splendid portfolio. In fact, it is only when he exposes himself to feeling that he at last is able to complete a painting of Nami in his mind, and even then, no mention is made of translating his mental images onto canvas. He concludes *Pillow of Grass*:

> The conductor ran toward us, slamming doors as he came. With the closing of each door, the gap widened between those who were leaving and those who were staying. Finally, Kyūichi's door slammed shut. The world was cut in two . . . Kyūichi stuck his head out the window. . . . [As the train departed], Nami looked after it in a daze. Strangely enough, her dazed look was replete with a sorrow I'd never seen. Patting Nami on the shoulder, I whispered, "That's it! That's it! Now that you show this feeling, you can become a painting." That instant, the picture in my mind was completed.[14]

Revealing in this passage that he does in fact depend on emotions (those of others if not his own) in order to create, the narrator undermines the theories of art he has been promoting throughout the novel. His imagination never lacked for images of Nami: unable to see Nami as a real person, he described her in many places as an apparition fluttering in and out of his line of vision and drew parallels between her and the Ophelia of British artist Sir John Everett Millais's (1829–96) painting *Ophelia* (1852). Thus, had he really not required human contact, the narrator of *Pillow of Grass* would have had no difficulty putting the final touches on the mental portrait of Nami and perhaps even would have created an actual painting.

Pillow of Grass mocks artists who insist on cutting themselves off from the world, concluding that artistic creation requires some degree of emotional connection. Taking up where Sōseki's novel leaves off, "Late-Blooming Cassia" not only draws attention to art's dependence on human relationships but also explores the paradox of art's ability to bring people together only to take a back seat to personal interactions. Weng's discovery of scholarship on Yu's writing, not to mention Yu's writing itself, leads to the reunion of the former classmates and to new friendships with Weng's family members, particularly his sister Lian. At the same time, however, art is explicitly critiqued as a poor substitute for direct interaction.

In the letter to Yu that opens "Late-Blooming Cassia," Weng remarks that on one of his infrequent trips into town he stumbled on some books on Yu and, his curiosity aroused, purchased everything he could find by and about his old friend. The more he read, the more he wanted to revive their friendship:

Passing by a bookstore, I happened to see several books about you, biographies and criticism, and when I went inside and inquired, I learned that you'd written as many as eight or nine books. I bought all your books and all the books about you, and went home to read. Reading these materials, it seemed as though I saw you the way you were when we were last together, more than a decade ago, laughing and talking. I couldn't resist. I read them all once, and then again, and the more I read the more I wanted to write you, the more I wanted to see you again.[15]

From its opening pages, "Late-Blooming Cassia" depicts the magic of art as stemming not from its origins in the nonhuman, as Sōseki's narrator would have us believe, but instead from its power to draw people together, old friends and strangers alike. No matter how much Weng reads about Yu's life, and no matter how many of Yu's own words he absorbs, Weng declares that he only will be satisfied when he can see Yu for himself, and talk to him, and include him in his wedding.

Yu also longs to renew their friendship and the following day makes the journey to Weng's home. Waiting for his friend to return, he admires the exquisite calligraphy that covers the walls of Weng's living room. But personal contact quickly supersedes art:

I stepped back into the living room and looked at the calligraphy and the paintings on the walls, reminded of what Weng Zesheng had described in his letter. It was a feast for the eyes—each of the hanging scrolls was exquisite. This room was nothing at all like the ordinary living rooms of country folk. The most striking work for me was a piece of calligraphy by Chen Hao [1839–1919] titled "On Returning Home." The bright colors and graceful strokes were like Dong Xiangguang's [1555–1630], but even more delicate. Just a glance around the living room revealed that the Weng family had had a passion for learning for generations. But before I had the chance to look at all the scrolls, a shout suddenly erupted from beyond the door behind me. "Yu, Yu, my good friend! You got here so soon!"[16]

Such joyous reunions cannot be taken for granted, yet they ultimately are no real surprise. More significant is the instant connection between Yu and Weng's sister Lian, whose very name is a homophone of the Chinese verb "link" (*lian*). Unlike Sōseki's narrator, who extrapolates volumes on Nami from the tidbits he overhears, in essence displacing the woman Nami with an imaginary character, Yu learns about Lian from her brother, who talks about her at length in his letter and in conversation, and it is only after spending some time with her in the mountains that Yu begins to feel a connection. To be sure, he is unable to see her as an adult, much less as an equal; despite her confidence, physical stamina, and knowledge of the mountains, not to mention her status as a widow abused by her former in-laws, he repeatedly likens her to a child and talks about her "innocence" and "purity." Yet Yu gets to know Lian on a more personal level than Sōseki's narrator gets to know Nami. Even more important, personal connections with Lian repeatedly trump art.

The morning after his reunion with Weng, Yu and Lian—at Weng's urging—head deeper into the mountains. Yu's thoughts, like those of Sōseki's narrator, frequently turn to artistic works and other writings, but art is easily displaced by human interaction:

We didn't talk for a bit. I was thinking about the German writer [Wilhelm] Jensen's [1837–1911] novel *Die braune Erica* [Brown Erica, 1868]. The English writer [William Henry] Hudson [1841–1922] copied this novel in his creation *Green Mansions* [1904]. Both novels are about cute innocent girls who grow up in the wilderness, and both heroines suffer in the end. I was lost in thought for quite a while, but she very naturally, standing behind me, put her plump hand on my shoulder.[17]

Moreover, unlike Sōseki's narrator, Yu does not use artistic works to barricade himself against heartfelt communication. Instead, he comments on the great disparity between reading and interacting. For instance, listening to Lian detail the plant and animal life surrounding West Lake, Yu is reminded of Gilbert White's (1720–93) *Natural History and Antiquities of Selborne* (1789), a series of letters that lyrically describe the flora and fauna of Hampshire, England. But Yu quickly concedes that listening to Lian speak is more moving than reading:

No matter how small a bird, insect, blade of grass, or tree, she not only knew its name but also when it hatched, when it migrated, when it chirped, when it shed its shell, when it flowered, when it bore fruit, the color of its flowers, and the taste of its fruit, etc. She spoke in such an interesting and thorough manner that I felt as though I were reading G. White's *Natural History and Antiquities of Selborne*. But White's book wasn't nearly as natural and stimulating. To listen to her clear and unhurried voice, to watch her red lips—which seemed to have been reddened by nature with colorfast lipstick—together with her own special way of smiling, added feeling to the information and added charm to book learning. We slowly walked and talked, and after less than an hour I was in a trance, crazy for her, as though I had become a young man again.[18]

Similarly, Yu declares that lunch with Lian after their long hike is better than anything in Dryden: "The lunch I shared with her atop Five Clouds Mountain was better for me than Alexander's feast as imagined by the English poet [John] Dryden [1631–1700, in "Alexander's Feast" (1697)]. And in terms of mental fulfillment, harmony, and appetite, I'm afraid that Alexander's feast didn't hold a candle to mine."[19] Evoking yet distancing himself from Sōseki's *Pillow of Grass*, suggesting that his is no "copy" (as he claims Hudson's *Green Mansions* is of Jensen's *Brown Erica*), the narrator of "Late-Blooming Cassia" repeatedly depicts interacting with others as more satisfying than engaging with art. This despite his great affection for and knowledge of the latter.

But Yu longs to continue writing, and after attending his friend's wedding, he heads back down the mountain; "Late-Blooming Cassia" concludes with the young artist bound for his writing desk in Shanghai. For Yu, creating art requires separating himself from human contact; declining Weng's invitation to spend several additional days on the mountain, he claims that he needs to go away to finish his story. But Yu makes no secret of the importance of the ties he has forged with Weng and his family, drawing the curtain on "Late-Blooming Cassia" with a scene that closely echoes and yet significantly transforms the final passage of *Pillow of Grass*:

Weng Zesheng and his sister took me to the station. When the signal blew and white steam rose from the locomotive, I stretched both my hands out the window. I took Zesheng's hand in one, and his sister's hand in the other, and held them very tightly. The whistle sounded and the train moved. They followed alongside the train for quite a bit. I also stuck my head out of the window and called to them. . . . The train moved farther and farther away, and the people on the platform who had come to see off passengers returned home. But I could still see the two of them standing at the eastern end of the platform, waving to me in the sunlight.[20]

Pillow of Grass and "Late-Blooming Cassia" both conclude with a train leaving a station. But whereas the train in Sōseki's novel creates a gulf between people, its slamming door suddenly "cutting the world in two," parting in Yu Dafu's short story is prolonged. Nami and Kyūichi can only fix their eyes on each other as the young man's train chugs out of the station and out of sight, but Yu, Weng, and Lian hold hands and then gaze at one another indefinitely. Lacunae in the Chinese narration highlight the close ties among the three characters, ties that even the moving train cannot sever; of course, the three have to release their physical grip at some point and cannot remain visible to one another forever, but "Late-Blooming Cassia" makes no mention of hands unclasping and in fact concludes with much waving and gazing.

Near the conclusion of *Pillow of Grass*, the narrator has harsh words for trains, which he believes are enemies of humanity:

> Whenever I see the violent way trains thrust along, indiscriminately regarding all people as freight, I look at the people cooped up in the train cars, and at the iron cars that care not a bit for the individual's selfhood, and I think, "Watch out, watch out. It's dangerous not to pay attention." Modern civilization is full of very visible dangers. The train that blindly forges ahead in the darkness is one example.[21]

The narrator's depiction of trains as carving up the landscape with no regard for humanity ironically parallels the very artistic process he has been advocating, one where artists, embracing the nonhuman, remove themselves from human interactions. It also points to the dangerous ramifications of such an attitude. The train in *Pillow of Grass* will take Kyūichi on the first leg of his journey to the Manchurian battlefield, a place the narrator describes as a different world, "a world far, far away, where men work in the stench of gunpowder, where they slip in blood and blindly tumble, and where loud noises fill the skies."[22] The novel implies that at least part of what allows such an environment to come into existence, grow, and even flourish is nothing less than refusing to engage with the world outside the self, a process in which art can, but need not necessarily be, complicit.

Yu Dafu's story transforms into literature the vision of human relationships to which Sōseki's narrator simply points at the conclusion of his novel. "Late-Blooming Cassia" reveals the joy that can be found when people get to know each other as people, or at least as more than figments of one another's imaginations, when tools—including the pen and the train—connect people rather than isolate them. On the other hand, like "A Small Incident," Yu Dafu's story leaves some disturbing loose ends. Taking place in the fall of 1932, not long after the Japanese established a puppet regime in Manchuria (May 15, 1932), and intertextualizing a novel that refers explicitly to Japanese military activities in northeastern China, "Late-Blooming Cassia" is audibly silent on questions of empire. Both Yu and Weng were educated in Japan and reminisce on their experiences there, but they do not speak of recent Japanese incursions. The focus on renewing their relationship, and, in the case of Yu, forging ties with

Lian, in some ways obscures the bigger picture. The train itself becomes a tubular bubble that provides Yu safe passage between bubbles (his study in Shanghai and Weng's mountain refuge, to which he pledges to return the following year), rather than forcing him to confront the potential disintegration of his homeland. In some ways, "Late-Blooming Cassia" paradoxically reveals the artist who seemed to have everything, who successfully integrated career and relationships, as even more naïve than his Japanese predecessor.

Families and Societies

Like Lu Xun's "A Small Incident" and Yu Dafu's "Late-Blooming Cassia," the Korean writer Yŏm Sangsŏp's novel *Three Generations* (1931) and the Chinese writer Ba Jin's novel *Family* (1933) highlight more deeply intertwined relationships than the Japanese novel they intertextualize, Shimazaki Tōson's *Family* (1911). But rather than focusing primarily on interpersonal connections, *Three Generations* and Ba Jin's *Family* spotlight not only intrafamilial relationships but also the interconnectedness of the family and society; both the Chinese and Korean narrators depict characters who are more committed than their Japanese counterparts to making a difference both within and outside the walls of the family compound. The Japanese *Family*, the Chinese *Family*, and the Korean *Three Generations* have much in common: all three focus on the crumbling of the conventional family in a rapidly changing society and explore the experiences of the younger generation as it tries to carve out a place for itself in unfamiliar territory. Yŏm Sangsŏp's and Ba Jin's third-person narrators cleverly allude to Tōson's novel while deliberately establishing their distance. Unlike the protagonists of "A Small Incident" and "Late-Blooming Cassia," whose connections with others—while bringing them joy or at least something to think about—have little impact on society, characters in *Family* and *Three Generations* make a difference, and stand on the brink of making an even greater difference, in their societies. But their accomplishments in these arenas do not come easily, and both novels highlight the ambiguity of personal sacrifices—of oneself and others—made in the name of liberation, progress, and community.

Crumbling Walls

Ba Jin's deep involvement with Western literatures, particularly those from nineteenth-century Europe, is well known.[23] But he was also an avid reader of contemporary Japanese literature, and his interpretive, interlingual, and intertextual transculturations of this corpus reveal significant tensions vis-à-vis the cultural products of China's semi-colonial oppressor and wartime opponent. Tōson's works were among his most significant interpretive and intertextual targets, as the intertitularity of his novels *New Life* (1932), *Family* (1933), and *Spring* (1938) suggests; this trio inverts Tōson's *Spring* (1908), *Family* (1911), and *New Life* (1919).[24] Interestingly, in a conversation with Ba Jin during the latter's visit to Japan in 1980, the Japanese writer Kinoshita Junji reminded his Chinese friend that he was only a young boy when Tōson published *Family*, "his novel with the same title as yours." But lest Ba Jin think that he was implying that the Chinese writer's prose was a mere imitation of Tōson's, Kinoshita quickly emphasized their differences: "When we compare the plot of Tōson's tale with your autobiographical novel, we clearly understand their opposition."[25] Kinoshita's anxiety is palpable. But unlike many instances of intertitularity, where a literary work appropriates the title of a celebrated text but the title continues to be associated primarily with the first text, particularly if it has appeared in translation, Ba Jin's *Family* preempted Tōson's *Family* from becoming the East Asian *Family*.

Both *Family* novels focus on families crumbling in the face of radical economic and social change. Tōson's *Family*, which takes place between 1898 and 1910, describes a Japanese family whose town on the Nakasendō—once a busy post road linking Kusatsu (near Kyoto) with Edo (Tokyo)—is becoming increasingly isolated; Ba Jin's novel describes a Chinese family living in Chengdu (the capital of Sichuan province in southwest China) in the turbulent May Fourth period.[26] But the Chinese *Family*'s challenges to the Japanese *Family* establish the considerable distance between these two texts. The Chinese novel differentiates itself from its Japanese predecessor in two principal ways. First, it mocks the closed walls, the interiorized narration, of Tōson's *Family*. It is more concerned than its Japanese predecessor with depicting the harsh landscape outside the home. Although not apolitical, Tōson's narrator frequently narrows his gaze to the downfall of the Koizumi and Hashimoto families.[27] Ba Jin's narrator, on the other hand, magnifies the crises facing the Gao family by contextualizing its stagnation more rigorously. Second, the gloom and doom of Tōson's novel are replaced in Ba Jin's *Family* with ambition and fervor. Characters in the Chinese novel are not immune to suffering and failure, but *Family* proposes that defiance, rebellion, and revolt are not futile. It argues that positive change can be enacted when there is willingness to engage with society beyond the walls of the family compound. Like many colonial and semicolonial texts, Ba Jin's novel flouts the resignation to fate exhibited by Japanese literary characters.[28]

The ambivalent relationship between the narrator of Ba Jin's *Family* and his Japanese predecessor is evident from the opening sections of the Chinese novel. Tōson's novel begins inside the hectic yet relatively enclosed Hashimoto kitchen:

> The kitchen of the Hashimoto home was bustling with lunch preparations. Usually, six male employees, from chief clerk down to shop boy, had to be fed. But now there were also guests from Tokyo. Including the family, there were thirteen who had to be served. . . . The hearth was spacious, the cabinets glossy, and the floor clean. Food was readily brought from the kitchen and served here. From the dark garrets hung sooty bamboo pothooks, and below a fire burned, even in summer. Gentle beams of light entered the old-fashioned, dignified building through a high window, and clear blue sky was visible through an open panel.[29]

In contrast, the Chinese *Family* begins outside, the "bustling" kitchen transformed into a raging snowstorm through which the Gao brothers must forge; it is only in the second chapter that Juehui and Juemin actually enter the gates of the family compound. The novel starts off:

> The wind was blowing hard, and snowflakes, dancing in the air like cotton fluff from a torn quilt, floated down aimlessly all around. . . .
>
> On the street pedestrians and sedan-chair carriers struggled in vain against the wind and snow, shrinking away. The snow was falling heavier and heavier. It filled the sky, falling everywhere. It fell on umbrellas, on the sedan-chairs, on the reed hats of the sedan-chair carriers and on the faces of the pedestrians. . . .
>
> Roaring sorrowfully, the wind mixed with the sound of footsteps in the snow, creating strange music. This music irritated the pedestrians. And, it seemed to warn them, the wind and snow will rule the world for a long time; the bright and beautiful spring sun never will return. . . .
>
> Only one hope spurred on the pedestrians struggling on these secluded streets—they soon would return to their warm, well-lit homes.[30]

Reversing Tōson's novel, the narrator of the Chinese *Family* signals that his text, although titled *Family*, also will explore the storms that rage outside the home. On the whole, Ba Jin's narrator paints a very different picture of responses to oppressive family dynamics. Tōson's characters tend to turn inward and succumb to their perceived fates, muddle through, or channel whatever rebellious instincts they might possess into unproductive enterprises. Ba Jin's characters—although not paragons of virtue, some even responsible for the deaths of those they love—courageously travel to the river that rushes outside their home to see where it might take them, not content simply to listen to it babble away. The distant brook of the Japanese *Family*, the description of which Tōson famously claimed was based on impressions from listening to it from afar, is transformed into the rushing torrent of Ba Jin's *Jiliu sanbuqu* (Torrent Trilogy), of which *Family* is the opening novel.[31]

Degradation and decline are the norm in the Japanese *Family*. To be sure, some life grows amid this deterioration. Gardens continue to flourish and the Koizumi daughters are said to grow like young grass within the disintegrating house. But the girls all perish; sons are born, but their fate is uncertain. At one point, the leading character Koizumi Sankichi tells his wife Oyuki that everything they have done for the family has had unanticipated consequences, that all their toil has resulted in nothing more than additional dependents. The marriage satisfies neither, and the couple flounders helplessly, doing very little to improve their situation. Moreover, those in Tōson's *Family* who choose to rebel do not think about the consequences of their behavior and often hurt the very individuals they are trying to help.

Whereas a powerful and mostly unrelieved gloom governs Tōson's *Family*, the struggle for autonomy begins early in the Chinese *Family*, where no matter how bleak things become, the characters tend to learn something from their mistakes and continue to press forward. In both the Chinese and Japanese novels, the younger generation longs for freedom of thought, expression, and action, but the characters in Ba Jin's *Family* pursue these goals more aggressively than their Japanese counterparts. To be sure, this approach at times comes at great cost to them and those they cherish. But Ba Jin's *Family* demonstrates that the oppressive family system, believed by many to have played a prominent role in China's deterioration, need not be a death sentence; the text argues that although conventions cannot be eradicated completely—at least not at present—this is no excuse for individuals not to question authority both inside and outside the home, rebel when necessary, and create their own pathways.

Breaking free from entrenched customs is not easy, and the narrator of Ba Jin's *Family*, while romanticizing several episodes including Mingfeng's drowning and Juehui's escape from his hometown, also exposes unnecessary sacrifices. Although committed to the cause of individual liberty and actively involved in the youth movement, Juehui has yet to learn the basics of human relationships. He is so wrapped up in revolutionary activities outside the home that he does not grant Mingfeng the few minutes she asks of him, during which she had hoped to tell him that she was about to be sold as a concubine; had he been willing to listen, he likely could have saved her from this fate. Instead, she drowns herself, and while the narrator expresses sympathy, he also is quick to point out that her death changes nothing in the family dynamic: Mingfeng is simply replaced. Ba Jin's novel reveals the high price paid for national reform but suggests that it is not as steep as the cost of people detaching themselves from society.

The final paragraphs of Ba Jin's *Family* echo and transform those of Tōson's. In Tōson's novel, Sankichi and Oyuki are unable to sleep, obsessed with thoughts of the body of a family member as it is transported from the hospital to the crematorium; in addition, a pregnant Oyuki wonders if she will be the next to die, 33 being an unlucky age for women. The text concludes before daybreak: "They dozed for a bit, but again awoke. 'Oyuki, What time is it? Isn't the sun coming up? They're probably cremating Shōta's body now,' said Sankichi as he opened one of the storm doors. He imagined that Shōta's body was being moved from the hospital in Nagoya to the crematorium before night was over. Outside it was still dark."[32]

This darkness reemerges in the opening pages of Ba Jin's *Family*, where the sun has set on a swirling snowstorm. But the novel concludes at daybreak, the dawn of a new day and the dawn of new life for Juehui. His sister-in-law has just died in childbirth, a death anticipated at the conclusion of the Japanese *Family*, but this death is what finally awakens her husband Juexin to the validity of his brothers' (Juehui and Juemin) protests against the patriarchal system; this death allows him at least to begin to take seriously their arguments instead of following his usual course of action, which is merely to bow to "fate." Moreover, the body in motion in Ba Jin's novel is not a corpse heading to a crematorium, as in Tōson's *Family*, but rather the very alive and perhaps excessively hopeful Juehui on a boat headed for Shanghai:

A new emotion gradually took hold of him. He didn't know whether it was happiness or sorrow. But he knew beyond the shadow of a doubt that he was leaving his family. In front of him was endless green water. This water swept him constantly forward, taking him to an unfamiliar city. . . . This water, this blessed water, was carrying him from the home he had known for eighteen years to a city and people he did not know. . . . He turned and looked back for the last time and gently said "Goodbye." And then he turned again and watched the green water that endlessly rushed forward, stopping not for an instant.[33]

Unlike Tōson's characters, Juehui takes advantage of the speeding torrent, using it for the final leg of his physical escape from his family, an escape already underway in the opening passage of the Chinese novel. Halfway through *Family*, the narrator declares that all the new ideas Qin (a young female revolutionary) has obtained from Ibsen's social dramas and the writings of the Japanese feminist poet Yosano Akiko vanish from her mind, replaced by terror at current events. Just as the narrator of *Family* declares Yosano's (and Ibsen's) elegant words useless in contemporary struggles, so too does he cast aside Tōson's novel, revealing its picture of the family to be woefully inadequate.

Writing in the early 1930s about May Fourth fervor that had peaked more than a decade before, Ba Jin remarked in the preface to the *Torrent Trilogy* that although he had been surrounded by darkness without bounds, he had never been alone and had never been without hope. Rather, he declared, "No matter where I am, I always see the torrent of life in turbulence, creating its own path. . . . It cannot stop, and there is nothing that can hold it back."[34] Published in the dark days of Japan's attacks on China, portraying events of an earlier and in some ways more innocent time, *Family* reminded readers of what once was, at least in memory, and what might come again. Engaging in intertitularity, it also established once and for all the Chinese *Family*, against which no translation of Tōson's novel could hope to compete. The significance of this displacement should not be underestimated.

Breaking Apart the Family

Yŏm Sangsŏp's novel *Three Generations* explores clashes among generations, classes, and ideologies in late 1920s Seoul. The confrontation with Tōson's *Family* is more subtle here than in Ba Jin's novel: the title *Three Generations* strongly suggests a family, but it does not immediately evoke a celebrated literary predecessor, nor is the novel's manipulation of Tōson's motifs as obvious. But like its Chinese counterpart, Yŏm Sangsŏp's novel differentiates itself from Tōson's *Family* not only by depicting characters more engaged with their societies but also by devoting more narrative space to the landscape outside the family compound.

Yŏm Sangsŏp lived in Japan for about a decade (1912–20, 1926–28), during which time he read Japanese literature and befriended Japanese writers, including members of the White Birch Society such as Arishima Takeo, Shiga Naoya, and Yanagi Muneyoshi (Sōetsu, 1889–1961).[35] He wrote essays on Japanese literature, some of which—like those of many colonial and semicolonial East Asian writers—critique what he perceived as the narrow vision of the Japanese literary establishment. In addition, he intertextualized Japanese literature in his own creative work, including writings by Arishima, Kunikida Doppo, and Shimazaki Tōson. His reconfiguration of Tōson's *Family* in *Three Generations* is particularly noteworthy for its project of redefining the East Asian family novel. Yŏm Sangsŏp was one of the few East Asian colonial and semicolonial writers to talk explicitly about the impact of Japanese literature on his own work. In the essay "Reminiscences on a Literary Youth" (1955), for instance, he reveals, "I was in Japan at the height of naturalism and there is no denying that the works of its representative writers had an extraordinary influence on my thought and style."[36] But this "influence" was not a passive flow: Yŏm Sangsŏp's oeuvre dynamically engages with Japanese and other predecessors.

Like Ba Jin's and Tōson's novels, *Three Generations* highlights the depravity and decay of the conventional family. The novel focuses on the Cho family, a relatively prosperous clan with a corrupt patriarch who dies near the end of the tale, a son (Sanghun) who has studied in the United States and converted to Christianity, and a grandson (Dŏkgi) who is a student in Japan frequently home on extended visits. Many passages in *Three Generations* are directly concerned with the three generations of the novel's title. Incidents surrounding proper protocol for ancestral ceremonies, the patriarch's attempts to keep Dŏkgi under his control, and the drama—which involves the Japanese authorities—of passing the key to the family safe from the patriarch directly to Dŏkgi, thereby skipping over Sanghun, are some of the most gripping episodes in Yŏm Sangsŏp's novel. Like Tōson's *Family*, *Three Generations* depicts the conventional family as very confining, particularly for the educated younger generations who unlike their elders do not have the authority to bend rules at will.

Yet the tightly interwoven Cho family is not the only entwined network examined in *Three Generations*: both the narrator and the protagonist of Yŏm Sangsŏp's novel are more concerned than their Japanese counterparts with the ties that bind both family members and the family itself to society. The departure from *Family* is evident from the opening passage of *Three Generations*. Whereas the Japanese novel begins with lunch in the busy Hashimoto kitchen, its Korean counterpart moves quickly from in front of the inner quarters (where Dŏkgi has been packing for his upcoming trip to Japan), to the outer quarters (where Dŏkgi meets up with his friend Kim Pyŏnghwa), and then outside the family compound (where Dŏkgi and Pyŏnghwa enjoy a drink in town).[37] Titled "Two Friends," the first section concentrates on Dŏkgi's interactions with his pal. This pattern repeats itself throughout the novel, the narrator interweaving storylines about the Chos with those about other families. In fact, *Three Generations* concludes with Dŏkgi's plans to return to Japan thwarted yet again, but rather than giving the last word to his multiple responsibilities vis-à-vis his family, the narrator concludes with his realization that "taking care of [the impoverished factory worker] P'ilsun and her mother was his duty and responsibility."[38]

Yŏm Sangsŏp's novel argues that connections and obligations extend beyond the family, and most readily across class lines; Dŏkgi's closest friends hover on the verge of starvation while he enjoys a comfortable lifestyle, although—as he is quick to add—one that pales next to what the Japanese enjoy.[39] *Three Generations* depicts relationships outside the family as just as complex and troubled as those within: verbal arguments—among relatives, friends, enemies, and strangers—make up the bulk of the dialogue. Indeed, Yŏm Sangsŏp's narrator portrays traumas and tragedies as passing through family walls in both directions, implicating virtually everyone, including the Japanese, who by the late 1920s seemed a permanent fixture on the Korean landscape. Like Tōson's *Family*, *Three Generations* concludes on a sorrowful note, although there is less resignation in the Korean story. The radius of human interactions grows considerably from Tōson's *Family* to *Three Generations*, but not without regret, and not without consequence, for both the individual and society. Would Dŏkgi's contributions to both his family and society be even greater were he able to return to Japan, with its resources and educational opportunities? By remaining closer to home—at least for the time being—does he ultimately deprive himself and his society of reaching their full potential? These questions, like many others, are left unanswered.

The Individual and the Nation

Just as Ba Jin's *Family* and Yŏm Sangsŏp's *Three Generations* reconfigure Tōson's *Family* in a way that accentuates the interdependence of the individual, the patriarchal family, and society at large, other East Asian colonial and semicolonial reconfigurations of Japanese literature trump Japanese texts that minimize if not omit the nation in their dissection of personal trials. Implicitly differentiating local circumstances from those in Japan, they point to the difficulties of discussing individual hardships without implicating the nation as a whole. In so doing, they not only accentuate the crises facing their societies but also recast relationships between individuals and their homelands as more intertwined than in the Japanese creative texts they intertextually reconfigure. These relationships often are uncomfortable and unbalanced. For one, they almost always are framed negatively: the country is blamed for personal hardships but rarely is perceived as abetting personal success. Furthermore, they are almost always one-sided, with the nation shouldering the blame and emphasis on individual agency unusual. Becoming at once wider and more rigid, the filigreed relationships in these intertextual weavings point to a double burden on colonial and semicolonial societies. Two excellent examples of this phenomenon are Zhou Zuoren's intertextualization of the Japanese writer Senge Motomaro's poem "Hae" (Flies, 1919) in his poem and essay of the same title (1920, 1924) and Yu Dafu's recasting of Satō Haruo's novella *Den'en no yūutsu* (Rural Melancholy, 1918) in "Sinking" (1921).

The Battle of the Flies

A member of the Japanese White Birch Society known for his humanistic verse, Senge Motomaro caught the attention of Zhou Zuoren, who translated and intertextually reconfigured several of his poems, including "Flies."[40] Both Senge's "Flies" and Zhou Zuoren's Chinese poem of the same title, published the following year, talk about flies, but whereas the focus of Senge's poem is relatively narrow, the Chinese poem implicates all of China.[41] Senge's poet describes a trash collector and his wife moving a cart of garbage; flies surround the wife when she stops to wipe sweat from her brow. The poet reacts strongly to this sight: "anger welled up within me as I watched / nothing is as hateful as those flies that infest corpses." This is in contrast to the trash collector, who several lines later is said to be oblivious to the buzzing cloud that surrounds and taunts him like a group of children mocking a beggar. The poet concludes, "that kind of person will go to heaven / but we will go to hell," suggesting that the trash collector's suffering has not been in vain.

In the Chinese "Flies," the poet also makes no secret of his hatred of these insects. He begins by claiming that although he has it in him to love a diverse array of animals, he cannot love flies: "We speak of love, / love all living beings. / But I—don't think I can love them all. / I can love wolves and monster serpents, / and I can love pigs that live in mountain forests. / But I cannot love flies. / I abhor them, I curse them." But the Chinese poet does not stop here. He launches into a diatribe on the horrors of flies, explaining just why they are so hateful, and calls for their destruction: "Flies big and small, / destroyers of beauty and life, / Flies—good friends of the Chinese! / I curse you, may you all be annihilated / by the power of the darkest, darkest magic / exceeding the power of mankind." Zhou Zuoren's poem appropriates the title and subject of Senge's "Flies" to accentuate the dangers facing China. Plagued by destructive friends—the fly that carries disease, as well as the larger "flies" of Japan and Western nations, not to mention homegrown parasites— powers that the poet suggests cannot be dissipated except by a superhuman force, China is depicted as on the brink of collapse. In the Chinese poem, the Japanese image of an impoverished garbage collector and his wife attacked by flies becomes one of flies attacking, and potentially destroying, the beauty and life of an entire nation. As in much colonial and semicolonial intertextualization of Japanese literature, the focus is broadened to address the plight of the home-land.

But the critique did not stop here. Several years after publishing "Flies," Zhou Zuoren wrote an essay by the same name, "Cangying" (Flies, 1924), which further exposes the complexity of his relationship with Senge's poem.[42] This sketch first describes how he and his friends enjoyed playing with flies when they were young and specu-lates that children have enjoyed games with flies for thousands of years. Then Zhou Zuoren explains the circumstances behind the composition of the poem "Flies" and summarizes human reactions to flies:

We now have been baptized by science and know that flies can spread germs, so today we resent these insects. Three years ago, when I was sick and hospitalized, I wrote a poem. Here's the second half:

> Flies big and small,
> destroyers of beauty and life.
> Flies—good friends of the Chinese!
> I curse you, may you all be annihilated
> by the power of the darkest, darkest magic
> exceeding the power of mankind

But actually, the most evil thing about flies is another bad addiction of theirs: they like to crawl on and lick people's faces, hands, and feet. Ancient peoples gave it the beautiful name 'inhaling beauty.' . . . Many people marveled at the fly's persistence and daring.[43]

Later in the essay "Flies," Zhou Zuoren cites a haiku by the famed Tokugawa poet Kobayashi Issa (1763–1827) that calls for mercy on the fly since it is just "rubbing its hands, rubbing its legs." Zhou Zuoren declares that after reading Kobayashi's verse, "I often feel ashamed of my own poem about flies," and he confesses that he "will never be able to reach that level of sensibility."[44] Superior in artistry and sentiment, at least in the eyes of the modern Chinese poet, the Tokugawa verse evokes shame. But in so doing it paradoxically tightens solidarity with none other than Senge Motomaro's Japanese poem.

The insect that in Zhou Zuoren's poem "Flies" is the "destroyer of beauty and life" is revealed in his essay "Flies" to have a long history in literature and thought as the embodiment of beauty and life, a belief that has been compromised by modern science. Having suffered from an illness he believes was caused at least in part by flies, Zhou Zuoren explains why his feelings toward these insects differ from those of poets of old. He is not entirely comfortable with his perceptions, despite their scientific foundations, but also recognizes that there can be no turning back. Yet by openly polyintertextualizing his work, citing numerous examples of the early aestheticization of flies, Zhou Zuoren's essay ironically reveals his view of the fly in his poem "Flies" as closer to that of Senge's "Flies" than to the sentiments of early Chinese, Japanese, and Europeans. The twentieth-century Chinese poet shares more with his Japanese counterpart than he does with his earlier self, not to mention with poets of times past. On the other hand, although the gulf between the modern Chinese poet and his Japanese counterpart shrinks with the essay "Flies," it does not disappear. Creating a poem similar to Senge's "Flies," yet intensifying feelings of anger and hatred in addition to implicating China for maintaining friendships with such ruthless foreign powers, the poem "Flies" broadens the context from two garbage collectors (as depicted in Senge's poem) to China itself, and in so doing underlines the dangers facing his nation. On the other hand, as is often the case in intertextualization, the poet offers no solution of his own, instead simply calling on some unknown super-human entity to destroy these supposedly evil creatures.

Individual and National Burial

The sash tying individual affliction to national decay is woven even more tightly in Yu Dafu's short story "Sinking" (1921) than in Zhou Zuoren's "Flies." Intertextually confronting Satō Haruo's novella *Rural Melancholy* (1918), the narrator of "Sinking" describes an emotionally distraught young man whose self-imposed isolation from society—both as a child in China and a young man in Japan—belies the robust tethers binding him to his homeland. "Sinking" expands the perspective from a despondent Japanese artist hiding in the countryside to a gloomy Chinese student/artist preoccupied with the vision of a deteriorating China. One of Satō's most famous texts, *Rural Melancholy* is the story of *kare* (the Japanese pronoun "he"), a young poet from Tokyo who moves to the country with his wife and pets; his quest for peace is frustrated by hallucinations, hypochondria, loneliness, and numbing boredom. The novella fittingly concludes with the despairing refrain "Oh Rose, thou art sick," taken from the first line of William Blake's (1757–1827) poem "The Sick Rose" (1794). One of Yu Dafu's best known works, "Sinking" is the story of *ta* (the Chinese pronoun "he"), a self-conscious young Chinese literary man attending school in Japan; after completing his preparatory studies in Tokyo he moves to the outskirts of Nagoya. There he becomes increasingly isolated; frustrated by unfulfilled sexual desires and convinced that the Japanese he meets taunt him behind his back, he chastises both himself and China. At the end of the story, he walks along the shoreline, about to commit suicide, and calls out to China, urging it to become rich and strong. But one of the great paradoxes of "Sinking" is that despite the protagonist's expressed concern with China's deterioration—in contrast with the relative apathy toward current events displayed by Satō's protagonist—he indicates that he will end his life in Japan rather than return to China and use his newly acquired knowledge to help his homeland. His repeated evocation of an ailing China is in fact a smoke-screen masking insecurities that date back to childhood, long before he was conscious of "China" as such.

Scholarship comparing *Rural Melancholy* and "Sinking" abounds, fueled both by the texts' many similarities and by the close friendship between Satō Haruo and Yu Dafu, which began while Yu Dafu was living in Japan but came to a sudden halt in 1938.[45] Before their falling out, Yu Dafu made no secret of his admiration for Satō, and for *Rural Melancholy* in particular. He once commented, "I respect Satō Haruo more than any other modern Japanese writer. Zhou Zuoren has translated some of his fiction, but not his greatest masterpieces. We must conclude that of his writings, his best work is his breakout novel *Rural Melancholy*."[46] Yu Dafu once declared that all literary works are "autobiographies of their authors," and numerous parallels have been drawn between his often intensely personal oeuvre and the Japanese I-novel. But there is one fundamental difference, and that is concern—or at least expressed concern—with the nation. The echoes of *Rural Melancholy* in "Sinking" are unmistakable, but the protagonist of the latter text appears significantly more anxious about China than his counterpart does about Japan. On the other hand, however sincere this concern, it is cut short by the protagonist's emotional paralysis.

In the preface to "Sinking" Yu Dafu refers to the short story as a "dissection of hypochondria," a phrase that accurately describes *Rural Melancholy* as well. The structures of the two texts have much in common. Their protagonists are enthusiastic readers and writers of literature who suffer from imagined illnesses; they both hail from villages with dramatic landscapes, are the prodigal sons of their families, and have difficulty relating to others, particularly women. Isolated and unhappy with life in the city, they move to the countryside, and finding peace unattainable, they quickly deteriorate. Yet in the end these and other similarities between the two only accentuate their differences.

The opening section of "Sinking" reveals the closeness of its ties with *Rural Melancholy*, while simultaneously giving an early indication of the distance between the Chinese story and the Japanese novella. In both, the sun shines brightly, its light dazzling, timeless, and eternal, illuminating an isolated protagonist. *Rural Melancholy* opens with a poem by Edgar Allen Poe, giving both the Japanese translation and the original English: "I dwelt alone / In a world of moan, / And my soul was a stagnant tide."[47] Similarly, the narrator of "Sinking" opens with, "He recently had been feeling pitifully lonely. . . . The barrier separating him from everyone else got higher and higher."[48] In both texts, attention quickly turns to the natural world, but the foliage that envelops the protagonist in *Rural Melancholy* cannot protect his Chinese counterpart.

Satō's novella contains multiple descriptions of its protagonist's new garden. In this seemingly untamed landscape, dense and unyielding trees and plants compete with one another for sunlight, and those defeated in the struggle quickly wither away. Branches mingle to create a vaulted space, and foliage forms a green canopy through which the narrator views distant hills. *Rural Melancholy* begins with its protagonist walking on a country road, remembering similar journeys, but he generally is surrounded by greenery, some of which bears the human touch, but most of which is all-encompassing wild growth:

The untended garden grew thick in midsummer. All the trees stretched their roots into the ground as deep as they could to draw up power from the soil. The trees wore leaves on every side to soak up their fill of sunlight. . . . To bathe in as much sunlight as possible, to grow larger, every tree thrust out its branches. . . . The lush branches and leaves of the many different types of vegetation, the entire garden, were just like the melancholy of wild hair hanging down from a madman's lead-colored forehead. The invisible weight of the vegetation pushed on the narrow garden from above and made one feel as though the building in the middle were surrounded and squashed by its perimeter.[49]

The tables are turned in "Sinking." As a child in China, the protagonist of this short story regularly withdrew to his room, but in Japan he has no such refuge. After starting school on the outskirts of Nagoya, he rents a deserted cottage surrounded by trees, perhaps hoping to emulate his Japanese literary predecessor. But still unsatisfied, he travels, and each journey is replete with reminders—most self-inflicted—that he is a Chinese man living in Japan. There is no escape to a wild garden, no darkness that obscures nationality, at least in his eyes. The question of national identity, indeed survival, has become too pressing, and no matter where he goes, this young Chinese man cannot, or rather refuses to, find or create an enclosed space.

The protagonist's obsession with roses in *Rural Melancholy* is transformed in "Sinking" into obsession with China. Roses are the Japanese protagonist's favorite flower, and he reminds the reader how they have been heralded by poets the world over. But in Satō's novella, they are crushed by a profusion of plants from both Japan and the West that attack from above and below; the leaves and flowers that manage to survive are punctured by tiny insects. Try as he might, Satō's character cannot save his roses. China's fate, as depicted by the young protagonist in "Sinking," is remarkably similar. Once the revered heart of East Asia, China now is being attacked from all sides. Chinese youth, despite promising revenge on those who disparage their nation, believe themselves powerless to stop its decline.

Satō's protagonist slowly disintegrates into himself in the final sections of *Rural Melancholy*. Discovering that insects have blanketed his roses, he blurts out, "Oh Rose, thou art sick," a phrase that repeats itself nearly a dozen times before the novella draws to a close. Interestingly, he does not recite the remainder of Blake's poem, which describes the actual destruction of the rose: "O Rose, thou art sick: / The invisible worm / That flies in the night, / In the howling storm, // Hath found out thy bed / Of crimson joy; / And his dark secret love / Does thy life destroy."[50] But simply seeing the insects attack his roses is enough to send him over the edge. The novella concludes with the protagonist fruitlessly trying to light a lamp, an unknown voice in hot pursuit: "He struck another match. 'Oh Rose, thou art sick!' No matter how many he struck, no matter how many he struck. 'Oh Rose, thou art sick!' Wherever was that voice coming from? Was it a divine revelation? Was it a prophecy? In any case, the words chased him. Forever, forever. . . ."[51]

In "Sinking," the decomposing roses of *Rural Melancholy* are recast as the decaying country of China. Yu Dafu's young protagonist initially is concerned with why China has not grown rich and strong; early in the story, he scribbles in his diary: "Why did I bother to come to Japan? Why did I bother to come here to pursue my studies? Now that you've come to Japan, is it any surprise that the Japanese scorn you? China, oh China! Why have you not become wealthy and strong? I can bear it no longer."[52] Later, terrified that he will have to confess to a waitress that he is an abhorred "Shinajin" (a pejorative for "Chinese"), he again asks China why it has not grown strong. But in the final lines of the story, no longer asking China why it has not reformed, he begs his country to become rich and powerful and gives it a compelling reason to do so: "Wiping away his tears, he stood still and gave a lengthy sigh. He then said, with many pauses, 'Motherland, oh motherland! You are the cause of my death. Quickly become rich, become strong! Many of your children continue to suffer.' "[53] Whereas *kare* disintegrates, *ta* makes a final plea to his nation, but he does not acknowledge that he might play a role in helping China become "rich and strong" like Japan.

As in Zhou Zuoren's intertextualization of Senge Motomaro's verse, Yu Dafu's story appropriates many elements of Satō's framework, at once demonstrating affinity for the Japanese text and emphasizing that the Chinese story cannot be told the same way. Whereas in Senge's "Flies" and Satō's *Rural Melancholy* insects eat away at life, more powerful foes penetrate China's borders, necessitating a fundamentally different narrative. But despite the attention given to the plight of the nation, and the calls in Yu Dafu's narrative for it to become wealthy and strong, virtually no mention is made of just how the nation is to achieve these lofty goals, much less the place of the intellectual in this process. Far from offering hope, webs here do little more than bind puzzled people to sinking nations.

Perspectives on Relationships Transcending Nations

The intertextualization of Senge's "Flies" in Zhou Zuoren's "Flies" and Satō's *Rural Melancholy* in Yu Dafu's "Sinking" expands the narrative scope of the Japanese texts by articulating concerns with national destiny yet depicting awareness of potential catastrophe as having little effect on empirical conditions. Other more proactive colonial and semicolonial textual contact involving the homeland reconceptualizes relationships—particularly those between Japanese and the colonized/semicolonized—that transcend nations. This transculturation proposes parity within solidarity. Early twentieth-century Chinese, Korean, and Taiwanese creative works transpose Japanese narratives that romanticize personal relationships transcending national origin, particularly proletarian writings that advocate a camaraderie rich on the surface but often lacking in deeper substance. In other words, they deconstruct texts that embody a fundamental paradox of the Japanese proletarian movement: Japanese proletarian intellectuals simultaneously reached out to and both subordinated and criticized the nationalism of colonial and semicolonial revolutionaries. By reclaiming colonial and semicolonial voices silenced or distorted in Japanese literary works, Chinese, Korean, and Taiwanese intertextual reconfigurations of Japanese proletarian literature propose strategies of resilience that challenge not only their Japanese predecessors but also texts—including Zhou Zuoren's "Flies" and Yu

Dafu's "Sinking" — that wallow in despair closer to home. The most famous example of this phenomenon is the intertextualization of Nakano Shigeharu's poem "Shinagawa Station in the Rain" (February 1929) in the Korean writer and revolutionary Im Hwa's poem "Yokohama Pier under the Umbrella" (September 1929). Another key confrontation occurs between the Taiwanese writer Yang Kui's short story "The Paperboy" (1934) and the leading Japanese proletarian writer Kobayashi Takiji's novella *Kani kōsen* (Cannery Boat, 1929).

Reclaiming Voices and Rectifying Revolutionaries

Im Hwa's "Yokohama Pier under the Umbrella" (September 1929) intertextualizes both Nakano Shigeharu's censored poem "Shinagawa Station in the Rain" (February 1929) and this poem's Korean translation (May 1929), discussed in Chapter 4. Critics often read "Yokohama Pier under the Umbrella" as a "response" to "Shinagawa Station in the Rain," but Im Hwa's poem is better interpreted as actively negotiating with textual predecessors.[54] Im Hwa, who lived in Japan from 1929 to 1931 and was a friend of Nakano's, was a passionate reader of Japanese literature from childhood, consuming texts by Nakano, Ikuta Shungetsu, Miyoshi Jūrō (1902–58), Moriyama Kei, and Ueda Bin. He published some of his work in Japanese periodicals, including Nakano's *Proletarian Arts*, the principal journal of the Japanese proletarian literary movement.[55] "Shinagawa Station in the Rain" and "Yokohama Pier under the Umbrella" both take place on rainy days at Japanese transportation hubs and describe the painful separation of friends and loved ones; they also anticipate the return of Korean revolutionaries to Japan. "Shinagawa Station in the Rain" features an anonymous Japanese revolutionary who calls on several Korean comrades who have been expelled from Japan (in preparation for the enthronement of the Shōwa emperor, November 10, 1928) to hurry back to the metropole and threaten if not assassinate the emperor. Similarly, in "Yokohama Pier under the Umbrella" the poet is a Korean revolutionary about to be deported to Korea who reassures his Japanese girlfriend that although he now is being forced to leave Japan, he and his comrades will return. However, the Korean poet does not simply echo the Japanese poet's conviction (replicated in the poem's Korean translation) that the exiled Koreans one day will return to Japan with a dramatic flourish. Asserting a voice and a presence denied his counterpart in both the Japanese- and Korean-language versions of "Shinagawa Station in the Rain," the Korean poet problematizes several of his predecessors' assumptions. He challenges their portrayal of Koreans as hollow and frozen beings, shadows marked only by piercing eyes, fevered cheeks, and deadly weapons. "Yokohama Pier under the Umbrella" presents Koreans as more human, as individuals who love and who suffer loss, and who have their own vision of revolution and the future. Moreover, the Korean poet ridicules the expectations voiced in "Shinagawa Station in the Rain" that the return of Koreans to Japan, albeit guaranteed, will be independent of the actions of their Japanese counterparts. Underlining the responsibilities of the Japanese proletariat, he argues for greater Japanese and Korean cooperation than is expressed in "Shinagawa Station in the Rain."[56] At certain points in the poem, in fact, he points to the artificiality of divisions along national lines. On the other hand, demonstrating the ambivalence of much intra-empire textual contact, "Yokohama Pier under the Umbrella" also seems resigned to the very imperial authority that is challenged in Nakano's poem and even more deeply undercut by its Korean translation.

Like many autoethnographic texts, "Yokohama Pier under the Umbrella" depicts colonial peoples as more human than do the writings it intertextualizes. The water imagery of the early stanzas of "Shinagawa Station in the Rain" contrasts both Korea and Japan, and Koreans and Japanese: Korea is portrayed as a frozen wilderness, whereas Japan is depicted as more fluid and life-sustaining. The rain of Nakano's title is echoed in the first stanza, where several Koreans board the train at Shinagawa in the rain. In the fourth through the seventh stanzas, the poet speaks in turn of the ocean, pigeons, and Korean revolutionaries as "wet with rain," of eyes and lights in the "spraying rain," and of rain "pouring" onto the sidewalk, "falling" onto the dark sea, and "disappearing" from the Koreans' feverish young cheeks.[57] The contrast with the third stanza is significant: "The rivers in your country [Korea] freeze in the cold winter / Your rebel [Korean] hearts freeze at the moment of departure."[58] Here, Koreans are soaked with (Japanese) rain while their hearts remain icy. The narrator deepens his dehumanization of the drenched and departing Koreans by implying that their "burning" black eyes might be reflections of a "green [harbor] signal," not the products of inner passion. Koreans are presented as little more than "black shadows" that pass through the entrance gate, objects in white clothing that flutters in the dark corridor.

Such images are undermined in Im Hwa's poem. Declaring in the opening stanza, "My heart blazes with the fire of sadness at being separated and anger at being chased away," Im Hwa's Korean revolutionary challenges the assertion of the Japanese revolutionary of "Shinagawa Station in the Rain" and its Korean translation that "your rebel [Korean] hearts freeze at the moment of departure."[59] Throughout "Yokohama Pier under the Umbrella," Im Hwa's Korean activist highlights his strong feelings for his Japanese girlfriend and his dedication to the revolutionary cause:

> I for you and you for me
> And those people for you and you for those people
> Why did we pledge our lives . . .
> There was no reason
> No karma between us
> Moreover, you are a foreign girl, I am a man from the colony
> However — the one reason
> Was that you and I, we simply were laboring siblings
> So for only one purpose we
> lives from two different countries ate the same rice
> and you and I lived in love.[60]

Even though their love at times appears more formulaic than flaming, in the Korean poem both the Korean revolutionary and his Japanese lover emerge as more human than the disappearing shadows featured in Nakano's poem. The romantic tie between colonizer and colonized further accentuates the possibilities of solidarity between revolutionaries of the two nations.[61]

Im Hwa's Korean revolutionary stresses joint responsibility, emphasizing that the Japanese need to do more than simply wait for Korean revolutionaries to sweep back to the metropole. "Yokohama Pier under the Umbrella" advises Japanese on the roles they are to play in the proletarian movement — topics not addressed in "Shinagawa Station in the Rain," where the narrator suggests that they need do little more than wait for the return of their "front and rear shields" and celebrate the Korean attack on the emperor. In the Korean poem, the poet tells his girlfriend to keep busy helping recently freed prisoners, child laborers, and others in need. But unlike Nakano's poem and its Korean translation, which assign revolutionary duties based on ethnicity, "Yokohama Pier under the Umbrella" for the most part speaks simply of revolutionaries. For instance, the Korean poet predicts that demonstrations will "flow down the street" in his absence but does not specify just who is demonstrating.[62] Explicitly referring to both Japan and Korea as "foreign lands," the Korean revolutionary alludes to his isolation from both sites, but he also points to the arbitrary nature of the national categories that his predecessors take for granted.

"Yokohama Pier under the Umbrella" thus offers a very different vision of the relationship between Japanese and Korean revolutionaries from that provided in "Shinagawa Station in the Rain." Cleverly intertextualizing essential motifs inscribed in the Japanese poem, the Korean revolutionary challenges the ingrained assumptions articulated by a Japanese writer who, although generally compassionate toward Koreans, still failed to understand their struggles both in Japan and at home and thus was unable to define a course of action amenable to revolutionaries of both nations.[63] The narrator of "Yokohama Pier under the Umbrella" redefines friendships between Koreans and Japanese as mutually beneficial relationships between politically aware cohorts, where one party is not dehumanized for the glory of the other.

On the other hand, by not calling for overt rebellion, "Yokohama Pier under the Umbrella" undermines its predecessors' challenge to the imperial status quo. Im Hwa's Korean revolutionary mentions exhibitions of revolutionary fervor, speaking, for instance, of "young men's speeches" that "pour like flames on the heads of laborers."[64] This marks a notable change from "Shinagawa Station in the Rain," where a gloomy Japan is portrayed as soaked through with a rain that almost certainly would extinguish burning flames. And the revolutionary even urges his girlfriend, when she no longer can tolerate the injustices heaped on her jailed comrades, to hurl her pale skin against "that face" and "that head."[65] This appeal resembles a line near the end of "Shinagawa Station in the Rain": "Thrust up and hold `` jaw."[66] It also resembles this line's Korean translation: "Precisely at his veX aim the sickleX."[67] But these echoes are quickly subverted. The Korean revolutionary claims that when he and his comrades return to Yokohama, his girlfriend might "bury [her] cute head in [his] chest and try crying, try laughing."[68] The laughing and crying that in "Shinagawa Station in the Rain" and its Korean translation were to have taken place in the "ecstasy of burning [revenge]" now are a private affair. Love replaces rather than complements revolution; "Yokohama Pier under the Umbrella" at the end lessens potential for their symbiosis. And so the text that destabilizes prejudices against colonial subjects propagated by Nakano's poem and reinforced by the poem's

Korean translation does so while resigning itself to the imperial authority that is challenged in Nakano's poem and even more deeply rejected by its Korean translation.[69]

Revolutionizing Revolutionaries

Where Im Hwa realigned the distorted, Yang Kui resuscitated the silenced. The revolutionary Taiwanese writer's short story "The Paperboy" (1934) intertextually transposes the leading Japanese proletarian writer Kobayashi Takiji's novella *Cannery Boat* to add colonial voices to discourse on transnational proletarian solidarity. An intellectual deeply concerned with social injustice, Kobayashi became active in the Japanese proletarian movement in the 1920s and quickly caught the attention of revolutionary writers from across East Asia, who interpretively, interlingually, and intertextually transculturated many of his essays and creative works. Some Chinese, Korean, and Taiwanese writers got to know Kobayashi personally and wrote movingly on the injustice of his brutal murder in 1933 by Japanese police.[70] Kobayashi's most lauded publication, *Cannery Boat* is based on an exposé he read in the mid-1920s on abused cannery-boat workers who sued their captain after returning to port.[71] This novella follows a diverse group of seamen—fishers, farmers, factory workers, miners, and students—as they leave the port of Hakodate in southern Hokkaido on the Hakkō Maru for waters off the Soviet Union's Kamchatka Peninsula (northeast of Hokkaido, partway to Alaska), where they fish for crabs. Treated ruthlessly by their captain, the sadistic Asakawa whose every move is in turn dictated by "capitalist bosses," and inspired by Soviet propaganda, the men launch small-scale rebellions; *Cannery Boat* concludes with their resolution to join together in a mass strike, which, the narrator reveals in the postscript, not only "succeeded beyond anyone's imagination," but also was replicated on other ships.[72]

Like many Japanese proletarian literary works, *Cannery Boat* depicts both a transnational proletariat and the injustices of imperialism. The crew of the Hakkō Maru listens eagerly to stories of encounters with Russian farmers relayed by fishers who spent several days on Kamchatka after being washed ashore in a storm. The Russians they met treated them kindly and, aided by a Chinese interpreter, also encouraged them not to fear the Soviet Union as did their leaders (Japanese authorities were terrified that the Bolshevik revolution would spread to Japan), but instead to embrace the proletarian cause and take pride in themselves as workers. In addition to alluding to the possibility of Soviet-Sino-Japanese solidarity, the narrator also criticizes the Japanese imperialist project, likening the ravaging of Hokkaido and Sakhalin to that of colonial Korea and Taiwan: "There, as in the colonies of Korea and Taiwan, they could exploit workers to an absurd degree, knowing they would never have to explain themselves."[73] Soon thereafter, he reveals that Korean laborers employed in Japan—mistreated by Japanese bosses and coworkers—suffer more abuse than their Japanese counterparts. But despite these gestures, the main thrust of *Cannery Boat* is the bonding of Japanese workers who have been victimized by their government's incessant calls for increased production to fuel imperial ambitions. In fact, the narrator goes so far as to call the Japanese laborers "colonials": "In Japan [*naichi*], the laborers who refused to be killed joined together and resisted the capitalists. But the 'colonial' [*shokuminchi*] laborers [Japanese working in Hokkaido and Sakhalin] were completely isolated from all this. Their suffering was unbearable. But each time they fell over and got up, they found that, just like snowballs—they were burdened with yet another layer of suffering."[74] Japanese laborers, whether or not working in Japan proper, were subjected to many of the same abuses as their Korean and Taiwanese counterparts. But to call them "colonials" risks obscuring the deeper indignity of Japan's imperial project more than it strengthens imperial-colonial worker solidarity.

Yang Kui, familiar with a broad spectrum of Japanese writing and no stranger to the Japanese literary world, intertextualizes *Cannery Boat* in "The Paperboy."[75] Narrated in the first person, "The Paperboy" resuscitates the colonial voices silenced in Kobayashi's novella. Picking up on his predecessor's reference to a film featuring a newsboy who becomes a model factory worker and whose dedication leads to financial security, "The Paperboy" focuses on a young Taiwanese boy in Japan who after weeks of searching for employment finally lands a job working for a newspaper agency and morphs quickly into a proletarian hero. Yang Kui's story reveals Taiwanese-Japanese unity in suffering and in struggle: the Japanese student Tanaka comes to the rescue, helping the narrator financially and giving him much needed encouragement, while—in passages censored from the 1934 version of this story—Japanese proletarian leaders embrace his perspective, and he becomes something of a celebrity. Here, interaction replaces comparison. Unlike *Cannery Boat*, where the narrator draws only cursory parallels between working conditions in Japan and those in its colonies (Sakhalin, Korea, and Taiwan), "The Paperboy" depicts Japanese and Taiwanese as working closely together, both suffering as one in the trenches and collectively rejoicing in the spirit of international revolution, at least in Japan; the story concludes with the narrator returning alone to Taiwan to inaugurate a revolution in the colony, suggesting that this is a battle the Taiwanese will have to fight alone. Furthermore, the narrator not surprisingly discusses injuries inflicted by Japan on Taiwan. Again unlike *Cannery Boat*, which mentions Taiwan and Korea only in passing, "The Paperboy" gives a vivid portrait of Japanese as well as local Taiwanese exploitation of the island and its resources.

In notes penned in 1929, Kobayashi expressed concern over Japan's exploitation of its colonies and commented that in *Cannery Boat* he had tried to represent the "typical exploitation of colonies and undeveloped territory."[76] Elsewhere, he declared that because the exploited and tortured Chinese and Japanese proletariat shared a similar plight, fate, and emotions, his novella, as the revolutionary expression of the Japanese proletariat, also could inspire the Chinese proletariat.[77] But Kobayashi's concern with China and the colonies, like that of most Japanese proletarian writers, frequently rang hollow in the ears of colonial and semicolonial revolutionaries who hungered for more than what for them sometimes appeared to be a stale rhetoric of inclusion. Arrested in 1927 for demonstrating with Korean protestors in Tokyo, Yang Kui was deeply sympathetic to the plight of the impoverished across the empire, and in "The Paperboy" this empathy extends to the Japanese themselves. In this fashion, literature of the colonized also advanced an agenda of community different from that of the hegemonic state with its scripted pan-Asianism.

The textual contact discussed in this chapter, taking place in the 1920s and 1930s — the heyday of transculturation in twentieth-century East Asian literary contact nebulae — is only a small subset of colonial and semicolonial East Asian negotiation with what many Chinese, Korean, and Taiwanese writers perceived as their Japanese counterparts' distorted perceptions of how individuals fit into the vast networks of the family, town, nation, and ultimately, world.[78] Most intertextual reconfigurations challenge the relative social separation articulated or implied in modern Japanese literary antecedents, depicting tighter human networks than those in metropolitan predecessors.

But whether rectifying Japanese portrayals of relationships between Japanese and Chinese, Koreans, and Taiwanese, or contrasting relationships among Japanese with those among Chinese, Koreans, and Taiwanese, the interpersonal and intrasocietal relationships found in these intertextualizations are suffused with ambiguity. Distances collapse, but then what? Are things transformed? Do things really change at all? Some characters, like the first-person narrator of Lu Xun's short story "A Small Incident," are not as quick as their Japanese predecessors to dismiss encounters with strangers, but they are so stunned at their physical and metaphorical collisions with them that they do little more than reminisce, not moving much beyond the supposedly transformative moment. Likewise, the first-person narrator of Yu Dafu's short story "Late-Blooming Cassia" forges deeper friendships than his Japanese predecessor, yet in the end elongates his bubble rather than moving outside it. Other voices, like the poet of Zhou Zuoren's "Flies" and the first-person narrator of Yu Dafu's "Sinking," are more conscious of the difficulties facing their nations than are the voices in the Japanese narratives they intertextually reconfigure. But their concern, rather than translating into action, stops with vacuous demands that ultimately relieve them of further responsibility: in "Flies," the poet calls on a magical power, one explicitly "exceeding the power of mankind," to fix China's ills, whereas the protagonist of "Sinking," about to commit suicide in Japan, simply calls on China to become rich and strong. Although written in the first person, suggesting that its protagonist is not yet deceased, "Sinking" holds out little hope that the supposedly engaged intellectual actually will devote his talents to helping reform his homeland. These and other intertextual reworkings of Japanese literature depict strong ties binding people to one another, to communities, and to nations; but these ties, despite allowing for important insights into human experience, do not necessarily lead to resistance against the banal and the corrupt, let alone the continued eroding of national sovereignty. If anything, they increase vulnerability by giving the illusion of engagement.

To be sure, not all Chinese, Korean, and Taiwanese intertextual transculturations that reconceptualize the relationships depicted in Japanese creative works are this pessimistic. Ba Jin's *Family* and Yŏm Sangsŏp's *Three Generations* feature young men determined to have a hand in reforming their societies. Likewise, Im Hwa's "Yokohama Pier under the Umbrella" and Yang Kui's "The Paperboy" focus on eager young revolutionaries. But ironically, these creative works abandon their characters in transit, cutting them loose as they float, in some cases literally, toward possibility: we leave the Korean revolutionaries of "Yokohama Pier under the Umbrella" about to begin their circle tour from Japan to Korea and back, where they presumably will rejoin an intra-empire proletarian struggle; Ba Jin's Juehui departing home for Shanghai, where he presumably will join with likeminded youths to rejuvenate China; and the narrator of "The Paperboy" approaching Taiwan, where he presumably will launch a proletarian revolution singlehandedly. For his part, Dŏkgi longs to sail off to Japan to wrap up his education there; although *Three Generations* concludes with his declaring it his duty to help the impoverished P'ilsun, there is no word of his abandoning his plans, which have been some time in the making, to sail back to Kyoto. Possibility is alive in these texts, and their earlier successes suggest these characters will not sink into oblivion. But there is no denying the precarious vessel on which the narrative twilight turns to darkness.

Portrayals of suffering and relationships, probing the cores of human experience, are among the most significant targets of intertextual recasting as writers work to establish their own cultural capital and authority. Equally (if not more) consequential are intertextualizations that, while not silent on questions of colonial and semicolonial suffering and relationships, negotiate even more aggressively with imperial depictions of human agency. The next chapter takes up the dynamics of culpability, accountability, obligation, persistence, and change in early twentieth-century intra–East Asian intertextual transculturation.

EIGHT

Questions of Agency:
Raising Responsibility, Parodying
Persistence, and Rethinking Reform

Questions concerning human agency — responsibility, endurance, and ultimately the ability to (bring about) change — underlie much intertextualization that reconceptualizes suffering and relationships. But some textual contact prioritizes concern with agency. To be sure, most literature deals to at least a limited degree with issues of personal and societal flexibility (the ability both to change and to be changed), persistence (working to maintain or to change the status quo), and responsibility (accountability, culpability, and obligation). Yet dynamic intertextualization, particularly when confrontational, frequently accentuates these anxieties as texts grapple with their own positionalities vis-à-vis literary predecessors. Embodying the ambiguities of creative agency, dynamic intertextualization provides fertile territory for examining the paradoxes of human agency.

This tendency exists in literatures from around the world. The Chinese exile writer Gao Xingjian's (1940–) drama *Chezhan* (The Bus Stop, 1983) engages actively with the dynamics of endurance in both Samuel Beckett's (1906–89) *En attendant Godot* (Waiting for Godot, 1952) and Lu Xun's "Guoke" (The Passerby, 1925); for its part, the Japanese writer Ōe Kenzaburō's novel *A Personal Matter* (1964) likewise sets up numerous parallels with Jean-Paul Sartre's *Nausea* (1938), but stresses questions of responsibility. Yet vigorously tackling issues of human agency—whether via reworking the discussions of literary predecessors (Gao Xingjian) or greatly amplifying them (Ōe Kenzaburō)—is especially noticeable in intertextual transculturation in spaces of significantly unbalanced power relationships.

Probing responsibility, persistence, and possibilities of change has special import in contexts of political and social oppression, where peoples are deprived of autonomy and where modes of collaboration, acquiescence, and resistance often fuse. Colonialism is one of the most abject forms of surrender of one people to another; it also is one of the most ruthless types of cultural abuse of one people by another. Semicolonialism, the multinational yet fragmented political, economic, and cultural domination such as China experienced, also entails exploitation and demands submission. Unable to escape from outside control, colonial and semicolonial peoples frequently find it impossible to sustain outright resistance; complicity and even collaboration often seem the only means of survival. Concerns with agency, present in every society, frequently rise to the forefront in (semi)colonial and post(semi)colonial discourse.[1] And these concerns are particularly acute in contacts with texts by metropolitan writers, key embodiments of metropolitan cultural capital and often authority. Obvious examples include the West Indian novelist Jean Rhys's intertextual recasting of Charlotte Brontë's *Jane Eyre* (1847) in *Wide Sargasso Sea* (1966) and the reconfiguration of Joseph Conrad's *Heart of Darkness* (1902) in the Sudanese novelist Tayeb Salih's *Season of Migration to the North* (1966), both of which highlight the agency of the formerly silenced. In contrast, T'itsian T'abidze (1895–1937), a founder of Georgian poetic modernism, greatly reduces this agency. His poem "Me qachaghemba momk'les aragvze" (I Was Killed by Bandits on the Aragvi, 1920s) displaces the "heroic masculinity of the folk tradition" as enunciated by Georgian literary texts and even more importantly by the Russian Romantic poet Mikhail Lermontov (1814–41) in *Mtsyri* (The Novice, 1839) and *Demon* (1829–41), with "the poet's morbid sensitivity, pessimism, and infinite vulnerability to fate."[2] Providing an interesting twist is the Cuban novelist Alejo Carpentier's *The Harp and the Shadow* (1979), which reinvents the imperial aggressor, featuring an incapacitated Christopher Columbus who grapples with his responsibility for the suffering he inflicted on the Americas.

In intra–East Asian literary contact nebulae as well, colonial and semicolonial creative writers intertextualized Japanese literature to probe the degree to which persons and societies have control over their lives and futures. As discussed in the preceding two chapters, while not denying the horrors of foreign exploitation, many re-castings highlight the local origins of suffering and depict it as virtually inevitable. Equally foreboding is textual transposition that, by drawing attention to human interdependence, depicts characters who—despite their greater concern for the world beyond themselves than their Japanese counterparts—nevertheless are powerless to bring about change or whom the text abandons as they are en route to effecting change. The thickest gloom, however, enshrouds intertextual reconfigurations that focus on agency. It is here that possibilities for change that would alleviate suffering—facilitated by assumptions of responsibility and unwavering persistence—are most deeply interrogated. Frequently, such creative recastings manipulate existing discussions of agency, but they also regularly interject concerns with agency into the narrative.

Early twentieth-century East Asian intertextualizations of modern Japanese literature explore questions of agency in three principal ways: by replacing or augmenting Japanese obsession with fate with increased attention to responsibility; by featuring characters with more stamina than their Japanese counterparts despite harsher conditions; and by depicting characters grappling with greater corruption than their Japanese predecessors. Responsibility is explored, but suffering only multiplies; endurance, leading to Sisyphean struggles, is invoked only to be parodied; and attempts at social criticism are mocked, compromising the possibility of reform. Together, intertextualizations of Japanese literature that draw attention to human agency provide an ominous vision of the colonial and semicolonial future. Of course many Chinese, Korean, and Taiwanese creative works offer such a vision without directly engaging with metropolitan textual products. But those that do—implicitly or explicitly differentiating conditions in their lands from those in Japan and emending Japanese depictions of colonial and semicolonial peoples—are especially significant, through their mere existence, in embodying colonial and semicolonial agency vis-à-vis the cultural products of the imperial power, and, through their manner of reconfiguration, in problematizing such agency vis-à-vis the future of their societies.

Challenging Fate, Raising Responsibility

Concepts of fate abound in a broad array of folk beliefs, religions, philosophies, and literatures. Peter Hill has observed:

Awareness of [our] ultimately grim lot can readily give rise to feelings that each individual is driven to destruction and death by some inexorable force or fate that also determines the individual's life-term. . . . It is easy to feel that many important events in life happen to, or more correctly come upon the individual from the outside or the beyond: the individual has little or no power to control or change these. . . . When faced with life's endless inexplicabilities, belief in an ineluctable and all-pervasive power was a highly seductive option. Such attitudes may well be universal and probably date from earliest times.[3]

Some texts put forward extreme positions, portraying fate either as obliterating entirely the possibility of independent action or as something that can be overcome completely with sufficient effort. In *The Iliad*, for instance, Hera proposes saving Achilles from the Trojans but notes that "afterward he must suffer what the Fates spun out / on the doomed fighter's life line drawn that day / his mother gave him birth."[4] This sentiment is repeated in *The Odyssey*, where Alcinous comments that after Odysseus returns home he must "suffer all that Fate / and the overbearing Spinner spun out on his life line / the very day his mother gave him birth."[5] In contrast, Albert Camus asserts in "Le mythe de Sisyphe" (The Myth of Sisyphus, 1942): "The lucidity that was to be his torture also crowns his victory; there is no fate that cannot be surmounted by scorn."[6] Similarly, in the essay "Fate," Ralph Waldo Emerson (1803–82) argues, "Intellect annuls fate. So far as a man thinks, he is free."[7] As gripping as these statements are, most explorations of the control human beings have over their lives are more ambiguous.

Discussions of fate and agency appear frequently in early twentieth-century East Asian literatures, as in most literatures.[8] A small subset stem from dynamic intra-empire intertextualization. Stories by the Korean writers Hyŏn Chin-gŏn and Kim Dong-in provide some of the most striking examples of this phenomenon. Hyŏn Chin-gŏn's "Sul kwŏnhanŭn sahoe" (A Society That Drives You to Drink, 1921) and "Fire" (1925) and Kim Dong-in's "Paettaragi" (The Seaman's Chant, 1921) manipulate the fixation on fate and repression of human agency found in the Japanese writer Tayama Katai's novella *The End of Jūemon* (1902), as well as in his colleague Kunikida Doppo's short stories "Unmeironsha" (The Fatalist, 1902) and "Jonan" (Woman Trouble, 1903). Focusing to a greater degree than their Japanese precursors on questions of responsibility, including accountability, culpability, and obligation, they give darker assessments of human potential and agency.

Like Doppo, Katai played an axial role in the development of modern Japanese literature. One of Japan's most prominent naturalist writers, he is best known for his novel *The Quilt* (1907) and for launching what later was referred to as the I-novel, fiction that claimed to expose writers' sordid thoughts and immoral acts. Exchange students in Japan snatched up Katai's oeuvre, and his texts were interpretively, interlingually, and intertextually transculturated in China and Korea.[9] Hyŏn Chin-gŏn, one of the pacesetters of the twentieth-century Korean short story and a master of realism, lived in Japan from 1912 to 1919; his diary indicates that he grew fond of Western and Japanese literature while there, and his creative products dynamically rework a broad array of Japanese prose.[10]

Battles between Fate and Responsibility

Doppo's "The Fatalist" (1902) and Hyŏn Chin-gŏn's "A Society That Drives You to Drink" (1921) both feature characters who obsessively bemoan their lack of agency. Takahashi Shinzō spends the majority of "The Fatalist" describing to *jibun* (the reflexive pronoun, here meaning "I" or "myself")—a man he approaches on the beach—how fate has cursed his life; he asserts repeatedly that there is no escape from the "demon of fate." "A Society That Drives You to Drink" focuses on *namp'yŏn* ("husband"), a man who repeatedly blames not fate but "Korean society" for leaving him no choice but to numb his mind with alcohol and who claims that the only way to survive life in Korea is to stumble around in a drunken stupor. "A Society That Drives You to Drink" complicates Shinzō's obsession with fate by placing greater emphasis on human agency, that is to say personal, social, and societal responsibility. In addition, by concentrating explicitly on Korean society as opposed to society in general, "A Society That Drives You to Drink" encapsulates the dilemma of colonial subjects stymied not only by foreign oppression but also by the seeming inability of their own people to take responsibility or act responsibly, that is to say, to exert agency.

Frustrated that her husband has become an alcoholic, *namp'yŏn*'s wife asks him who is forcing him to drink. She assumes that anger, or perhaps the local dandies, are to blame. But he implicates Korean society: "What drives me to drink isn't fury, and it's not the dandies. It's this society that drives me to drink. It's this Korean society that forces me to drink. Do you get it? It's my good fortune to have been born in Korea, since if I'd been born in another country I wouldn't be able to drink."[11] Unlike Shinzō, who holds a supernatural power accountable for his numerous difficulties, *namp'yŏn* instead fingers society as the culprit, and fate—paradoxically—as making life in this society somewhat more endurable. *Namp'yŏn* accentuates the difficulties of living in Korea, telling his wife: "You just don't understand. People are suffocating. What I'm trying to say is that if you remain sober you can't survive a single day in this society. You'll vomit blood and die, or you'll fall in the water and drown. I'm telling you, your chest gets clogged up and you choke. You suffocate."[12]

In his conversation with his wife, *namp'yŏn* reveals that he is particularly disturbed by Korean selfishness:

Say we organize a club. If we listen to those who come together to join this club what do we hear but assertions that the people come first, that society comes first. . . . But do you know what happens in just two days, in just two days? . . . Night and day [the members of the club] tear into each other and try to demolish each other. What's the result of all this? What actually gets done? And it's not just clubs—corporations, associations. . . . The society we Korean guys have organized is made up entirely of pieces like this. What can one do in a society like this?[13]

Namp'yŏn declares Koreans responsible for the disintegration of their own society and country.

But condemning society is one thing and striving to transform it is another. *Namp'yŏn* reveals that a number of Koreans, despairing of the status quo, have made earnest attempts to reform their society. Unsuccessful in these endeavors, many have convinced themselves that alcohol is the only answer:

The guy who tries to do something is an idiot. The guy who is really with it just throws up blood and dies—there's nothing he can do to stop it. If it doesn't go like this, he has nothing but booze. Not so long ago I decided to do something, and I really tried to do it. But it all came to naught. I was a fool. I don't drink because I want to. . . . The only thing one can do in this society is become a drunk.[14]

"A Society That Drives You to Drink" ultimately depicts social responsibility (in this case the individual's obligations to society) as no match for societal responsibility (in this case society's culpability).

The protagonists of "The Fatalist" and "A Society That Drives You to Drink" both portray themselves as bereft of agency, at the mercy of powers beyond their control. By replacing "fate" with "Korean society," the Korean short story impresses on the reader both the immediacy and the human face of the origins of suffering. Yet significantly, neither immediacy nor the presence of a human face facilitates reform. Societal culpability is acknowledged, but social accountability and obligation, while initially concerns, eventually fall by the wayside, making change virtually impossible.

Fighting Back with Fire

"A Society That Drives You to Drink" replaces Shinzō's fixation on the controlling hand of fate with *namp'yŏn's* obsession with the grasp of Korean society. Hyŏn Chin-gŏn's later short story "Fire" (1925) similarly undermines the emphasis in the Japanese writer Tayama Katai's *The End of Jūemon* (1902) on the controlling hand of fate by highlighting Korean societal responsibility, especially the abuses inherent in the traditional Korean family system. To be sure, the plot of "Fire" more closely resembles that of Anton Chekhov's (1860–1904) short story "Sleepy" (1888) and Katherine Mansfield's (1888–1923) short story "The-Child-Who-Was-Tired" (1910) than it does *The End of Jūemon*. Like "Sleepy" and "The-Child-Who-Was-Tired," "Fire" features a girl in her early teens enslaved to an abusive family; no longer able to endure their cruelty, she destroys what she believes to be, but in fact is not, the source of her pain.[15] On the other hand, the intertextualization of Katai is more significant than that of Chekhov and Mansfield. Whereas Hyŏn Chin-gŏn dynamically appropriates elements from "Sleepy" and "The-Child-Who-Was-Tired" to heighten artistic capital and narrative intensity, he actively confronts *The End of Jūemon* to focus on questions of responsibility. Hyŏn Chin-gŏn's protagonist Sun-i (a young woman with an abusive husband and mother-in-law) and Katai's protagonist Jūemon (a man suffering from elephantiasis) both are victims of physical and verbal abuse who are driven to arson. Jūemon convinces his young lover to burn down multiple buildings in his village; Sun-i sets fire to the room where her husband has raped her repeatedly. Yet unlike *jibun*, the secondary narrator of *The End of Jūemon* who explores at length fate's role in the destruction of Jūemon, the narrator of "Fire" holds society accountable for the demise of Sun-i.[16] The narrator of "Fire" reveals society and especially family as more powerful and blameworthy than any superhuman force.

Jibun is shocked to learn that an arsonist is plaguing the beautiful village his friends call home. He expends considerable energy contemplating why this man takes such drastic measures and concludes that Jūemon has no control over his behavior: "I was sure that Jūemon's congenital defects shaped part of his basic lawlessness and that his disposition had a large impact on his crimes."[17] After Jūemon's murder, *jibun* speaks explicitly of the troubled man's fate: "Above all, he was fated to be unable to escape his hometown, a mountain village that . . . holds traditional practices in tremendous esteem."[18] Although *jibun* speaks occasionally of societal culpability and is distressed that no one in the village feels sympathy for Jūemon, his primary concern is dissecting this man's character.

Conversely, the narrator of the Korean story "Fire," describing the events of a single day in Sun-i's life, shifts the spotlight to societal responsibility, familial culpability in particular. "Fire" begins:

> Sun-i, who was just fourteen and had come to her husband's home a little over a month ago, was deep in sleep. Yet she felt as if she were going to be asphyxiated. It was as though a large rock were pressing down on her, and she were suffocating. . . . Her waist and hips throbbed, as though they were being cleaved off, ripped into shreds, and crushed to pieces. The throbbing, burning, blistering pain was unbearable. It was as though a rod had been thrust up her insides to her chest, and the sharp pain caused her mouth to open with a snap and her body to jerk up.[19]

The previous night, hundreds of miles from her birth family, Sun-i had attempted to escape her vicious husband by hiding in the barn, but he had dragged her back to the house and raped her. The day "Fire" takes place, Sun-i's mother-in-law abuses her, yelling at her for small infractions and beating her severely for breaking some dishes. Believing that if the room disappears so will the abuse, the young bride retaliates by setting fire to the space where her husband has repeatedly assaulted her. Her reasoning is painfully naïve; trying to escape her husband by burning his property will almost certainly prove futile.

In contrast with his Japanese counterpart, the narrator of "Fire" does not analyze Sun-i's "natural" disposition and does not question what about her character led her to commit arson; providing virtually no information about Sun-i apart from her identity as an abused spouse, the narrator suggests that anyone in her situation would feel similarly compelled. The narrator of the Korean text—although speaking only of Sun-i—points to the brutality of the traditional Korean marriage system, which required girls to leave home at an early age and live at the mercy of often ruthless husbands and vicious mothers-in-law.[20] Thus "Fire," like "A Society That Drives You to Drink," calls greater attention to societal responsibility than its Japanese predecessors and implicates Korean society in particular. But as before, exposing societal responsibility has little effect on social conditions; Sun-i is even less likely than *namp'yŏn* to improve her own situation, let alone inspire a revolution.

Fate, Obligation, and Accountability

In their intertextual transculturations of Japanese creative works, the Korean stories "A Society That Drives You to Drink" and "Fire" both shift the focus from fate to societal responsibility. Conversely, the Korean writer Kim Dong-in's short story "The Seaman's Chant" intertextualizes Doppo's story "Woman Trouble" to move the spotlight from obsession with fate to social responsibility. In other words, the question shifts from the extent to which society determines the trajectory of individual lives to the responsibilities of individuals within society. "Woman Trouble" also addresses personal accountability and obligation, but matters of responsibility — particularly the responsibility of the primary and secondary witnesses of a crime — are more prominent in "The Seaman's Chant."[21]

The storylines and narrative structures of "The Seaman's Chant" and "Woman Trouble" are conspicuously similar. A nameless man — *jibun* (the reflexive pronoun, as above) in "Woman Trouble" and *na* (the personal pronoun "I") in "The Seaman's Chant" — unexpectedly hears beautiful music, approaches the performer, and asks him to tell his story. The majority of "Woman Trouble" and "The Seaman's Chant," both of which are framed narratives, consists of the life histories these musicians — Shūzō (a nearly blind *shakuhachi* player) and the anonymous singer *kŭ* (the pronoun "he") — relate to *jibun* and *na*. Shūzō and *kŭ* tell their interlocutors about the grave difficulties they experienced with women and describe three incidents of "woman trouble" that involve abandonment by or of women. Shūzō and *kŭ* also mention that, no longer involved with women, they migrate from town to town, bereft of home and loved ones. After narrating their stories, the musicians perform a final number and walk away. "Woman Trouble" and "The Seaman's Chant" conclude with *jibun* and *na* continuing their journeys, their reactions to the stories they have just been told drowned out by Shūzō's and *kŭ*'s plaintive notes.[22]

"Woman Trouble" parodies obsession with fate and exposes the fallacy of unilaterally blaming misfortune on destiny. Throughout his life, Shūzō has used fate to predict, explain, and rationalize the many complications of his relationships with women. When he was a child, Shūzō's mother took him to a fortuneteller, who after look- ing carefully at his face concluded: "Nope, don't worry. This child has a wonderful physiognomy, so he'll enjoy a successful career. But he'll have one problem, and that will be with women. If for the rest of his life he's careful in his dealings with women, he'll certainly en- joy a magnificent existence."[23] Shūzō and his mother erroneously in- terpreted "being careful" with women as "fearing" all women, and he followed what he believed was the diviner's command to the let- ter. Ironically, Shūzō's fear of women – exacerbated by his mother's many lectures on their "evils" – caused more problems than it solved and complicated otherwise pleasurable relationships.

Shūzō makes several feeble attempts to deflect attention from his fate, occasionally claiming personal responsibility for his dysfunc- tional relationships. For instance, at one point he tells *jibun*, "I've had so much woman trouble not because of my nature [as the fortuneteller had suggested] but because I am gentle and inexperienced."[24] Yet claims of gentleness and lack of experience simply reinforce the notion that his "woman trouble" has been fated: not only is being "gentle" part of one's nature, but Shūzō after all is not inexperienced. "Woman Trouble" portrays a man so convinced that he was fated to experience "woman trouble" that he failed to exert subjective autonomy, and so his became a self-fulfilling prophecy. Nonethe- less, the greater ramifications of Shūzō's failure to exert agency are not explored in Doppo's story; after Shūzō completes his tale he simply plays another song filled with nostalgia, sorrow, and eternal resentment.

Questions of responsibility loom larger in the Korean writer Kim Dong-in's "The Seaman's Chant," which engages intertextually with Doppo's "Woman Trouble." Although the Korean and Japanese sto- ries follow similar trajectories, the protagonist of "The Seaman's Chant" is more brutal than his Japanese counterpart. Including a vio- lent character allows the narrator of "The Seaman's Chant" to ex- plore the accountability of both perpetrators and witnesses of crimes.[25] *Kŭ* tells *na* – the nameless traveler whose summary of *kŭ*'s adventures occupies the bulk of "The Seaman's Chant" – that he re- peatedly struck his wife and was responsible for her death. He also reveals that his temper flared at the slightest provocation and that he beat his brother and sister-in-law for criticizing him. In the past, both *kŭ* and those who witnessed or were told about his crimes ascribed his behavior to fate, and so now does *na*. In fact, one of the most significant differences between "Woman Trouble" and "The Seaman's Chant" is the latter's emphasis on the sizable roles played by spectators (in this case *kŭ*'s brother, sister-in-law, and other villagers) and by secondary witnesses (in this case *na*) in the transmission and interpretation of events. Intertextually reconfiguring "Woman Trouble," "The Seaman's Chant" argues that aversion to accepting responsibility is not exclusive to the criminal but rather is shared with witnesses, often with deadly ramifications.

Kŭ is quick to blame fate. At the beginning of the story he responds to *na*'s question as to why he has not visited his hometown for several decades with the following declaration: "Well that's just the way life is. Do things ever turn out the way you want them to? . . . Fate is so powerful."[26] This comment is one of the few of *kŭ*'s that *na* cites directly, thus emphasizing *kŭ*'s refusal to claim responsibility. *Kŭ*'s occasional gestures toward accountability are undermined by his subsequent behavior. He spends years traveling the seas gaining sympathy from strangers via his *paettaragi*, a seaman's chant that laments the long separations between sailors and their wives; the *paettaragi* turns his confession into an easy ploy for evading responsibility.

Yet the burden of responsibility does not fall solely on *kŭ*, who reveals to *na* that few in his village did anything to assist his wife, and that even after her beaten body washed ashore, he was not held accountable for her death. It is true that when they heard *kŭ* physically abusing his wife, *kŭ*'s brother and his brother's wife attempted to defuse the situation. But even after the body of *kŭ*'s wife was discovered, *kŭ*'s brother did not censure *kŭ* and instead simply looked at him reproachfully, "as though he wanted to ask, 'Brother, what have you done?'"[27] For their part, the other villagers ignored the serious crimes taking place in their midst. *Na* tells the reader that they deemed the relationship between *kŭ* and his wife somewhat strange — not because he beat her, ironically enough, but rather because the two appeared to be so in love. But even if they really had no inkling of the brutal acts that regularly took place in *kŭ*'s home, *kŭ*'s neighbors were aware of his wife's early and violent death. Still, they did not chastise *kŭ*, much less charge him with a crime. They instead simply mourned with him.

Kŭ's neighbors were unable or unwilling to hold him accountable for his crimes, but *na* goes one step farther and explicitly exonerates *kŭ*, referring several times in the final paragraphs of "The Seaman's Chant" to *kŭ*'s story as the "fateful narrative of his life" (*sukmyŏng jŏk kyŏnghŏmdam*). Kim Dong-in's short story concludes with the imagined strains of the *paettaragi* drowning out memories of the "fateful tale." *Na* remarks that immediately after hearing *kŭ*'s story, both the song and the tale circle through his mind and keep him awake at night; *na* gives every indication that they resonate with equal volume. But as early as the following morning, memories of the *paettaragi* so overwhelm recollections of the tale that *na* makes no mention of the latter. A year later, *na* speaks of *kŭ* as leaving behind both "a fateful tale and a sorrowful *paettaragi*."[28] Yet, as happened the day after hearing *kŭ*'s tale, *na* quickly focuses his attention on the sorrowful *paettaragi*, forgetting the tragedy of *kŭ*'s wife. "The Seaman's Chant" thus reveals how relying on fate to explain a crime can contribute both to the escalation and to the romanticization of violence, regardless of whether fate is invoked by the perpetrator of a crime, by an eyewitness, or by someone who learns about it only after the act. In so doing, Kim Dong-in's short story raises issues of responsibilities to society not addressed in its Japanese predecessor.

In their dynamic intertextualization of Japanese literature, the Korean stories "A Society That Drives You to Drink," "Fire," and "The Seaman's Chant" go beyond Japanese obsessions with fate by provoking deeper queries about responsibility. In so doing, they disclose microcosms of the self-inflicted injustices pervading lands under Japanese control and also highlight lacunae in the cultural products of their Japanese oppressors. But they offer few answers. Responsibility both social and societal is acknowledged, and probed, but suffering seems only to intensify.

Parodying Persistence

In addition to undermining Japanese obsession with fate, intraempire intertextualizations of Japanese literature that explore questions of agency also look closely at human endurance. The ability to persist, to forge ahead despite everything, is often a prerequisite to transforming individuals and societies. But results are not guaranteed, and struggle for the sake of struggle, while in some instances ennobling, often is symptomatic of feckless strength.

Parodying Faith in Human Endurance

Early twentieth-century Chinese, Korean, and Taiwanese literary works that transculturate Japanese creative texts frequently feature characters who, although tormented or nearly numbed by despair, paradoxically express greater hope and aspiration, that is to say faith in human endurance, than their Japanese predecessors. In fact, some colonial and semicolonial texts depict characters who sink into even more profound despondency than those in the Japanese writings they rework—in part because of the additional burden of foreign political oppression—yet who display more grit and determination than their Japanese antecedents. At the same time that Chinese, Korean, and Taiwanese texts underline the resilience of subjugated peoples in the face of great hardship, they also implicitly critique the cowardice of the Japanese characters who, although granted untold advantages, believe they have little potential and insist on feeling sorry for themselves.

One important example is the intertextualization of Akutagawa's stories "A Fool's Life" (1927) and "Cogwheels" (1927) in Yi Sang's short story "Wings" (1936).[29] An accomplished poet and prose writer who composed in both Korean and Japanese, Yi Sang was one of Korea's leading modernists and a fan of Japanese literature; he wrote as early as 1932 that he was fascinated by Akutagawa's oeuvre.[30] Although most of his encounters with Japanese literature took place in Korea, his artistic creations abound with traces and often intertextualizations of Japanese, Western, and Chinese literary works.[31]

"A Fool's Life," "Cogwheels," and "Wings" all feature an emasculated and desperate writer with an unbearable home life who is obsessed by wings: his own imagined wings, the wings of animals (dead and alive), metal wings, and pictures of wings. Over the course of these stories, wings—mechanisms of flight and potential implements of escape—become remote from the human body and nearly impossible to utilize. Wings metamorphose both within and among texts: from wings of soaring butterflies that transform into easily destroyed "artificial wings" and then into the limbs of preserved animals ("A Fool's Life"), to the externalized metallic airfoils that support planes and the subject of frightening visual and auditory hallucinations, both of which struggle to supplant the less technologically advanced cogwheels ("Cogwheels"), and finally to vanished and yearned-for body parts that have been replaced by Japanese architectural structures ("Wings").

These stories also portray words—mechanisms that allow for cerebral flight and facilitate intellectual escape—as coming increasingly from outside the individual and nearly impossible to harness. In "A

Fool's Life," reading the works of earlier writers provides the protagonist with some comfort but gradually increases his anxiety;
writing offers only slight reprieve and frequently exacerbates feelings
of confinement. Although in "Cogwheels" writing provides some
solace, the words the narrator reads circulate in his mind as randomly
and as menacingly as do wings, and they contribute to his eventual
paralysis. But by the conclusion of Yi Sang's "Wings," the dictionary
has been emptied: the narrator imagines flipping through a lexicon
of endless blank white pages. The absence of words and wings in
"Wings" is particularly noticeable when compared with the proliferation of these instruments in Akutagawa's stories.

Examining how depictions of wings (natural and artificial) and
words (reading and writing, foreign and native) are transformed both
within and among Akutagawa's and Yi Sang's stories — primarily to
emphasize the increasing despair of the intellectual antihero as he
moves from a mechanized society to the colonial landscape — suggests
the distress experienced by many educated early twentieth-century
East Asians. These intellectuals feared that the penetration of mechanical modernity, not to mention the invading colonial power, far
from providing greater opportunities, ultimately would leave them
with nowhere to go and nothing to say; lacking necessary expertise,
they worried they would be rendered obsolete. "A Fool's Life" depicts
manufactured words (literary works) as increasingly threatening;
images of words and wings on the attack are intensified in "Cogwheels." By "Wings," artificial words and wings no longer are the
primary concern. This story presents the other side of modernity —
an emasculated colonial intellectual stripped of his language and his
wings by the very mechanized forces that created the menacing
words and wings depicted in "Cogwheels." Yet the narrator's initial
timidity is precisely what puts his eventual display of courage in bold
relief.

Shattering Illusions

The third-person narrator of "A Fool's Life," a semi-autobiographical
story published shortly after Akutagawa's suicide, focuses on *kare*
(the pronoun "he"), a writer and enthusiastic reader. The 51 loosely
linked short sections of this text describe recent episodes in *kare's* life
and underline his despair. *Kare* claims he has no desire to live, and
although he maintains his passion for work, he finds it increasingly
difficult to write; in addition, over the course of the narrative, he de-

teriorates mentally and physically and his family life becomes more and more precarious. *Kare* demonstrates little faith in human potential; he believes that the yellowed moth-eaten wings he sees on a stuffed swan in a junk shop symbolize what has become of his life. "A Fool's Life" concludes with *kare*'s descent into a drug-induced haze that allows him only brief periods of lucidity. Featuring a protagonist confronted by a mechanical society that he believes gives him little room to soar, "A Fool's Life" draws attention to the intellectual's increasing spatial and psychological confinement: here the "natural" wings of a less technologically savvy era are banished to junk shops and stuffed with synthetic materials, while the proliferating words of other writers leave scant room for his own.

Kare's road to flight is indirect, and although he eventually is allowed to roam in his reveries, his moment of ecstasy is all too brief, and he tumbles back to earth and literally into shackles. The journey begins when *kare*—reading an English dictionary—stumbles across the English words "talaria" (winged shoes), "tale" (narrative), and "talipot" (a palm tree that blossoms only once every seven decades). *Kare* is transfixed by these words and daydreams about blossoms soaring above the remote seas. He later encounters flight, the touch of a butterfly's wings leaving a lasting impression: "In wind filled with the scent of seaweed, a butterfly flashed. That instant he felt the touch of the butterfly's wings on his dry lips. The dust the wings imprinted on his lips still glittered years later."[32]

Having been brushed by flight, the next step is actually to fly. The narrator claims that Voltaire—through *Candide*, a satire of excessive optimism—has "supplied *kare* with artificial wings"; the narrator imagines that *kare* uses these wings to fly above the earth and that he hurtles toward the sun like a modern-day Icarus, seemingly forgetting what happened to the ancient Greek:

Voltaire had provided him with artificial wings. *Kare* spread out these artificial wings and easily soared up to the sky. At the same time, the joys and sorrows of life, bathed in the light of intellect, sank below his eyes. He let irony and smiles fall over shabby towns and ascended through unobstructed space, straight for the sun. He seemed to have forgotten that the sun's rays had burned wings identical to these and sent an ancient Greek falling to a watery death.[33]

Voltaire's words provide *kare* with wings and he floats above the earth, yet the next section, ironically entitled "Kase" (Shackles, the grounding of flight), finds *kare* chained to his publisher and his family.

Wings do not reappear until much later in the story, and then only as the sallow and bedraggled appendages of a mounted swan in a junk shop. The narrator notes: "He happened to see a stuffed swan in a second-hand store. It stood with neck erect, its wings yellowed and eaten by moths. Reflecting back on his life, he felt tears and cold laughter welling up inside him."[34] *Kare's* fall is nearly complete. The following section of "A Fool's Life" aptly is entitled "Toriko" (Prisoner) and the final and concluding section "Haiboku" (Defeat). Our last image of *kare* is of a man high on Veronal whose hand shakes constantly and who lives from day to day in semidarkness. "A Fool's Life" replaces flapping wings with trembling hands.

Words also are problematized in this short story. *Kare's* textual inheritance is oppressive: literary works circulate ominously in "A Fool's Life," now that improved technology has made books even more widely accessible and further jammed bookstore shelves. Indeed, references to *kare* reading appear more frequently than those of him writing. The narrator suggests that all words have been used, or abused; he asks where there is space, or rather whether there is space, for *kare* to make his mark. Although writing occasionally allows *kare* to deflect crises and teaches him something about himself, it remains a perilous activity. For instance, toward the conclusion of "A Fool's Life," *kare* sets out to compose an autobiography. Yet this text brings him little fulfillment. No sooner has he completed his manuscript—which he ironically entitles "A Fool's Life"—than he goes to a junk shop where he sees the stuffed swan with decrepit wings. This swan clearly symbolizes what he has become: a lifeless animal under attack. Bereft of wings and crowded out by the words of others, *kare* is rendered immobile.

Bombarding the reader with a multiplicity of texts, the narrator of "A Fool's Life" depicts writing as only exacerbating depression. The proliferation of books by other writers simply adds to *kare's* anxiety. Confronted by a hostile environment, *kare* abandons his struggle and finds refuge in drugged semiconsciousness.

Assailed by Words, Wheels, and Wings

"Cogwheels" is narrated in the first person by *boku* (the personal pronoun "I"), an anxious author who spends considerable time alone in his hotel room attempting to write. He often remarks that he feels strange, ill, or depressed; he has frequent hallucinations—especially of cogwheels and wings—and is disturbed by objects as banal as his overcoat. Books and foreign words are particularly menacing. *Boku*'s symptoms improve slightly after he returns home, thanks to increased medication and the presence of his family. Yet his peace is short-lived, and he soon finds himself swallowed by anxiety, believing that forces beyond his control are manipulating him. Filled with despair and on the brink of committing suicide, *boku* concludes "Cogwheels" claiming that he does not have the strength to continue writing; he asks whether there really is no one who "will come and strangle me in my sleep."[35]

Throughout, *boku* presents himself as overwhelmed by wheels, words, and wings. Virtually obliterating the possibility of flight, words and wings in this text are more ominous than those in "A Fool's Life," where Voltaire's words granted *kare* a tragic ride above the earth, and *kare*'s own words reduced his identity to that of a hapless swan. *Boku* goes a step further in "Cogwheels," depicting his words as fizzling out and being superseded almost completely by the words of his literary predecessors, competitors that flood the marketplace and leave little shelf space for newcomers. Similarly, the stuffed natural wings in "A Fool's Life" are replaced in "Cogwheels" by mechanical instruments, while even *boku*'s repeated and haunting hallucinations of cogwheels are replaced by silver wings. Hallucinations of artificial wings and the implied loss of real ones accentuate his already biting despair and leave him little choice but to relinquish his pen. Words have the potential to provide wings in "A Fool's Life," but in "Cogwheels" they are silenced by cogwheels and then by factory-produced wings, the technological attack on the intellectual coming from all directions.

Boku depicts himself as repeatedly subjected to hallucinations of flight-inducing appendages and airfoils. Pictures of airplane wings frequently obstruct his vision and disturb him deeply, as does the sight of an actual airplane—still a novelty in Japan in the mid-1920s. The initial appearance of wings in "Cogwheels" is fairly innocuous: *boku* says he hears flapping wings outside his door, and he dismisses these sounds as emanating from a guest's pet bird. Yet the situation quickly becomes more menacing: the flapping returns in the third section of "Cogwheels," where *boku* is so disturbed by the "sound of wings" that he leaps from his bed. Later in the story, *boku* has no sooner articulated his desire to flee than a small white advertising sign depicting an automobile tire with wings startles him. The wings gain the upper hand in this competition between wings and wheels;

boku thinks not of cogwheels (as had been his habit) but rather of Icarus and his "artificial wings":

If only my nerves were as strong as those of ordinary people. But for that to happen I had to go somewhere. To Madrid, to Rio, to Samarkand. Then a small white sign hanging on the eaves of a shop suddenly made me uneasy. It showed the trademark of wings painted on a tire. This reminded me of the ancient Greek supported by artificial wings. He flew high into the sky only to have his wings burned by the sun's rays, and in the end he drowned in the ocean. To Madrid, to Rio, to Samarkand—how could I not scoff at this dream of mine.[36]

Unlike *kare*, whose readings of Voltaire provided him with the wings to lurch toward the sun oblivious of Icarus's plight and to enjoy the fleeting trip while it lasted, *boku* recalls only Icarus's tragic plummet to the earth and rejects the notion that travel will improve his state of mind. Beset with mechanized words and wings, *boku* cannot conceive of the possibility of flying solo.

Images of artificial wings also disturb *boku* and trigger hallucinations. Smoking an Airship cigarette, he comments, "Artificial wings rose once again before my eyes."[37] Actual planes prove even more troubling. While visiting his in-laws *boku* is agitated by a low-flying plane, which reminds him of Airship cigarettes. Later that day cogwheels again fill *boku*'s vision but quickly are supplanted by wings:

About half an hour later, I was upstairs lying on my back, eyes firmly closed, with a terrible headache. Then a single wing of silver feathers folded like scales began to appear from behind my eyelids. It was in fact reflected clearly on my retina. I opened my eyes and looked up at the ceiling, and confirming there was nothing like that to be seen, I shut them once again. But the silver wing was reflected in the darkness. Then I suddenly remembered that there had also been wings on the radiator cap of the car in which I recently had ridden.[38]

This is *boku*'s final hallucination. Mechanical wings—whether seen or imagined—imprison him ever deeper within himself. As in "A Fool's Life" they are partly responsible for sapping the energy on which he depended for writing.

The words of *boku*'s literary predecessors are even more portentous than the new technology of airplane wings, textual antecedents a larger menace here than in "A Fool's Life." *Boku* not only finds foreign words difficult to assimilate, he also extracts little solace from reading. Foreign words are scattered throughout "Cogwheels," written in *katakana* and Roman letters, and *boku* frequently imagines the worst when he hears them. For instance, he picks up the telephone and is confronted with a voice that repeats a word that sounds like "mole." Even after he hangs up, the word "mole" (rodent) weighs on his mind: "Mole—*Mole*. . . . . . Mole is English for moguramochi. The association was not a happy one for me. But several seconds later *Mole* became *la mort*. La mort—death in French—immediately made me anxious. Death had closed in on my sister's husband, and now it seemed to close in on me."[39] Another verbal association occurs when *boku* looks at fruit through the glass door of a closed restaurant and thinks he overhears one man say to another, "It's tantalizing." After flagging a taxi, the words "Tantalizing,—*tantalizing*—*Tantalus*—*Inferno*" run through *boku*'s mind, and he likens himself to Tantalus, surrounded by food and drink that he is not allowed to consume:

Tantalus was I myself—gazing at fruit through the glass door . . . I felt that everything was a lie. Politics, business, art, science—all of these were for me nothing more than various colors of enamel, hiding this awful life. I gradually began to feel suffocated and opened the cab's window. But the sensation that something was strangling my heart didn't go away.[40]

Exposure to foreign vocabulary leaves *boku* literally gasping for breath.

Reading also proves traumatic. Although on one occasion *boku* speaks of going to a bookstore seeking "spiritual tonic," he generally is either overwhelmed or disappointed by the books he finds. *Kare* also feels threatened by some of the texts he reads, but they are not as menacing to him as are those that confront *boku*. Both protagonists visit the Maruzen bookstore, but the differences in their experiences indicate large disparities between the two. "A Fool's Life" begins with the narrator's description of *kare* on the second floor. The narrative is relatively straightforward: *kare* is on a ladder looking for new books, and he discovers titles by de Maupassant, Baudelaire, Strindberg, Ibsen, Shaw, and Tolstoy. As the sun sets, he is surrounded by Nietzsche, Verlaine, the brothers Goncourt, Dostoevsky, Hauptmann, and Flaubert. The separation from the beginning of the third section of "Cogwheels"—which also takes place at nightfall on the second floor of Maruzen—is striking. *Boku* is anxious even before entering the store, and opening books once inside only adds to his apprehension. One of the books

contained an insert depicting a row of cogwheels that had eyes and noses just like those of human beings. (It was a collection of drawings done by mental patients that had been assembled by some German.) I sensed a rebellious feeling rising in my melancholy, and like a crazy and desperate gambler, I opened one book after another. Yet for some reason, almost every book had hidden in it several needles, either in the text or the illustrations.[41]

As Seiji Lippit has observed, "The bounded and ordered world of literature found in the first episode of *A Fool's Life* has disintegrated [in "Cogwheels"] into an open and indefinite urban landscape."[42] Hardly offering *boku* comfort, literary works from both Japan and abroad generally disturb his sensibilities and either frustrate him or make him feel woefully inadequate. Although reading Shiga Naoya's *An'ya kōro* (Dark Night's Passing, 1921–37) provides *boku* with temporary relief, the novel creates more problems than it solves:

> I lay down on the bed and began to read *Dark Night's Passing*. I sensed each of the hero's spiritual struggles acutely. Comparing myself to the hero, I felt foolish and began to cry. At the same time, the tears brought me peace. But this did not last long. My right eye again began to sense those half-transparent cogs. The cogs, turning incessantly as always, gradually increased in number.[43]

Later, on the brink of despair, *boku* sits down with Dostoevsky's *Crime and Punishment* (1866), but the volume has been bound haphazardly, and the first page to which he turns actually comes from Dostoevsky's later *The Brothers Karamazov* (1880): "I continued reading, unable to stop. But before I had finished a single page, I felt my entire body trembling. [I had opened to the story of] Ivan being tormented by the Devil. . . . Ivan, Strindberg, de Maupassant, and myself in this room. Only sleep could save me now. Yet before I knew it there wasn't a single sleeping pill remaining."[44]

Attacked by words from other pens, *boku*'s one hope appears to be his own writing. Whereas *kare*'s texts enable him only to find kinship with a mounted swan, writing temporarily helps *boku*. Tortured by his unexpected encounter with *The Brothers Karamazov* and fresh out of sleeping pills, *boku* turns to his manuscript: "With a courage born of despair, I had some coffee brought in and decided to move my pen frantically. Two pages, five pages, seven pages, ten pages — in an instant the manuscript was finished. I filled the story with supernatural animals. One of these animals was a self-portrait."[45] Although here *boku* does not comment on how he feels about writing, earlier in "Cogwheels" he expresses guarded satisfaction at finishing his manuscripts. *Boku* also describes the joy writing brings him:

I sat at the desk by the window and began another story. I too thought it strange just how quickly the pen ran across the paper of my manuscript. However, after a few hours it stopped, as if someone invisible were restraining me. I couldn't help getting up from my seat and walking around the room. My megalomania now was at its peak. With a savage joy, I felt as though I had no parents, no wife, and no children. I felt that the only thing I had was the life that flowed from my pen.[46]

Yet writing cannot save *boku* from the onslaught of words (from foreign tongues and textual predecessors), cogwheels, and wings. He concludes "Cogwheels" by acknowledging defeat and pleading for someone to put him out of his misery: "I don't have the strength to continue writing. It's indescribably painful to live with this mental state. Isn't there someone who could strangle me in my sleep?"[47] Life in a rapidly mechanizing society, in which interpersonal relations appear to be attenuating, holds no hope or promise for him, nor do drugs any longer offer relief. Like Akutagawa himself, at this point in his life *boku* can seek release only in death. *Boku* abandons hope completely, the story arguing that by 1927 wheels and especially wings and mass-produced words—the latter two then epitomes of the mechanized modern—not only were incapable of liberating the intellectual but also were at least partly responsible for driving him, gasping for breath, into a corner.

Abandoning Words and Faith

Like the protagonists in Akutagawa's stories, *na* ("I"), the first-person narrator of "Wings," is a young isolated intellectual whose personal life is in disarray.[48] Even more of a hermit than *kare* or *boku*, he spends most of his life lying in bed, hiding under the covers, while his wife works outside the home during the day and at night serves male customers in her half of their room. *Na* has not lost all interest in the world outside his four walls, and after his wife physically and verbally abuses him, he considers leaving home for good. "Wings" concludes with *na* standing on top of a Japanese department store in Seoul—an emblem of Japanese architectural, consumerist, and cultural penetration of Korea by the mid-1930s—calling on his "wings" to regrow and allow him to fly once again. "Wings" exchanges *kare*'s and *boku*'s myopic pessimism with cautious faith. The individual who initially appeared to be the least likely of the three protagonists examined here to emerge out of the shadows is in fact the most determined to forge a new life. Yet "Wings" also suggests that there is very little chance he will be able to do so.

Whereas the first-person narrator of "Cogwheels" is an intellectual assaulted by external words and wings that attack from all directions, *na* focuses on the loss of more intrinsic words and wings, namely his native Korean and his ability to function both outside and within his bedcovers. In so doing, he presciently foreshadows the heightened verbal and physical constraints imposed by Japan on Korea after 1938. *Na* explicitly portrays his words and wings as having been dislocated: wings from shoulders and words from the dictionary. *Na's* circumstances are even more desperate than those of *boku* or *kare*; his reconfigurations of vital images from his literary predecessors show the extent of his depression and decay. Yet the conclusion of "Wings" finds *na* exerting more agency than *kare* or *boku*. *Na's* pervasive sense of helplessness puts his struggles in the final paragraphs of "Wings" in sharp relief; there is no certainty of release, yet *na* refuses to surrender in the face of psychological oppression and spatial confinement. On the other hand, *na's* repeated pleas for something anatomically impossible—"sprouting wings"— also illuminate the futility of his struggle. It is one thing to hope to fly, physically or metaphorically, and then to take the necessary steps to actualize flight, and another to insist that nonexistent body parts start growing.[49]

The first line of "Wings," recasting the stuffed swan of "A Fool's Life," opens with a question to the reader: "Do you know of the stuffed genius?"[50] Whereas in Akutagawa's story *kare's* life flashes before him as he stares at a stuffed swan with decaying wings, here *na* implies not only that he has become the stuffed specimen but also that his wings have been removed. When he wakes up, he says he feels like an amorphous pillow "filled with shredded cotton and buckwheat husks."[51] At the end of "Wings," the wings exist only in memory: the "natural" if unusable wings preserved on a stuffed swan in "A Fool's Life" and mechanized in "Cogwheels" now are portrayed as relics of the past. Moreover, whereas *kare* and *boku* both entertain visions of flying through the heavens, in Yi Sang's prose it is the globe, not the individual, hurtling through space, *na* commenting that he lives on a planet racing through the cosmos with lightning speed.[52]

In fact, unlike his Japanese predecessors, *na* must beg for wings. He stands on the roof of the Mitsukoshi Department Store in Seoul, a colonial structure that also represents the "modern consumerist life of leisure" where Korean *yangban* elites spend even more lavishly than the Japanese, spurred on by the popular catchphrase "Today the Imperial Theatre, tomorrow Mitsukoshi."[53] *Na* gazes first at the ineffectual movements of the pedestrians down below and then at the soaring high-rise products of modernity nearby. The people on the street clamor like fowl: "It seemed as though they all had spread their four limbs and were flapping them as chickens do."[54] These flailing folks flap but have no wings, and they quickly are submerged in a carbonated modernity: "All kinds of glass, steel, marble, banknotes, and ink seemed to boil up and bubble over into a moment of tremendous racket. It was truly an extremely dizzying noontime."[55] Although *na* does not mention books explicitly, the overflowing ink to which he refers perhaps comes from the thousands of one-yen editions (*enpon*) the Japanese businessman Bandō Kyōgo is reported to have spread out in the plaza behind Mitsukoshi on his 1932 visit to Seoul.[56]

Confronted with ineffective human flapping and longing to rise above construction materials, money, and desk supplies, if not Japanese books, *na* declares that his armpits suddenly have begun to itch precisely where his artificial wings once grew. Several lines later, he concludes "Wings" with a desperate plea for his wings, natural or artificial, to emerge again:[57] "Wings! Sprout once again. Let's fly. Let's fly. Let's fly. Let's fly just once more. Let's try to fly just once more."[58] *Na*'s desperation grows increasingly acute. Using the hortatory form of the verb *nalda* (to fly), *na* is purposely ambiguous as to who/what he would like to accompany him: is he simply calling on his wings to accompany him in flight, or is he also imploring the flapping crowd below to join him in his travels?

The absence of physical wings in "Wings" is particularly noteworthy considering not only the title of this short story but also the prevalence of wings (actual and imagined) in the creative works it intertextualizes. Yet the loss of wings is only the beginning. Even if *na*'s wings were to heed his call and sprout again, and if they then allowed him to fly, where could he travel? At this point in the narrative, *na*—having liberated himself from months of imprisonment in his own home—is at a higher altitude than ever before, but he is standing on a Japanese edifice; longing to fly on his own, he wants to break free from the colonial structure, as well as the colonial books below. But he is the first to admit that he has nowhere to go.[59]

Na not only is deprived of wings and a destination, he also is stripped of words: after commenting on the flapping limbs of the people below, he imagines flipping blank pages of the (Korean) dictionary. Words were not always so difficult to come by. In the opening section of "Wings," *na* likens words to checker pieces, stating that whenever nicotine seeps into his roundworm-infested stomach, a sheet of white paper is ready in his head, and on this sheet he arranges words of wit and paradox like pieces of *paduk* (Korean checkers). Words begin as a game, but they quickly vanish; later *na* states that when he cannot fall asleep he composes poems in his head that disappear like so many bubbles. Thus it is not surprising that in the final scene of "Wings," immediately before he calls on his wings to grow, *na* envisions turning empty pages. The dictionary *na* imagines is an implicit and dramatic reconfiguration of the one *kare* peruses in "A Fool's Life." *Kare*'s forays into the lexicon lead him to imagine a blossom soaring in the firmament, while *na*'s plunge into the dictionary results in comments on the "erasure" of the words "hope" and "ambition," and soon he begs for the return of his wings.

The paradox is conspicuous. Officially sanctioned words—words deemed appropriate by the authorities for inclusion in the dictionary—have been expunged, but not the sentiments suggested by these words. *Na* laments the loss of the words "hope" and "ambition," but it is precisely these sentiments that he exhibits most forcefully in the final section of "Wings" by begging his wings to return. Although he is trapped within a "silent soliloquy," *na* articulates clearly his loss of language and of flight.[60] *Na*'s former wings might never return, but he manages to create his own "wings," in the form of the story "Wings," a text that rather than drawing attention to the suppression and destruction of the autonomous subject in colonial Korea instead bears witness to his robust persistence.[61]

"Wings" ends with *na* stripped of wings and words, yet he remains outside, not collapsing in darkened rooms like *kare* and *boku*. He thus undergoes the greatest transformation of the three protagonists examined here: from a man imprisoned under his bedcovers to one standing on the top of a shrine to capitalist consumer culture in the bright sunshine begging to fly. *Na* demonstrates that deleting words from a dictionary cannot obliterate their essence and cannot prevent their being acted out, by an individual or a society, even under a strict colonial regime. Presenting himself as bereft of words and wings, *na* is in a situation that contrasts starkly with that of his

Japanese counterparts. The plights of *kare* and *boku* appear trivial in comparison to his own. Yet at the same time that he emblematizes the emasculation of the colonial subject, *na* also reverses the slide into deeper desperation exhibited by the protagonists of "A Fool's Life" and "Cogwheels," captured in Akutagawa's texts by the increasing externalization of words and wings. Instead, *na* underlines colonial resilience, the capacity of colonial subjects—despite overwhelming odds—to attempt to overcome the loss of limbs and language even if the scars throb with pain, even if "hope," "ambition," and every other linguistic construction have been erased by a force majeure from the lexicon of their native language.[62]

Akutagawa's "A Fool's Life" and "Cogwheels" and the Korean writer Yi Sang's "Wings"—threaded together by multiple dynamic intertexts—highlight the decline of the intellectual suffering from positional anxiety. The three protagonists harbor strong doubts and insecurities over their place in an increasingly mechanized and/or authoritarian world. In contrast with Lu Xun's parody of the man who is all talk and no action, captured in Juansheng's obsession with wings and words in "Regret for the Past: Juansheng's Notes," the narrators of "A Fool's Life" and "Cogwheels" explore the mounting burdens on the intellectual brought about by the progressive mechanization of society; the protagonists of the Japanese stories gradually are stripped of confidence and resign themselves to paralysis. "Wings" moves the question of place and space to the colonial context—an environment overtaken by foreign words and edifices—where belief in persistence is even more difficult to maintain. Yet it is the colonial subject who comments on the absence of the words "hope" and "ambition" and ultimately emerges from his shell, exhibits these sentiments, and in so doing expresses his faith in human perseverance. Whether *na* has any chance against progressive modernity, not to mention repressive colonialism, is doubtful—after all, the people he sees in the street below are deprived of wings and are capable only of gyrating their limbs in an unbalanced struggle with the rising technological edifices of the colonizer. There is no indication that *na*'s struggles will be any different from theirs, although his appear more self-conscious and therefore painful.

Standing Firm in Hallucinations and Dreams

As they intertextualize Japanese creative works featuring trapped persons desperately trying to escape their fetters and reclaim personhood, early twentieth-century Chinese, Korean, and Taiwanese writings often depict characters who are more persistent and less easily defeated than their Japanese predecessors. Such colonial and semicolonial literary works frequently portray people of all backgrounds who continue their struggles long after their Japanese counterparts relinquish or are forced to relinquish their efforts. In fact, many Chinese, Korean, and Taiwanese texts that reconfigure Japanese struggles to reclaim self and space also put characters in environments more treacherous than those found in their Japanese counterparts. In so doing, they simultaneously emphasize not only the nightmarish aspects of colonial and semicolonial landscapes, as opposed to more benign Japanese settings, but also the tenacity of oppressed peoples in the face of insurmountable odds. Yet they additionally reveal the high price of persistence by portraying conflicts as interminable, continuing even in death. Just as the final curtain of Yi Sang's "Wings" goes down with *na* begging for wings that will never sprout, other colonial and semicolonial works give a cross section of what is assumed to be an eternal struggle. Human perseverance is not so much celebrated as it is parodied and pitied.

Several imporant examples occur in the intertextualization of sections of Sōseki's *Ten Nights of Dreams* (1908) in Lu Xun's collection of prose poems *Wild Grass* (1927). Lu Xun was part of the first wave of Chinese Sōseki aficionados, living in Sōseki's former house near the Hongō campus of Tokyo Imperial University, reading Sōseki's serialized novels in Japanese newspapers, and transculturating Sōseki's oeuvre interpretively, interlingually, and intertextually. In an essay written several years before his death, Lu Xun reminisced on his time in Japan, commenting that as a young man "My favorite authors were the Russian N. Gogol and the Pole H. Sienkiewicz [1846–1916], and the Japanese writers Natsume Sōseki and Mori Ōgai."[63] Lu Xun engaged actively with Sōseki's oeuvre for most of his life, transposing everything from the canonical to the all but forgotten.

While writing *Wild Grass* between 1924 and 1927, Lu Xun also was translating essays by Kuriyagawa Hakuson. Not surprisingly, allusions to Hakuson's works are prominent in *Wild Grass*, especially in Lu Xun's treatment of dreams. Yet episodes in *Wild Grass* enjoy even more significant relationships with those in *Ten Nights of Dreams*.[64] Both collections consist of loosely connected surrealistic vignettes arranged in ostensibly chronological order, generally presented either as dreams/nightmares or hallucinations. Removing the events they portray from the empirical world allows the narrators of these two collections to explore more freely the subconscious and engage in provocative experiments with language.

The surreal landscape of *Wild Grass* is even more exaggerated and menacing than that of *Ten Nights of Dreams*, reflecting more clearly than Lu Xun's "Regret for the Past: Juansheng's Notes" the chaos of mid-1920s China, which was reeling from both the Nationalist government's failure to unify the country and the May Fourth Movement's failure to enact enduring change.[65] As though the chasms, forests, burning sun, attacking pigs, and missing spouses of *Ten Nights of Dreams* were not enough, characters in *Wild Grass* must contend with a landscape where nightmares have been magnified, a landscape replete with towering mountains, skies flooded with frozen clouds, forests of ice, endless dust, infinite wastelands, underground fires, wilderness abutting hell, bombing missions, and talking corpses.

Compared with the characters in *Ten Nights of Dreams*, those of *Wild Grass* are at a distinct disadvantage. But the latter also display more courage. Just as Yi Sang's "Wings" features a protagonist whose defeats and triumphs surpass those of his Japanese predecessors, so too several sections of *Wild Grass* present characters grappling with a landscape more severe than that displayed in *Ten Nights of Dreams* who nevertheless continue with their struggles; *Wild Grass* depicts a reality that accentuates the macabre in Sōseki's landscape, yet one in which human persistence flourishes. At the same time, the narrator of Lu Xun's text reveals human perseverance to be just as much a curse as a blessing. *Wild Grass* abounds with dynamic intertexts from *Ten Nights of Dreams*; reappropriating elements of its Japanese predecessor, the Chinese text affirms human endurance while also questioning its purpose in the face of interminable suffering.

The most dramatic reworkings of the sketches in *Ten Nights of Dreams* included in *Wild Grass* appear in the play "The Passerby" and the prose poem "Zheyang de zhanshi" (This Kind of Warrior). "The Passerby" features a traveler who refuses to rest despite his painful bleeding feet and the endless wilderness spreading out before him; he contrasts with the traveler in "Dainanaya" (The Seventh Night), a young man confronted with an endless ocean, who is so bored that he commits suicide.[66] Similarly, "This Kind of Warrior" depicts a fighter who refuses to surrender, raising his lance repeatedly in both life and death. Although Shōtarō, the warrior's Japanese counterpart in "Daijūya" (The Tenth Night), also repeatedly strikes down his "enemies" (attacking pigs), he eventually falls into a chasm and is rescued, but by whom or what we are not told. "The Passerby" and "This Kind of Warrior" offer their characters little relief from suffering while at the same time highlighting their endurance, particularly when compared with their Japanese predecessors. On the other hand, they are denied the silence of death granted the figures in the Japanese text and instead appear condemned to fight forever. Cross-cultural intertextual comparison of these sections highlights their faith in — and ridicule of — human perseverance.

The journeys depicted in "The Seventh Night" and "The Passerby" are described as infinite and nearly impossible to bear. *Jibun*, the narrator of "The Seventh Night," begins:

> I'm riding on some big ship. This ship pushes forward without a moment's rest, day after day and night after night, vomiting black smoke and cutting the waves. The noise is tremendous. But I don't know where we're going. I just know that the sun emerges from the bottom of the sea like burning tongs. It rises just above the high mast, hangs there briefly, and then before you know it overtakes the big ship and goes on ahead. Then, it sizzles like burning tongs and sinks back down to the bottom of the sea. Every time it sets, the blue waves in the distance boil to a dark red. The ship makes a tremendous racket as it chases the sun's path. But it never catches up.[67]

Similarly, when in "The Passerby" someone identified only as Laoweng (old man) asks Guoke (the passerby) where he is from and where he is going, he replies:

> I don't know [where I'm from]. I've been walking like this for as long as I can remember. . . . I don't know [where I'm going]. I've been walking like this for as long as I can remember, walking to a place, a place up ahead. I remember only that I've walked a long way and that I now have arrived here. I'll push on that way (he points west), up ahead![68]

Both *jibun* and Guoke emphasize the lack of a precise destination and claim they have little choice but to travel west. Here "The Seventh Night" and "The Passerby" allude not to the Buddhist Western Paradise but rather to Japan's and China's respective turns to the West, which dominated early twentieth-century East Asian intellectual discourse. Yet in *Ten Nights of Dreams*, Japanese Westernization is portrayed as plowing forward with great momentum, leaving little room for individual enterprise (the boat has sailed and the individual can do nothing but ride along), whereas *Wild Grass* suggests that the Chinese have more ground to cover and need to display more initiative. Indeed, while *jibun*, carried along by a powerful boat, has the relative luxury of dying of boredom, Guoke—pulled by a "voice from up ahead"—must exert himself to the point of exhaustion and damages his feet so badly he can barely walk. Here, as in much of his writing, Lu Xun pinpoints the difficulties facing Chinese determined to liberate themselves from their past and implicitly calls attention to the relative comfort Japanese seem to have taken for granted for decades.

"The Seventh Night" concludes with *jibun* committing suicide by throwing himself off the ship and into the sea. Guoke, on the other hand, refuses to bury himself in oblivion. Laoweng offers him refuge and attempts to persuade him to rest at least temporarily, but although he is tempted to stay, Guoke determines that he must move on:

LAOWENG: It's because you don't rest that you're too weak to carry anything. If you'd rest for a bit you'd be ok.
GUOKE: That's right. A rest. . . . . . (He thinks to himself, then wakes up with a start and listens attentively.) No, I can't! It would be better for me to go.
LAOWENG: You don't want to rest?
GUOKE: I want to rest.
LAOWENG: Then you should rest a bit.
GUOKE: But I can't. . . . . .
LAOWENG: You still think it would be better for you to go on?
GUOKE: Yes, I'd better go on.[69]

Guoke is adamant about pressing forward, telling Laoweng: "I have to keep going. If I go back, there's not a place without celebrities, a place without landlords, a place without banishment and cages, a place without superficial smiles, a place without hypocritical tears. I hate them. I'm not going back!"[70] When his interlocutor tells him that if he returns he might be welcomed with heartfelt tears and compassion, Guoke declares that he has no desire to see these tears or to be pitied and again asserts that he has no choice but to press on.

In its implicit reconfiguration of "The Seventh Night," "The Passerby" emphasizes the greater determination and resilience of the Chinese than the Japanese. But to what purpose? There is no indication that the passerby ever will reach a destination; the play suggests that he will stagger on indefinitely. His determination to fight to the end despite his severely disadvantaged position distinguishes him from his Japanese counterparts. Yet his tenacity also raises questions about resilience: is the passerby a hero for continuing to press forward, or is he a wretched fool for devoting his life to incessant travel? This play both celebrates and parodies earnest determination.

Whereas "The Passerby" features a man who travels through exhaustion, "This Kind of Warrior," reconfiguring Sōseki's "The Tenth Night," goes one step farther; it narrates the story of a warrior who continues to fight through both fatigue and death. The anonymous fighter of "This Kind of Warrior" and Shōtarō of "The Tenth Night" repeatedly raise long cylindrical weapons to club their enemies, but while Sōseki's character is eventually defeated, even death does not deter Lu Xun's warrior. In "The Tenth Night," *jibun* relates the story of Shōtarō, a dapper man distinguished by his relaxed attitude and panama hat. A woman whom Shōtarō had offered to help took him to the edge of a cliff and told him to jump off. When he politely refused, she informed him that pigs would lick him until he obeyed her orders. Shōtarō chose to stand his ground and used his walking stick to hit every one of the myriad snouts pressing toward him. The pigs at first retreated with barely an oink, but their sheer numbers in the end defeated Shōtarō: "For seven days and six nights Shōtarō struck the pigs' snouts, displaying a courage born of desperation. But his vitality at last was exhausted and his hands grew limp like wet noodles. And in the end he was licked by a pig and tumbled over the precipice."[71] Here *jibun* describes an individual who, determined not to surrender, single-mindedly repeats what appears to be the only available course of action, yet his struggle gets him nowhere and he surrenders.

Implicitly redeploying Shōtarō, "This Kind of Warrior" portrays an anonymous fighter faced with obstacles more treacherous than lusty pigs. Whereas the pigs, swarming by the thousands, are clearly visible, the warrior's enemy is elusive; "nothingness" has replaced masses of swine. The warrior's opponent also is more deadly; the narrator remarks that the enemy even uses nodding "as a weapon to kill without bloodshed."[72] Yet despite the ferocity and elusiveness of his opponents, the Chinese warrior does not wait for "nothingness" to launch an attack but instead chooses to walk into the "battle lines of nothingness."[73] He also demonstrates remarkable tenacity after the fight has begun. Dodging lethal nods and enough flags, banners, and overcoats to smother a platoon, the warrior repeatedly "raises his lance," a phrase repeated five times in this two-page prose poem and always prefaced by "but," indicating its counterintuitivity; the warrior continues to raise his lance and walk into the line of battle even after "nothingness" enjoys a temporary victory. The narrator depicts the warrior as growing old and dying in the "lines of nothingness," fighting until the end of his days. His death initially appears to signal defeat, the narrator remarking: "He is not a warrior after all, and nothingness is the victor. In this place we hear no war cry: peace. Peace. . . . . . ." Yet Lu Xun's prose poem concludes: "But he raises his lance!"[74] The warrior continues to fight, even in death; there is no mention of victory, but neither is there talk of defeat.

"This Kind of Warrior" expresses more faith in human persistence than its Japanese predecessor. Yet it also poses questions concerning endless struggle. The warrior's ability to survive death and continue fighting leaves open the possibility of eventual victory, but it also prolongs his suffering and condemns him to a seeming eternity of raising his lance. Like "The Passerby," "This Kind of Warrior" interrogates human perseverance, celebrating and parodying eternal struggle.[75]

In "The Myth of Sisyphus," Albert Camus argues that we must believe that Sisyphus, the epitome of the individual condemned to seemingly endless and meaningless struggle, is content: "He is superior to his fate. He is stronger than his rock. . . . I leave Sisyphus at the foot of the mountain! One always rediscovers one's burden. . . . [But] Sisyphus also determines that all is well. . . . The fight itself toward the summits is enough to fill a man's heart. We must imagine Sisyphus happy."[76] Some of the struggles depicted in Yi Sang's "Wings" and Lu Xun's *Wild Grass* resemble those of Sisyphus: characters bravely raise their voices and their weapons and press forward despite all obstacles, without assurance that their movements will benefit anyone, least of all themselves. Yet it is difficult to imagine the characters in these colonial and semicolonial texts as "happy." *Na* is doomed to wish endlessly for wings, Guoke to walk forever, and the fighter to raise his lance eternally. The colonial and semicolonial texts examined here assign to human persistence the task of keeping the doors of opportunity from swinging shut. Yet they and numerous other literary works intertextualizing metropolitan predecessors also suggest that if the threshold is never crossed, if there is nothing beyond struggle, and if human potential is not realized, the agony of existence is only prolonged. "Wings" and *Wild Grass* portray colonial and semicolonial characters as continuing to fight, but they also intimate that if the struggle never actualizes its possibility, then it might be in vain.

Rethinking Individual, Social, and National Reform

Silencing critical voices arguably delivers some of the most brutal blows to the possibility of constructive change. Even more unnerving than seemingly endless suffering, fruitless relationships, feckless responsibility, misplaced faith in endurance, or hopeless battles that continue after death is the smothering of criticism.

Colonial and semicolonial intra–East Asian intertextualization of Japanese literature underlines the difficulties of effecting meaningful social change outside the metropole. This is especially true of revolutionary works, including the recasting of Kobayashi Takiji's *Fuzai jinushi* (The Absentee Landlord, 1929) in the Chinese writer Wu Zuxiang's story "Eighteen Hundred Piculs" (1934) and in the Taiwanese writer Yang Kui's story "Oni seibatsu" (Conquering the Demon, 1936). *The Absentee Landlord,* "Eighteen Hundred Piculs," and "Conquering the Demon" all discuss the "awakening" of the impoverished, who although initially believing themselves the victims of fate eventually realize that they have some voice in reclaiming their lives. Yet "Eighteen Hundred Piculs" and "Conquering the Demon" depict the revolutionary path as strewn with even more landmines than those encountered by the characters in *The Absentee Landlord.*

Similarly, the Japanese proletarian writer Hayashi Fusao's story "Mayu" (Cocoons, 1929) and the Chinese revolutionary writer Mao Dun's story "Spring Silkworms" (1932) both reveal the human cost of silk production: "Cocoons" exposes the treacherous conditions in Japanese silk mills, while "Spring Silkworms" focuses on the fate of Chinese who harvest silkworms. Yet "Spring Silkworms" not only addresses how Japan's penetration of China has exacerbated the suffering of Chinese farmers and workers but also subtly vitiates the revolutionary romanticism articulated near the conclusion of "Cocoons." There, *boku,* the first-person narrator, records the reaction of his friend Sakai when he learns that his mother has died in the mill:

> But I will not give up hope. . . . There was not just one cocoon! My mother was not the only one who suffered! In just this country of ours, how many millions, no, tens of millions of people are having their lives sucked from them. . . . I know the enemy I must fight. . . . I suddenly remembered how in middle school I brandished my knife against a guy who bullied me. But the road I'm going to take from now on is not a mean and nasty one like that.[77]

The short story "Cocoons" exposes some of the great injustices confronting Japanese workers, but as this extract shows, it also features a character who believes that he is embarking on a noble path and that wrongs can be righted. In contrast, the narrator of "Spring Silkworms" depicts characters who cannot find a buyer for their goods; the story concludes with the simple observation that the villagers have struggled in vain. Like many transculturations of Japanese literature, "Spring Silkworms" underlines the increased suffering of colonial and semicolonial peoples and the great difficulties of effecting change.

Yet even more damning than Wu Zuxiang's "Eighteen Hundred Piculs," Yang Kui's "Conquering the Demon," and Mao Dun's "Spring Silkworms," are Lu Xun's "The True Story of Ah Q" (1921), early twentieth-century China's most famous short story, and Lao She's novel *City of Cats* (1933), which has been called "the most savage indictment of China ever penned by a Chinese."[78] Intertextualizing Natsume Sōseki's celebrated novel *I Am a Cat* (1906), "The True Story of Ah Q" not only depicts a society in a state of greater decay but also removes its critical voice: this story replaces the perceptive *wagahai*, a pompous cat who insightfully critiques human society, with the arrogant Ah Q, a bumbling and inarticulate man who longs to join the "revolution." In contrast, intertextualizing Akutagawa's novella *Kappa* (Kappa, 1927) with a depiction of a Chinese social critic who perceptively dissects other cultures but ignores the severe decay of his own country, *City of Cats* deflects and defeats critical voices. In so doing, "The True Story of Ah Q" and *City of Cats* evoke the profound hopelessness of early twentieth-century China vis-à-vis Japan.

Removing the Critic

Interactions with Sōseki's writing are readily apparent in *Wild Grass*, but Lu Xun's engagement with the Meiji writer's oeuvre is even more significant in his intertextualizing of the latter's *I Am a Cat* in "The True Story of Ah Q." Lu Xun's story resembles the Polish writer Henryk Sienkiewicz's *Szkice węglem* (Charcoal Sketches, 1876), which Lu Xun and Zhou Zuoren translated between 1908 and 1909; *Sachem* (1883), which Zhou Zuoren translated in 1912; and "Bartek Zwycięzka" (Bartek the Conqueror, 1882), as well as Gogol's "Shinel" (Overcoat, 1842) and "Zapiski sumasshedshego" (Madman's Diary). To be sure, "The True Story of Ah Q" more closely resembles "Charcoal Sketches" and "Bartek the Conqueror" than it does *I Am a Cat*. But where he appropriates Sienkiewicz, Lu Xun confronts Sōseki.[79]

I Am a Cat and "The True Story of Ah Q" both depict societies filled with selfish, ignorant people who hurt others indiscriminately. Yet *wagahai* is concerned with a nation whose citizens lose themselves in pompous intellectual discussions, inebriated with the European philosophies that flowed into Japan with the Meiji Restoration, while the narrator of "The True Story of Ah Q" critiques a nation whose citizens lose themselves in their past, whose 1911 revolution seems to have done little more than reinforce the status quo. But "The True Story of Ah Q" does more than depict a society in greater crisis than the Japan of *I Am a Cat*. It also removes one of the last hopes for such a society: it compromises the insightful critical voice that, no matter how distant from its target, at least has the potential to transform attitudes and behaviors.

From his opening lines, the narrator of "The True Story of Ah Q" establishes parallels between his story and *I Am a Cat* while also stressing the greater hardships faced by Ah Q and his contemporaries, and by the writer brave enough to tackle Ah Q's biography. For instance, the problem of naming looms large at the beginning of both texts, but the difficulties *wagahai* articulates in *I Am a Cat* are magnified in the novel's Chinese transculturation. Sōseki's cat opens his manuscript with the simple announcement "I am a cat; I still don't have a name," and the absence of a name haunts *wagahai* until his death.[80] In contrast, lamenting his ignorance of Ah Q's surname and place of birth, the narrator of "The True Story of Ah Q" claims that he does not even know the characters for Ah Q's first name, or what to title his manuscript:

For several years I've been hoping to write the true story of Ah Q. . . . But no sooner had I taken up my pen than I realized the tremendous difficulties in writing this mortal work. The first was what to name it. . . . There are many names for biographies: official biographies, autobiographies, unauthorized biographies, legends, supplementary biographies, family histories, sketches. . . . . . but sadly none of these fit. . . . The second difficulty was that a biography like this really should begin with something along the lines of "So-and-so, also called so-and-so, was from such-and-such a place." But I really wasn't sure of Ah Q's surname. . . . The third difficulty was that I didn't know how to write Ah Q's first name. . . . The fourth difficulty was Ah Q's birthplace. . . . The only thing that comforts me is that the character 'Ah' is absolutely correct.[81]

The ambiguity of his background has more serious consequences for Ah Q than *wagahai*: the cat is mistreated by his owners but is not persecuted by the feline population, while Ah Q is shunned by nearly everyone in part because of his dubious origins; his insecurity concerning his origins also contributes to much of his erratic behavior, which in turn isolates him further. The narrator of "The True Story of Ah Q" thus establishes an instant link with *I Am a Cat* while simultaneously underlining the differences between circumstances discussed in his text and those in the Japanese novel it intertextually manipulates.

"The True Story of Ah Q" also reworks humorous passages from *I Am a Cat* to highlight Ah Q's vulnerability. Both texts include episodes where their protagonists are caught with stolen food hanging from their bodies, but *wagahai* comes across as comic and Ah Q desperate. Near the beginning of his narrative, *wagahai* describes an unfortunate incident with a New Year's treat: he bites into a rice cake sitting in his owner's bowl, it sticks firmly in his teeth, and everyone in the household has a good laugh watching him struggle vigorously to free himself; someone finally pulls the rice cake from his mouth and all returns to normal. Ah Q has an analogous experience: he steals four turnips from a convent, stuffs them in his jacket until it bulges, and is chased away. The most important difference is that while *wagahai* is drawn to the rice cake out of curiosity, Ah Q steals the turnips because he is starving; *wagahai* becomes a source of much amusement for his owners, whereas Ah Q is reprimanded sternly for his criminal activities. Ah Q's difficulties proliferate in "The True Story of Ah Q" in ways that *wagahai* could hardly have imagined.

The concluding scenes of these prose works also are conspicuously similar—the curtains close with the deaths of *wagahai* and Ah Q, but the latter's is more brutal. For much of their lives, *wagahai* and Ah Q have used their powerful imaginations to reshape empirical events in their favor, yet only *wagahai* is able to do to so until the very end; he drowns believing he has found peace, while Ah Q is executed believing he is in hell. *Wagahai*, who transforms drowning in a jar he cannot escape into a religious experience, determines to drift off peacefully, but not before taking some drastic measures:

I gradually begin to feel comfortable . . . I simply feel comfortable. No, I can't really say that I feel comfortable. I've cut off the sun and moon, pulverized heaven and earth, and entered into a mysterious peace . . . I'm dying and attaining this peace. This peace can be obtained only in death. Namu Amida Butsu, Namu Amida Butsu. Thank you, thank you.[82]

Chanting the Nenbutsu—a requirement for rebirth in the Pure Land—*wagahai* imagines that he at last has found peace. Describing his own death, impossible if one is actually dead, the cat reveals his narrative as a fictional reverie. His imagination has saved him once again.

The narrator of "The True Story of Ah Q" also concludes with images of pulverization, but there is no peace for Ah Q; unlike the cat who dreamed of shattering heaven and earth, Ah Q feels as though he himself has been shattered. Accused of robbing the Zhao family, Ah Q is sentenced to death. He is dragged before a crowd that devours him with their eyes:

Ah Q took another look at the shouting people. That instant, his thoughts spun around in his head like a whirlwind. Four years ago, at the foot of the mountain, he met a starving wolf that followed him not too close and not too far, wanting to eat his flesh. . . . He had never forgotten the wolf's eyes, fierce yet cowardly . . . that seemed to pierce his body from a distance. Now he saw eyes that were even more frightening than the wolf's, eyes scarier than any he had ever seen, dull yet penetrating eyes that not only had already chewed his words but also wanted to chew something beyond his body, following not too close and not too far. . . . All turned to black, there was buzzing in his ears, and he felt as though his entire body was being scattered in all directions like tiny pieces of dust.[83]

Throughout his life, Ah Q has had the uncanny ability to put a favorable spin on many of the difficulties he encounters, by lying either to himself or to others. He does not so much see a silver lining in every cloud as create a clear sky out of one filled with dark thunderheads. Eagerly embracing the few compliments that come his way, Ah Q dismisses without a second thought the many criticisms with which he is bombarded. And true to form, Ah Q remains calm while being carried to the execution ground, having convinced himself that all people—at some point in their lives—have their heads cut off. He also declares, like many criminals before him, that he will return. Yet the roar of the crowd overpowers his imagination, and Ah Q finds himself turned to dust. Far from the peaceful scene, however contrived, at the conclusion of *I Am a Cat*, the spectacle of Ah Q's death reeks of cruelty and violence. While *wagahai* is treated to visions of Amida's paradise, Ah Q finds himself in hell. Ah Q is not allowed to fade into the sunset, interpreting this as his final victory. His mind has no defense against the bullets that destroy his body.

Transposing key episodes from *I Am a Cat*, the narrator of "The True Story of Ah Q" aligns his text with Sōseki's. In so doing, he sets up an implicit contrast between conditions in early twentieth-century China and those in Japan. But muting *wagahai*'s critical voice, the narrator of "The True Story of Ah Q" also reveals reform as facing greater obstacles. The greatest difference between *wagahai* and Ah Q, aside from *wagahai*'s being a cat (although one that can write in Japanese) and Ah Q a human being (who often slinks around like a cat), is *wagahai*'s ability to articulate coherent critiques of human society.

To be sure, regardless of how "human" he sounds in print, *wagahai* cannot vocalize his assessment of human society, much less converse with the people he critiques; his insightfulness remains inaudible to the people he encounters, who see him as a nonverbal cat. Yet *wagahai* — even if he does die in the jar — leaves a written record.[84] The mere presence of this record offers no guarantees, yet its existence leaves open the potential for change. In "The True Story of Ah Q," that door is effectively closed. Although he often complains that he is being mistreated and longs to join the "revolution," Ah Q offers few insightful analyses of his society and none as penetrating as those of *wagahai*. Furthermore, writing some time after Ah Q's death, the narrator of "The True Story of Ah Q" reveals that Ah Q has been all but forgotten. The biography of Ah Q itself brims with social criticism. Yet the transfer of the critical voice from a character in the text to an outsider who synthesizes material a decade after the fact encapsulates the increased helplessness of the society depicted in Lu Xun's short story. *Wagahai* is at best a marginal figure, but the world of *I Am a Cat* at least contains a critical voice.

Nonalien Communities of Aliens

Featuring a drinking or more likely drunken cat, the original cover of Lao She's novel *City of Cats* (1933) is eerily reminiscent of the original cover of *I Am a Cat*, and there are many other similarities between the two novels. Drunk on reverie leaves (*miye*, here a euphemism for opium), the Cat-people (*maoren*) of *City of Cats* resemble Sōseki's feline narrator as he drifts off to a "great peace" at the conclusion of his critique of Japanese society. Yet harshly indicting China, Lao She's novel reveals the Chinese as considerably worse off than the Japanese, their suffering longer lasting and more intense. Even more significant than Lao She's reworking of *I Am a Cat*, however, is his intertextual transposing of Akutagawa's novella *Kappa* (1927).

Lao She was one of early twentieth-century China's most accomplished playwrights and fiction writers. He also enjoyed favor with wartime and especially postwar Japanese readers and was warmly welcomed when he took his first trip to Japan in 1965.[85] Although he did not know Japanese, Lao She read broadly and chances are high that he was familiar with *Kappa*, which was translated into Chinese in 1928 and enjoyed some popularity on the mainland.[86] *City of Cats* has been likened to a number of Western classics, everything from H. G. Wells's (1866–1946) *The First Men in the Moon* (1901), a comparison made by Lao She himself, to Jonathan Swift's (1667–1745) *Gulliver's Travels* (1726), Aristophanes' (c. 448–380 BCE) *Birds* (414 BCE), François Rabelais' (1494–1553) early sixteenth-century *La vie de Gargantua et de Pantagruel* (The Life of Gargantua and Pantagruel), and Dante's early fourteenth-century *Divina commedia* (Divine Comedy).[87] It shares much with these and other predecessors, particularly its narrative structure and trenchant satirizing of contemporary society. The similarities with Wells's novel are especially prominent. Both narratives feature human travel to another terrestrial body and discovery of a corrupt semihuman people who have much in common with their earthly counterparts, including opiate addiction; in Lao She's novel, Wells's Selenites—insect-like moon people—become Mars-dwelling Cat-people. The voice exposing human society's "irrational violence [and] . . . insatiable aggressions" that is silenced in the final pages of *The First Men in the Moon* remains quiet in *City of Cats*, the latter novel pointing to the great difficulties of engaging in constructive dialogue, much less reform.[88] But written in the wake of the Japanese assassination of Zhang Zuolin in 1928, the seizure of Manchuria in 1931, and the violent Japanese response to Chinese boycotts in Shanghai in 1932, the intertextualization of the Japanese *Kappa* in *City of Cats*—although similar in some ways to that of *The First Men in the Moon*, including the manipulation of the critical voice—is in many places more intricate and overall is more consequential than that of the Western texts to which it alludes. Lao She's novel not only underlines the severity of Chinese decay vis-à-vis its semicolonial oppressor, but it also strikes a fatal blow to the possibility of reform by highlighting the impotence of even the best-educated and most perceptive social critics.

Unlike *I Am a Cat* and "The True Story of Ah Q," which both take place in the human world, *Kappa* and *City of Cats* describe the discoveries of human travelers who land accidentally in a semihuman realm that closely resembles their own countries, become harsh critics of this supposedly alien society, and end up returning home. *City of Cats* elaborates on several important episodes in *Kappa* but problematizes the future of the critical voice to a greater degree than its Japanese predecessor. Through his travels and interactions with the Kappa, *boku*, the first-person narrator of Akutagawa's text, sharpens his understanding—and criticism—not only of this subterranean society but also of the Japanese.[89] On the other hand, *wo*, the first-person narrator of Lao She's text, is so preoccupied with giving detailed and thought-provoking critiques of Cat Country that he fails to recognize the reflections of Cat Country and China in each other. *City of Cats* also points to the defeat of the critical voice, introducing Xiaoxie (Little Scorpion), a Cat-person who although a vocal and perceptive critic is overwhelmed by the decay engulfing his country. *Kappa* too addresses the value and efficacy of criticism, but this question occupies a more central space in *City of Cats*.

In scenes with striking parallels, *boku* and *wo* describe their dramatic falls and their encounters with a human-like society. The Kappa and the Cat-people even share several physical features: both have unusual foreheads and glide through space so as to baffle the human imagination, and neither wears clothing. Both represent only one of several warring groups in their realms, the underworld in *Kappa* and Mars in *City of Cats*. The Japanese and Chinese narrators are active critics of these alien societies. They also compare life at home with life in the land they visit. Yet these structural similarities belie the differences between *Kappa* and *City of Cats*: the latter's portrayal of greatly increased suffering and decay, not to mention the deflecting and defeating of the social critic.

Conditions in Kappaland are severe. *Boku* learns that unemployed Kappa workers are killed and eaten. As his new friends inform him: "We slaughter them and eat their flesh as meat." The Kappa justify this behavior by arguing that they actually are showing compassion: "The state spares them [the unemployed] the trouble of starving to death or suicide. It's just a whiff of poison gas so there's no real pain involved."[90] In another telling scene, a Kappa about to be born announces that he does not want to come into the world: he is afraid not only of the defects he will inherit from his father but also of the evil that runs rampant throughout Kappaland. But life in Kappaland is comfortable compared with life in Cat Country; reconfiguring scenes from *Kappa*, *City of Cats* underlines the greater degeneracy and decay of the Cat-people. *City of Cats* also magnifies certain incidents that take place in *Kappa*, including the threatened collapse of housing in *Kappa* that in *City of Cats* actually comes to pass; the destructive, although avoidable, family life of the Kappa that in *City of Cats* has become inevitable; and the "borrowing" of the "foreign" that in *Kappa* is little more than an annoyance but in *City of Cats* is fingered as responsible for destroying the education system. In addition, Cat Country is full of horrors that the Kappa likely could not have imagined. The narrator speaks at length of greed and rudeness that have reached epidemic proportions, of unimaginable dirt and squalor, of wretched living conditions, and of the pointless murder of countless Cat-people. As *wo* comments halfway through the novel: "Filth, disease, chaos, idiocy, darkness—these are the traits of this civilization."[91] Moreover, although the Kappa are able to thwart their bellicose neighbors the Otters, the Cat-people are destroyed by an invading army.

Boku and *wo* both harshly critique these semihuman societies. Yet *City of Cats* deflects the critical voice where it matters most: whereas *boku* points to the many parallels between contemporary Japan and Kappaland, *wo* adamantly insists that there exists a vast gulf between Cat Country and China. Not long after arriving in Kappaland, *boku* decisively announces: "needless to say, there's no real difference between this country's [Kappaland's] civilization and civilization in human countries, at least Japanese civilization."[92] Throughout, *boku* makes no secret of his disgust with both human beings and Kappa. The tables are turned in *City of Cats*, where *wo* mercilessly criticizes the Cat-people but creates a virtually impenetrable verbal halo around China. He defines the civilization of the Cat-people in terms of filth, disease, and chaos but declares his homeland China "glorious" and "wondrous." Shedding tears of homesickness after being captured by the Cat-people, *wo* ironically calls out, "Bright China, mighty China, land where there's no brutality or torture."[93] He echoes these sentiments at the conclusion of *City of Cats*, remarking that six months after witnessing the destruction of the Cat-people, he returned "to my mighty, bright, and free China."[94] *Wo* describes China proper as a more appealing place than *boku* does Japan. Furthermore, unlike the Kappa, who are familiar with life on earth and are quick to remind *boku* that theirs is not the only degenerate society, the Cat-people seem to know little about China and cannot undermine *wo*'s assertions. Not a claim to Chinese superiority vis-à-vis Japan, *wo*'s defense of his homeland instead exposes the loss of perspective that can plague even the most devoted researcher.

The resemblances between Cat Country and China are unmistakable. As Lao She pointed out and contemporary readers instantly recognized, everything from Cat Country's reverie leaves and crowded streets to wasted educations, corrupt politicians/warlords, and foreign enclaves had counterparts in 1920s and 1930s China. *Wo* is well aware of what can happen to a people for whom lethargy is the behavior and reverie leaves the drug of choice, but he shows no inclination to apply the same sharp scalpel to his homeland that he does to the Cat-people. After catching sight of Cat City, *wo* had declared: "I hoped to use my stay in Cat Country to understand fully the inner workings of this one civilization and thus enhance my experience of life."[95] *Wo* enhances his experiences, but not his perceptions of his homeland. *City of Cats* intertextualizes Akutagawa Ryūnosuke's novella *Kappa* in a way that foregrounds a paradox haunting many societies: those most skilled at dissecting "foreign" infections frequently are less aware of the epidemics erupting closer to home. Lao She's novel draws attention to China's decay at the same time that it parodies local obliviousness to this degeneration.

But more than simply deflecting critical voices, *Cat Country* also exposes their defeat. Despite his continued concern with dissecting the social ills of the Cat-people, *wo* is powerless when it comes to halting their destruction. So too is Xiaoxie, a homegrown critic. Although full of keen insights, Xiaoxie is rendered nearly powerless by the chaos engulfing his country, and he can hope only for a quick death. Neither Xiaoxie nor *wo* is able to serve as anything more than a critical observer and analyst of the Cat-people's demise; although armed with local and recently transplanted critics, Cat Country is beyond help. Unable to untangle the confusion plaguing the minds of the vast majority of their compatriots, critics like Xiaoxie are exposed as ineffective and in some ways responsible for the chaos spreading through their nation.

What do *Kappa* and *City of Cats* augur for the future, and for reform in particular? The Japanese novella leaves open the potential, however remote, of eventual reform — the mental patient longs to tell and retell his story, and it is possible that someone listening to his tale actually will do something to begin to right some of the wrongs he exposes. *City of Cats*, on the other hand, not only outlines the annihilation of Cat Country but also denies China the possibility of reform. A society retains the potential for reform as long as it maintains its critical voices, but *City of Cats* depicts China as lacking this essential resource; *wo* is perceptive and eloquent in his discussions of the woes plaguing Cat Country but appears blind to the degeneration of China. As a reconfiguration of Akutagawa's *Kappa*, Lao She's *City of Cats* not only points to the increased degeneration and squalor of early twentieth-century China as compared with Japan, but it also insinuates that although many Chinese have become experts at dissecting the ills plaguing other societies, they are unable — or perhaps simply unwilling — to acknowledge the imminent disasters facing their own country. *City of Cats* raises poignant questions about the ability of a society to reform when even those with the most finely tuned critical skills refuse to acknowledge the need for change. Akutagawa's novella and Lao She's novel both highlight the marginalization of the social critic, but while the Japanese text leaves open the chance of reform, the Chinese text effectively shuts the lid on this possibility. The one hope is that readers, spotting the contradictions of *wo*'s argument, will be awakened to the urgent need to do what they can to improve conditions in China, before the novel's imagined community of China becomes Cat Country.

Abrasive satires of Chinese society like Lu Xun's "The True Story of Ah Q" and Lao She's novel *City of Cats* silence the critical voices that resonate in the Japanese literary works that they intertextualize. In so doing, they not only underscore the additional suffering experienced by Chinese, but also suggest that reform is a remote possibility at best. Duration, even more than intensity, is depicted as the hallmark of human agony.

Literature deals extensively with questions of agency even as it embodies many of its paradoxes. It explores what say people have in shaping their lives; what say societies have in shaping their presents, pasts, and futures; to what extent both individuals and societies are governed by forces beyond their control; and how fate and agency are blurred in human experience. But constantly grappling with predecessors, contemporaries, and successors from diverse cultural fields, literary works themselves assert and deny varying degrees of agency. Considering the depth and breadth of imperial Japanese expansion into surrounding areas of East Asia and the painful loss of sovereignty experienced by its neighbors in the early twentieth century, it is not surprising that these issues come to the fore both in and through semicolonial Chinese and colonial Korean and Taiwanese transculturations of modern Japanese literature.

A little more than a year after the Marco Polo Bridge Incident on July 7, 1937, which marked the beginning of total war between China and Japan, a teenage member of the Taiwanese Atayal tribe was caught in a raging storm, slipped off a bridge, and fell into the turbulent waters of the Nan-ao River in northeastern Taiwan. She was never heard from again. The disappearance of Sayon Hayon on September 27, 1938 likely would have gone unnoticed outside her village were it not for what she was carrying: the luggage of a Japanese teacher summoned to Taipei to enlist in the Japanese army. Not taken for granted, Sayon's accidental sacrifice for imperial Japan quickly became a cause célèbre, told and retold in a variety of artistic media to inspire Taiwanese and others under Japanese control to give their all to Japan, and in some cases to encourage Japanese to welcome colonial peoples into the imperial fold. Whereas multiple deaths at a bridge outside Beijing widened irreparably the political chasm between Japanese and Chinese, a single death at a bridge in rural Taiwan blurred boundaries between Japanese and Taiwanese, at least in imperial rhetoric. The Japanese writer Murakami Genzō's play *Bell of Sayon* (1941), for instance, describes Sayon as someone who had metamorphosed from "a young aboriginal girl" into a "brave, praiseworthy graceful Japanese woman."[96] Intertextualizing *Bell of Sayon*, the Taiwanese writer Wu Mansha's *Bell of Sayon: A Tale of Patriotism* (1943) — which Wu claimed was based on a performance of Murakami's *Bell of Sayon* — stresses Sayon's patriotism even more emphatically.[97] The Japanese film *Sayon no kane* (Bell of Sayon, 1943), building on Wu Mansha's and especially Murakami's versions of the story, and made for Japanese consumption, provides yet a different perspective, emphasizing Japan's benevolent rule of the island.[98]

Loss of life can represent the ultimate surrendering of agency. But for Sayon, as for many constructed martyrs, this surrender multiplied as her story spread around East Asia, making its way into movie theaters, paintings, theatrical performances, songs, stories, and even textbooks. Were Sayon somehow to have survived the accident and eventually made her way home, she would not have recognized herself, nor would she have been recognized by others, so vast the gap between the many cultural reconfigurations of Sayon and Sayon the young woman. On the other hand, attaching ever greater significance to her death, the multiple creative recastings of her life increasingly bestowed her with agency. They transformed Sayon from a traveler who slipped off a bridge into a hero of the Japanese empire.

Similar things can be said of Japanese texts in motion, and particularly the corpus of Japanese literature transculturated by early twentieth-century Chinese, Korean, and Taiwanese writers. (Semi)colonial intertextualization of Japanese literary works often compromised the agency of imperial cultural products at the same time that it augmented their presence in East Asian cultural spheres. Chinese, Korean, and Taiwanese intertextualization likewise frequently performed (semi)colonial agency at the same time that it affirmed metropolitan cultural capital. Transposed fragments from modern Japanese literature are scattered throughout the literatures of colonial and semicolonial East Asia, where they sometimes are unmistakable, but more often than not form nuanced nebulae of intertextual transculturation. Intertextualizing Japanese literature by focusing on questions of suffering, relationships, and agency, colonial and semicolonial East Asian writers, like their counterparts around the world, sought to reform their societies and carve out new artistic positions vis-à-vis not only their own heritages and Western forms, but also imperial Japanese culture.

EPILOGUE

Postwar Intra–East Asian Dialogues and the Future of Negotiating Transculturally

The more we examine East Asian cultures, the more the diversity and complexity of their deep interconnections become apparent and the clearer it is that dividing this region's creative output along national and linguistic lines can hinder our understanding of its vibrant artistic production. This is just as true for the decades since World War Two as it was for the colonial period and in fact for most of East Asia's history. Conventional focuses on postwar East-West cultural negotiations, intra–East Asian popular culture flows, as well as East Asian depictions of East Asian "others," do not do justice to the dynamic and extensive intra–East Asian postcolonial/postsemicolonial transculturation taking place in the region. The parallels between East Asia now and a century ago are striking: extensive intra-regional language learning, travel, foreign study, friendships and networks, and transculturation of a wide variety of cultural products. But today the playing field is more even; China, South Korea, and Taiwan have been free of direct Japanese control for decades, and they enjoy strong economies and increased standards of living.

Buzzwords like Gross National Cool, Japan Cool, and MASK (manga, anime, sushi, karaoke) for Japan, and Korean Boom and Korean Wave (and backwash) for South Korea, have orbited energetically in recent years.[1] Yet the proliferation of Pokémon and the seductions of singers and soaps from Seoul represent only one segment of intra–East Asian cultural negotiation. The future of humanistic scholarship on East Asian societies lies partly in understanding a broader range of cultural phenomena in a regional and global perspective. A key part of this endeavor will be analyzing the dynamics of literary contact nebulae.

Intra-East Asian travel and readerly, writerly, and textual contact did not end with removal of Japanese troops from China and departure of Japanese colonial authorities from Korea and Taiwan after World War Two. The decolonization of nearly all of the twentieth-century European empires was protracted, bitter, and traumatic. The decolonization of Japan, on the other hand, instigated when it accepted the Potsdam Declaration on August 14, 1945, was total and uncontested; Japan's withdrawal from China, Korea, and Taiwan took place as quickly as was logistically possible. But decolonization and the return of Japanese to Japan did not bring true autonomy for any part of East Asia: Japan, China, Korea, and Taiwan all were rapidly sucked into Cold War rivalries. The Japanese underwent neocolonialism, in the form of American occupation, which ended in April 1952 except for Okinawa, where it officially ended in May 1972. Korea was divided along the 38th parallel in 1945, Japanese control replaced in the north by the Soviet Union's "guiding hand" and in the south by American occupation.[2] Separate regimes were created in 1948, and the two Koreas engaged in a bloody civil war between 1950 and 1953. In China, civil war followed the departure of Japanese and other foreign powers, the Guomindang (KMT) backed by the United States and the Communist Party backed by the Soviet Union. When the People's Republic of China (PRC) was established in 1949, the Chinese enjoyed relatively greater independence than their East Asian neighbors. Even so, they relied heavily on the Soviet Union for economic support and technical expertise until the Sino-Soviet rift in 1960. Decolonization in Taiwan meant the transfer of control from Japan to China; the KMT occupation of the island after 1947 was ruthless and encountered strong resistance. After meeting defeat on the mainland in 1949 at the hands of Communist troops, the KMT made Taiwan the new home of the Republic of China.

Cold War tensions combined with the traumatic colonial and semi-colonial past severely hampered the reestablishment of relations among East Asian regimes, and diplomatic recognition, slow to arrive, did not extinguish antagonisms, some of which linger to this day. Japan and South Korea normalized relations in 1965, but the two nations continue to argue about how Japan's colonization of Korea should be represented in textbooks, whether the prime minister of Japan should visit the Yasukuni Shrine memorializing Japan's war dead, what role the Japanese military played in forcing Korean women into sexual slavery as "comfort women," who has legitimate claim to the islets Takeshima/Dokdo, and how to conduct diplomacy toward North Korea. Japan and China normalized relations in 1972, at which time Japan also recognized the PRC's jurisdiction in Taiwan. But the mainland remains troubled over Japanese atrocities in World War Two: the spring of 2005 was marked by large anti-Japanese demonstrations in Beijing and other Chinese cities, and the two countries currently are competing for oil-drilling rights in nearby waters (the oil-rich shelf off the Diaoyutai/Senkaku Islands in the East China Sea) and for natural resources around the world. Although Taiwanese memories of Japanese oppression are not as strong as those of Chinese and Koreans, largely because of China's and Korea's much longer histories as autonomous (although deeply interconnected) cultures, Japanese-Taiwanese relations are not free from strain. China and North Korea established diplomatic ties almost immediately, but China and South Korea did not resume relations until 1992. For their part, the two Koreas remain officially at war, nearly six decades after the opening shots of the Korean War, while Taiwan is self-governing yet legally a part of the PRC, its future status still uncertain. Considering these geopolitical conditions, it is no surprise that after the mass repatriations in the months following Japanese surrender, the movement of peoples that characterized the first half of the twentieth century slowed considerably. Except for the traffic across the Yalu River between China and North Korea, intra–East Asian travel did not revive until the end of the twentieth century, when the heaviest restrictions at last were lifted.

Yet textual travel relies only in small part on human travel, and despite strict government controls, intra–East Asian literary contact continued on a modest scale in the first decades after Japan's surrender. Most Korean and Taiwanese writers in the early postwar period were products of the Japanese colonial education system and many had studied in Japan; similarly, a number of Chinese writers also had studied in Japan and forged ties with Japanese counterparts. Direct communication among the literary worlds of East Asia declined for several decades, as Chinese, Korean, and Taiwanese writers involved with Japan during the (semi)colonial period were replaced through retirement, death, or exile by others with little Japan experience. But transculturation persisted, and twenty years after World War Two, a resurgence began that has continued virtually unabated. Today one can walk into any large bookstore or library in China, South Korea, and Taiwan and find shelves of translations and studies of Japanese literature. Likewise, the space in Japanese bookstores and libraries dedicated to the literatures of China, Korea, and Taiwan is increasing, as is the space in Chinese, Korean, and Taiwanese bookstores and libraries devoted to one another's literatures. More recently, intellectuals from several East Asian nations discussed establishing an East Asian Publishing Network—a contact nebula with several centers "to foster the exchange and utilization of information and ideas among publishing professionals throughout East Asia."[3]

Chinese, Japanese, Korean, and Taiwanese literatures have all served as such extensive spaces of intra–East Asian transculturation since the mid-twentieth century that, like *Empire of Texts in Motion*, my book *Texts in Turmoil: Reimagining Regions and Worlds* (now in preparation) is necessarily selective, not comprehensive. Analyzing Japanese, Korean, and above all Taiwanese postwar transculturations of Lu Xun's oeuvre alone could fill volumes. The determined cosmopolitanism of many contemporary East Asian writers makes untangling intertextual and other networks particularly challenging. But on the whole, the outbound vectors of Japanese literature across East Asia have remained the speediest, broadest, and most controversial. Educated in the Japanese language, if not in Japan itself, many early postwar East Asian writers possessed at least limited proficiency in Japanese and continued to be intrigued by Japanese literature; for some, liberation only made it more fascinating. The renowned South Korean novelist Pak Wansŏ (1931–) points out the popularity of foreign literature in the immediate postwar period and the irony of continued Korean dependence on Japanese translations:

As the Japanese who had lost the war were returning home, all sorts of household items came out on the market, and among these many were books. Not to mention the books of well-known Japanese writers that I had always wanted to read, complete sets of famous writers and world literature were on the streets for sale and these at such low price attracted more buyers than any other object. . . . The Japanese translations and their selections continued to influence us long after the country's liberation, regardless of our anti-Japanese sentiments.[4]

Pak Wansŏ notes that many Koreans "despised Japanese literature as stereotyped and shallow," but she dismisses this as "probably the customary response of a population who had just been liberated from colonialism." She freely admits to her own enthrallment with this corpus:

I was part of the generation whose literary sensibilities had been formed through Japanese. It is true that even to bring up Japanese colonialism is repulsive. But I was in fact more fascinated by Japanese novels after the liberation, thinking it fortunate that the liberation came when I could speak Japanese almost as fluently as a native speaker. . . . There can't be any better language than Japanese to express the pathos of life contained in the commonplaces of the everyday, the unobtrusive grain of life, the foreboding of death and decimation. . . . Even after Korea became liberated and independent, the influence of the language [and literature] of the dominant nation was persistent and all-powerful.[5]

Such sentiments, expressed nearly six decades after liberation, expose the strength and stamina of cultural products whose movements seldom parallel but often intersect political discourse.

Pak Wansŏ's observations concerning the Japanese language in Korea notwithstanding, one of the greatest differences between the postwar East Asian literary landscape and that of other postcolonial sites is the place of the language of the former imperial power. Most postcolonial writers have chosen or have had little choice but to write in the languages of their former colonizers, even if they were born after decolonization. To be sure, postwar Korean and Taiwanese writers, primarily those educated under Japanese colonialism, often incorporate Japanese expressions into their novels, plays, poems, and short stories; a handful—most notably haiku and *tanka* proponents in Korea and Taiwan—continue to write at least some of their work in Japanese.[6] Moreover, increasing numbers of Chinese, Koreans, and Taiwanese are studying Japanese both at home and in Japan. But with the exception of those raised in Japan or who have lived there for many years, postwar Chinese, Koreans, and Taiwanese—first under the duress of postwar political circumstances and then by simple inertia—generally have not used Japanese as a language of creative composition.

Yet they have continued engaging intensely with Japanese literature. Despite the great vitality of postcolonial studies, with the exception of negotiations with Japanese bestsellers, postwar Chinese, Korean, and Taiwanese transculturation of Japanese literature has received scant scholarly attention; postwar Japanese engagement with Chinese, Korean, and Taiwanese literatures has been even more neglected, while Sino-Korean and Taiwanese-Korean interpretive, interlingual, and intertextual transculturation is scarcely acknowledged. Like their predecessors during the colonial period, postwar intra–East Asian critical commentaries, adaptations, translations, and intertextualizations are likely to prove fertile fields of inquiry as their numbers continue to rise and as East Asian nations become more economically and politically interdependent.[7]

Postwar interpretive and interlingual transculturation of Japanese literature had a sluggish start but was revitalized in the early 1960s and took off after Kawabata Yasunari became the first East Asian writer to win the Nobel Prize in Literature (1968). Kawabata was the most frequently translated Japanese writer in South Korea in the 1960s; fifteen translations of his novel *Yukiguni* (Snow Country, 1935–47) were published during that decade alone, eight of them in 1968.[8] Nobel Prize aside, the popularity of *Snow Country* in South Korea is noteworthy considering the circumstances surrounding its production and distribution among wartime Japanese. During World War Two, the novel was popular among Japanese colonizers and soldiers throughout East Asia, primarily for its nostalgic evocations of the Japanese homeland.[9] Moreover, although critics generally have accepted Kawabata's claim that he never became a blind worshipper of Japanese militarism, he was an ardent supporter of World War Two, and his own writings clearly show that his disengagement from Japanese imperialism took place in the late 1940s.[10] It is likely that *Snow Country* has been translated repeatedly in South Korea not only because it is one of Kawabata's representative works and one of the texts that won him the Nobel Prize, but also because its depiction of a relatively ahistorical landscape—the very feature that attracted so many worldwide to this text—gave South Korean translators the opportunity to expose the complicity of the Japanese literary establishment in the war effort, not only by their active propagandizing but also by their silence and escapism.

Some in China have suggested that Japan essentially rigged the 1968 Nobel Prize competition.[11] Yet Kawabata remains a favorite of writers and translators there. As the preeminent Chinese avant-garde novelist Yu Hua (1960–) recently declared, "I chose what I read of twentieth-century literature on the grounds of whether it had won the Nobel Prize or not. The first Kawabata I read was from the Zhejiang selection of Nobel Prize–winning works."[12] But while Japan's two recipients of the Nobel Prize in Literature—Kawabata and Ōe Kenzaburō (1994)—are admired across East Asia, the most popular Japanese writer in the region by far is Murakami Haruki. In fact, when

Ōe visited Beijing in 2000, he found Chinese writers, scholars, and readers alike more interested in Murakami.[13] Murakami's *Noruwei no mori* (Norwegian Wood, 1987), a novel on a university student's troubled relationships with women, is his most popular work in East Asia. Translations of Murakami's *Hitsuji o meguru bōken* (A Wild Sheep Chase, 1989) and the three-volume *Nejimakidori kuronikuru* (Wind-Up Bird Chronicle, 1995) also are bestsellers; the former touches on Japanese violence in East Asia, while the latter includes graphic depictions of Japanese wartime atrocities on the Manchurian-Mongolian border.[14] These discussions of Japanese actions on the continent resonate with the concerns of many contemporary Chinese, Koreans, and Taiwanese, but they represent only one subset of the many features of Murakami's oeuvre that attract readers across East Asia.[15] In the preface to a volume of Murakami's work in translation completed in the mid-1990s, the Taiwanese writer Lai Mingzhu indicated that many of his readers were frustrated by the slow speed with which Murakami was being translated.[16] Today, translations of Murakami, together with those of the newest generation of Japanese writers, abound in East Asia, and they are read by millions. In fact, some Chinese, Korean, and Taiwanese writers bemoan the popularity of their Japanese rivals. As the South Korean writer Chŏng Yihyŏn (1972–) has lamented, "Even friends who don't read my books raced through [Japanese writer] Kaori Ekuni's [1964–] new book."[17]

East Asian translation and study of Japanese literary products are greater today than at any time since the early twentieth century. Contemporary Japanese writers, Murakami in particular, have received the most critical attention, but in the last several decades Chinese, Koreans, and Taiwanese have translated an even greater variety of Japanese novels, plays, poems, and short stories than their early twentieth-century counterparts. Most remarkable is the large assortment of pre-twentieth century Japanese literary works, everything from the eighth-century *Collection of Ten Thousand Leaves* to nineteenth-century drama that, after centuries of virtual neglect, at last are being consumed and discussed by Chinese, Korean, and Taiwanese readers.

But what about the literary legacy? East Asian writers from the 1950s through the new millennium have been actively intertextualizing Japanese literature in their own creative texts, and some have talked openly of the impact of this corpus on their work. One of the most intriguing forms of intertextualization has been intertitularity:

postwar Chinese, Korean, and Taiwanese writers have given their texts the same or very similar names as celebrated Japanese literary products, everything from the *Collection of Ten Thousand Leaves* to early twentieth-century poetry by Hagiwara Sakutarō and prose by Arishima Takeo, mid-twentieth century novels and short stories by Kawabata Yasunari and Ōba Minako (1930–2007), and late-twentieth century stories by Yoshimoto Banana (1964–). Sometimes there is little relationship between textual bodies packaged under identical or nearly identical titles, suggesting simple coincidence. Yet often there is more to these relationships, particularly when a canonical Japanese work is involved. At times, intertitularity indicates solidarity, at times it asserts cultural legitimacy, at times it undermines textual predecessors, among many creative strategies. It occurs within and across all genres and borders, misplacing, displacing, and replacing creative antecedents even while calling greater attention to them. But, like most forms of intertextualization, this phenomenon has especially complex implications when it occurs in the context of uneven power relationships or, as is true of East Asia today, the memory of such relationships.

One of the most interesting examples of postcolonial East Asian engagement with Japanese creative texts via intertitularity is the Korean writer Hwang Sunwŏn's (1915–2000) *K'ain ŭi huye* (Descendants of Cain, 1954), which reworks Arishima Takeo's *Kain no matsuei* (Descendants of Cain, 1917). Both texts explore the human capacity for cruelty within the triadic relationship of the landlord, the landlord's agent, and the tenant farmer. Arishima's novella depicts a world nearly devoid of compassion in which a tenant farmer, abused by his landlord and fellow tenants, forever remains a vicious and destitute migrant. Hwang's novel briefly mentions the appalling living conditions of tenant farmers, but one of its most interesting features is that it contrasts a passively sympathetic landlord with his ruthless estate agent, only to expose the similar malevolent effect each has on society.

Like much confrontational intertextuality of the colonial era, Hwang Sunwŏn's novel uses intertexts to emphasize the relative intensity of Korean suffering: whereas Arishima's Japanese protagonist and his family lose their home, the Korean protagonist and his relatives, in effect, lose their country. But directly tying his novel to a Japanese work written nearly 40 years earlier allowed Hwang Sunwŏn to create a text that, although grounded firmly in recent events —

the novel discusses the division of Korea following Japanese defeat and the impending communist takeover of North Korea—expresses solidarity with its Japanese predecessor and on a more fundamental level underscores the continued plight of all humanity. Published in South Korea in the aftermath of the Korean War and less than a decade after liberation from Japan, the Korean *Descendants of Cain* nevertheless does more than deplore the cruelties of communism and colonialism. The novel explores the fallibility of even the most seemingly benign individuals and underlines the ubiquity of brutality and destructiveness; it undercuts the slim hopes for humanity to which the Japanese *Descendants of Cain* alludes. Although repeatedly differentiating itself from its Japanese predecessor, the Korean *Descendants of Cain* in the end more often upholds than critiques Arishima's novella. Providing sympathetic portrayals of both Koreans and Japanese, Hwang Sunwŏn's text stresses their common fate. All, it suggests, are the descendants of Cain.[18]

Different dynamics are at play in the Japanese-language *Taiwan Man'yōshū* (Taiwan Collection of Ten Thousand Leaves, 1981–93), compiled by the Taiwanese physician Kohō Banri (Wu Jiantang, 1926–99) and published in Japan. Asserting Taiwanese cultural legitimacy in the wake of the Japanese recognition of the PRC and continued exclusion of Taiwanese *tanka* from anthologies of poetry in Japanese, the *Taiwan Collection of Ten Thousand Leaves* explicitly positions itself to rival both the Japanese *Shōwa Man'yōshū* (Shōwa Collection of Ten Thousand Leaves, 1979–80) and the eighth-century *Collection of Ten Thousand Leaves*. Specifying place (Taiwan) as opposed to period (Shōwa), the anthology argues for recognizing Taiwan as a cultural center apart from both China and Japan, albeit one inhabited by (Taiwanese) poets with a Japanese education who, in Kohō's words, "borrow the *tanka* form of the *Collection of Ten Thousand Leaves* to lay bare their life's breath."[19] This late twentieth-century struggle for legitimacy vis-à-vis both China and Japan was a replay of colonial-period dynamics, but as before, one that positioned Taiwanese as continually attempting to catch up with their East Asian neighbors.

Many poems in the *Taiwan Collection of Ten Thousand Leaves* intertextualize Japanese predecessors. But just as interesting a feature of the Taiwanese collection is its emphasis on the Taiwanese poets themselves. The *Taiwan Collection of Ten Thousand Leaves* is arranged by author, not by subject and period as is the Shōwa collection. The prose passages that surround and in some cases overwhelm the *tanka* generally do not discuss poetry, instead giving detailed personal information such as the poet's educational, employment, and publishing history, as well as connections with Japan. These mini-biographies, present in neither the *Collection of Ten Thousand Leaves* nor the *Shōwa Collection of Ten Thousand Leaves*, make Kohō's anthology much more a "who's who" than a "what's what" of Taiwanese poetry. They present the poems as products of individual Taiwanese who, despite their ties with Japan, are more than the heirs of a so-called Japanese pulse. In so doing, the mini-biographies undermine the emphasis in the collection's prefaces and commentaries on the *Taiwan Collection of Ten Thousand Leaves* as the expression of hearts infused with Japaneseness. The biographies also have the added benefit of bulking up the collection, since by any count Taiwanese *tanka* poets and their creations are greatly outnumbered by their Japanese counterparts.

Another prominent example of postwar intra–East Asian textual contact involving intertitularity is the Taiwanese writer Zhu Tianxin's Chinese-language novella *Ancient Capital* (1996). Whereas the intertitularity in *Descendents of Cain* expresses solidarity, and in Kohō Banri's volume it asserts Taiwanese cultural legitimacy, in the Taiwanese *Ancient Capital* it subordinates Kawabata's novel *Ancient Capital* (1962). The Japanese *Ancient Capital*, one of the three works for which Kawabata won the Nobel Prize, is the story of a young woman separated from her twin sister at birth and briefly reunited with her years later. Kawabata's novel interweaves personal struggles with lyric and informative descriptions of Kyoto and its many temples, shrines, and festivals. Some parts of the Japanese *Ancient Capital* read more like a travel guide than a work of fiction. Its Taiwanese counterpart, on the other hand, reconfigures the confrontations with bloodline depicted in Kawabata's novel as confrontations with both cultural identities and physical and literary spaces.

The narrator of the Taiwanese novella is a second-generation Chinese mainlander in Taiwan who is a 1990s *flâneur* of both Taipei and Kyoto and a reader of texts from around the world, including Japanese literature and maps. Disoriented in contemporary Taipei, she portrays Kyoto as a more desirable city, a place she feels at home, with its "twin"—colonial Taipei—a close, if ambivalent, second. At the same time that it venerates Japan's cultural capital (Kyoto), in part because it is a repository of things Chinese, Zhu Tianxin's *Ancient Capital* severely compromises Japanese cultural capital. The Taiwanese novella interweaves and then undermines passages from Kawabata's *Ancient Capital*, ultimately displacing the text itself. Citing Kawabata's final lines well before its own conclusion, the Taiwanese *Ancient Capital* points to the inadequacies of the Japanese narrative in guiding the Taiwanese project; there is, Zhu Tianxin's novella implies, much more to say, much additional ground to be covered.

Most critics of the Taiwanese *Ancient Capital* highlight the narrator's polyintertextuality (the novella cites and alludes to a variety of predecessors) and explore her convoluted construction and deconstruction of multiple cultural identities. Underappreciated in this process are the novella's intertitularity and the interwoven passages from Kawabata's novel. The shuffled citations from the Japanese *Ancient Capital*, brief snippets in no particular order, signify the Taiwanese *Ancient Capital's*—and in effect the postcolonial—subordination of a locally and internationally venerated Japanese cultural product. After all, not only was Kawabata the first East Asian writer to receive the Nobel Prize, but he also has retained star status in China and Taiwan. His *Ancient Capital* has enjoyed particular acclaim. By the time Zhu Tianxin published her novella in 1996, Kawabata's had been translated into Chinese at least six times; it has remained a popular object of transculturation into the twenty-first century. The narrator of the Taiwanese *Ancient Capital* thus boldly performs vivisection on a literary work that is flourishing, indeed multiplying, outside its country of origin; her combination of fragmented explicit intertextuality (citation of passages, in Chinese translation, from Kawabata's novel) and intertitularity asserts Taiwanese creative authority. This novella, the narrator declares, is the Taiwanese "old [textual] capital," not the Japanese book (Kawabata's *Ancient Capital*) parading around in Chinese clothes (translation).[20]

There is no denying the large presence of American, European, and other non–East Asian literatures in postwar East Asian creative production. But the postcolonial and postsemicolonial East Asian literary landscape—like its prewar and wartime counterparts—also is one of remarkably nuanced, sometimes subtle and sometimes trenchant, intra–East Asian transcultural negotiation. Complicating matters is an increased reliance on translations. Since not many Chinese, Korean, and Taiwanese writers educated in the postwar decades know Japanese, their intertextualizations of Japanese literature are often as much recastings of local transculturations, mostly translations but at times intertextualizations, as they are of the "original" Japanese novels, plays, poems, and short stories themselves. This is just as true of other postcolonial and postsemicolonial intra–East Asian intertextual vectors.

Scholarship on intra–East Asian cultural contacts has emphasized pre-twentieth century sinocentrism and early twenty-first century popular culture flows. Studies of twentieth-century intra–East Asian relationships have emphasized geopolitical concerns. These dominant narratives obscure the vibrant intra–East Asian cultural and particularly literary transculturation that took place throughout the turbulent 1900s and continues into the new millennium; China, Japan, Korea, and Taiwan all remain active sites of intra–East Asian travel, as well as linguistic, readerly, writerly, and textual contact. Studying East Asian literatures and cultures in geographic isolation can impose artificial frameworks that impede our comprehension of this dynamic part of the world. Examining them together opens broad perspectives appropriate to the lively transcultural interaction that has long characterized the region.

Empire of Texts in Motion exposes and analyzes a multitude of creative networks and contact nebulae, but much work remains. Building on the recent boom in scholarship on habitually disregarded peoples, cultural products, and intracultural dynamics, we need to devote further attention to processes of circulation, dislocation, manipulation, reconfiguration, and transculturation. Discovering and analyzing local, subnational, national, regional, and global networks and nebulae will better illuminate the dynamism of the world's cultural landscapes, and ultimately the complex texture of human experience, across time and space.

Reference Matter

Notes

Introduction

1. Sylvia Spitta, *Between Two Waters*, p. 24. Spitta focuses on the transformation of both Spanish cultures and those indigenous to Latin America. Cf. Anuradha Dingwaney, "Introduction: Translating 'Third World' Cultures," p. 8; Fernando Ortiz, *Contrapunteo cubana del tabaco y el azúcar*, p. xi; Phyllis Peres, *Transculturation and Resistance in Lusophone African Narrative*, p. 10; Mary Louise Pratt, *Imperial Eyes*, p. 7; Ángel Rama, *Transculturación narrativa en América Latina*.

2. The concept of "cultural capital" is loosely adapted from Pierre Bourdieu, "The Forms of Capital."

3. Nineteenth- and twentieth-century empires were the largest, the most organized, and the most regulated regimes in human history. By the early twentieth century, they together controlled a substantial majority of the earth's surface and population. Edward Said, *Culture and Imperialism*, pp. 8, 221. See also Komagome Takeshi, "Colonial Modernity for an Elite Taiwanese, Lim Bo-seng," pp. 141-42. The term *semicolonial* designates the multinational yet fragmented political, economic, and cultural domination of China by Japan and numerous Western nations (including Russia/the Soviet Union), from the mid-nineteenth to the mid-twentieth centuries. Scholars have proposed several other terms, including *multiple colonialism* (Paul A. Cohen), *hypercolony* (Ruth Rogaski), and *politically compromised* (Selçuk Esenbul), but *semicolonial* best describes China's situation. Paul A. Cohen, *Discovering History in China*, pp. 144-45; Selçuk Esenbul, "Japan's Global Claim to Asia and the World of Islam," pp. 1140-70; Ruth Rogaski, *Hygienic Modernity*, pp. 15-16.

4. Mary Louise Pratt, *Imperial Eyes*, p. 7.

5. Mary Louise Pratt, *Imperial Eyes*, p. 8. Mireille Rosello's notion of "performative encounters" likewise acknowledges the interactive and improvisational dimensions of these contacts, although for her they are "exceptional

moment[s]" rather than common occurrences. See her *France and the Maghreb*, p. 1.

6. Transcultural artistic contacts also have been discussed as phenomena of spaces "in-between" or as performing and embodying "in-betweenness." See, for instance, Anuradha Dingwaney, "Introduction," pp. 8–9; Lital Levy, "Self-Portraits of the Other," pp. 343–402; Steven Ungar, "Writing in Tongues," pp. 132–33. As these scholars aptly demonstrate, some encounters clearly position themselves or are positioned "in-between" (languages, literatures, peoples, cultures, etc.). See also Régine Robin, *La Québécoite*, p. 69. But I prefer the more nuanced flexibility offered by the phrase "contact nebulae," which can indicate creative and physical spaces both between and among.

7. Cf. Roland Barthes, *S/Z*, p. 10. Barthes uses the neologisms "readerly" (*le lisible*) and "writerly" (*le scriptible*) to refer to texts, distinguishing between "classic" texts and those that make the reader "no longer a consumer, but a producer." Linguistic, readerly, writerly, and textual interactions also occur among peoples and cultural products in more balanced power relations, but the focus here is on these contacts in empire and postimperial spaces, interpreted broadly.

8. Japan colonized Taiwan in 1895 and Korea in 1910. It never formally colonized China, but it subjected the mainland to severe cultural, economic, political, and military pressure from the end of the nineteenth century to the mid-twentieth. Japan seized Manchuria (northeast China) in 1931, and in 1932 proclaimed it the nominally independent state of Manchukuo. But in fact Manchukuo was Japan's puppet state, an informal, de facto colony. Mariko Asano Tamanoi, "Introduction," p. 8. The Japanese did not speak of the people of occupied Manchuria as Chinese and even referred to the Chinese language as *Manwen* (Manchu). Norman Smith, "Wielding Pens as Swords," p. 47. Occupied Manchuria was a site of vibrant transculturation, but its artistic fields were dwarfed by those of China proper.

9. Tony Ballantyne and Antoinette Burton warn of the pitfalls inherent in the terms "the West," "Asia," and the like, "not only because each of those categories tends to homogenize the geographical region it evokes, but equally because all of those places have been interdependent from the fourteenth century onward, if not before" ("Introduction: Bodies, Empires, and World Histories," p. 2). Gayatri Spivak problematizes conceptualizations of "Asia" in "Other Asias" and *Other Asias* (pp. 209–38), while Atsuko Ueda summarizes constructions of "Asia" and the "West" in Meiji Japan (1868–1912) in *Concealment of Politics, Politics of Concealment*, pp. 15–20. See also Sun Ge, "How Does Asia Mean?"; Wang Hui, "The Politics of Imagining Asia." Pascale Casanova discusses intra-European literary hierarchies in *The World Republic of Letters*.

10. See David L. Curley, "Maharaja Krisnacandra, Hinduism, and Kingship in the Contact Zone of Bengal," pp. 85–117; Madeleine Dobie, "Translation in the Contact Zone"; Karsten Fitz, *Negotiating History and Culture*, pp. 32–42; Renée Green, ed., *Negotiations in the Contact Zone*; Noreen Groover Lape, *West of the Border*, pp. 1–18; Katie Pickles and Myra Rutherdale, eds., *Contact Zones*; Susanne Reichl, *Cultures in the Contact Zone*, pp. 1–8, 40–45.

11. Examples are Bill Ashcroft et al., *Post-colonial Studies*; Bill Ashcroft et al., *The Empire Writes Back*; Homi K. Bhabha, *The Location of Culture*; Nicholas Harrison, *Postcolonial Criticism*; Padmini Moniga, ed., *Contemporary Postcolonial Theory*; Patrick Williams and Laura Chrisman, eds., *Colonial Discourse and Postcolonial Theory*. A common and valid critique of postcolonial perspectives is that they tend "to maintain Europe as an inevitable reference point" and "to overemphasize and overgeneralize from the British empire." Nicholas Harrison, "Life on the Second Floor," p. 342. See also Frederick Cooper, "Postcolonial Studies and the Study of History," pp. 409–11. Scholars breaking away from the West-Rest paradigm include Lital Levy in her discussion of Palestinian Arab writers publishing in Hebrew; the contributors to François Lionnet and Shu-mei Shih's edited volume on "minor transnationalism" (distinguished from both the rhizome of Gilles Deleuze and Félix Guattari and the postnational "flexible" norms of citizenship of Arjun Appadurai, May Joseph, and Aihwa Ong); and Harsha Ram in his examination of Russian-Georgian literary dialogues. Levy, "Self-Portraits of the Other"; François Lionnet and Shu-mei Shih, "Introduction"; Ram, "Towards a Cross-cultural Poetics of the Contact Zone," pp. 63–89. As Lital Levy notes, in Arab Jewish writings in both Hebrew and Arabic "the signs of transculturation [are most evident] in the writers' efforts to delineate and articulate their own subjectivity, a process fraught with East-West tension." But the struggle for subjective presence and authority "was directed not only at the West but at the dominant groups within the *nahḍha* and *haskala* (Muslim and Christian Arabs and European Jews, respectively)" ("Jewish Writers in the Arab East," pp. 89–90, 99).

12. As Christopher L. Miller soberly reminds us, "In the context of the slave trade, encounter meant war and capture; movement was a forced march in chains and a Middle Passage without return; hybridity came from rape" (*The French Atlantic Triangle*, p. ix).

13. Equally important are inter-(post)imperial networks, a phenomenon discussed briefly in following chapters. See also Tejaswini Niranjana, "Alternative Frames?"

14. I examine twentieth-century Japanese negotiations with Chinese, Korean, and Taiwanese literatures, and Chinese, Korean, and Taiwanese engagement with one another's literatures at length in "Cultures and Texts in Motion," pp. 311–91, 743–841. See also Karen Thornber, "Transspatializing Texts and Transtextualizing Spaces in Literary Contact Nebulae."

15. Simon Gikandi, *Maps of Englishness*, pp. xv, 225. This phenomenon is not unique to (post)imperial spaces. See, for instance, Toni Morrison's discussion in *Playing in the Dark* of the centrality of the black presence in white American constructions of identity.

16. Alexander Des Forges gives several examples of this phenomenon in *Mediasphere Shanghai*, pp. 20–21, 29–43.

17. To give one example, during the colonial period the Japanese government encouraged Japanese writers and other artists and intellectuals to spend time in China, occupied Manchuria, Korea, and Taiwan, but as educators or travelers, not as students. An interesting exception is the Japanese ethnolo-

gist Kano Tadao (1906–45), whose fascination with mountains and insects was part of what prompted him to attend high school in Taiwan. Kano Tadao, *Yama to kumo to banjin to*, p. 33.

18. See, for instance, Lúcia Sá's study *Rain Forest Literatures* on the impact of indigenous texts, however mediated, on canonical Latin American literature.

19. Bill Ashcroft et al., *The Empire Writes Back*, p. 6. Most scholarship focuses on postcolonial literary interactions. One exception is Paul Giles, *Transatlantic Insurrections*, which examines how in the decades surrounding the American Revolution British and American literatures "became kinds of 'secret sharers' . . . twisting and intertwining with each other in mutually disorienting ways" (p. 2). See also Rachel Feldhay Brenner, *Inextricably Bonded*.

20. See, for instance, Joshua Fogel, *Articulating the Sinosphere*, Maria Rosa Menocal, *The Arabic Role in Medieval Literary History*, and Claudine Salmon, ed., *Literary Migrations*. Scholars increasingly are recognizing the importance of examining together literary Chinese writings by Chinese, Japanese, and Koreans. The *jōdai bungaku* (ancient Japanese literature) project at the University of Tokyo, for instance, seeks to "rethink ancient Japanese literature" as "part of an East Asian classical tradition" (http://fusehime.c.u-tokyo.ac.jp/eastasia/e/theme/index.html. Accessed November 28, 2008).

21. Ronald P. Toby, *State and Diplomacy in Early Modern Japan*, p. 234. See also Harry Harootunian, "The Function of China in Tokugawa Thought," pp. 9–36.

22. Peter Kornicki, *The Book in Japan*, p. 15.

23. For more on the translation and introduction of Chinese vernacular fiction in Japan see Ma Zuyi and Ren Rongzhen, *Hanji waiyishi*, pp. 514–38. See also Dai Yan, "*Jiandeng xin hua* he *Jiandeng yu hua* zai Riben de liuchuan ji qi yingxiang," pp. 195–207; Tanaka Yūko, "Kinsei Nihon to Ajia no bungaku," pp. 37–52; Yan Shaotang and Wang Xiaoping, *Zhongguo wenxue zai Riben*; and Jonathan Zwicker, *Practices of the Sentimental Imagination*, pp. 125–68. For more on eighteenth-century Japanese writing in the Chinese vernacular, see Emanuel Pastreich, "The Projection of Quotidian Japan on the Chinese Vernacular," pp. 1–2.

24. See James Lewis, "Beyond *Sakoku*," p. 30; Hong Sŏn-p'yo, "Korean Painting of the Late Chosŏn Period in Relation to Japanese Literati Painting," p. 18. See also Burglind Jungmann, *Painters as Envoys*.

25. Korean accounts include those by An Chongsu, Kang Posŏng, Kim Kisu, Pak Yŏnghyo, and Song Hŏnbin. See Kim Sunjŏn, "Sŏgu ŭi ch'unggyŏk kwa Han-Il munhak ŭi taeŭng yangsang," p. 138 and Kim T'aejun, "*Ildong kiyu wa Sŏyu kyŏnmun*," pp. 70–100. Chinese accounts include those by Huang Zunxian, Fu Yunlong, Wang Tao, and Yao Wendong. See Lin Qingzhang's three-volume *Jindai Zhongguo zhishifenzi zai Riben* for more on modern Chinese intellectuals in Japan.

26. Yun Ch'iho, *Yun Ch'iho ilgi 3*, pp. 195, 204. Yun Ch'iho wrote this part of his diary in English.

27. Western nations also altered their assessments of Japan, a nation they had seen as a "backward, Oriental country, far removed from the dynamic

achievements of European civilization" (Daniel Botsman, *Punishment and Power*, p. 6). Yet, as Botsman additionally notes, at the same time that "Westerners continued to express admiration for Japan's achievements . . . they found it difficult to abandon the idea that modern civilization was a uniquely European [phenomenon]" (pp. 224–25). See also Susan J. Napier, *From Impressionism to Anime*, p. 15.

28. Guo Moruo, "Zhuozi de tiaowu," p. 139, quoted in Kondō Haruo, "Chūgoku bundan to ryūnichi gakusei," p. 25; and Ching-mao Cheng, "The Impact of Japanese Literary Trends on Modern Chinese Writers," p. 63. Chinese writers educated or spending significant time in Japan include Lu Xun (1881–1936), Ouyang Yuqian (1889–1962), and Zhou Zuoren (1885–1967) in the late Qing, followed by Cheng Fangwu (1897–1984), Guo Moruo, Tian Han (1898–1968), Yu Dafu (1896–1945), and Zhang Ziping (1893–1959) in the 1910s. Others traveled to Japan after the 1919 May Fourth Movement, such as Feng Zikai (1898–1975), Li Chuli (1900–94), Mu Mutian (1900–79), Xia Yan (1900–95), and Xie Liuyi (1898–1945). More went to Japan after the Guomindang (Nationalist Party) purge of communists in April 1927, including Hu Feng (1903–85), Jiang Guangci (1901–31), Lei Shiyu (1911–96), and Mao Dun (1896–1981). Ba Jin (1904–2005), Du Xuan (1914–2004), and others spent time in Japan in the mid-1930s. Most Chinese writers who studied in Japan were men, but several important Chinese women writers with Japan experience include Qiu Jin (1875–1907), who lived there from 1903 to 1906; Bai Wei (1894–1987), who lived there for eight years beginning in 1918; and Xie Bingying (1906–2000), who went in 1931 and again in 1935. See Jia Zhifang's list in "Zhongguo liuri xuesheng yu Zhongguo xiandai wenxue," pp. 179–81. See also Jia Zhifang, "Zhongguo liuri xuesheng yu Zhongguo xiandai wenxue," pp. 1–20 and Kondō Haruo, *Gendai Chūgoku no sakka to sakuhin*, pp. 93–203.

29. These include Dan Di (1916–92), Mei Niang (1920–), and Wu Ying (1915–61). Norman Smith, *Resisting Manchukuo*, pp. 59, 68–70. For more on Mei Niang's time in Japan see also Xu Naixiang and Huang Wanhua, *Zhongguo kangzhan shiqi lunxianqu wenxueshi*, pp. 375–77.

30. Yi Injik (1862–1916), Ch'oe Namsŏn (1890–1957), and Yi Kwangsu (1892–1950), arriving in the first decade of the twentieth century, were some of the earliest Korean creative artists to study in Japan. They were followed in later years by important novelists and short-story writers including Ch'ae Mansik (1902–50), Chang Hyŏkju (1905–98), Chu Yohan (1900–79), Hwang Sunwŏn (1915–2000), Hyŏn Chin-gŏn (1900–43), Kim Dong-in (1900–51), and Kim Saryang (1914–50). Writers active in the Korean proletarian literature movement such as Im Hwa (1908–53), Kim Kijin (1903–85), Pak Yŏnghŭi (1901–50), Yi Pukman (1907–59), and Yi Kiyŏng (1896–1945) also had considerable Japan experience. Finally, Korean female literary artists who studied in Japan include the prose writers Kim Ilyŏp (1896–1971) and Pak Hwasŏng (1904–88), the poet Yi Changhŭi (1900–29), and the poet and prose writer Na Hyesŏk (1896–1946). See Shirakawa Yutaka (Sirakkawa Yuttakka), "Hanguk kŭndae munhak ch'och'anggi ŭi Ilbonjŏk yŏnghyang"; Hotei Toshihiro, "Kaidai," pp. 3–7; Kamiya Tadataka, "Senjika no Chōsen bungakukai to Nihon." Major

contributors to colonial Taiwanese literature who studied in Japan include Long Yingzong (1911–99), Lü Heruo (1914–51), Wang Changxiong (1916–2000), Yang Kui (1905–85), Zhang Shenqie (1904–65), Zhang Wenhuan (1909–78), and Zhou Jinbo (1920–96). See Fujii Shōzō, "Senzenki Taiwan sakka no Tokyo ryūgaku taiken ni kansuru keifuteki kenkyū," p. 3. Nearly all of colonial Taiwan's prominent writers were men. For more on the small numbers of Taiwanese female writers see Mei-yao Chen, "Gender, Race, and Nation in Modern Japanese and Taiwanese Literatures" and Qiu Guifen, "Zhimin jingyan yu Taiwan (nuqing) xiaoshuo shixue fangfa chutan."

31. Joshua Fogel, *The Literature of Travel in the Japanese Rediscovery of China,* p. 251.

32. The Japanese distinguished between *kokugo* (lit. national language) and *Nihongo* (lit. Japanese), with *kokugo* as "the official, constructed [and sacred] language shared by the community of native speakers in mainland Japan (*naichi*)" and *Nihongo*, at least in the 1930s and 1940s, a "'potential' common language for Greater East Asia (*tōa kyōtsūgo*)." Faye Kleeman, "The Boundaries of the Japaneseness between '*Nihon bungaku*' and '*Nihongo bungaku*,'" p. 378.

33. Douglas Reynolds, *China, 1898–1912,* p. 111; Xu Minmin, *Senzen Chūgoku ni okeru Nihongo kyōiku;* See Heng Teow, *Japan's Cultural Policy Toward China.*

34. Faye Kleeman, *Under an Imperial Sun,* p. 122. See also Chen Peifeng, "Rizhi shiqi Taiwan hanwenmaizhong de xiangxiang"; Huang Mei-e, "Wenti yu guoti"; Tang Haoyi (Tō Kō-un), "Nihon tōchiki Taiwan sakka"; and Tarumi Chie, "1930 nendai Taiwan bungaku." Some (post)colonial writers have written "between languages in order to destabilize hierarchies of the colonial period" (Steven Ungar, "Writing in Tongues," p. 132).

35. Although she does not use these terms, for more on readerly, writerly, and textual contact in other imperial spaces, see Priya Joshi's examination in *In Another Country* of Indian consumption of English fiction in the nineteenth century and Indian novelistic production in the late nineteenth and twentieth centuries.

36. Japanese literature was available almost exclusively in Japan and read and reworked almost solely by Japanese before the late nineteenth century. Peter Kornicki, *The Book in Japan,* pp. 277–319. For exceptions see Lin Wenyueh, "Literary Interflow between Japan and China," p. 188; Wang Xiaoping, *Jindai Zhong-Ri wenxue jiaoliushi gao,* pp. 405–12.

37. In recent years scholars also have begun looking more closely at the transculturation of Japanese literature in Latin America and Africa by such figures as the Nobel Prize–winning Colombian writer Gabriel García Márquez (1927–).

38. Harish Trivedi, *Colonial Transactions,* p. 120; Leo Ou-fan Lee, *The Romantic Generation of Modern Chinese Writers,* p. 277.

39. For more on settler colonialism and how it undermined distinctions between "colonizers" and "colonized" see Caroline Elkins and Susan Pedersen, eds., *Settler Colonialism in the Twentieth Century* and Gregor Muller, *Colonial Cambodia's "Bad Frenchmen."*

40. Peter Duus, "Japan's Wartime Empire," pp. xii–xiii. See also Ramon H. Myers and Mark R. Peattie, eds., *The Japanese Colonial Empire.* Japan's pelagic empire was also extensive. As William Tsutsui notes, "On the eve of Pearl Harbor [it] stretched from the Bering Sea to the Antarctic, along the coastlines of virtually every Asian country, from the pearl beds off of Darwin, Australia, to the trawling grounds of the Gulf of California" ("The Pelagic Empire," pp. 10–11).

41. See Carter Eckert et al., *Korea Old and New*, pp. 254–75.

42. Minami Jirō, "Renmei honrai no shimei," pp. 57–58, cited in Jun Uchida, "'Brokers of Empire,'" pp. 483–84.

43. Kim Kyuch'ang (Kim Kyoo Chang), "Chosŏn-ŏgwa simal kwa Il-ŏ kyoyuk ŭi yŏksajŏk paegyŏng (1)," p. 16. Kim follows this with ten articles in subsequent issues of *Sŏul Kyoyuk Taehak nonmunjip* on Japanese-language education and the Korean language in colonial Korea. See also Kim Kyuch'ang, "Iljeha ŏn-ŏ kyoyuk chŏngch'aek ŭi chedosajŏk koch'al (1)," pp. 509–49; Kawamura Minato, *Umi o watatta Nihongo*, pp. 131–55; and Chiho Sawada, "Cultural Politics in Imperial Japan and Colonial Korea," pp. 94–113. For more on the relationship between Japanese-language education and other Japanese policies in Korea see Komagome Takeshi, *Shokuminchi teikoku Nihon no bunka tōgō*, pp. 75–125, 191–234.

44. Fong Shiaw-Chian has estimated that by 1944 more than 70 percent of Taiwanese were able to communicate in Japanese ("Hegemony and Identity in the Colonial Experience of Taiwan," p. 174). See also Fujii Shōzō, *Taiwan bungaku kono hyakunen*, p. 31.

45. The other national languages were Manchu and Mongolian. Before 1937, Japanese often was studied as a "foreign" language in Manchuria, but circumstances changed significantly after the outbreak of the second Sino-Japanese War (1937–45). Yamamuro Shin'ichi, *Manchuria under Japanese Domination*, pp. 211–12. See also Ōkubo Akio, "Wei Manzhouguo hanyu zuojia de yuyan huanjing yu wenxue wenbenzhong de yuyan yingyong."

46. Han Sŏkjŏng, Review of Yamamuro, *Manchuria under Japanese Domination*, p. 110, citing Han Sŏkjŏng, *Manjuguk kŏn-guk ŭi chae haesŏk: koeroeguk ŭi kukga hyogwa*; Y. Tak Matsusaka, "Managing Occupied Manchuria," p. 135.

47. Ronald Robinson, "The Eccentric Idea of Imperialism, With or Without Empire," cited in Peter Duus, "Japan's Informal Empire in China," pp. xvii–xviii. For recent overviews of (semi)colonial collaboration and its legacies see Timothy Brook, *Collaboration*, "Collaboration in the History of Wartime East Asia," and "Collaboration in the Postwar"; Prasenjit Duara, "Collaboration and the Politics of the Twentieth Century"; Han Sŏkjŏng, "On the Question of Collaboration in South Korea"; and Heonik Kwon, "Excavating the History of Collaboration." Public demonstrations against Japanese rule did continue, among the most notable of which were the March First Movement (1919) and the Kwangju student protests (1929) in Korea. Deborah Solomon, "Taking it to the Streets."

48. Carter Eckert et al., *Korea Old and New*, p. 320.

49. Im Chongguk discusses these and other incentives in *Shinnichi bungakuron*. See also Sŏ Yŏnho, *Sikminji sidae ŭi ch'in-ilgŭk yŏn-gu*; Xu Naixiang and Huang Wanhua, *Zhongguo kangzhan shiqi*, pp. 673–78; Yi Sugyŏng (Yi Sookyung), "Shokuminchiki no Kin Kichin [Kim Kijin] oyobi kanren chishikijin kenkyū," pp. 105–11.

50. Tarumi Chie summarizes Japanese-language Taiwanese literature in *Taiwan no Nihongo bungaku*. Examinations of Japanese-language Korean literature include Hotei Toshihiro (Hot'ei T'osihiro), "Ilje malgi Ilbon-ŏ sosŏl ŭi sŏjihakjŏk yŏn-gu"; Im Chŏnhye (Im Jon Hye), *Nihon ni okeru Chōsenjin no bungaku no rekishi*, pp. 233–41; Tamura Hideaki, *Shokuminchiki ni okeru Nihongo bungaku to Chōsen*. See also Jonathan Glade, "Assimilation through Resistance," pp. 42–43.

51. Gilles Deleuze and Félix Guattari, *Kafka*, pp. 29–50.

52. Even assertions of artistic prerogative often have political undertones. For instance, when asked in 1940 why he did not write creative texts in Japanese, the Chinese writer Gu Ding (1916–64), who lived in occupied Manchuria, responded, "Of course it's not because I'm not capable [of writing in Japanese]. But Japanese doesn't have the poetic qualities of Chinese. . . . It's only when writing fiction that I really don't want to use Japanese." *Xinchao* (July 1, 1941), cited in Huang Wanhua, "Shilun Yiwenzhipai de chuangzuo," pp. 217–18.

53. For more on this phenomenon in Arab literature, see Shai Ginsburg, "'The Rock of Our Very Existence,'" p. 188. For more on the implications of language choice see Sharon Mosingal Bell, "In the Shadow of the Father Tongue," pp. 51–74; Vincente L. Rafael, *The Promise of the Foreign*, pp. 19–20.

54. During the second half of the colonial period, Taiwanese wrote much of their literature in a mixture of Chinese and Hokkien. Michelle Yeh, "Frontier Taiwan," p. 18.

55. See John Hunter Boyle, *China and Japan at War*; Timothy Brook, *Collaboration*; David Barrett and Larry N. Shyu, *Chinese Collaboration with Japan*.

56. Edward Gunn, *Unwelcome Muse*, p. 4. See also Poshek Fu, *Passivity, Resistance, and Collaboration*; Norman Smith, *Resisting Manchukuo*, p. 55; Frederic Wakeman Jr., "Hanjian," pp. 298–341.

57. Norman Smith, "Wielding Pens as Swords," pp. 81–82. See also Kazeta Eiki, "Wei Manzhouguo wenyi zhangye de fazhan."

58. See Rana Mitter, *The Manchurian Myth* and Prasenjit Duara, *Sovereignty and Authenticity*.

59. Lydia Liu, "The Translator's Turn," p. 1056. See also Edward Gunn, *Rewriting Chinese*, pp. 185–294. Kim Ch'aesu compares the Japanese and Korean *genbun itchi* movements in *Hanguk kwa Ilbon ŭi kŭndae ŏnmun-ilch'ich'e hyŏngsŏng kwajŏng*. For more on *genbun itchi* and other language movements in colonial Taiwan, including debates concerning Taiwanese dialects and the Chinese vernacular, see Faye Kleeman, *Under an Imperial Sun*, pp. 147–53; Peng Hsiao-yen, "Colonialism and the Predicament of Identity," pp. 235–37. As Indra Levy has noted, the impetus of the *genbun itchi* movement in Japan was the "siren call of Western vernacular writing" (*Sirens of the Western Shore*, p. 4).

60. For more on this phenomenon in China see especially Lydia Liu, *Translingual Practice*, pp. 265–374; Sanetō Keishū, *Chūgokujin Nihon ryūgakushi*, pp. 331–407. Edward Gunn explores resistance to these neologisms before the May Fourth Movement in *Rewriting Chinese*, pp. 36–61. For more on neologisms in Korea, see Ch'oe Kyŏng-ok, *Hanguk kaehwagi kŭndae oerae hanjaŏ ŭi suyong yŏn-gu*; Paek Namdŏk (Paek Nam Deok), "19 seikimatsu Kankokujin ryūgakusei ni juyō sareta Nihon kanjigo no shosō," "19 seikimatsu Kankokujin ryūgakusei ni yoru Nihon kanjigo no ryūnyū," pp. 51–69, and "20 seiki shotō ni okeru zainichi Kankokujin ryūgakusei no Nihongo no juyō," pp. 221–30; Andre Schmid, *Korea between Empires*, p. 399; Yi Hanbyŏn, "Sŏyu kyŏnmun e pat-adŭlyŏjin Ilbon ŭi hanjaŏ e taehayŏ." For more on this phenomenon in Taiwan, see Bert Scruggs, "Collective Consciousness and Individual Identities in Colonial Taiwan Fiction," pp. 55, 64–65. A number of these neologisms also were incorporated into Vietnamese. See Shawn Frederick McHale, *Print and Power*, pp. 11, 32; Guy Faure and Laurent Schwab, *Japan and Vietnam*.

61. The term *moga* refers to progressive young women in 1920s Japan who, thanks to their conspicuous clothing and association with cafés, dance halls, and neon lights, were transformed into symbols of the "modern" and appeared frequently in creative writing. For transculturations of the *moga* in Korea and Taiwan see Jina Kim, "The Materializing and Vanishing Modern Girl." Shu-mei Shih discusses the modern girl in China in "Gender, Race, and Semicolonialism," p. 947, and *The Lure of the Modern*, pp. 292–99. For more on the *moga* in Japan and Japanese literature, see William Gardner, *Advertising Tower*, pp. 144–68; Barbara Hamill Satō, "The *Moga* Sensation," pp. 363–81, and *The New Japanese Woman*, pp. 45–77; Miriam Silverberg, "The Café Waitress Serving Modern Japan," pp. 208–25, and *Erotic Grotesque Nonsense*, pp. 51–72. The modern girl was an international phenomenon. See, for instance, Judith Henchy, "Vietnamese New Women and the Fashioning of Modernity," pp. 121–38; Alys Eve Weinbaum et al., eds., *The Modern Girl around the World*.

62. E. Taylor Atkins, "The Dual Career of 'Arirang,'" p. 646. Kim Brandt explores the engagement of Japanese intellectuals and folk art aficionados such as Yanagi Muneyoshi (1889–1961) with Korean folk art, arguing that "Japanese appreciation of Korean art . . . not only reflected Japanese colonial power but also helped to shape and augment it" (*Kingdom of Beauty*, p. 3). With the exception of Atkins's and Brandt's work, most scholarship on early twentieth-century intra–East Asian artistic networks focuses on Chinese, Korean, and Taiwanese transculturation of Japanese cultural products. For more on the adaptation of Japanese art and art history in semicolonial China, see Aida Yuen Wong, *Parting the Mists*, and "Inventing Eastern Art in Japan and China." For more on the adaptation of Japanese music in colonial Korea, see Hilary Finchum-Sung, "New Folksongs," pp. 10–20; Young Mee Lee, "The Beginnings of Korean Pop," pp. 1–9; Pak Ch'anho, "Shokuminchika no Chōsen to sono zanshi," pp. 190–217. See also Shinada Yoshikazu, *Kŭndae Hanguk kwa Ilbon ŭi min-yo ch'angch'ul*, and Se-Mi Oh, "Oral/Aural Community."

63. Lindsay Proudfoot and Michael Roche, "Introduction," p. 4. Tony Ballantyne and Antoinette Burton likewise use the metaphor of the web "to em-

phasize interconnected networks of contact and exchange without downplaying the very real systems of power and domination such networks had the power to transport [in empire]. . . . Empires, like webs, were fragile and prone to crises where important threads were broken or structural nodes destroyed, yet also dynamic, being constantly remade and reconfigured" ("Introduction," p. 3).

64. The catalogs of many libraries, including those of the governorsgeneral in Korea and Taiwan, as well as major university collections, are reprinted in Katō Kiyofumi's fourteen-volume *Kyūshokuminchi toshokan zōsho mokuroku*, devoted to Japanese libraries in Korea, and his nine-volume *Kyūshokuminchi toshokan zōsho mokuroku: Taiwan hen*, devoted to libraries in Taiwan. For more on Japanese libraries in early twentieth-century East Asia, see Nihon Toshokan Kyōkai, ed., *Kindai Nihon toshokan no ayumi*, pp. 844–66. For more on Japanese libraries in colonial Korea, see Kukrip Chung-ang Tosŏgwan, ed., *Kukrip Chung-ang Tosŏgwan sa*; Miyamoto Masaaki, "Kaidai," pp. 417–23; Ujigō Tsuyoshi, "Kindai Kankoku toshokanshi no kenkyū: kaikaki kara 1920 nendai made," pp. 1–22, and "Kindai Kankoku toshokanshi no kenkyū: shokuminchiki o chūshin ni," pp. 1–28. For more on libraries in colonial Taiwan, see Guojia Tushuguan Qishinian Jishi Bianji Weiyuanhui, ed., *Guojia Tushuguan qishi nian jishi*, and Katō Kiyofumi, "Kaidai," pp. 497–501.

65. Xu Naixiang and Huang Wanhua, *Zhongguo kangzhan shiqi*, p. 40; Jin Huanji, "Dongbei lunxian shiqi de Haerbin wentan," pp. 195–205.

66. Chiho Sawada, "Cultural Politics," pp. 182–88. On the other hand, as James R. Brandon reveals in *Kabuki's Forgotten War*, kabuki writers penned more than 150 plays promulgating imperial ideology, and kabuki troupes entertained Japanese in occupied Manchuria, China, and Korea. For more on the experiences of Japanese theater troupes in wartime China, see Hayasaka Takashi, *Senji engei imondan "Warawashi-tai" no kiroku*.

67. I discuss the intricacies of this phenomenon in "Cultures and Texts in Motion," pp. 142–43.

68. For more on the inroads made by Japanese bookstores in Taiwan, see Kawahara Isao, *Taiwan shinbungaku undō no tenkai*, pp. 249–97. See also Han Weijun et al., eds., *Taiwan shudian fengqing*; Jiang Xingjun, *Feixing Taipei*; Munetake Asako and Ozaki Hatsuki, *Nihon no shoten hyakunen*, pp. 500–503; Murasaki Nagaaki, *Hachijūnen no kaikoroku*; and Zhuan Yue'an, *Duyutou de jiushudian ditu*.

69. See, for instance, Alexis Dudden, *Japan's Colonization of Korea*; Sean Hawkins, *Writing and Colonialism*; Edward Said, *Culture and Imperialism*. Said argues that the power to narrate or to block narration is one of the principal ties between culture and imperialism (p. xiii). Cf. Shefali Chandra, "Mimicry."

70. This contrasts sharply with the Japanese government's use of film. As Michael Baskett argues in *The Attractive Empire*, "the Japanese film industry was integral to Japan's imperial enterprise from 1895 to 1945 and not simply a byproduct of mobilization for Japan's wars in Asia." Baskett also explores how the Japanese government "used film education programs to assimilate

indigenous Taiwanese populations while at the same time combating the undermining influence of Chinese films" (pp. 3, 14–20).

71. Marlene J. Mayo, "Introduction," p. 15. See also Barak Kushner, *The Thought War*, pp. 80–82; Ben-Ami Shillony, *Politics and Culture in Wartime Japan*, pp. 116–20; Bert Winther-Tamaki, "From Resplendent Signs to Heavy Hands."

72. Faye Kleeman, *Under an Imperial Sun*, p. 44.

73. Faye Kleeman, "The Poetics of Colonial Nostalgia," p. 3. See also Tanaka Masuzō and Miyashita Kyōko, eds., "Tokushū haijin to kajin no Ajia chizu," pp. 2–89.

74. Faye Kleeman, *Under an Imperial Sun*, p. 2. Edward Gunn summarizes the resolutions adopted at these conferences and notes the limited effect they had on literary output (*Unwelcome Muse*, pp. 32–34). See also Ōmura Masuo, "Dai Tōa Bungakusha Taikai to Chōsen," pp. 783–805; Ben-Ami Shillony, *Politics and Culture*, pp. 118–19; Norman Smith, *Resisting Manchukuo*, pp. 51–52, and "Wielding Pens as Swords," pp. 85–89. For more on pan-Asianism in general, see Sven Saaler and J. Victor Koschmann, eds., *Pan-Asianism in Modern Japanese History*.

75. One of the many ironic incidents at these meetings was the Japanese writer Kataoka Teppei's (1894–1944) denunciation of Lu Xun's brother Zhou Zuoren as "an obstacle to the literary movement to found the ideals of Greater East Asia." Zhou Zuoren had long played an active role in introducing Japanese literature and culture to Chinese, but in wartime essays rebutted Japanese propaganda. Edward Gunn, *Unwelcome Muse*, pp. 151–71.

76. Gila Ramras-Rauch, *The Arab in Israeli Literature*, p. 198, quoted in Lital Levy, "Self Portraits of the Other," p. 383. The Moroccan writer Abdelkebir Khatibi (1938–2009) expresses similar sentiments: "A foreign tongue is not added to the native tongue as a simple palimpsest, but transforms it. . . . Dividing myself, reincarnating myself — in the other's language. Henceforth, little by little, my native tongue becomes foreign to me" ("Diglossia," p. 158). For more on the ambiguities of "native language" and "mother tongue," see Ri Kenji, *Chōsen kindai bungaku to nashonarizumu*, pp. 75–100; Naoki Sakai, "Introduction," pp. 1–38, and *Translation and Subjectivity*, pp. 20–21.

77. Tony Barnstone, "Introduction," p. 35. Thanks to Steven Yao for alerting me to this statement. Like that of a number of Chinese émigré writers, Ha Jin's work is censored in China. See Min Lee, "Writer Ha Jin." The anxiety can work both ways, with readers at times uncertain what to make of literature written in "their" language by "outsiders" or literature by "insiders" written in an "outside" language. For different perspectives on the pitfalls of the obsession with national identities, cultures, and literatures, see Marcel Cornis-Pope and John Neubauer, eds., *History of the Literary Cultures of East-Central Europe*.

78. Tawada Yōko (1960–), a native speaker of Japanese who has lived in Germany most of her adult life and published extensively in both Japanese and German, uses the term "exophony" to refer to those who "step outside of their mother tongue." Reiko Tachibana, "Tawada Yōko's Quest for Exo-

phony," p. 153. See also Tawada Yōko, *Ekusophonī*. Prominent examples of Chinese exophonic writers in addition to Ha Jin include François Cheng (Cheng Baoyi, 1929–), who moved to France in 1948 and was elected to the Académie française in 2002, the first person of Asian heritage so honored; and Dai Sijie (1954–), author of the bestselling novel *Balzac et la Petite Tailleuse chinoise* (Balzac and the Little Chinese Seamstress, 2000), who moved to France in 1984. See Karen Thornber, "French Discourse in Chinese, in Chinese Discourse in French."

79. These include texts by writers for whom Japanese is a "native" language, such as *Zainichi* (resident Korean) writers. These also include texts by writers forced to learn Japanese, particularly early twentieth-century Koreans and Taiwanese. Additionally, these include texts by writers who learned Japanese at least somewhat voluntarily later in life, such as Ian Hideo Levy (1950–) and Yang Yi (1964–). Levy was born in the United States, spent part of his childhood in Taiwan, and learned Japanese as a third language when living in Japan with his family as a teenager; he was nominated for the prestigious Akutagawa Prize in 1996. Yang Yi was raised in Harbin, China and first went to Japan in 1987 as a student knowing little Japanese; she has lived there ever since and in 2008 was awarded the Akutagawa Prize for her *Toki ga nijimu asa* (A Morning When Time Blurs). She is the first nonnative speaker to earn the award since its establishment in 1935 (Yamauchi Tadashi, "Portrait of Yang Yi," p. 51).

80. As Yang Yi declared, "I don't have much sense of my novels as Japanese literature. I'd just like them to be read by a lot of people" ("Breaking the Literary Language Barrier," p. 50). See also my "Translating, Intertextualizing."

81. As David Damrosch has argued, "All works cease to be the exclusive products of their original culture once they are translated; all become works that only 'began' in their original language" (*What Is World Literature?*, p. 22). Taking Damrosch's argument one step farther, many works in fact "begin" in spaces far distant from their "original language." For his part, Itamar Even-Zohar maintains that translated literature is an active system within literary polysystems ("The Position of Translated Literature within the Literary Polysystem," pp. 117–27). Likewise, just as interpretive and intertextual transculturations allow works to become part of additional cultures, interpretations and intertextualizations are active systems within literary polysystems.

82. The Chinese language, with its multiple mutually unintelligible dialects, is the most obvious case, but what we understand as the "Japanese language" itself has several major and a number of minor dialects. Moreover, xenoglossia (multilingualism, Sprachmischung [mixing languages]) is a hallmark of much "Japanese-language" literature. "Japanese-language" texts contain numerous "foreign" expressions, particularly English, but also Portuguese, Chinese, Korean, and so on. For instance, the Japanese proletarian poet Oguma Hideo (1901–40) not only included Korean-language expressions in his work, but gave one of his poems—"Changjang ch'uya" (Long, Long Autumn Nights, 1935)—a Korean-language title, although the poem is written

primarily in Japanese. Yang Yi notes, "I like to think that by incorporating Chinese [into my Japanese-language fiction] I might be able to expand Japanese literature, at least a little bit. . . . I think the flavor of my writing is like Japanese cuisine prepared in a Chinese style. Some people reading my fiction might think I've added hot pepper—but in any case, it's an original dish" ("Breaking the Literary Language Barrier," pp. 50, 51). Likewise, Japanese-language expressions are readily found in "foreign" languages/literatures. The term xenoglossia here is taken from Suga Keijirō, "Translation, Exophony, Omniphony," pp. 21–33. For more on the concept of Sprachmischung, see Claudio Guillén, *The Challenge of Comparative Literature*, pp. 272–73. Tessa Morris-Suzuki discusses questions of nationality in the Japanese empire in "Migrants, Subjects, Citizens." For more on the hybrid and relational nature of cultures, see Edouard Glissant, *Poétique de la relation*. The Japanese government's current Japanesque Modern initiative provides an interesting perspective on understandings of cultural identity. Cf. Hashiya Hiroshi, *Teikoku Nihon to shokuminchi toshi*.

83. Victor Brombert, *In Praise of Antiheroes*, p. 2.

Chapter 1

1. Homi K. Bhabha, "Signs Taken for Wonders," p. 144.

2. See Gauri Viswanathan, *Masks of Conquest*; Harish Trivedi, *Colonial Transactions*, p. 27. For more general comments on the authority of books see Sandra Pouchet Paquet, "Foreword," p. xvii.

3. Poonam Trivedi, "Introduction," pp. 13–15.

4. Anita Desai, "Various Lives," p. 12.

5. Cyril Lionel Robert James, *Beyond a Boundary*, pp. 27, 37, 43.

6. Ye Shitao, *Yige Taiwan laoxiu zuojia de wuling niandai*, pp. 12–13, 36.

7. Fujii Shōzō, "Lu Xun in Textbooks and Classes of Chinese," pp. 24–25.

8. David Pollack, *Reading Against Culture*, p. 41.

9. See Doi Shunsho, "Shinkokujin no gakuseigeki," p. 115; Ihara Seiseien, "Shinkokujin no gakuseigeki," p. 113; Nakamura Tadayuki, "Chunliushe yishi gao 1," p. 41, cited in Siyuan Liu, "The Impact of *Shinpa* on Early Chinese *Huaju*," pp. 344–45.

10. Guo Moruo, "Zhongguoren dique shi tiancai," p. 762.

11. Nayoung Aimee Kwon, "Translated Encounters and Empire," p. 199, citing an advertisement for the series in the *Osaka mainichi Chōsenban*, June 11, 1934. As Kwon notes, the series aimed to "subsume Korean culture in the Japanese language for the consuming passions of Japanese readers" (p. 203).

12. Cited in Kajii Noboru, "Gendai Chōsen bungaku e no Nihonjin no taiō (2)," p. 111.

13. See both volumes of Kawabata Yasunari et al., eds., *Manshūkoku kakuminzoku sōsaku senshū*.

14. Norman Smith, *Resisting Manchukuo*, pp. xii, 57.

15. Zhong Ruifang, ed., *Lü Heruo riji*, p. 294.

16. Chang Chilin, "Taiwan puroretaria bungaku no tanjō," p. 12.

17. Also significant in this context is the emotional epistolary contact between the Korean writer Kim Saryang and the Taiwanese writer Long Yingzong. See Shimomura Sakujirō, *Bungaku de yomu Taiwan*, pp. 210–12.

18. Zhong Lihe, *Zhong Lihe shujian*, p. 135.

19. Quoted in Li Zhengwen, "Lu Xun zai Chaoxian," p. 34.

20. Xu Naixiang and Huang Wanhua, *Zhongguo kangzhan shiqi lunxianqu wenxueshi*, p. 376. Xiao Jun's (1908–51) anti-Japanese *Bayue de xiangcun* (Village in August, 1935) was one of the many Chinese literary works readers from occupied Manchuria could access in Japan more easily than at home. Mei Niang, "Songhua jiang de buyu," pp. 230–33, cited in Norman Smith, *Resisting Manchukuo*, p. 70. Dan Di makes similar remarks in "Riji Chao," cited in Norman Smith, "Wielding Pens as Swords," p. 114.

21. Although most intra–East Asian writerly contacts took place in East Asia, some occurred in other parts of the world, including the relationship in Paris between the Chinese writer Xu Xu (1908–80) and the Japanese writer Asabuki Tomiko (1917–2005), who communicated with each other in French. Frederick Green, "Re-appropriating *zhiguai*."

22. Norman Smith, *Resisting Manchukuo*, p. 27.

23. Hu Shi, "Riben Dongjing suo jian Zhongguo xiaoshuo shumu ti'an xu," quoted in Zhang Shaochang, "Women weishenme yao yanjiu Riben," pp. 2–3.

24. Zhou Zuoren, *Lu Xun de gujia*, p. 295.

25. Xie Bingying, *Nubing zizhuan*, p. 260.

26. Jennifer Robertson, "Preface," p. xi. Robertson's focus is Taiwanese doctors educated in Japan, but her observations hold true for colonial and semicolonial professionals in general.

27. David Der-wei Wang, "The Lyrical in Epic Time," lecture at Harvard University, February 9, 2007.

28. Jiang Wenye, "Jūsetsukai [Shichahai] no natsumatsuri," p. 50.

29. Jiang Wenye, "'Mei' ni yosuru joshi," p. 4.

30. Jiang Wenye, "'Mei' ni yosuru kōda," p. 123.

31. Kim Dong-in, "Mundan 30 nyŏn ŭi chach'oe," p. 432.

32. Chu Yohan played a pioneering role in the Korean free-verse movement in the 1920s; in the 1940s he wrote pro-Japanese propaganda poetry.

33. Kim Dong-in, "Mundan 30 nyŏn ŭi chach'oe," pp. 432–33. Thanks to John Kim for assistance with the translation of this section.

34. Sanetō Keishū, *Chūgokujin Nihon ryūgakushi* (n.p.). Figures vary widely, but Sanetō's generally are accepted as the most reliable. More than 900 pages, the *Nihon ryūgaku Chūka Minkoku jinmeichō* is the most complete list of Chinese studying in Japan during the first four decades of the twentieth century. Kōain, ed., *Nihon ryūgaku Chūka Minkoku jinmeichō*.

35. Roger F. Hackett estimates that there were as many as 13,000 Chinese students in Japan in 1906 (*Chinese Students in Japan*, p. 142).

36. Li Yu-ning, *The Introduction of Socialism into China*, p. 108.

37. Chung Chai-sik, "Changing Korean Perceptions of Japan on the Eve of Modern Transformation," pp. 39–50. See also M. J. Rhee, *The Doomed Empire*, p. 39; Andre Schmid, *Korea between Empires*, pp. 103–13.

38. Fukuzawa's attitudes changed dramatically after the failed coup d'etat (*Kapsin Chŏngbyŏn*) of December 4, 1884. For more on Fukuzawa's complex relationships with Korea, see Kinebuchi Nobuo, *Fukuzawa Yukichi to Chōsen*. See also Albert M. Craig, *Civilization and Enlightenment*.

39. Carter Eckert et al., *Korea Old and New*, p. 275; Andre Schmid, *Korea Between Empires*, p. 109, citing figures from the *Tae-guk hakbo*, 6:12, recorded in Kim Kiju, *Hanmal chaeil Hanguk yuhaksaeng ŭi minjok undong*. For more on Korean students in Japan at the end of the Chosŏn dynasty, see Abe Hiroshi, "Kyūkanmatsu no Nihon ryūgaku (1)," pp. 63–83; "Kyūkanmatsu no Nihon ryūgaku (2)," pp. 95–116; "Kyūkanmatsu no Nihon ryūgaku (3)," pp. 103–27.

40. Carter Eckert et al., *Korea Old and New*, p. 275. Kim Sunjŏn gives very different figures in "Sŏgu ŭi ch'unggyŏk," p. 145.

41. George De Vos and Changsoo Lee, "The Colonial Experience," pp. 31–57; Chaeil Hanguk Yuhaksaeng Yŏnhaphoe, *Ilbon yuhak 100 nyŏnsa*, p. 59. For more on the experiences of Korean students in Japan, see *Ilbon yuhak 100 nyŏnsa*, pp. 67–253.

42. Michael Weiner, *The Origins of the Korean Community in Japan*, p. 62. For more on Koreans in Japan during the colonial period, see Abe Kazuhiro, "Race Relations and the Capitalist State," pp. 35–60; Naitou Hisako, "Korean Forced Labor in Japan's Wartime Empire," pp. 90–98; Yi Yu-hwan, *Zainichi Kankokujin gojūnenshi*.

43. See Bruce Cumings, *The Origins of the Korean War*, pp. 53–61.

44. For a breakdown of Taiwanese students by majors, see Wu Wenxing, *Riju shiqi Taiwan shehui lingdao jieceng zhi yanjiu*, pp. 122–23.

45. See E. Patricia Tsurumi, *Japanese Colonial Education in Taiwan*, pp. 126–29; Harry J. Lamley, "Taiwan Under Japanese Rule," p. 230. Lamley estimates that at the conclusion of World War Two, between 20,000 and 30,000 Taiwanese lived in Japan (p. 230). For slightly different figures see Lai Ruiqin, "Nihon tōchiki no Taiwan bungaku ni okeru ryūgaku taiken," pp. 3–6.

46. Tōa Keizai Chōsakyoku, *The Manchoukuo Year Book*, p. 685; Interdepartmental Committee for the Acquisition of Foreign Publications, *The Manchoukuo Year Book 1942*, p. 665.

47. For more on Chinese writers who studied in Kyushu, see Iwasa Masaaki, ed., *Chūgoku gendai bungaku to Kyushu*. See also Yokoyama Hiroaki, *Nagasaki ga deatta kindai Chūgoku*.

48. See Tian Han, "Lixiang de ziwei," cited in Heiner Frühauf, "Urban Exoticism and Its Sino-Japanese Scenery," p. 167. Michelle Yeh lists a number of modern Chinese poets who did study in Europe and the United States ("'There Are No Camels in the Koran,'" p. 15).

49. In a symbolic show of solidarity, on the first night of his visit to Japan in May 2008, Chinese President Hu Jintao (1942–) shared a meal with Japanese Prime Minister Fukuda Yasuo (1936–) at the Matsumotorō Restaurant in Hibiya Park, Tokyo, a favorite spot of Sun Yat-sen, and the place where the latter established important personal ties with Japanese. Seima Oki, "Hu Visits Sun Yat-sen's Favorite Eatery," p. 3. For more on the role of exchange students in the 1911 revolution, see Kojima Yoshio, *Ryūnichi gakusei no shingai*

kakumei. See also Michael Gasster, *Chinese Intellectuals and the Revolution of 1911*; Marius Jansen, "Japan and the Chinese Revolution of 1911," pp. 339–74, and *The Japanese and Sun Yat-sen*; and John E. Schrecker, "The Reform Movement of 1898 and the Meiji Restoration as Ch'ing-i Movements," pp. 96–106. Many Chinese, including the leaders of the Tongmenghui, also were deeply inspired by the Meiji Restoration (1868). See Peng Zezhou, *Chūgoku no kindaika to Meiji ishin* and Douglas Reynolds, *China, 1898–1912*. Sun Yat-sen and other Chinese developed friendships in Japan with activists from a variety of backgrounds, including the Philippine revolutionary Mariano Ponce (1863–1918). See Kimura Ki, *Nunobikimaru*.

50. Chow Tse-tsung, *The May Fourth Movement*, pp. 32–33. For more on the relationship between Chinese and Japanese Marxism, see Chen Yingnian, "Jindai Riben sixiangjia zhuzuo zai Qingmo Zhongguo de jiejue he chuanbo," pp. 262–82; Joshua Fogel, *Ai Ssu-ch'i's Contribution to the Development of Chinese Marxism*; Germaine Hoston, "A 'Theology' of Liberation?" pp. 165–221; Ishikawa Yoshihiro, "Chinese Marxism in the Early 20th Century and Japan," pp. 24–34; Ō Eishō and Takahashi Tsuyoshi, *Shū Onrai* [Zhou Enlai] *to Nihon*.

51. Robert A. Scalapino and Chong-sik Lee, *Communism in Korea*, vol. 1, pp. 134–35; Carter Eckert, *Korea Old and New*, p. 275. For more on the development of the Korean communist movement and its connections with Japan, see Robert A. Scalapino and Chong-sik Lee, *Communism in Korea*; Richard Mitchell, *The Korean Minority in Japan*, pp. 60–66; Dae-Sook Suh, *The Korean Communist Movement*.

52. Pak Kyŏng-sik, *Zainichi Chōsenjin undōshi 8/15 kaihōmae*, p. 221, cited in Samuel Perry, "Korean as Proletarian," p. 283.

53. These include Count Sakatani Yoshirō (1863–1941), Kinoshita Tomosaburō, Nagata Hidejirō (1876–1933), and the Reverend Uemura Masahisa (1857–1925). Count Sakatani was president of the Dai Nihon Heiwa Kyōkai (Greater Japan Peace Association), Kinoshita was the president of Meiji University, Nagata was a member of the House of Peers, and Reverend Uemura was principal of Tokyo Theological College. Ann M. F. Heylen, "Taiwanese Students in Metropolitan Tokyo." For more on Taiwanese activism in Japan, see Tarumi Chie, *Ryo Kakujaku* [Lü Heruo] *kenkyū*, pp. 36–41; E. Patricia Tsurumi, *Japanese Colonial Education in Taiwan*, pp. 177–211.

54. Theodore Jun Yoo, *The Politics of Gender in Colonial Korea*, pp. 1–2. The dramatist Kim Ujin, who graduated from Waseda University with a degree in English, should not be confused with the adapter of Tokutomi Roka's novel *Hototogisu* (The Cuckoo, 1899) with whom he shared his name.

55. Norman Smith, *Resisting Manchukuo*, p. 60. For more on Mei Niang's and Dan Di's writings see Kishi Yōko, *Chūgoku chishikijin no hyakunen*, pp. 180–210.

56. For more on Chinese women in Japan, see Ishii Yōko, "Chūgoku joshi ryūgakusei meibo," pp. 49–69; Misaki Hiroko, "Tōkyō Joi Gakkō," pp. 63–72; Mary Rankin, "The Emergence of Women at the End of the Ch'ing," pp. 49–53; Sanetō Keishū, *Chūgokujin Nihon ryūgakushi*, pp. 75–79 and *Chūgoku ryūgakusei shidan*, pp. 31–32; Norman Smith, *Resisting Manchukuo*; Ellen Widmer, "For-

eign Travel through a Woman's Eyes," pp. 763–91; Zhou Yichuan, "Minguo qianqi liuri xueshengzhong de nuxing." For more on Taiwanese women in Japan, see E. Patricia Tsurumi, *Japanese Colonial Education in Taiwan*, p. 126. Some of the East Asian women educated in Japan in the early twentieth century later wrote accounts of their experiences, giving fascinating perspectives on women's lives in the metropole. See, for instance, Han Youtong,"Tōdai Hōgakubu kenkyūshitsu de no gonenkan," in Jinmin Chūgoku Zasshisha, ed., *Waga seishun no Nihon: Chūgoku chishikijin no Nihon kaisō*, pp. 113–25.

57. I give a number of examples of this phenomenon and list relevant scholarship in "Cultures and Texts in Motion," pp. 131, 150–223. See also Michael Baskett, *The Attractive Empire*, which discusses the intertwining of the Japanese, Chinese (particularly occupied Manchurian), Korean, and Taiwanese film spheres.

58. More than six hundred political novels and novels with similar themes were published during the 1880s. John Pierre Mertz, *Novel Japan*, p. 245. The Freedom and Popular Rights Movement called for citizens' rights, representative assemblies, and a constitutional government. For a comprehensive study of the political novel, see Yanagida Izumi's three-volume *Seiji shōsetsu kenkyū*.

59. Zhou Zuoren, *Lu Xun de gujia*, p. 315. Lu Xun himself remarked that Chinese students in Tokyo "generally read the newspapers as soon as we woke up. Most students read the *Asahi shinbun* and the *Yomiuri shinbun*" ("Fan Ainong," p. 504). For more on Lu Xun's engagement with foreign literature, see Fujian Shifan Daxue Zhongwenxi, ed., *Lu Xun lun waiguo wenxue*, pp. 513–29; Patrick Hanan, "The Technique of Lu Hsun's Fiction," pp. 53–96.

60. Yi Kwangsu, *Ilgi*, p. 16.

61. Yi Kwangsu, "Kim Kyŏng," pp. 569–70.

62. Chu Yohan, "*Ch'angjo* sidae ŭi mundan," p. 135.

63. Yŏm Sangsŏp, "Munhak so-nyŏn sidae ŭi hoesang," p. 215.

64. Yu Dafu, "Wuliunian lai chuangzao shenghuo de huigu," p. 178. Yu Dafu lived in Japan from 1913 to 1922 and wrote this essay in 1927.

65. Tian Han, "Xuezi," p. 103. For more on Tian Han's experiences in Japan, see Chen Huiwen, "Tian Han zai Riben," pp. 195–226; Itō Toramaru et al., eds., *Tian Han zai Riben*; Luo Liang, "Theatrics of Revolution."

66. Muramatsu Shōfū, "Fushigi na miyako 'Shanhai,'" p. 23.

67. Zhang Shenqie, "Dui Taiwan xinwenxue luxian de yi ti'an," pp. 83–84. Zhang Shenqie also was involved in staging *Gold Demon* in Japan.

68. See Zhong Ruifang, ed., *Lü Heruo riji*.

69. Remarks by Walter Lew, referring to family members. "Korea's 'Early Modern': Colonial Literature and the Constellation of History," conference at Rutgers University, November 5–6, 2004.

70. See Kim T'aesaeng's remarks in "*Nakano Shigeharu shishū* to no deai," pp. 112–17. Cf. Mark Gamsa, *Chinese Translation*, p. 219.

71. These include Chŏn Yŏngt'aek (1898–1968), Chu Yohan, and Kim Dong-in from Korea and Cheng Fangwu (1897–1984), Guo Moruo, Tian Han, Yu Dafu, and Zhang Ziping from China. For more on the background of the

Chinese Creation Society see Xiaobing Tang and Michel Hockx, "The Creation Society (1921–30)," pp. 103–17.

72. Cited in Tarumi Chie, *Ryo Kakujaku* [Lü Heruo] *kenkyū*, p. 43. Theirs was similar to an earlier call by Wu Kunhuang, Zhang Wenhuan, and Wang Baiyuan: "Our culture circle is composed of young Taiwanese in Tokyo interested in the liberal arts (things like literature, the fine arts, film, music, and theater) and in the problems of Taiwanese culture. . . . We have to construct true Taiwanese culture with our own hands" (ibid., p. 42).

73. For more on the proliferation of Chinese publications in Japan see Huang Fuqing (Huang Fu-ch'ing), *Chinese Students in Japan in the Late Ch'ing Period*, pp. 271–75; Sanetō Keishū, *Chūgokujin Nihon ryūgakushi*, pp. 417–21, and "Nitchū jānarizumu no kōshō," pp. 895–903; Wang Xiangrong, *Zhongguo de jindaihua yu Riben*, pp. 66–70. For more on Korean publications in Japan, see Chang Duk-sun, "Literary Magazines in the Past," p. 19; Shirakawa Yutaka (Sirakkawa Yuttakka), "Hanguk kŭndae munhak," p. 12; Kim Hakdong, *Hanguk kaehwagi shiga yŏn-gu*, pp. 110–11. For more on Taiwanese publications in Japan, see Nakajima Toshirō, *Riju shiqi Taiwan wenxue zazhi zongmu*.

74. Zhang Fugui and Jin Conglin, *Zhong-Ri jinxiandai wenxue guanxi bijiao yanjiu*, p. 217.

75. Du Xuan, "Sensō zen'ya no seishun," p. 169. For more on Akita Ujaku's support of Chinese left-wing theater, see Zhang Fugui and Jin Conglin, *Zhong-Ri jinxiandai wenxue*, pp. 217–19.

76. Tian Han, *Qiangwei zhi lu*, p. 29.

77. For more on Satō Haruo and Yu Dafu's relationship, especially in the context of other interwar Sino-Japanese literary exchanges, see Christopher T. Keaveney, *Beyond Brushtalk*, pp. 117–28; "Satō Haruo's 'Ajia no ko,' " pp. 21–31.

78. Hu Feng, *Hu Feng huiyi lu*, p. 4. See also Hu Feng's 1933 article on his impressions of Akita Ujaku, "Qiutian Yuque [Akita Ujaku] yinxiang ji," pp. 255–64.

79. Norman Smith, *Resisting Manchukuo*, p. 60.

80. Some writers, such as Mei Niang, also published Chinese-language work in Japan.

81. Wang Min, "Remembering Huang Ying," pp. 42–54.

82. Ikezawa Miyoshi and Uchiyama Kayo, eds., *Mō ichido haru ni seikatsu dekiru koto o*, p. 14.

83. Lei Shiyu, "Wo zai Riben canjia zuoyi shige yundong de rizi," p. 14.

84. Onchi Terutake, "Jo," pp. 4–7.

85. Yang Dongguk lists the poetry Chu Yohan published in Japanese periodicals in "Shu Yōkan [Chu Yohan] to Nihon kindaishi," supplement, pp. i–iv.

86. Chu Yohan, "Ch'angjo sidae ŭi mundan," p. 135. For more on Chu Yohan's time in Japan and relationships with Japanese writers, see Chŏng Hanmo, "Hanguk hyŏndae sisa (B)," pp. 113–20; Sim Wŏnsŏp (Shim Won-Sup), "Chu Yohan ŭi ch'ogi munhak kwa sasang ŭi hyŏngsŏng yŏn-gu"; Yang Dongguk, "Shu Yōkan [Chu Yohan] to Nihon kindaishi"; and Yokoyama Keiko, "Chu Yohan ŭi Il-ŏ si chakp'um e kwanhan yŏn-gu."

87. Cited by Hong Chŏngsŏn (Hon Jonson), "Heiwa to kokumin no yūai no tame ni sasageta shōgai," p. 125.

88. For more on Chŏng Chiyong's time in Japan see Yoshikawa Nagi, *Chōsen saisho no modanisuto Chon Jiyon* [Chŏng Chiyong], pp. 29–143.

89. Im Chŏnhye (Im Jon Hye, Nin Tenkei), *Nihon ni okeru Chōsenjin*, pp. 177–80. For more on the literary activities of Korean proletarian writers in Japan, see Yi Hanch'ang (Lee Han-chang), "Haebang chŏn chaeil Chosŏn-in sahoe-juŭijadŭl ŭi munhak hwaldong," pp. 349–73.

90. See Kim Pyŏngch'ŏl, *Segye munhak pŏn-yŏk sŏji mokrok ch'ongram*, pp. 81–88.

91. Kajii Noboru lists the contents of the special issues in "Gendai Chōsen bungaku e no Nihonjin no taiō (2)," pp. 95–98, 113–15. For more on writing by Koreans in Japanese, see Im Chŏnhye (Im Jon Hye, Nin Tenkei), *Nihon ni okeru Chōsenjin*, pp. 177–232; Kim Yunsik, "Hanguk chakga ŭi Ilbon-ŏ chakp'um," pp. 270–78. Kim Yunsik discusses the connections between the Korean and Japanese literary fields in the 1940s in *Kizuato to kokufuku*, pp. 55–77.

92. See Chang Hyŏkju, "Gakidō," pp. 5–47.

93. For more on Kim Saryang's early years in Japan see Shirakawa Yutaka, *Shokuminchiki Chōsen no sakka to Nihon*, pp. 34–82.

94. Scholarship on Kim Soun's close ties to the Japanese literary world includes Im Yongt'aek (Imu Yonteku), *Kin So-un* [Kim Soun] *Chōsen shishū no sekai* and "Nikkan kindaishi no hikaku bungakuteki ikkōsatsu"; Kitahara Tsuzuru, *Shijin*, pp. 13–18.

95. For more on Yi Injik and Japanese theater, see Tajiri Hiroyuki (Tajiri Hiroyukki), *Yi Injik yŏn-gu*, pp. 157–80.

96. For more on Taiwanese theatrical activities in Japan see Shi Wanwu, Lin Boqiu and Zeng Xianzhang, *Zhang Weixian*, pp. 46–55.

97. Chang Chilin, "Taiwan puroretaria bungaku," pp. 187–91.

98. Fujii Shōzō, "Senzenki Taiwan sakka," pp. 3–15, and *Taiwan bungaku kono hyakunen*, pp. 127–62; Tarumi Chie, *Ryo Kakujaku* [Lü Heruo] *kenkyū*, pp. 141–44.

99. See Xie Huizhen, "Toransu nashonaru tsūshin: Taiwan kara mita Yokomitsu Riichi," pp. 12–13.

100. Ch'en Ming-t'ai, "Modernist Poetry in Prewar Taiwan," p. 96.

101. Mushakōji Saneatsu, "Shū Sakujin [Zhou Zuoren] to watakushi," p. 11. For more on Zhou Zuoren, Mushakōji, and the Japanese New Village movement, see Yu Yaoming, *Shū Sakujin* [Zhou Zuoren] *to Nihon kindai bungaku*, pp. 185–205; Itō Noriya, "'Watakushi' to iu chūzuri sōchi," pp. 6–8. Other Chinese with an abiding interest in the New Village movement included Li Dazhao and Qu Qiubai (1899–1935), both leading figures in the Chinese Communist Party. Inspired by Mushakōji's work, Zhou Zuoren established his own New Village movement in China in the 1920s; he also was a longtime aficionado of Yanagita Kunio's thought. See Prasenjit Duara, "Local Worlds," p. 32.

102. "Taiwan Bunren Tōkyō Shibu daiikkai sawakai," p. 30.

103. Ming-Cheng M. Lo, *Doctors within Borders*, pp. 126–29.

104. Cited in Ogasawara Masaru, "Nakano Shigeharu to Chōsen (2)," p. 117.

105. Satō Haruo, "Chōsen no shijintō o naichi no shidan ni mukaen to suru no ji," pp. 4–9.

106. Muramatsu Shōfū, "Fushigi na miyako 'Shanhai,'" p. 24.

107. See Sim Wŏnsŏp, "1910 nyŏndae 'yŏrogujo' hyŏng sŏsa wa nangman-jŏk sŏjŏngsi e nat'a-nan Ilbon yuhaksaeng mun-indŭl ŭi Tae Han-Il ŭisik e taehayŏ," pp. 18–35.

108. Marius Jansen, "Japanese Views of China During the Meiji Period," pp. 182–83.

109. Yu Dafu, Yu Dafu quanji, vol. 12, pp. 3–4.

110. Xie Bingying, Nubing zizhuan, pp. 234–38.

111. Sanetō Keishū, Kindai Nitchū kōshō shiwa, p. 257.

112. Sung-sheng Yvonne Chang, Literary Culture in Taiwan, p. 58.

113. Yi Kwangsu, "Ai ka," pp. 24–25.

114. Ibid., p. 26.

115. See Na Tohyang, "Yŏ ilbalsa," pp. 137–43; Pak T'aewŏn, "Ttakhan saramdŭl," pp. 133–49. Janet Poole discusses this phenomenon in Korea in "Colonial Interiors," pp. 74–82.

116. Chinese, Koreans, and Taiwanese continued writing about the experiences of (semi)colonial intellectuals in Japan long after decolonization. An excellent example is Chang Hyŏkju's (Noguchi Kakuchū) autobiographical novel Arashi no uta (Poem in the Storm, 1975). See John Treat, "Collaboration and Colonial Modernity."

117. Lu Xun, "Tengye xiansheng," p. 498. The relationship between Lu Xun and Mr. Fujino has attracted considerable critical attention. See, for instance, Fujino Sensei to Ro Jin [Lu Xun] Kankōkai, ed., Fujino sensei to Ro Jin [Lu Xun]; Sakai Tatsuo, "Ro Jin [Lu Xun] to Fujino Sensei no jūkyūkagetsu (3)."

118. Lu Xun, "Tengye xiansheng," p. 502.

119. Yu Dafu, "Chenlun," p. 31.

120. The Taiwanese writer Bai Xianyong's (1937–) short story "Zhijiage [Chicago] zhi si" (Chicago Death, 1964) similarly features a despondent Taiwanese exchange student (Wu Hanhun) who envisions himself drowning in Lake Michigan the day after earning his Ph.D. in English literature from the University of Chicago. "Chicago Death" replaces perceived Japanese prejudices with actual (presumably American) chauvinism, a woman he meets at a bar declaring she will call him "Tokyo," even though he is Chinese. This is because "It doesn't matter. You Easterners all look about the same. Hard to distinguish" ("Zhijiage zhi si," p. 264).

121. Yu Dafu, "Chenlun," p. 35.

122. Yang Kui, "Shinbun haitatsufu," p. 61.

123. Ibid., p. 64.

124. Wu Zhuoliu, Ajia no koji, pp. 78–79.

125. Ibid., p. 79.

126. Ibid., p. 83.

127. Lo Chengchun, "Long Yingzong yanjiu," p. 239, quoted in Leo Ching, *Becoming "Japanese,"* p. 129.

128. Julia Lovell, *The Politics of Cultural Capital*, p. 68. See James F. English, *The Economy of Prestige*, for more on the politics of cultural prizes.

129. Kim Saryang, "Haha e no tegami," quoted in An Ushiku (An Usik), *Kin Shiryō* [Kim Saryang], p. 95.

130. Quoted in An Ushiku, *Kin Shirō* [Kim Saryang], p. 99.

131. Chang Hyŏkju, "Watakushi ni taibō suru hitobito e," pp. 299–300.

132. "Preface," in Kokusai Bunka Shinkōkai, ed., *Introduction to Contemporary Japanese Literature*, p. iii.

133. Kataoka Yoshikazu, " 'Kwon to yû otoko' (A Man Called Kwon)," pp. 419–21.

134. Yi Sang, "Donggyŏng," p. 97. Yi Sang provides a very distorted vision of Japanese department stores.

135. Ibid., pp. 95–96.

136. Guo Moruo, "Wo de tongnian," p. 31.

137. Huang Mei-e, "Wenxue xiandaixing de yizhi yu chuanbo."

138. Yang Kui, *E mama yao chujia*, quoted in Faye Kleeman, *Under an Imperial Sun*, pp. 162–63. Yang Kui credited his Japanese schoolteacher Numakawa Sadao, who allowed him to use his private library, with introducing him to modern Japanese literature and translations of Western literature (p. 172).

139. Ann Lee, "The Representation of the Colonial State and Popular Forces as Proponents of Social Reform and Modernization in the Novel *Taeha* [The Great River] (1939)," p. 363.

140. Uchiyama Kanzō, *Kakōroku*, p. 145. Uchiyama's bookstore later relocated to Suzuran-dōri in Tokyo; it now specializes in books from China. Uchiyama and his store are even featured in *manga*. See Minami Ippei, *Uchiyama Kanzō no shōgai*. See also Ōta Naoki, *Densetsu no Nitchū bunka saron*.

141. See Zhang Guangzheng, "Zhang Wojun yu Zhong-Ri wenhua jiaoliu," p. 88.

142. See Edward Mack, "Marketing Japan's Literature in Its 1930s Colonies," pp. 134–41, and "The Value of Literature," pp. 195–98.

143. Zhang Xiangshan, "Bungaku ni akekureta hibi," p. 153. Zhang studied in Japan from 1933 to 1937.

144. On the other hand, few Chinese or Korean writers went to Taiwan, much less interacted significantly with Taiwanese writers there, and few Chinese or Taiwanese writers went to Korea, much less interacted significantly with Korean writers there.

145. For more on this phenomenon, see Daqing Yang, "Between Lips and Teeth," pp. 58–93.

146. Yun Yunjin, "Chung-Han hyŏndae munhak kyoryu kwan-gye e taehan yakganhan koch'al," p. 367; and Yin Yunzhen, "Zhongguo xinwenxue de dongjin xuqu," pp. 110–22.

147. Cited in Ma Zuyi and Ren Rongzhen, *Hanji waiyishi*, p. 609. For more on Yi Yuksa's relationship with Lu Xun, see Kim Hakhyŏn, "Kōya no shijin," pp. 529–41.

148. Interesting in this context is Kim Kwanggyun's (1914–93) poem "Ro Sin [Lu Xun]," which depicts Lu Xun as someone who can understand the poet's sorrows. For more on Lu Xun's relationships with Koreans, see Yang Zhaoquan, *Zhong-Chao guanxishi lunwenji*, pp. 484–97. Kim Sijun (Kin Shi-jun) summarizes Lu Xun's references to encounters with Koreans in "Chūgoku ni ryūbōsuru Kankoku chishikijin to Ro Jin [Lu Xun]," pp. 9–21. For more on early twentieth-century Sino-Korean literary friendships in general, see Yang Zhaoquan, *Zhong-Chao guanxishi lunwenji*, pp. 483–530.

149. For more on Taiwanese writers in Beijing, see Okada Hideki, "Rinkan jiki Beijing bundan no Taiwan sakka sanjūshi," pp. 167–88; and Shimomura Sakujirō, "Shō Riwa [Zhong Lihe] no 'Chūgoku taiken' ni tsuite," pp. 93–97.

150. See, for instance, Joshua Fogel's list of prominent early twentieth-century Japanese literary figures who wrote on their travels to the mainland ("Guest Editor's Introduction," pp. 3–5). See also Fogel's *The Literature of Travel*, especially pp. 250–96.

151. For more on Japanese-Taiwanese theater contacts during the latter part of the colonial period see Qiu Kinliang, "Zai Tai Ribenren xijujia yu Taiwan xiju."

152. As Joseph R. Allen has commented, "Even as they moved closer to 'becoming Japanese,' the Taiwanese elite held close to qualities of their 'Chineseness,' often represented by [classical] literary arts. From their perspective, there must have been a good deal of irony in the Japanese regard for classical Chinese language and literature" ("Taipei Park," p. 182; see also p. 181).

153. Xi Mi (Michelle Yeh), "Ranshao yu feiyue," p. 54. See also Ye Di, "Riju shidai Taiwan shitan de chaoxianshi zhuyi yundong," pp. 21–34, cited in Michelle Yeh, "Modern Poetry of Taiwan," p. 563.

154. See Christopher Keaveney, *Beyond Brushtalk*, pp. 23–43. Writerly contacts in Shanghai provide an interesting contrast with those among jazz musicians there, a subject that recently has garnered increased critical attention. As E. Taylor Atkins has commented, the interacting musicians were "*all* invaders (Americans, Japanese, Russians, Filipinos, etc.); and the natives (the Chinese) [were] really peripheral to the interaction. . . . For Japanese musicians, Shanghai represented a rite of authentication and initiation into the jazz culture, an alternative experience, and a stepping stone to fame and fortune in the homeland's entertainment industry. . . . It was the closest access to American performers that Japanese would have before 1945" (*Blue Nippon*, pp. 84–86).

155. Uchiyama is said to have treated everyone equally, regardless of nationality (Koizumi Yuzuru, *Ro Jin* [Lu Xun] *to Uchiyama Kanzō*, p. 97; Uchiyama Kanzō, *Kakōroku*, p. 113; Yoshida Hiroji, *Ro Jin* [Lu Xun] *no tomo*, p. 91).

156. Other Japanese periodicals in China included, in Shanghai, the *Shanhai nippō* (Shanghai Daily Report), *Shanhai nichinichi shinbun* (Shanghai Daily News), *Shanhai mainichi shinbun* (Shanghai Daily News), and, in Harbin, the *Harubin nichinichi shinbun* (Harbin Daily News), *Harubin tsūshin* (Harbin Report), and *Teikoku tsūshin* (Imperial Report).

157. For instance, the Literary Collective was supported by the Japanese critic Kobayashi Hideo (1902–83), the novelist Abe Tomoji (1903–73), and the

playwright Kishida Kunio (1890–1954). The leading Manchuria-based Chinese writer Liang Shanding (1914–96) criticized his colleagues in the Literary Collective for selling out to the Japanese (Prasenjit Duara, "Local Worlds," p. 32; Norman Smith, *Resisting Manchukuo*, pp. 46–48). Gu Ding, a key player in the group Chronicle of the Arts, was particularly close with Japanese writers. For more on Japanese literature and Manchuria, see Annika Culver, "'Between Distant Realities,'" particularly p. 178; Kawamura Minato, *Bungaku kara miru 'Manshū,'* and *Ikyō no Shōwa bungaku.*

158. See Annika Culver, "'Between Distant Realities'" for more on the contrasts between the independent exchanges of the 1920s and these more calculated arrangements (pp. 425–26).

159. This information on Kaji appears in Takashi Yoshida, *The Making of the "Rape of Nanking,"* pp. 34–35. For more on Japanese pacifist writers in China during the war, see Lü Yuanming, "Zaihua Riben fanzhan wenxue lun," pp. 39–94. Jin Conglin discusses Chinese-Japanese literary relations during the war in "Kang-Ri zhanzheng shiqi de Zhong-Ri wenxue guanxi," pp. 325–38.

160. The Nationalist Party, on the other hand, was no fan of *Three Brothers* and suspended performance of this play, declaring that it "had a bad influence on Chinese soldiers" (Lü Yuanming, "Zaihua Riben fanzhan wenxue lun," p. 52).

161. Although now known primarily for his novel *Nanjing* (1939), Ah Long also was an accomplished poet. See, for instance, Ah Long, *Ā Ron* [Ah Long] *shishū.*

162. Ken Sekine, "A Verbose Silence in 1939 Chongqing," p. 9. I discuss the relationship among Ah Long's *Nanjing* and writings by Hino and Ishikawa in Chapter 6. For more on the participation of Japanese writers in the anti-Japanese movement in China, see Lü Yuanming, *Chūgokugo de nokosareta Nihon bungaku,* and "Lun Lu Dixuan [Kaji Wataru] zai Zhongguo kangzhan shiqi de chuangzuo," pp. 179–92.

163. "Chōsen Bunjin Kyōkai ga tanjō," cited in Jun Uchida, "'Brokers of Empire,'" p. 510.

164. Kim Yunsik, "1940 nen zengo zai Sōru [Seoul] Nihonjin no bungaku katsudō," p. 238. Satō Kiyoshi led the poetry circle at the *Keijō nippō* (Keijō Daily).

165. Takeuchi Yoshimi, "Bunka inyū no hōhō," p. 103.

166. Peng Hsiao-yen, "Colonialism and the Predicament of Identity," p. 231. Nishikawa's relationships with Taiwanese writers provide an interesting comparison with those of Nakanishi Inosuke, particularly the latter's ties with Yang Kui. See Tarumi Chie, "Nakanishi Inosuke *Taiwan kenmonki* shokō." For more on Japanese writers in Taiwan see Nakajima Toshirō, "Nihon tōchiki Taiwan bungaku kenkyū."

167. For more on Nakamura's and Satō's stories see Faye Kleeman, *Under an Imperial Sun,* pp. 29–34, 38–41. Robert Tierney discusses these phenomena in "Ethnography, Borders and Violence," pp. 89–110 and "Going Native," pp. 115–29.

168. See Satō Haruo, "Jokaisen kidan," pp. 254–75.

169. Natsume Sōseki, *Nikki – danpen*, p. 65, and "Man-Kan tokoro dokoro," p. 235, quoted in Jay Rubin, "Sōseki [Natsume Sōseki]," pp. 369–70. See also Mariko Tamanoi, *Memory Maps*, pp. 39–44.

170. Akutagawa Ryūnosuke, "Shanhai yūki," pp. 21, 24. For more on mendicancy in China, see Hanchao Lu, *Street Criers*.

171. Akutagawa Ryūnosuke, "Shanhai yūki," p. 10.

172. Early twentieth-century Asakusa was a vibrant space of corporeal pleasure. See Miriam Silverberg, *Erotic Grotesque Nonsense*, pp. 177–79.

173. Simon Gikandi, *Maps of Englishness*, p. 115.

174. Takagi Ichinosuke, "Koten no sekai," pp. 20–21. Thanks to Jason Webb for bringing Takagi's comments to my attention.

175. Tanizaki Jun'ichirō, "Shanhai kōyūki," pp. 564–65, 569, 571, 577.

176. Maruyama Noboru, "Lu Xun in Japan," p. 224.

177. See Karen Thornber, "Cultures and Texts in Motion," pp. 46–110.

Part I

1. For instance, prefaces, afterwords, and other commentaries often accompany or include translations and adaptations, while some transculturations blend translation and adaptation.

2. Sandra Bermann's remarks on translation also hold true for adaptation and literary criticism ("Introduction," p. 2).

3. Susan Bassnett and André Lefevere's remarks concerning translation also apply to adaptation and literary criticism ("Introduction," p. 7).

4. Lawrence Venuti, *The Translator's Invisibility*, p. 310.

5. See, for instance, Haroldo de Campos, "Da Tradução como Criação e como Critica," pp. 31–48.

6. Yunte Huang, *Transpacific Displacement*, p. 4.

7. J. M. Coetzee, *Doubling the Point*, p. 88.

8. Lawrence Venuti, *The Scandals of Translation*, p. 4; Susan Bassnett and Harish Trivedi, "Introduction," p. 2. Scholarship on the manipulative properties of translation abounds. For a summary see Edwin Gentzler and Maria Tymoczko, "Introduction," pp. xi–xxviii. For discussions that address the interplay between translation and intertextuality, see Harsha Ram, "Towards a Cross-cultural Poetics of the Contact Zone" and Karen Thornber, "Early Twentieth-Century Intra–East Asian Literary Contact Nebulae."

9. Tejaswini Niranjana, *Siting Translation*, pp. 3, 21. See also Lawrence Venuti, *The Scandals of Translation*, pp. 165–70.

10. Anuradha Dingwaney, "Introduction," p. 6.

11. Shaden Tageldin, "Disarming Words," p. 2. See also Eric Cheyfitz, *The Poetics of Imperialism*.

12. See José Rizal, *Noli Me Tángere*, pp. 205–13. Vicente L. Rafael discusses the implications of this scene and others like it in *Contracting Colonialism*, pp. 1–3, 212–19, and "Language, Identity, and Gender in Rizal's *Noli*," pp. 110–40.

13. Korean interpretive and interlingual transculturation of contemporary Chinese literature was significant but did not approach that of Japanese litera-

ture. For more on this phenomenon see Karen Thornber, "Cultures and Texts in Motion," pp. 345-51, and "Transspatializing Texts and Transtextualizing Spaces."

14. Vicente L. Rafael, *Contracting Colonialism*, p. 211.

15. Carlos Fuentes, "Las dos orillas," pp. 18-19.

16. Ibid., p. 58. For more on translation and resistance in "Las dos orillas," see Paul Jay, "Translation, Invention, Resistance," pp. 405-31.

17. Carlos Fuentes, "Las dos orillas," pp. 55-56.

18. Michael Cronin, "History, Translation, Postcolonialism," p. 35. See also Poonam Trivedi's remarks on translation as "an act of measuring up to the might of the master language . . . a compensatory act for the loss of political power" ("Introduction," p. 16).

19. For more on the "long tail" marketplace, see Chris Anderson, *The Long Tail*.

20. Edwin Gentzler and Maria Tymoczko, "Introduction," p. xix.

21. Lawrence Venuti, *The Translator's Invisibility*, pp. 307-8.

Chapter 2

1. Stephen Owen, *Readings in Chinese Literary Thought*, p. 3. One striking example is Vladimir Nabokov's (1899-1977) four volume "translation" of Pushkin's *Eugene Onegin* (1832), the bulk of which in fact is commentary of various kinds, not translation. See Aleksandr Pushkin, *Eugene Onegin*.

2. Chang Chilin, "Taiwan Puroretaria bungaku no tanjō," p. 63. For more on the Japanese reception of "The Paperboy," see Chang Chilin, "Taiwan Puroretaria bungaku," pp. 57-76; Kawamura Minato, *Sakubun no naka no Dai Nihon teikoku*; Faye Kleeman, *Under an Imperial Sun*, pp. 164-65; Tokunaga Sunao et al., " 'Shinbun haitatsufu' ni tsuite," p. 291.

3. "Taiwan Bunren Tōkyō Shibu daiikkai sawakai," pp. 24-30.

4. Lai Minghong, "Shokuminchi bungaku o shidō seyo," quoted in Shimomura Sakujirō, *Bungaku de yomu Taiwan*, p. 12.

5. Kishi Yamaji, "Taiwan no sakka ni nozomu koto," p. 36. For additional Japanese writings on Taiwanese literature see Matsunaga Masayoshi, "Guanyu Riben de Taiwan wenxue yanjiu," pp. 239-40; Sun Lichuan and Wang Shunhong, *Riben yanjiu Zhongguo xiandangdai wenxue lunzhu suoyin*, p. 323.

6. Norman Smith, *Resisting Manchukuo*, p. 49.

7. Huang Shide, "Xiaoshuo de renwu miaoxie."

8. For instance, in the mid-1930s, Taiwanese exchange students in Japan visited Guo Moruo and published articles in his honor in *Taiwan bungei* (Taiwan Literature) and other venues. The visits of Chinese writers to Japan also prompted discussions in Japanese periodicals including Shang Weiyang's "Hui Yu Dafu ji," pp. 60-65.

9. Yun Yunjin summarizes Korean engagement with Chinese literature and Chinese engagement with Korean literature in *Han-Chung munhak pigyo yŏn-gu*.

10. Yang Paekhwa draws the title of the first article from Cheng Fangwu's famous essay "Cong wenxue geming dao geming wenxue" (From Literary Revolution to Revolutionary Literature, 1928). Other key players in introducing modern Chinese literature to Korea were Chŏng Naedong (1903–85) and Kim T'aejun (1905–49).

11. *Writing* was led by Yi T'aejun (1904–?), a prolific novelist and master of the short story, who studied in Japan in the late 1920s. Publication of "Selections of Battlefront Literature" coincided with Yi T'aejun's noted "Munjang ŭi kojŏn, hyŏndae, ŏnmun-ilch'i" (Writing's Past, Present, and *Genbun itchi*, 1940), a treatise on writing in Korean.

12. "China hangjŏn chakga ŭi haengbang," pp. 143–45. Ozaki's text occupies the top two-thirds and "The Whereabouts of Chinese Resistance Writers" the lower third of three pages in this issue.

13. See Yang Paekhwa, "Ho Chŏk [Hu Shi] ssi rŭl chungsim ŭ ro han Chungguk ŭi munhak hyŏkmyŏng," parts 1–4. See also Aoki Masaru, "Ko Teki [Hu Shi] o chūshin ni uzumaite iru bungaku kakumei," parts 1–3.

14. Takeuchi Yoshimi, "Hōhō to shite no Ajia," pp. 92–94.

15. See, for instance, Sun Lichuan and Wang Shunhong, *Riben yanjiu Zhongguo*; Watanabe Kazutami, "Senjika jūnen no Chūgoku to Nihon (1)"; Watanabe Kazutami, "Senjika jūnen no Chūgoku to Nihon (2)."

16. Kaneko Mitsuharu, "Nanshi no geijutsukai," reprinted in Itō Toramaru, *Tian Han zai Riben*, pp. 203–6.

17. Aoki Masaru, "Ko Teki [Hu Shi] o chūshin ni (3)," pp. 218–19; "Ko Teki [Hu Shi] o chūshin ni (2)," p. 123. Maruyama Noboru also notes this discrepancy in "Lu Xun in Japan," pp. 216–17.

18. Richard Calichman, *What Is Modernity?*, pp. x–xi.

19. For more on the reception of Lu Xun in Japan see Kondō Haruo, *Gendai Chūgoku*, pp. 17–28; Maruyama Noboru, *Aru Chūgoku tokuhain*; Sun Lichuan and Wang Shunhong, *Riben yanjiu Zhongguo*, pp. 98–154.

20. Kirk A. Denton, "General Introduction," pp. 1–2. For more on early twentieth-century East Asian literary criticism see Marián Gálik, *The Genesis of Modern Chinese Literary Criticism*; Hijikata Teiichi, *Kindai Nihon bungaku hyōronshi*; Im Hŏn-yŏng and Hong Chŏngsŏn, eds., *Hanguk kŭndae pip'yŏngsa ŭi chaengjŏm*; Karatani Kōjin, ed., *Kindai Nihon no hihyō*; Kim Hye-ni, *Hanguk kŭnhyŏndae pip'yŏng munhaksa yŏn-gu*; Yoshida Seiichi, *Kindai bungei hyōronshi*.

21. Mikami Sanji (1865–1939) and Takatsu Kuwasaburō's (1864–1921) two-volume *Nihon bungakushi* (History of Japanese Literature, 1890) was Japan's first comprehensive literary history (Tomi Suzuki, "*The Tale of Genji*, National Literature, Language, and Modernism," p. 250).

22. Dennis Washburn, *Translating Mt. Fuji*, p. 84. In Europe, the Romantic concept of "original genius," with which many Meiji intellectuals were familiar, dates to the turn of the nineteenth century. See Judith Ryan and Alfred Thomas, "Preface," p. x.

23. Ibid., p. 73. Rupert Cox, ed., *The Culture of Copying in Japan* provides additional perspectives on questions of "originality" as they relate to Japan.

24. One exception is the Chinese monk Mingkong's commentary on the Japanese regent Shōtoku Taishi's (574–622) discussion of Chinese translations of a Sanskrit sūtra. Hanayama Shinshō, *Shōmangyō gisho no Jōgūōsen ni kansuru kenkyū*, pp. 46–49, cited in Peter Kornicki, *The Book in Japan*, pp. 306–7.

25. For more on Huang Zunxian's *Poems on Miscellaneous Subjects from Japan* and *Treatises on Japan*, see Satō Tamotsu, "Kō Junken [Huang Zunxian] to Nihon," pp. 55–76; Richard John Lynn, "Aspects of Meiji Culture," "Early Modern Cross-Cultural Perspectives," "Huang Zunxian," and "Literary Critical Writings of Huang Zunxian in Japan." Thanks to Richard Lynn for sharing these papers with me.

26. See Richard John Lynn, "'This Culture of Ours' and Huang Zunxian's Literary Experiences in Japan," pp. 113–38.

27. Huang Zunxian, *Riben zashi shi*, p. 674.

28. Ibid., pp. 672–73.

29. Richard John Lynn, "Aspects of Meiji Culture," p. 4.

30. See Wang Xiangyuan, *Dongfang geguo wenxue zai Zhongguo*, p. 317.

31. These include Tsubouchi Shōyō, Higuchi Ichiyō, Futabatei Shimei, Ozaki Kōyō, Kōda Rohan (1867–1947), Kitamura Tōkoku (1868–94), Kunikida Doppo, Natsume Sōseki, Mori Ōgai, Nagai Kafū, and Tanizaki Jun'ichirō. Published in the revolutionary journal *Xin qingnian* (New Youth), "The Development of Japanese Literature in the Last Thirty Years" was the first of many essays Zhou Zuoren wrote on Japanese literature.

32. During the 1920s and 1930s examinations of Japanese literature were published in a range of Chinese periodicals, including *Kaiming* (Enlightenment), *Wenxue zhoubao* (Literature Weekly), *Xiandai wenxue* (Modern Literature), *Xiandai wenxue pinglun* (Modern Literature Commentary), *Xiaoshuo shijie* (Fiction World), *Xiaoshuo yuebao* (Fiction Monthly), *Wenxue* (Literature), *Wenyi xinwen* (Literary News), and *Zuojia* (Writers). See Ōdaka Iwao, "Shina bundan ni oyoboshita Nihon bungaku ronsho," pp. 82–86; Wang Xiangyuan, *Dongfang geguo wenxue*, pp. 317–32.

33. Xie Liuyi discusses most of the major figures and schools of late nineteenth- and early twentieth-century Japanese literature and appends a detailed bibliography of sources on Japanese literature. For more on Xie Liuyi's engagement with Japanese literature see Nakamura Fumiko, "Nihon kindai bungaku ni okeru Chūgoku bungaku to no kōryū," pp. 265–89.

34. During these years Chinese published articles on Japanese literature in journals such as *Riben yanjiu* (Japan Research), *Wenyi zazhi* (Literary Magazine), *Yecao* (Wild Grass), *Zhongguo wenxue* (Chinese Literature), and *Zhongguo wenyi* (Chinese Literature). *Chinese Literature* was established in September 1939 in occupied Beijing. Although financed by Japanese, it was edited and published by Zhang Shenqie, a Taiwanese writer and translator living in China. See Huang Yingzhe, "Zhang Shenqie de zhengzhi yu wenxue," pp. 41–43.

35. Sŏ Dusu, "Ilbon munhak ŭi t'ŭkjil," pp. 4–16.

36. Zhang Wojun, "Riben wenxue jieshao yu fanyi," pp. 449–50.

37. Tian Han, "Shiren yu laodong wenti," parts 1 and 2. Bonnie McDougall summarizes this essay in _The Introduction of Western Literary Theories into Modern China_, pp. 88–108.

38. Tian Han, "Shiren yu laodong wenti," part 1, p. 1.

39. Tian Han, "Shiren yu laodong wenti," part 2, p. 94, citing Ikuta Shungetsu's _Atarashiki shi no tsukurikata_ (The Making of New Poetry, 1919), a treatise on poetics. See Ikuta Shungetsu, _Atarashiki shi no tsukurikata_, pp. 335–475.

40. Tian Han, "Shiren yu laodong wenti," part 2, p. 98.

41. Ibid., p. 98.

42. Qiu Gengguang, "Chuangzuo dongji yu biaoxian wenti," pp. 2–4.

43. Ibid., p. 2.

44. See Kuriyagawa Hakuson, _Kumon no shōchō_ (Symbol of Suffering, 1921).

45. Qiu Gengguang, "Chuangzuo dongji yu biaoxian wenti," p. 4.

46. For more on Ba Jin's time in Japan see Fujii Shōzō, _Tōkyō Gaigo Shinagobu_, pp. 97–146; Jin Mingquan, _Zhongguo xiandai zuojia yu Riben_, pp. 239–53; Yamaguchi Mamoru, "Ha Kin [Ba Jin] no Nihon taizai ni kansuru kiroku," pp. 55–68; Zhao Changyou (Jō Chan'ū), "Ha Kin [Ba Jin] no Nihonkan oyobi Nihonjinzō," pp. 86–98. For general studies of Ba Jin's time abroad in France, Japan, and Korea and the impact of these experiences on his thought and writing see Olga Lang, _Pa Chin and His Writings_; Mao-sang Ng, "Ba Jin and Russian Literature," pp. 67–92, and _The Russian Hero in Modern Chinese Fiction_, pp. 181–218.

47. Ba Jin, "Ji duan bu gongjing de hua," p. 512.

48. Ibid., p. 514.

49. In _New Life_, Tōson describes his affair with his niece, escape to France, return to Japan, and continuation of the relationship. See Shimazaki Tōson, _Shinsei_, pp. 190–511.

50. Ba Jin, "Ji duan bu gongjing de hua," p. 515.

51. Zhang Wojun, "Guanyu Daoqi Tengcun [Shimazaki Tōson]," p. 168. Zhang Wojun began serializing his translation of _Before the Dawn_ in the first issue of the _Guoli Huabei bianyiguan guankan_ (October 1942); his translation includes substantial explanatory notes.

52. Zhou Zuoren, "Daoqi Tengcun [Shimazaki Tōson] xiansheng," p. 4. The journal _Japan Research_ included a commemorative section on Tōson in its October 1943 issue, which contains essays on and translations of his work.

53. Ba Jin, "Ji duan bu gongjing de hua," p. 515. For more on Ba Jin's critiques of Japanese literature see Ono Shinobu, "Wenxue bu neng tuoli rensheng er ying tong qi jinmi xianglian," pp. 126–38. See also Masuda Wataru, "Chūgokujin no mita Nihon bungaku," pp. 146–55. Olga Lang lists the Japanese writers Ba Jin discussed in his essays and fiction in _Pa Chin and His Writings_, p. 331.

54. Ba Jin also translated Japanese literature. See Liu Chunying, "Yi tashan zhi shi de beizhuang jingli," p. 315.

55. Ba Jin, "Wenxue shenghuo wushi nian," p. 4. Interestingly, the transcript of a conversation between Ba Jin and the Japanese writer Kinoshita Junji (1914–2006) that took place during Ba Jin's visit to Japan in April 1980 finds

Kinoshita adding Tōson to this roster: "Ba Jin, in your lecture, you said that the Japanese writers you liked or who had influenced you were Natsume Sōseki, Tayama Katai, Arishima Takeo, Akutagawa Ryūnosuke, and Mushakōji Saneatsu. You also said that in addition to these, one other writer was Shimazaki Tōson" (Ōbayashi Shigeru and Kitabayashi Masae, eds., "Kinoshita Junji to no kaiwa," p. 329). The transcript does not provide Ba Jin's response to this comment. For more on Ba Jin's postwar experiences in Japan, see Ba Jin, *Haiwai xingji*, pp. 81–208.

56. Ōbayashi Shigeru and Kitabayashi Masae, eds., "Kinoshita Junji to no kaiwa," p. 338.

57. Particularly intriguing in this regard are Ba Jin's essays on Hiroshima and Nagasaki, where he reveals that he has been thinking about the atomic bombings for decades and applauds the resilience of the survivors; he claims they give him hope for humankind. See Ba Jin, "Changqi [Nagasaki] de meng," pp. 118–21, and "Fangwen Guangdao," pp. 63–69.

58. Ba Jin, "Ji duan bu gongjing de hua," p. 511. See also Akutagawa Ryūnosuke, "Chōkō yūki," p. 254.

59. Han Shiheng, "Xiandai Riben wenxue zagan," pp. 2–3.

60. Zhang Wojun, "Riben wenxue jieshao yu fanyi," p. 449.

61. Zhang Wojun, "Guanyu Daoqi Tengcun [Shimazaki Tōson]," p. 169.

62. Zhang Wojun, "Riben wenhua de zai renshi," pp. 199–200.

63. Ibid., p. 205.

64. Lu Xun, "*Yige qingnian de meng* yizhe xu," p. 521.

65. Lu Xun, "*Yige qingnian de meng* yizhe xu er," pp. 523–24. For more on Lu Xun's translation of *The Dream of a Certain Young Man*, see Yamada Keizō, *Ro Jin [Lu Xun] no sekai*, pp. 192–229. Although long an admirer of Mushakōji's work, Lu Xun did not meet him until 1936. See Maruyama Noboru, "Ro Jin [Lu Xun] to Mushakōji Saneatsu no menkai o megutte," pp. 4–7.

66. Zhou Zuoren, "Xu," p. 1.

67. Xie Liuyi, *Riben wenxueshi*, p. 1.

68. Ibid., pp. 1–2.

69. Im Hwa, "Chosŏn munhak yŏn-gu ŭi il kwaje," p. 377.

70. Ibid., p. 378.

71. Zhang Wojun, "Ping Juchi Kuan [Kikuchi Kan] jin zhu *Riben wenxue annei* [Nihon bungaku annai]," p. 161.

72. Zhang Wojun, "Riben wenhua de zai renshi," p. 197.

73. Xie Liuyi, *Riben wenxueshi*, p. 1.

74. Dennis Washburn, "Transition or Transformation?" p. 10. See also Washburn's *Translating Mount Fuji*.

75. Chu Yohan, "Ilbon kŭndae si ch'o," p. 76. This essay is devoted to Japanese poetry. The writer Pak Chonghwa's (1901–1981) two-page "Ajik al su ga ŏmnŭn Ilbon mundan ŭi ch'oegŭn kyŏnghyang—hyŏnmundan ŭi segyejŏk kyŏnghyang" (The Most Recent and Hitherto Unknown Trends of the Japanese Literary World: The Modern Literary World's Global Trends, 1924) is believed to have been the first Korean article discussing Japanese literature in general.

76. Hwang Sŏk-u, "Ilbon sidan ŭi idae kyŏnghyang," p. 76. Hwang Sŏk-u wrote a number of essays on modern Japanese literature and thought. See, for instance, his "Hyŏn Ilbon sasanggye ŭi t'ŭkjil kwa kŭ chujo" (Characteristics and Main Currents in the Thought of Modern Japan), included in the April 1923 issue of _Kaebyŏk_ (Creation).

77. Ham Ildon, "Myŏngch'i munhak sajŏk koch'al." Ham Ildon, who received a degree in literature from Tokyo Imperial University in 1929, was the only Japanese literature specialist in the Haeoe Munhak Yŏn-guhoe (Association for the Study of Foreign Literature), founded in Tokyo in 1925 by Korean students. Their journal, _Haeoe munhak_ (Foreign Literature), contains more than 60 translations of foreign works, many of which are based on Japanese translations, but only one of which is of a text originally written in Japanese; only one of _Foreign Literature_'s many essays concerns Japanese literature.

78. Yang Chichang, "Esupuri nūbō to shi seishin," p. 255. Cited in Ch'en Ming-t'ai, "Modernist Poetry in Prewar Taiwan," p. 104. See also Yang's essay "Joisuana [Joyceana]: Jeimusu Joisu [James Joyce] no bungaku undō" (Joyceana: The Literary Movement of James Joyce, 1936) in which he praises Japanese research on Joyce.

79. See Yang Chichang, "Xixie Shunsanliang [Nishiwaki Junzaburō] de shijie," p. 186.

80. Zhang Shenqie, "Dui Taiwan xinwenxue luxian de yi ti'an," pp. 80–82.

81. Lu Xun, "Houji," pp. 283–84.

82. Zhou Zuoren, "Riben jin sanshinian xiaoshuo zhi fada," p. 27.

83. In _Essence of the Novel_, Tsubouchi Shōyō first voices his disgust at the direction of Japanese literature and then outlines what writers, particularly novelists, should strive for in their work. Recent scholarship has debunked the notion that _Essence of the Novel_ is the "origin" of modern Japanese literature. See, for instance, Atsuko Ueda, _Concealment of Politics_, pp. 1–8, and "Meiji Literary Historiography." Wang Xiaoping examines Chinese discussions of this treatise in _Jindai Zhong-Ri wenxue_, pp. 258–63.

84. Milena Doleželová-Velingerová, "Fiction from the End of the Empire to the Beginning of the Republic," pp. 710–11.

85. Ch'oe Chaesŏ, "Tangmok Sunsam [Karaki Junzō] chŏ, _Kŭndae Ilbon munhak ŭi chŏngae_," p. 121.

86. Ibid., p. 126.

87. Hasegawa Nyozekan, _Nihonteki seikaku_.

88. By contrast, bibliographies are not provided for the two articles that follow "The Characteristics of Japanese Literature" and together make up the "Tongyang munhak ŭi chae pansŏng" (Reflecting Again on East Asian Literature) section of this issue of _Humanities Criticism_: Pae Ho's "China munhak ŭi t'ŭkjil: si wa sosŏl ŭi paljŏn" (The Characteristics of Chinese Literature: The Development of Poetry and the Novel) and Kim T'aejun, "Chosŏn munhak ŭi t'ŭkjil: t'ŭkhi Samguk sidae munhak ŭi Chosŏn chŏk t'ŭkjil ŭi punsŏk" (The Characteristics of Korean Literature: An Analysis Focusing on the Korean Characteristics of Literature from the Three Kingdoms Period).

89. Mary Hanneman emphasizes this aspect of Nyozekan's thought in "Hasegawa Nyozekan, Liberalism, and the Japanese National Character."

90. Hasegawa Nyozekan, *Nihonteki seikaku*, p. 9; Sŏ Dusu, "Ilbon munhak ŭi t'ŭkjil," pp. 5–6.

91. Zhang Wojun, "*Aiyu* [Aiyoku] yizhe yinyan," pp. 357–58.

92. Zhang Wojun, "Ping Juchi Kuan [Kikuchi Kan] jin zhu *Riben wenxue annei* [Nihon bungaku annai]," p. 162.

93. Kikuchi Hiroshi (Kan), *Nihon bungaku annai*, p. 234.

94. See Xie Liuyi, *Riben wenxueshi*, pp. 131–51.

95. Cited in Wang Xiangyuan, *Ershi shiji Zhongguo de Riben fanyi wenxue shi*, p. 61.

96. Zhang Shifang, *Zhanshi Riben wentan*, p. 51.

97. Zhang Shenqie, *Tan Riben, shuo Zhongguo*, pp. 146–58.

98. Lei Shiyu, *Riben wenxue jianshi*, p. 1.

Chapter 3

1. Richard Jacquemond, "Translation and Cultural Hegemony," p. 141.

2. Martina Ghosh-Schellhorn, "'Uneasy lies the head,'" p. 44. See Welcome Msomi, "*uMabatha*," pp. 168–87; William Shakespeare, *The Tragedy of Macbeth*, pp. 1227–61.

3. James Gibbs and Christine Matzke, "'accents yet unknown,'" p. 16.

4. Janet Suzman, "South Africa in *Othello*," pp. 23–24.

5. Many critics are silent on this inherent ambiguity. See, for instance, Richard Jacquemond's discussion of naturalizing foreign literary products as a declaration of cultural independence in Egypt and Michael Etherton's comments on Africans "taking over" the convention of "'reworking' the great dramatic works of the past." Richard Jacquemond, "Translation and Cultural Hegemony," p. 142; Michael Etherton, *The Development of African Drama*, p. 102, cited by Daniel Fischlin and Mark Fortier, "*uMabatha*, Welcome Msomi," p. 166.

6. For more on translations of T. S. Eliot into Hindi, and the work of Vishnu Khare in particular, see Harish Trivedi, *Colonial Transactions*, pp. 88–100.

7. Irene Eber, "Introduction," p. 15.

8. Lawrence Venuti, *The Scandals of Translation*, p. 184.

9. Ohsawa Yoshihiro, "Amalgamation of Literariness," p. 137. Recent comments by the bestselling Japanese writer and translator Murakami Haruki (1949–) highlight the close connections between translation and creative writing. See "'Breakfast at Tiffany's' Helped Inspire Murakami to Write for His Daily Bread."

10. Also interesting in this context are texts that advertise themselves as translations or adaptations of writings that upon further investigation do not appear to have ever existed.

11. Munshi Ratna Chand, *Bharamajalak Natak*, pp. 39–40, quoted in Harish Trivedi, *Colonial Transactions*, p. 30.

12. Rainer Schulte and John Biguenet's remarks on translation in the Roman Empire and the Renaissance apply to many contexts. See Rainer Schulte and John Biguenet, eds., *Theories of Translation*, p. 2.

13. Reuben Brower's comments on the attitudes of Shakespeare and his generation toward ancient literature are applicable to many writers. See Reuben Brower, *Mirror on Mirror*, p. 10.

14. Important exceptions are Hu Feng's volumes *Shanling – Chaoxian Taiwan duanpian xiaoshuo ji* (Mountain Spirit: Collection of Short Stories from Korea and Taiwan, 1936) and *Ruoxiao minzu xiaoshuoji* (Collection of Stories from Weak Countries, 1936). Both include translations of Yang Kui's "The Paperboy" and texts by Chang Hyŏkju. Some Taiwanese urged their compatriots to show more initiative in spreading their literature beyond the island's shores. Zhang Xingjian's article "Hon'yaku bungaku ni tsuite" (On Translated Literature, 1942) discusses translation in Taiwan and presses for the translation of Japanese-language Taiwanese literature into other languages, particularly Chinese. He boldly concludes, "the translation of the [Japanese-language] works of our country into Chinese is our mission, and we must never forget this" (p. 9). But not many heeded his call.

15. Sources on early twentieth-century Japanese-language translations of Korean literature include Im Chŏnhye (Nin Tenkei), "Nihon ni hon'yaku, shōkai sareta Chōsen bungaku ni tsuite," pp. 14-20; Ōmura Masuo and Hotei Toshihiro, *Chōsen bungaku kankei Nihongo bunmyaku mokuroku*.

16. The theater luminaries Akita Ujaku and Murayama Tomoyoshi and the Korean writers Chang Hyŏkju and Yu Chin-o (1906-87) edited the *Selected Works of Korean Literature*; these writers all had participated in the 1938 conference "Chōsen bunka no shōrai to genzai" (The Future and Present of Korean Culture), organized by Hayashi Fusao. For more on this meeting and its implications, see Tamura Hideaki, "1939 nen Chōsen shokuminchi bungaku no tenkanten," pp. 238-45.

17. For more on Korean writers' translation of their literature in the late 1930s and early 1940s see Shirakawa Yutaka, *Shokuminchi Chōsen no sakka*, pp. 184-85.

18. Shakuo Shunjō, *Chōsen oyobi Manshū* (February 1916), p. 1, and *Chōsen* (November 1911), pp. 12-13, quoted in Jun Uchida, "'Brokers of Empire,'" p. 159; Aoyagi Tsunatarō, *Chōsen tōchiron*, pp. 58, 64, 229, quoted in Jun Uchida, "'Brokers of Empire,'" p. 159.

19. Jun Uchida, "'Brokers of Empire,'" p. 153. In this they were similar to nineteenth-century English translators of Arabic and Indian literatures, who through their rewritings of colonial texts often underlined hierarchies.

20. Korean audiences, on the other hand, were quite critical of productions of this play. For more on Japanese recreations of Chang Hyŏkju's adaptation of *The Tale of Spring Fragrance*, see Shirakawa Yutaka, *Shokuminchiki Chōsen no sakka*, pp. 191-222. Nayoung Aimee Kwon explores the differences between Japanese and Korean versions and receptions of *The Tale of Spring Fragrance* in "Translated Encounters and Empire," pp. 103-80. Kwon rightly demonstrates how this play performs the breakdown of harmonious assimilation.

21. Susan Bassnett and Harish Trivedi, "Introduction," p. 6.

22. For more on Taiwanese negotiation with Chinese literature before the May Fourth Movement, see Yang Ruoping, *Taiwan yu dalu wenxue guanxi jianshi*, pp. 96–131.

23. Sanetō Keishū gives statistics on Japanese translations of Chinese classics in *Zhongguo yi Riben shu zonghe mulu*, p. 94. See also Ma Zuyi and Ren Rongzhen, *Hanji waiyishi*, pp. 515–46; Yan Shaotang and Wang Xiaoping, *Zhongguo wenxue zai Riben*, pp. 282–316.

24. At times, translation was collaborative. For instance, Lu Xun added 85 footnotes to Yamagami Masayoshi's (1896–1938) 1931 translation of "The True Story of Ah Q." Maruyama Noboru, "Lu Xun in Japan," p. 219.

25. For instance, Mei Niang and Gu Ding, two of occupied Manchuria's most celebrated writers, both translated Japanese literature.

26. See Nagai Enoko, "Gendai Chūgoku bungaku hon'yaku no hyakunen."

27. The most obvious examples are Kawabata's two anthologies *Selected Works by Each of the Races of Manchuria*.

28. Long Yingzong, "Papaya no aru machi," p. 62.

29. Maruyama Noboru, "Lu Xun in Japan," p. 223. Inoue's "complete works" included translations of only two of Lu Xun's short-story collections.

30. The following paragraph is based on Okada Hideki, "Hon'yakusha Ōuchi Takao no jirenma," and "The Realities of Racial Harmony," pp. 61–90. For more on Ōuchi's time in Shanghai see his articles in *Shokō* 4–13 (July 1, 1929–April 1, 1930).

31. Andre Schmid, *Korea between Empires*, pp. 55–100. In 1894, *hangul* displaced Chinese as Korea's national script; Koreans dropped literary Chinese in large part because of its associations with China. Henry Em, "Minjok as a Modern and Democratic Construct," p. 351.

32. For more on Yang Paekhwa and early twentieth-century Korean translations of Chinese literature, see Yi Sŏkho (Lee Sukho), "Chungguk munhak chŏnsinja ro sŏ ŭi Yang Paekhwa," pp. 117–31; Mōri Makiko, "1920 nendai ni okeru Chōsenjin no Chūgoku bunka ninshiki ni tsuite."

33. Quoted by Mōri Makiko, "1920 nendai ni okeru Chōsenjin," pp. 22, 60.

34. Yun Ilsu (Yoon Il-Soo) lists translations of Chinese plays into Korean between 1923 and 1936 in "Chunggukgŭk ŭi Hanguk suyong yangsang e kwanhan yŏn-gu," p. 140.

35. For more on Korean translations of Chinese literature during the war, see Ma Zuyi and Ren Rongzhen, *Hanji waiyishi*, p. 609; Pak Chae-u (Park Jae-woo), "Kankoku ni okeru Chūgoku gendai bungaku kenkyūshi no sobyō," pp. 296–318.

36. For more on Japanese adaptations of Western literature see J. Scott Miller, *Adaptations of Western Literature in Meiji Japan*. Cf. Hiroko Cockerill, *Style and Narrative in Translations*. On the other hand, Japanese and Korean writers had been producing close renditions of Chinese literature off and on for centuries; parts of the twelfth-century Japanese *Kara monogatari* (Tales of China), for instance, are fairly faithful to Chinese texts.

37. The volume became more popular and was reprinted several times in following decades, after Lu Xun and Zhou Zuoren had become household names and readers grown accustomed to more faithful translations.

38. Lawrence Venuti, *The Scandals of Translation*, pp. 184–85.

39. See, for instance, Theresa Hyun's discussion of translation debates in early twentieth-century Korea in "The Lover's Silence, The People's Voice," pp. 157–59.

40. Gérard Genette discusses this phenomenon more generally in *Seuils*.

41. Autoethnographic refers "to instances in which colonized subjects undertake to represent themselves in ways that *engage with* the colonizer's own terms. . . . [A]utoethnograhic texts are [those constructed] in response to or in dialogue with those metropolitan representations" (Mary Louise Pratt, *Imperial Eyes*, p. 9).

42. See, for instance, Todd A. Henry, "Respatializing Chosŏn's Royal Capital," pp. 15–38.

43. As discussed in Part II, in the 1920s and 1930s intertextual transculturations took up the slack of negotiating difference between Japan and its colonial and semicolonial areas.

44. For more on this phenomenon, see Karen Thornber, "Early Twentieth-Century Intra–East Asian Literary Contact Nebulae."

45. Tarumoto Teruo, "Qingmo minchu de fanyi xiaoshuo," p. 163; Sanetō Keishū (Shiten Huixiu) et al., eds., *Zhongguo yi Riben shu*, p. 72 Between 1840 and 1920 the majority of translations (of literature) into Chinese were of English-language creative works, with French-language texts a distant second. Both Tarumoto and Sanetō group together creative texts from Great Britain and the United States.

46. Unless otherwise noted, figures on the translation of Korean literature are taken from Table 1 in Yi Myŏnghŭi, "Ilmunhak pŏn-yŏksŏ ŭi pyŏnch'ŏn kwajŏng e kwanhan yŏn-gu," pp. 77–78. Yi Myŏnghŭi estimates that Koreans produced nearly 2,400 volumes of literature in translation between 1895 and 1945, of which approximately 125 (5 percent of the total) were rewritings of late nineteenth- and early twentieth-century Japanese literature. These numbers do not include the many translations published in colonial Korean periodicals. For more on the latter, see Kim Pyŏngch'ŏl, *Segye munhak pŏn-yŏk*, pp. 3–88. Estimates vary widely on the number of colonial Korean translations of Japanese literature, and no scholar has yet attempted a comprehensive study of Korean translations of Japanese literature along the lines of Wang Xiangyuan, *Ershi shiji Zhongguo* or Kuroko Kazuo and Kang Dongyuan, *Nihon kingendai bungaku no Chūgokugoyaku sōran* for Chinese translations. In *Hanguk kŭndae pŏn-yŏk munhaksa yŏn-gu*, Kim Pyŏngch'ŏl, one of Korea's most prolific scholars in the field of translation studies, discusses Korean translations of literature between the late-nineteenth and mid-twentieth centuries. Surprisingly, although he includes the translations of Japanese texts published before the colonial period, as in *Segye munhak pŏn-yŏk*, he omits Korean translations of Japanese literature published after annexation. Chapters 4–6 in *Hanguk kŭndae pŏn-yŏk*, which discuss translation from the 1920s to 1945, have

separate sections on translations from a variety of literatures, but do not mention those from the Japanese.

47. See Yu Yue, ed., *Dongying shixuan* (1883). Yu Yue was also interested in Chinese-language poems by Japanese women, and the fortieth volume of his anthology is devoted to their work. For more on his engagement with Japanese literature, see Wang Xiaoping, *Jindai Zhong-Ri wenxue*, pp. 412–20. Yao Wendong edited the *Chongjiu denggao shi* (Poems for the Double Nine Festival, 1882), a collection of poems composed by Japanese intellectuals invited to a poetry gathering in Ueno, Tokyo by Li Shuchang (1837–98), Chinese minister to Japan. He also compiled several collections of Japanese poetry and prose at his own initiative, including *Mojiang xiuxi shi* (Poems Composed at the Sumida River, 1883), *Haiwai tongwenji* (Collection of Foreign Literature, 1888), and *Guisheng zengyan* (Words of Encouragement for My Departure, 1889). Fully 10 volumes of his planned 22-volume series *Dongcha ershierzhong mulu* (Series on Japanese Studies in Twenty-two Volumes) were to be devoted to Japanese literature; Yao Wendong also spoke of compiling a trilogy of Chinese-language prose written in Japan between ancient times and the Meiji period with a volume each of pre-seventeenth-century prose, Tokugawa prose, and Meiji prose. See Benjamin Wai-ming Ng, "Yao Wendong (1852–1927) and Japanology," pp. 8–22.

48. Yao Wendong, *Qingdai liuqiu jilu xuji*, p. 190, quoted in Benjamin Wai-ming Ng, "Yao Wendong (1852–1927) and Japanology," p. 11.

49. Sanetō Keishū, *Chūgokujin Nihon ryūgakushi*, p. 283. Scholarship on Chinese translation history is extensive. See, for instance, Sin-wai Chan, *A Chronology of Translation in China and the West from the Legendary Period to 2004*; Eva Hung, "Translation in China," pp. 67–107; Ma Zuyi, *Zhongguo fanyi jianshi*, and *Zhongguo fanyishi*; Lawrence Wang-chi Wong, "From 'Controlling the Barbarians' to 'Wholesale Westernization,'" pp. 109–34. Lin Kenan summarizes the history of translation in China, arguing that translation always has played an important role in promoting social change. But like most who have written on translation in China, he does not examine Chinese translation of Japanese texts. Lin Kenan, "Translation as a Catalyst for Social Change in China," pp. 160–83.

50. Liang Qichao, "Qingdai xueshu kai lun," p. 71, quoted in Philip Huang, *Liang Ch'i-ch'ao and Modern Chinese Liberalism*, p. 43.

51. See Sanetō Keishū, *Chūgoku Nihon ryūgakushi*, pp. 259–73; Paula Harrell, *Sowing the Seeds of Change*, pp. 90–94.

52. According to one estimate, between 1840 and 1898 Chinese adapted only seven titles of Western creative writing. See Chen Pingyuan, *Ershi shiji Zhongguo xiaoshuoshi*, vol. 1, p. 24. Even more notably, between 1660 and 1895 the Chinese apparently adapted only three Japanese literary works (Sanetō Keishū [Shiten Huixiu] et al., eds., *Zhongguo yi Riben shu*, p. 49).

53. Tarumoto Teruo, "A Statistical Survey of Translated Fiction," p. 39. Cf. Aying, *Wan Qing xiaoshuo shi*.

54. See Patrick Hanan, *Chinese Fiction of the Nineteenth and Early Twentieth Centuries*, especially pp. 144–61. Also intriguing is the case of the Qing editor,

writer, and translator Xu Nianci's (1875–1908) story "Xin Faluo xiansheng tan" (A New Account of Mr. Windbag, 1905), an adaptation of a Japanese short story by Iwaya Sazanami (1870–1933), itself an adaptation of the fictional adventures of the German Baron Münchhausen (1720–97). See David Wang, *Fin-de-Siècle Splendor*, pp. 295–301; Takeda Masaya, "Donghai Juewo Xu Nianci xiaokao," pp. 313–25.

55. See Keiko Kockum, *Japanese Achievement, Chinese Aspiration*, pp. 187–88. For more on trends in Chinese rewriting see David Pollard, ed., *Translation and Creation*.

56. Liang Qichao's adaptation of Shiba Shirō's (Tōkai Sanshi, 1852–1922) political novel *Kajin no kigū* (Chance Meetings with Beautiful Women, 1885–97) was a popular topic of discussion among Vietnamese reformers and was readapted into Vietnamese by the reformer Phan Châu Trinh (1872–1926), who met Liang in Japan in 1905. In his text, which readapts only up to the first part of Chapter 9, Phan not only omits several references to the "glory" of France but also reconfigures a song on longing to visit Japan with one on visiting Vietnam; furthermore, his adaptation is entirely in verse. Vĩnh Sính, "'Elegant Females' Re-Encountered," pp. 195–206. Other writings by Liang Qichao and by the Chinese reformer Kang Youwei (1858–1927) and revolutionary Sun Yat-sen (1866–1925) also were popular in early twentieth-century Vietnam. See David G. Marr, *Vietnamese Tradition on Trial*.

57. See Nakajima Toshirō's two-part annotated index of late Qing adaptations and translations, "Bansei no hon'yaku shōsetsu" nos. (1) and (2). Kondō Haruo, *Gendai Chūgoku*, pp. 103–93; Kuroko Kazuo and Kang Dongyuan, *Nihon kingendai bungaku*, pp. 10–228; and Wang Xiangyuan, *Ershi shiji Zhongguo*, pp. 407–94, include the most complete lists of Chinese translations of Japanese literature. Kondō covers Chinese adaptations and translations of Japanese literature published both in journals and newspapers and as separate volumes through the 1940s, and both Wang and Kuroko and Kang cover volumes of Japanese literature in Chinese translation published between the late nineteenth and late twentieth centuries. None of these indexes is complete. For an additional précis of early twentieth-century Chinese translation of Japanese literature see Zhang Zhongliang, *Wusi shiqi de fanyi wenxue*, pp. 109–73.

58. See the first appendix in Wang Xiangyuan, *Ershi shiji Zhongguo*, pp. 407–84.

59. Later in 1903, an anonymous writer translated *Kakan'ō* (Song Thrushes among the Flowers, 1887), the sequel to *Plum Blossoms in the Snow*. Nakamura Tadayuki discusses the publication history of the Chinese versions of *Chance Meetings with Beautiful Women* and *Inspiring Instances of Statesmanship* in "Chūgoku bungei ni oyoboseru Nihon bungei no eikyō," pp. 86–152. Scholars are divided on the identity of the rewriter of *Inspiring Instances of Statesmanship*, but many believe it was Liang Qichao; whether Liang Qichao was in fact the translator of *Chance Meetings with Beautiful Women* is also a matter of some debate.

60. Liang Qichao, "Yi yin zhengzhi xiaoshuo xu," pp. 53–54.

61. The domestic novel focused on "model" wifely behavior but gave women only limited opportunities to reshape imposed ideals of married life. This genre emerged around 1900, when the Meiji government was concerned with defining the "family" and women's place in it. See Kathryn Ragsdale, "Marriage, the Newspaper Business, and the Nation-State," pp. 229-55.

62. See Hiroko Willcock, "Meiji Japan and the Late Qing Political Novel," pp. 1-28. Seven of China's first hundred *huaju* (spoken realistic dramas popular in the early twentieth century) actually were adaptations of plays from Japan. Zheng Zhengqiu, *Xinju kaozheng baichu*, quoted in Wang Xiangyuan, *Ershi shiji Zhongguo*, p. 34.

63. See Kim Pyŏngch'ŏl, *Hanguk kŭndae pŏn-yŏk*, pp. 18-151; Ann Lee, "The Early Writings of Yi Gwang-su," pp. 263-64.

64. For more on the relationship between *Diavola* and its Japanese adaptation, see Ian McArthur and Mio Bryce, "Names and Perspectives in Sute-Obune."

65. Kim Pyŏngch'ŏl summarizes Korean translation and adaptation of foreign literary works between 1895 and 1910 in *Hanguk kŭndae pŏn-yŏk*, pp. 303-9. The total number of rewritings of literary works Kim Pyŏngch'ŏl lists for this period differs from Yi Myŏnghŭi's figure in "Ilmunhak pŏn-yŏksŏ," yet there is no reason to doubt the validity of Kim Pyŏngch'ŏl's observation that many Korean translations were based on Japanese translations. See also Sin Kŭnjae (Shin Keun-jae), "20 segi ch'oyŏp ŭl chŏnhuhan Han-Il chisik-in ŭi munhwa isik e taehan koch'al," pp. 158-59; Theresa Hyun, *Writing Women in Korea*, pp. 21-22, for additional estimates. Sin and Hyun both emphasize the large numbers of retranslations of Japanese texts.

66. See Kim Sunjŏn, *Han-Il kŭndae sosŏl ŭi pigyo munhakjŏk yŏn-gu*, pp. 135-54.

67. Sin Kŭnjae (Shin Konje), *Nikkan kindai shōsetsu no hikaku kenkyū* is an excellent introduction to Korean adaptations of Japanese literature. See also Han Kwangsu, *Nihon kindai shōsetsu no Kankoku ni okeru hon'an ni kansuru kenkyū*.

68. See Yang Sŭngguk (Yang Seung-Goog), "1910 nyŏndae sinp'agŭk," pp. 62-64, for more on the connections between drama and the novel in 1910s Korea.

69. The Japanese began building theaters in Korea in 1907, two years after making the nation a protectorate, and numerous Japanese theatrical groups representing several forms of drama went to Korea to perform for the growing resident Japanese population as well as colonial Koreans. Hong Sŏn-yŏng (Hon Sonyon) discusses Japanese theatrical travels to colonial Korea in "1910 nen zengo no Sōru [Seoul] ni okeru Nihonjingai no engeki katsudō," pp. 70-90. See also Kwŏn Chŏnghŭi, "Haehyŏp ŭl nŏm ŭn 'kukmin munhak,'" pp. 38-56; Yang Sŭngguk, "1910 nyŏndae Hanguk sinp'agŭk," pp. 20-42.

70. Marius B. Jansen, *The Making of Modern Japan*, pp. 433-34.

71. See Theodore Huters, "A New Way of Writing," pp. 243-76, and "From Writing to Literature," pp. 51-96.

72. Tōkai Sanshi, *Kajin no kigū*, pp. 20–21; Liang Qichao, *Jiaren qiyu*, p. 14, and *Qing yi bao* 1:5, *Qing yi bao quanbian*, p. 313.

73. See Atsuko Sakaki, "*Kajin no kigū*," p. 101; Catherine Vance Yeh, "Zeng Pu's 'Niehai Hua,'" p. 163.

74. See Catherine Vance Yeh, "Zeng Pu's 'Niehai Hua,'" pp. 159–60.

75. See Ōmura Masuo, "Ryō Keichō [Liang Qichao] oyobi *Kajin no kigū*," pp. 114–16.

76. Liang Qichao, *Jiaren qiyu*, p. 220, quoted also by Ōmura Masuo, "Ryō Keichō [Liang Qichao] oyobi *Kajin no kigū*," p. 116; and in part by Lawrence Wang-chi Wong, "'The Sole Purpose Is to Express My Political Views,'" pp. 113–14.

77. For more on melodrama in *The Cuckoo* and its contemporaries, see Ken Ito, *An Age of Melodrama*.

78. Wang Xiangyuan, *Ershi shiji Zhongguo*, pp. 36–37. Wang Xiangyuan does not give the dates of Chinese performances of *The Cuckoo*. See also Sin Kŭnjae (Shin Keun-jae), *Han-Il kŭndae munhak ŭi pigyo yŏn-gu*, p. 100. For more on Chinese reception of Roka's novel see Kondō Haruo, *Gendai Chūgoku*, pp. 131–34; Kwŏn Bodŭrae (Kwon Boduerae), "Hanguk, Chungguk, Ilbon," pp. 373–404; Nakamura Tadayuki, "Tokutomi Roka to gendai Chūgoku bungaku," pp. 1–28.

79. For statistics on Lin Shu see Yu Qiuhong, "Lin Shu fanyi zuopi kaoshuo," p. 403, cited in Lawrence Wang-chi Wong, "From 'Controlling the Barbarians' to 'Wholesale Westernization,'" p. 125.

80. Tokutomi Roka, *Hototogisu*, p. 267; *Nami-ko: A Realistic Novel*, p. 74; *Burugui*, p. 35.

81. Tokutomi Roka, *Hototogisu*, p. 340; *Nami-ko*, p. 193; *Burugui*, p. 15.

82. Tokutomi Roka, *Hototogisu*, p. 355; *Nami-ko*, p. 218; *Burugui*, p. 26.

83. Tokutomi Roka, *Hototogisu*, p. 397; *Nami-ko*, p. 283; *Burugui*, p. 55.

84. Tokutomi Roka, *Burugui*, p. 55.

85. Tokutomi Roka, *Hototogisu*, p. 397; *Nami-ko*, p. 283.

86. Tokutomi Roka, *Burugui*, p. 55.

87. Marius B. Jansen, *The Making of Modern Japan*, p. 433.

88. See also Lin Shu's remarks several chapters earlier, following the lengthy scene of the battle on the Yellow Sea, where he speaks of the violence of battle and talks about his translation of *The Cuckoo*. Tokutomi Roka, *Burugui*, pp. 27–28.

89. Interesting in this context is that explicit talk of "our country" in the Chinese *Cuckoo* occurs not in the text itself but in the translators' additions. Roka's *Cuckoo* refers to Japan as "our country" and China as "the enemy," while the body of the Chinese *Cuckoo* refers to Japan as "Japan," but retains China's identity as "the enemy."

90. See Lin Shu, "Xu," pp. 1–3.

91. One notable exception was the Korean translation of the Japanese novelist Emi Suiin's (1869–1934) essay "Urusan yuki" (Visiting Ulsan, 1906). The translation was penned by Korean students in Japan almost immediately after the essay's release there and published in 1907 in the *Taehan Yuhaksaenghoe*

hakbo (Bulletin of the Korean Foreign Student Group), a journal put out by Korean students in Japan and also distributed in Korea. In this essay, Emi has glowing words for the Korean landscape but disparages the Korean people. Rather than restructuring his comments to suit better the tastes of their Korean audience, his Korean translators believed it imperative to make such attitudes public. See Im Chŏnhye (Nin Tenkei), "Chōsen ni hon'yaku, shōkai sareta Nihon bungaku ni tsuite," pp. 35–52.

92. As one Japanese government publication declared in 1940, 30 years after colonization, "It is the primitive charms of Korea which appeal most" (Japan Kokusai Kankōkyoku, *Japan Pictorial, Le Japon illustré, Japan in Bildern*), n.p.

93. Suehiro Tetchō, *Setchūbai*, p. 325.

94. Ibid., p. 325.

95. Gu Yŏnhak, *Sŏljungmae*, p. 13.

96. See the discussion of the Yi dynasty in Carter Eckert et al., *Korea Old and New*, pp. 107–253.

97. Carter Eckert et al., *Korea Old and New*, p. 232.

98. Natsume Sōseki, "Dainanaya," pp. 118–19.

99. Mark E. Caprio, "Assimilation Rejected," p. 130. Most of the approximately 40 periodicals published in the 1910s were short lived. See Todd A. Henry, "Sanitizing Empire," p. 642.

100. The many similarities between *Observations from a Journey to the West* and *Conditions in the West* were not readily acknowledged until the 1970s, presumably for political reasons, but since then have attracted considerable critical attention in both Japan and Korea.

101. Andre Schmid, *Korea between Empires*, p. 111.

102. See Yi Hansŏp (I Hansoppu), "*Seiyū kenmon* [Sŏyu kyŏnmun] no kanjigo ni tsuite," pp. 39–50; Yi Hanbyŏn, "*Sŏyu kyŏnmun* e pat-adŭlyŏjin Ilbon ŭi hanjaŏ e taehayŏ," pp. 85–107.

103. See Yu Kilchun, "*Sŏyu kyŏnmun* sŏ," pp. 3–8. Yu Kilchun easily could have written *Observations from a Journey to the West* in Chinese. Like other intellectuals of his generation, he had been trained in the Chinese classics and wrote poetry in Chinese. See Hŏ Sŏng-il (Huh Sung-il), "Kanshi bunshū ni arawareta Yu Kitsushun [Yu Kilchun] no kaika ishiki," pp. 59–79.

104. Yu Kilchun, *Sŏyu kyŏnmun*, p. 404. For more on Yu Kilchun's notions of civilization, particularly as compared with those of Fukuzawa, see Kim T'aejun (Kimu Tejun), "*Seiyū kenmon* [Sŏyu kyŏnmun] to *Seiyō jijō*," pp. 122–30. Many of the products to which Yu Kilchun refers later were displayed at the 1900 Paris Universal Exposition. See Daniel Kane, "Display at Empire's End," pp. 41–66.

105. Fukuzawa had been a great supporter of Korea in the early 1880s: he played an instrumental role in the 1883 founding of Korea's first modern newspaper, invited dozens of Koreans to study at Keiō Gijuku, gave crucial assistance to Kim Okgyun, Pak Yŏnghyo, and other reformers involved in the 1884 failed coup d'état, and offered the nine survivors of the Korean reform party assistance when they escaped to Japan later that year. Yet Fukuzawa's

attitudes toward Korea changed in the mid-1880s. Frustrated with Korea's failure to turn itself around more quickly, he abandoned his project of "enlightening" the country and instead called for Japanese leadership and hegemony in East Asia. See In Kwan Hwang, "The Korean Reform Movement of the 1880s and Fukuzawa Yukichi," pp. 216–20. In his famous essay "Datsu-a ron" (Shedding Asia, 1885), Fukuzawa argues that Japanese should not wait for Chinese and Korean enlightenment but instead should treat these countries as Westerners treat them. For more on Fukuzawa's writings on Korea, see Kinebuchi Nobuo, *Fukuzawa Yukichi to Chōsen*. See also Atsuko Ueda's summaries in "Colonial Ambivalence and the Modern Shōsetsu," pp. 188–91, and *Concealment of Politics*, pp. 108–11.

106. The founder, together with Yun Paeknam (1888–1954), of the troupe Munsusŏng (est. 1912), Cho Iljae frequently staged his textual adaptations.

107. "Yŏn-yegye," p. 3, quoted in Han Kwangsu, *Nihon kindai shōsetsu*, p. 18.

108. Kikuchi Yūhō, *Ono ga tsumi*, p. 687.

109. See Cho Iljae, *Ssang-oknu*, January 31, February 1, 2, 4, 1913.

110. Kōain, ed., *Nihon ryūgaku*, pp. 308–13.

111. Hahm Chaibong, "Civilization, Race, or Nation?" p. 35.

112. See Sin Kŭnjae (Shin Konje), *Nikkan kindai shōsetsu*, p. 201.

113. Ken Ito summarizes Japanese performances of *The Cuckoo* in Japan in "The Family and the Nation in Tokutomi Roka's *Hototogisu*," p. 491. Yang Sŭngguk (Yang Seung-Gook) lists plays in the Korean repertory between 1912 and 1919 in "1910 nyŏndae Hanguk sinp'agŭk," pp. 12–20.

114. The phrase "unapologetic nationalism" is Ken Ito's. As Ito also notes, "*Hototogisu* is a text that allows its reader to 'think the empire.' It is no accident that the battle scenes employ the rhetoric of 'our fleet' and the 'enemy.' For this is a text that posits a narratee that is 'us,' the Japanese of the turn of the century beginning to imagine the empire" ("The Family and the Nation in Tokutomi Roka's *Hototogisu*," pp. 530, 532).

115. See Cho Iljae, *Pulyŏgwi*.

116. See Kim Ujin, *Yuhwau* (1912), and *Yuhwau* (1968), quoted in Sin Kŭnjae (Shin Konje), *Nikkan kindai shōsetsu*, p. 265.

117. See Kim Sunjŏn, *Han-Il kŭndae sosŏl*, pp. 217–22; Sin Kŭnjae (Shin Kunjae), *Nikkan kindai shōsetsu*, p. 261.

118. Sŏn-u Il, *Tugyŏngsŏng*, pp. 505–6.

119. Han Kwangsu, *Nihon kindai shōsetsu*, p. 389. *Long Teary Dream* was serialized in the *Daily News* between May and October 1913 and was first performed on stage in July 1913. It was serialized a second time in 1914, again in the *Daily News*, and eventually was performed by every major theater company. See Yang Sŭngguk (Yang Seung-Gook), "1910 nyŏndae Hanguk sinp'agŭk," pp. 12–20, 50–51; William E. Henthorn, "The Early Days of Western-Inspired Drama in Korea," p. 207.

120. See Ozaki Kōyō, *Konjiki yasha*; Cho Iljae, *Changhanmong*. As was true of its presentation of *A Pair of Jeweled Tears*, the *Daily News* lists Cho Iljae as the "author" (*chŏ*), not the adapter or translator, of *Long Teary Dream*, which it

classifies as "new fiction." See, for instance, the advertisement announcing this novel's forthcoming serialization in the *Daily News*, May 11, 1913, p. 3.

121. For more on questions of morality in *The Gold Demon* and on contemporary understandings of love and money, see Ken Ito, *An Age of Melodrama*, pp. 86–139.

Chapter 4

1. Jonathan D. Spence, *The Search for Modern China*, p. 301.

2. Quoted by Paek Ch'ŏl et al., "Hanguk sinmunhak e kkich'in oeguk munhak ŭi yŏnghyang e kwanhan yŏn-gu," p. 15. *Gloom* is the story of a man who falls in love with his wife's half-sister and after being denied her affections winds up a beggar.

3. Decades after the war, the Taiwanese writer Ye Shitao noted that growing up in colonial Taiwan in the 1930s he read both the Chinese classics and contemporary Chinese literature, including Lu Xun's famed "The True Story of Ah Q" and Yu Dafu's popular "Sinking," in Japanese translation (Ye Shitao, *Yige Taiwan laoxiu zuojia*, p. 13).

4. Guo Moruo, "Yizhe shu," p. 1. *Pillow of Grass* appealed to Chinese readers in part because of the Japanese narrator's admiration for classical Chinese poetry. The narrator's comment that "Japan produces its works of art with the attitude of a pickpocket" additionally struck a chord in many East Asian observers of Japan. See Natsume Sōseki, *Kusamakura*, p. 506; *Caozhen*, p. 108.

5. Zhang Wojun, "*Liming zhi qian* [Yoake mae] shang zai liming zhi qian," p. 172.

6. See Chapter 2 and Han Shiheng, "Xiandai Riben wenxue zagan (daixu)," pp. 1–26.

7. Akutagawa Ryūnosuke, "Nihon shōsetsu no Shinayaku," p. 255.

8. Eguchi Kan, "Nihon puroretaria bungaku no Shinayaku to sono yakusha," p. 62. This essay summarizes Chinese translations of Japanese proletarian literature circa 1934. Eguchi's comments are similar to those of Tanizaki, discussed in Chapter 2.

9. Zhang Wojun, "Guanyu Daoqi Tengcun [Shimazaki Tōson]," p. 164.

10. See Nakanishi Inosuke, *Neppū*.

11. Im Chŏnhye (Nin Tenkei), "Chōsen ni hon'yaku," pp. 41–43. Makimoto Kusurō's (1898–1956) *Akai hata: Puroretaria dōyōshū* (Red Flag: Proletarian Collection of Children's Songs, 1930) includes a similar gesture to Korean readers and translators. As Samuel Perry has commented, this text "not only has its cover written in the Korean alphabet, but also prints as its very first song one translated into Korean by Im Hwa. . . . Makimoto's understanding of the importance of the Korean language for Korean educators and his effort to dignify it within Japanese proletarian print culture can certainly be seen as an act of solidarity and encouragement, one consistent with the proletarian imagination of a community beyond the borders of 'Japan' and the Japanese language" ("Aesthetics for Justice," pp. 179–80). See also Makimoto Kusurō, *Akai hata*.

12. Uchiyama Kanzō, *Kakōroku*, pp. 193–94.

13. Kondō Haruo lists several dozen early twentieth-century Chinese publishing houses that released volumes of Japanese literature in Chinese translation, all but three of which were located in Shanghai (*Gendai Chūgoku*, pp. 103–5).

14. Tang Yuemei, "Zhong-Ri wenxue jiaoliu de guoqu he xianzai," p. 188. See also Kondō Haruo's index in *Gendai Chūgoku*, pp. 105–93. For more on May Fourth Chinese translations of Japanese literature, see Zhang Zhongliang, *Wusi shiqi de fanyi wenxue*, pp. 109–73.

15. See the first and second appendices in Wang Xiangyuan, *Ershi shiji Zhongguo*, pp. 407–94.

16. Kim Pyŏngch'ŏl lists translations of foreign literatures published in Korean journals during the colonial period, but does not include translations of Japanese literature. See *Segye munhak pŏn-yŏk soji*, pp. 6–88.

17. Although during the war years some Koreans published Japanese-language translations of foreign (non-Japanese) literatures in Japanese journals, publication of Korean-language translations in Korean journals also appeared in surprising numbers. See Kim Pyŏngch'ŏl, *Segye munhak pŏn-yŏk*, pp. 79–88.

18. Huang Mei-e, "Wenxue xiandaixing," p. 29.

19. Wang Xiangyuan, *Ershi shiji Zhongguo*, p. 394.

20. Zhang Shenqie published his *Xiandai Riben duanpian mingzuo xuan* (Collection of Famous Modern Japanese Stories, 1942) in Beijing; this volume includes a translation by Zhang Wojun. Zhang Wojun's early translations appear in the *Taiwan People's News*, but from the late 1920s until 1945, his work came out primarily in Chinese periodicals.

21. Early twentieth-century Chinese translated nearly one-fourth of Akutagawa's oeuvre. Naturalist writers translated by Chinese include Shimazaki Tōson and Tayama Katai, and White Birch Society writers include Mushakōji Saneatsu, Shiga Naoya, and Arishima Takeo. Chinese also translated the Japanese leftist writers and literary critics Aono Suekichi, Eguchi Kan, Katagami Noburu (1884–1928), Kobayashi Takiji, Kurahara Korehito, and Moriyama Kei, as well as collections of the translated works of leftist writers Akita Ujaku, Fujimori Seikichi, Hayama Yoshiki, Hayashi Fusao, Hirabayashi Taiko (1905–72), and Nakano Shigeharu. Japanese modernist and neosensationalist writers translated into Chinese at this time include Kataoka Teppei, Satō Haruo, and Yokomitsu Riichi. For more on Chinese translation of Japanese modernists/neosensationalists, see Qian Xiaobo, "Modanizumu no juyō to keishō"; Shu-mei Shih, *The Lure of the Modern*, pp. 242–43.

22. The first of these was Lu Xun and Zhou Zuoren's *Collection of Modern Japanese Stories* (1923), which included translations of texts by Natsume Sōseki, Kikuchi Kan, Akutagawa Ryūnosuke, Mushakōji Saneatsu, Arishima Takeo, Kuriyagawa Hakuson, and nine other Japanese writers. In his preface, Zhou Zuoren praises the Japanese arrival on the world literary marquee. Lu Xun and Zhou Zuoren were two of early twentieth-century China's most active translators of Japanese and other literatures. For more on their contributions,

see Wang Yougui, *Fanyijia Zhou Zuoren*; Fujian Shifan Daxue Zhongwenxi, ed., *Lu Xun lun waiguo wenxue*, pp. 513–29; Mark Gamsa, *Chinese Translation of Russian Literature*; Lennart Lundberg, *Lu Xun as a Translator*.

23. Texts translated include plays, poetry, and prose by Akutagawa Ryūnosuke, Arishima Takeo, Hayama Yoshiki, Higuchi Ichiyō, Kikuchi Kan, Kunikida Doppo, Masamune Hakuchō, Mushakōji Saneatsu, Shiga Naoya, Natsume Sōseki, Tokuda Shūsei, Shimazaki Tōson, and Yokomitsu Riichi.

24. Some of the more popular Japanese dramatists translated into Chinese at this time included Akita Ujaku, Arishima Takeo, Fujimori Seikichi, Kikuchi Kan, and Mushakōji Saneatsu.

25. For more on Kim Okgyun's interactions with Japanese, see Kŭm Pyŏngdong, *Kin Gyokkin* [Kim Okgyun] *to Nihon*. While in Japan in the late 1800s, Kim Okgyun grew familiar with the Japanese political novel, and he even wrote a postface for and appeared as a character in Tōkai Sanshi's *Chance Meetings with Beautiful Women* (1885–97), one of Meiji Japan's most important political novels. Likewise, the preface to Ku In-am's novel *Kobore ume* (Scattered Plum Blossoms, 1894) indicates that this *yuan sosŏl* (transmitted novel) is based on tales told by Kim Okgyun. *Scattered Plum Blossoms* eerily resembles Suehiro Tetchō's political novel *Plum Blossoms in the Snow* (1886), revealing that Koreans were reading Japanese political novels more than a decade before Korean writers began adapting them and creating their own political fiction. See Iida Saburō, "Jijo," p. 2.

26. Yu Yaoming discusses Zhou Zuoren's engagement with Japanese poetry in *Shū Sakujin* [Zhou Zuoren] *to Nihon*, pp. 45–83, 125–84.

27. For more on this phenomenon, see Han Sŭngmin (Han Seung-min), "Han-Il ch'och'anggi sangjingjuŭi si toip-yangsang pigyo yŏn-gu," pp. 101–42; Kim Ŭnjŏn (Kim Ŭn-jŏn), "Kim Ŏk ŭi P'urangsŭ sangjingjuŭi suyong yangsang"; Im Yŏngt'aek, "Kim Ŏk ŭi si e nat'a-nan Ilbonjŏk yoso," pp. 335–48.

28. For more on Chinese translations of Japanese literary theory see Wang Jinhou, *Wusi xinwenxue yu waiguo wenxue*, pp. 120–32.

29. Wang Xiangyuan, *Ershi shiji Zhongguo*, p. 61. Books and essays on literature by Natsume Sōseki, Hagiwara Sakutarō, Kuriyagawa Hakuson, Honma Hisao, Miyajima Shinzaburō (1892–1934), and others found a wide readership in Chinese translation.

30. For more on Chinese translations of Lafcadio Hearn, see Liu Anwei (Ryū Gan'i), *Koizumi Yakumo to kindai Chūgoku*.

31. Zhang Xiangshan talks about reading a diverse array of classical Japanese literature while in school in Japan in "Bungaku ni akekureta hibi," pp. 158–60.

32. Yi Pyŏngdo, "Kyubang munhak," p. 41.

33. For a summary of Chinese reception of classical Japanese literature, see Wang Xiangyuan, *Dongfang geguo wenxue*, pp. 165–87. Zhou Zuoren was one of the most active Chinese translators of classical Japanese literature; by the mid-1920s, he had translated not only a number of haiku and other short poems but also ten *kyōgen* (medieval comic plays, lit. wild words), and one part of Yoshida Kenkō's (1283–1350) *zuihitsu* (lit. random jottings) *Tsurezure-*

gusa (Essays in Idleness, published posthumously). For more on Zhou Zuoren and classical Japanese literature, see Wu Honghua (Go Kōka), *Shū Sakujin to Edo shomin bungei*. In 1936, the eminent Chinese short-story writer Yu Dafu translated six additional sections of *Essays in Idleness*.

34. Michael Holquist, "Introduction, Corrupt Originals," p. 18.

35. For more on Kim Hoyŏng and Yi Pukman, see Ogasawara Masaru, "Nakano Shigeharu to Chōsen (2)," pp. 102–18.

36. Editors employed several strategies in attributing authorship to rewritings: they listed both the "original writer" and the "adapter"/"translator"; they explicitly indicated or implied that the translator was the "original writer" (as noted in Chapter 3); or, as happened with the Korean translation of Nakano's poem, they gave the name of the writer but not that of the translator. The latter two tactics smudged texts' interlingual backgrounds.

37. Nakano Shigeharu, "Ame no furu Shinagawa eki" (1929), p. 82; "Pi nal-i nŭn P'umch'ŏn-yŏk," p. 69.

38. Nakano Shigeharu, "Ame no furu Shinagawa eki" (1959), p. 93; "Ame no furu Shinagawa eki" (1996), p. 114.

39. Nakano Shigeharu, "Ame no furu Shinagawa eki" (1929), p. 83.

40. Nakano Shigeharu, "Pi nal-i nŭn P'umch'ŏn-yŏk," p. 69. Thanks to John Kim for assistance translating into English the Korean translation of Nakano's poem.

41. Chŏng Sŭng-un (Jeong Seung Un), "Nakano Shigeharu, 'Ame no furu Shingawa eki,'" pp. 353–55; Kim Yunsik, *Im Hwa yŏn-gu*, p. 244.

42. Mizuno Naoki, "'Ame no furu Shinagawa eki' no jijitsu shirabe," pp. 97–105.

43. Cf. Chŏng Sŭng-un (Jeong Seung Un), "Nakano Shigeharu, 'Ame no furu Shingawa eki'."

44. Nakano Shigeharu, "Ame no furu Shinagawa eki" (1959), p. 94; "Ame no furu Shinagawa eki" (1996), p. 115. For tables comparing published versions of Nakano's poem (14 in Japanese, 1 in Korean) see Chŏng Sŭng-un, *Nak'ano Sigeharu ŭi pi naeri nŭn Sinagawa yŏk*, pp. 269–86.

45. The appendix includes a mistranslation of the Korean version, depicting the poet as explicitly commanding Korean revolutionaries to stab the emperor (1996, p. 550). Postwar editions of Japanese creative works replace many earlier *fuseji* with words, but tend to eschew rhetoric maligning the emperor.

46. Norbert Schaffeld, "'I need some answers William,'" p. 5. For more on this topic, see James Gibbs and Christine Matzke, "'accents yet unknown,'" pp. 22–26. Tobias Banda, Chairman of the Censorship Board in Malawi, was apparently not perturbed "by the fact that the victim of the central plot [in *Julius Caesar*] was a head of state." He told Gibbs in the 1970s that "he did not bother to read texts by such writers as Sophocles and Shakespeare . . . What could be more worthy of reverence—and performance—than a play by the undisputed master of English about one of the noblest Romans of them all" (p. 23). *Julius Caesar* was censored elsewhere in Africa, including Ethiopia. For more on the vagaries of imperial Japanese censorship, see Sari Kawana, *Murder Most Modern*, pp. 151–59. Not surprisingly, some East Asian writers

explicitly parodied censors/censorship in their own creative work, including Tanizaki in "Ken'etsukan" (The Censor, 1921) and Yi Sang in "Shuppanhō" (Publications Law, 1932).

47. See Nakano Shigeharu, "Ame no furu Shinagawa eki" (1929), p. 83; "Pi nal-i nŭn P'umch'ŏn-yŏk," p. 69.

48. Nakano Shigeharu, "'Ame no furu Shinagawa eki' no koto," p. 78.

49. The final years of the empire most Japanese writers belonged to the Nihon Bungaku Hōkokukai (Japanese Literature Patriotic Association), established in May 1942 by the Naikaku Jōhōkyoku (Cabinet Information Bureau), which sponsored the collection and publication of patriotic texts. For more on Japanese writers' wartime activities, see Ben-Ami Shillony, *Politics and Culture in Wartime Japan*, pp. 110–33. For more on Chinese publishing during the war years, see Xiong Fu et al., eds., *Zhongguo kang-Ri zhanzheng shiqi dahoufang chubanshi*.

50. As in previous years, translations were published in periodicals and anthologies, as well as in separate volumes. Xu Naixiang and Huang Wanhua, *Zhongguo kangzhan shiqi*, pp. 350–51. In 1944 and 1945, for instance, the journal *Japan Research*, founded in Beijing in September 1943 and intended as an "introduction to Japan," carried translations of drama and fiction by Doppo, Futabatei, Kikuchi, Hakuchō, Sōseki, Shūsei, Tanizaki, and Tōson; explanatory notes are appended to some of these translations. See Zhang Shaochang's comments concerning the purpose of *Japan Research* in "Women weishenme yao yanjiu Riben," p. 5. In Manchuria, Chinese writers and translators like Gu Ding stressed the importance of making Japanese literature available to readers of Chinese. Wang Xiangyuan, *Ershi shiji Zhongguo*, p. 175. See also Lü Qinwen, "Dongbei lunxianqu de wailai wenxue yu xiangtu wenxue," in Yamada Keizō and Lü Yuanming, eds., *Zhong-Ri zhanzheng yu wenxue*, p. 133.

51. Qian Daosun published translations of poems from the *Collection of Ten Thousand Leaves* and Nie Changzhen a translation of the *Notes from a Ten Foot Square Hut* in 1943 and 1944 in *Japan Research*. Substantial notes accompany these translations. In addition, in 1942 a Chinese translation of part of the *Record of Ancient Matters* was published in Manchuria in the journal *Chronicle of the Arts*.

52. For more on Chinese engagement with Japanese antiwar literature, and Kaji Wataru's writings in particular, see Jin Conglin, "Kang-Ri zhanzheng shiqi," p. 332; Lü Yuanming, "Zaihua Riben fanzhan wenxue lun," pp. 39–94.

53. In August 1938, the Japanese Board of Information (Naikaku Jōhōbu, later Naikaku Jōhōkyoku) established the first Pen Squadron (Pen Butai), which sent literary figures to the front to write about conditions there and the sacrifices of the nation's soldiers. During the war, Japanese periodicals including the *Asahi shinbun* likewise sent creative writers to battlefields across Asia and the South Pacific. While in China and Manchuria, Japanese writers also met with Japanese civilians and local residents. Taiwanese did not translate Japanese battlefront literature to the same degree as Chinese and Koreans largely because a greater percentage of Taiwanese could read these texts in the original; Taiwanese also had access to Chinese translations.

54. David M. Rosenfeld, *Unhappy Soldier*, p. 8.

55. During the 1930s and 1940s, Wu Zhefei also translated several English and Japanese books on literature and politics.

56. Genette gives several examples of this phenomenon in *Seuils*, pp. 9–10.

57. Haruko Taya Cook, "The Many Lives of *Living Soldiers*," p. 156; Haruko Taya Cook and Theodore F. Cook, *Japan at War*, p. 65.

58. See Ishikawa Tatsuzō, *Ikiteiru heitai, Chūō kōron (rinji zōkan)*, pp. 274–350, cited in Daqing Yang, "Convergence or Divergence?" p. 857.

59. Haruko Taya Cook discusses the publication history of *Living Soldiers* in Japan in "The Many Lives of *Living Soldiers*," pp. 149–75. Seemingly more troubling to the Police Bureau than the content of *Living Soldiers* was the failure of the *Central Review* editors to consult with them on last-minute changes. Richard H. Mitchell, *Censorship in Imperial Japan*, p. 289. Ironically, these changes removed some of the more controversial lines from the manuscript.

60. Ishikawa Tatsuzō, "Shi," p. 1. Most dramatically, the 1945 version replaces the final two lines of the 1938 version (two lines of censorship marks) with two chapters focusing on a misogynistic Japanese soldier.

61. See, for instance, Haruko Taya Cook, "The Many Lives of *Living Soldiers*"; Fujii Sadakazu, *Kotoba to sensō*, p. 48.

62. Chinese and Taiwanese writers had been translating Ishikawa's oeuvre since the early 1930s, so it is likely that Ishikawa was aware of the Chinese translations of his novella. But it is doubtful that he wrote *Living Soldiers* with Chinese readers in mind. This contrasts with cases like that of the Guatemalan activist Rigoberta Menchú, whose testimony is, in the words of David Damrosch, "a prime example of a work consciously produced within an international setting, intended from the start to circulate beyond the author's national sphere. It is a book that couldn't even have been published in Guatemala, whose government was suppressing any publications critical of its genocidal policies" (*What Is World Literature?*, p. 231).

63. The *Great American Evening News* and the *Huamei wanbao* (Chinese-American Evening News) were the "only overt challenges to Japanese censorship [in Shanghai]." Poshek Fu, *Passivity, Resistance, and Collaboration*, p. 32.

64. *Living Soldiers* also appears to have been translated into English at this time. In his preface to Xia Yan's translation of *Living Soldiers*, Kaji Wataru notes that he recently heard that a Japanese person living in the United States had translated Ishikawa's novel into English and that this translation "aroused the terror of the military fascists" ("Xu," p. 685). Zhang Shifang also mentions this translation in *Zhanshi Riben wentan*, p. 12. For more on Xia Yan's wartime experiences see Xia Yan, *Pen to sensō*. For more on the Chinese translation of *Living Soldiers* and other works of Japanese literature during the war years, see Liu Chunying (Ryū Shun'ei), "Kōnichi sensōki no Chūgoku ni okeru Nihon bungaku no hon'yaku," pp. 291–300; Wang Xiangyuan, *Ershi shiji Zhongguo*, pp. 171–93. Ishikawa Tatsuzō, and *Living Soldiers* in particular, have remained popular with Chinese-language translators. To give just two examples, Zhong Qingan and Ou Xilin published a translation of the novel in 1987 in Beijing and Liu Musha a translation in 1995 in Taipei.

65. Bai Mu, "Yizhe xu," p. 1.

66. Ishikawa Tatsuzō, *Ikiteiru heitai* (1938), p. 1. The 1945 version of *Living Soldiers* places this note at the end of the novella, omits the note's first sentence, and changes "everything . . . is fiction" to "much is fiction." The writer does not explicitly admit to reporting "fact," but he no longer hides completely behind declarations of "fiction." See Ishikawa Tatsuzō, *Ikiteiru heitai* (1945), p. 178.

67. Zhang Shifang, *Zhanshi Riben wentan*, pp. 9–10.

68. Cited by Lin Huanping in "Lun 1938 nian de Riben wenxuejie," *Wenyi chendi* 2:12, quoted in Wang Xiangyuan, *Ershi shiji Zhongguo*, p. 182.

69. Wu Zhefei, "Yizhe de hua," p. 1

70. Hino Ashihei, *Mai yu bingdui*, p. i.

71. Nishimura's essay appeared in the November 1939 Korean edition of *Modern Japan*. See Im Chŏnhye (Nin Tenkei), "Chōsen ni hon'yaku," p. 47. By the time he translated *Wheat and Soldiers* into Korean, Nishimura Shintarō had been involved with Korean affairs for decades. See, for instance, *Il-Sŏn hoehwa chŏngt'ong* (1917), his 700-page language textbook for Koreans studying Japanese.

72. Nobuhara Satoshi's Korean-language preface to Nishimura's translation indicates that this text was translated, with Hino's consent, for "those of our peninsular compatriots who don't know the national language [Japanese]" ("Sŏ," p. 3). Nishimura's translation was in such demand that it was reissued nine times between July 8 and August 15, 1939 alone.

73. Liu Yusheng, "Huaixiang ji," p. 157, quoted in Poshek Fu, *Passivity, Resistance, and Collaboration*, p. 149.

74. See Hino Ashihei, *Mugi to heitai*, p. 121; *Mai yu bingdui*, p. 14.

75. Hino Ashihei, *Mugi to heitai*, p. 205; *Mai yu bingdui*, p. 64.

76. Hino Ashihei, *Mugi to heitai*, pp. 206–7; *Mai yu bingdui*, p. 65.

77. When Chinese translations of Japanese battlefront literature do depict Chinese waving the Japanese flag or having on their person other Japanese insignia, the surrounding narrative (in both the Japanese text and its Chinese translation) indicates that possession of these emblems does not signify Chinese support of Japan. In *Earth and Soldiers*, the Japanese narrator is quick to reveal his suspicion that those waving flags are in fact Chinese soldiers or spies. Hino Ashihei, *Tsuchi to heitai*, pp. 114–15, *Tu yu bingdui*, pp. 52–53. In *Living Soldiers*, the peasants wearing Rising Sun armbands are described as simply a downtrodden people submitting to their conquerors, as they have for generations. Ishikawa Tatsuzō, *Ikiteiru heitai*, p. 9; *Weisi de bing* (Bai Mu, Shanghai Zazhishe), p. 6; *Weisi de bing* (Bai Mu, *Damei wanbao*, March 18, 1938); *Weisi de bing* (Xia Yan), p. 693.

78. Hino Ashihei, *Mugi to heitai*, p. 199; *Mai yu bingdui*, p. 60.

79. Hino Ashihei, *Mugi to heitai*, p. 143; *Mai yu bingdui*, p. 30.

80. An excellent example of the latter occurs midway through the novel, where the narrator describes an encounter with a young Chinese man in a bookstore who notices him pick up some texts by Su Manshu (1884–1918), a poet with a Japanese mother and Chinese father who was born in Japan, lived

in China as a child, studied in Tokyo, and wrote primarily in Chinese. The young Chinese man in *Flowers and Soldiers* laments that with all the talk of forming a "new East Asian culture" people will forget about such border-crossing pioneers as Su Manshu (Hino Ashihei, *Hana to heitai*, p. 352).

81. Hino Ashihei, *Hana to heitai*, p. 295; "Chŏnjang ŭi chŏngwŏl," p. 113.

82. Hino Ashihei, *Hana to heitai*, pp. 295–96; "Chŏnjang ŭi chŏngwŏl," pp. 114–15.

83. See, for instance, Hino Ashihei, *Mugi to heitai*, p. 172; *Mai yu bingdui*, pp. 50–51.

84. Hino Ashihei, *Mugi to heitai*, p. 188; "Pori wa pyŏngjŏng," p. 219.

85. Hayashi Fumiko, *Sensen*, p. 29; "Chŏnjang ŭi todŏk," p. 181.

86. Hayashi Fumiko, *Sensen*, p. 91.

87. Ibid., pp. 91–92.

88. Hino Ashihei, *Tsuchi to heitai*, pp. 147–50; "'Hŭlk kwa pyŏngdae' e sŏ," pp. 159–60.

89. Hino Ashihei, *Tsuchi to heitai*, pp. 61–68; "Chŏkjŏn sangryuk," pp. 177–78.

90. Hino Ashihei, *Tsuchi to heitai*, p. 61; "Chŏkjŏn sangryuk," p. 177.

91. Hino Ashihei, *Tsuchi to heitai*, p. 61; "Chŏkjŏn sangryuk," p. 178.

92. Hino Ashihei, *Tsuchi to heitai*, p. 63; "Chŏkjŏn sangryuk," p. 178.

93. Hino Ashihei, *Tsuchi to heitai*, p. 68; "Chŏkjŏn sangryuk," p. 178.

94. Hino Ashihei, *Tsuchi to heitai*, p. 69.

95. See Hino Ashihei, *Mugi to heitai*, p. 142; *Mai yu bingdui*, p. 30. Interestingly, the Chinese translation dehumanizes this prisoner by deleting the background information on him that Hino provides.

96. Ishikawa Tatsuzō, *Ikiteiru heitai* (1938), p. 25; *Weisi de bing* (Bai Mu, Shanghai Zazhishe), p. 18; *Weisi de bing* (Bai Mu, *Damei wanbao*, March 22, 1938); *Weisi de bing* (Xia Yan), p. 704. Xia Yan takes a different approach to Ishikawa's censored references to Japanese women, replacing Ishikawa's remark that "he [a man around 50] had recently brought over Japanese •••••••" with "he recently had brought over to China Japanese prostitutes." See *Ikiteiru heitai* (1938), p. 103; *Weisi de bing* (Xia Yan), p. 756.

97. Ishikawa Tatsuzō, *Ikiteiru heitai* (1938), p. 27; *Weisi de bing* (Bai Mu, Shanghai Zazhishe), p. 21; *Weisi de bing* (Bai Mu, *Damei wanbao*, March 23, 1938). Here Xia Yan closely follows Ishikawa's marks. See *Weisi de bing* (Xia Yan), p. 706.

98. Ishikawa Tatsuzō, *Ikiteiru heitai* (1938), p. 25; *Huozhe de bingdui*, p. 45, quoted in Zhang Shifang, *Zhanshi Riben wentan*, p. 10.

99. Ishikawa Tatsuzō, *Ikiteiru heitai* (1938), p. 86; *Weisi de bing* (Xia Yan), p. 745. Xia Yan replaces "Chiang Kai-shek" with "XXX" but "Soong Meiling" with "XXling."

100. This diminishing of violence by its victims provides an interesting comparison with the normalization and routinization of violence on the part of its perpetrators. See, for instance, Hannah Arendt, *Eichmann in Jerusalem*.

101. Hino Ashihei, *Mugi to heitai*, p. 138; *Mai yu bingdui*, p. 27.

102. Hino Ashihei, *Mugi to heitai*, p. 193; *Mai yu bingdui*, p. 58.

103. Hino Ashihei, *Mugi to heitai*, pp. 172–73; *Mai yu bingdui*, pp. 50–51.

104. Hino Ashihei, *Mugi to heitai*, pp. 203–4; *Mai yu bingdui*, p. 63.

105. Ishikawa Tatsuzō, *Ikiteiru heitai* (1938), p. 69; *Huozhe de bingdui*, p. 114, quoted in Zhang Shifang, *Zhanshi Riben wentan*, p. 11.

106. Ishikawa Tatsuzō, *Weisi de bing* (Bai Mu, *Damei wanbao*, March 18, 1938); *Weisi de bing* (Bai Mu, Shanghai Zazhishe), p. 4.

107. Ishikawa Tatsuzō, *Weisi de bing* (Bai Mu, *Damei wanbao*, March 23, 1938); *Weisi de bing* (Bai Mu, Shanghai Zazhishe), p. 21.

108. One telling exception is Xia Yan's deletion of Ishikawa's claim that Chinese soldiers in Nanjing, having littered the streets with their discarded uniforms, are hiding among civilian refugees and thus are making it increasingly difficult for Japanese soldiers "to dispose of just the actual [Chinese] soldiers." Ishikawa, *Ikiteiru heitai* (1938), p. 86; *Weisi de bing* (Xia Yan), p. 744. Here Xia Yan masks both Japanese atrocities in Nanjing and the partial culpability of Chinese soldiers in the murder of Chinese civilians.

109. Ishikawa Tatsuzō, *Weisi de bing* (Bai Mu, *Damei wanbao*, March 18, 1938).

110. Bai Mu, "Yizhe xu," p. 2.

111. Discussions of the Nanjing Massacre also appear in the creative output of Chinese émigré writers, including François Cheng. The narrator of Cheng's *Le dit de Tianyi* (The Saying of Tianyi, 1998) comments: "1937 . . . In Nanking alone, in the several weeks after they took the city, unleashed soldiers succeeded in killing more than two hundred thousand people. They killed them with knives, buried entire groups alive, or machined-gunned indiscriminately" (p. 48). See as well Shouhua Qi's recent historical novel *When the Purple Mountain Burns*, which describes the experiences of Chinese and foreigners in Nanjing between December 12 and December 18, 1937.

112. For more on the publication history of *Nanjing Blood Sacrifice*, see Michael Berry, "A History of Pain," pp. 72–86, and *A History of Pain*, pp. 142–53; Ken Sekine, "A Verbose Silence in 1939 Chongqing," and "Ā Ron [Ah Long] no yonjūdai ni okeru tokuisei ni kansuru kōsatsu," pp. 195–208. For more on Nanjing as a repressed topic of reportage and creative production, see Takashi Yoshida, *The Making of the "Rape of Nanking"*; Joshua Fogel, ed., *The Nanjing Massacre in History and Historiography*. Interesting parallels can be drawn between repression of literary depictions of atrocity in China and Taiwan. For more on the latter, see Sylvia Li-chun Lin, *Representing Atrocity in Taiwan*. The troubled history of Japanese literature of the atomic bomb, a creative corpus produced in large quantities but shunned by readers and critics alike, provides a telling counterpoint with that of Chinese literature on Nanjing and Taiwanese literature on the February 28 (1947) Incident. See Karen Thornber, "Responsibility and Japanese Literature of the Atomic Bomb."

113. Jing Tsu, *Failure, Nationalism, and Literature*, p. 7.

Chapter 5

1. Meyer Howard Abrams, *A Glossary of Literary Terms*, p. 285. See also Graham Allen, *Intertextuality*; and Mary Orr, *Intertextuality*.

2. The understanding of intertextuality as massaging literary works into textual bodies comes from Kwame Anthony Appiah, *In My Father's House*, p. 150.

3. Gérard Genette, *Palimpsestes*, p. 16.

4. Michael Worton and Judith Still, *Intertextuality*, p. 2. See Julia Kristeva, "Word, Dialogue and Novel," pp. 34–61.

5. Quoted by Walter Jackson Bate, *The Burden of the Past and the English Poet*, pp. 3–4.

6. David Damrosch, ed., *The Longman Anthology, World Literature*, vol. A, p. 88. See also David Damrosch, *The Buried Book*, especially pp. 3, 212.

7. D. A. Russell, "De Imitatione," p. 1.

8. Quoted idem., p. 1. See also Petrarch's (1304–74) advice to Boccaccio (1313–75) that "a proper imitator should take care that what he writes resembles the original without reproducing it. The resemblance . . . should be the resemblance of a son to his father" (quoted in Thomas M. Greene, *The Light in Troy*, pp. 95–96).

9. Harold Bloom, *The Anxiety of Influence*, p. 30. See also John T. Hamilton's discussion of Pindaric interpretation, and the thematization of Pindaric obscurity in particular, in *Soliciting Darkness*.

10. Atsuko Sakaki, "*Kajin no kigū*," p. 102.

11. Robert H. Brower and Earl Miner, *Japanese Court Poetry*, p. 506.

12. Ann Louise Huss, "Old Tales Retold," p. 30.

13. For more on the revision and rewriting of Chinese vernacular fiction, see Martin W. Huang, ed., *Snakes' Legs*.

14. Stanley Sultan, *Eliot, Joyce, and Company*, p. 6.

15. Claudio Guillén, *The Challenge of Comparative Literature*, p. 57.

16. See Alison Boulanger, "Influence or Confluence," pp. 18–47.

17. Andrew Plaks, "Full-length *Hsiao-shuo* and the Western Novel," p. 176.

18. Zong-qi Cai, *Configurations of Comparative Poetics*, pp. 254–55.

19. Takayuki Yokota-Murakami, *Don Juan East/West*, pp. 155–56.

20. Benjamin Lawson, "Federated Fancies," pp. 39, 46. Emphasis mine.

21. Sari Kawana elucidates this dynamic as it pertains to the detective novel in *Murder Most Modern*, pp. 19–25. Cf. Mark Silver, *Purloined Letters*.

22. See Mieke Bal, *Quoting Caravaggio*, pp. 8–9, cited by Atsuko Sakaki, *Obsessions with the Sino-Japanese Polarity in Japanese Literature*, p. 8.

23. Christopher Ricks, *Allusion to the Poets*, p. 1.

24. Ibid., p. 4.

25. The byline of "Behind the Papering of the Four-and-a-half Mat Room" declares the story a "*gesaku* by Kinpu Sanjin," and in the first preface the narrator claims that while airing his boxes he found a text by Kinpu Sanjin entitled "Behind the Papering," which he copied. Yet the second preface portrays Kinpu Sanjin not as the author but rather as a character who discovers a manuscript buried in his new house. It is this manuscript that allegedly provides the body of "Behind the Papering of the Four-and-a-half Mat Room." See Kinpu Sanjin [Nagai Kafū], "Yojōhan no fusuma no shitabari," pp. 177–85; and Tsuge Tanehiko, ed., "Yojōhan fusuma no shitabari,"

pp. 66–78. Kirsten Cather discusses this story and the controversy it fostered in "The Great Censorship Trials of Literature and Film in Postwar Japan," pp. 254–73.

26. See Julia Kristeva, *Revolution in Poetic Language*, p. 60.

27. M. Keith Booker, *Joyce, Bakhtin, and the Literary Tradition*, p. 10. Booker notes that while many scholars have pointed out the "what" of Joyce's intertextual sources, and some the "how," "surprisingly little has been done to illuminate the 'so what' of Joyce's intertextual poetics."

28. Claudio Guillén, *The Challenge of Comparative Literature*, pp. 56–57. For more on the "flow" implied by the term "influence," see Ronald Primeau, "Introduction," pp. 3–12. Jay Clayton and Eric Rothstein summarize the evolution of the influence paradigm in literary criticism in "Figures in the Corpus," pp. 3–36.

29. The notion of the writer being held hostage is from Stanley Sultan, *Eliot, Joyce, and Company*, p. 6.

30. Janet Ng, *The Experience of Modernity*, p. 15. Cf. Ángel Rama, "Literature and Culture," p. 137.

31. See, for instance, Shu-mei Shih's discussion of Chinese and Japanese neosensationalism in *The Lure of the Modern* and Christopher T. Keaveney's examination of the Chinese appropriation of the Japanese *shishōsetsu* (I-novel) in *The Subversive Self in Modern Chinese Literature*, as well as Margaret Hillenbrand's comparison of postwar Japanese and Taiwanese fiction in *Literature, Modernity, and the Practice of Resistance*. For more on structural and generic intertextuality in the colonial and semicolonial context, see Mary Layoun, *Travels of a Genre*.

32. Miryam Sas, *Fault Lines*, p. 38.

33. Cf. Henry Peyre, *French Literary Imagination and Dostoevsky and Other Essays*, pp. 93–114.

34. Udo Hebel outlines various forms of allusion in "Towards a Descriptive Poetics of *Allusion*," pp. 135–64. For more on "figures on loan," see Theodore Ziolkowski, *Varieties of Literary Thematics*, pp. 123–51. For more on the significance of intertitularity, see Wolfgang Karrer, "Titles and Mottoes as Intertextual Devices," pp. 122–34; Leo H. Hoek, *La marque du titre*, and *Titres, toiles et critique d'art*; Michael Seidel, "Running Titles," pp. 34–50.

35. Stephen Snyder, *Fictions of Desire*, p. 65.

36. Ibid., pp. 8, 65. See Susan Napier, *From Impressionism to Anime* for more on Western fantasies of Japan in the Madame Butterfly archetype (pp. 101–11). In this context, it would be interesting to examine further the paradox of the defeated nation as source of cultural authority exhibited in early twentieth-century Japanese emulation of Russian literature and the impact of this dynamic on the relationship between Russian and Japanese literatures following the Russo-Japanese War. Cf. J. Thomas Rimer, ed., *A Hidden Fire*.

37. For more on the Internet in the circulation of avant-garde poetry in China, see Michael Day, "Online Avant-Garde Poetry in China Today."

38. Antoine and Bird also share fiery red hair and have girlfriends obsessed with experiencing "perfect moments." The parallels between Bird's encounter

with the ginkgo tree as he pedals madly to the hospital and Antoine's encounter with the chestnut tree are particularly noteworthy. Gabriel García Márquez's *Memoria de mis putas tristes* (Memories of My Melancholy Whores) is more explicit, opening with a quotation (translated into Spanish) from Kawabata's *Nemureru bijo* (House of the Sleeping Beauties, 1961) that the narrator notably twists. See Kawabata, *Nemureru bijo*; Márquez, *Memoria de mis putas tristes*. Cf. Márquez, "El avión de la bella durmiente" (Airplane of the Sleeping Beauty, 1982), where the narrator identifies closely with his Japanese counterpart (*Doce Cuentos peregrinos*, pp. 79–89).

39. Joseph Conrad, *Heart of Darkness*, p. 62.

40. Ōe Kenzaburō, *Kojinteki na taiken*, p. 205.

41. *The Woman in the Dunes* also draws from Franz Kafka's (1883–1924) oeuvre. See also Karen Thornber, "Ecoambivalence, Ecoambiguity."

42. Henry Louis Gates, Jr., *The Signifying Monkey*, pp. 255–56.

43. Sandra M. Gilbert and Susan Gubar, *The Madwoman in the Attic*, p. xxi. Gilbert and Gubar distinguish between the masculine "anxiety of influence" and the feminine "anxiety of authorship," the latter referring to the seemingly more collaborative relationship of women writers with female predecessors.

44. For instance, the South African writer Sol Plaatje's (1876–1932) *Native Life in South Africa* (1914) was modeled in part on W. E. B. Du Bois's (1868–1963) *The Souls of Black Folk* (1903). For more on this phenomenon, see Laura Chrisman, *Rereading the Imperial Romance*, pp. 18–19.

45. Françoise Lionnet, "Transcolonial Translations, Shakespeare in Mauritius," pp. 201–21.

46. William Butler Yeats, "Introduction," pp. vii, xiii. For more on Tagore's relationships with East Asian intellectuals, see Stephen Hay, *Asian Ideas*.

47. Elleke Boehmer, *Empire, the National, and the Postcolonial*, p. 8.

48. Anthony Appiah, *In My Father's House*, p. 150.

49. Suzanne Hagedorn, *Abandoned Women*, pp. 21–22. Additional discussions of the relationship between Brontë's and Rhys's novels include Mary Lou Emery, *Jean Rhys at 'World's End'*; Monika Kaup, *Mad Intertextuality*; Gayatri Chakravorty Spivak, "Three Women's Texts and a Critique of Imperialism," pp. 243–61.

50. Cf. Marián Galik, *Milestones in Sino-Western Literary Confrontation*. Galik uses the term "confrontation" to refer to encounters, not oppositions.

51. A particularly noteworthy exception is the Japanese *nō* drama *Haku Rakuten* (Bai Juyi), which portrays the famed Chinese poet Bai Juyi (772–846) in a seaside encounter with Japanese gods, including the god of Japanese poetry, Sumiyoshi no Kami. Embodying the creative power of a land where "all living things have the gift of song," the Japanese gods flap their sleeves so powerfully that Bai Juyi is driven back to China, his poetry deemed no longer relevant to Japan. See *Haku Rakuten*, pp. 305–8.

52. Robert Hollander, *Boccaccio's Dante and the Shaping Force of Satire*, pp. 10, 44.

53. Matsuo Bashō, *Oku no hosomichi*, p. 81.

54. Ibid., p. 84.

55. John Foster, "Starting with Dostoevsky's Double," pp. 14–19.

56. Ibid., p. 16.

57. Robert Hegel, "Rewriting the Tang," pp. 159–60.

58. Howard Hibbett, *The Chrysanthemum and the Fish*, p. 52. See also Howard Hibbett, *The Floating World in Japanese Fiction*, p. 92.

59. For more on the relationship between Futabatei Shimei's and Hayashi Fumiko's *Floating Clouds*, see Karen Thornber, "Roaming Clouds, Memories, and Texts," pp. 411–23.

60. Elisa Martí-López, *Borrowed Words*, p. 32.

61. The tendency to define postcolonial literatures as simply "writing back" is particularly troubling. See Byron Caminero-Santangelo's examination of this issue in *African Fiction and Joseph Conrad*, pp. 1–29. See also Réda Bensmaïa, *Experimental Nations*.

62. For more on confrontations with the narrative act in the work of Hara Tamiki and Charlotte Delbo, see Karen Thornber, "When the Protagonist Is Death," pp. 105–12. Similarly, as Sandra Gilbert notes, "combatant poets reshaped the traditional pastoral elegy into the skeptical poetry of mourning with which we are familiar today" (*Death's Door*, pp. 378–79). In contrast, some literature of atrocity explores how aesthetic pleasure can serve as a survival mechanism, arguing that texts like Marcel Proust's (1871–1922) *À la recherche du temps perdu* (Remembrance of Things Past, 1913–27) can "offer a useful means of imaginative escape from the worst conditions" (Brett Ashley Kaplan, " 'The Bitter Residue of Death,' " p. 335).

63. Graham Allen, *Intertextuality*, p. 163. See also Patricia S. Yaeger, " 'Because a Fire Was in My Head,' " pp. 955–73.

64. Sandra Gilbert and Susan Gubar, *The Madwoman in the Attic*, pp. 86–87. See also Páraic Finnerty's discussion of nineteenth-century women writers' literary relationships with Shakespeare in *Emily Dickinson's Shakespeare*, pp. 95–116.

65. See Tsushima Yūko, *Chōji*; Ōe Kenzaburō, *Kojinteki na taiken*.

66. Yunte Huang, *Transpacific Displacement*, p. 133. See also Yunte Huang, "Pidginizing Chinese," pp. 205–20.

67. Michael Molasky draws these parallels in his review of Melissa Wender, *Lamentation as History*, pp. 257–58. Also noteworthy in this context is the American writer Helena María Viramontes's (1954–) novel *Under the Feet of Jesus* (1995), which intertextualizes John Steinbeck's (1902–68) *The Grapes of Wrath* (1939) in part to call attention to added perils of the Mexican American migrant experience.

68. W. H. New, "Colonial Literatures," p. 110. Examples include the Australian writers Charles Harpur (1813–68) and Henry Kendall (1839–82) and the Canadian writers Charles Sangster (1822–93) and Charles Heavysege (1816–76).

69. *The Harp and the Shadow* depicts an incapacitated Christopher Columbus reflecting on his life, ashamed of his obsession with gold and the dreadful consequences of this obsession; substituting human flesh for elusive metal, he was responsible for inaugurating the slave trade. See Alejo Carpentier, *El arpa y la sombra*. *The Harp and the Shadow* is the prototype of Latin American

writings on the "discovery" and conquest of the Americas. Thomas Christensen and Carol Christensen, "Translator's Preface," p. xii. Other recent literary reconfigurations of the discovery and conquest of the Americas include novels by Miguel Ángel Asturias (1899–1974), Carlos Fuentes (1928–), Gabriel García Márquez, João Ubaldo Ribeiro (1941–), and Abel Posse (1934–).

70. Sharon Lubkemann Allen, "Metamorphosis." Veríssimo's "Metamorphosis" reverses Franz Kafka's story of the same title (Die Verwandlung, 1915) and concludes by asserting "Kafka means nothing to cockroaches."

71. Elleke Boehmer, *Colonial and Postcolonial Literature*, pp. 173–74.

72. W. H. New, "Colonial Literatures," pp. 108–9.

73. Gayatri Spivak, "Three Women's Texts," p. 243.

74. Edward Said, *Culture and Imperialism*, p. 62. See also Aimé Césaire's comments on the "novelists of civilization" in his *Discours sur le colonialisme*.

75. Elleke Boehmer, "Introduction," p. xxx. See also Bill Ashcroft et al., *The Empire Writes Back*.

76. Shu-mei Shih's observations concerning intertextuality in Sinophone articulations hold true for transcultural intertextualization more generally, particularly intertextualization that rectifies stereotypes: "The Sinophone's favorite modes . . . tend to be intertextual: satire, irony, paradox, bricolage, collage, and others. This intertextuality, however, is not simply rewriting or reinvention, but a means to construct new identities and cultures" (*Visuality and Identity*, pp. 35–36).

77. As Edward Said has noted, Salih's work is "far less schematic and ideologically embittered" than Naipaul's, "a novel of genuine post-colonial strength and passion" ("Embargoed Literature," p. 102). See Joseph Conrad, *Heart of Darkness*; Chinua Achebe, *Things Fall Apart*; V. S. Naipaul, *A Bend in the River*; Tayeb Salih, *Season of Migration to the North*.

78. See William Shakespeare, *The Tempest*, pp. 1537–68.

79. Aimé Césaire, *Une tempête; d'après "La tempête" de Shakespeare*, p. 28. The Barbadian writer George Lamming (1927–) similarly grapples with *The Tempest* in several texts, including *Water with Berries* (1972) and *The Pleasures of Exile* (1960). The subject of the latter, he declares, is "the migration of the West Indian writer, as colonial and exile, from his native kingdom, once inhabited by Caliban, to the tempestuous island of Prospero's and his language" (p. 13). For more on reconfigurations of *The Tempest*, see Chantal Zabus, *Tempests after Shakespeare*. (Post)colonial writers also targeted Shakespeare's *Othello*. The Sudanese Mustafa Sa'eed, one of the principal characters in Salih's *Season of Migration to the North*, kills his European wife just like Shakespeare's Othello, with whom he explicitly identifies. Yet as one critic has noted, "if Othello allowed, through weakness, baseness or fate, his mind to be overcome by his own poetry and passions, Mustafa will have his vengeance with his mind. . . . Othello, overcome by passion and Iago, forgets his reason. That reason, coldly ironic and unrelenting, finely honed, becomes Mustafa's weapon" (Barbara Harlow, "Sentimental Orientalism," pp. 78–79). Cf. *The Tragedy of Othello the Moor of Venice*, pp. 1090–136.

80. In *Jane Eyre*, Bertha's brother describes her as "daughter of Jonas Mason, merchant, and of Antoinetta his wife, a Creole" (Charlotte Brontë, *Jane Eyre*, p. 343), while Rochester declares that she "came of a mad family:–idiots and maniacs through three generations! Her mother, the Creole, was both a mad woman and a drunkard!" (p. 345). In nineteenth-century usage the word "creole" referred to both whites and blacks born in the West Indies, but passages throughout *Jane Eyre* emphasize Bertha's dark coloring. See Susan Meyer, "'Indian Ink,'" pp. 43–74.

81. Jane Eyre declares, "What it was, whether beast or human being, one could not, at first sight, tell: it groveled, seemingly on all fours; it snatched and growled like some strange wild animal: but it was covered with clothing; and a quantity of dark, grizzled hair, wild as a mane, hid its head and face . . . the maniac bellowed: she parted her shaggy locks from her visage, and gazed wildly at her visitors. I recognized well that purple face,–those bloated features" (Charlotte Brontë, *Jane Eyre*, p. 346).

82. Mary Lou Emery, *Jean Rhys at 'World's End,'* p. 15. See Charlotte Brontë, *Jane Eyre*, and Jean Rhys, *Wide Sargasso Sea*. The South African writer Sol Plaatje's historical novel *Mhudi* (1913) similarly rewrites Henry Rider Haggard's (1856–1925) "zulu epic" *Nada the Lily* (1892); *Mhudi* revises the Haggardian imperial romance, revealing stereotyping as a human construction by situating "African women as self-determining subjects of a potential oppositional political culture, one that critiques African patriarchy and its attendant notions of sexual difference along with white colonialism" (Laura Chrisman, *Rereading the Imperial Romance*, p. 186).

83. See Nakano Shigeharu, "Ame no furu Shinagawa eki" (1929); Im Hwa, "Usan pat-ŭn Yok'ohama ŭi pudu," pp. 66–70.

84. See Chen Duxiu, "Dikang li," n.p., cited in Paul B. Foster, *Ah Q Archaeology*, p. 54.

85. Ena C. Vulor, *Colonial and Anti-Colonial Discourses*, p. 144. See Mohammed Dib, *La Grande maison*, *L'Incendie*, and *Le Métier à tisser*.

86. Arabs represented less than one-fourth of the population of Oran and had neither voting rights nor citizenship (Martha O'Nan, "Biographical Context and Its Importance to Classroom Study," p. 108).

87. An excellent example of this phenomenon is the Australian writer Peter Carey's (1940–) novel *Jack Maggs* (1997), which intertextually recasts Charles Dickens's (1812–70) *Great Expectations* (1860). Carey's novel employs interfigurality and rewrites Dickens's banished criminal Abel Magwitch as Jack Maggs: both men are deported to Australia, where they make their fortune and sponsor a young man from home, Phillip Pirrip (Pip) in *Great Expectations* and Henry Phipps in *Jack Maggs*. But Maggs plays a more significant role in *Jack Maggs* than Magwitch in *Great Expectations*, and he exposes the underside of London society more effectively than his literary predecessor. See Charles Dickens, *Great Expectations*; Peter Carey, *Jack Maggs*.

88. J. M. Coetzee, *Foe*, p. 23.

89. This narrative move is particularly intriguing in light of the analysis by Radhika Jones of how novels like *Foe* not only contest cultural imperialism,

but also formally engage with their genre's own past and with questions of authorship, reception theory, and canonization ("Required Rereading").

90. Much has been written on the depiction of China and Chinese in modern Japanese literature. See, for instance, Atsuko Sakaki, *Obsessions with the Sino-Japanese Polarity in Japanese Literature*; Muramatsu Sadataka et al., eds., *Kindai Nihon bungaku ni okeru Chūgokuzō*; Sofue Shōji's series of articles in *Zhongguoyu* 99–110 (April 1968–March 1969). For depictions of Chinese in Japanese wartime film, see Peter B. High, *The Imperial Screen*, pp. 276–85. The Li Xianglan (Yamaguchi Yoshiko) phenomenon is particularly interesting in this regard: Yamaguchi, known in Japan by her screen name Ri Kōran (Li Xianglan), was a tremendously popular bilingual Japanese actress born in Manchuria who in numerous films played a Chinese beauty "happily subordinate to the dashing head-of-family Japanese male" (Sharalyn Orbaugh, *Japanese Fiction of the Allied Occupation*, p. 220). Yamaguchi's Japanese identity was not revealed until after the war. Discussions of Korea and Koreans in modern Japanese literature include Pak Ch'un-il, *Kindai Nihon bungaku ni okeru Chōsenzō*; Gu Inmo (Ku In-mo), "Tank'a [tanka] ro kŭrin Chosŏn ŭi p'ungsokji (fūzokushi)," pp. 214–36; Takasaki Ryūji, "Nihonjin bungakusha no mita Chōsen," pp. 133–37; Yi Sŏn-ok, "Ilje kangjŏmgi chŏnhu Ilbon munhak e nat'a-nan Hanguksang." There also are numerous articles on the portrayal of Korea and Koreans in the works of individual Japanese writers. For Japanese depictions of Taiwan and Taiwanese, see Faye Kleeman, *Under an Imperial Sun*. William Tyler summarizes depictions of non-Japanese in Japanese modernist fiction in *Modanizumu*, pp. 171–77.

91. William Gardner, *Advertising Tower*, p. 68.

92. Sven Saaler, "Pan-Asianism in Modern Japanese History," p. 3.

93. Homi Bhabha defines colonial mimicry as "the desire for a reformed, recognizable Other, *as a subject of a difference that is almost the same, but not quite*," and as such "one of the most elusive and effective strategies of colonial power and knowledge" (*The Location of Culture*, p. 122).

94. Cited in G. D. Killman, "Chinua Achebe," p. 16. See also Bernth Lindfors, ed., *Conversations with Chinua Achebe*, pp. 7–10; and Kim Soonsik, "Chinua Achebe's *Things Fall Apart* as a Counter-Conradian Discourse on Africa," pp. 333–55.

95. Chinua Achebe, *Things Fall Apart*, p. 5. Cf. Joyce Cary, *Mister Johnson*. For more on language in *Things Fall Apart*, see Catherine Lynette Innes, "Language, Poetry and Doctrine in *Things Fall Apart*," pp. 111–25.

96. William Butler Yeats, "The Second Coming," pp. 89–90.

97. See Romanus Okey Muoneke, *Art, Rebellion and Redemption*, pp. 100–101.

98. Catherine Lynette Innes, *Chinua Achebe*, p. 35.

99. Chinua Achebe, *Things Fall Apart*, p. 3.

100. Ji Xian was born and raised in China, went to Japan in 1936 (where he studied poetry and art), returned to China in 1937, and in 1948 moved to Taiwan; he has been living in the United States since 1976.

101. Miró likely was aware of Hagiwara's poem, considering Hagiwara's ties with European surrealists and the popularity of his anthology.

102. See Ji Xian, "Fei yue de quan," p. 82; Hagiwara Sakutarō, "Kanashii tsukiyo," p. 41. Xi Mi discusses the relationship between Miró's painting, Ji Xian's poem, and the Taiwanese writer Chen Li's (1954–) poem of the same title "Fei yue zhi quan" (Dog Howling at the Moon, 1990). See *Xiandangdai shiwen lu*, pp. 13–23. She examines, among other things, how the differences between Ji Xian's and Chen Li's output reflect not only disparities in the personal circumstances of the two artists but developments in Taiwanese poetry more generally.

103. Anna Mundow, "The Interview with Chimamanda Ngozi Adichie," p. E7.

104. For more on Li Kuixian's involvement with the Japanese poetry world, see his essay "Dongjing shiji," pp. 110–11.

105. Natsume Sōseki, *Wagahai wa neko de aru*, p. 11; Lin Huanzhang, "Wo shi mao, bu!" p. 145.

106. In the words of David Damrosch, "world literature" refers to a "subset of the plenum of literature," those texts that "circulate beyond their culture of origin, either in translation or in their original language. . . . a work only has an *effective* life as world literature whenever, and wherever, it is actively present within a literary system beyond that of its original culture" (*What Is World Literature?*, p. 4). Furthermore, as Pascale Casanova has noted, "Since the position of each national space in the world structure depends on its relative degree of autonomy, which in turn is a function of its volume of literary capital, and so ultimately of its age, the world of letters must be conceived as a composite of the various national literary spaces, which are themselves bipolar and differentially situated in the world structure according to the relative attraction exerted upon them by its national and international poles, respectively" (*The World Republic of Letters*, p. 108).

107. Henri Peyre, *French Literary Imagination*, p. 94.

108. Although my focus is on literature for adults, significant ties also exist among early twentieth-century East Asian children's literatures. For more on this phenomenon see Ōtake Kiyomi (Oot'ak'e K'iyomi), *Han-Il adong munhak kwan-gyesa sosŏl*.

109. David Wang, "Translating Modernity," p. 312. See also Shimizu Ken'ichirō, "Ryō Keichō [Liang Qichao] to 'teikoku kanbun,'" pp. 22–37; Wang Hongzhi, "Zhuanyu fabiao ququ zhengjian," pp. 172–205. Nakamura Tadayuki discusses connections among *The Future of New China*, Shiba Shirō's *Chance Meetings with Beautiful Women* (1885–97), and Yano Ryūkei's *Inspiring Instances of Statesmanship* (1884), Japan's two other major political novels, in "*Shin Chūgoku miraiki* [Xin Zhongguo weilaiji] kōsetsu," pp. 65–93.

110. An Kuksŏn went to Japan in 1894, where he studied politics. For more on the connections between "Record of the Conference of Birds and Beasts" and Japanese novels, see Im Kwŏnhwan, " 'Kŭmsu hoeŭi rok' ŭi chaeraejŏk wŏnch'ŏn e taehayŏ," pp. 631–44; Kim Sunjŏn, *Han-Il kŭndae sosŏl ŭi pigyo munhakjŏk yŏn-gu*, pp. 86–105. An Kuksŏn's creative texts also reconfigure classical Chinese and Korean literature, as well as writings by Liang Qichao.

111. For instance, the Korean writer Ch'oe Ch'ansik's (1881–1951) *Kŭmgang-mun* (The Gate of Kumgang, 1914) alludes heavily to Suehiro Tetchō's *Plum Blossoms in the Snow*. See Kim Sunjŏn (Kim Soon-Jeun), "Ch'oe Chansik ŭi *Sŏl-jungmae* ŭi suyŏng yangt'ae pigyo yŏn-gu," pp. 137–65; Kim Sunjŏn, "Kan-Nichi kaikaki shōsetsu no hikaku bungakuteki kenkyū," pp. 239–53.

112. Don Price, *Russia and the Roots of the Chinese Revolution*, p. 122.

113. *Touch Me Not* originally was published in Spanish while José Rizal was studying in Europe.

114. Scholarship linking Lu Xun's creative texts with Japanese literary works abounds; an excellent starting point is Fujii Shōzō, *Ro Jin* [Lu Xun] *jiten*, pp. 216–24.

115. Samuel Perry comments on the ties between "Hell of Hungry Spirits" and "Here and There in Manchuria and Korea" in "Aesthetics for Justice," pp. 254–55.

116. See Fujiishi Takayo, "Kim Namch'ŏn no 'Shi' [Si] to Akutagawa Ryū-nosuke no 'Yabu no naka,'" pp. 220–31.

117. Fujiya Kawashima, "A Shared Vision in Taishō Japan and Revolutionary China," p. 123. Kawashima discusses the ties between Ye Shengtao's novel *Ni Huanzhi* (Schoolmaster Ni Huanzhi, 1928) and the arguments of the White Birch Society. For more on the connections between Chinese writers and the White Birch Society, see Liu Lishan, *Riben baihuapai yu Zhongguo zuojia*.

118. Interestingly, Taiwanese texts with naturalist tendencies contain fewer intertexts from Japanese literature than do their Chinese or Korean counterparts. For a discussion of naturalism in Taiwan, including the Taiwanese introduction of Western naturalism, see Nai-huei Shen, "The Age of Sadness," pp. 32–40.

119. Similarly, Kim Dong-in's "Paettaragi" (The Seaman's Chant, 1921) reworks Doppo's "Jonan" (Woman Trouble, 1903) to pose more penetrating questions of responsibility, while Hyŏn Chin-gŏn's "Sul kwŏnhanŭn sahoe" (A Society That Drives You to Drink, 1921) reworks Doppo's "Unmeironsha" (The Fatalist, 1902), turning the focus to the ambiguous tension between social and societal responsibility.

120. Despite their obvious connections, and Ba Jin's demonstrated engagement—via interpretive and interlingual transculturation—with Japanese literature, few critics have explored the connections between Tōson's *Family* and Ba Jin's *Family*. To the best of my knowledge, no one has discussed the relationship between Tōson's and Ba Jin's other like-titled works.

121. Similarly, Chŏn Yŏngt'aek's short story "Dok-yak ŭl masinŭn yŏin" (The Woman Who Took Poison, 1921) confronts Hōmei's acclaimed novel of the same title, *Dokuyaku o nomu onna* (1914), while Yŏm Sangsŏp's short story "Ijŭl su ŏmnŭn saram dŭl" (Unforgettable People, 1924) confronts Doppo's story of the same title ("Wasureenu hitobito," 1899).

122. Tanizaki Jun'ichirō, "Shanhai kōyūki," p. 567.

123. Hu Qiuyuan, "Riben wuchan wenxue zhi guoqu yu xianzai," cited in Sanetō Keishū, *Chūgokujin Nihon ryūgakushi kō*, pp. 164–65.

124. Some of the most intriguing connections are between Xia Yan's drama *Shanghai wuyan xia* (Under Shanghai Eaves, 1937), which portrays Shanghai tenement dwellers who are "rescued" by a young Communist, and Fujimori's plays *Gisei* (Sacrifice) and *Meian* (Light and Darkness). Like many East Asian proletarian literary texts, *Under Shanghai Eves* also intertextually recasts Maxim Gorky's (1868–1936) *The Lower Depths* (1902), which was adapted for the Chinese stage. For more on the ties between texts by Xia Yan and Fujimori Seikichi, see Jin Mingquan, *Zhongguo xiandai zuojia*, pp. 120–37.

125. Chinese, Korean, and Taiwanese revolutionary writers also frequently reconfigured Japanese proletarian literary theory in their discussions of socialist realism and popularization (*taishūka*). The prominent Korean proletarian critics An Mak (1910–?), Han Hyo (1912–?), Kim Kijin, Kim Namch'ŏn, Paek Ch'ŏl (1908–1985), and Pak Yŏnghŭi reconstructed theories by Aono Suekichi, Itō Einosuke, Kobayashi Takiji, Kurahara Korehito, and Moriyama Kei. In China, essays by Hu Feng, Jiang Guangci, and Li Chuli closely resemble those by Aono Suekichi, Fukumoto Kazuo (1894–1983), and Kurahara Korehito. Chinese, Korean, and Taiwanese revolutionary critics habitually used Japanese thought as a springboard to further their political agenda.

126. Liu Na'ou was born to a Taiwanese father and Japanese mother and was raised in Japan but generally is considered a Chinese writer because of his numerous literary and cinematic activities in Shanghai. Kataoka Teppei's "Shikijō bunka" (Culture of Lust), translated into Chinese by Liu Na'ou, was one of the most frequently reconfigured Japanese neosensationalist texts; its echoes resound in stories by Mu Shiying, Shi Zhecun, and Liu Na'ou. See Jin Mingquan, *Zhongguo xiandai zuojia*, pp. 153–66. Other Chinese, Korean, and Taiwanese writers, including Tian Han, viewed the modern city from a more nostalgic perspective and reworked the poetry of Kitahara Hakushū and Kinoshita Mokutarō (1885–1945). Heiner Frühauf, "Urban Exoticism and Its Sino-Japanese Scenery," p. 163. Tanizaki's writings on the "Return to Japan" also attracted Chinese modernists. For instance, Shi Zhecun's essay "Xiaoshuo zhong de duihua" (Dialogues in Fiction, 1937) cites extensively from Tanizaki's postscript to the novella *Shunkin shō* (Portrait of Shunkin, 1933). Shu-mei Shih, *The Lure of the Modern*, pp. 367–68.

127. Xun Si, "Mu Shiying," pp. 231–32, cited in Shu-mei Shih, *The Lure of the Modern*, pp. 305–6. See also Anthony Wan-hoi Pak, "The School of New Sensibilities (Xin'ganjuepai) in the 1930s." Mu Shiying additionally reconfigured texts by Akutagawa, including "In a Grove," which he skillfully reworked in "Benbu xinwenlan bianjishili yizha feigaoshang de gushi" (A Story Cobbled Together from a Bundle of Rejected Articles in a Newsroom of Our City, 1934). Several of Mu Shiying's characters read Japanese literature, including one in the short story "Wuyue" (May, 1933) and the femme fatale in the short story "Bei dangzuo xiaoqianpin de nanzi" (Men Kept as Playthings, 1932). Shu-mei Shih, *The Lure of the Modern*, pp. 331–32; Zhang Yingjin, *The City in Modern Chinese Literature & Film*, p. 168. For more on relationships among Japanese and Chinese neosensationalist texts, see Jin Mingquan, *Zhongguo xiandai zuojia*,

pp. 153–66; Peng Hsiao-yen, *Haishang shuo qingyu*, pp. 65–103; Qian Xiaobo, "Nihon to Chūgoku no shinkankakuha bungaku no hikaku kenkyū ni tsuite."

128. Wu Yongfu, for instance, claimed his creative texts were influenced by Yokomitsu's output (Xie Huizhen, "Toransu nashonaru tsūshin," p. 13).

129. Korean intertextualizations of modern Japanese poetry began in the early twentieth century with Ch'oe Namsŏn's reworkings of Japanese railroad songs.

130. William Gardner, *Advertising Tower*, pp. 76–77. For more on the use of *kana* in modernist texts, see William Tyler, *Modanizumu*, pp. 177–81.

131. See Miki Rofū, "Sariyuku gogatsu no shi," pp. 22–23; Chu Yohan, "Samidare no asa," pp. 6–7.

132. Many of the poems included in *The Blue Cat* appeared in other venues before the publication of this collection. For more on Japanese intertexts in early twentieth-century Korean poetry, see Pak Ch'ŏlsŏk, "Hanguk kŭndaesi ŭi Ilbonsi yŏnghyang yŏn-gu," pp. 17–40, "Han-Il kŭndaesi ŭi pigyo munhakjŏk yŏn-gu," pp. 29–62.

133. For more on Zhou Zuoren and Japanese poetry, see Yu Yaoming, *Shū Sakujin* [Zhou Zuoren] *to Nihon kindai bungaku*. Zhou Zuoren was particularly drawn to Japanese colloquial poetry and read both poems written in this style and poetic treatises such as Ikuta Shungetsu's *Atarashiki shi no tsukurikata* (Making New Poetry, 1918) and Muroo Saisei's *Atarashii shi to sono tsukurikata* (New Poetry and Its Making, 1925).

134. In *Resisting Manchukuo*, for instance, Norman Smith aptly demonstrates how in their fiction Chinese women writers in Manchuria denounced the Japanese state's ideals of "good wives and wise mothers." But Smith does not explore the possible connections between these condemnations and those in the writings of Japanese feminists, with which many Manchuria-based writers were familiar.

135. Quoted in Shu Zhongtian, "*Luse de gu* yu xiangtu wenxue," p. 225.

136. Liang Shanding's *Luse de gu* (Green Valley, 1942) was embraced by Japanese authorities and translated quickly into Japanese, although passages were censored. See Prasenjit Duara, "Local Worlds." For more on Doppo, Tōson, Satō, and native place literature in Japan, see Stephen Dodd, *Writing Home*.

137. Shimomura Sakujirō examines the ties between Murakami's and Wu Mansha's texts in "Reverse Exportation from Japan of the Tale of 'The Bell of Sayon,'" pp. 279–93. Another important focus of intertextualization in 1940s Taiwan was Japanese historical fiction on the island, including Nishikawa Mitsuru's famed "Sekikanki" (Record of the Red Fort, 1940), which Zhou Jinbo later claimed impacted his own story "Kyōshū" (Nostalgia, 1943). Nakajima Toshirō, "Zhou Jinbo xinlun," p. 16.

138. Studies of the ties between plays by Tian Han and those by Japanese playwrights include Saji Toshihiko, "Chūgoku wageki undōshi tenbyō," pp. 37–59; Wang Xiangyuan, *Zhong-Ri xiandai wenxue bijiaolun*, pp. 303–15. Tian Han also reconfigured films by Tanizaki, including the latter's *Jasei no in* (Lust of the White Serpent, 1921), in his script for *Hubian chunmeng* (Spring Dream

on the Lakeside, 1927), which he based on the Japanese writer Ueda Akinari's *Ugetsu monogatari* (Tales of Moonlight and Rain, 1776). Ueda's text itself derives in part from a story by the Chinese writer Feng Menglong (1574–1645). For more on Tian Han and Japanese film, see Zhang Zhen, *An Amorous History of the Silver Screen*, p. 256.

139. For more on the relationship between works by Kim Ujin and Arishima Takeo, see Yi Sikmi (Lee Jik Mi), "Kim Ujin hŭigok ŭi pigyo munhakjŏk yŏn-gu."

140. Mizuno Naoki, "'Ame no furu Shinagawa eki' no Chōsengo yaku o megutte," pp. 6–7; Takagawa Mayumi, "Nakano Shigeharu ron," pp. 82–89.

141. "The Fan of Hunan" tells the story of a Japanese doctor's trip to Hunan, where one of his former classmates offers him food that has been soaked in the blood of a fallen hero and declares that if he eats it he will never fall ill. Lu Xun includes a similar scene in "Medicine." "Medicine" and "Juriano Kichisuke" have strikingly similar endings. For more on the impact of Lu Xun's writing on Akutagawa, see Hō Shun'yō, "Akutagawa Ryūnosuke to Ro Jin [Lu Xun]," pp. 161–65; Sakai Tōyōo, "Jiechuan Longzhijie [Akutagawa Ryūnosuke] yu Lu Xun," pp. 39, 59–64; Sekiguchi Yasuyoshi, *Tokuhain Akutagawa Ryūnosuke*; and Takenaka Gen'ichi, "Jiechun Longzhijie [Akutagawa Ryūnosuke] yu Zhongguo," pp. 193–99.

142. For more on the parallels between early twentieth-century Chinese and Korean literatures, see Ho Kyegŏn, "Han-Chung yangguk ŭi kŭndae ch'ogi munhak pigyo yŏn-gu"; Jin Ying Yu, "Han-Chung kŭndae sosŏl ŭi hwakrip kwajŏng pigyo yŏn-gu"; Xu Shixu, "Han-Zhong xinwenxueshi zhi fenqi bijiao," pp. 87–94.

143. See Yang Ruoping, *Taiwan yu dalu wenxue*, pp. 164–66.

144. For more on the impact of Lu Xun's writing on Lai He, see Lin Ruiming, "Lu Xun yu Lai He," pp. 79–94. For more on the impact of Lu Xun's writing on Zhong Lihe see Ye Zhenzhen, "Liangge 'Guxiang,'" pp. 95–119.

145. See, for instance, U Imgŏl, *Hanguk kaehwagi munhak kwa Yang Kyech'o [Liang Qichao]* and "Hanguk kaehwagi munhak e kkich'in Yang Kyech'o [Liang Qichao] ŭi yŏnghyang yŏn-gu"; Yŏp Kŏn-gon, *Yang Kyech'o [Liang Qichao] wa ku Hanmal munhak*, and "Yang Kyech'o [Liang Qichao] wa ku Hanmal munhak."

146. For more on the ties between Korean and Chinese writers, see Yu Yŏa, *Hanguk kwa Chungguk hyŏndae sosŏl ŭi pigyo yŏn-gu*. For a brief comparison of the Chinese and Korean New Culture Movements, see also Zhao Binghuan, "Han-Zhong xinwenhua yundong zhi fayuandi," pp. 64–73, and Guo Moruo's comments on the plight of Koreans in Japan in *Nihon bōmeiki*, pp. 221–26.

147. See, for instance, Shirakawa Yutaka, "Shokuminchiki Chōsen to Taiwan no Nihongo bungaku shōkō," pp. 61–84. For a comparison of the development of proletarian thought and literature in Taiwan and Korea, see Tseng Tienfu, *Hanguk p'ŭromunhak kwa ŭi pigyo rŭl t'onghae pon Ilje Taeman chwaik munhak yŏn-gu*.

Chapter 6

1. Theodor W. Adorno, *Aesthetic Theory*, p. 27, quoted in Harold Schweizer, *Suffering and the Remedy of Art*, p. 3. See also Ramu Nagappan, *Speaking Havoc*, pp. 3–21.

2. See Bonnie Roos, "Anselm Kiefer and the Art of Allusion," p. 24.

3. Jing Tsu, *Failure, Nationalism, and Literature*, p. 15. Peter Zarrow talks at length about suffering in early twentieth-century China in *China in War and Revolution*. See also Michael Berry, "A History of Pain" and *A History of Pain*; Eric Hayot, *The Hypothetical Mandarin*; and David Der-wei Wang, *The Monster that Is History*. Dorothy Ko discusses pain and meaning in late nineteenth- and early twentieth-century China in "The Subject of Pain," pp. 478–503.

4. For more on the question of happiness in narratives of suffering, see Vivasvan Soni, "Trials and Tragedies," pp. 119–39.

5. Elaine Scarry, *The Body in Pain*, p. 11.

6. For more on the relationship between intertextuality and plagiarism, see Christiane Chaulet-Achour, "Writings as Exploratory Surgery," pp. 89–108; Marilyn Randall, *Pragmatic Plagiarism*.

7. For more on Yang Chichang's time in Tokyo, including copies of his early poems, see Huang Jianming, "Rizhi shiqi Yang Chichang ji qi wenxue yanjiu."

8. Sakamoto Etsurō was affiliated with the leading literary journals *Poetry and Poetics* and *Bungaku rebyū* (Literary Review). A fan of German poetry from childhood, he also published criticism on this genre. He enjoyed limited recognition among Chinese, Korean, and Taiwanese writers studying in Japan.

9. Sakamoto Etsurō, "Aki no umi," p. 110.

10. Yang Chichang, "Aki no umi," p. 112.

11. "Show Window," "Paved Road," and "Hot Monocle 5" are from Kitasono's collection *Hi no sumire* (Violet of Fire), which was not published until 1939, but the poems themselves predate Yang Chichang's "Burning Cheeks." Kitasono, who included the work of colonial writers in his literary journals, was Japan's "flamboyant and controversial avant-garde leader . . . whose activity spanned the middle fifty years of the twentieth century and left an indelible mark on poetry written in the international idiom" (John Solt, *Shredding the Tapestry of Meaning*, p. 1).

12. Yang Chichang, "Moeru hoo," p. 112.

13. Kitasono Katsue, "Kazarimado," pp. 205–6.

14. Kitasono Katsue, "Hodō," p. 206. "Paved Road" resembles the French poet Guillaume Apollinaire's (1880–1918) famous "Le Pont Mirabeau" (The Mirabeau Bridge, 1913).

15. Kitasono Katsue, "Atsui monokuru 5," pp. 209–10.

16. Writing about the painful experiences of the colonized via negative description was a hallmark of Yang Chichang's poetry more generally. See Joyce C. H. Liu, "The Importance of Being Perverse," pp. 93–112.

17. Donald Keene, *Dawn to the West*, p. 271.

18. For more on Hwang Sŏk-u's literary activities, including his time in Japan, see Han Sŭngmin (Han Seung-min), "Han-Il ch'och'anggi sangjingjuŭi toip-yangsang pigyo yŏn-gu," pp. 251–303.

19. Hwang Sŏk-u, "Pyŏkmo ŭi myo," p. 16.

20. Hagiwara Sakutarō, "Aoneko," pp. 143–44.

21. Several critics have drawn attention to the ties between Hwang Sŏk-u's "Cat with Blue Hair" and Charles Baudelaire's (1821–67) poems on cats in *Les fleurs du mal* (Flowers of Evil, 1857): "Le Chat" (Cat), "Le Chat" (Cat), and "Les Chats" (Cats). Baudelaire's obsession with cats, like that of many of his contemporaries, is well known. It is likely that Hwang Sŏk-u drew from Baudelaire's oeuvre, but the intertextualization of Hagiwara's "Blue Cat" in Hwang's "Cat with Blue Hair" is more significant than that of Baudelaire's poems, which are concerned less with the "sad history of humankind" than with the sad history of the lovelorn poet. See Charles Baudelaire, *Les fleurs du mal*, pp. 47–48, 66–67, 85.

22. Mikiso Hane explores the ambiguous "modernity" of early twentieth-century Japan in *Peasants, Rebels, and Outcastes*. See also Andrew Gordon, *A Modern History of Japan*, pp. 144–54.

23. Jonathan D. Spence, *The Search for Modern China*, pp. 375–85. Life in occupied areas of China was no easier. Poshek Fu describes Shanghai in the early 1940s as a "dark world" of "constant fear, poverty, uncertainty, and misery. During the 45 months of total occupation, Shanghai became a hell on earth. The economy collapsed and inflation went wild. Hoarding and black-marketeering thrived; massive unemployment was accompanied by widespread hunger. Anxiety about survival became a way of life in Shanghai" (*Passivity, Resistance, and Collaboration*, p. 122). See also J. G. Ballard's descriptions of wartime Shanghai in his autobiography *Miracles of Life*, pp. 3–62.

24. Janet Poole, "Colonial Interiors," p. 77. Chinese writers also appropriated this trope. See, for instance, Yu Dafu's short story "Chunfeng chenzui de wanshang" (Intoxicating Spring Nights, 1923), pp. 260–73.

25. See Pak T'aewŏn, "Ttakhan saramdŭl," pp. 133–49; Tayama Katai, *Futon*, pp. 7–55.

26. Mikiso Hane, *Peasants, Rebels, and Outcastes*, p. 33.

27. Jay Rubin, "Kunikida Doppo," pp. 2–3, 155–56. Although few paid attention to Doppo's texts during his most productive years (1896–1903), younger writers began in 1906 to turn to his works for inspiration.

28. In addition to Kim Dong-in, colonial and semicolonial writers who intertextualized Doppo's oeuvre in their own creative work include Lu Xun and the Korean writers Chŏn Yŏngt'aek, Kim Saryang, Yi Kwangsu, Yŏm Sang-sŏp, and Yu Chin-o (1906–87). Chŏng Kwiryŏn (Chō Kiren, Jeong Gwi-ryun) has written extensively on Korean emulation of Doppo's oeuvre. See, for instance, "Kunikida Doppo to wakaki Kankoku kindai bungakusha no gunzō" and numerous articles in *Bungaku kenkyū ronshū*, *Chōsen gakuhō*, *Hikaku bungaku*, and *Kindai bungaku*. See also Yaegashi Aiko, "Hanguk kŭndae sosŏl kwa Kukmokjŏn Dokbo [Kunikida Doppo]," pp. 697–714.

29. For more on Kim Dong-in's time in Japan, see Kim Ch'unmi (Kim Choon Mie), "Kim Dong-in yŏn-gu," esp. pp. 297–300; Shirakawa Yutaka (Sirakkawa Yuttakka), "Hanguk kŭndae munhak."

30. Kunikida Doppo, "Gyūniku to bareisho," p. 366.

31. Kim Dong-in, "Kamja," p. 364.

32. Ibid., p. 364.

33. Kunikida Doppo, "Gyūniku to bareisho," p. 384.

34. For more on Zhou Zuoren's ties to the Japanese literary world, see Chapters 1, 4, and 5.

35. Tanizaki talks about his impressions of Zhou Zuoren in "Reisei to yūkan," pp. 23–27.

36. Zhou Zuoren, "Ruce dushu," p. 509.

37. Ibid., p. 510.

38. Ibid., pp. 510–11. Cf. Erica Jong, *Fear of Flying*, pp. 25–26.

39. Zhou Zuoren, "Ruce dushu," p. 511.

40. Ibid., pp. 511–12.

41. Tanizaki Jun'ichirō, "In'ei raisan," pp. 515–57.

42. See Chapter 1 for more on Tanizaki's friendships with Chinese writers and his visits to China.

43. For more on sanitation in the Japanese colonial and semicolonial imperium, see Ruth Rogaski, *Hygienic Modernity*.

44. As John K. Gillespie summarizes, "Yokomitsu disparaged [the naturalist] approach to literature as trivial; there was more to artistic literary creation, he was convinced, than prosaically cataloguing facts. And he planted himself firmly against the increasingly popular proletarian literary forays, feeling that such politically laden works, by their insistence on dividing mankind into social classes, defeated the aims of art and failed to grasp fundamental humanity" ("Yokomitsu Riichi's Two Machines," p. 229).

45. For more on this phenomenon, see Zhang Zhang, "Zhang Tianyi yu waiguo wenxue," p. 195.

46. Zhang Tianyi, "Chouhen," p. 95.

47. Yokomitsu Riichi, "Jikan," pp. 191–92.

48. Zhang Tianyi, "Chouhen," p. 85.

49. Leo Ou-fan Lee, *Shanghai Modern*, pp. xi–xii, 3–7. See also Laikwan Pang, "The Collective Subjectivity of Chinese Intellectuals and Their Café Culture in Republican Shanghai," pp. 24–42. For alternative visions of early twentieth-century Shanghai, see Hanchao Lu, *Beyond the Neon Lights*; Jeffrey Wasserstrom, *Global Shanghai*; Meng Yue, *Shanghai and the Edges of Empires*. Christian Henriot and Wen-hsin Yeh's edited volume *In the Shadow of the Rising Sun* explores the economy, politics, and culture of Shanghai under Japanese occupation.

50. For more on Japanese literary works that take on Shanghai, see Zhao Mengyun, *Shanhai bungaku zanzō*. Also interesting in this context are the Japanese-born British author Kazuo Ishiguro's (1954–) novel *When We Were Orphans* (2000) and screenplay for *The White Countess* (2005). Numerous scholars have examined the place of Shanghai in modern Chinese literature. See, for

instance, Alexander Des Forges, *Mediasphere Shanghai*; Heiner Fruehauf, "Urban Exoticism in Modern and Contemporary Chinese Literature," pp. 133–64; Leo Ou-fan Lee, *Shanghai Modern*; Shu-mei Shih, *The Lure of the Modern*. For a general overview of the city in modern Chinese narrative, see Zhang Yingjin, *The City in Modern Chinese Literature and Film*.

51. Yokomitsu was one of the many celebrated Japanese writers who attended the dinner party arranged by the prominent Japanese publisher Kikuchi Kan for Mu Shiying on his visit to Japan in 1939. Mu Shiying reportedly shared with Yokomitsu his frustration with the Japanese literary world's seeming abandonment of neosensationalism and embrace of imperialist propaganda, but he is said to have resolved to work with Japanese writers for peace. Such dreams soon were shattered: a Guomindang agent assassinated Mu Shiying the following year. The September 1940 issue of the Japanese journal *Bungakukai* (Literary World), appearing several months after Mu Shiying's murder, carried a special section that provides some insight into how Mu was received by Japanese writers. See particularly Yokomitsu Riichi, "Mu Shiying shi no shi," pp. 174–75, cited in Shu-mei Shih, *The Lure of the Modern*, pp. 260, 334–38. See also Anthony Wan-hoi Pak, "The School of New Sensibilities (Xin'ganjuepai) in the 1930s," pp. 48–49.

52. Edward Gunn discusses the stylistic innovations of "Shanghai Foxtrot," as well as this story's recovery of several archaic forms, in *Rewriting Chinese*, pp. 125–26, 256–57.

53. Mu Shiying, "Shanghai de hubuwu," pp. 256–57. "Sonata" appears in English. Leo Lee notes that the reason neither Mu Shiying nor Liu Na'ou explicitly referred to Yokomitsu's *Shanghai* might have been that this novel was published after the neosensationalist school had disbanded and some of its members had turned to proletarian literature. Yet, as Lee stresses, "traces of Mu's imitation can still be discerned" (*Shanghai Modern*, p. 316).

54. Mu Shiying, "Shanghai de hubuwu," p. 257. Here Mu Shiying is referring to *Zhongguo yijiusanyi* (China 1931), a novel he hoped to write but never did. "Shanghai Foxtrot" was to be a fragment of this text, hence its full title "Shanghai hubuwu (yige duanpian)," or "Shanghai Foxtrot (a fragment)."

55. Gregory Golley, *When Our Eyes No Longer See*, pp. 135–36.

56. See Yokomitsu Riichi, *Shanhai*, p. 5; Mu Shiying, "Shanghai de hubuwu," p. 249.

57. Yokomitsu Riichi, *Shanhai*, p. 5.

58. Alexander Des Forges discusses the circular construction of "Shanghai Foxtrot" in *Mediasphere Shanghai*, pp. 156–58.

59. See, for instance, the opening lines of Mao Dun's massive novel *Ziye* (Midnight, 1933).

60. Mu Shiying, "Shanghai de hubuwu," p. 255.

61. Horst Bredekamp, "Artists as Criminals and the Concept of Absolutism."

62. Edward Lucie-Smith, ed., *The Faber Book of Art Anecdotes*, pp. 14–15, 80. See also Eric Michaud's discussion of the conviction of many artists that art is a "sublime mission that demands fanaticism" and how in certain situations

artists are held to different standards (*The Cult of Art in Nazi Germany*, pp. 2–17).

63. As William Tyler comments, "The Tattooer" and "Hell Screen" often are seen as "the beginnings of opposition to the literary school of Naturalism (*shizenshugi*) and the narrative style of the I-novel, which emphasized flat, unvarnished, and sincere depiction in contrast to the new, spectacle-driven narrative style of the modernists" (*Modanizumu*, p. 25).

64. In this they are reminiscent of Edgar Allen Poe's short story "The Oval Portrait" (1845), the tale of an obsessed artist who sacrifices his wife to paint her portrait.

65. Kim Dong-in's later "Kwanghwasa" (Mad Painter, 1935) explores similar questions, intertextually reworking these Japanese stories, and Tanizaki's "The Tattooer" in particular. See Karen Thornber, "Cultures and Texts in Motion," pp. 674–78. Several critics have noted similarities between Oscar Wilde's (1854–1900) novel *The Picture of Dorian Gray* (1890) and Kim Dong-in's two stories on violent artists, but *The Picture of Dorian Gray* depicts violence as facilitated by the work of art rather than, as "Mad Flame Sonata," "Mad Painter," and the Japanese stories speculate, as art's principal stimulus. Also important in this context are the Korean writer Yi Cheha's (1938–) lengthy novel *Kwanghwasa* (Mad Painter, 1986), which intertextualizes Kim Dong-in's story, and Mishima Yukio's kabuki play *Jigokuhen* (Hell Screen, 1953), which adapts Akutagawa's story. See also the American writer Ingrid J. Parker's novel *The Hell Screen* (2003) and Alvin Lu's (1969–) novel *The Hell Screens* (2000), set in Taipei.

66. Kim Dong-in, "Kwang-yŏm sonat'a," p. 51. In the opening paragraphs of "Mad Flame Sonata," the first-person narrator denies that his story took (or is taking) place in Korea but gives his protagonist a Korean name, suggesting that the story has a Korean connection after all. Significant too is the narrator's insinuation that Korea is decades behind Europe, a sentiment harbored by numerous early twentieth-century East Asian intellectuals: "It's fine if the reader thinks that the events of the tale I now am about to write happened somewhere in Europe. It's okay too if the reader thinks they might happen in Korea 40 or 50 years from now. These events might have happened somewhere on earth, might be happening now, or might happen in the future; all the reader needs to know is that they are possible. It's fine if the reader thinks of the hero of my story, Paek Sŏngsu, as an Albert, a Jim, a Mr. Hu, or a Mr. Kimura. It doesn't matter. The reader just needs to recognize that this is happening in the human world, with a man as the hero. That having been said, I begin my story" (p. 33).

67. Ibid., p. 35.

68. Akutagawa Ryūnosuke, "Jigokuhen," p. 157.

69. Yang Kui was only one of many colonial and semicolonial writers to reconfigure Sōseki's oeuvre intertextually. Others include, from China, Feng Zikai (1898–1975), Lao She, Lu Xun, Yu Dafu, and Zhou Zuoren. For more on Yang Kui's time in Japan and interactions with Japanese writers and literature, see Chapters 1 and 5.

70. For more on literary conscription, including the background of "Behind Increased Production," see Douglas Fix, "Conscripted Writers, Collaborating Tales?" pp. 19–41.

71. Yang Kui, "Zōsan no kage ni," p. 3.

72. Natsume Sōseki, *Kōfu*, pp. 335–36. The narrator's portrayal of miners echoes many early twentieth-century Japanese intellectuals' depictions of rural Japanese. See, for instance, Mikiso Hane, *Peasants, Rebels, and Outcastes*, pp. 34–36.

73. Natsume Sōseki, *Kōfu*, p. 463.

74. "Behind Increased Production" is not quite the "idyllic picture" of Taiwanese mining that some critics have claimed. See, for instance, Angelina C. Yee, "Constructing a Native Consciousness," p. 88.

75. Yang Kui, "Zōsan no kage ni," p. 6.

76. Douglas Fix, "Conscripted Writers," p. 25. Cf. Émile Zola, *Germinal*.

77. Ah Long, *Nanjing xueji*, pp. 222–23.

78. Ibid., p. 3.

79. Ibid., pp. 190–91. Most passages on the abuse of Chinese women in the "original" *Nanjing* were censored in the 1987 publication of the novel (Ken Sekine, "A Verbose Silence in 1939 Chongqing," p. 8). In *Orphan of Asia* (1945), the Taiwanese writer Wu Zhuoliu likewise speaks of the abuse of women from Jin Ling Women's University, revealing the soldiers' callousness. A young soldier tells the protagonist Taiming: "When we entered Nanjing, the refugee camps were teeming with female students from Jin Ling University. We had our pick. . . . [But] we didn't touch them. The battalion that arrived afterward, however, had older men in it, and they apparently made good work of the girls. What a missed opportunity!" (p. 219).

80. Ah Long, *Nanjing xueji*, p. 215.

81. Jonathan D. Spence, *The Search for Modern China*, p. 423. Ah Long was one of the few if not the only Chinese writer to expose the gruesome consequences of the Chinese scorched earth policy (Michael Berry, "A History of Pain," p. 80; *A History of Pain*, p. 148).

82. For more on the relationship between Ah Long's novel and Hino Ashihei's trilogy, as well as work by Tagore, see Akiyoshi Kukio, "Ā Ron [Ah Long] to Hino Ashihei no sensō bungaku."

83. Zhou Zuoren, "Sifa," p. 162.

84. See Masaoka Shiki, "Shigo," pp. 510–19.

85. Zhou Zuoren, "Sifa," p. 162.

Chapter 7

1. The principal contrast between Japanese naturalism and its offspring the I-novel on the one hand, and self-referential Chinese, Korean, and Taiwanese fiction on the other, generally is seen as the tendency of the latter to address broader social and national concerns. This tendency holds true for other intra–East Asian textual relationships.

2. Several critics have commented on the structural similarities between "Tangerines" and "A Small Incident." See, for instance, Aoyagi Tatsuo, "Akutagawa Ryūnosuke to kindai Chūgoku josetsu," pp. 157–77; Zhang Lei, *Akutagawa Ryūnosuke to Chūgoku*, pp. 39–98.

3. Akutagawa Ryūnosuke, "Mikan," p. 233.

4. Ibid., p. 233.

5. Lu Xun, "Yijian xiaoshi," p. 49.

6. Akutagawa Ryūnosuke, "Mikan," p. 235.

7. Thanks to Perry Link for alerting me to this interpretation of "A Small Incident."

8. Lu Xun, "Yijian xiaoshi," p. 54.

9. Ba Jin, "Yijian xiaoshi," p. 162.

10. Ibid., p. 163. See also Zhang Tianyi, "Yijian xiaoshi," pp. 297–320.

11. Natsume Sōseki, *Kusamakura*, pp. 417–18.

12. Ibid., p. 425.

13. Ibid., p. 521.

14. Ibid., pp. 584–85.

15. Yu Dafu, "Chiguihua," p. 697.

16. Ibid., p. 709.

17. Ibid., p. 718.

18. Ibid., p. 717.

19. Ibid., p. 722.

20. Ibid., p. 727.

21. Natsume Sōseki, *Kusamakura*, p. 582.

22. Ibid., p. 584. For more on railways as rupture in early twentieth-century Japanese literature, see Stephen Dodd, *Writing Home*, pp. 106–12.

23. Olga Lang summarizes these relationships in *Pa Chin and His Writings*, pp. 218–54.

24. For more on Ba Jin's criticism of Japanese literature and Tōson in particular, see Chapter 2. Also interesting in this context is the Manchuria-based writer Gu Ding's novel *Xinsheng* (New Life, 1944), which speaks of relationships with Japanese counterparts.

25. Ōbayashi Shigeru and Kitabayashi Masae, eds., "Kinoshita Junji to no kaiwa," p. 329.

26. For more on Chengdu at this time, see Di Wang, *Street Culture in Chengdu* and *The Teahouse*. For more on travel in Tokugawa Japan, see Constantine Vaporis, *Breaking Barriers*. See also Mary Elizabeth Berry, *Japan in Print*.

27. Michael Bourdaghs discusses the politics of Tōson's *Family* in *The Dawn That Never Comes*, pp. 77–113.

28. For more on this phenomenon, see Chapter 8.

29. Shimazaki Tōson, *Ie*, p. 159.

30. Ba Jin, *Jia*, p. 3.

31. The trilogy consists of *Family* (1932), *Spring* (1938), and *Qiu* (Fall, 1940).

32. Shimazaki Tōson, *Ie*, p. 425.

33. Ba Jin, *Jia*, pp. 427–28.

34. See Ba Jin, "*Jiliu* zongxu," pp. iii–iv.

35. For more on Yŏm Sangsŏp's experiences in Japan, see Shirakawa Yutaka (Sirakkawa Yuttakka), "Hanguk kŭndae munhak," pp. 38–45.

36. Yŏm Sangsŏp, "Munhak so-nyŏn sidae ŭi hoesang," p. 215. Yŏm Sangsŏp also acknowledges this influence in "Na wa *P'yeho sidae*," p. 210.

37. See Yŏm Sangsŏp, *Samdae*, pp. 11–16.

38. Ibid., pp. 417–18.

39. See ibid., pp. 42–51.

40. Zhou Zuoren published a translation of Senge's "Flies" in 1920. For more on his involvement with Senge's works, see Yu Yaoming, *Shū Sakujin* [Zhou Zuoren] *to Nihon kindai bungaku*, pp. 125–51. Reconfigurations of Japanese dramas, essays, novels, poems, and short stories appear throughout Zhou Zuoren's oeuvre. For more on his engagement with Japan and Japanese textual products, see Chapters 1, 2, 3, and 6.

41. See Senge Motomaro, "Hae," p. 125; Zhou Zuoren, "Cangying," in *Zhou Zuoren zibian wenji* 9, p. 24.

42. It is possible that the essay "Flies" was motivated in part by the publication of Yokomitsu Riichi's short story "The Fly" (Hae, 1923), which echoes Senge's and Zhou Zuoren's poems but returns the focus to impoverished individuals. See Yokomitsu Riichi, "Hae," pp. 191–95.

43. Zhou Zuoren, "Cangying," in *Zhou Zuoren ji* 1, pp. 99–100.

44. Ibid., p. 101.

45. For more on Satō Haruo and Yu Dafu's relationship, see Chapter 1.

46. Cited by Oda Takeo, *Iku Tatsufu* [Yu Dafu] *den*, pp. 48–49.

47. Satō Haruo, *Den'en no yūutsu*, p. 3.

48. Yu Dafu, "Chenlun," p. 1.

49. Satō Haruo, *Den'en no yūutsu*, pp. 10–11.

50. William Blake, "The Sick Rose," in *Blake*, p. 223. An earlier, slightly different version of "The Sick Rose" appeared in *Poems from the Notebook* (1792). *Blake*, p. 166.

51. Satō Haruo, *Den'en no yūutsu*, p. 50.

52. Yu Dafu, "Chenlun," p. 8.

53. Ibid., p. 35.

54. The notes appended to "Yokohama Pier under the Umbrella" in the *Im Hwa chŏnjip* (The Complete Works of Im Hwa, 2000) refer to this text as a "response" to Nakano's poem ("Usan pat-ŭn Yok'ohama ŭi pudu," p. 70). See also Kim Yunsik, *Im Hwa yŏn-gu*, p. 247; Ōmaki Fujio, "Nakano Shigeharu to Chōsen," p. 108.

55. Im Hwa once remarked that he learned of Nakano while growing up in Korea, reading Japanese journals such as *Central Review* and *Reconstruction*. Cited in Han Kyejŏn [Han Kye Jeon] et al., "1930 nyŏndae Hanguk munhak ŭi pigyo munhakjŏk yŏn-gu," p. 38. In an August 1933 article, Im Hwa spoke explicitly of his admiration for Nakano's poetry. Cited in Ko Yŏngja [Ko Young-Ja], "Nakano Shigeharu to Rin Wa [Im Hwa]," p. 192.

56. Gayatri Spivak addresses similar concerns in *Critique of Postcolonial Reasoning*, where she censures the tendency to view subalterns as potential sources of change.

57. Nakano Shigeharu, "Ame no furu Shinagawa eki" (1929), pp. 82–83.

58. Ibid., p. 82.

59. Im Hwa, "Usan pat-ŭn Yok'ohama ŭi pudu," p. 66; Nakano Shigeharu, "Ame no furu Shinagawa eki" (1929), p. 82.

60. Im Hwa, "Usan pat-ŭn Yok'ohama ŭi pudu," p. 67.

61. In fact, the Japanese government supported romantic relations between colonized and colonizer, proclaiming marriages between Koreans and Japanese patriotic acts; couples who intermarried received official recognition. Kimberley Kono notes that when Nashimoto Masako and Yi Ŭn (Prince Yŏng), members of the Japanese and Korean royalty, married only a year after the March First Movement (1919), their union was described as a stellar example of *naisen chōwa* (harmonious relations between Japanese and Koreans) and *naisen ittai* (Japan and Korea as one body), popular slogans in the colonial period ("Writing Imperial Relations," pp. 96–99). On the other hand, a conservative faction of the imperial bureaucracy strongly resisted this union, believing it antithetical to Japan's imperial myth (Christine Kim, "Imperial Hangover," p. 2). Intermarriage appears frequently in colonial-period Japanese literature, but rarely without exposing the darker underbelly of this phenomenon. See, for instance, Sakaguchi Reiko (1914–), "Tokeisō" (Passionflower, 1943); Yuasa Katsue (1910–82), "Natsume" (Jujube, 1937); Yokota Fumiko (1909–85), "Koibumi" (Love Letter, 1942). Writing by Koreans on the theme "Japanese-Korean romance" (*naesŏn yŏn-ae*) also flourished. See, for instance, Ōya Chihiro, "Chapji 'Naesŏn ilch'e' e nat'a-nan naesŏn kyŏlhon ŭi yangsang yŏn-gu," 271–72. Cited by Christine Kim, "Imperial Hangover," p. 4.

62. Im Hwa, "Usan pat-ŭn Yok'ohama ŭi pudu," p. 68.

63. Nakano's concern with the future of Korea was reflected in *Proletarian Arts*, which contained numerous articles on Korea and texts by Koreans. See Ogasawara Masaru, "Nakano Shigeharu to Chōsen (1)," pp. 162–64; Takagawa Mayumi, "Nakano Shigeharu ron," pp. 78–98. For more on the ties between Nakano and Korean revolutionaries, see Chapters 1 and 4.

64. Im Hwa, "Usan pat-ŭn Yok'ohama ŭi pudu," p. 69.

65. Ibid., p. 69.

66. Nakano Shigeharu, "Ame no furu Shinagawa eki" (1929), p. 83.

67. Nakano Shigeharu, "Pi nal-i nŭn P'umch'ŏn-yŏk" (1929), p. 69.

68. Im Hwa, "Usan pat-ŭn Yok'ohama ŭi pudu," p. 69.

69. Im Hwa's transposition of Nakano's "Shinagawa Station in the Rain" and especially of the Japanese poem's Korean translation provides an interesting comparison with Aimé Césaire's reconfiguration of the French writer Prosper Mérimée's (1803–70) influential short story "Tamango" (1829) in his *Cahier d'un retour au pays natal* (Notebook of a Return to My Native Land, 1939). Césaire likewise rewrites a bloody massacre as a bloodless revolt: "Working intertextually, as he so often does in the *Cahier*, Césaire is able to recuperate and rehabilitate . . . [the image] of a ship full of revolted slaves . . . rescuing the image from the corrosive, disabling irony with which Mérimée had covered it" (Christopher L. Miller, *The French Atlantic Triangle*, p. 222). Yet Césaire's text, unlike Im Hwa's, depicts the slaves as "standing / and / free."

70. For more on Chinese fascination with Kobayashi, see Lu Yuanming, *Riben wenxue lunshi jianji Zhong-Ri bijiao wenxue,* pp. 269–72; Shirakaba Bungakukan Takiji Raiburarī, ed., *Ima Chūgoku ni yomigaeru Kobayashi Takiji no bungaku.* For more on Kobayashi and Korea, see Izu Toshihiko, "Teikoku-shugi to bungaku." Kobayashi's work currently is enjoying a resurgence of popularity in Japan, with publishers experiencing sales "almost unheard of" for a work from that period ("1929 Proletarian Novel Hits Home with Workers," p. 3). See also Norma Field, "Commercial Appetite and Human Need."

71. Kobayashi also was inspired by the Japanese proletarian writer Hayama Yoshiki's groundbreaking novel *Umi ni ikiru hitobito* (People Who Live on the Sea, 1926), which exposes the cruel treatment of workers on a ship carrying coal along Japan's coast.

72. Kobayashi Takiji, *Kani kōsen,* p. 126.

73. Kobayashi Takiji, *Kani kōsen,* p. 58. Japan seized all of Sakhalin in the final days of the Russo-Japanese War, and although forced to return the northern part of the island to Russia as part of the Portsmouth Peace Treaty, Japan administered the southern part, which it called Karafuto, as a colony until the end of World War Two.

74. Kobayashi Takiji, *Kani kōsen,* p. 63.

75. For more on Yang Kui's experiences in Japan, interactions with Japanese writers, and engagement with Japanese literature, see Chapters 1, 5, and 6.

76. Kobayashi Takiji, *Teihon Kobayashi Takiji zenshū* 14, p. 50.

77. Cited in Lu Yuanming, *Riben wenxue lunshi jianji Zhong-Ri bijiao wenxue,* p. 270.

78. Chinese, Korean, and Taiwanese writers also intertextualized one another's literary works to provide different perspectives on these and other relationships. For instance, the Taiwanese writer Lai He recasts Lu Xun's short story "Hometown" in his short story "Guijia" (Returning Home, 1932) to underline the deeper connections of a Taiwanese intellectual to his place of origin than is true of his Chinese counterpart, despite or perhaps because of Japanese colonialism. For more on this recasting, see Karen Thornber, "Cultures and Texts in Motion," pp. 570–79.

Chapter 8

1. Josna E. Rege discusses this phenomenon in *Colonial Karma.*

2. Harsha Ram, "Towards a Cross-cultural Poetics of the Contact Zone," p. 81. Interestingly, as Ram also notes, in his Russian translation of this poem Boris Pasternak reversed many of these changes, attenuating T'itsian's "personal pessimism . . . and the skepticism about the efficacy of the poet's role" (p. 85). Georgia was incorporated into the Soviet Union in 1922 and did not regain independence until 1991.

3. Peter Hill, *Fate, Predestination and Human Action in the Mahābhārata,* pp. 195, 197. Dalya Cohen-Mor makes similar comments in *A Matter of Fate,* p. 239. For more on global understandings of fate, see Helmer Ringgren, ed., *Fatalistic Beliefs in Religion, Folklore, and Literature.* The term "fate" generally

differs in nuance from chance, destiny, divine intervention, fortune, luck, providence, and other similar terms, yet all imply that what has happened, is happening, and will happen ultimately is beyond the individual's, and often human, control.

4. Homer, *The Iliad*, p. 507.

5. Homer, *The Odyssey*, p. 186.

6. Albert Camus, "Le mythe de Sisyphe," p. 166.

7. Ralph Waldo Emerson, "Fate," p. 27.

8. I list a variety of examples from East Asia in "Cultures and Texts in Motion," pp. 625–26. See also Sabina Knight, *The Heart of Time*; and Christopher Lupke, ed., *The Magnitude of Ming*.

9. East Asian writers whose texts allude to Katai's work include Lu Xun, Yu Dafu, Hyŏn Chin-gŏn, and Kim Dong-in. For more on the impact of Katai's work across East Asia, see An Yŏnghŭi, "Han-Il kŭndae sosŏl e nat'a-nan ko-paekch'e tamron ŭi chŏn-gae," pp. 103–26; Tomonaga Nori, "Pigyo munhak-jŏk ŭ ro pon Chŏnsan Katae [Tayama Katai] wa Hyŏn Chin-gŏn," pp. 381–401. For more on Doppo's life, oeuvre, and impact on colonial and semicolonial writers, see Chapters 5 and 6.

10. These include texts by Futabatei Shimei, Kunikida Doppo, Iwano Hō-mei, Natsume Sōseki, Shiga Naoya, Shimazaki Tōson, and Tayama Katai. For further discussion of the connections between Hyŏn Chin-gŏn's texts and Japanese literature, see Chŏng Inmun, "Hyŏn Chin-gŏn ch'ogi sosŏl kwa Il-bon munhak kwa ŭi kwanryŏn yangsang," pp. 155–73. For more on Kim Dong-in's life, work, and connections with Japanese writers and literature, see Chapters 1, 5, and 6. Kim Dong-in lived in Japan from 1914 to 1919.

11. Hyŏn Chin-gŏn, "Sul kwŏnhanŭn sahoe," p. 230.

12. Ibid., pp. 232–33.

13. Ibid., p. 231.

14. Ibid., pp. 231–32.

15. Hyŏn Chin-gŏn was an avid reader of Chekhov and was familiar with "Sleepy," but it is unclear whether he was aware of "The-Child-Who-Was-Tired." Mansfield's and Chekhov's stories are so similar that she was accused of plagiarism. See Anton Chekhov, "Sleepy," pp. 75–82; Katherine Mansfield, "The Child-Who-Was-Tired," pp. 71–80.

16. The voice of the primary narrator of *The End of Jūemon* is heard only in the opening sentences, where he mentions a gathering of intellectuals discussing the Russian novelist Ivan Turgenev (1818–83). *Jibun*, the secondary narrator, comments that thinking about Turgenev has reminded him of a man he met who could have come directly from one of the Russian writer's short stories. The remainder of *The End of Jūemon* consists of *jibun*'s summary of his experiences.

17. Tayama Katai, *Jūemon no saigo*, p. 367.

18. Ibid., p. 381.

19. Hyŏn Chin-gŏn, "Pul," p. 206.

20. For more on the Korean system of *minmyŏnŭri*, see Theodore Jun Yoo, *The Politics of Gender in Colonial Korea*, pp. 172–76.

21. Secondary witnesses are those who learn about a crime after it has been committed. For more on the relationship between the work of Doppo and that of Kim Dong-in, and the ties between "The Seaman's Chant" and both "Woman Trouble" and "The Fatalist" in particular, see Chong Inmun, "Kim Dong-in ŭi Ilbon kŭndae munhak suyong yŏn-gu," pp. 135–54. See also Chapters 1, 5, and 6.

22. The framework of "Woman Trouble" and "The Seaman's Chant" echoes that of the celebrated Tang poet Bai Juyi's "Pipa xing" (Song of the Lute): a man hears stirring music, approaches the performer, and learns the sad story of the performer's life. But whereas "Woman Trouble" and "The Seaman's Chant" focus almost entirely on the musician's story, the "Song of the Lute" mixes in the narrator's own laments.

23. Kunikida Doppo, "Jonan," p. 219.

24. Ibid., p. 225.

25. Kim Dong-in's later "Mad Flame Sonata" (1929) does the same in its reconfiguration of Akutagawa's "Hell Screen" (1918). See Chapter 6 for more on the reworking of Japanese literature in "Mad Flame Sonata."

26. Kim Dong-in, "Paettaragi," p. 192.

27. Ibid., p. 198.

28. Ibid., p. 200.

29. All three stories draw from Lu Xun's "Regret for the Past: Juansheng's Notes" (1925). See Karen Thornber, "Cultures and Texts in Motion," pp. 684–721. "Wings" also intertextualizes such creative works as Yu Dafu's short story "Intoxicating Spring Nights" (1923), satirizing the unemployed intellectual's repeated attempts to portray himself as more deserving of pity than the truly destitute.

30. Hwang Sŏksung (Hwang Seock-Soong), "Kaech'ŏn Ryongjigae [Akutagawa Ryūnosuke] ŭi munhak kwa Yi Sang ŭi sosŏl," p. 186.

31. Yi Sang did not travel to Japan until September 1936, less than a year before his death. His work has been likened to that of the Japanese modernist writers Akutagawa Ryūnosuke, Kitasono Katsue, Ogata Kamenosuke (1900–42), and Yokomitsu Riichi, as well as a plethora of European writers, particularly Jean Cocteau (1889–1963).

32. Akutagawa Ryūnosuke, "Aru ahō no isshō," p. 47.

33. Ibid., p. 48.

34. Ibid., p. 65.

35. Akutagawa Ryūnosuke, "Haguruma," p. 85.

36. Ibid., pp. 74–75.

37. Ibid., p. 76.

38. Ibid., p. 84. The car in question is likely a Rolls Royce, which for nearly a century sported a sculpture of a flying woman, the Spirit of Ecstasy by Charles Robinson Sykes. In the 1930s, several other car manufacturers adorned their products with wings (Jerry Garrett, "Civil War?" p. D9).

39. Ibid., p. 69. Italics here indicate the use of Western-language words in the Japanese text.

40. Ibid., p. 55.

41. Ibid., p. 57

42. Seiji M. Lippit, *Topographies of Japanese Modernism*, p. 56.

43. Akutagawa Ryūnosuke, "Haguruma," pp. 62–63.

44. Ibid., pp. 77–78.

45. Ibid., p. 78.

46. Ibid., p. 68.

47. Ibid., p. 85.

48. Several scholars have examined the close relationship between Yi Sang's "Wings" and Akutagawa's "A Fool's Life" and "Cogwheels." See, for instance, O Yumi, "Yi Sang munhak ŭi oeraejŏk yoso yŏn-gu," pp. 205–43; Hwang Sŏksung (Hwang Seock-Soong), "Kaech'ŏn Ryongjigae [Akutagawa Ryūnosuke] ŭi munhak kwa Yi Sang ŭi sosŏl." Chang Hyejŏng (Chang Hae-jung) examines the relationship between "Cogwheels" and another of Yi Sang's stories — "Silhwa" (Losing Flowers, 1939) — in "Ak'ut'agawa (Akuta-gawa) wa Yi Sang munhak e nat'a-nan 'ŭisik ŭi hŭ-rŭm' ki-pŏp."

49. The Korean writer Kim Yongho (1912–73) gives another alternative in his poem "Nalgae (II)" (Wings (II), 1952), which features a poet having climbed a ladder that Time has removed and asking his mother why she "forgot to give me wings" (Kim Yongho, "Nalgae (II)," p. 183). See also Kim Yongho's poem "Nalgae (I), 1954" (p. 163). Both poems appear in his collection *Nalgae (Kim Yongho si chŏnjip*, pp. 149–203).

50. Yi Sang, "Nalgae," p. 149.

51. Ibid., p. 155.

52. Ibid., p. 160.

53. Kazumi Ishii, "*Josei*," p. 8; Jun Uchida, "'Brokers of Empire,'" pp. 125–26. For more on the colonial transformation of Korean city space, see Todd A. Henry, "Respatializing Chosŏn's Royal Capital," pp. 15–38; Hong Seong-tae, "From Mount Baekak to the Han River," pp. 121–35.

54. Yi Sang, "Nalgae," p. 176.

55. Ibid., p. 176.

56. For more on Bandō and his activities in Korea, see Chapter 1.

57. Although *na* first explicitly laments the loss of his artificial wings (*in-gong ŭi nalgae*), when he calls for wings (*nalgae*) to grow (*tutda*) in the penultimate line of "Wings" without referring to them as either "natural" or "artificial," he suggests that at one time he might have possessed more "natural" wings.

58. Yi Sang, "Nalgae," p. 176.

59. Contemporary writing that intertextually reconfigures Yi Sang's "Wings" also draws attention to this absence, including Kim Sŏkhŭi's (1952-) "Yi Sang ŭi nalgae" (Yi Sang's Wings, 1988) and Ha Sŏngran's (1967-) "Ch'on-nong nalgae" (Waxen Wings, 1999). "Yi Sang's Wings" focuses on a writer named Yi Sang, whose life initially resembles *na*'s. After discovering that he can fly, the fictional Yi Sang wreaks havoc on society. But he eventually retreats to his bedding; flying grants him a variety of freedoms, but he makes little progress. Kim Sŏkhŭi's narrator undermines *na*'s perseverance by positing flying as only a beginning and suggesting that possibilities of growth are com-

promised. See "Yi Sang ŭi nalgae," pp. 10–30. Bruce Fulton discusses the relationship between "Yi Sang's Wings" and "Wings" in "Wings and Wiggles," pp. 65–75. "Waxen Wings" features a young woman who, taking up hang gliding, finally attains the flight she has been dreaming of since childhood, when her teacher feared she would jump off the roof (perhaps like *na*). But a sudden gust of wind interrupts her jump from a mountain cliff, and despite everything she loses a leg. Time literally stops for her, the narrator announcing in the opening and closing sections that "it is always 3:14." Her first attempt to "fly" after her accident—by jumping off a swing that she has propelled to its maximum height—results in her body landing in a heap on the ground; for its part, her prosthetic leg flies out from under her skirt, hits a seesaw, and drops to the ground. She awakens in the ICU, able only to imagine half of her body hanging (rather than flying) in the air.

60. Henry Em refers to "Wings" as the first-person narrator's "silent soliloquy" because *na* does not say anything in the narrative ("Yi Sang's *Wings* Read as an Anti-colonial Allegory," p. 106).

61. Cf. Idem.

62. The conclusion of "Wings" also differentiates this story from the Japanese modernist writer Yokomitsu Riichi's short story "Tori" (Bird, 1930). Having suffered numerous relationship woes, the narrator of "Bird" takes an airplane ride with his wife and reaches his own "epiphany." He states that he "has become a bird" and that his wings "hit the mountains"; he concludes with the claim that he and his wife are now remarried ("Tori," pp. 344–56). *Na* is denied such a joyous, albeit escapist, ending.

63. Lu Xun, "Wo zenme zuoqi xiaoshuo lai," p. 511. Lu Xun was particularly fascinated with Sōseki's sense of humor and his "dilettante" (*yoyū*) style. See Wang Xiangyuan, *Zhong-Ri xiandai wenxue bijiaolun*, pp. 234–44.

64. For more on Hakuson's popularity in China, see Chapter 4. For more on the impact of Hakuson's essays on Lu Xun's writing and thought in particular, see Aiura Takashi, *Chūgoku bungaku ronkō*, pp. 41–86. Discussions of the similarities between *Ten Nights of Dreams* and *Wild Grass* include Lin Cong, "Ro Jin [Lu Xun] no *Yecao* ni okeru Sōseki no *Yume jūya* no eikyō," pp. 35–48; Li Guodong (Ri Kokutō), *Ro Jin [Lu Xun] to Sōseki no hikaku bungakuteki kenkyū*, pp. 128–44; Wang Xiangyuan, *Zhong-Ri xiandai wenxue bijiaolun*, pp. 336–46.

65. A compelling example of the magnification of the grotesque in *Wild Grass* takes place in "Mujiewen" (The Epitaph), which intertextualizes "Daiichiya" (The First Night), the first section of *Ten Nights of Dreams*, to underline the horrors of death.

66. "The Passerby" also reconfigures "Daisan'ya" (The Third Night) and "Daiyon'ya" (The Fourth Night), but the recasting of "The Seventh Night" is the most dramatic.

67. Natsume Sōseki, "Dainanaya," p. 118.

68. Lu Xun, "Guoke," pp. 189–90.

69. Ibid., p. 193.

70. Ibid., p. 191.

71. Natsume Sōseki, "Daijūya," p. 122.

72. Lu Xun, "Zheyang de zhanshi," p. 214.

73. Ibid., p. 214.

74. Ibid., p. 215.

75. In *Wild Grass*, the nonhuman also fights through death and nothingness. "Qiuye" (Autumn Night) depicts a tree that refuses to remain still even when stripped of its fruit and foliage and left for dead: "The straightest and longest branches, rigid as iron, silently stab the strange high sky, making it glitter and blink devilishly. They pierce the full moon in the sky, turning it pale and ill at ease . . . [they] stab the strange high sky, determined to take its life" (Lu Xun, "Qiuye," p. 163). For another vision of life after death in *Wild Grass*, see Lu Xun's "Sihou" (After Death), the section that precedes "This Kind of Warrior."

76. Albert Camus, "Le mythe de Sisyphe," pp. 165, 168.

77. Hayashi Fusao, "Mayu," p. 11.

78. C. T. Hsia, *A History of Modern Chinese Fiction*, p. 546. See also David Der-wei Wang, *Fictional Realism in Twentieth-Century China*, p. 139.

79. In 1922, Zhou Zuoren claimed that the "origin of the technique" of "The True Story of Ah Q" lay in the work of Gogol and Sienkiewicz, while texts by Ōgai and Sōseki exerted a "considerable influence." He mentions specifically "The Overcoat," "The Madman's Diary," "Charcoal Sketches," "Sachem," *I Am a Cat*, and Ōgai's "Chinmoku no tō" (Tower of Silence, 1910). Zhou Zuoren, "A Q zhengzhuan," p. 227; Patrick Hanan, "The Technique of Lu Hsun's Fiction," p. 57. See Henryk Sienkiewicz, "Bartek the Conqueror," pp. 85–141. David Der-wei Wang draws attention to late Qing echoes in "The True Story of Ah Q" in *Fin-de-Siècle Splendor*, pp. 245–46.

80. Natsume Sōseki, *Wagahai wa neko de aru*, p. 11.

81. Lu Xun, "A Q zhengzhuan," pp. 83–88.

82. Natsume Sōseki, *Wagahai wa neko de aru*, pp. 580–81.

83. Lu Xun, "A Q zhengzhuan," p. 131.

84. *Wagahai*'s death is doubtful considering the eloquence with which he describes it; the narrative suggests that he either imagined his death or was rescued just in time.

85. For more on the reception of Lao She in Japan, see Meng Zeren, "Yin zai Riben de shenshen de zuji," pp. 215–24.

86. The 1928 translation of *Kappa* was reissued in 1936; another translation of *Kappa* was published in 1941.

87. See Hao Changhai, "Lao She yu waiguo wenxue," p. 1010, cited in David Der-wei Wang, *Fictional Realism in Twentieth-Century China*, p. 136. *City of Cats* also might have served as an inspiration for Val Lewton's (1904–51) horror film *Cat People* (1942).

88. H. G. Wells, *The First Men in the Moon*, p. 262.

89. *Kappa* actually contains two first-person narrators. The text opens with a preface by *boku*, who tells the reader that what follows is the story narrated to him by Patient No. 23 of a Japanese mental hospital. At the beginning of the

first chapter, *boku* turns the text over to this man, who also refers to himself as *boku*.

90. Akutagawa Ryūnosuke, *Kappa*, p. 125.

91. Lao She, *Maochengji*, p. 223.

92. Akutagawa Ryūnosuke, *Kappa*, p. 107.

93. Lao She, *Maochengji*, p. 153.

94. Ibid., p. 298.

95. Ibid., p. 195.

96. Shimomura Sakujirō, "Reverse Exportation from Japan," p. 285. See Murakami Genzō, *Sayon no kane*, pp. 49–66.

97. See Wu Mansha, *Shayang de zhong*. See also Wu Mansha's article on his version of *Bell of Sayon*, "*Shayang de zhong* xiaoshuo kanxing de qianyan," pp. 17–18. The previous year, Wu Mansha published a poem on Sayon, "Shayang de zhong" (Bell of Sayon, July 1942), that provides an interesting foretaste of the 1943 text.

98. Emilie Yueh-yu Yeh and Darrell William Davis, *Taiwan Film Directors*, p. 16. The role of Sayon was played by Yamaguchi Yoshiko (screen name Ri Kōran). Shimomura Sakujirō anthologizes the various versions of the Sayon story and provides much helpful information in "*Sayon no kane*" *kankei shiryō-shū*.

Epilogue

1. Consumers in East Asia at times are more familiar with cultural products from elsewhere in the region than with those from closer to home. For instance, many Hong Kongers know more about Japanese *manga* than they do about Hong Kong film, which has a greater following in Shanghai than in Hong Kong (Leo Ou-fan Lee, "City between Worlds").

2. Carter Eckert et al., *Korea Old and New*, p. 336.

3. Yim Kyung Taek et al., "Roundtable: What Is an East Asia Publishing Network?" Thanks to Henry Smith for bringing this network to my attention.

4. Pak Wansŏ (Wan-Suh Park), "The Act of Writing in a Postcolonial Situation," pp. 476–77.

5. Ibid., pp. 478–79.

6. Most postwar Japanese-language poetry writing in Korea has been clandestine. See Choe Sang-hun, "Japanese Poetry Persists in Korea, Despite Disapproval," p. A10.

7. For instance, the leaders of China, Japan, and South Korea held their first-ever trilateral summit on December 12, 2008.

8. Between 1961 and 1995, *Snow Country* was translated into Korean nearly 50 times.

9. Charles Cabell, "Kawabata Yasunari," p. 159.

10. Ibid., p. 162. See also Charles Cabell, "Maiden Dreams."

11. See Julia Lovell, *The Politics of Cultural Capital*, p. 139.

12. Quoted ibid., p. 112. See also pp. 139–41.

13. Lin Shaohua, "Murakami Haruki no bungaku sekai to Chūgoku gendai seinen no seishin kōzō," p. 109.

14. See Murakami Haruki, *Hitsuji o meguru bōken, Nejimakidori kuronikuru,* and *Noruwei no mori.*

15. See Fujii Shōzō, *Murakami Haruki no naka no Chūgoku* for more on the place of China in Murakami's work and Rebecca Suter, *The Japanization of Modernity* for more on Murakami as cultural mediator.

16. Lai Mingzhu, "Yixu," p. 7.

17. "Young Women Spearhead Japanese Literary Wave." See Shibata Motoyuki et al., eds., *A Wild Haruki Chase* for more on Murakami's popularity across East Asia. The Taehan Ch'ulp'an Munhwa Hyŏphoe (Korean Publishers Association) estimates that in 2006, 42 percent of all translated books were translations from Japanese to Korean. Some South Korean literary critics attribute the popularity of Japanese literature in Korea in part to shortcomings in contemporary Korean literature (Yang Sun Jin, "South Korean Literary Market Hurt by Cyberspace, Japanese Novels," p. 22).

18. See Arishima Takeo, *Kain no matsuei,* pp. 87–128; Hwang Sunwŏn, *K'ain ŭi huye,* pp. 171–364. Hwang received a degree in English from Waseda University in Tokyo in 1939; his adviser was Tanizaki Jun'ichirō's brother Seiji, whom he described as a "major influence" on him.

19. Kohō Banri, "Maegaki," p. 11.

20. See Kawabata Yasunari, *Koto,* pp. 229–435; Zhu Tianxin, *Gudu,* pp. 151–233.

Works Cited

Abe Hiroshi. "Kyūkanmatsu no Nihon ryūgaku (1): shiryōteki kōsatsu." *Han* 3:5 (May 1974), pp. 63-83.

———. "Kyūkanmatsu no Nihon ryūgaku (2): shiryōteki kōsatsu." *Han* 3:6 (June 1974), pp. 95-116.

———. "Kyūkanmatsu no Nihon ryūgaku (3): shiryōteki kōsatsu." *Han* 3:7 (July 1974), pp. 103-27.

Abe Kazuhiro. "Race Relations and the Capitalist State: A Case Study of Koreans in Japan, 1917 through the Mid-1920s." *Korean Studies* 7 (1983), pp. 35-60.

Abrams, Meyer Howard. *A Glossary of Literary Terms*, 6th ed. Fort Worth, TX: Harcourt Brace College Publishers, 1993.

Achebe, Chinua. *Things Fall Apart*. London: Heinemann Educational Books, 1958.

Adorno, Theodor W. *Aesthetic Theory*. London: Routledge and Kegan Paul, 1984. Translated by C. Lenhardt.

Ah Long. *Ā Ron* [Ah Long] *shishū*. Tokyo: Doyō Bijutsusha, 1997. Translated by Akiyoshi Kukio.

———. *Nanjing xueji*. Beijing: Renmin Wenxue Chubanshe, 1987.

Aiura Takashi. *Chūgoku bungaku ronkō*. Tokyo: Miraisha, 1990.

Akiyoshi Kukio. "Ā Ron [Ah Long] to Hino Ashihei no sensō bungaku: Ā Ron [Ah Long] no sakuhin *Nankyō* [Nanjing] o jiku to shite," in *Ā Ron* [Ah Long] *shishū*. Tokyo: Doyō Bijutsusha, 1997. Translated by Akiyoshi Kukio. Pp. 264-97.

Akutagawa Ryūnosuke. "Aru ahō no isshō," in *Akutagawa Ryūnosuke zenshū* 16. Tokyo: Iwanami Shoten, 1977. Pp. 37-67.

———. "Chōkō yūki," in *Akutagawa Ryūnosuke zenshū* 11. Tokyo: Iwanami Shoten, 1996. Pp. 251-63.

———. "Haguruma," in *Akutagawa Ryūnosuke zenshū* 15. Tokyo: Iwanami Shoten, 1997. Pp. 40-85.

——. "Jigokuhen," in *Akutagawa Ryūnosuke zenshū* 3. Tokyo: Iwanami Shoten, 1996. Pp. 156–201.

——. *Kappa*, in *Akutagawa Ryūnosuke zenshū* 14. Tokyo: Iwanami Shoten, 1996. Pp. 102–72.

——. "Mikan," in *Akutagawa Ryūnosuke zenshū* 4. Tokyo: Iwanami Shoten, 1996. Pp. 231–36.

——. "Nihon shōsetsu no Shinayaku," in *Akutagawa Ryūnosuke zenshū* 7. Tokyo: Iwanami Shoten, 1978. Pp. 253–55.

——. "Shanhai yūki," in *Akutagawa Ryūnosuke zenshū* 8. Tokyo: Iwanami Shoten, 1996. Pp. 6–65.

Allen, Graham. *Intertextuality*. New York: Routledge, 2000.

Allen, Joseph R. "Taipei Park: Signs of Occupation." *Journal of Asian Studies* 66:1 (February 2007), pp. 159–99.

Allen, Matthew and Rumi Sakamoto, eds. *Popular Culture, Globalization and Japan*. New York: Routledge, 2006.

Allen, Sharon Lubkemann. "Metamorphosis: From Dostoevsky & Machado de Assis to Verrissimo, Lispector & Pelevin." Paper given at the American Comparative Literature Association Annual Conference, Princeton University, March 24, 2006.

Amyuni, Mona Takieddine, ed. *Season of Migration to the North by Tayeb Salih: A Casebook*. Beirut: American University of Beirut, 1985.

An Ushiku (An Usik). *Kin Shiryō* [Kim Saryang]: *sono teikō no shōgai*. Tokyo: Iwanami Shoten, 1972.

An Yŏnghŭi. "Han-Il kŭndae sosŏl e nat'a-nan ko-paekch'e tamron ŭi chŏngae: Tayama Kat'ai [Tayama Katai], Yiwano Homei [Iwano Hōmei], Kim Dong-in," in Saegusa Toshikatsu (Saegusa Tosik'assŭ), ed. *Hanguk kŭndae munhak kwa Ilbon*. Seoul: Somyŏng Ch'ulp'an, 2003. Pp. 103–26.

Anderson, Chris. *The Long Tail: Why the Future of Business Is Selling Less of More*. New York: Hyperion, 2006.

Anzai Ikurō and Yi Sukyŏng, eds. *Kurarute undō to Tanemaku Hito: hansen bungaku undō "Kurarute" no Nihon to Chōsen de no tenkai*. Tokyo: Ochanomizu Shobō, 2000.

Aoki Masaru. "Ko Teki [Hu Shi] o chūshin ni uzumaite iru bungaku kakumei (1)." *Shinagaku* 1:1 (September 1920), pp. 11–26.

——. "Ko Teki [Hu Shi] o chūshin ni uzumaite iru bungaku kakumei (2)." *Shinagaku* 1:2 (October 1920), pp. 112–30.

——. "Ko Teki [Hu Shi] o chūshin ni uzumaite iru bungaku kakumei (3)." *Shinagaku* 1:3 (November 1920), pp. 199–219.

Aoyagi Tatsuo. "Akutagawa Ryūnosuke to kindai Chūgoku josetsu (hitotsu)." *Kantō Gakuen Daigaku kiyō* 18 (March 1991), pp. 157–77.

Aoyagi Tsunatarō. *Chōsen tōchiron*. Seoul: Chōsen Kenkyūkai, 1923.

Appiah, Kwame Anthony. *In My Father's House: Africa in the Philosophy of Culture*. New York: Oxford University Press, 1992.

Arendt, Hannah. *Eichmann in Jerusalem: A Report on the Banality of Evil*. New York: The Viking Press, 1963.

Arishima Takeo. *Kain no matsuei*, in *Arishima Takeo zenshū* 3. Tokyo: Chikuma Shobō, 1979. Pp. 87–128.

Armstrong, Charles K. et al., eds. *Korea at the Center: Dynamics of Regionalism in Northeast Asia*. Armonk, NY: M. E. Sharpe, 2006.

Ashcroft, Bill et al. *The Empire Writes Back: Theory and Practice in Post-Colonial Literatures*. New York: Routledge, 2002.

——. *Post-colonial Studies: The Key Concepts*. New York: Routledge, 2000.

Atkins, E. Taylor. *Blue Nippon: Authenticating Jazz in Japan*. Durham, NC: Duke University Press, 2001.

——. "The Dual Career of 'Arirang': The Korean Resistance Anthem That Became a Japanese Pop Hit." *Journal of Asian Studies* 66:3 (August 2007), pp. 645–87.

Aying. *Wan Qing xiaoshuo shi*. Shanghai: Shangwu Yinshuguan, 1937.

Ba Jin. "Changqi [Nagasaki] de meng," in *Tan suo ji, Suixianglu* 2. Beijing: Renmin Wenxue Chubanshe, 1986. Pp. 118–21.

——. "Fangwen Guangdao," in *Tan suo ji, Suixianglu* 2. Beijing: Renmin Wenxue Chubanshe, 1986. Pp. 63–69.

——. *Haiwai xing ji: 1979–1984 nian chufang riji ji suixiang*. Shanghai: Shanghai Shehui Kexueyuan Chubanshe, 2005.

——. *Ha Kin [Ba Jin] shasaku shōgai*. Sendai: Bungei Tōhoku Shinsha, 1999.

——. "Ji duan bu gongjing de hua," in *Ba Jin quanji* 12. Beijing: Renmin Wenxue Chubanshe, 1986. Pp. 511–15.

——. *Jia*, in *Ba Jin quanji* 1. Beijing: Renmin Wenxue Chubanshe, 1986. Pp. 1–434.

——. "Jiliu zongxu," in *Ba Jin quanji* 1. Beijing: Renmin Wenxue Chubanshe, 1986. Pp. iii–iv.

——. "Wenxue shenghuo wushi nian," in *Ba Jin xuanji* 1. Chengdu: Sichuan Renmin Chubanshe, 1982. Pp. 1–12.

——. "Yijian xiaoshi," in *Ba Jin wenji* 8. Beijing: Renmin Wenxue Chubanshe, 1959. Pp. 158–64.

Bai Mu. "Yizhe xu," in Ishikawa Tatsuzō, *Weisi de bing*. Shanghai: Zazhishe, 1938. Pp. 1–2.

Bai Xianyong. "Zhijiage zhi si," in *Bai Xianyong duanpian xiaoshuo xuan*. Fuzhou: Fujian Renmin Chubanshe, 1982. Pp. 256–69.

Bal, Mieke. *Quoting Caravaggio: Contemporary Art, Preposterous History*. Chicago, IL: University of Chicago Press, 1999.

Ballantyne, Tony and Antoinette Burton. "Introduction: Bodies, Empires, and World Histories," in Tony Ballantyne and Antoinette Burton, eds., *Rethinking Colonial Encounters in World History*. Durham, NC: Duke University Press, 2005. Pp. 1–15.

——, eds. *Rethinking Colonial Encounters in World History*. Durham, NC: Duke University Press, 2005.

Ballard, J. G. *Miracles of Life: Shanghai to Shepperton*. London: Fourth Estate, 2008.

Barnett, Richard B., ed. *Rethinking Early Modern India*. New Delhi: Manohar Publishers and Distributors, 2002.

Barnstone, Tony. "Introduction: Chinese Poetry through the Looking Glass," in Tony Barnstone, ed. *Out of the Howling Storm: The New Chinese Poetry.* Hanover, NH: Wesleyan University Press, University Press of New England, 1993. Pp. 1–38.

——, ed. *Out of the Howling Storm: The New Chinese Poetry.* Hanover, NH: Wesleyan University Press, University Press of New England, 1993.

Barrett, David and Larry N. Shyu. *Chinese Collaboration with Japan, 1932–1945: The Limits of Accommodation.* Stanford, CA: Stanford University Press, 2000.

Barthes, Roland. *S/Z.* Paris: Éditions du Seuil, 1970.

Baskett, Michael. *The Attractive Empire: Transnational Film Culture in Imperial Japan.* Honolulu, HI: University of Hawai'i Press, 2008.

Bassnett, Susan and André Lefevere, eds. *Constructing Cultures: Essays on Literary Translation.* Philadelphia, PA: Multilingual Matters, 1998.

——. "Introduction: Where Are We in Translation Studies?" in Susan Bassnett and André Lefevere, eds. *Constructing Cultures: Essays on Literary Translation.* Philadelphia, PA: Multilingual Matters, 1998. Pp. 1–11.

Bassnett, Susan and Harish Trivedi. "Introduction: Of Colonies, Cannibals and Vernaculars," in Susan Bassnett and Harish Trivedi, eds. *Post-Colonial Translation: Theory and Practice.* New York: Routledge, 1999. Pp. 1–18.

——, eds. *Post-Colonial Translation: Theory and Practice.* New York: Routledge, 1999.

Bate, Jonathan et al., eds. *Shakespeare and the Twentieth Century: The Selected Proceedings of the International Shakespeare Association World Congress, Los Angeles, 1996.* Newark, DE: University of Delaware Press, 1998.

Bate, Walter Jackson. *The Burden of the Past and the English Poet.* Cambridge, MA: Belknap Press, 1970.

Baudelaire, Charles. "Le Chat," in *Les fleurs du mal.* Paris: Union générale d'éditions, 1994. Pp. 47–48.

——. "Le Chat," in *Les fleurs du mal.* Paris: Union générale d'éditions, 1994. Pp. 66–67.

——. "Les Chats," in *Les fleurs du mal.* Paris: Union générale d'éditions, 1994. P. 85.

Beijingshi Shehui Kexue Yanjiusuo Guoji Wenti Yanjiushi, ed. *Zhong-Ri wenhua yu jiaoliu* 1. Beijing: Zhongguo Zhanwang Chubanshe, 1984.

Beijingshi Zhong-Ri Wenhua Jiaoliushi Yanjiuhui, ed. *Zhong-Ri wenhua jiaoliushi lunwenji.* Beijing: Renmin Chubanshe, 1982.

Bell, Sharon Mosingal. "In the Shadow of the Father Tongue: On Translating the Masks in J.-S. Alexis," in Anuradha Dingwaney and Carol Maier, eds. *Between Languages and Cultures: Translation and Cross-Cultural Texts.* Pittsburgh, PA: University of Pittsburgh Press, 1995. Pp. 51–74.

Bensmaïa, Réda. *Experimental Nations: Or, the Invention of the Maghreb.* Princeton, NJ: Princeton University Press, 2003.

Berger, Anne-Emmanuelle, ed. *Algeria in Others' Languages.* Ithaca, NY: Cornell University Press, 2002.

Bermann, Sandra. "Introduction," in Sandra Bermann and Michael Wood, eds. *Nation, Language, and the Ethics of Translation*. Princeton, NJ: Princeton University Press, 2005. Pp. 1–10.

Bermann, Sandra and Michael Wood, eds. *Nation, Language, and the Ethics of Translation*. Princeton, NJ: Princeton University Press, 2005.

Berry, Mary Elizabeth. *Japan in Print: Information and the Nation in the Early Modern Period*. Berkeley, CA: University of California Press, 2006.

Berry, Michael. "A History of Pain: Literary and Cinematic Mappings of Violence in Modern China." Ph.D. dissertation, Columbia University, 2004.

———. *A History of Pain: Literary and Cinematic Mappings of Violence in Modern China*. New York: Columbia University Press, 2008.

Bhabha, Homi K. *The Location of Culture*. New York: Routledge Classics, 2004.

———. "Signs Taken for Wonders: Questions of Ambivalence and Authority under a Tree Outside Delhi, May 1817." *Critical Inquiry* 12:1 (Autumn 1985), pp. 144–65.

Blake, William. "The Sick Rose," in *Songs of Experience*, in *Blake: The Complete Poems*. New York: Longman, 1989. P. 223.

Bloom, Harold. *The Anxiety of Influence: A Theory of Poetry*. New York: Oxford University Press, 1997.

———, ed. *Charlotte Brontë's Jane Eyre*. New York: Chelsea House, 2007.

Boehmer, Elleke. *Colonial and Postcolonial Literature: Migrant Metaphors*. New York: Oxford University Press, 2005.

———. *Empire, the National, and the Postcolonial, 1890–1920: Resistance in Interaction*. New York: Oxford University Press, 2002.

———, ed. *Empire Writing: An Anthology of Colonial Literature, 1870–1918*. Oxford, UK: Oxford University Press, 1998.

———. "Introduction," in Elleke Boehmer, ed. *Empire Writing: An Anthology of Colonial Literature, 1870–1918*. Oxford, UK: Oxford University Press, 1998. Pp. xv–xxxvi.

Boitani, Piero. *Winged Words: Flight in Poetry and History*. Chicago, IL: University of Chicago Press, 2007.

Booker, M. Keith. *Joyce, Bakhtin, and the Literary Tradition: Toward a Comparative Cultural Poetics*. Ann Arbor, MI: University of Michigan Press, 1995.

Botsman, Daniel V. *Punishment and Power in the Making of Modern Japan*. Princeton, NJ: Princeton University Press, 2005.

Boulanger, Alison. "Influence or Confluence: Joyce, Eliot, Cohen and the Case for Comparative Studies." *Comparative Literature Studies* 39:1 (2002), pp. 18–47.

Bourdaghs, Michael. *The Dawn That Never Comes: Shimazaki Tōson and Japanese Nationalism*. New York: Columbia University Press, 2003.

Bourdieu, Pierre. "The Forms of Capital," in John G. Richardson, ed. *Handbook of Theory and Research for the Sociology of Education*. Westport, CT: Greenwood Press, 1986. Pp. 241–58. Translated by Richard Nice.

Boyle, John Hunter. *China and Japan at War, 1937–1945: The Politics of Collaboration*. Stanford, CA: Stanford University Press, 1972.

Brandon, James R. *Kabuki's Forgotten War, 1931–1945*. Honolulu, HI: University of Hawai'i Press, 2008.

Brandt, Kim. *Kingdom of Beauty: Mingei and the Politics of Folk Art in Imperial Japan*. New York: Columbia University Press, 2007.

" 'Breakfast at Tiffany's' Helped Inspire Murakami to Write for His Daily Bread." Interview with the *Mainichi shinbun*. http://mdn.mainichi.jp/culture/features/news. Accessed May 30, 2008.

"Breaking the Literary Language Barrier: Yang Yi, Ian Hideo Levy." *Japan Echo* (December 2008), pp. 49–51. Translated from "Nihongo de tsumugu imi to yorokobi." *Asahi Shinbun* (August 3, 2008), p. 21.

Bredekamp, Horst. "Artists as Criminals and the Concept of Absolutism." Lecture at Harvard University, November 14, 2005.

Brenner, Rachel Feldhay. *Inextricably Bonded: Israeli, Arab, and Jewish Writers Re-visioning Culture*. Madison, WI: University of Wisconsin Press, 2003.

Brombert, Victor. *In Praise of Antiheroes: Figures and Themes in Modern European Literature 1830–1980*. Chicago, IL: University of Chicago Press, 1999.

Brontë, Charlotte. *Jane Eyre*. New York: Doubleday, 1997.

Brook, Timothy. "Collaboration in the History of Wartime East Asia." *Japan Focus*, July 4, 2008.

——. "Collaboration in the Postwar." *Japan Focus*, July 4, 2008.

——. *Collaboration: Japanese Agents and Local Elites in Wartime China*. Cambridge, MA: Harvard University Press, 2005.

Brower, Reuben. *Mirror on Mirror: Translation, Imitation, Parody*. Cambridge, MA: Harvard University Press, 1974.

Brower, Robert H. and Earl Miner. *Japanese Court Poetry*. Stanford, CA: Stanford University Press, 1961.

Brydon, Diana and Irena R. Makaryk, eds. *Shakespeare in Canada: 'a world elsewhere'?* Toronto, ON: University of Toronto Press, 2002.

Cabell, Charles. "Kawabata Yasunari," in Jay Rubin, ed. *Modern Japanese Writers*. New York: Charles Scribner's Sons, 2001. Pp. 149–67.

——. "Maiden Dreams: Kawabata Yasunari's Beautiful Japanese Empire." Ph.D. dissertation, Harvard University, 1999.

Cai, Zong-qi. *Configurations of Comparative Poetics: Three Perspectives on Western and Chinese Literary Criticism*. Honolulu, HI: University of Hawai'i Press, 2002.

Calichman, Richard. *What Is Modernity? Writings of Takeuchi Yoshimi*. New York: Columbia University Press, 2005.

Caminero-Santangelo, Byron. *African Fiction and Joseph Conrad: Reading Postcolonial Intertextuality*. Albany, NY: State University of New York Press, 2005.

Camus, Albert. "Le mythe de Sisyphe," in *Le mythe de Sisyphe: Essai sur l'absurde*. Paris: Éditions Gallimard, 1942. Pp. 162–68.

Cancalon, Elaine D. and Antoine Spacagna, eds. *Intertextuality in Literature and Film: Selected Papers from the Thirteenth Annual Florida State University Conference on Literature and Film*. Gainesville, FL: University of Florida Press, 1994.

Caprio, Mark E. "Assimilation Rejected: The Tong'a ilbo's Challenge to Japan's Colonial Policy in Korea," in Li Narangoa and Robert Cribb, eds. *Imperial Japan and National Identities in Asia, 1895–1945.* New York: Routledge Curzon, 2003. Pp. 129–45.

Carey, Peter. *Jack Maggs.* Boston, MA: Faber and Faber, 1997.

Carpentier, Alejo. *El arpa y la sombra.* Mexico: Siglo XXI Editores, 1979.

———. *The Harp and the Shadow.* San Francisco, CA: Mercury House, Inc., 1990. Translated by Thomas Christensen and Carol Christensen.

Cary, Joyce. *Mister Johnson.* London: J. M. Dent, 1995.

Casanova, Pascale. *The World Republic of Letters.* Cambridge, MA: Harvard University Press, 2004. Translated by M. B. DeBevoise.

Cather, Kirsten. "The Great Censorship Trials of Literature and Film in Postwar Japan." Ph.D. dissertation, University of California, Berkeley, 2004.

Césaire, Aimé. *Discours sur le colonialisme.* Paris: Présence Africaine, 1958.

———. *Une tempête; d'après "La tempête" de Shakespeare. Adaptation pour un théâtre nègre.* Paris: Editions du Seuil, 1969.

Chaeil Hanguk Yuhaksaeng Yŏnhaphoe, ed. *Ilbon yuhak 100 nyŏnsa.* Tokyo: Chaeil Hanguk Yuhaksaeng Yŏnhaphoe, 1988.

Chaibong, Hahm. "Civilization, Race, or Nation? Korean Visions of Regional Order in the Late Nineteenth Century," in Charles K. Armstrong et al., eds. *Korea at the Center: Dynamics of Regionalism in Northeast Asia.* Armonk, NY: M. E. Sharpe, 2006. Pp. 35–50.

Chan, Sin-wai. *A Chronology of Translation in China and the West from the Legendary Period to 2004.* Hong Kong: Chinese University Press, 2008.

Chand, Munshi Ratna. *Bharamajalak Natak.* Lucknow: Nawal Kishore Press, 1882.

Chandra, Shefali. "Mimicry, Masculinity, and the Mystique of Indian English: Western India, 1870–1900." *Journal of Asian Studies* 68:1 (February 2009), pp. 199–225.

Chang Chilin. "Taiwan puroretaria bungaku no tanjō: Yō Ki [Yang Kui] to 'Dai Nihon teikoku.'" Ph.D. dissertation, University of Tokyo, 2000.

Chang Duk-sun. "Literary Magazines in the Past." *Korea Journal* 2:8 (August 1962), pp. 19–21, 45.

Chang Hyejŏng (Chang Hae-jung). "Ak'ut'agawa (Akutagawa) wa Yi Sang munhak e nat'a-nan 'ŭisik ŭi hŭ-rŭm' ki-pŏp: 'T'opnipak'u' [Haguruma] wa 'Silhwa' rŭl chungsim ŭ ro." *Il-ŏ Ilmunhak yŏn-gu* 62:2 (August 2007), pp. 107–24.

Chang Hyŏkju. "Gakidō," in Nan Bujin and Shirakawa Yutaka, eds. *Chō Kakuchū* [Chang Hyŏkju] *Nihongo sakuhinsen.* Tokyo: Bensei Shuppan, 2003. Pp. 5–47.

———. "Watakushi ni taibō suru hitobito e: Tokunaga Sunao shi ni okuru tegami," in Nan Bujin and Shirakawa Yutaka, eds. *Chō Kakuchū* [Chang Hyŏkju] *Nihongo sakuhinsen.* Tokyo: Bensei Shuppan, 2003. Pp. 296–301.

Chang, Sung-sheng Yvonne. *Literary Culture in Taiwan: Martial Law to Market Law.* New York: Columbia University Press, 2004.

Chang Yun-shik et al., eds. *Korea between Tradition and Modernity: Selected Papers from the Fourth Pacific and Asian Conference on Korean Studies.* Vancouver, BC: University of British Columbia, Institute of Asian Research, 1998.

Chaulet-Achour, Christiane. "Writings as Exploratory Surgery: Yambo Ouologuem's *Bound to Violence*," in Christopher Wise, ed. *Yambo Ouologuem: Postcolonial Writer, Islamic Militant.* Boulder, CO: Lynne Rienner Publishers, 1999. Pp. 89–108.

Chekhov, Anton. "Sleepy," in *Motley Tales and a Play.* New York: Doubleday, 1998. Pp. 75–82.

Chen Huiwen. "Tian Han zai Riben," in Lin Qingzhang, ed. *Jindai Zhongguo zhishifenzi zai Riben* 3. Taipei: Wanjuanlou Tushu Gufen Youxian Gongsi, 2003. Pp. 195–226.

Chen, Kuan-Hsing and Chua Beng Huat, eds. *The Inter-Asia Cultural Studies Reader.* New York: Routledge, 2007.

Chen, Mei-yao. "Gender, Race, and Nation in Modern Japanese and Taiwanese Literatures: A Comparative Study of Women's Literary Production." Ph.D. dissertation, University of British Columbia, 2005.

Ch'en Ming-t'ai. "Modernist Poetry in Prewar Taiwan: Yang Ch'ih-ch'ang, the Feng-ch'e (Le Moulin) Poetry Society, and Japanese Poetic Trends." *Taiwanese Literature: English Translation Series* 2 (December 1997), pp. 93–118.

Chen Peifeng. "Rizhi shiqi Taiwan hanwenmaizhong de xiangxiang: diguo, zhimindi hanwen, Zhongguo baihuawen, Taiwan huawen." Paper given at the Teikokushugi to Bungaku Conference, Aichi University, August 1–3, 2008. Reprinted in the conference handout, pp. 143–74.

Chen Pingyuan. *Ershi shiji Zhongguo xiaoshuoshi* 1. Beijing: Beijing Daxue Chubanshe, 1989.

Chen Yingnian. "Jindai Riben sixiangjia zhuzuo zai Qingmo Zhongguo de jiejue he chuanbo," in Beijingshi Zhong-Ri Wenhua Jiaoliushi Yanjiuhui, ed. *Zhong-Ri wenhua jiaoliushi lunwenji.* Beijing: Renmin Chubanshe, 1982. Pp. 262–82.

Cheng, Ching-mao. "The Impact of Japanese Literary Trends on Modern Chinese Writers," in Merle Goldman, ed. *Modern Chinese Literature in the May Fourth Era.* Cambridge, MA: Harvard University Press, 1977. Pp. 63–88.

Cheng, François. *Le dit de Tianyi.* Paris: Albin Michel, 1998.

Cheyfitz, Eric. *The Poetics of Imperialism: Translation and Colonization from The Tempest to Tarzan.* Philadelphia, PA: University of Pennsylvania Press, 1997.

"China hangjŏn chakga ŭi haengbang." *Munjang* 2:2 (February 1940), pp. 143–45.

Ching, Leo. *Becoming "Japanese": Colonial Taiwan and the Politics of Identity Formation.* Berkeley, CA: University of California Press, 2001.

Cho Iljae. *Changhanmong, Maeil sinbo,* May 13, 1913–October 1, 1913.

———. *Pulyŏgwi.* Tokyo: Keiseisha Shoten, 1912.

———. *Ssang-oknu, Maeil sinbo,* July 17, 1912–February 4, 1913.

Ch'oe Chaesŏ. "Tangmok Sunsam [Karaki Junzō] chŏ, *Kŭndae Ilbon munhak ŭi chŏn-gae.*" *Inmun p'yŏngnon* 1:1 (October 1939), pp. 121–26.

Ch'oe Kyŏng-ok. *Hanguk kaehwagi kŭndae oerae hanjaŏ ŭi suyong yŏn-gu.* Seoul: J & C, 2003.

Choe Sang-hun. "Japanese Poetry Persists in Korea, Despite Disapproval." *New York Times*, March 27, 2008, p. A10.

Chŏng Hanmo. "Hanguk hyŏndae sisa (B): Yohan ŭi si wa Ilbon ŭi kŭndae si." *Hyŏndae sihak* 4:11 (November 1972), pp. 113–20.

Chŏng Inmun. "Hyŏn Chin-gŏn ch'ogi sosŏl kwa Ilbon munhak kwa ŭi kwan-ryŏn yangsang." *Guk-ŏ gukmunhak* 10 (December 1990), pp. 155–73.

——. "Kim Dong-in ŭi Ilbon kŭndae munhak suyong yŏn-gu." Ph.D. disser-tation, Dong-A University, 1994.

Chŏng Kwiryŏn (Chō Kiren, Jeong Gwi-ryun). "Kunikida Doppo to wakaki Kankoku kindai bungakusha no gunzō." Ph.D. dissertation, Tsukuba Uni-versity, 1997.

Chŏng Sŭng-un (Jeong Seung Un). "Nakano Shigeharu, 'Ame no furu Shina-gawa eki' no saikaishaku (1): 'nukumori' o chūshin ni." *Ilbon-ŏ munhak* 12 (2002), pp. 351–75.

——. *Nak'ano Sigeharu* [Nakano Shigeharu] *ŭi pi naeri nŭn Sinagawa* [Shina-gawa] *yŏk.* Seoul: Ch'op'an Palhaeng, 2006.

"Chōsen Bunjin Kyōkai ga tanjō." *Keijō nippō*, October 30, 1939.

Chow Tse-tsung. *The May Fourth Movement: Intellectual Revolution in Modern China, 1915–1924.* Stanford, CA: Stanford University Press, 1960.

Chrisman, Laura. *Rereading the Imperial Romance: British Imperialism and South African Resistance in Haggard, Schreiner, and Plaatje.* New York: Oxford Uni-versity Press, 2000.

Christensen, Thomas and Carol Christensen. "Translator's Preface: Discover-ing Alejo Carpentier," in Alejo Carpentier. *The Harp and the Shadow.* San Francisco, CA: Mercury House, 1990. Translated by Thomas Christensen and Carol Christensen. Pp. xi–xiv.

Chu Yohan. "Ch'ang jo sidae ŭi mundan." *Chayu munhak* 1:1 (1956), pp. 134–37.

——. "Ilbon kŭndae si ch'o." *Ch'ang jo* 1:1 (February 1919), pp. 76–80.

——. "Samidare no asa." *Bungei zasshi* (October 1916), reprinted in Yang Dongguk, "Shu Yōkan [Chu Yohan] to Nihon kindaishi." Ph.D. disserta-tion, University of Tokyo, 1997. Pp. 6–7.

Chung Chai-sik. "Changing Korean Perceptions of Japan on the Eve of Mod-ern Transformation: The Case of Neo-Confucian Yangban Intellectuals." *Korean Studies* 19 (1995), pp. 39–50.

Clayton, Jay and Eric Rothstein. "Figures in the Corpus: Theories of Influence and Intertextuality," in Jay Clayton and Eric Rothstein, eds. *Influence and Intertextuality in Literary History.* Madison, WI: University of Wisconsin Press, 1991. Pp. 3–36.

——, eds. *Influence and Intertextuality in Literary History.* Madison, WI: Uni-versity of Wisconsin Press, 1991.

Cockerill, Hiroko. *Style and Narrative in Translations: The Contribution of Futa-batei Shimei.* Manchester, UK: St. Jerome Publishing, 2006.

Coetzee, J. M. *Doubling the Point: Essays and Interviews.* Cambridge, MA: Har-vard University Press, 1992.

——. *Foe*. London: Secker and Warburg, 1986.

Cohen, Paul A. *Discovering History in China*. New York: Columbia University Press, 1984.

Cohen, Paul A. and Merle Goldman, eds. *Ideas Across Cultures: Essays on Chinese Thought in Honor of Benjamin I. Schwartz*. Cambridge, MA: Harvard University Press, 1990.

Cohen-Mor, Dalya. *A Matter of Fate: The Concept of Fate in the Arab World as Reflected in Modern Arabic Literature*. New York: Oxford University Press, 2001.

Conrad, Joseph. *Heart of Darkness*, in *Heart of Darkness and The Secret Sharer*. New York: The New American Library of World Literature, 1959. Pp. 57–142.

Cook, Haruko Taya. "The Many Lives of *Living Soldiers*: Ishikawa Tatsuzō and Japan's War in Asia," in Marlene J. Mayo et al., eds. *War, Occupation, and Creativity: Japan and East Asia, 1920–1960*. Honolulu, HI: University of Hawai'i Press, 2001. Pp. 149–75.

Cook, Haruko Taya and Theodore F. Cook. *Japan at War: An Oral History*. New York: The New Press, 1992.

Cooper, Frederick. "Postcolonial Studies and the Study of History," in Ania Loomba et al., eds. *Postcolonial Studies and Beyond*. Durham, NC: Duke University Press, 2005. Pp. 401–22.

Cornis-Pope, Marcel and John Neubauer, eds. *History of the Literary Cultures of East-Central Europe*, 3 vols. Philadelphia, PA: John Benjamins Publishing Company, 2007.

Cox, C. Brian, ed. *African Writers* 1. New York: Charles Scribner's Sons, 1997.

Cox, Rupert, ed. *The Culture of Copying in Japan: Critical and Historical Perspectives*. New York: Routledge, 2008.

Craig, Albert M. *Civilization and Enlightenment: The Early Thought of Fukuzawa Yukichi*. Cambridge, MA: Harvard University Press, 2009.

Cronin, Michael. "History, Translation, Postcolonialism," in Sherry Simon and Paul St.-Pierre, eds. *Changing the Terms: Translating in the Postcolonial Era*. Ottawa, ON: University of Ottawa Press, 2000. Pp. 33–52.

Cruz, Laura, ed. *Making Sense Of: Dying and Death*. Oxford, UK: The Inter-Disciplinary Press, 2004.

Culver, Annika. "'Between Distant Realities': The Japanese Avant-Garde, Surrealism, and the Colonies, 1924–1943." Ph.D. dissertation, University of Chicago, 2007.

Cumings, Bruce, ed. *Chicago Occasional Papers on Korea*. Select Papers 6. Chicago, IL: The Center for East Asian Studies, University of Chicago, 1991.

——. *The Origins of the Korean War*. Princeton, NJ: Princeton University Press, 1981.

Curley, David L. "Maharaja Krisnacandra, Hinduism, and Kingship in the Contact Zone of Bengal," in Richard B. Barnett, ed. *Rethinking Early Modern India*. New Delhi: Manohar Publishers and Distributors, 2002. Pp. 85–117.

Dai Sijie. *Balzac et la petite tailleuse chinoise*. Paris: Gallimard, 2000.

Dai Yan. "*Jiandeng xin hua* he *Jiandeng yu hua* zai Riben de liuchuan ji qi ying-xiang," in Beijingshi Zhong-Ri Wenhua Jiaoliushi Yanjiuhui, ed. *Zhong-Ri wenhua jiaoliushi lunwenji.* Beijing: Renmin Chubanshe, 1982. Pp. 195–207.

Damrosch, David. *The Buried Book: The Loss and Rediscovery of the Great Epic of Gilgamesh.* New York: Henry Holt and Company, 2006.

——. *What Is World Literature?* Princeton, NJ: Princeton University Press, 2003.

——, ed. *The Longman Anthology, World Literature*, vol. A. New York: Longman, 2004.

Dan Di. "Riji Chao." *Dongbei wenxue yanjiu shiliao* 6 (1987), pp. 173–80.

Day, Michael. "Online Avant-Garde Poetry in China Today," in Christopher Lupke, ed. *New Perspectives on Chinese Poetry.* New York: Palgrave Macmillan, 2008. Pp. 201–17.

de Campos, Haroldo. "Da Tradução como Criação e como Critica," in *Metalinguagem e Outras Metas: Ensaios de Teoria e Crítica Literária.* São Paolo: Perspectiva, 1992. Pp. 31–48.

de Courtivron, Isabelle, ed. *Lives in Translation: Bilingual Writers on Identity and Creativity.* New York: Palgrave Macmillan, 2003.

Deleuze, Gilles and Félix Guattari. *Kafka: Pour une literature mineure.* Paris: Éditions de Minuit, 1975.

del Sarto, Ana et al., eds. *The Latin American Cultural Studies Reader.* Durham, NC: Duke University Press, 2004.

Deng Keyun, ed. *Lu Xun shouce.* Shanghai: Bolan Shuju, 1946.

Denton, Kirk A. "General Introduction," in Kirk A. Denton, ed. *Modern Chinese Literary Thought: Writings on Literature, 1893–1945.* Stanford, CA: Stanford University Press, 1996. Pp. 1–61.

——, ed. *Modern Chinese Literary Thought: Writings on Literature, 1893–1945.* Stanford, CA: Stanford University Press, 1996.

Denton, Kirk A. and Michel Hockx, eds. *Literary Societies of Republican China.* New York: Lexington Books, 2008.

Des Forges, Alexander. *Mediasphere Shanghai: The Aesthetics of Cultural Production.* Honolulu, HI: University of Hawai'i Press, 2007.

Desai, Anita. "Various Lives," in Isabelle de Courtivron, ed. *Lives in Translation: Bilingual Writers on Identity and Creativity.* New York: Palgrave Macmillan, 2003. Pp. 11–17.

De Vos, George and Changsoo Lee. "The Colonial Experience, 1910–1945," in Changsoo Lee and George De Vos, eds. *Koreans in Japan: Ethnic Conflict and Accommodation.* Berkeley, CA: University of California Press, 1981. Pp. 31–57.

Dib, Mohammed. *La Grande maison.* Paris: Éditions du Seuil, 1952.

——. *L'Incendie.* Paris: Éditions du Seuil, 1954.

——. *Le Métier à tisser.* Paris: Éditions du Seuil, 1957.

Dickens, Charles. *Great Expectations.* New York: Penguin, 1996.

Dingwaney, Anuradha. "Introduction: Translating 'Third World' Cultures," in Anuradha Dingwaney and Carol Maier, eds. *Between Languages and Cultures: Translation and Cross-Cultural Texts.* Pittsburgh, PA: University of Pittsburgh Press, 1995. Pp. 3–15.

Dingwaney, Anuradha, and Carol Maier, eds. *Between Languages and Cultures: Translation and Cross-Cultural Texts*. Pittsburgh, PA: University of Pittsburgh Press, 1995.

Dobie, Madeleine. "Translation in the Contact Zone: Antoine Galland's *Mille et une nuits: contes arabes*," in Saree Makdisi and Felicity Nussbaum, eds. *The Arabian Nights in Historical Context: Between East and West*. New York: Oxford University Press, 2008. Pp. 25–49.

Dodd, Stephen. *Writing Home: Representations of the Native Place in Modern Japanese Literature*. Cambridge, MA: Harvard University Asia Center, 2004.

Doi Shunsho. "Shinkokujin no gakuseigeki." *Waseda bungaku* 7 (1907), pp. 114–18.

Doleželová-Velingerová, Milena. "Fiction from the End of the Empire to the Beginning of the Republic (1897–1916)," in Victor Mair, ed. *The Columbia History of Chinese Literature*. New York: Columbia University Press, 2001. Pp. 697–731.

Du Xuan. "Sensō zen'ya no seishun," in Jinmin Chūgoku Zasshisha, ed. *Waga seishun no Nihon: Chūgoku chishikijin no Nihon kaisō*. Tokyo: Tōhō Shoten, 1982. Pp. 164–74.

Duara, Prasenjit. "Collaboration and the Politics of the Twentieth Century." *Japan Focus*, July 4, 2008.

——. "Local Worlds: The Poetics and Politics of the Native Place in Modern China." *South Atlantic Quarterly* 99:1 (Winter 2000), pp. 13–45.

——. *Sovereignty and Authenticity: Manchukuo and the East Asian Modern*. Lanham, MD: Rowman and Littlefield Publishers, 2003.

Dudden, Alexis. *Japan's Colonization of Korea: Discourse and Power*. Honolulu, HI: University of Hawai'i Press, 2005.

Duus, Peter. "Japan's Informal Empire in China, 1895–1937: An Overview," in Peter Duus et al., eds. *The Japanese Informal Empire in China, 1895–1937*. Princeton, NJ: Princeton University Press, 1989. Pp. xi–xxix.

——. "Japan's Wartime Empire: Problems and Issues," in Peter Duus, Ramon H. Myers, and Mark R. Peattie, eds. *The Japanese Wartime Empire, 1931–1945*. Princeton, NJ: Princeton University Press, 1996. Pp. xi–xlvii.

Duus, Peter, Ramon H. Myers, and Mark R. Peattie, eds. *The Japanese Informal Empire in China, 1895–1937*. Princeton, NJ: Princeton University Press, 1989.

——, eds. *The Japanese Wartime Empire, 1931–1945*. Princeton, NJ: Princeton University Press, 1996.

Eber, Irene. "Introduction: The Fountain of Living Waters," in Marián Gálik, ed. *Influence, Translation, and Parallels: Selected Studies on the Bible in China*. Sankt Augustin, Germany: Monumenta Serica Institute, 2004. Pp. 9–21.

Eckert, Carter et al. *Korea Old and New: A History*. Seoul: Ilchokak Publishers, 1990.

Eguchi Kan. "Nihon puroretaria bungaku no Shinayaku to sono yakusha." *Bungaku hyōron* 1:10 (October 1934), pp. 62–68.

Elkins, Caroline and Susan Pedersen, eds. *Settler Colonialism in the Twentieth Century: Projects, Practices, Legacies*. New York: Routledge, 2005.

Em, Henry. "Minjok as a Modern and Democratic Construct: Sin Ch'aeho's Historiography," in Gi-Wook Shin and Michael Robinson, eds. *Colonial Modernity in Korea.* Cambridge, MA: Harvard University Asia Center, 1999. Pp. 336–61.

——. "Yi Sang's *Wings* Read as an Anti-colonial Allegory." *Muae* 1 (1995), pp. 105–11.

Emerson, Ralph Waldo. "Fate," in *The Conduct of Life, The Collected Works of Ralph Waldo Emerson* 6. Boston, MA: Houghton, Mifflin and Company, 1898.

Emery, Mary Lou. *Jean Rhys at 'World's End': Novels of Colonial and Sexual Exile.* Austin, TX: University of Texas Press, 1990.

English, James F. *The Economy of Prestige: Prizes, Awards, and the Circulation of Cultural Value.* Cambridge, MA: Harvard University Press, 2005.

Esenbul, Selçuk. "Japan's Global Claim to Asia and the World of Islam: Transnational Nationalism and World Power, 1900–1945." *American Historical Review* 109:4 (October 2004), pp. 1140–70.

Etherton, Michael. *The Development of African Drama.* New York: Africana Publishing Company, 1982.

Even-Zohar, Itamar. "The Position of Translated Literature within the Literary Polysystem," in James S. Holmes et al., eds. *Literature and Translation: New Perspectives in Literary Studies.* Leuven: Acco, 1978. Pp. 117–27.

Fairbank, John K. and Kwang-ching Liu, eds. *The Cambridge History of China, vol. 11, Late Ch'ing 1800–1911, 2.* New York: Cambridge University Press, 1980.

Faure, Guy and Laurent Schwab. *Japan and Vietnam: A Relation under Influences.* Honolulu, HI: University of Hawai'i Press, 2008.

Feng Weiqun et al., eds. *Dongbei lunxian shiqi wenxue guoji xueshu yantaohui lunwenji.* Shenyang: Shenyang Chubanshe, 1992.

Feuerwerker, Albert, Rhoads Murphey, and Mary Clabaugh Wright, eds. *Approaches to Modern Chinese History.* Berkeley, CA: University of California Press, 1967.

Field, Norma. "Commercial Appetite and Human Need: The Accidental and Fated Revival of Kobayashi Takiji's *Cannery Ship.*" *Japan Focus*, February 22, 2009.

Finchum-Sung, Hilary. "New Folksongs: *Shin Minyo* of the 1930s," in Keith Howard, ed. *Korean Pop Music: Riding the Wave.* Folkestone, Kent: Global Oriental, 2006. Pp. 10–20.

Finnerty, Páraic. *Emily Dickinson's Shakespeare.* Amherst, MA: University of Massachusetts Press, 2006.

Fischlin, Daniel and Mark Fortier, eds. *Adaptations of Shakespeare: A Critical Anthology of Plays from the Seventeenth Century to the Present.* London: Routledge, 2000.

——. "*uMabatha*, Welcome Msomi," in Daniel Fischlin and Mark Fortier, eds. *Adaptations of Shakespeare: A Critical Anthology of Plays from the Seventeenth Century to the Present.* London: Routledge, 2000. Pp. 164–87.

Fitz, Karsten. *Negotiating History and Culture: Transculturation in Contemporary Native American Fiction.* New York: Peter Lang, 2001.

Fix, Douglas. "Conscripted Writers, Collaborating Tales? Taiwanese War Stories." *Harvard Studies on Taiwan: Papers of the Taiwan Studies Workshop* 2 (1998), pp. 19–41.

Fogel, Joshua. *Ai Ssu-ch'i's Contribution to the Development of Chinese Marxism.* Cambridge, MA: Council on East Asian Studies, Harvard University, 1987.

———. *Articulating the Sinosphere: Sino-Japanese Relations in Space and Time.* Cambridge, MA: Harvard University Press, 2009.

———. "Guest Editor's Introduction." *Chinese Studies in History* 30:4 (Summer 1997), pp. 3–5.

———. *The Literature of Travel in the Japanese Rediscovery of China, 1862–1945.* Stanford, CA: Stanford University Press, 1996.

———, ed. *The Nanjing Massacre in History and Historiography.* Berkeley, CA: University of California Press, 2000.

Fong Shiaw-Chian. "Hegemony and Identity in the Colonial Experience of Taiwan, 1895–1945," in Liao Ping-hui and David Der-wei Wang, eds. *Taiwan under Japanese Colonial Rule, 1895–1945: History, Culture, Memory.* New York: Columbia University Press, 2006. Pp. 160–83.

Foster, John. "Starting with Dostoevsky's Double: Bakhtin and Nabokov as Intertextualists," in Elaine D. Cancalon and Antoine Spacagna, eds. *Intertextuality in Literature and Film: Selected Papers from the Thirteenth Annual Florida State University Conference on Literature and Film.* Gainesville, FL: University of Florida Press, 1994. Pp. 9–20.

Foster, Paul B. *Ah Q Archaeology: Lu Xun, Ah Q, Ah Q Progeny and the National Character Discourse in Twentieth Century China.* Lanham, MD: Lexington Books, 2006.

Fruehauf, Heiner. "Urban Exoticism in Modern and Contemporary Chinese Literature," in Ellen Widmer and David Der-wei Wang, eds. *From May Fourth to June Fourth: Fiction and Film in Twentieth-Century China.* Cambridge, MA: Harvard University Press, 1993. Pp. 133–64.

Frühauf, Heiner. "Urban Exoticism and Its Sino-Japanese Scenery, 1910–1923." *Asian and African Studies* 6 (1997), pp. 126–68.

Fu, Poshek. *Passivity, Resistance, and Collaboration: Intellectual Choices in Occupied Shanghai 1937–1945.* Stanford, CA: Stanford University Press, 1993.

Fuentes, Carlos. "Las dos orillas," in *El naranjo, o los círculos del tiempo.* Mexico: Alfaguara Literaturas, 1993. Pp. 9–60.

Fujian Shifan Daxue Zhongwenxi, ed. *Lu Xun lun waiguo wenxue.* Beijing: Waiguo Wenxue Chubanshe, 1982.

Fujii Sadakazu. *Kotoba to sensō.* Tokyo: Ōtsuki Shoten, 2007.

Fujii Shōzō. "Lu Xun in Textbooks and Classes of Chinese: A Study of the Introduction of Modern Chinese Literature before the War in Japan," in Earl Roy Miner and Haga Tōru, eds. *Contents of the ICLA '91 Tokyo Proceedings: The Force of Vision 4: Translation and Modernization.* Tokyo: University of Tokyo Press and International Comparative Literature Association, 1995. Pp. 18–26.

———. *Murakami Haruki no naka no Chūgoku.* Tokyo: Asahi Shinbunsha, 2007.

———. *Ro Jin* [Lu Xun] *jiten.* Tokyo: Sanseidō, 2002.

——. "Senzenki Taiwan sakka no Tōkyō ryūgaku taiken ni kansuru keifuteki kenkyū." *Kenkyū seika hōkokusho* (March 1999), pp. 3–16.

——. *Taiwan bungaku kono hyakunen.* Tokyo: Tōhō Shoten, 1998.

——. *Tōkyō Gaigo Shinagobu: kōryū to shinryaku no hazama de.* Tokyo: Asahi Shinbusha, 1992.

Fujiishi Takayo. "Kim Namch'ŏn no 'Shi' [Si] to Akutagawa Ryūnosuke no 'Yabu no naka': Shiten ni tsuite," in Ōtani Morishige Hakushi Koki Kinen Chōsen Bungaku Ronsō Kankō Iinkai, ed. *Ōtani Morishige hakushi koki kinen: Chōsen bungaku ronsō.* Tokyo: Hakuteisha, 2002. Pp. 220–31.

Fujino Sensei to Ro Jin [Lu Xun] Kankōkai, ed. *Fujino sensei to Ro Jin [Lu Xun].* Sendai: Tōhoku Daigaku, 2007.

Fulton, Bruce. "Wings and Wiggles: Four Intertextual Korean Stories." *Acta Koreana* 8:2 (July 2005), pp. 65–75.

Galef, David, ed. *Second Thoughts: A Focus on Rereading.* Detroit, MI: Wayne State University Press, 1998.

Gálik, Marián. *The Genesis of Modern Chinese Literary Criticism (1917–1930).* London: Curzon Press, 1980. Translated by Peter Tkáč.

——. *Milestones in Sino-Western Literary Confrontation (1898–1979).* Wiesbaden: Otto Harrassowitz, 1986.

——, ed. *Influence, Translation, and Parallels: Selected Studies on the Bible in China.* Sankt Augustin, Germany: Monumenta Serica Institute, 2004.

Gamsa, Mark. *Chinese Translation of Russian Literature: Three Studies.* Boston, MA: Brill, 2008.

Gardner, William. *Advertising Tower: Japanese Modernism and Modernity in the 1920s.* Cambridge, MA: Harvard University Asia Center, 2006.

Garrett, Jerry. "Civil War? Done That. Now We're Re-Enacting Hood Ornaments." *New York Times*, August 1, 2005, p. D9.

Gasster, Michael. *Chinese Intellectuals and the Revolution of 1911: The Birth of Modern Chinese Radicalism.* Seattle, WA: University of Washington Press, 1969.

Gates, Henry Louis, Jr. *The Signifying Monkey: A Theory of Afro-American Literary Criticism.* New York: Oxford University Press, 1988.

Genette, Gérard. *Palimpsestes: La littérature au second degré.* Paris: Éditions du Seuil, 1982.

——. *Seuils.* Paris: Éditions du Seuil, 1987.

Gentzler, Edwin and Maria Tymoczko. "Introduction," in Maria Tymoczko and Edwin Gentzler, eds. *Translation and Power.* Amherst, MA: University of Massachusetts Press, 2002. Pp. xi–xxviii.

Ghosh-Schellhorn, Martina. "'Uneasy lies the head…': South African Encounters with the Bard," in Norbert Schaffeld, ed. *Shakespeare's Legacy: The Appropriation of the Plays in Post-Colonial Drama.* Trier: Wissenschaftlicher Verlag Trier, 2005. Pp. 37–51.

Gibbs, James and Christine Matzke. "'accents yet unknown': Examples of Shakespeare from Ghana, Malawi and Eritrea," in Norbert Schaffeld, ed. *Shakespeare's Legacy: The Appropriation of the Plays in Post-Colonial Drama.* Trier: Wissenschaftlicher Verlag Trier, 2005. Pp. 15–36.

Gikandi, Simon. *Maps of Englishness: Writing Identity in the Culture of Colonialism.* New York: Columbia University Press, 1996.

Gilbert, Sandra M. *Death's Door: Modern Dying and the Ways We Grieve.* New York: W. W. Norton, 2006.

Gilbert, Sandra M. and Susan Gubar. *The Madwoman in the Attic: The Woman Writer and the Nineteenth-Century Literary Imagination.* New Haven, CT: Yale University Press, 1979.

Giles, Paul. *Transatlantic Insurrections: British Culture and the Formation of American Literature, 1730–1860.* Philadelphia, PA: University of Pennsylvania Press, 2001.

Gillespie, John K. "Yokomitsu Riichi's Two Machines," in Hiroshi Nara, ed. *Inexorable Modernity: Japan's Grappling with Modernity in the Arts.* Lanham, MD: Lexington Books, 2007. Pp. 229–54.

Ginsburg, Shai. "'The Rock of Our Very Existence': Anton Shammas's *Arabesques* and the Rhetoric of Hebrew Literature." *Comparative Literature* 58:3 (Summer 2006), pp. 187–204.

Glade, Jonathan. "Assimilation through Resistance: Language and Ethnicity in Kim Saryang's 'Hikari no naka ni.'" *Southeast Review of Asian Studies* 29 (2007), pp. 41–55.

Glissant, Edouard. *Poétique de la relation.* Paris: Gallimard, 1990.

Golley, Gregory. *When Our Eyes No Longer See: Realism, Science, and Ecology in Japanese Literary Modernism.* Cambridge, MA: Harvard University Asia Center, 2008.

Gordon, Andrew. *A Modern History of Japan: From Tokugawa Times to the Present.* New York: Oxford University Press, 2003.

Green, Frederick. "Re-appropriating *zhiguai*: Xu Xu (1908–1980) and the Search for a Chinese Romanticism." Paper presented at the New England Regional Conference for the Association for Asian Studies, October 18, 2008.

Green, Renée, ed. *Negotiations in the Contact Zone.* Lisbon: Assírio & Alvim, 2003.

Greene, Thomas M. *The Light in Troy: Imitation and Discovery in Renaissance Poetry.* New Haven, CT: Yale University Press, 1982.

Gu Inmo (Ku In-mo). "Tank'a [tanka] ro kŭrin Chosŏn ŭi p'ungsokji (fūzoku-shi): Sisan Sŏngung [Ichiyama Morio] p'yŏn, *Chosŏn p'ungt'o kajip* [Chōsen fūshi kashū] (1935) e taehayŏ." *Sai* 1 (November 2006), pp. 214–36.

Gu Yŏnhak. *Sŏljungmae,* in *Hanguk sinsosŏl chŏnjip* 6. Seoul: Ŭryu Munhwasa, 1968. Pp. 13–58.

Guillén, Claudio. *The Challenge of Comparative Literature.* Cambridge, MA: Harvard University Press, 1993.

Gunn, Edward. *Rewriting Chinese: Style and Innovation in Twentieth-Century Chinese Prose.* Stanford, CA: Stanford University Press, 1991.

———. *Unwelcome Muse: Chinese Literature in Shanghai and Peking, 1937–1945.* New York: Columbia University Press, 1980.

Guo Moruo. *Nihon bōmeiki.* Toyko: Hōsei Daigaku Shuppankyoku, 1958. Translated by Komine Kimichika.

——. "Wo de tongnian," in *Guo Moruo xuanji* 3. Beijing: Renmin Wenxue Chubanshe, 1997. Pp. 1–30.

——. "Yizhe shu," in *Caozhen*. Shanghai: Huali Shudian, 1930. Pp. 1–9.

——. "Zhongguoren dique shi tiancai," in *Guo Moruo lun chuangzuo*. Shanghai: Wenyi Chubanshe, 1983. Pp. 762–64.

——. "Zhuozi de tiaowu," in Hong Kong Literary Research Association, ed. *Zhongguo xinwenxue daxi xubian* 1. Hong Kong, 1968.

Guojia Tushuguan Qishinian Jishi Bianji Weiyuanhui, ed. *Guojia Tushuguan qishi nian jishi*. Taipei: Guojia Tushuguan, 2003.

Ha Sŏngran. "Ch'onnong nalgae," in *Yŏpjip yŏja*. Seoul: Ch'angjak kwa Pip'yŏngsa, 1999. Pp. 115–40.

Hackett, Roger F. *Chinese Students in Japan, 1900–1910*. Cambridge, MA: Harvard University Press, 1949.

Hagedorn, Suzanne. *Abandoned Women: Rewriting the Classics in Dante, Boccaccio, & Chaucer*. Ann Arbor, MI: University of Michigan Press, 2004.

Hagiwara Sakutarō. "Aoneko," in *Hagiwara Sakutarō zenshū* 1. Tokyo: Chikuma Shobō, 1978. Pp. 143–44.

——. "Kanashii tsukiyo," in *Hagiwara Sakutarō zenshū* 1. Tokyo: Chikuma Shobō, 1978. P. 41.

Hahm, Chaibong. "Civilization, Race, or Nation? Korean Visions of Regional Order in the Late Nineteenth Century," in Charles K. Armstrong et al., eds. *Korea at the Center: Dynamics of Regionalism in Northeast Asia*. Armonk, NY: M. E. Sharpe, 2006. Pp. 35–50.

Haku Rakuten, in *Nihon koten bungaku taikei* 41. Tokyo: Iwanami Shoten, 1958. Pp. 305–8.

Ham Ildon. "Myŏngch'i munhak sajŏk koch'al." *Haeoe munhak* 2 (July 1927).

Hamilton, John T. *Soliciting Darkness: Pindar, Obscurity, and the Classical Tradition*. Harvard Studies in Comparative Literature 47. Cambridge, MA: Harvard University Press, 2003.

Hammond, Marlé and Dana Sajdi, eds. *Transforming Loss into Beauty: Essays on Arabic Literature and Culture in Honor of Magda al-Nowaihi*. Cairo: American University in Cairo Press, 2008.

Han Kwangsu. *Nihon kindai shōsetsu no Kankoku ni okeru hon'an ni kansuru kenkyū, Senshū jinbun ronshū* 57 (1995).

Han Kyejŏn [Han Kye Jeon] et al. "1930 nyŏndae Hanguk munhak ŭi pigyo munhakjŏk yŏn-gu." *Pigyo munhak* 14 (December 1989), pp. 9–116.

Han Shiheng. "Xiandai Riben wenxue zagan (daixu)," in *Xiandai Riben xiaoshuo*. Shanghai: Chunchao Shuju, 1929. Pp. 1–26.

Han Sŏkjŏng. *Manjuguk kŏn-guk ŭi chae haesŏk: koeroeguk ŭi kukga hyogwa, 1932–1936*. Pusan: Dong-A University Press, 2007.

——. "On the Question of Collaboration in South Korea." *Japan Focus*, July 4, 2008.

——. Review of Yamamuro Shin'ichi, *Manchuria under Japanese Domination*. *Journal of Japanese Studies* 34:1 (Winter 2008), pp. 109–14.

Han Sŭngmin (Han Seung-min). "Han-Il ch'och'anggi sangjingjuŭi si toip-yangsang pigyo yŏn-gu: chŏngsinja ŭi yŏkhal kwa chŏn-gae kwajŏng ŭl chungsim ŭ ro." Ph.D. dissertation, Dongdŏk Women's University, 2001.

Han Weijun et al., eds. *Taiwan shudian fengqing*. Taipei: Shengzhi, 2000.

Han Youtong. "Tōdai Hōgakubu kenkyūshitsu de no gonenkan," in Jinmin Chūgoku Zasshisha, ed. *Waga seishun no Nihon: Chūgoku chishikijin no Nihon kaisō*. Tokyo: Tōhō Shoten, 1982. Pp. 113-25.

Hanan, Patrick. *Chinese Fiction of the Nineteenth and Early Twentieth Centuries*. New York: Columbia University Press, 2004.

———. "The Technique of Lu Hsun's Fiction." *Harvard Journal of Asiatic Studies* 34 (1974), pp. 53-96.

Hanayama Shinshō. *Shōmangyō gisho no Jōgūōsen ni kansuru kenkyū*. Tokyo: Iwanami Shoten, 1944.

Hane, Mikiso. *Peasants, Rebels, and Outcastes: The Underside of Modern Japan*. New York: Pantheon Books, 1982.

Hanneman, Mary Louise. "Hasegawa Nyozekan, Liberalism and the Japanese National Character: An Intellectual Biography." Ph.D. dissertation, University of Washington, 1991.

Hao Changhai. "Lao She yu waiguo wenxue," in Zeng Guangcan and Wu Huaibin, eds. *Lao She yanjiu ziliao* 2. Beijing: Beijing Shiyue Wenyi Chubanshe, 1985. Pp. 1000-1015.

Harlow, Barbara. "Sentimental Orientalism: *Season of Migration to the North* and *Othello*," in Mona Takieddine Amyuni, ed. *Season of Migration to the North by Tayeb Salih: A Casebook*. Beirut: American University of Beirut, 1985. Pp. 75-79.

Harootunian, Harry. "The Function of China in Tokugawa Thought," in Akira Iriye, ed. *The Chinese and the Japanese: Essays in Political and Cultural Interactions*. Princeton, NJ: Princeton University Press, 1980. Pp. 9-36.

Harrell, Paula. *Sowing the Seeds of Change: Chinese Students, Japanese Teachers, 1895-1905*. Stanford, CA: Stanford University Press, 1992.

Harrison, Nicholas. *Postcolonial Criticism: History, Theory, and the Work of Fiction*. Malden, MA: Blackwell Publishers, 2003.

———. "Life on the Second Floor." Review of Haun Saussy, ed. *Comparative Literature in an Age of Globalization*. *Comparative Literature* 59:4 (2007), pp. 332-48.

Hasegawa Nyozekan. *Nihonteki seikaku*. Tokyo: Iwanami Shoten, 1938.

Hashiya Hiroshi. *Teikoku Nihon to shokuminchi toshi*. Tokyo: Yoshikawa Kōbunkan, 2004.

Hawkins, Sean. *Writing and Colonialism in Northern Ghana: The Encounter between the LoDagaa and "the World on Paper."* Toronto, ON: University of Toronto Press, 2002.

Hay, Stephen N. *Asian Ideas of East and West: Tagore and His Critics in Japan, China, and India*. Cambridge, MA: Harvard University Press, 1970.

Hayasaka Takashi. *Senji engei imondan "Warawashi-tai" no kiroku: geinintachi ga mita Nitchū sensō*. Tokyo: Chūō Kōron Shinsha, 2008.

Hayashi Fumiko. "Chŏnjang ŭi todŏk." *Munjang* 1:4 (May 1939), p. 181.

———. *Sensen*. Tokyo: Asahi Shinbunsha, 1938.

Hayashi Fusao. "Mayu," in *Gendai Nihon shōsetsu taikei* 42. Tokyo: Kawade Shobō, 1949. Pp. 5–11.

Hayot, Eric. *The Hypothetical Mandarin: Sympathy, Modernity, and Chinese Pain*. New York: Oxford University Press, 2009.

Hebel, Udo. "Towards a Descriptive Poetics of *Allusion*," in Heinrich F. Plett, ed. *Intertextuality*. New York: Walter de Gruyter, 1991. Pp. 135–64.

Hegel, Robert. "Rewriting the Tang: Humor, Heroics, and Imaginative Reading," in Martin W. Huang, ed. *Snakes' Legs: Sequels, Continuations, Rewritings, and Chinese Fiction*. Honolulu, HI: University of Hawai'i Press, 2004. Pp. 159–89.

Henchy, Judith. "Vietnamese New Women and the Fashioning of Modernity," in Kathryn Robson and Jennifer Yee, eds. *France and "Indochina": Cultural Representations*. Lanham, MD: Lexington Books, 2005. Pp. 121–38.

Henriot, Christian and Wen-hsin Yeh, eds. *In the Shadow of the Rising Sun: Shanghai under Japanese Occupation*. Cambridge, UK: Cambridge University Press, 2004.

Henry, Todd A. "Respatializing Chosŏn's Royal Capital: The Politics of Japanese Urban Reforms in Early Colonial Seoul, 1905–1919," in Timothy R. Tangherlini and Sallie Yea, eds. *Sitings: Critical Approaches to Korean Geography*. Honolulu, HI: University of Hawai'i Press, 2008. Pp. 15–38.

———. "Sanitizing Empire: Japanese Articulations of Korean Otherness and the Construction of Early Colonial Seoul, 1905–1919." *Journal of Asian Studies* 64:3 (August 2005), pp. 639–75.

Henthorn, William E. "The Early Days of Western-Inspired Drama in Korea." *Yearbook of Comparative and General Literature* 15 (1966), pp. 204–13.

Heylen, Ann M. F. "Taiwanese Students in Metropolitan Tokyo: Debating the Chinese Language and the Formation of the 'Taiwan National Movement' in the 1920s." http://www.riccibase.com/docfile/eth-tw14.htm. Accessed October 22, 2006.

Hibbett, Howard. *The Chrysanthemum and the Fish: Japanese Humor Since the Age of the Shoguns*. Tokyo: Kodansha International, 2002.

———. *The Floating World in Japanese Fiction*. New York: Grove Press, 1959.

High, Peter B. *The Imperial Screen: Japanese Film Culture in the Fifteen Years' War, 1931–1945*. Madison, WI: University of Wisconsin Press, 1995.

Hijikata Teiichi. *Kindai Nihon bungaku hyōronshi*. Tokyo: Shōshinsha, 1948.

Hill, Peter. *Fate, Predestination and Human Action in the Mahābhārata: A Study in the History of Ideas*. New Delhi: Munshiram Manoharlal Publishers, 2001.

Hillenbrand, Margaret. *Literature, Modernity, and the Practice of Resistance: Japanese and Taiwanese Fiction, 1960–1990*. Boston, MA: Brill, 2007.

Hino Ashihei. "Chŏkjŏn sangryuk." *Munjang* 1:3 (April 1939), pp. 177–78.

———. "Chŏnjang ŭi chŏngwŏl." *Munjang* 1:10 (November 1939), pp. 113–15.

———. *Hana to heitai*, in Niwa Fumio, Hino Ashihei shū, *Shōwa bungaku zenshū* 46. Tokyo: Kadokawa Shoten, 1954. Pp. 295–381.

———. " 'Hŭlk kwa pyŏngdae' e sŏ." *Munjang* 1:2 (March 1939), pp. 159–60.

———. *Mai yu bingdui*. Shanghai: Zazhishe, 1938. Translated by Wu Zhefei.

——. *Mugi to heitai. Kaizō* 2:8 (August 1938), pp. 103–214.

——. *Pori wa pyŏng jŏng.* Seoul: Chōsen Sōtokufu, Maeil Sinbosa, 1939. Translated by Nishimura Shintarō.

——. "'Pori wa pyŏngjŏng' e sŏ." *Munjang* 3:2 (February 1941), pp. 214–19.

——. *Tsuchi to heitai.* Tokyo: Kaizōsha, 1938.

——. *Tu yu bingdui.* Beijing: Dongfang Shudian, 1939. Translated by Jin Gu.

Hō Kisei, ed. *Shū Sakujin* [Zhou Zuoren] *sensei no koto.* Tokyo: Kōfūkan, 1944.

Ho Kyegŏn. "Han-Chung yangguk ŭi kŭndae ch'ogi munhak pigyo yŏn-gu: sinmunhak sigi rŭl chungsim ŭ ro." Ph.D. dissertation, Seoul National University, 1980.

Hō Shun'yō. "Akutagawa Ryūnosuke to Ro Jin [Lu Xun]: 'Konan no ōgi' to 'Kusuri' [Yao] o chūshin to shite," in Yasukawa Sadao Sensei Koki Kinen Ronbunshū Iinkai, ed. *Yasukawa Sadao sensei koki kinen: Kindai Nihon bungaku no shosō.* Tokyo: Meiji Shoin, 1990. Pp. 161–65.

Hŏ Sŏng-il (Huh Sung-il). "Kanshi bunshū ni arawareta Yu Kitsushun [Yu Kilchun] no kaika ishiki." *Bukkyō Daigaku Sōgō Kenkyūjo kiyō bessatsu* (March 2003), pp. 59–79.

Hoek, Leo H. *La marque du titre: Dispositifs sémiotiques d'une pratique textuelle.* New York: Mouton, 1981.

——. *Titres, toiles et critique d'art: Déterminants institutionnels du discours sur l'art au dix-neuvième siècle en France.* Amsterdam: Rodopi, 2001.

Hollander, Robert. *Boccaccio's Dante and the Shaping Force of Satire.* Ann Arbor, MI: University of Michigan Press, 1997.

Holmes, James S. et al., eds. *Literature and Translation: New Perspectives in Literary Studies.* Leuven: Acco, 1978.

Holquist, Michael. "Introduction, Corrupt Originals: The Paradox of Censorship." *Proceedings of the Modern Language Association* 109:3 (May 1994), pp. 14–25.

Homer. *The Iliad.* New York: Penguin Books, 1990. Translated by Robert Fagles.

——. *The Odyssey.* New York: Viking, 1996. Translated by Robert Fagles.

Hong Chŏngsŏn (Hon Jonson). "Heiwa to kokumin no yūai no tame ni sasageta shōgai," in Anzai Ikurō and Yi Sukyŏng, eds. *Kurarute undō to Tanemaku Hito: hansen bungaku undō "Kurarute" no Nihon to Chōsen de no tenkai.* Tokyo: Ochanomizu Shobō, 2000. Pp. 124–60.

Hong Kong Literary Research Association, ed. *Zhongguo xinwenxue daxi xubian* 1. Hong Kong, 1968.

Hong Seong-tae. "From Mount Baekak to the Han River: A Road to Colonial Modernization." *Traces: A Multilingual Journal of Cultural Theory and Translation* 3 (2004), pp. 121–35. Translated by Kang Nae-hui.

Hong Sŏn-p'yo. "Korean Painting of the Late Chosŏn Period in Relation to Japanese Literati Painting." *Korea Journal* 20:5 (May 1980), pp. 17–24.

Hong Sŏn-yŏng (Hon Sonyon). "1910 nen zengo no Sōru [Seoul] ni okeru Nihonjingai no engeki katsudō: Nihongo shinbun *Keijō shinpō* no engeiran o chūshin ni," in Tsukuba Daigaku Kindai Bungaku Kenkyūkai, ed. *Meijiki zasshi media ni miru "bungaku."* Tsukuba: Tsukuba Daigaku Kindai Bungaku Kenkyūkai, 2000. Pp. 70–90.

Hoston, Germaine. "A 'Theology' of Liberation? Socialist Revolution and Spiritual Regeneration in Chinese and Japanese Marxism," in Paul A. Cohen and Merle Goldman, eds. *Ideas Across Cultures: Essays on Chinese Thought in Honor of Benjamin I. Schwartz.* Cambridge, MA: Harvard University Press, 1990. Pp. 165–221.

Hotei Toshihiro (Hot'ei T'osihiro). "Ilje malgi Ilbon-ŏ sosŏl ŭi sŏjihakjŏk yŏngu." *Munhak sasang* 280 (April 1996), pp. 44–78.

———. "Kaidai," in Ōmura Masuo and Hotei Toshihiro, eds. *Chōsen bungaku kankei Nihongo bunken mokuroku: 1882.4–1945.8.* Tokyo: Ryokuin Shobō, 1997. Pp. 3–7.

Howard, Keith, ed. *Korean Pop Music: Riding the Wave.* Folkestone, Kent: Global Oriental, 2006.

Hsia, C. T. *A History of Modern Chinese Fiction.* Bloomington, IN: Indiana University Press, 1999.

Hu Feng. *Hu Feng huiyi lu.* Beijing: Renmin Wenxue Chubanshe, 1993.

———. "Qiutian Yuque [Akita Ujaku] Yinxiangji." *Hu Feng quanji.* Wuhan: Hubei Renmin Chubanshe, 1999. Pp. 255–64.

Huang Fuqing (Huang Fu-ch'ing). *Chinese Students in Japan in the Late Ch'ing Period.* Tokyo: The Centre for East Asian Cultural Studies, 1982.

Huang Jianming. "Rizhi shiqi Yang Chichang ji qi wenxue yanjiu." Master's thesis, Guoli Chenggong University, 2002.

Huang, Martin W., ed. *Snakes' Legs: Sequels, Continuations, Rewritings, and Chinese Fiction.* Honolulu, HI: University of Hawai'i Press, 2004.

Huang Mei-e. "Wenti yu guoti: Riben wenxue zai Rizhi shiqi Taiwan hanyu wenyan xiaoshuozhong de kuajie xinglu—wenhua fanyi yu shuxie cuozhi." Paper given at the Teikokushugi to Bungaku Conference, Aichi University, August 1–3, 2008. Reprinted in the conference handout, pp. 278–304.

———. "Wenxue xiandaixing de yizhi yu chuanbo: Rizhi shidai Taiwan chuantong wenren dui shijie wenxue de jieshou, fanyi yu moxie." Paper given at the Taiwan Literature International Conference, Academia Sinica, Taiwan, July 15, 2004. Reprinted in the conference handout compiled by Peng Hsiao-yen.

Huang, Philip. *Liang Ch'i-ch'ao and Modern Chinese Liberalism.* Seattle, WA: University of Washington Press, 1972.

Huang Shide. "Xiaoshuo de renwu miaoxie." *Di yi xian,* January 6, 1934.

Huang Wanhua. "Shilun Yiwenzhipai de chuangzuo," in Feng Weiqun et al., eds. *Dongbei lunxian shiqi wenxue guoji xueshu yantaohui lunwenji.* Shenyang: Shenyang Chubanshe, 1992. Pp. 208–23.

Huang Yingzhe. "Zhang Shenqie de zhengzhi yu wenxue," in *Zhang Shenqie quanji* 4. Taipei: Wenjing Chubanshe, 1998. Pp. 27–46.

Huang, Yunte. "Pidginizing Chinese," in Doris Sommer, ed. *Bilingual Games: Some Literary Investigations.* New York: PalgraveMacmillan, 2003. Pp. 205–20.

——. *Transpacific Displacement: Ethnography, Translation, and Intertextual Travel in Twentieth-Century American Literature*. Berkeley, CA: University of California Press, 2002.

Huang Zunxian. *Riben zashi shi*, in *Zuo xiang shijie congshu* 3. Changsha: Yuelu Shushe, 1985. Pp. 535–813.

Hung, Eva and Judy Wakabayashi, eds. *Asian Translation Traditions*. Northampton, MA: St. Jerome Publishing, 2005.

——. "Translation in China—An Analytical Survey: First Century B.C.E. to Early Twentieth Century," in Eva Hung and Judy Wakabayashi, eds. *Asian Translation Traditions*. Northampton, MA: St. Jerome Publishing, 2005. Pp. 67–107.

Huss, Ann Louise. "Old Tales Retold: Contemporary Chinese Fiction and the Classical Tradition." Ph.D. dissertation, Columbia University, 2000.

Huters, Theodore. "From Writing to Literature: The Development of Late Qing Theories of Prose." *Harvard Journal of Asiatic Studies* 47:1 (June 1987), pp. 51–96.

——. "A New Way of Writing: The Possibilities for Literature in Late Qing China, 1895–1908." *Modern China* 14:3 (July 1988), pp. 243–76.

Hwang Sŏksung (Hwang Seock-Soong). "Kaech'ŏn Ryongjigae [Akutagawa Ryūnosuke] ŭi munhak kwa Yi Sang ŭi sosŏl." *Sangmyŏng Yŏja Taehakkyo nonmunjip* 30 (1992), pp. 183–98.

Hwang Sŏk-u. "Hyŏn Ilbon sasanggye ŭi t'ŭkjil kwa kŭ chujo." *Kaebyŏk* (April 1923), pp. 25–46.

——. "Ilbon sidan ŭi idae kyŏnghyang." *P'yehŏ* 1:1 (July 1920), pp. 76–98.

——. "Pyŏkmo ŭi myo." *P'yehŏ* 1:1 (July 1920), p. 16.

Hwang Sunwŏn. *K'ain ŭi huye*, in *Hwang Sunwŏn chŏnjip* 6. Seoul: Munhak kwa Chisŏngsa, 1995. Pp. 171–364.

Hyŏn Chin-gŏn. "Pul," in *Unsu choŭn nal: Hyŏn Chin-gŏn tanp'yŏnjip*. Seoul: Ŭlyu Munhwasa, 1975. Pp. 206–16.

——. "Sul kwŏnhanŭn sahoe," in *Unsu choŭn nal: Hyŏn Chin-gŏn tanp'yŏnjip*. Seoul: Ŭlyu Munhwasa, 1975. Pp. 217–35.

Hyun, Theresa. "The Lover's Silence, The People's Voice: Translating Nationalist Poetics in the Colonial Period in Korea," in Eva Hung and Judy Wakabayashi, eds. *Asian Translation Traditions*. Northampton, MA: St. Jerome Publishing, 2005. Pp. 155–68.

——. *Writing Women in Korea: Translation and Feminism in the Colonial Period*. Honolulu, HI: University of Hawai'i Press, 2004.

Ihara Seiseien. "Shinkokujin no gakuseigeki." *Waseda bungaku* 7 (1907), pp. 108–14.

Iida Saburō. "Jijo," in Ku In-am, *Kobore ume: Kin Gyokkin* [Kim Okgyun] *ian*. Tokyo: Hōrinkan, 1894. Pp. 1–2.

Ikezawa Miyoshi and Uchiyama Kayo, eds. *Mō ichido haru ni seikatsu dekiru koto o: teikō no romanshugi shijin Rei Sekiyu* [Lei Shiyu] *no hansei*. Tokyo: Chōryū Shuppansha, 1995.

Ikuta Shungetsu. *Atarashiki shi no tsukurikata*, in *Ikuta Shungetsu zenshū* 9. Tokyo: Iizuka Shobō, 1981. Pp. 335–475.

Im Chongguk. *Shinnichi bungakuron.* Tokyo: Kōrei Shorin, 1976. Translated by Ōmura Masuo.

Im Chŏnhye (Nin Tenkei). "Chōsen ni hon'yaku, shōkai sareta Nihon bungaku ni tsuite (1907–1945)." *Kaikyō* 10 (May 1981), pp. 35–52.

—— (Nin Tenkei). "Nihon ni hon'yaku, shōkai sareta Chōsen bungaku ni tsuite." *Chōsen kenkyū* 44 (October 1965), pp. 14–20.

—— (Im Jon Hye, Nin Tenkei). *Nihon ni okeru Chōsenjin no bungaku no rekishi: 1945 made.* Tokyo: Hōsei Daigaku Shuppankyoku, 1994.

Im Hŏn-yŏng and Hong Chŏngsŏn, eds. *Hanguk kŭndae pip'yŏngsa ŭi chaeng- jŏm.* Seoul: Tongsŏngsa, 1986.

Im Hwa. "Chosŏn munhak yŏn-gu ŭi il kwaje: Sin munhaksa ŭi pangbŏp- non," in *Im Hwa chŏnjip* 2. Seoul: Pagijŏng, 2001. Pp. 371–85.

——. "Usan pat-ŭn Yok'ohama ŭi pudu," in *Im Hwa chŏnjip* 1. Seoul: Pagijŏng, 2000. Pp. 66–70.

Im Kwŏnhwan. "'Kŭmsu hoeŭi rok' ŭi chaeraejŏk wŏnch'ŏn e taehayŏ." *Koryŏ Taehakkyo ŏ-mun nonch'ong* 19–20 (September 1977), pp. 631–44.

Im Yŏngt'aek. "Kim Ŏk ŭi si e nat'a-nan Ilbonjŏk yoso: chŏnggam kwa unryul ŭl chungsim ŭ ro." *Ilbon munhwa hakbo* 7 (August 1999), pp. 335–48.

—— (Imu Yonteku). *Kin So-un* [Kim Soun] *Chōsen shishū no sekai: sokoku sō- shitsusha no shishin.* Tokyo: Chūō Kōron Shinsha, 2000.

——. "Nikkan kindaishi no hikaku bungakuteki ikkōsatsu: Kin Soun [Kim Soun] yaku Chōsen shishū o chūshin ni." Ph.D. dissertation, University of Tokyo, 1995.

In Kwan Hwang. "The Korean Reform Movement of the 1880s and Fukuzawa Yukichi." Ph.D. dissertation, Washington University in St. Louis, 1975.

Innes, Catherine Lynette. *Chinua Achebe.* New York: Cambridge University Press, 1990.

——. "Language, Poetry and Doctrine in *Things Fall Apart,*" in Catherine Lynette Innes and Bernth Lindfors, eds. *Critical Perspectives on Chinua Achebe.* Washington, DC: Three Continents Press, 1978. Pp. 111–25.

Innes, Catherine Lynette, and Bernth Lindfors, eds. *Critical Perspectives on Chinua Achebe.* Washington, DC: Three Continents Press, 1978.

Interdepartmental Committee for the Acquisition of Foreign Publications. *The Manchoukuo Year Book 1942.* Hsinking: The Manchoukuo Year Book Co., 1942.

International Congress of the P.E.N. Clubs. *The Voice of the Writer 1984: Collected Papers of the 47th International P.E.N. Congress in Tokyo.* Tokyo: Kodansha, 1986.

Iriye, Akira, ed. *The Chinese and the Japanese: Essays in Political and Cultural Interactions.* Princeton, NJ: Princeton University Press, 1980.

Ishii, Kazumi. "*Josei:* A Magazine for the 'New Woman.'" *Intersections: Gender, History and Culture in the Asian Context* 11 (August 2005), pp. 1–17.

Ishii Yōko. "Chūgoku joshi ryūgakusei meibo, 1901–1919." *Shingai kakumei kenkyū* 2 (March 1982), pp. 49–69.

Ishikawa Tatsuzō. *Huozhe de bingdui.* Shanghai: Wenzhai, 1938. Translated by Zhang Shifang.

———. *Ikiteiru heitai. Chūō kōron* 53:3 (March 1938), pp. 1–105.

———. *Ikiteiru heitai.* Tokyo: Kawade Shobō, 1945.

———. *Ikiteiru heitai. Chūō kōron (rinji zōkan): gekidō no Shōwa bungaku* (November 1997), pp. 274–350.

———. "Shi," in *Ikiteiru heitai.* Tokyo: Kawade Shobō, 1945. Pp. 1–3.

———. *Weisi de bing, Damei wanbao,* March 18–April 8, 1938. Translated by Bai Mu.

———. *Weisi de bing.* Shanghai: Zazhishe, 1938. Translated by Bai Mu.

———. *Weisi de bing,* in *Xia Yan quanji* 14. Hangzhou: Zhejiang Wenyi Chubanshe, 2005. Pp. 683–757. Translated by Xia Yan.

Ishikawa Yoshihiro. "Chinese Marxism in the Early 20th Century and Japan." *Sino-Japanese Studies* 14 (April 2002), pp. 24–34.

Ito, Ken. *An Age of Melodrama: Family, Gender, and Social Hierarchy in the Turn-of-the-Century Japanese Novel.* Stanford, CA: Stanford University Press, 2008.

———. "The Family and the Nation in Tokutomi Roka's *Hototogisu.*" *Harvard Journal of Asiatic Studies* 60:2 (2000), pp. 489–536.

Itō Noriya. " 'Watakushi' to iu chūzuri sōchi: Shū Sakujin [Zhou Zuoren] no Nihongo sōsaku," in Ro Jin [Lu Xun] Ronshū Henshū Iinkai, ed. *Ro Jin* [Lu Xun] *to dōjidaijin.* Tokyo: Kyūko Shoin, 1992. Pp. 6–8.

Itō Toramaru et al., eds. *Kindai bungaku ni okeru Chūgoku to Nihon: kyōdō kenkyū Nitchū bungaku kōryūshi.* Tokyo: Kyūko Shoin, 1986.

———. *Tian Han zai Riben.* Beijing: Renmin Wenxue Chubanshe, 1997.

Iwasa Masaaki, ed. *Chūgoku gendai bungaku to Kyūshū: ikoku, seishun, sensō.* Fukuoka: Kyūshū Daigaku Shuppankai, 2005.

Izu Toshihiko. "Teikokushugi to Bungaku: Kankoku de Kobayashi Takiji o yomu." *Ilbon-ŏ munhak* 36 (March 2008), pp. 3–18.

Jacquemond, Richard. "Translation and Cultural Hegemony: The Case of French-Arabic Translation," in Lawrence Venuti, ed. *Rethinking Translation: Discourse, Subjectivity, Ideology.* New York: Routledge, 1992. Pp. 139–58.

James, Cyril Lionel Robert. *Beyond a Boundary.* London: Hutchinson, 1963.

Jansen, Marius. "Japan and the Chinese Revolution of 1911," in John K. Fairbank and Kwang-ching Liu, eds. *The Cambridge History of China,* vol. 11, *Late Ch'ing 1800–1911, 2.* New York: Cambridge University Press, 1980. Pp. 339–74.

———. *The Japanese and Sun Yat-sen.* Cambridge, MA: Harvard University Press, 1954.

———. "Japanese Views of China During the Meiji Period," in Albert Feuerwerker, Rhoads Murphey, and Mary Clabaugh Wright, eds. *Approaches to Modern Chinese History.* Berkeley, CA: University of California Press, 1967. Pp. 163–89.

———. *The Making of Modern Japan.* Cambridge, MA: The Belknap Press of Harvard University Press, 2000.

Japan Kokusai Kankōkyoku. *Japan Pictorial, Le Japon illustré, Japan in Bildern.* Tokyo: Board of Tourist Industry, Japanese Government Railways, 1940?

Jay, Paul. "Translation, Invention, Resistance: Rewriting the Conquest in Carlos Fuentes's 'The Two Shores.'" *Modern Fiction Studies* 43:2 (Summer 1997), pp. 405-31.

Ji Xian. "Fei yue de quan," in *Ji Xian zixuanji*. Taipei: Liming Wenhua Shiye Gongsi, 1978. P. 82.

Jia Zhifang. "Zhongguo liuri xuesheng yu Zhongguo xiandai wenxue." *Zhongguo bijiao wenxue* 1 (1991), pp. 1-20.

———. "Zhongguo liuri xuesheng yu Zhongguo xiandai wenxue," in Wang Zhuo, ed. *Zhong-Ri bijiao wenxue yanjiu ziliaohui*. Hangzhou: Zhongguo Meiyi Xueyuan Chubanshe, 2002. Pp. 166-83.

Jiang Wenye. "Jūsetsukai [Shichahai] no natsumatsuri," in *Pekin mei*. Tokyo: Seigodō, 1942. P. 50.

———. "'Mei' ni yosuru joshi," in *Pekin mei*. Tokyo: Seigodō, 1942. P. 4.

———. "'Mei' ni yosuru kōda," in *Pekin mei*. Tokyo: Seigodō, 1942. P. 123.

Jiang Xingjun. *Feixing Taipei: guang shudian*. Taipei: Zhengzhong Shuju, 2002.

Jiang Zide (Chiang Chi-der), ed. *Zhimindi jingyan yu Taiwan wenxue*. Taipei: Yuan Liu Chuban Gongsi, 2000.

Jin Conglin. "Kang-Ri zhanzheng shiqi de Zhong-Ri wenxue guanxi," in Yamada Keizō and Lü Yuanming, eds. *Zhong-Ri zhanzheng yu wenxue: Zhong-Ri xiandai wenxue de bijiao yanjiu*. Changchun: Dongbei Shifan Daxue Chubanshe, 1992. Pp. 325-38.

Jin Huanji. "Dongbei lunxian shiqi de Haerbin wentan," in Yamada Keizō and Lü Yuanming, eds. *Zhong-Ri zhanzheng yu wenxue: Zhong-Ri xiandai wenxue de bijiao yanjiu*. Changchun: Dongbei Shifan Daxue Chubanshe, 1992. Pp. 195-205.

Jin Mingquan. *Zhongguo xiandai zuojia yu Riben*. Ji'nan: Shandong Wenyi Chubanshe, 1993.

Jin Ying Yu. "Han-Chung kŭndae sosŏl ŭi hwakrip kwajŏng pigyo yŏn-gu: Yŏm Sangsŏp, Hyŏn Chin-gŏn kwa Ro Sin [Lu Xun] ŭi sosŏl ŭl chungsim ŭ ro." Ph.D. dissertation, Hanguk Kyowŏn University, 2003.

Jinmin Chūgoku Zasshisha, ed. *Waga seishun no Nihon: Chūgoku chishikijin no Nihon kaisō*. Tokyo: Tōhō Shoten, 1982.

Jones, Radhika. "Required Reading, or How Contemporary Novels Respond to the Canon." Ph.D. dissertation, Columbia University, 2008.

Jong, Erica. *Fear of Flying*. New York: Holt, Rinehart and Winston, 1973.

Joshi, Priya. *In Another Country: Colonialism, Culture, and the English Novel in India*. New York: Columbia University Press, 2002.

Jungmann, Burglind. *Painters as Envoys: Korean Inspiration in Eighteenth-Century Japanese Nanga*. Princeton, NJ: Princeton University Press, 2004.

Kaji Wataru. "Xu," in Ishikawa Tatsuzō, *Weisi de bing, Xia Yan quanji* 14. Hangzhou: Zhejiang Wenyi Chubanshe, 2005. Pp. 685-87.

Kajii Noboru. "Gendai Chōsen bungaku e no Nihonjin no taiō (2): 'Chōsen' tokushū to bungaku (1910-1945)." *Toyama Daigaku Jinbungakubu kiyō* 5 (1981), pp. 93-115.

Kamens, Edward, ed. *The Cambridge History of Japanese Literature* (forthcoming).

Kamiya Tadataka. "Senjika no Chōsen bungakukai to Nihon: 'Naisen ittai' ni tsuite." *Hokkaidō Bunkyō Daigaku* 9 (March 2008), pp. 13–24.

Kan Tokusan [Kang Tŏksang] Sensei Koki Taishoku Kinen Ronbunshū Kankō Iinkai, ed. *Nitchō kankei shi ronshū: Kan Tokusan [Kang Tŏksang] sensei koki taishoku kinen.* Tokyo: Shinkansha, 2003.

Kane, Daniel. "Display at Empire's End: Korea's Participation in the 1900 Paris Universal Exposition." *Sungkyun Journal of East Asian Studies* 4:2 (2004), pp. 41–66.

Kaneko Mitsuharu. "Nanshi no geijutsukai." *Shūkan Asahi*, November 28, 1926. Reprinted in Itō Toramaru, ed., *Tian Han zai Riben.* Beijing: Renmin Wenxue Chubanshe, 1997. Pp. 203–6.

Kanhaeng Wiwŏnhoe, ed. *Han-Chung munhak pigyo yŏn-gu: Hŏ Hoil kyosu chŏngnyŏn t'oeim ki-nyŏm nonmunjip.* Seoul: Kukhak Charyowŏn, 1997.

Kano Tadao. *Yama to kumo to banjin to: Taiwan kōzan kikō.* Tokyo: Bun'yūsha, 2002.

Kaplan, Brett Ashley. " 'The Bitter Residue of Death': Jorge Semprun and the Aesthetics of Holocaust Memory." *Comparative Literature* 55:4 (Fall 2003), pp. 320–37.

Karaki Junzō. *Kindai Nihon bungaku no tenkai.* Tokyo: Kōga Shoin, 1939.

Karatani Kōjin, ed. *Kindai Nihon no hihyō: Meiji Taishō hen.* Tokyo: Fukutake Shoten, 1992.

Karrer, Wolfgang. "Titles and Mottoes as Intertextual Devices," in Heinrich F. Plett, ed. *Intertextuality.* New York: Walter de Gruyter, 1991. Pp. 122–34.

Kataoka Yoshikazu. " 'Kwŏn to iu otoko' [A Man Called Kwŏn] 1933, By Cho Kok Chu," in Kokusai Bunka Shinkōkai, ed. *Introduction to Contemporary Japanese Literature.* Tokyo: Kokusai Bunka Shinkōkai, 1939. Pp. 419–21.

Katō Kiyofumi. "Kaidai," in Katō Kiyofumi, ed. *Kyūshokuminchi toshokan zōsho mokuroku: Taiwan hen* 9. Tokyo: Yumani Shobō, 2004–5. Pp. 497–501.

——, ed. *Kyūshokuminchi toshokan zōsho mokuroku*, 14 vols. Tokyo: Yumani Shobō, 1998–2004.

——, ed. *Kyūshokuminchi toshokan zōsho mokuroku: Taiwan hen*, 9 vols. Tokyo: Yumani Shobō, 2004–5.

Kaup, Monika. *Mad Intertextuality: Madness in Twentieth-Century Women's Writing.* Trier: Wissenschaftlicher Verlag Trier, 1993.

Kawabata Yasunari. *Koto*, in *Kawabata Yasunari zenshū* 18. Tokyo: Shinchōsha, 1980. Pp. 229–435.

—— et al., eds. *Manshūkoku kakuminzoku sōsaku senshū* 1. Tokyo: Sōgensha, 1942.

—— et al., eds. *Manshūkoku kakuminzoku sōsaku senshū* 2. Tokyo: Sōgensha, 1944.

——. *Nemureru bijo.* Tokyo: Shinchōsha, 1967.

——. *Yukiguni.* Tokyo: Kadokawa Shoten, 1968.

Kawahara Isao. *Taiwan shinbungaku undō no tenkai: Nihon bungaku to setten.* Tokyo: Kenbun Shuppan, 1997.

Kawamura Minato. *Bungaku kara miru 'Manshū': 'gozoku kyōwa' no yume to genjitsu.* Tokyo: Yoshikawa Kōbunkan, 1998.

———. *Ikyō no Shōwa bungaku: "Manshū" to kindai Nihon*. Tokyo: Iwanami Shoten, 1990.

———. *Sakubun no naka no Dai Nihon teikoku*. Tokyo: Iwanami Shoten, 2000.

———. *Umi o watatta Nihongo: shokuminchi no "kokugo" no jikan*. Tokyo: Seidosha, 1994.

Kawana, Sari. *Murder Most Modern: Detective Fiction and Japanese Culture*. Minneapolis, MN: University of Minnesota Press, 2008.

Kawashima, Fujiya. "A Shared Vision in Taishō Japan and Revolutionary China: A Quest for the Perfect Community." *Ajia bunka kenkyū* 23 (March 1997), pp. 119–36.

Kazeta Eiki. "Wei Manzhouguo wenyi zhangye de fazhan," in Feng Weiqun et al., eds. *Dongbei lunxian shiqi wenxue guoji xueshu yantaohui lunwenji*. Shenyang: Shenyang Chubanshe, 1992. Pp. 156–81.

Keaveney, Christopher T. *Beyond Brushtalk: Sino-Japanese Literary Exchange in the Interwar Period*. Hong Kong: Hong Kong University Press, 2009.

———. "Satō Haruo's 'Ajia no ko' and Yu Dafu's Response: Literature, Friendship, and Nationalism." *Sino-Japanese Studies* 13:2 (March 2001), pp. 21–31.

———. *The Subversive Self in Modern Chinese Literature: The Creation Society's Reinvention of the Japanese Shishōsetsu*. New York: Palgrave Macmillan, 2004.

Keene, Donald. *Dawn to the West: Japanese Literature in the Modern Era – Poetry, Drama, Criticism*. New York: Holt, Rinehart and Winston, 1984.

Kellman, Steven G., ed. *Approaches to Teaching Camus's The Plague*. New York: Modern Language Association of America, 1985.

Khatibi, Abdelkebir. "Diglossia," in Anne-Emmanuelle Berger, ed. *Algeria in Others' Languages*. Ithaca, NY: Cornell University Press, 2002. Pp. 157–60.

Kihŏn Son Rakbŏm Sŏnsaeng Hoegap Ki-nyŏn Nonmunjip Kanhaeng Wiwŏnhoe, ed. *Kihŏn Son Rakbŏm sŏnsaeng hoegap kin-yŏn nonmunjip*. Seoul: Kihŏn Son Rakbŏm Sŏnsaeng Hoegap Kin-yŏn Nonmunjip Kanhaeng Wiwŏnhoe, 1972.

Kikuchi Hiroshi (Kan). *Nihon bungaku annai*. Tokyo: Modan Nipponsha, 1938.

Kikuchi Yūhō. *Ono ga tsumi*, in *Kikuchi Yūhō zenshū* 1. Tokyo: Nihon Tosho Sentā, 1997.

———. *Ssang-oknu*, *Maeil sinbo*, July 17, 1912–February 4, 1913. Adaptation of *Ono ga tsumi* by Cho Iljae.

Killman, G. D. "Chinua Achebe," in C. Brian Cox, ed. *African Writers* 1. New York: Charles Scribner's Sons, 1997. Pp. 15–36.

Kim Ch'aesu. *Hanguk kwa Ilbon ŭi kŭndae ŏnmun-ilch'ich'e hyŏngsŏng kwajŏng*. Seoul: Pogosa, 2002.

Kim, Christine. "Imperial Hangover: The Chosŏn Monarchy in Republican Korea, 1945–1965." Lecture at Harvard University, December 11, 2008.

Kim Ch'unmi (Kim Choon Mie). "Kim Dong-in yŏn-gu: pigyo munhakjŏk koch'al." Ph.D. dissertation, Korea University, 1984.

Kim Dong-in. "Kamja," in *Kim Dong-in chŏnjip* 7. Seoul: Hongja Ch'ulp'ansa, 1964. Pp. 363–70.

———. "Kwang-yŏm sonat'a," in *Kwang-yŏm sonat'a oe*. Seoul: Chosŏn Ilbosa, 1988. Pp. 33–51.

———. "Mundan 30 nyŏn ŭi chach'oe," in *Kim Dong-in p'yŏngnon chŏnjip*. Seoul: Samyŏngsa, 1984. Pp. 421–511.

———. "Paettaragi," in *Kim Dong-in jip 7*. Seoul: Hongja Ch'ulp'ansa, 1956. Pp. 188–200.

Kim Hakdong. *Hanguk kaehwagi shiga yŏn-gu*. Seoul: Simunhaksa, 1981.

Kim Hakhyŏn. "Kōya no shijin: Li Rikushi [Yi Yuksa] Chōsen bungaku to Ro Jin [Lu Xun]." *Bungaku* 44:4 (1976), pp. 529–41.

Kim Hye-ni. *Hanguk kŭn-hyŏndae pip'yŏng munhaksa yŏn-gu*. Seoul: Wŏrin, 2003.

Kim, Jina. "The Materializing and Vanishing Modern Girl: The Circulation of Urban Literary Modernity in Colonial Korea and Taiwan." Ph.D. dissertation, University of Washington, 2005.

Kim Kiju. *Hanmal chaeil Hanguk yuhaksaeng ŭi minjok undong*. Seoul: Nut'i Namu, 1993.

Kim Kwanggyun. "Ro Sin [Lu Xun]." *Sinch'ŏnji*, March 4, 1947.

Kim Kyuch'ang (Kim Kyoo Chang). "Chosŏn-ŏgwa simal kwa Il-ŏ kyoyuk ŭi yŏksajŏk paegyŏng (1): Iljeha ŭi ŏn-ŏ kyoyuk chŏngch'aek nongo (Ki-il)." *Sŏul Kyoyuk Taehak nonmunjip* 1 (1968), pp. 7–44.

———. "Iljeha ŏn-ŏ kyoyuk chŏngch'aek ŭi chedosajŏk koch'al (1): Iljeha taehan ŏn-ŏ kyoyuk chŏngch'aeksa sŏsŏl," in Kihŏn Son Rakpŏm Sŏnsaeng Hoegap kin-yŏn Nonmunjip Kanhaeng Wiwŏnhoe, ed. *Kihŏn Son Rakpŏm sŏnsaeng hoegap kin-yŏn nonmunjip kanhaeng*. Seoul: Kihŏn Son Rakpŏm Sŏnsaeng Hoegap kin-yŏn Nonmunjip Wiwŏnhoe, 1972. Pp. 509–49.

Kim Pyŏngch'ŏl. *Hanguk kŭndae pŏn-yŏk munhaksa yŏn-gu*. Seoul: Ŭryu Munhwasa, 1975.

———. *Segye munhak pŏn-yŏk sŏji mokrok ch'ongram (1895–1987)*. Seoul: Gukhak Charyowŏn, 2002.

Kim Sijun (Kin Shi-jun). "Chūgoku ni ryūbōsuru Kankoku chishikijin to Ro Jin [Lu Xun]." *Ajia yūgaku* 25 (March 2001), pp. 9–21.

Kim Sŏkhŭi. "Yi Sang ŭi nalgae," in *Yi Sang ŭi nalgae: Kim Sŏkhŭi ch'ang jak sosŏljip*. Seoul: Silch'ŏn Munhaksa, 1989. Pp. 10–30.

Kim Soonsik. "Chinua Achebe's *Things Fall Apart* as a Counter-Conradian Discourse on Africa." *Pigyo munhak* 25 (2000), pp. 333–55.

Kim Soun, ed. *Nyūshoku no kumo*. Tokyo: Kawade Shobō, 1940.

Kim Sunjŏn (Kim Soon-Jeun). "Ch'oe Chansik ŭi *Sŏljungmae* ŭi suyŏng yang-t'ae pigyo yŏn-gu: chakp'um *Kŭmgangmun* ŭl chungsim ŭ ro." *Yongbong nonch'ong* 22 (December 1993), pp. 137–65.

———. *Han-Il kŭndae sosŏl ŭi pigyo munhakjŏk yŏn-gu*. Seoul: T'aehaksa, 1998.

——— (Kim Soon-Jeon). "Kan-Nichi kaikaki shōsetsu no hikaku bungakuteki kenkyū." *Ilbon munhwa hakbo* 11 (August 2001), pp. 239–53.

———. "Sŏgu ŭi ch'unggyŏk kwa Han-Il munhak ŭi taeŭng yangsang." *Ilbon kŭndae munhak: yŏn-gu wa pip'yŏng* (May 2002), pp. 121–50.

Kim T'aejun. "Ildong kiyu wa *Sŏyu kyŏnmun*: sŏdurŭm kwa chiriham ŭi pigyo munhwaron." *Pigyo munhak* 16 (December 1991), pp. 70–100.

——— (Kimu Tejun). "*Seiyū kenmon* [Sŏyu kyŏnmun] to *Seiyō jijō*: hikaku bunkateki kenkyū no tame no mondai teiki." *Han* 6:5 (May 1977), pp. 122–30.

Kim T'aesaeng. "*Nakano Shigeharu shishū* to no deai." *Sanzenri* 21 (February 1980), pp. 112–17.

Kim, Uchang, ed. *Writing Across Boundaries: Literature in the Multicultural World*. Elizabeth, NJ: Hollym International, 2002.

Kim Ujin. *Yuhwau*. Tokyo: Tōyō Shoin, 1912.

——. *Yuhwau*, in *Hanguk sinsosŏl chŏnjip 6*. Seoul: Ŭryu Munhwasa, 1968. Pp. 221–69.

Kim Ŭnjŏn (Kim Ŭn-jŏn). "Kim Ŏk ŭi P'ŭrangsŭ sangjingjuŭi suyong yangsang." Ph.D. dissertation, Seoul National University, 1984.

Kim Yongho. *Nalgae*, in *Kim Yongho si chŏnjip*. Seoul: Taegwang Munhwasa, 1983. Pp. 149–203.

——. "Nalgae (I)," in *Kim Yongho si chŏnjip*. Seoul: Taegwang Munhwasa, 1983. P. 162.

——. "Nalgae (II)," in *Kim Yongho si chŏnjip*. Seoul: Taegwang Munhwasa, 1983. P. 183.

Kim Yunsik. "1940 nen zengo zai Sōru [Seoul] Nihonjin no bungaku katsudō: *Kokumin bungaku* shi to kanren shite," in Ōe Shinobu et al., eds. *Kindai Nihon to shokuminchi 7: bunka no naka no shokuminchi*. Tokyo: Iwanami Shoten, 1993. Pp. 231–51.

——. "Hanguk chakga ŭi Ilbon-ŏ chakp'um: Il-ŏro ssŭn chakp'umdŭl kwa kŭ munje chŏm." *Munhak sasang* 145 (September 1974), pp. 270–78.

——. *Im Hwa yŏn-gu*. Seoul: Munhak Sasanga, 1989.

——. *Kizuato to kokufuku: Kankoku no bungakusha to Nihon*. Tokyo: Asahi Shinbunsha, 1975. Translated by Ōmura Masuo.

Kimura, Hiroshi. *The Kurillian Knot: A History of Japanese-Russian Border Negotiations*. Stanford, CA: Stanford University Press, 2008. Translated by Mark Ealey.

Kimura Ki. *Nunobikimaru: Firipin dokuritsugun hiwa*. Tokyo: Kōbunsha, 1981.

Kinebuchi Nobuo. *Fukuzawa Yukichi to Chōsen: Jiji shinpō shasetsu o chūshin ni*. Tokyo: Sairyūsha, 1997.

King, Bruce, ed. *New National and Post-Colonial Literatures: An Introduction*. New York: Oxford University Press, 1996.

Kinpu Sanjin [Nagai Kafū]. "Yojōhan no fusuma no shitabari," in Yagiri Tadayuki, ed. *Naze "Yojōhan fusuma no shitabari" wa meisaku ka*. Tokyo: San'ichi Shobō, 1995. Pp. 177–85.

Kishi Yamaji. "Taiwan no sakka ni nozomu koto." *Taiwan shinbungaku* 1 (1936), pp. 36–37.

Kishi Yōko. *Chūgoku chishikijin no hyakunen: bungaku no shiza kara*. Tokyo: Waseda Daigaku Shuppanbu, 2004.

Kitahara Tsuzuru. *Shijin – sono kyozō to jitsuzō: chichi Kin So-un* [Kim Soun] *no baai*. Tokyo: Sōrinsha, 1986.

Kitasono Katsue. "Atsui monokuru 5," in *Kitasono Katsue zenshishū*. Tokyo: Chūsekisha, 1983. Pp. 209–10.

——. "Hodō," in *Kitasono Katsue zenshishū*. Tokyo: Chūsekisha, 1983. P. 206.

——. "Kazarimado," in *Kitasono Katsue zenshishū*. Tokyo: Chūsekisha, 1983. Pp. 205–6.

Kleeman, Faye. "The Boundaries of the Japaneseness between '*Nihon bungaku*' and '*Nihongo bungaku*,' " in *Proceedings of the Association for Japanese Literary Studies* 1 (2000), pp. 377–88.

——. "The Poetics of Colonial Nostalgia: A Case for *Taiwan Man'yōshū*." *Proceedings of the Association for Japanese Literary Studies* 3 (Summer 2002), pp. 2–11.

——. *Under an Imperial Sun: Japanese Colonial Literature of Taiwan and the South.* Honolulu, HI: University of Hawai'i Press, 2003.

Knight, Sabina. *The Heart of Time: Moral Agency in Twentieth-Century Chinese Fiction.* Cambridge, MA: Harvard University Asia Center, 2006.

Ko, Dorothy. "The Subject of Pain," in David Der-wei Wang and Shang Wei, eds. *Dynastic Crisis and Cultural Innovation: From the Late Ming to the Late Qing and Beyond.* Cambridge, MA: Harvard University Asia Center, 2005. Pp. 478–503.

Ko Yŏngja [Ko Young-Ja]. "Nakano Shigeharu to Rin Wa [Im Hwa]." *Chŏnnam Taehakkyo yongbong nonch'ong* 21 (December 1991), pp. 191–208.

Kōain, ed. *Nihon ryūgaku Chūka Minkoku jinmeichō, Kōain chōsa shiryō* 9. Tokyo: Kōain, 1940.

Kobayashi Takiji. *Kani kōsen*, in *Kani kōsen*. Tokyo: Senkisha, 1929. Pp. 1–126.

——. *Teihon Kobayashi Takiji zenshū* 14. Tokyo: Shin Nihon Shuppansha, 1969.

Kockum, Keiko. *Japanese Achievement, Chinese Aspiration: A Study of the Japanese Influence on the Modernization of the Late Qing Novel.* Löberöd, Sweden: Plus Ultra, 1990.

Kohō Banri. "Maegaki," in Kohō Banri, ed. *Taiwan Man'yōshū* 1. Tokyo: Shūeisha, 1994. Pp. 8–11.

——, ed. *Taiwan Man'yōshū* 1. Tokyo: Shūeisha, 1994.

Koizumi Yuzuru. *Ro Jin [Lu Xun] to Uchiyama Kanzō.* Tokyo: Tosho Shuppan, 1989.

Kojima Yoshio. *Ryūnichi gakusei no shingai kakumei.* Tokyo: Aoki Shoten, 1989.

Kokusai Bunka Shinkōkai, ed. *Introduction to Contemporary Japanese Literature.* Tokyo: Kokusai Bunka Shinkōkai, 1939.

——. "Preface," in Kokusai Bunka Shinkōkai, ed. *Introduction to Contemporary Japanese Literature.* Tokyo: Kokusai Bunka Shinkōkai, 1939. Pp. iii–iv.

Komagome Takeshi. "Colonial Modernity for an Elite Taiwanese, Lim Boseng: The Labyrinth of Cosmopolitanism," in Liao Ping-hui and David Der-wei Wang, eds. *Taiwan under Japanese Colonial Rule, 1895–1945: History, Culture, Memory.* New York: Columbia University Press, 2006. Pp. 141–59.

——. *Shokuminchi teikoku Nihon no bunka tōgō.* Tokyo: Iwanami Shoten, 1996.

Kondō Haruo. "Chūgoku bundan to ryūnichi gakusei." *Tōzai* (April 1947), pp. 25–30.

——. *Gendai Chūgoku no sakka to sakuhin.* Tokyo: Shinsen Shobō, 1949.

Kono, Kimberly. "Writing Imperial Relations: Romance and Marriage in Japanese Colonial Literature." Ph.D. dissertation, University of California, Berkeley, 2001.

Kornicki, Peter. *The Book in Japan: A Cultural History from the Beginnings to the Nineteenth Century.* Leiden: Brill, 1998.

Kratoska, Paul H., ed. *Asian Labor in the Wartime Japanese Empire: Unknown Histories*. Armonk, NY: M. E. Sharpe, 2005.

Kristeva, Julia. *Revolution in Poetic Language*. New York: Columbia University Press, 1984. Translated by Margaret Waller.

———. "Word, Dialogue and Novel," in Toril Moi, ed. *The Kristeva Reader*. New York: Columbia University Press, 1986. Pp. 34–61.

Ku In-am. *Kobore ume: Kin Gyokkin* [Kim Okgyun] *ian*. Tokyo: Hōrinkan, 1894.

Kukrip Chung-ang Tosŏgwan, ed. *Kukrip Chung-ang Tosŏgwan sa*. Seoul: Kukrip Chung-ang Tosŏgwan, 1973.

Kŭm Pyŏngdong. *Kin Gyokkin* [Kim Okgyun] *to Nihon: sono tainichi no kiseki*. Tokyo: Ryokuin Shobō, 1991.

Kunikida Doppo. "Gyūniku to bareisho," in *Kunikida Doppo zenshū* 2. Tokyo: Gakushū Kenkyūsha, 1969. Pp. 361–88.

———. "Jonan," in *Kunikida Dopposhū, Nihon gendai bungaku zenshū* 18. Tokyo: Kōdansha, 1962. Pp. 215–29.

———. "Unmeironsha," in *Kunikida Doppo zenshū* 3. Tokyo: Gakushū Kenkyūsha, 1964. Pp. 143–73.

Kuriyagawa Hakuson. *Kumon no shōchō*. Tokyo: Kaizōsha, 1924.

Kurokawa Sō, ed. *Gaichi no Nihon bungakusen 3*. Tokyo: Shinjuku Shobō, 1996.

Kuroko Kazuo and Kang Dongyuan. *Nihon kingendai bungaku no Chūgokugoyaku sōran*. Tokyo: Bensei Shuppan, 2006.

Kushner, Barak. *The Thought War: Japanese Imperial Propaganda*. Honolulu, HI: University of Hawai'i Press, 2006.

Kwŏn Bodŭrae (Kwon Boduerae). "Hanguk, Chungguk, Ilbon ŭi kŭndaejŏk munhak kae-nyŏm mit munhak-ŏ hyŏngsŏng (1): sosŏl *Pulyŏgui* [Hototogisu] ŭi ch'angjak mit pŏn-yŏk—pŏn-an yangsang ŭl chungsim ŭ ro." *Taedong munhwa yŏn-gu* 2 (June 2003), pp. 373–404.

Kwŏn Chŏnghŭi. "Haehyŏp ŭl nŏm ŭn 'kukmin munhak': Chosŏn e sŏ ŭi *Pulyŏgwi* suyong yangsang," in Saegusa Toshikatsu (Saegusa Tosik'assŭ), ed. *Hanguk kŭndae munhak kwa Ilbon*. Seoul: Somyong, 2003. Pp. 38–56.

Kwon, Heonik. "Excavating the History of Collaboration." *Japan Focus*, July 4, 2008.

Kwon, Nayoung Aimee. "Translated Encounters and Empire: Colonial Korea and the Literature of Exile." Ph.D. dissertation, University of California, Los Angeles, 2007.

Lai Mingzhu. "Yixu," in *Yu jian 100% de nu hai*. Taipei: Shibao Wenhua Chuban Qiye Gufen Youxian Gongsi, 1995. Pp. 5–8.

Lai Ruiqin. "Nihon tōchiki no Taiwan bungaku ni okeru ryūgaku taiken." *Chūgoku gengo bunka kenkyū* 5 (2005), pp. 1–28.

Lamley, Harry J. "Taiwan Under Japanese Rule, 1895–1945: The Vicissitudes of Colonialism," in Murray A. Rubinstein, ed. *Taiwan: A New History*. Armonk, NY: M. E. Sharpe, 1999. Pp. 201–60.

Lamming, George. *The Pleasures of Exile*. New York: Schocken Books, 1984.

———. *Water with Berries*. New York: Holt, Rinehart and Winston, 1971.

Lang, Olga. *Pa Chin and His Writings: Chinese Youth Between the Two Revolutions*. Cambridge, MA: Harvard University Press, 1967.

Lao She. *Maocheng ji*, in *Lao She quanji* 2. Beijing: Renmin Wenxue Chubanshe, 1999. Pp. 143–298.

Lape, Noreen Groover. *West of the Border: The Multicultural Literature of the Western American Frontiers*. Athens, OH: Ohio University Press, 2000.

Lawson, Benjamin. "Federated Fancies: Balzac's *Lost Illusions* and Melville's *Pierre*," in Elaine D. Cancalon and Antoine Spacagna, eds. *Intertextuality in Literature and Film: Selected Papers from the Thirteenth Annual Florida State University Conference on Literature and Film*. Gainesville, FL: University of Florida Press, 1994. Pp. 37–47.

Layoun, Mary. *Travels of a Genre: The Modern Novel and Ideology*. Princeton, NJ: Princeton University Press, 1990.

Lee, Ann. "The Early Writings of Yi Gwang-su." *Korea Journal* 42:2 (Summer 2002), pp. 241–78.

———. "The Representation of the Colonial State and Popular Forces as Proponents of Social Reform and Modernization in the Novel *Taeha* [The Great River] (1939)," in Chang Yun-sik et al., eds. *Korea Between Tradition and Modernity: Selected Papers from the Fourth Pacific and Asian Conference on Korean Studies*. Vancouver, BC: Institute of Asian Research, University of British Columbia, 1998. Pp. 361–82.

Lee, Changsoo and George De Vos, eds. *Koreans in Japan: Ethnic Conflict and Accommodation*. Berkeley, CA: University of California Press, 1981.

Lee, Leo Ou-fan. "City between Worlds." Lecture at Harvard University, June 24, 2008.

———, ed. *Lu Xun and His Legacy*. Berkeley, CA: University of California Press, 1985.

———. *The Romantic Generation of Modern Chinese Writers*. Cambridge, MA: Harvard University Press, 1973.

———. *Shanghai Modern: The Flowering of a New Urban Culture in China, 1930–1945*. Cambridge, MA: Harvard University Press, 1999.

Lee, Min. "Writer Ha Jin Says He Wants to Visit Native China but Is Frustrated by Censorship." *Daily Yomiuri Online*, July 27, 2008.

Lee, Young Mee. "The Beginnings of Korean Pop: Popular Music during the Japanese Occupation Era (1910–45)," in Keith Howard, ed. *Korean Pop Music: Riding the Wave*. Folkestone, Kent: Global Oriental, 2006. Pp. 1–9.

Lei Shiyu. *Riben wenxue jianshi*. Hebei: Hebei Jiaoyu Chubanshe, 1992.

———. *Sabaku no uta*. Tokyo: Zensōsha, 1935.

———. "Wo zai Riben canjia zuoyi shige yundong de rizi." *Riben wenxue* 1 (January 1982), pp. 11–17.

Levy, Indra. *Sirens of the Western Shore: The Westernesque Femme Fatale, Translation, and Vernacular Style in Modern Japanese Literature*. New York: Columbia University Press, 2006.

Levy, Lital. "Jewish Writers in the Arab East: Literature, History, and the Politics of Enlightenment, 1863–1914." Ph.D. dissertation, University of California, Berkeley, 2008.

———. "Self-Portraits of the Other: Toward a Palestinian Poetics of Hebrew Verse," in Marlé Hammond and Dana Sajdi, eds. *Transforming Loss into*

Beauty: Essays on Arabic Literature and Culture in Honor of Magda al-Nowaihi. Cairo: American University in Cairo Press, 2008. Pp. 343–402.

Lewis, James. "Beyond *Sakoku*: The Korean Envoy to Edo and the 1719 Diary of Shin Yu-han." *Korea Journal* 25:11 (November 1985), pp. 22–41.

Li Guodong (Ri Kokutō). *Ro Jin* [Lu Xun] *to Sōseki no hikaku bungakuteki kenkyū: higekisei to bunka dentō.* Tokyo: Meiji Shoin, 2001.

Li Kuixian. "Dongjing shiji," in *Li Kuixian wenji* 8. Taipei: Xingzhengyuan Wenhua Jianshi Weiyuanhui, 2002. Pp. 110–11.

Li Yu-ning. *The Introduction of Socialism into China.* New York: Columbia University Press, 1971.

Li Zhengwen. "Lu Xun zai Chaoxian." *Shijie wenxue* 157 (1981), pp. 32–42.

Liang Shanding, ed. *Xiao Jun jinian ji.* Shenyang: Chufeng Wenyi Chubanshe, 1990.

Liang Qichao. *Qing yi bao quanbian.* Yokohama: Xinminshe, 1898–1901.

——. "Qingdai xueshu kai lun," in *Yinping shi hoji* 34. Shanghai: 1932.

——. "Yi yin zhengzhi xiaoshuo xu." *Qing yi bao* 1 (November 11, 1898), pp. 53–54.

Liao Ping-hui and David Der-wei Wang, eds. *Taiwan under Japanese Colonial Rule, 1895–1945: History, Culture, Memory.* New York: Columbia University Press, 2006.

Lin Cong. "Ro Jin [Lu Xun] no *Yecao* ni okeru Sōseki no *Yume jūya* no eikyō: 'Kakyaku' [Guoke] to 'Dainanaya' o megutte." *Hikaku bungaku* 32 (1989), pp. 35–48.

Lin Huanzhang. "Wo shi mao, bu!" *The Chinese Pen (Taiwan)* 31:3 (September 2003), p. 145.

Lin Kenan. "Translation as a Catalyst for Social Change in China," in Maria Tymoczko and Edwin Gentzler, eds. *Translation and Power.* Amherst, MA: University of Massachusetts Press, 2002. Pp. 160–83.

Lin Qingzhang, ed. *Jindai Zhongguo zhishifenzi zai Riben,* 3 vols. Taipei: Wanjuanlou Tushu Gufen Youxian Gongsi, 2003.

Lin Ruiming. "Lu Xun yu Lai He," in Nakajima Toshirō, ed. *Taiwan xinwenxue yu Lu Xun.* Taipei: Qianwei Chubanshe, 1999. Pp. 79–94.

Lin Shaohua. "Murakami Haruki no bungaku sekai to Chūgoku gendai seinen no seishin kōzō," in Wa-Kan Hikaku Bungakukai and Zhong-Ri Bijiao Wenxuehui, eds. *Shinseiki no Nitchū bungaku kankei: sono kaiko to tenbō.* Tokyo: Bensei Shuppan, 2003. Pp. 107–22.

Lin Shu. "Xu," in *Burugui: Aiqing xiaoshuo.* Shanghai: Shangwu Yinshuguan, 1908. Translated by Lin Shu and Wei Yi. Pp. 1–3.

Lin, Sylvia Li-chun. *Representing Atrocity in Taiwan: The 2/28 Incident and the White Terror in Fiction and Film.* New York: Columbia University Press, 2007.

Lin Wen-yueh. "Literary Interflow between Japan and China," in Japan P.E.N. Club, ed. *The Voice of the Writer 1984: Collected Papers of the 47th International P.E.N. Congress in Tokyo.* Tokyo: Kodansha International, 1986. Pp. 184–93.

Lindfors, Bernth, ed. *Conversations with Chinua Achebe.* Jackson, MS: University Press of Mississippi, 1997.

Lionnet, Françoise. "Transcolonial Translations, Shakespeare in Mauritius," in Françoise Lionnet and Shu-mei Shih, eds. *Minor Transnationalism*. Durham, NC: Duke University Press, 2005. Pp. 201–21.

Lionnet, Françoise and Shu-mei Shih. "Introduction," in Françoise Lionnet and Shu-mei Shih, eds. *Minor Transnationalism*. Durham, NC: Duke University Press, 2005.

——, eds. *Minor Transnationalism*. Durham, NC: Duke University Press, 2005.

Lippit, Seiji M. *Topographies of Japanese Modernism*. New York: Columbia University Press, 2002.

Liu Anwei (Ryū Gan'i). *Koizumi Yakumo to kindai Chūgoku*. Tokyo: Iwanami Shoten, 2004.

Liu Boqing et al., eds. *Riben xuezhe Zhongguo wenxue yanjiu yicong* 4. Changchun: Jilin Jiaoyu Chubanshe, 1990.

Liu Chunying (Ryū Shun'ei). "Kōnichi sensōki no Chūgoku ni okeru Nihon bungaku no hon'yaku," in Yamada Keizō and Lü Yuanming (Ro Genmei), eds. *Jūgonen sensō to bungaku: Nitchū kindai bungaku no hikaku kenkyū*. Tokyo: Tōhō Shoten, 1991. Pp. 291–300.

——. "Yi tashan zhi shi de beizhuang jingli," in Yamada Keizō and Lü Yuanming, eds. *Zhong-Ri zhanzheng yu wenxue: Zhong-Ri xiandai wenxue de bijiao yanjiu*. Changchun: Dongbei Shifan Daxue Chubanshe, 1992. Pp. 303–24.

Liu, Joyce C. H. "The Importance of Being Perverse: China and Taiwan, 1931–1937," in David Der-wei Wang and Carlos Rojas, eds. *Writing Taiwan: A New Literary History*. Durham, NC: Duke University Press, 2007. Pp. 93–112.

Liu Lishan. *Riben baihuapai yu Zhongguo zuojia*. Shenyang: Liaoning Daxue Chubanshe, 1995.

Liu, Lydia. "The Translator's Turn: The Birth of Modern Chinese Language and Fiction," in Victor Mair, ed. *The Columbia History of Chinese Literature*. New York: Columbia University Press, 2001. Pp. 1055–66.

——. *Translingual Practice: Literature, National Culture, and Translated Modernity – China, 1900–1937*. Stanford, CA: Stanford University Press, 1995.

Liu, Siyuan. "The Impact of *Shinpa* on Early Chinese *Huaju*." *Asian Theatre Journal* 23:2 (Fall 2006), pp. 342–55.

Liu Yusheng. "Huaixiang ji." *Fengyu tan* 6 (October 1943).

Lo Chengchun. "Long Yingzong yanjiu," in *Long Yingzong ji, Taiwan zuojia quanji: Riju shidai* 9. Taipei: Qianwei Chubanshe, 1991. Pp. 233–307.

Lo, Ming-Cheng M. *Doctors within Borders: Profession, Ethnicity, and Modernity in Colonial Taiwan*. Berkeley, CA: University of California Press, 2002.

Loomba, Ania et al., eds. *Postcolonial Studies and Beyond*. Durham, NC: Duke University Press, 2005.

Long Yingzong. "Papaya no aru machi," in Kawahara Isao, ed. *Nihon tōchiki Taiwan bungaku Taiwanjin sakka sakuhinshū* 3. Tokyo: Ryokuin Shobō, 1999. Pp. 11–68.

Lovell, Julia. *The Politics of Cultural Capital: China's Quest for a Nobel Prize in Literature*. Honolulu, HI: University of Hawai'i Press, 2006.

Lu, Alvin. *The Hell Screens*. New York: Four Walls Eight Windows, 2000.

Lu, Hanchao. *Beyond the Neon Lights: Everyday Shanghai in the Early Twentieth Century.* Berkeley, CA: University of California Press, 1999.

——. *Street Criers: A Cultural History of Chinese Beggars.* Stanford, CA: Stanford University Press, 2005.

Lü Qinwen. "Dongbei lunxianqu de wailai wenxue yu xiangtu wenxue," in Yamada Keizō and Lü Yuanming, eds. *Zhong-Ri zhanzheng yu wenxue: Zhong-Ri xiandai wenxue de bijiao yanjiu.* Changchun: Dongbei Shifan Daxue Chubanshe, 1992. Pp. 127–59.

Lu Xun. "A Q zhengzhuan," in *Lu Xun ji.* Guangzhou: Huacheng Chubanshe, 2000. Pp. 83–135.

——. "Fan Ainong," in *Lu Xun ji.* Guangzhou: Huacheng Chubanshe, 2000. Pp. 504–13.

——. "Guoke," in *Yecao,* in *Lu Xun quanji* 1. Beijing: Renmin Wenxue Chubanshe, 1981. Pp. 188–94.

——. "Houji," in *Lu Xun yiwenji* 3. Beijing: Renmin Wenxue Chubanshe, 1959. Pp. 283–84.

——. "Qiuye," in *Yecao, Lu Xun quanji* 1. Beijing: Renmin Wenxue Chubanshe, 1981. Pp. 162–64.

——. "Shangshi: Juansheng de shouji," in *Lu Xunji.* Guangzhou: Huacheng Chubanshe, 2001. Pp. 276–96.

——. "Sihou," in *Yecao, Lu Xun quanji* 1. Beijing: Renmin Wenxue Chubanshe, 1981. Pp. 209–13.

——. "Tengye xiansheng," in *Lu Xun ji.* Guangzhou: Huacheng Chubanshe, 2000. Pp. 497–503.

——. "Wo zenme zuoqi xiaoshuo lai," in *Lu Xun quanji* 4. Shanghai: Renmin Wenxue Chubanshe, 1981. Pp. 511–15.

——. "Yige qingnian de meng yizhe xu," in *Lu Xun yiwen ji* 2. Beijing: Renmin Wenxue Chubanshe, 1959. Pp. 521–22.

——. "Yige qingnian de meng yizhe xu er," in *Lu Xun yiwen ji* 2. Beijing: Renmin Wenxue Chubanshe, 1959. Pp. 523–24.

——. "Yijian xiaoshi," in *Lu Xun ji.* Guangzhou: Huacheng Chubanshe, 2000. Pp. 49–53.

——. "Zheyang de zhanshi," in *Yecao, Lu Xun quanji* 1. Beijing: Renmin Wenxue Chubanshe, 1981. Pp. 214–15.

Lü Yuanming. *Chūgokugo de nokosareta Nihon bungaku: Nitchū sensō no naka de.* Tokyo: Hōsei Daigaku Shuppankyoku, 2001. Translated by Nishida Masaru.

——. "Lun Lu Dixuan [Kaji Wataru] zai Zhongguo kangzhan shiqi de chuangzuo." *Zhongguo bijiao wenxue* 1 (1991), pp. 179–92.

——. *Riben wenxue lunshi jianji Zhong-Ri bijiao wenxue.* Changchun: Dongbei Shifan Daxue Chubanshe, 1992.

——. "Zaihua Riben fanzhan wenxue lun," in Yamada Keizō and Lü Yuanming, eds. *Zhong-Ri zhanzheng yu wenxue: Zhong-Ri xiandai wenxue de bijiao yanjiu.* Changchun: Dongbei Shifan Daxue Chubanshe, 1992. Pp. 39–94.

Lucie-Smith, Edward, ed. *The Faber Book of Art Anecdotes.* London: Faber and Faber, 1992.

Lundberg, Lennart. *Lu Xun as a Translator: Lu Xun's Translation and Introduction of Literature and Literary Theory, 1903–1936.* Stockholm: Orientaliska Studier, Stockholm University, 1989.

Luo Liang. "Theatrics of Revolution: Tian Han (1898–1968) and the Cultural Politics of Performance in Modern China." Ph.D. dissertation, Harvard University, 2006.

Lupke, Christopher, ed. *The Magnitude of Ming: Command, Allotment, and Fate in Chinese Culture.* Honolulu, HI: University of Hawai'i Press, 2005.

——, ed. *New Perspectives on Chinese Poetry.* New York: Palgrave Macmillan, 2008.

Lynn, Richard John. "Aspects of Meiji Culture Represented in the Poetry and Prose of Huang Zunxian's *Riben zashi shi* (1877–1882)." Paper given at the International Research Center for Japanese Studies Workshop, Santa Barbara, January 26–27, 2001.

——. "Early Modern Cross-Cultural Perspectives: the *Poems on Miscellaneous Subjects from Japan* of Huang Zunxian." Unpublished manuscript.

——. "Huang Zunxian (1848–1905) and His Association with Meiji Era Japanese Literati *Bunjin*." Unpublished manuscript.

——. "Literary Critical Writings of Huang Zunxian in Japan (1877–1882)." Unpublished manuscript.

——. "'This Culture of Ours' and Huang Zunxian's Literary Experiences in Japan (1877–1882)." *Chinese Literature: Essays, Articles, Reviews* 19 (December 1997), pp. 113–38.

Ma Zuyi. *Zhongguo fanyi jianshi: "Wusi" yundong yiqian bufen.* Beijing: Zhongguo Duiwai Fanyi Chuban Gongsi, 1984.

——. *Zhongguo fanyishi.* Hankou: Hubei Jiaoyu Chubanshe, 1999.

Ma Zuyi and Ren Rongzhen. *Hanji waiyishi.* Hankou: Hubei Jiaoyu Chubanshe, 1997.

Mack, Edward. "Marketing Japan's Literature in Its 1930s Colonies." *Bulletin of the Bibliographical Society of Australia & New Zealand* 28:1, 2 (2004), pp. 134–41.

——. "The Value of Literature: Cultural Authority in Interwar Japan." Ph.D. dissertation, Harvard University, 2002.

Mair, Victor, ed. *The Columbia History of Chinese Literature.* New York: Columbia University Press, 2001.

Makdizi, Saree and Felicity Nussbaum, eds. *The Arabian Nights in Historical Context: Between East and West.* New York: Oxford University Press, 2008.

Makimoto Kusurō. *Akai hata: Puroretaria dōyōshū.* Tokyo: Kōgyokudō, 1930.

Mansfield, Katherine. "The Child-Who-Was-Tired," in *In a German Pension.* London: Hesperus Press Limited, 2003. Pp. 71–80.

Mao Dun. *Ziye.* Beijing: Renmin Wenxue Chubanshe, 1984.

Márquez, Gabriel García. "El avión de la bella durmiente," in *Doce Cuentos peregrines.* Mexico: Editorial Diana, 1992. Pp. 79–89.

——. *Memoria de mis putas tristes.* New York: Alfred A. Knopf, 2004.

Marr, David G. *Vietnamese Tradition on Trial, 1920–1945.* Berkeley, CA: University of California Press, 1981.

Martí-López, Elisa. *Borrowed Words: Translation, Imitation, and the Making of the Nineteenth-Century Novel in Spain.* Lewisburg, PA: Bucknell University Press, 2002.

Maruyama Noboru. *Aru Chūgoku tokuhain: Yamagami Masayoshi to Ro Jin* [Lu Xun]. Tokyo: Chūō Kōronsha, 1976.

——. "Lu Xun in Japan," in Leo Ou-fan Lee, ed. *Lu Xun and His Legacy.* Berkeley, CA: University of California Press, 1985. Pp. 216–42.

——. "Ro Jin [Lu Xun] to Mushakōji Saneatsu no menkai o megutte." *Shunjū* 147 (August/September 1973), pp. 4–7.

Masaoka Shiki. "Shigo," in *Shiki zenshū* 12. Tokyo: Kōdansha, 1975. Pp. 510–19.

Masuda Wataru. "Chūgokujin no mita Nihon bungaku, Ha Kin [Ba Jin] no hihyō." *Shin Chūgoku* 12 (1947), pp. 146–55.

Matsunaga Masayoshi. "Guanyu Riben de Taiwan wenxue yanjiu." *Chungguk hyŏndae munhak* 7 (May 1993), pp. 239–52.

Matsuo Bashō. *Oku no hosomichi,* in *Bashō bunshū, Nihon koten bungaku taikei* 46. Tokyo: Iwanami Shoten, 1971. Pp. 69–99.

Matsusaka, Y. Tak. "Managing Occupied Manchuria, 1931–1934," in Peter Duus, Ramon H. Myers, and Mark R. Peattie, eds. *The Japanese Wartime Empire, 1931–1945.* Princeton, NJ: Princeton University Press, 1996. Pp. 97–135.

Mayo, Marlene J. "Introduction," in Marlene J. Mayo and J. Thomas Rimer, eds. *War, Occupation, and Creativity: Japan and East Asia, 1920–1960.* Honolulu, HI: University of Hawai'i Press, 2001. Pp. 1–42.

Mayo, Marlene J., and J. Thomas Rimer, eds. *War, Occupation, and Creativity: Japan and East Asia, 1920–1960.* Honolulu, HI: University of Hawai'i Press, 2001.

McArthur, Ian and Mio Bryce. "Names and Perspectives in Sute-Obune: A Meiji-Era Adaptive Translation of the Mary Braddon Mystery Novel, *Diavola.*" *The International Journal of the Humanities* 5:3 (2007), pp. 141–52.

McDougall, Bonnie. *The Introduction of Western Literary Theories into Modern China, 1919–1925.* Tokyo: The Centre for East Asian Cultural Studies, 1971.

McHale, Shawn Frederick. *Print and Power: Confucianism, Communism, and Buddhism in the Making of Modern Vietnam.* Honolulu, HI: University of Hawai'i Press, 2008.

Mei Niang. "Songhua jiang de buyu," in Liang Shanding, ed. *Xiao Jun jinian ji.* Shenyang: Chufeng Wenyi Chubanshe, 1990. Pp. 230–33.

Meng Yue. *Shanghai and the Edges of Empires.* Minneapolis, MN: University of Minnesota Press, 2006.

Meng Zeren. "Yin zai Riben de shenshen de zuji: Lao She zai Riben de diwei." *Xin wenxue shiliao* 1 (1982), pp. 215–24.

Menocal, Maria Rosa. *The Arabic Role in Medieval Literary History.* Philadelphia, PA: University of Pennsylvania Press, 1987.

Mertz, John Pierre. *Novel Japan: Spaces of Nationhood in Early Meiji Narrative, 1870–88.* Ann Arbor, MI: Center for Japanese Studies, University of Michigan, 2003.

504 Works Cited

Meyer, Susan. "'Indian Ink': Colonialism and the Figurative Strategy of *Jane Eyre*," in Harold Bloom, ed. *Charlotte Brontë's Jane Eyre*. New York: Chelsea House, 2007. Pp. 43–74.

Michaud, Eric. *The Cult of Art in Nazi Germany*. Stanford, CA: Stanford University Press, 2004. Translated by Janet Lloyd.

Miki Rofū. "Sariyuku gogatsu no shi," in *Miki Rofū zenshū* 1. Mitaka: Miki Rofū Zenshū Kankōkai, 1974. Pp. 22–23.

Miller, Christopher L. *The French Atlantic Triangle: Literature and Culture of the Slave Trade*. Durham, NC: Duke University Press, 2008.

Miller, J. Scott. *Adaptations of Western Literature in Meiji Japan*. New York: Palgrave, 2001.

Minami Ippei. *Uchiyama Kanzō no shōgai: Nitchū yūkō no kakehashi: manga*. Ibara: Senjin Kenshōkai, 2008.

Minami Jirō. "Renmei honrai no shimei: giron yorimo jikkō e." *Sōdōin* 1:2 (July 1939), pp. 57–58.

Miner, Earl Roy and Haga Tōru, eds. *Contents of the ICLA '91 Tokyo Proceedings: The Force of Vision 4: Translation and Modernization*. Tokyo: University of Tokyo Press and International Comparative Literature Association, 1995.

Misaki Hiroko. "Tōkyō Joi Gakkō, Tōkyō Joshi Igaku Senmon Gakkō Chūgokujin ryūgakusei meibo: 1908 nen kara 1942 nen made." *Shingai kakumei kenkyū* 8 (December 1988), pp. 63–72.

Mishima Yukio. *Jigokuhen*, in *Mishima Yukio zenshū* 21. Tokyo: Shinchōsha, 1976. Pp. 7–32.

Mitchell, Richard H. *Censorship in Imperial Japan*. Princeton, NJ: Princeton University Press, 1983.

——. *The Korean Minority in Japan*. Berkeley, CA: University of California Press, 1967.

Mitter, Rana. *The Manchurian Myth: Nationalism, Resistance, and Collaboration in Modern China*. Berkeley, CA: University of California Press, 2000.

Miyamoto Masaaki. "Kaidai," in Katō Kiyofumi, ed. *Kyūshokuminchi toshokan zōsho mokuroku* 14. Tokyo: Yumani Shobō, 1998–2004. Pp. 417–23.

Mizuno Naoki. "'Ame no furu Shinagawa eki' no Chōsengo yaku o megutte," in *Nakano Shigeharu zenshū* 3. Tokyo: Chikuma Shobō, 1977. Pp. 6–7.

——. "'Ame no furu Shinagawa eki' no jijitsu shirabe." *Sanzenri* 21 (1980), pp. 97–105.

Molasky, Michael. Review of Melissa Wender, *Lamentation as History: Narratives by Koreans in Japan, 1965–2000*. *Journal of Japanese Studies* 33:1 (Winter 2007), pp. 257–58.

Mommsen, Wolfgang J. and Jürgen Osterhammel, eds. *Imperialism and After*. Boston, MA: Allen and Unwin, 1986.

Moniga, Padmini, ed. *Contemporary Postcolonial Theory: A Reader*. New York: Oxford University Press, 1997.

Mōri Makiko. "1920 nendai ni okeru Chōsenjin no Chūgoku bunka ninshiki ni tsuite." Master's thesis, University of Tokyo, 1999.

Morris-Suzuki, Tessa. "Migrants, Subjects, Citizens: Comparative Perspectives on Nationality in the Prewar Japanese Empire." *Japan Focus*, August 28, 2008.

Morrison, Toni. *Playing in the Dark: Whiteness and the Literary Imagination.* Cambridge, MA: Harvard University Press, 1992.

Mostow, Joshua et al., eds. *The Columbia Companion to Modern East Asian Literature.* New York: Columbia University Press, 2003.

Msomi, Welcome. "*uMabatha*," in Daniel Fischlin and Mark Fortier, eds. *Adaptations of Shakespeare.* London: Routledge, 2000. Pp. 168–87.

Mu Shiying. "Shanghai de hubuwu," in *Mu Shiying xiaoshuo quanji.* Beijing: Zhongguo Wenlian Chuban Gongsi, 1995. Pp. 249–59.

Muller, Gregor. *Colonial Cambodia's "Bad Frenchmen": The Rise of French Rule and the Life Story of Thomas Caraman, 1840–87.* New York: Routledge, 2006.

Mundow, Anna. "The Interview with Chimamanda Ngozi Adichie." *Boston Sunday Globe*, October 8, 2006, p. E7.

Munetake Asako and Ozaki Hatsuki. *Nihon no shoten hyakunen: Meiji Taishō Shōwa no shuppan hanbai shōshi.* Tokyo: Seiseisha, 1991.

Muoneke, Romanus Okey. *Art, Rebellion and Redemption: A Reading of the Novels of Chinua Achebe.* New York: Peter Lang, 1994.

Murakami Genzō. *Sayon no kane, Kokumin engeki* 1:10 (December 1941), pp. 49–66.

Murakami Haruki. *Hitsuji o meguru bōken.* Tokyo: Kōdansha, 1990.

———. *Nejimakidori kuronikuru.* Tokyo: Shinchōsha, 1995.

———. *Noruwei no mori.* Tokyo: Kōdansha, 1991.

Muramatsu Sadataka et al., eds. *Kindai Nihon bungaku ni okeru Chūgokuzō.* Tokyo: Yūhikaku, 1975.

Muramatsu Shōfū. "Fushigi na miyako 'Shanhai.'" *Chūō kōron* 38:9 (August 1923), pp. 1–57.

Murasaki Nagaaki. *Hachijūnen no kaikoroku: kioku o tadotte.* Tokyo: Nishida Shoten, 1983.

Mushakōji Saneatsu. "Shū Sakujin [Zhou Zuoren] to watakushi," in Hō Kisei, ed. *Shū Sakujin [Zhou Zuoren] sensei no koto.* Tokyo: Kōfūkan, 1944. Pp. 1–22.

Myers, Ramon H. and Mark R. Peattie, eds. *The Japanese Colonial Empire, 1895–1945.* Princeton, NJ: Princeton University Press, 1984.

Na Tohyang. "Yŏ ilbalsa," in *Na Tohyang chŏnjip* 1. Seoul: Jipmundang, 1988. Pp. 137–43.

Nagai Enoko. "Gendai Chūgoku bungaku hon'yaku no hyakunen." Ph.D. dissertation, Fu Jen Catholic University, 2000.

Nagappan, Ramu. *Speaking Havoc: Social Suffering & South Asian Narratives.* Seattle, WA: University of Washington Press, 2005.

Naipaul, V. S. *A Bend in the River.* New York: Random House, 1989.

Naitou Hisako. "Korean Forced Labor in Japan's Wartime Empire," in Paul H. Kratoska, ed. *Asian Labor in the Wartime Japanese Empire: Unknown Histories.* Armonk, NY: M. E. Sharpe, 2005. Pp. 90–98.

Nakajima Toshirō. "Bansei no hon'yaku shōsetsu: Kayaku Nichibun shōsetsu hennen mokuroku shokō (1)." *Senriyama bungaku ronshū* 15 (April 1976), pp. 96–111.

———. "Bansei no hon'yaku shōsetsu: Kayaku Nichibun shōsetsu hennen mokuroku shokō (2)." *Senriyama bungaku ronshū* 16 (October 1976), pp. 75–89.

———. *Nihon tōchiki Taiwan bungaku: bungei hyōronshū 1.* Tokyo: Ryokuin Shobō, 2001.

———. "Nihon tōchiki Taiwan bungaku kenkyū: Nihonjin sakka no keifu — shikon no hyōhaku — Nagasaki Hiroshi (Yamagata hen)." *Gifu Seitoku Gakuen Daigaku kiyō* 47 (2008), pp. 49–75.

———. *Riju shiqi Taiwan wenxue zazhi zongmu: renming suoyin.* Taipei: Qianwei Chubanshe, 1995.

———. "Zhou Jinbo xinlun," in *Zhou Jinbo ji.* Taipei: Qianwei, 2002. Pp. 1–23.

Nakajima Toshirō, ed. *Taiwan xinwenxue yu Lu Xun.* Taipei: Qianwei Chubanshe, 1999.

Nakamura Fumiko. "Nihon kindai bungaku ni okeru Chūgoku bungaku to no kōryū: Tanizaki Jun'ichirō — Sha Muitsu [Xie Liuyi], Den Kan [Tian Han], Kaku Matsujaku [Guo Moruo], Ōyō Yosen [Ouyang Yuqian] nado." *Aichi Kenritsu Daigaku Gaikokugobu kiyō* 32 (2000), pp. 265–89.

Nakamura Tadayuki. "Chūgoku bungei ni oyoboseru Nihon bungei no eikyō (3)." *Taidai bungaku* 8:2 (August 1943), pp. 86–152.

———. "Chunliushe yishi gao 1: Xian gei Ouyang Yuqian xiansheng." *Xiju* 3 (2004), pp. 32–45.

———. "*Shin Chūgoku miraiki* [Xin Zhongguo weilaiji] kōsetsu: Chūgoku bungei ni oyoboseru Nihon bungei no eikyō no ichirei." *Tenri Daigaku gakuhō* 1:1 (May 1949), pp. 65–93.

———. "Tokutomi Roka to gendai Chūgoku bungaku (1)." *Tenri Daigaku gakuhō* 1:2–3 (October 1949), pp. 1–28.

Nakanishi Inosuke. *Neppū.* Tokyo: Heibonsha, 1928.

Nakanishi Susumu and Matsumura Masaie, eds. *Nihon bungaku to gaikoku bungaku: nyūmon hikaku bungaku.* Tokyo: Eihōsha, 1991.

Nakano Shigeharu. "Ame no furu Shinagawa eki." *Kaizō* 11:2 (February 1929), pp. 82–83.

———. "Ame no furu Shinagawa eki," in *Nakano Shigeharu zenshū 1.* Tokyo: Chikuma Shobō, 1959. Pp. 92–94.

———. "Ame no furu Shinagawa eki," in *Nakano Shigeharu zenshū 1.* Tokyo: Chikuma Shobō, 1996. Pp. 113–15.

———. "'Ame no furu Shinagawa eki' no koto," in *Nakano Shigeharu zenshū 22.* Tokyo: Chikuma Shobō, 1975. Pp. 77–78.

———. "Pi nal-i nŭn P'umch'ŏn-yŏk." *Musanja* 3:1 (May 1929), p. 69.

Nan Bujin and Shirakawa Yutaka, eds. *Chō Kakuchū* [Chang Hyŏkju] *Nihongo sakuhinsen.* Tokyo: Bensei Shuppan, 2003.

Napier, Susan J. *From Impressionism to Anime: Japan as Fantasy and Fan Cult in the Mind of the West.* New York: Palgrave Macmillan, 2007.

Nara, Hiroshi, ed. *Inexorable Modernity: Japan's Grappling with Modernity in the Arts.* Lanham, MD: Lexington Books, 2007.

Narangoa, Li and Robert Cribb, eds. *Imperial Japan and National Identities in Asia, 1895–1945*. New York: Routledge Curzon, 2003.

Natsume Sōseki. *Caozhen*. Shanghai: Huali Shudian, 1930. Translated by Guo Moruo.

———. "Dainanaya," in *Yume jūya, Natsume Sōseki shū, Meiji bungaku zenshū 55*. Tokyo: Chikuma Shobō, 1971. Pp. 118–19.

———. "Daijūya," in *Yume jūya, Natsume Sōseki shū, Meiji bungaku zenshū 55*. Tokyo: Chikuma Shobō, 1971. Pp. 121–22.

———. *Kōfu*, in *Sōseki bungaku zenshū 4*. Tokyo: Shūeisha, 1970. Pp. 211–467.

———. *Kusamakura*, in *Sōseki bungaku zenshū 2*. Tokyo: Shūeisha, 1970. Pp. 417–585.

———. "Man-Kan tokoro dokoro," in *Natsume Sōseki zenshū 12*. Tokyo: Iwanami Shoten, 1999. Pp. 227–351.

———. *Nikki – danpen*, in *Natsume Sōseki zenshū 19*. Tokyo: Iwanami Shoten, 1999.

———. *Wagahai wa neko de aru*, in *Sōseki bungaku zenshū 1*. Tokyo: Shūeisha, 1970.

New, W. H. "Colonial Literatures," in Bruce King, ed. *New National and Post-Colonial Literatures: An Introduction*. New York: Oxford University Press, 1996. Pp. 102–19.

Ng, Benjamin Wai-ming. "Yao Wendong (1852–1927) and Japanology in Late Qing China." *Sino-Japanese Studies* 10:2 (April 1998), pp. 8–22.

Ng, Janet. *The Experience of Modernity: Chinese Autobiography of the Early Twentieth Century*. Ann Arbor, MI: University of Michigan Press, 2003.

Ng, Mao-sang. "Ba Jin and Russian Literature." *Chinese Literature: Essays, Articles, Reviews* 3:1 (January 1981), pp. 67–92.

———. *The Russian Hero in Modern Chinese Fiction*. Albany, NY: State University of New York Press, 1988.

Nihon Toshokan Kyōkai, ed. *Kindai Nihon toshokan no ayumi: chihō hen – Nihon Toshokan Kyōkai sōritsu hyakunen kinen*. Tokyo: Nihon Toshokan Kyōkai, 1992.

"1929 Proletarian Novel Hits Home with Workers." *Daily Yomiuri* (May 3, 2008), p. 3.

Niranjana, Tejaswini. "Alternative Frames? Questions for Comparative Research in the Third World," in Kuan-Hsing Chen and Chua Beng Huat, eds. *The Inter-Asia Cultural Studies Reader*. New York: Routledge, 2007. Pp. 103–14.

———. *Siting Translation: History, Post-Structuralism, and the Colonial Context*. Berkeley, CA: University of California Press, 1992.

Nishimura Shintarō. *Il-Sŏn hoehwa chŏngt'ong*. Seoul: Kyŏngsŏng Ilbonsa, 1917.

Nobuhara Satoshi. "Sŏ," in *Pori wa pyŏng jŏng*. Seoul: Chōsen Sōtokufu, Maeil Sinbosa, 1939. P. 3.

Ō Eishō and Takahashi Tsuyoshi. *Shū Onrai [Zhou Enlai] to Nihon: kunō kara hishō e no seishun*. Tokyo: Hakuteisha, 2002.

O Yumi. "Yi Sang munhak ŭi oeraejŏk yoso yŏn-gu." *Kwanak ŏ-munhak yŏn-gu* 1 (October 1976), pp. 205–43.

Ōbayashi Shigeru and Kitabayashi Masae, eds. "Kinoshita Junji to no kaiwa," in *Ha Kin* [Ba Jin] *shasaku shōgai*. Sendai: Bungei Tōhoku Shinsha, 1999. Pp. 326–41.

Oda Takeo. *Iku Tatsufu* [Yu Dafu] *den: sono shi to ai to Nihon*. Tokyo: Chūō Kōronsha, 1975.

Ōdaka Iwao. "Shina bundan ni oyoboshita Nihon bungaku ronsho." *Shomotsu tenbō* 3:11 (November 1941), pp. 82–86.

Ōe Kenzaburō. *Kojinteki na taiken, Ōe Kenzaburō zensakuhin 6*. Tokyo: Shinchōsha, 1966. Pp. 203–370.

Ōe Shinobu et al., eds. *Kindai Nihon to shokumichi 7: bunka no naka no shokuminchi*. Tokyo: Iwanami Shoten, 1993.

Ogasawara Masaru. "Nakano Shigeharu to Chōsen (1): Nihon mondai to shite no Chōsen." *Kikan zainichi bungei mintō* 2:3 (May 1988), pp. 149–64.

——. "Nakano Shigeharu to Chōsen (2): 'Ame no furu Shinagawa eki' o meguru jōkyō." *Kikan zainichi bungei mintō* 2:4 (September 1988), pp. 102–18.

Oguma Hideo. *Oguma Hideo zen shishū*. Tokyo: Shichōsha, 1965.

Oh, Se-Mi. "Oral/Aural Community: Language Play and Gramophone in Colonial Korea." Lecture at Harvard University, February 5, 2009.

Ohsawa Yoshihiro. "Amalgamation of Literariness: Translations as a Means of Introducing European Literary Techniques to Modern Japan," in Eva Hung and Judy Wakabayashi, eds. *Asian Translation Traditions*. Northampton, MA: St. Jerome Publishing, 2005. Pp. 135–51.

Okada Hideki. "Hon'yakusha Ōuchi Takao no jirenma." *Shūka* 6 (December 30, 1993).

——. "The Realities of Racial Harmony: The Case of the Translator Ōuchi Takao." *Acta Asiatica* 72 (1997), pp. 61–90.

——. "Rinkan jiki Beijing bundan no Taiwan sakka sanjūshi," in Shimomura Sakujirō et al., eds. *Yomigaeru Taiwan bungaku: Nihon tōchiki no sakka to sakuhin*. Tokyo: Tōhō Shoten, 1995. Pp. 167–88.

Oki, Seima. "Hu Visits Sun Yat-sen's Favorite Eatery." *Daily Yomiuri*, May 9, 2008, p. 3.

Ōkubo Akio. "Wei Manzhouguo hanyu zuojia de yuyan huanjing yu wenxue wenbenzhong de yuyan yingyong." Paper given at the Teikokushugi to Bungaku Conference, Aichi University, August 1–3, 2008. Reprinted in the conference handout, pp. 199–224.

Ōmaki Fujio. "Nakano Shigeharu to Chōsen." *Shakai bungaku* 14 (2000), pp. 105–9.

Ōmura Masuo and Hotei Toshihiro. *Chōsen bungaku kankei Nihongo bunmyaku mokuroku 1882.4–1945.8*. Tokyo: Ryokuin Shobō, 1997.

——. "Dai Tōa Bungakusha Taikai to Chōsen." *Waseda shakai kagaku tōkyū* 34:3 (1989), pp. 783–805.

——. "Ryō Keichō [Liang Qichao] oyobi *Kajin no kigū*." *Waseda Hōgakkai jinbun ronshū* 11 (1973), pp. 103–33.

O'Nan, Martha. "Biographical Context and Its Importance to Classroom Study," in Steven G. Kellman, ed. *Approaches to Teaching Camus's The Plague*. New York: Modern Language Association of America, 1985. Pp. 102–9.

Onchi Terutake. "Jo," in Lei Shiyu, *Sabaku no uta*. Tokyo: Zensōsha, 1935. Pp. 4-7.

Ono Shinobu. "Wenxue bu neng tuoli rensheng er ying tong qi jinmi xianglian: Ba Jin de Riben wenxueguan," in Liu Boqing et al., eds. *Riben xuezhe Zhongguo wenxue yanjiu yicong* 4. Changchun: Jilin Jiaoyu Chubanshe, 1990. Pp. 126-38.

Orbaugh, Sharalyn. *Japanese Fiction of the Allied Occupation: Vision, Embodiment, Identity*. Leiden: Brill, 2007.

Orr, Mary. *Intertextuality: Debates and Contexts*. Malden, MA: Blackwell Publishing, 2003

Ortiz, Fernando. *Contrapunteo cubana del tabaco y el azúcar*. Caracas: Biblioteca Ayachucho, 1987.

Ōta Naoki. *Densetsu no Nitchū bunka saron: Shanhai – Uchiyama Shoten*. Tokyo: Heibonsha, 2008.

Ōtake Kiyomi (Oot'ak'e K'iyomi). *Han-Il adong munhak kwan-gyesa sosŏl*. Seoul: Ch'ŏng-un, 2006.

Ōtani Morishige Hakushi Koki Kinen Chōsen Bungaku Ronsō Kankō Iinkai, ed. *Ōtani Morishige hakushi koki kinen: Chōsen bungaku ronsō*. Tokyo: Hakuteisha, 2002.

Owen, Stephen. *Readings in Chinese Literary Thought*. Cambridge, MA: Council on East Asian Studies, Harvard University, 1992.

Ōya Chihiro. "Chapji 'Naesŏn ilch'e' e nat'a-nan naesŏn kyŏlhon ŭi yangsang yŏn-gu." *Sai* 1 (November 2006).

Ozaki Kōyō. *Konjiki yasha*. Tokyo: Shun'yōdō, 1907.

———. *Changhanmong*, *Maeil sinbo*, May 13, 1913-October 1, 1913. Adapted by Cho Iljae.

Paek Ch'ŏl et al. "Hanguk sinmunhak e kkich'in oeguk munhak ŭi yŏnghyang e kwanhan yŏn-gu (1): 1890 nyŏndae–1910 nyŏndae rŭl chungsim ŭ ro." *Chung-ang Taehakkyo ŏ-mun nonjip* 7 (February 1972), pp. 7-50.

Paek Namdŏk (Paek Nam Deok). "19 seikimatsu Kankokujin ryūgakusei ni juyō sareta Nihon kanjigo no shosō: *Shinmokukai kaihō* [Ch'inmokhoe hoebo]." *Ilbon-ŏ* 36 (March 2008), pp. 53-70.

———. "19 seikimatsu Kankokujin ryūgakusei ni yoru Nihon kanjigo no ryūnyū: *Shinmokukai kaihō* [Ch'inmokhoe hoebo] o shiryō to shita chōsa hōkoku." *Ilbon-ŏ munhak* 25 (June 2005), pp. 51-69.

———. "20 seiki shotō ni okeru zainichi Kankokujin ryūgakusei no Nihongo no juyō: bungakusha Ch'oe Namsŏn no baai." *Hiroshima Daigaku Daigakuin Kyōikugaku Kenkyūka kiyō* 54 (2005), pp. 221-30.

Pak, Anthony Wan-hoi. "The School of New Sensibilities (Xin'ganjuepai) in the 1930s: A Study of Liu Na'ou['s] and Mu Shiying's Fiction." Ph.D. dissertation, University of Toronto, 1995.

Pak Chae-u (Park Jaewoo). "Kankoku ni okeru Chūgoku gendai bungaku kenkyūshi no sobyō (1920-2000)." *Chūgoku* 15 (June 2000), pp. 296-318.

Pak Ch'anho. "Shokuminchika no Chōsen to sono zanshi: Nihonkyoku no hon'an kayō to 'Uese kayō' ronnan," in Kan Tokusan [Kang Tŏksang] Sensei Koki Taishoku Kinen Ronbunshū Kankō Iinkai, ed. *Nitchō kankei shi ronshū: Kan Tokusan* [Kang Tŏksang] *sensei koki taishoku kinen.* Tokyo: Shin-kansha, 2003. Pp. 190–217.

Pak Ch'ŏlsŏk. "Hanguk kŭndaesi ŭi Ilbonsi yŏnghyang yŏn-gu." *Guk-ŏ guk-munhak* 6 (October 1985), pp. 17–40.

———. "Han-Il kŭndaesi ŭi pigyo munhakjŏk yŏn-gu." *Guk-ŏ gukmunhak* 5 (December 1982), pp. 29–62.

Pak Chonghwa. "Ajik al su ga ŏmnŭn Ilbon mundan ŭi ch'oegŭn kyŏng-hyang: hyŏnmundan ŭi segyejŏk kyŏnghyang." *Kaebyŏk* 44 (February 1924), pp. 92–93.

Pak Ch'un-il. *Kindai Nihon bungaku ni okeru Chōsenzō.* Tokyo: Miraisha, 1969.

Pak Kyŏng-sik. *Zainichi Chōsenjin undōshi 8/15 kaihōmae.* Tokyo: San'ichi Sho-bō, 1979.

Pak T'aewŏn. "Ttakhan saramdŭl," in *Sosŏlga Kubo ssi ŭi iril.* Seoul: Kip'ŭn Saem, 1989. Pp. 133–49.

Pak Wansŏ (Wan-Suh Park). "The Act of Writing in a Postcolonial Situation," in Uchang Kim, ed. *Writing Across Boundaries: Literature in the Multicultural World.* Elizabeth, NJ: Hollym International, 2002. Pp. 466–85.

Pang, Laikwan. "The Collective Subjectivity of Chinese Intellectuals and Their Café Culture in Republican Shanghai." *Inter-Asia Cultural Studies* 7:1 (2006), pp. 24–42.

Paquet, Sandra Pouchet. "Foreword," in George Lamming, *The Pleasures of Exile.* Ann Arbor, MI: University of Michigan Press, 1992. Pp. vii–xxvii.

Parker, Ingrid J. *The Hell Screen.* New York: St. Martin's Minotaur, 2003.

Pastreich, Emanuel. "The Projection of Quotidian Japan on the Chinese Vernacular: The Case of Sawada Issai's 'Vernacular Tale of the Chivalrous Courtesan.'" *Occasional Papers in Japanese Studies.* Harvard University, Edwin O. Reischauer Institute of Japanese Studies. May 2002.

Peng Hsiao-yen. "Colonialism and the Predicament of Identity: Liu Na'ou and Yang Kui as Men of the World," in Liao Ping-hui and David Der-wei Wang, eds. *Taiwan under Japanese Colonial Rule, 1895–1945: History, Culture, Memory.* New York: Columbia University Press, 2006. Pp. 210–47.

———. *Haishang shuo qingyu: cong Zhang Ziping dao Liu Na'ou.* Taipei: Zhongy-ang Yanjiuyuan Zhongguo Wenzhe Yanjiusuo, 2001.

———, ed. *Piaobo yu xiangtu: Zhang Wojun shishi sishi zhounian jinian lunwenji.* Taipei: Xingzhengyuan Wenhua Jianshi Weiyuanhui, 1996.

Peng Zezhou. *Chūgoku no kindaika to Meiji ishin.* Kyoto: Dōhōsha Shuppanbu, 1976.

Peres, Phyllis. *Transculturation and Resistance in Lusophone African Narrative.* Gainesville, FL: University Press of Florida, 1997.

Perry, Samuel. "Aesthetics for Justice: Proletarian Literature in Japan and Colonial Korea." Ph.D. dissertation, University of Chicago, 2007.

———. "Korean as Proletarian: Ethnicity and Identity in Chang Hyŏk-chu's 'Hell of the Starving.'" *positions: east asia cultures critique* 14:2 (Fall 2006), pp. 279–309.

Peyre, Henry. *French Literary Imagination and Dostoevsky and Other Essays.* University, AL: University of Alabama Press, 1975.

Pickles, Katie and Myra Rutherdale, eds. *Contact Zones: Aboriginal and Settler Women in Canada's Colonial Past.* Vancouver, BC: University of British Columbia Press, 2005.

Plaks, Andrew. "Full-length *Hsiao-shuo* and the Western Novel: A Generic Reappraisal," in William Tay et al., eds. *China and the West: Comparative Literature Studies.* Hong Kong: Chinese University Press, 1980. Pp. 163-76.

Plett, Heinrich F., ed. *Intertextuality.* New York: Walter de Gruyter, 1991.

Pollack, David. *Reading Against Culture: Ideology and Narrative in the Japanese Novel.* Ithaca, NY: Cornell University Press, 1992.

Pollard, David, ed. *Translation and Creation: Readings of Western Literature in Early Modern China, 1840-1918.* Philadelphia, PA: John Benjamins Publishing Company, 1998.

Poole, Janet. "Colonial Interiors: Modernist Fiction of Korea." Ph.D. dissertation, Columbia University, 2004.

Pratt, Mary Louise. *Imperial Eyes: Travel Writing and Transculturation,* second edition. New York: Routledge, 2008.

Price, Don. *Russia and the Roots of the Chinese Revolution, 1896-1911.* Cambridge, MA: Harvard University Press, 1974.

Primeau, Ronald, ed. *Influx: Essays on Literary Influence.* Port Washington, NY: Kennikat Press, 1977.

———. "Introduction," in Ronald Primeau, ed. *Influx: Essays on Literary Influence.* Port Washington, NY: Kennikat Press, 1977. Pp. 3-12.

Proudfoot, Lindsay and Michael Roche. *(Dis)Placing Empire: Renegotiating British Colonial Geographies.* Burlington, VT: Ashgate Publishing Company, 2005.

———. "Introduction," in Lindsay Proudfoot and Michael Roche, eds. *(Dis)Placing Empire: Renegotiating British Colonial Geographies.* Burlington, VT: Ashgate Publishing Company, 2005. Pp. 1-11.

Pushkin, Aleksandr. *Eugene Onegin, A Novel in Verse by Aleksandr Pushkin, Translated from the Russian, with a Commentary, by Vladimir Nabokov.* New York: Bollingen Foundation, Pantheon Books, 1964.

Qi, Shouhua. *When the Purple Mountain Burns.* San Francisco, CA: Long River Press, 2005.

Qian Xiaobo. "Modanizumu no juyō to keishō: Chūgoku ni okeru Nihon shinkankakuha bungaku no hon'yaku o chūshin ni." *Gengo to kōryū* 11 (June 2008), pp. 87-102.

———. "Nihon to Chūgoku no shinkankakuha bungaku no hikaku kenkyū ni tsuite: seiritsu no haikei, hossoku no keii oyobi meimei no yurai o chūshin ni." *Gengo to kōryū* 10 (2007), pp. 95-109.

Qiu Gengguang. "Chuangzuo dongji yu biaoxian wenti." *Taiwan bungei* 1:1 (November 1934), pp. 2-4.

Qiu Guifen. "Zhimin jingyan yu Taiwan (nuqing) xiaoshuo shixue fangfa chutan," in Jiang Zide (Chiang Chi-der), ed. *Zhimindi jingyan yu Taiwan wenxue.* Taipei: Yuan Liu Chuban Gongsi, 2000. Pp. 85-112.

Qiu Kinliang. "Zai Tai Ribenren xijujia yu Taiwan xiju—yi Songju Taolou wei li." Paper given at the Teikokushugi to Bungaku Conference, Aichi University, August 1-3, 2008. Reprinted in the conference handout, pp. 442-60.

Rafael, Vicente L. *Contracting Colonialism: Translation and Christian Conversion in Tagalog Society under Early Spanish Rule*. Durham, NC: Duke University Press, 1993.

———. "Language, Identity, and Gender in Rizal's *Noli*." *Review of Indonesian and Malaysian Affairs* 18 (Winter 1984), pp. 110-40.

———. *The Promise of the Foreign: Nationalism and the Technics of Translation in the Spanish Philippines*. Durham, NC: Duke University Press, 2005.

Ragsdale, Kathryn. "Marriage, the Newspaper Business, and the Nation-State: Ideology in the Late Meiji Serialized *Katei shōsetsu*." *Journal of Japanese Studies* 24:2 (Summer 1998), pp. 229-55.

Ram, Harsha. "Towards a Cross-cultural Poetics of the Contact Zone: Romantic, Modernist, and Soviet Intertextualities in Boris Pasternak's Translations of T'itsian T'abidze." *Comparative Literature* 59:1 (Winter 2007), pp. 63-89.

Rama, Ángel. "Literature and Culture," in Ana del Sarto et al., eds. *The Latin American Cultural Studies Reader*. Durham, NC: Duke University Press, 2004. Pp. 120-52.

———. *Transculturación narrativa en América Latina*. México: Siglo Venintiuno Editores, 1982.

Ramras-Rauch, Gila. *The Arab in Israeli Literature*. Bloomington, IN: Indiana University Press, 1989.

Randall, Marilyn. *Pragmatic Plagiarism: Authorship, Profit, and Power*. Toronto, ON: University of Toronto Press, 2001.

Rankin, Mary. "The Emergence of Women at the End of the Ch'ing: The Case of Ch'iu Chin," in Margery Wolf and Roxane Witke, eds. *Women in Chinese Society*. Stanford, CA: Stanford University Press, 1975. Pp. 39-66.

Rege, Josna E. *Colonial Karma: Self, Action, and Nation in the Indian English Novel*. New York: Palgrave Macmillan, 2004.

Reichl, Susanne. *Cultures in the Contact Zone: Ethnic Semiosis in Black British Literature*. Trier: Wissenschaftlicher Verlag Trier, 2002.

Reynolds, Douglas. *China, 1898-1912: The Xinzheng Revolution and Japan*. Cambridge, MA: Harvard University Press, 1993.

Rhee, M. J. *The Doomed Empire: Japan in Colonial Korea*. Brookfield, VT: Ashgate, 1997.

Rhys, Jean. *Wide Sargasso Sea*. New York: W. W. Norton, 1999.

Ri Kenji. *Chōsen kindai bungaku to nashonarizumu: "teikō no nashonarizumu" hihan*. Tokyo: Sakuhinsha, 2007.

Richardson, John G., ed. *Handbook of Theory and Research for the Sociology of Education*. Westport, CT: Greenwood Press, 1986.

Ricks, Christopher. *Allusion to the Poets*. New York: Oxford University Press, 2002.

Rimer, J. Thomas, ed. *A Hidden Fire: Russian and Japanese Cultural Encounters, 1868-1926*. Stanford, CA: Stanford University Press, 1995.

———. *Japanese Art of the Modern Age*. Unpublished manuscript.

Ringgren, Helmer, ed. *Fatalistic Beliefs in Religion, Folklore, and Literature: Papers Read at the Symposium on Fatalistic Beliefs*. Stockholm: Almqvist & Wiksell, 1967.

Rizal, José. *Noli Me Tángere*. Honolulu, HI: University of Hawai'i Press, 1996. Translated by Ma. Soledad Lacson-Locsin.

Ro Jin [Lu Xun] Ronshū Henshū Iinkai, ed. *Ro Jin [Lu Xun] to dōjidaijin*. Tokyo: Kyūko Shoin, 1992.

Robertson, Jennifer. "Preface," in Ming-Cheng M. Lo. *Doctors within Borders: Profession, Ethnicity, and Modernity in Colonial Taiwan*. Berkeley, CA: University of California Press, 2002. Pp. xi–xii.

Robin, Régine. *La Québécoite*. Montreal: Éditions Typo, 1993.

Robinson, Ronald. "The Eccentric Idea of Imperialism, With or Without Empire," in Wolfgang J. Mommsen and Jürgen Osterhammel, eds. *Imperialism and After*. Boston, MA: Allen and Unwin, 1986. Pp. 267–89.

Robson, Kathryn and Jennifer Yee, eds. *France and "Indochina": Cultural Representations*. Lanham, MD: Lexington Books, 2005.

Rogaski, Ruth. *Hygienic Modernity: Meanings of Health and Disease in Treaty-Port China*. Berkeley, CA: University of California Press, 2004.

Roos, Bonnie. "Anselm Kiefer and the Art of Allusion: Dialectics of the Early *Margarete* and *Sulamith* Paintings." *Comparative Literature* 58:1 (Winter 2006), pp. 24–43.

Rosello, Mireille. *France and the Maghreb: Performative Encounters*. Gainesville, FL: University Press of Florida, 2005.

Rosenfeld, David M. *Unhappy Soldier: Hino Ashihei and Japanese World War II Literature*. Lanham, MD: Lexington Books, 2002.

Rosenthal, M. L., ed. *William Butler Yeats: Selected Poems and Three Plays*. New York: Macmillan Publishing Co., 1962.

Rubin, Jay. "Kunikida Doppo." Ph.D. dissertation, University of Chicago, 1970.

———, ed. *Modern Japanese Writers*. New York: Charles Scribner's Sons, 2001.

———. "Sōseki [Natsume Sōseki] 1867-1916," in Jay Rubin, ed. *Modern Japanese Writers*. New York: Charles Scribner's Sons, 2001. Pp. 349–84.

Rubinstein, Murray A., ed. *Taiwan: A New History*. Armonk, NY: M. E. Sharpe, 1999.

Russell, D. A. "De Imitatione," in David West and Tony Woodman, eds. *Creative Imitation and Latin Literature*. New York: Cambridge University Press, 1979. Pp. 1–16.

Ryan, Judith and Alfred Thomas, eds. *Cultures of Forgery: Making Nations, Making Selves*. New York: Routledge, 2003.

———. "Preface," in Judith Ryan and Alfred Thomas, eds. *Cultures of Forgery: Making Nations, Making Selves*. New York: Routledge, 2003. Pp. ix–xiv.

Sá, Lúcia. *Rain Forest Literatures: Indigenous Texts and Latin American Culture*. Minneapolis, MN: University of Minnesota Press, 2004.

Saaler, Sven. "Pan-Asianism in Modern Japanese History: Overcoming the Nation, Creating a Region, Forging an Empire," in Sven Saaler and J. Victor Koschmann, eds. *Pan-Asianism in Modern Japanese History: Colonialism, Regionalism and Borders.* New York: Routledge, 2007. Pp. 1–18.

Saaler, Sven, and J. Victor Koschmann, eds. *Pan-Asianism in Modern Japanese History: Colonialism, Regionalism and Borders.* New York: Routledge, 2007.

Saegusa Toshikatsu (Saegusa Tosik'assŭ), ed. *Hanguk kŭndae munhak kwa Ilbon.* Seoul: Somyong, 2003.

Said, Edward. *Culture and Imperialism.* New York: Alfred A. Knopf, 1994.

——. "Embargoed Literature," in Anuradha Dingwaney and Carol Maier, eds. *Between Languages and Cultures: Translation and Cross-Cultural Texts.* Pittsburgh, PA: University of Pittsburgh Press, 1995. Pp. 97–102.

Saji Toshihiko. "Chūgoku wageki undōshi tenbyō: wageki sōzōki no tenkai to akusen kutō." *Tōyō bunka* 65 (March 1985), pp. 37–59.

Sakai, Naoki, Brett de Bary, and Iyotani Toshio, eds. *Deconstructing Nationality.* Ithaca, NY: East Asia Program, Cornell University, 2005.

——. "Introduction: Nationality and the Politics of the 'Mother Tongue,'" in Naoki Sakai, Brett de Bary, and Iyotani Toshio, eds. *Deconstructing Nationality.* Ithaca, NY: East Asia Program Cornell University, 2005. Pp. 1–38.

——. *Translation and Subjectivity: On "Japan" and Cultural Nationalism.* Minneapolis, MN: University of Minnesota Press, 1997.

Sakai Tatsuo. "Ro Jin [Lu Xun] to Fujino Sensei no jūkyūkagetsu (3): kaibōzu no tensaku o megutte." *Kikan Chūgoku* 92 (2008), pp. 19–28.

Sakai Tōyōo. "Jiechuan Longzhijie [Akutagawa Ryūnosuke] yu Lu Xun: tan 'Zhiliyanuo Jizhu' [Juriano Kichisuke] yu 'Yao' zhong de xugou zhi hua." *Shandong shiyuan yuebao* 54 (1981), pp. 39, 59–64.

Sakaki, Atsuko. "*Kajin no kigū*: The Meiji Political Novel and the Boundaries of Literature." *Monumenta Nipponica* 55:1 (Spring 2000), pp. 83–108.

——. *Obsessions with the Sino-Japanese Polarity in Japanese Literature.* Honolulu, HI: University of Hawai'i Press, 2005.

Sakamoto Etsurō. "Aki no umi," in *Teihon Sakamoto Etsurō zenshishū.* Tokyo: Yayoi Shobō, 1971. Pp. 110–11.

Salih, Tayeb. *Season of Migration to the North.* Portsmouth, NH: Heinemann, 1970. Translated by Denys Johnson-Davies.

Salmon, Claudine, ed. *Literary Migrations: Traditional Chinese Fiction in Asia (17–20th Centuries).* Beijing: International Culture Publishing Corporation, 1987.

Sanetō Keishū. *Chūgoku ryūgakusei shidan.* Tokyo: Daiichi Shobō, 1981.

——. *Chūgokujin Nihon ryūgakushi.* Tokyo: Kuroshio Shuppan, 1960.

——. *Chūgokujin Nihon ryūgakushi kō.* Tokyo: Nikka Gakkai, 1939.

——. *Kindai Nitchū kōshō shiwa.* Tokyo: Shunjūsha, 1973.

——. "Nitchū jānarizumu no kōshō." *Bungaku* 21:9 (1953), pp. 895–903.

—— (Shiten Huixiu) et al., eds. *Zhongguo yi Riben shu zonghe mulu.* Hong Kong: Zhongwen Daxue Chubanshe, 1980.

Sas, Miryam. *Fault Lines: Cultural Memory and Japanese Surrealism.* Stanford, CA: Stanford University Press, 1999.

Satō, Barbara Hamill. "The *Moga* Sensation: Perceptions of the *Modan Gāru* in Japanese Intellectual Circles During the 1920s." *Gender & History* 5:3 (Fall 1993), pp. 363–81.

———. *The New Japanese Woman: Modernity, Media, and Women in Interwar Japan.* Durham, NC: Duke University Press, 2003.

Satō Haruo. "Chōsen no shijintō o naichi no shidan ni mukaen to suru no ji," in Kim Soun, ed. *Nyūshoku no kumo.* Tokyo: Kawade Shobō, 1940. Pp. 4–9.

———. *Den'en no yūutsu,* in *Satō Haruo shū, Gendai Nihon bungaku taikei* 42. Tokyo: Chikuma Shobō, 1979. Pp. 3–50.

———. "Jokaisen kidan," in *Satō Haruo shū, Gendai Nihon bungaku taikei* 42. Tokyo: Chikuma Shobō, 1979. Pp. 254–75.

Satō Tamotsu. "Kō Junken [Huang Zunxian] to Nihon," in Itō Toramaru et al., eds. *Kindai bungaku ni okeru Chūgoku to Nihon: kyōdō kenkyū Nitchū bungaku kōryūshi.* Tokyo: Kyūko Shoin, 1986. Pp. 55–76.

Saussy, Haun, ed. *Comparative Literature in an Age of Globalization.* Baltimore, MD: Johns Hopkins University Press, 2006.

Sawada, Chiho. "Cultural Politics in Imperial Japan and Colonial Korea: Reinventing Assimilation and Education Policy, 1919–1922." Ph.D. dissertation, Harvard University, 2003.

Scalapino, Robert A. and Chong-sik Lee. *Communism in Korea,* 2 vols. Berkeley, CA: University of California Press, 1987.

Scarry, Elaine. *The Body in Pain: The Making and Unmaking of the World.* New York: Oxford University Press, 1985.

Schaffeld, Norbert. "'I need some answers William': Shakespeare and Post-Colonial Drama," in Norbert Schaffeld, ed. *Shakespeare's Legacy: The Appropriation of the Plays in Post-Colonial Drama.* Trier: Wissenschaftlicher Verlag Trier, 2005. Pp. 1–13.

———, ed. *Shakespeare's Legacy: The Appropriation of the Plays in Post-Colonial Drama.* Trier: Wissenschaftlicher Verlag Trier, 2005.

Schmid, Andre. *Korea between Empires, 1895–1919.* New York: Columbia University Press, 2002.

Schrecker, John E. "The Reform Movement of 1898 and the Meiji Restoration as Ch'ing-i Movements," in Akira Iriye, ed. *The Chinese and the Japanese: Essays in Political and Cultural Interactions.* Princeton, NJ: Princeton University Press, 1980. Pp. 96–106.

Schulte, Rainer and John Biguenet. "Introduction," in Rainer Schulte and John Biguenet, eds. *Theories of Translation: An Anthology of Essays from Dryden to Derrida.* Chicago, IL: University of Chicago Press, 1992. Pp. 1–10.

———, eds. *Theories of Translation: An Anthology of Essays from Dryden to Derrida.* Chicago, IL: University of Chicago Press, 1992.

Schweizer, Harold. *Suffering and the Remedy of Art.* Albany, NY: State University of New York Press, 1997.

Scruggs, Bert. "Collective Consciousness and Individual Identities in Colonial Taiwan Fiction." Ph.D. dissertation, University of Pennsylvania, 2003.

Seidel, Michael. "Running Titles," in David Galef, ed. *Second Thoughts: A Focus on Rereading.* Detroit, MI: Wayne State University Press, 1998. Pp. 34–50.

Sekiguchi Yasuyoshi. *Tokuhain Akutagawa Ryūnosuke: Chūgoku de nani o mita no ka.* Tokyo: Mainichi Shinbunsha, 1997.

Sekine, Ken. "Ā Ron [Ah Long] no yonjūdai ni okeru tokuisei ni kansuru kō-satsu." *Nihon Chūgoku gakkaihō* 51 (1999), pp. 195–208.

———. "A Verbose Silence in 1939 Chongqing: Why Ah Long's *Nanjing* Could Not Be Published." MCLC Resource Center, 2004. http://mclc.osu.edu/rc/pubs/sekine.htm. Accessed December 23, 2005.

Senge Motomaro. "Hae," in *Senge Motomaro zenshū* 1. Tokyo: Yayoi Shobō, 1964. P. 125.

Shakespeare, William. *The Tempest,* in Sylvan Barnet, ed. *The Complete Signet Classic Shakespeare.* New York: Harcourt Brace Jovanovich, 1972. Pp. 1537–68.

———. *The Tragedy of Macbeth,* in Sylvan Barnet, ed. *The Complete Signet Classic Shakespeare.* New York: Harcourt Brace Jovanovich, 1972. Pp. 1227–61.

———. *The Tragedy of Othello the Moor of Venice,* in Sylvan Barnet, ed. *The Complete Signet Classic Shakespeare.* New York: Harcourt Brace Jovanovich, 1972. Pp. 1090–1136.

Shang Weiyang. "Hui Yu Dafu ji." *Taiwan shinbungaku* 2:2 (January 1937), pp. 60–65.

Shen, Nai-huei. "The Age of Sadness: A Study of Naturalism in Taiwanese Literature under Japanese Colonization." Ph.D. dissertation, University of Washington, 2003.

Shi Wanwu. *Lin Boqiu.* Taipei: Guoli Taipei Yishu Daxue, 2003.

Shibata Motoyuki et al., eds. *A Wild Haruki Chase: sekai wa Murakami Haruki o dō yomu ka.* Tokyo: Bungei Shunjū, 2006.

Shih, Shu-mei. "Gender, Race, and Semicolonialism: Liu Na'ou's Urban Shanghai Landscape." *Journal of Asian Studies* 55:4 (November 1996), pp. 934–56.

———. *The Lure of the Modern: Writing Modernism in Semicolonial China, 1917–1937.* Berkeley, CA: University of California Press, 2001.

———. *Visuality and Identity: Sinophone Articulations across the Pacific.* Berkeley, CA: University of California Press, 2007.

Shillony, Ben-Ami. *Politics and Culture in Wartime Japan.* New York: Oxford University Press, 1981.

Shimazaki Tōson. *Ie,* in *Shimazaki Tōson shū, Chikuma gendai bungaku taikei* 9. Tokyo: Chikuma Shobō, 1977. Pp. 159–425.

———. *Shinsei,* in *Shimazaki Tōson shū, Chikuma gendai bungaku taikei* 8. Tokyo: Chikuma Shobō, 1975. Pp. 190–511.

Shimizu Ken'ichirō. "Ryō Keichō [Liang Qichao] to 'teikoku kanbun': 'shin-buntai' no tanjō to Meiji Tokyo no media bunka." *Ajia yūgaku* 13 (February 2002), pp. 22–37.

Shimomura Sakujirō. *Bungaku de yomu Taiwan: shihaisha, gengo, sakkatachi.* Tokyo: Tabata Shoten, 1994.

———. "Reverse Exportation from Japan of the Tale of 'The Bell of Sayon': The Central Drama Group's Taiwanese Performance and Wu Man-sha's *The Bell of Sayon,*" in Liao Ping-hui and David Der-wei Wang, eds. *Taiwan un-*

der *Japanese Colonial Rule, 1895–1945: History, Culture, Memory.* New York: Columbia University Press, 2006. Pp. 279–93.

——. *"Sayon no kane" kankei shiryōshū.* Tokyo: Ryokuin Shobō, 2007.

——. "Shō Riwa [Zhong Lihe] no 'Chūgoku taiken' ni tsuite." *Taiwan Bungaku Kenkyūkai kaihō* 8–9 (December 1984), pp. 93–97.

Shimomura Sakujirō et al., eds. *Yomigaeru Taiwan bungaku: Nihon tōchiki no sakka to sakuhin.* Tokyo: Tōhō Shoten, 1995.

Shin, Gi-Wook and Michael Robinson, eds. *Colonial Modernity in Korea.* Cambridge, MA: Harvard University Asia Center, 1999.

Shinada Yoshikazu. *Kŭndae Hanguk kwa Ilbon ŭi min-yo ch'angch'ul.* Seoul: Som-yŏng Ch'ulp'an, 2005.

Shirakaba Bungakukan Takiji Raiburarī, ed. *Ima Chūgoku ni yomigaeru Kobayashi Takiji no bungaku: Chūgoku Kobayashi Takiji kokusai shinpojiumu ronbunshū.* Tokyo: Higashi Ginza Shuppansha, 2006.

Shirakawa Yutaka (Sirakkawa Yuttakka). "Hanguk kŭndae munhak ch'och'anggi ŭi Ilbonjŏk yŏnghyang: mun-indŭl ŭi Ilbon yuhak ch'ehŏm ŭl chungsim ŭ ro (Yi Injik, Ch'oe Namsŏn, Yi Kwangsu, Kim Dong-in, Chŏn Yŏngtaek, Yŏm Sangsŏp, Hyŏn Chin-gŏn)." Ph.D. dissertation, Dongguk University, 1981.

——. *Shokuminchiki Chōsen no sakka to Nihon.* Okayama: Daigaku Kyōiku Shuppan, 1995.

——. "Shokuminchiki Chōsen to Taiwan no Nihongo bungaku shōkō: 1930–45 nen no shōsetsu o chūshin ni." *Nenpō Chōsengaku* 2 (March 1992), pp. 61–84.

Shirane, Haruo, ed. *Envisioning the* Tale of Genji: *Media, Gender, and Cultural Production.* New York: Columbia University Press, 2008.

Shu Zhongtian. "Luse de gu yu xiangtu wenxue," in Feng Weijun et al., eds. *Dongbei lunxian shiqi wenxue guoji xueshu yantaohui lunwenji.* Shenyang: Shenyang Chubanshe, 1992. Pp. 224–35.

Shui Yinping. *Kami no uo.* Tokyo: Kappa Shobō, 1985.

——. *Shui Yinping zuopinji.* Tainan: Tainan Shili Wenhua Zhongxin, 1995.

Sienkiewicz, Henryk. "Bartek the Conqueror," in *Charcoal Sketches, and Other Tales.* London: Angel Books, 1990. Pp. 85–141.

Silver, Mark. *Purloined Letters: Cultural Borrowing and Japanese Crime Literature, 1868–1937.* Honolulu, HI: University of Hawai'i Press, 2008.

Silverberg, Miriam. "The Café Waitress Serving Modern Japan," in Stephen Vlastos, ed. *Mirror of Modernity: Invented Traditions of Modern Japan.* Berkeley, CA: University of California Press, 1998. Pp. 208–25.

——. *Erotic Grotesque Nonsense: The Mass Culture of Japanese Modern Times.* Berkeley, CA: University of California Press, 2006.

Sim Wŏnsŏp. "1910 nyŏndae 'yŏrogujo' hyŏng sŏsa wa nangmanjŏk sŏjŏngsi e nat'a-nan Ilbon yuhaksaeng mun-indŭl ŭi Tae Han-Il ŭisik e taehayŏ: Chu Yohan, Na Kyŏngsŏk ŭi sanmun kwa Kim Yŏje, Kim Ŏk ŭi sŏjŏngsi rŭl chungsim ŭ ro." *Hanrim Ilbonhak yŏn-gu* 6 (December 2001), pp. 18–35.

—— (Shim Won-Sup). "Chu Yohan ŭi ch'ogi munhak kwa sasang ŭi hyŏngsŏng yŏn-gu." Ph.D. dissertation, Yonsei University, 1992.

Simon, Sherry and Paul St.-Pierre, eds. *Changing the Terms: Translating in the Postcolonial Era*. Ottawa, ON: University of Ottawa Press, 2000.

Sin Kŭnjae (Shin Keun-jae). "20 segi ch'oyŏp ŭl chŏnhuhan Han-Il chisik-in ŭi munhwa isik e taehan koch'al." *Il-ŏ Ilmunhak yŏn-gu* 2 (1981), pp. 133–64.

——. *Han-Il kŭndae munhak ŭi pigyo yŏn-gu*. Seoul: Il Cho Kak, 1995.

—— (Shin Konje). *Nikkan kindai shōsetsu no hikaku kenkyū: Tetchō, Kōyō, Roka to hon'an shōsetsu*. Tokyo: Meiji Shoin, 2006.

Sin Kyogyŏng. "Hwang Sŏk-u si yŏn-gu." *Sŏngsim ŏ-mun nonjip* 14–15 (February 1993), pp. 251–303.

Slaymaker, Doug, ed. *Yōko Tawada: Voices from Everywhere*. Lanham, MD: Lexington Books, 2007.

Smith, Norman. *Resisting Manchukuo: Chinese Women Writers and the Japanese Occupation*. Vancouver, BC: University of British Columbia Press, 2007.

——. "Wielding Pens as Swords: Chinese Women Writers and the Japanese Occupation of Manchuria, 1936–1945." Ph.D. dissertation, University of British Columbia, 2003.

Snyder, Stephen. *Fictions of Desire: Narrative Form in the Novels of Nagai Kafū*. Honolulu, HI: University of Hawai'i Press, 2000.

Sŏ Dusu. "Ilbon munhak ŭi t'ŭkjil." *Inmun p'yŏngnon* 2:6 (June 1940), pp. 4–16.

Sŏ Yŏnho. *Sikminji sidae ŭi ch'in-ilgŭk yŏn-gu*. Seoul: T'aehaksa, 1997.

Solomon, Deborah. "Taking It to the Streets: The 1929 Kwangju Student Protests and Their Repercussions for the Japanese Empire." Ph.D. dissertation, University of Michigan, 2009.

Solt, John. *Shredding the Tapestry of Meaning: The Poetry and Poetics of Kitasono Katue*. Cambridge, MA: Harvard University Asia Center, 1999.

Sommer, Doris, ed. *Bilingual Games: Some Literary Investigations*. New York: Palgrave Macmillan, 2003.

Soni, Vivasvan. "Trials and Tragedies: The Literature of Unhappiness (A Model for Reading Narratives of Suffering)." *Comparative Literature* 59:2 (Spring 2007), pp. 119–39.

Sŏn-u Il. *Tugyŏngsŏng*, in *Hanguk sinsosŏl chŏnjip* 5. Seoul: Ŭryu Munhwasa, 1968. Pp. 365–506.

Spence, Jonathan D. *The Search for Modern China*. New York: W. W. Norton, 1999.

Spitta, Silvia. *Between Two Waters: Narratives of Transculturation in Latin America*. Houston, TX: Rice University Press, 1995.

Spivak, Gayatri Chakravorty. *Critique of Postcolonial Reasoning: Toward a History of the Vanishing Present*. Cambridge, MA: Harvard University Press, 1999.

——. *Other Asias*. Malden, MA: Blackwell Publishing, 2008.

——. "Other Asias." *International House of Japan Bulletin* 28:1 (2008), pp. 2–20.

——. "Three Women's Texts and a Critique of Imperialism." *Critical Inquiry* 12:1 (1985), pp. 243–61.

Steinbeck, John. *The Grapes of Wrath*. New York: Penguin, 2006.

Suehiro Tetchō. *Setchūbai*, in *Meiji seiji shōsetsushū, Nihon kindai bungaku taikei* 2. Tokyo: Kadokawa Shoten, 1974. Pp. 321–431.

Suga Keijirō. "Translation, Exophony, Omniphony," in Doug Slaymaker, ed. *Yōko Tawada: Voices from Everywhere*. Lanham, MD: Lexington Books, 2007. Pp. 21–33.

Suh, Dae-Sook. *The Korean Communist Movement 1918–1948*. Princeton, NJ: Princeton University Press, 1967.

Sultan, Stanley. *Eliot, Joyce and Company*. New York: Oxford University Press, 1987.

Sun Ge. "How Does Asia Mean?," in Kuan-Hsing Chen and Chua Beng Huat, eds. *The Inter-Asia Cultural Studies Reader*. New York: Routledge, 2007. Pp. 9–65. Translated by Hui Shiu-Lun and Lau Kinchi.

Sun Lichuan and Wang Shunhong. *Riben yanjiu Zhongguo xiandangdai wenxue lunzhu suoyin, 1919–1989*. Beijing: Beijing Daxue Chubanshe, 1991.

Suter, Rebecca. *The Japanization of Modernity: Murakami Haruki between Japan and the United States*. Cambridge, MA: Harvard University Asia Center, 2008.

Suzman, Janet. "South Africa in *Othello*," in Jonathan Bate et al., eds. *Shakespeare and the Twentieth Century: The Selected Proceedings of the International Shakespeare Association World Congress, Los Angeles, 1996*. Newark, DE: University of Delaware Press, 1998. Pp. 23–40.

Suzuki, Tomi. "*The Tale of Genji*, National Literature, Language, and Modernism," in Haruo Shirane, ed. *Envisioning The Tale of Genji: Media, Gender, and Cultural Production*. New York: Columbia University Press, 2008. Pp. 243–87.

Tachibana, Reiko. "Tawada Yōko's Quest for Exophony: Japan and Germany," in Doug Slaymaker, ed. *Yōko Tawada: Voices from Everywhere*. Lanham, MD: Lexington Books, 2007. Pp. 153–68.

Tageldin, Shaden. "Disarming Words: Reading (Post)Colonial Egypt's Double Bond to Europe." Ph.D. dissertation, University of California, Berkeley, 2004.

Tagore, Rabindranath. *Gitanjali (Song Offerings)*. London: Macmillan and Co., 1913.

"Taiwan Bunren Tōkyō Shibu daiikkai sawakai." *Taiwan bungei* 2:4 (April 1935), pp. 24–30.

Tajiri Hiroyuki (Tajiri Hiroyukki). *Yi Injik yŏn-gu*. Seoul: Kukhak Charyowŏn, 2006.

Takagawa Mayumi. "Nakano Shigeharu ron: Chōsen mondai o chūshin ni." *Fuji Joshi Daigaku kokubungaku zasshi* 34 (December 1984), pp. 78–98.

Takagi Ichinosuke. "Koten no sekai." *Bunkyō no Chōsen* 16:7 (July 1940), pp. 18–25.

Takasaki Ryūji. "Nihonjin bungakusha no mita Chōsen: sakuhin nenpyō." *Kikan sanzenri* 28 (1979), pp. 133–37.

Takeda Masaya. "Donghai Juewo Xu Nianci xiaokao," in Wang Jiquan and Zhou Rongfang, eds. *Taiwan, Xianggang, haiwai xuezhe lun Zhongguo jindai xiaoshuo*. Nanchang: Baihuazhou Wenyi Chubanshe, 1991. Pp. 313–25.

Takenaka Gen'ichi. "Jiechun Longzhijie [Akutagawa Ryūnosuke] yu Zhongguo." *Zhongguo bijiao wenxue* 1 (1991), pp. 193–99.

Takeuchi Yoshimi. "Hōhō to shite no Ajia," in *Takeuchi Yoshimi zenshū* 5. Tokyo: Chikuma Shobō, 1981. Pp. 92–94.

———. "Bunka inyū no hōhō (Nihon bungaku to Chūgoku bungaku II): Ro Jin [Lu Xun] o chūshin ni," in *Takeuchi Yoshimi zenshū* 4. Tokyo: Chikuma Shobō, 1980. Pp. 115–27.

Tamanoi, Mariko Asano, ed. *Crossed Histories: Manchuria in the Age of Empire.* Honolulu, HI: University of Hawai'i Press, 2005.

———. "Introduction," in Mariko Asano Tamanoi, ed. *Crossed Histories: Manchuria in the Age of Empire.* Honolulu, HI: University of Hawai'i Press, 2005. Pp. 1–24.

Tamura Hideaki. "1939 nen Chōsen shokuminchi bungaku no tenkanten: Hayashi Fusao to Chōsen bungaku Nihongo sakuhin." *Ilbon-ŏ munhak* 20 (March 2004), pp. 229–45.

———. *Shokuminchiki ni okeru Nihongo bungaku to Chōsen.* Seoul: J&C, 2004.

Tanaka Masuzō and Miyashita Kyōko, eds. "Tokushū haijin to kajin no Ajia chizu." *Shuka* (Spring 2000), pp. 2–89.

Tanaka Yūko. "Kinsei Nihon to Ajia no bungaku," in Nakanishi Susumu and Matsumura Masaie, eds. *Nihon bungaku to gaikoku bungaku: nyūmon hikaku bungaku.* Tokyo: Eihōsha, 1991. Pp. 37–52.

Tang Haoyi (Tō Kō-un). "Nihon tōchiki Taiwan sakka—Rai Wa [Lai He]: hakuwashi to sono gengo shomondai." *Kikan Chūgoku* 92 (2008), pp. 61–71.

Tang, Xiaobing and Michel Hockx. "The Creation Society (1921–1930)," in Kirk A. Denton and Michel Hockx, eds. *Literary Societies of Republican China.* New York: Lexington Books, 2008. Pp. 103–36.

Tang Yuemei. "Zhong-Ri wenxue jiaoliu de guoqu he xianzai," in Beijingshi Shehui Kexue Yanjiusuo Guoji Wenti Yanjiushi, ed. *Zhong-Ri wenhua yu jiaoliu* 1. Beijing: Zhongguo Zhanwang Chubanshe, 1984. Pp. 183–202.

Tangherlini, Timothy R. and Sallie Yea, eds. *Sitings: Critical Approaches to Korean Geography.* Honolulu, HI: University of Hawai'i Press, 2008.

Tanizaki Jun'ichirō. "In'ei raisan," in *Tanizaki Jun'ichirō zenshū* 20. Tokyo: Chūō Kōronsha, 1970. Pp. 515–57.

———. "Reisei to yūkan: Shū Sakujin [Zhou Zuoren] shi no inshō," in Hō Kisei, ed. *Shū Sakujin [Zhou Zuoren] sensei no koto.* Tokyo: Kōfūkan, 1944. Pp. 23–27.

———. "Shanhai kōyūki," in *Tanizaki Jun'ichirō zenshū* 10. Tokyo: Chūō Kōronsha, 1970. Pp. 563–98.

Tarumi Chie. "Nakanishi Inosuke *Taiwan kenmonki* shokō." Paper given at the Teikokushugi to Bungaku Conference, Aichi University, August 1–3, 2008. Reprinted in the conference handout, pp. 238–50.

———. *Ryo Kakujaku [Lü Heruo] kenkyū: 1943 nen made no bunseki o chūshin to shite.* Tokyo: Kazama Shobō, 2002.

———. *Taiwan no Nihongo bungaku: Nihon tōchi jidai no sakkatachi.* Tokyo: Goryū Shoin, 1995.

———. "1930 nendai Taiwan bungaku ni okeru gengo mondai ni tsuite: kyōdo bungaku ronsō kara *Taiwan bungei* e." *Yokohama Kokuritsu Daigaku Ryūgakusei Sentā kyōiku kenkyū ronshū* 15 (2008), pp. 21–31.

Tarumoto Teruo. "Qingmo minchu de fanyi xiaoshuo: jing Riben zhuandao Zhongguo de fanyi xiaoshuo," in Wang Hongzhi, ed. *Fanyi yu chuangzuo: Zhongguo jindai fanyi xiaoshuolun.* Beijing: Beijing Daxue Chubanshe, 2000. Pp. 151–71.

———. "A Statistical Survey of Translated Fiction 1840–1920," in David Pollard, ed. *Translation and Creation: Readings of Western Literature in Early Modern China, 1840–1918.* Philadelphia, PA: John Benjamins Publishing Company, 1998. Pp. 37–43.

Tawada Yōko. *Ekusophonī: bogo no soto e deru tabi.* Tokyo: Iwanami Shoten, 2003.

Tay, William et al., eds. *China and the West: Comparative Literature Studies.* Hong Kong: Chinese University Press, 1980.

Tayama Katai. *Futon,* in *Tayama Katai, Iwano Hōmei, Chikamatsu Shūkō.* Tokyo: Chūō Kōronsha, 1970. Pp. 7–55.

———. *Jūemon no saigo,* in *Teihon Katai zenshū* 14. Tokyo: Teihon Katai Zenshū Kankōkai, 1937. Pp. 307–87.

Taylor, K. W. and John K. Whitmore, eds. *Essays into Vietnamese Pasts.* Ithaca, NY: Southeast Asia Program, Cornell University, 1995.

Teow, See Heng. *Japan's Cultural Policy Toward China, 1918–1931: A Comparative Perspective.* Cambridge, MA: Harvard University Press, 1999.

Thornber, Karen L. "Cultures and Texts in Motion: Reconfiguring Japan and Japanese Literature in Polyintertextual East Asian Contact Zones (Japan, Semicolonial China, Colonial Korea and Taiwan)." Ph.D. dissertation, Harvard University, 2006.

———. "Early Twentieth-Century Intra-East Asian Literary Contact Nebulae: Censored Japanese Literature in Chinese and Korean." *Journal of Asian Studies* 68:3 (August 2009).

———. "Ecoambivalence, Ecoambiguity, and Ecodegradation: Changing Environments of East Asian and World Literatures." Unpublished book manuscript.

———. "French Discourse in Chinese, in Chinese Discourse in French— Paradoxes of Chinese Francophone Émigré Writing." *Journal of Contemporary French and Francophone Literature* 13:2 (April 2009), pp. 223–32.

———. "Responsibility and Japanese Literature of the Atomic Bomb," in David Stahl and Mark Williams, eds. *Imag[in]ing the War in Japan: Aesthetic Confrontations with the Past* (Forthcoming, Brill).

———. "Roaming Clouds, Memories, and Texts: Confrontational Intertextuality and Hayashi Fumiko's *Ukigumo,*" in Eiji Sekine, ed. *Travel in Japanese Representational Culture: Its Past, Present and Future, Proceedings of the Association for Japanese Literary Studies* 8 (Summer 2007), pp. 411–23.

———. "Translating, Intertextualizing, and the 'Borders' of 'Japanese Literature.'" in Atsuko Ueda and Richard Okada, eds. *Literature and Literary Theory, Proceedings of the Association for Japanese Literary Studies* 9 (2008), pp. 76–92.

——. "Transspatializing Texts and Transtextualizing Spaces in Literary Contact Nebulae: The Case of Colonial Korea," in David McCann, ed. *City and Text in Colonial Korea* (Forthcoming, Harvard).

——. "When the Protagonist Is Death: Implicating Text and Reader in Trilogies of Auschwitz and Hiroshima," in Laura Cruz, ed. *Making Sense Of: Dying and Death*. Oxford, UK: The Inter-Disciplinary Press, 2004. Pp. 105-12.

Tian Han. "Lixiang de ziwei," in *Tian Han chuangzuo xuan*. Shanghai: Fanggu, 1936.

——. *Qiangwei zhi lu*. Shanghai: Taidong Tushuju, 1922.

——. "Shiren yu laodong wenti," part 1. *Shaonian Zhongguo* 1:8 (February 1920), pp. 1-36.

——. "Shiren yu laodong wenti," part 2. *Shaonian Zhongguo* 1:9 (March 1920), pp. 15-104.

——. "Xuezi," in *Tian Han sanwen ji*. Shanghai: Jindai Shudian, 1936.

Tierney, Robert. "Ethnography, Borders and Violence: Reading between the Lines in Satō Haruo's Demon Bird." *Japan Forum* 19:1 (2007), pp. 89-110.

——. "Going Native: Imagining Savages in the Japanese Empire." Ph.D. dissertation, Stanford University, 2005.

Tōa Keizai Chōsakyoku. *The Manchoukuo Year Book*. Tokyo: Kyoku, 1934.

Toby, Ronald P. *State and Diplomacy in Early Modern Japan: Asia in the Development of the Tokugawa Bakufu*. Princeton, NJ: Princeton University Press, 1984.

Tōkai Sanshi. *Kajin no kigū*, in *Meiji Taishō bungaku zenshū* 1. Tokyo: Shun'yōdō, 1930. Pp. 1-245.

——. *Jiaren qiyu*, in *Yinbingshi heji, zhuanji* 35. Shanghai: 1941. Pp. 1-220. Translated by Liang Qichao.

Tokunaga Sunao et al. " 'Shinbun haitatsufu' ni tsuite," in Nakajima Toshirō et al., eds. *Nihon tōchiki Taiwan bungaku: bungei hyōronshū* 1. Tokyo: Ryokuin Shobō, 2001. P. 291.

Tokutomi Roka. *Burugui: aiqing xiaoshuo*. Shanghai: Shangwu Yinshuguan, 1908. Translated by Lin Shu and Wei Yi.

——. *Hototogisu*, in *Nihon kindai bungaku taikei* 9. Tokyo: Kadokawa Shoten, 1972. Pp. 223-418.

——. *Nami-ko: A Realistic Novel*. Tokyo: The Yurakusha, 1905. Translated by Sakae Shioya and E. F. Edgett.

——. *Pulyŏgwi*. Tokyo: Keiseisha Shoten, 1912. Translated by Cho Iljae.

——. *Tugyŏngsŏng*, in *Hanguk sinsosŏl chŏnjip* 5. Seoul: Ŭryu Munhwasa, 1968. Adapted by Sŏn-u Il.

——. *Yuhwau*. Tokyo: Tōyō Shoin, 1912. Adapted by Kim Ujin.

——. *Yuhwau*, in *Hanguk sinsosŏl chŏnjip* 6. Seoul: Ŭryu Munhwasa, 1968. Pp. 221-69. Adapted by Kim Ujin.

Tomonaga Nori. "Pigyo munhakjŏk ŭ ro pon Chŏnsan Kadae [Tayama Katai] wa Hyŏn Chin-gŏn." *Il-ŏ Ilmunhak yŏn-gu* 13 (1988-1989), pp. 381-401.

Treat, John. "Collaboration and Colonial Modernity: On Jang Hyeokju's *Poem in the Storm*," in *Teikokushugi to Bungaku: shokuminchi Taiwan – Chūgoku sen-*

ryōku – *"Manshūkoku."* Paper given at the Teikokushugi to Bungaku Conference, Aichi University, August 1-3, 2008. Reprinted in the conference handout, pp. 130-41.

Trivedi, Harish. *Colonial Transactions: English Literature and India.* Calcutta: Papyrus, 1993.

Trivedi, Poonam and Dennis Bartholomeusz, eds. *India's Shakespeare: Translation, Interpretation, and Performance.* Newark, DE: University of Delaware Press, 2005.

———. "Introduction," in Poonam Trivedi and Dennis Bartholomeusz, eds. *India's Shakespeare: Translation, Interpretation, and Performance.* Newark, DE: University of Delaware Press, 2005. Pp. 13-43.

Tseng Tienfu. *Hanguk p'ŭromunhak kwa ŭi pigyo rŭl t'onghae pon Ilje Taeman chwaik munhak yŏn-gu.* Pusan: Sejong Ch'ulp'ansa, 2000.

Tsu, Jing. *Failure, Nationalism, and Literature: The Making of Modern Chinese Identity, 1895-1937.* Stanford, CA: Stanford University Press, 2005.

Tsuge Tanehiko, ed. "Yojōhan fusuma no shitabari." *Yuriika* 29:3 (March 1997), pp. 66-78.

Tsukuba Daigaku Kindai Bungaku Kenkyūkai, ed. *Meijiki zasshi media ni miru "bungaku."* Tsukuba: Tsukuba Daigaku Kindai Bungaku Kenkyūkai, 2000.

Tsurumi, E. Patricia. *Japanese Colonial Education in Taiwan, 1895-1945.* Cambridge, MA: Harvard University Press, 1977.

Tsushima Yūko. *Chōji.* Tokyo: Kawade Shobō, 1978.

Tsutsui, William M. "The Pelagic Empire: Reconsidering Japanese Expansionism." Paper given at the "Japan's Natural Legacies: Bodies and Landscapes Realized, Idealized, and Poisoned" conference, Montana State University, October 2, 2008.

Tyler, William. *Modanizumu: Modernist Fiction from Japan, 1913-1938.* Honolulu, HI: University of Hawai'i Press, 2008.

Tymoczko, Maria and Edwin Gentzler, eds. *Translation and Power.* Amherst, MA: University of Massachusetts Press, 2002.

U Imgŏl. "Hanguk kaehwagi munhak e kkich'in Yang Kyech'o [Liang Qichao] ŭi yŏnghyang yŏn-gu." Ph.D. dissertation, Sŏngkyun University, 2000.

———. *Hanguk kaehwagi munhak kwa Yang Kyech'o* [Liang Qichao]. Seoul: Pagijŏng, 2002.

Uchida, Jun. "'Brokers of Empire': Japanese Settler Colonialism in Korea, 1876-1945." Unpublished manuscript.

Uchiyama Kanzō. *Kakōroku.* Tokyo: Iwanami Shoten, 1961.

Ueda, Atsuko. "Colonial Ambivalence and the Modern Shōsetsu: *Shōsetsu shinzui* and De-Asianization." *Traces: A Multilingual Journal of Cultural Theory and Translation* 3 (2004), pp. 179-206.

———. *Concealment of Politics, Politics of Concealment: The Production of "Literature" in Meiji Japan.* Stanford, CA: Stanford University Press, 2007.

———. "Meiji Literary Historiography: The Production of 'Modern Japanese Literature.'" Ph.D. dissertation, University of Michigan, 1999.

Ueda, Atsuko and Richard Okada, eds. *Literature and Literary Theory, Proceedings of the Association for Japanese Literary Studies* 9 (2008).

Ujigō Tsuyoshi. "Kindai Kankoku toshokanshi no kenkyū: kaikaki kara 1920 nendai made." *Sankō shoshi kenkyū* 30 (September 1985), pp. 1–22.

———. "Kindai Kankoku toshokanshi no kenkyū: shokuminchiki o chūshin ni." *Sankō shoshi kenkyū* 34 (July 1988), pp. 1–28.

Ungar, Steven. "Writing in Tongues: Thoughts on the Work of Translation," in Haun Saussy, ed. *Comparative Literature in an Age of Globalization.* Baltimore, MD: Johns Hopkins University Press, 2006. Pp. 127–38.

Vaporis, Constantine. *Breaking Barriers: Travel and the State in Early Modern Japan.* Cambridge, MA: Council on East Asian Studies, Harvard University, 1994.

Venuti, Lawrence, ed. *Rethinking Translation: Discourse, Subjectivity, Ideology.* New York: Routledge, 1992.

———. *The Scandals of Translation: Towards an Ethics of Difference.* New York: Routledge, 1998.

———. *The Translator's Invisibility: A History of Translation.* New York: Routledge, 1995.

Vĩnh, Sính. " 'Elegant Females' Re-Encountered: From Tōkai Sanshi's *Kajin no kigū* to Phan Châu Trinh's *Giai Nhân Kỳ Ngộ Diên Ca*," in K. W. Taylor and John K. Whitmore, eds. *Essays into Vietnamese Pasts.* Ithaca, NY: Southeast Asia Program, Cornell University, 1995. Pp. 195–206.

Viramontes, Helena María. *Under the Feet of Jesus.* New York: Dutton, 1995.

Viswanathan, Gauri. *Masks of Conquest: Literary Study and British Rule in India.* New York: Columbia University Press, 1989.

Vlastos, Stephen, ed. *Mirror of Modernity: Invented Traditions of Modern Japan.* Berkeley, CA: University of California Press, 1998.

Vulor, Ena C. *Colonial and Anti-Colonial Discourses: Albert Camus and Algeria, An Intertextual Dialogue with Mouloud Mammeri, Mouloud Feraoun, and Mohammed Dib.* Lanham, MD: University Press of America, 2000.

Wa-Kan Hikaku Bungakukai and Zhong-Ri Bijiao Wenxuehui, eds. *Shinseiki no Nitchū bungaku kankei: sono kaiko to tenbō.* Tokyo: Bensei Shuppan, 2003.

Wakeman, Frederic, Jr. "*Hanjian* (Traitor)! Collaboration and Retribution in Wartime Shanghai," in Wen-hsin Yeh, ed. *Becoming Chinese: Passages to Modernity and Beyond.* Berkeley, CA: University of California Press, 2000. Pp. 298–341.

Wang, David Der-wei. *Fictional Realism in Twentieth-Century China: Mao Dun, Lao She, Shen Congwen.* New York: Columbia University Press, 1992.

———. *Fin-de-Siècle Splendor: Repressed Modernities of Late Qing Fiction, 1849–1911.* Stanford, CA: Stanford University Press, 1997.

———. "The Lyrical in Epic Time: On the Music and Poetry of Jiang Wenye." Lecture at Harvard University, February 9, 2007.

———. *The Monster That Is History: History, Violence, and Fictional Writing in Twentieth-Century China.* Berkeley, CA: University of California Press, 2004.

———. "Translating Modernity," in David Pollard, ed. *Translation and Creation: Readings of Western Literature in Early Modern China, 1840–1918*. Philadelphia, PA: John Benjamins Publishing Company, 1998. Pp. 303–29.

Wang, David Der-wei and Carlos Rojas, eds. *Writing Taiwan: A New Literary History*. Durham, NC: Duke University Press, 2007.

Wang, David Der-wei and Shang Wei, eds. *Dynastic Crisis and Cultural Innovation: From the Late Ming to the Late Qing and Beyond*. Cambridge, MA: Harvard University Asia Center, 2005.

Wang, Di. *Street Culture in Chengdu: Public Space, Urban Commoners, and Local Politics, 1870–1930*. Stanford, CA: Stanford University Press, 2003.

———. *The Teahouse: Small Business, Everyday Culture, and Public Politics in Chengdu, 1900–1950*. Stanford, CA: Stanford University Press, 2008.

Wang Hongzhi. "Zhuanyu fabiao ququ zhengjian: Liang Qichao he wanqing zhengzhi xiaoshuo de fanyi ji chuangzuo," in Wang Hongzhi, ed. *Fanyi yu chuangzuo: Zhongguo jindai fanyi xiaoshuo lun*. Beijing: Beijing Daxue Chubanshe, 2000. Pp. 172–205.

———, ed. *Fanyi yu chuangzuo: Zhongguo jindai fanyi xiaoshuo lun*. Beijing: Beijing Daxue Chubanshe, 2000.

Wang Hui. "The Politics of Imagining Asia: A Genealogical Analysis," in Kuan-Hsing Chen and Chua Beng Huat, eds. *The Inter-Asia Cultural Studies Reader*. New York: Routledge, 2007. Pp. 66–102. Translated by Matthew A. Hale.

Wang Jinhou. *Wusi xinwenxue yu waiguo wenxue*. Chengdu: Sichuan Daxue Chubanshe, 1996.

Wang Jiquan and Zhou Rongfang, eds. *Taiwan, Xianggang, haiwai xuezhe lun Zhongguo jindai xiaoshuo*. Nanchang: Baihuazhou Wenyi Chubanshe, 1991.

Wang Min. "Remembering Huang Ying: Chinese Poet and Admirer of Miyazawa Kenji." *Gaiko Forum* 6:1 (Spring 2006), pp. 42–54.

Wang Xiangrong. *Zhongguo de jindaihua yu Riben*. Hunan: Hunan Renmin Chubanshe, 1987.

Wang Xiangyuan. *Dongfang geguo wenxue zai Zhongguo: yijie yu yanjiushi shulun*. Nanchang: Jiangxi Jiaoyu Chubanshe, 2001.

———. *Ershi shiji Zhongguo de Riben fanyi wenxue shi*. Beijing: Beijing Shifan Daxue Chubanshe, 2001.

———. *Zhong-Ri xiandai wenxue bijiaolun*. Hunan: Hunan Jiaoyu Chubanshe, 1997.

Wang Xiaoping. *Jindai Zhong-Ri wenxue jiaoliushi gao*. Hunan: Hunan Wenyi Chubanshe, 1987.

Wang Yougui. *Fanyijia Zhou Zuoren*. Chengdu: Sichuan Renmin Chubanshe, 2001.

Wang Zhuo, ed. *Zhong-Ri bijiao wenxue yanjiu ziliaohui*. Hangzhou: Zhongguo Meiyi Xueyuan Chubanshe, 2002.

Washburn, Dennis. "Transition or Transformation? Developments in Late Nineteenth-Century Literature," in Edward Kamens, ed. *The Cambridge History of Japanese Literature* (Forthcoming).

———. *Translating Mt. Fuji*. New York: Columbia University Press, 2006.

Wasserstrom, Jeffrey. *Global Shanghai, 1850–2010: A History in Fragments*. New York: Routledge Curzon, 2009.

Watanabe Kazutami. "Senjika jūnen no Chūgoku to Nihon (1): Chūgoku Bungaku Kenkyūkai o megutte." *Shisō* 1010 (June 2008), pp. 6–34.

———. "Senjika jūnen no Chūgoku to Nihon (2): Chūgoku Bungaku Kenkyūkai o megutte." *Shisō* 1011 (July 2008), pp. 123–47.

Weinbaum, Alys Eve et al., eds. *The Modern Girl around the World: Consumption, Modernity, and Globalization*. Durham, NC: Duke University Press, 2008.

Weiner, Michael. *The Origins of the Korean Community in Japan: 1910–1923*. Manchester, UK: Manchester University Press, 1989.

Wells, H. G. *The First Men in the Moon*. Jefferson, NC: McFarland & Company, 1998.

West, David and Tony Woodman, eds. *Creative Imitation and Latin Literature*. New York: Cambridge University Press, 1979.

Widmer, Ellen. "Foreign Travel through a Woman's Eyes: Shan Shili's *Guimao lüxing ji* in Local and Global Perspective." *Journal of Asian Studies* 65:4 (November 2006), pp. 763–91.

Widmer, Ellen and David Der-wei Wang, eds. *From May Fourth to June Fourth: Fiction and Film in Twentieth-Century China*. Cambridge, MA: Harvard University Press, 1993.

Willcock, Hiroko. "Meiji Japan and the Late Qing Political Novel." *Journal of Oriental Studies* 33:1 (1995), pp. 1–28.

Williams, Patrick and Laura Chrisman, eds. *Colonial Discourse and Postcolonial Theory*. New York: Columbia University Press, 1994.

Winther-Tamaki, Bert. "From Resplendent Signs to Heavy Hands: Japanese Painting in War and Defeat, 1937–1952," in J. Thomas Rimer, ed. *Japanese Art of the Modern Age*. Unpublished manuscript.

Wise, Christopher, ed. *Yambo Ouologuem: Postcolonial Writer, Islamic Militant*. Boulder, CO: Lynne Rienner Publishers, 1999.

Wolf, Margery and Roxane Witke, eds. *Women in Chinese Society*. Stanford, CA: Stanford University Press, 1975.

Wong, Aida Yuen. "Inventing Eastern Art in Japan and China, ca. 1890s to ca. 1930s." Ph.D. dissertation, Columbia University, 1999.

———. *Parting the Mists: Discovering Japan and the Rise of National-Style Painting in Modern China*. Honolulu, HI: University of Hawai'i Press, 2006.

Wong, Lawrence Wang-chi. "From 'Controlling the Barbarians' to 'Wholesale Westernization': Translation and Politics in Late Imperial and Early Republican China, 1840–1919," in Eva Hung and Judy Wakabayashi, eds. *Asian Translation Traditions*. Northampton, MA: St. Jerome Publishing, 2005. Pp. 109–34.

———. " 'The Sole Purpose Is to Express My Political Views': Liang Qichao and the Translation and Writing of Political Novels in the Late Qing," in David Pollard, ed. *Translation and Creation: Readings of Western Literature in Early Modern China, 1840–1918*. Philadelphia, PA: John Benjamins Publishing Company, 1998. Pp. 105–26.

Worton, Michael and Judith Still. *Intertextuality: Theories and Practice*. New York: St. Martin's Press, 1990.

Wu Honghua (Go Kōka). *Shū Sakujin [Zhou Zuoren] to Edo shomin bungei*. Tokyo: Sōdosha, 2005.

Wu Mansha. *Shayang de zhong: aiguo xiaoshuo, Nanfang zazhishe*, March 1943.

———. "*Shayang de zhong* xiaoshuo kanxing de qianyan." *Nanfang*, April 1, 1943, pp. 17–18.

Wu Wenxing. *Riju shiqi Taiwan shehui lingdao jieceng zhi yanjiu*. Taipei: Zhengzhong Shuju, 1992.

Wu Zhefei. "Yizhe de hua," in Hino Ashihei, *Mai yu bingdui*. Shanghai: Zazhishe, 1938. Pp. 1–2.

Wu Zhuoliu. *Ajia no koji*. Tokyo: Shin Jinbutsu Ōraisha, 1973.

Xi Mi (Michelle Yeh). "Ranshao yu feiyue: 1930 niandai Taiwan de chaoxianshi shi." *Xinshi pinglun* 2 (2005), pp. 33–63.

———. *Xiandangdai shiwen lu*. Taipei: Lianhe Wenxue, 1998.

Xia Yan. *Pen to sensō*. Tokyo: Tōhō Shoten, 1988. Translated by Abe Yukio.

Xie Bingying. *Nubing zizhuan*, in *Xie Bingying wenji* 1. Hefei: Anhui Wenyi Chubanshe, 1999.

Xie Huizhen. "Toransu nashonaru tsūshin: Taiwan kara mita Yokomitsu Riichi—kenkyū no dōkō to jikiden deshi Wu Yongfu e no eikyō." *Yokomitsu Riichi Bungakukai kaihō* 13:3 (June 2008), pp. 12–13.

Xie Liuyi. *Riben wenxueshi*. Shanghai: Shanghai Shudian, 1991.

Xiong Fu et al., eds. *Zhongguo kang-Ri zhanzheng shiqi dahoufang chubanshi*. Chongqing: Chongqing Chubanshe, 1999.

Xu Minmin. *Senzen Chūgoku ni okeru Nihongo kyōiku*. Tokyo: Emutei Shuppan, 1996.

Xu Naixiang and Huang Wanhua. *Zhongguo kangzhan shiqi lunxianqu wenxueshi*. Fuzhou: Fujian Jiaoyu Chubanshe, 1995.

Xu Shixu. "Han-Zhong xinwenxueshi zhi fenqi bijiao," in Zhong-Han Wenhua Jijinhui, ed. *Di wu jie Zhonghan xuezhe huiyi lunwenji*. Taipei: Zhonghan Wenhua Jijinhui, 1983. Pp. 87–94.

Xun Si. "Mu Shiying," in Yang Zhihua, ed. *Wentan shiliao*. Shanghai: Zhonghua Ribaoshe, 1944. Pp. 231–32.

Yaegashi Aiko. "Hanguk kŭndae sosŏl kwa Kukmokjŏn Dokbo [Kunikida Doppo]." *Kŏnguk ŏ-munhak* 11–12 (April 1987), pp. 697–714.

Yaeger, Patricia S. "'Because a Fire Was in My Head': Eudora Welty and the Dialogic Imagination." *Publications of the Modern Language Association of America* 99:5 (October 1984), pp. 955–73.

Yagiri Tadayuki, ed. *Naze "Yojōhan fusuma no shitabari" wa meisaku ka*. Tokyo: San'ichi Shobō, 1995.

Yamada Keizō. *Ro Jin [Lu Xun] no sekai*. Tokyo: Taishūkan Shoten, 1977.

Yamada Keizō and Lü Yuanming (Ro Genmei), eds. *Jūgonen sensō to bungaku: Nitchū kindai bungaku no hikaku kenkyū*. Tokyo: Tōhō Shoten, 1991.

———, eds. *Zhong-Ri zhanzheng yu wenxue: Zhong-Ri xiandai wenxue de bijiao yanjiu*. Changchun: Dongbei Shifan Daxue Chubanshe, 1992.

Yamaguchi Mamoru. "Ha Kin [Ba Jin] no Nihon taizai ni kansuru kiroku." *Nihon Daigaku jinbun kagaku kenkyū kiyō* 39 (1990), pp. 55–68.

Yamamuro Shin'ichi. *Manchuria under Japanese Domination.* Philadelphia, PA: University of Pennsylvania Press, 2006. Translated by Joshua A. Fogel.

Yamauchi Tadashi. "Portrait of Yang Yi, 139th Akutagawa Prize Winner." *Japan Echo* (December 2008), pp. 51–52. Translated from "*Jinbutsu kōsaten, Yan I.*" *Chūō kōron* (September 2008), pp. 82–83.

Yan Shaotang and Wang Xiaoping. *Zhongguo wenxue zai Riben.* Guangzhou: Huacheng Chubanshe, 1990.

Yanagida Izumi. *Seiji shōsetsu kenkyū.* Tokyo: Shunjūsha, 1935–1939.

Yang Chichang. "Aki no umi," in Huang Jianming. "Rizhi shiqi Yang Chichang ji qi wenxue yanjiu." Master's thesis, Guoli Chenggong University, 2002. P. 112.

——. "Esupuri nūbō to shi seishin," in Shui Yinping. *Kami no uo.* Tokyo: Kappa Shobō, 1985.

——. "Joisuana [Joyceana]: Jeimusu Joisu [James Joyce] no bungaku undō," in Shui Yinping. *Kami no uo.* Tokyo: Kappa Shobō, 1985. Pp. 244–47.

——. "Moeru hoo," in Huang Jianming. "Rizhi shiqi Yang Chichang ji qi wenxue yanjiu." Master's thesis, Guoli Chenggong University, 2002. P. 112.

——. "Xixie Shunsanliang [Nishiwaki Junzaburō] de shijie: guanyu shiji *Ambarvalia,*" in *Shui Yinping zuopinji.* Tainan: Tainan Shili Wenhua Zhongxin, 1995. Pp. 185–86.

Yang, Daqing. "Between Lips and Teeth: Chinese-Korean Relations, 1910–1950," in Bruce Cumings, ed. *Chicago Occasional Papers on Korea.* Select Papers 6. Chicago, IL: The Center for East Asian Studies, University of Chicago, 1991. Pp. 58–93.

——. "Convergence or Divergence? Recent Historical Writings on the Rape of Nanjing." *American Historical Review* 104:3 (June 1999), pp. 842–65.

Yang Dongguk. "Shu Yōkan [Chu Yohan] to Nihon kindaishi." Ph.D. dissertation, University of Tokyo, 1997.

Yang Kui. *E mama yao chujia.* Taipei: Qianwei Chubanshe, 1985.

——. "Shinbun haitatsufu," in *Yang Kui quanji* 4. Taipei: Guoli Wenhua Zichan Baocun Yanjiu Zhongxin Choubeichu, 1998. Pp. 19–64.

——. "Zōsan no kage ni: nonki na jiisan no hanashi," in *Yang Kui quanji* 8. Taipei: Guoli Wenhua Zichan Baocun Yanjiu Zhongxin Choubeichu, 1998. Pp. 1–47.

Yang Paekhwa. "Ho Chŏk [Hu Shi] ssi rŭl chungsim ŭ ro han Chungguk ŭi munhak hyŏkmyŏng (1)." *Kaebyŏk* 5 (November 1920), pp. 53–60.

——. "Ho Chŏk [Hu Shi] ssi rŭl chungsim ŭ ro han Chungguk ŭi munhak hyŏkmyŏng (2)." *Kaebyŏk* 6 (December 1920), pp. 77–87.

——. "Ho Chŏk [Hu Shi] ssi rŭl chungsim ŭ ro han Chungguk ŭi munhak hyŏkmyŏng (3)." *Kaebyŏk* 7 (January 1921), pp. 139–44.

——. "Ho Chŏk [Hu Shi] ssi rŭl chungsim ŭ ro han Chungguk ŭi munhak hyŏkmyŏng (4)." *Kaebyŏk* 8 (February 1921), pp. 116–22.

Yang Ruoping. *Taiwan yu dalu wenxue guanxi jianshi, 1652–1949.* Shanghai: Shanghai Wenyi Chubanshe, 2004.

Yang Sŭngguk (Yang Seung-Gook). "1910 nyŏndae Hanguk sinp'agŭk ŭi rep'ŏt'ori yŏn-gu." *Hanguk kŭk-yesul yŏn-gu* 8 (June 1998), pp. 9–69.

——. "1910 nyŏndae sinp'agŭk kwa chŏnt'ong yŏnhŭi ŭi kwanryŏn yangsang." *Hanguk kŭk-yesul yŏn-gu* 9 (April 1999), pp. 47–68.

Yang Sun Jin. "South Korean Literary Market Hurt by Cyberspace, Japanese Novels." *Daily Yomiuri*, June 17, 2007. P. 22.

Yang Zhaoquan. *Zhong-Chao guanxishi lunwenji.* Beijing: Shijie Zhishi Chubanshe, 1988.

Yang Zhihua, ed. *Wentan shiliao.* Shanghai: Zhonghua Ribaoshe, 1944.

Yao Wendong. *Qingdai liuqiu jilu xuji.* Taipei: Taiwan Wenxian Congkan, 1972.

Yasukawa Sadao Sensei Koki Kinen Ronbunshū Iinkai, ed. *Yasukawa Sadao sensei koki kinen: kindai Nihon bungaku no shosō.* Tokyo: Meiji Shoin, 1990.

Ye Di. "Riju shidai Taiwan shitan de chaoxianshi zhuyi yundong: Fengche Shishe de shi yundong," in *Taiwan xiandaishi shilun.* Taipei: Wenxue Zazhishe, 1998. Pp. 21–34.

Ye Shitao. *Yige Taiwan laoxiu zuojia de wuling niandai.* Taipei: Qianwei Chubanshe, 1991.

Ye Zhenzhen. "Liangge 'Guxiang': Guanyu Lu Xun dui Zhong Lihe de yingxiang," in Nakajima Toshirō, ed. *Taiwan xinwenxue yu Lu Xun.* Taipei: Qianwei Chubanshe, 1999. Pp. 95–119.

Yeats, William Butler. "Introduction," in Rabindranath Tagore. *Gitanjali (song offerings).* London: Macmillan and Co., 1913. Pp. vii–xxii.

——. "The Second Coming," in M. L. Rosenthal, ed. *William Butler Yeats: Selected Poems and Three Plays.* New York: Macmillan Publishing Co., 1962. Pp. 89–90.

Yee, Angelina C. "Constructing a Native Consciousness: Taiwan Literature in the 20th Century." *China Quarterly* 165 (2001), pp. 83–101.

Yeh, Catherine Vance. "Zeng Pu's 'Niehai Hua' as a Political Novel: A World Genre in a Chinese Form." Ph.D. dissertation, Harvard University, 1990.

Yeh, Emilie Yueh-yu and Darrell William Davis. *Taiwan Film Directors: A Treasure Island.* New York: Columbia University Press, 2005.

Yeh, Michelle. "Frontier Taiwan: An Introduction," in Michelle Yeh and N. G. D. Malmqvist, eds. *Frontier Taiwan: An Anthology of Modern Chinese Poetry.* New York: Columbia University Press, 2001. Pp. 1–53.

——. "Modern Poetry of Taiwan," in Joshua Mostow et al., eds. *The Columbia Companion to Modern East Asian Literature.* New York: Columbia University Press, 2003. Pp. 561–69.

——. "'There Are No Camels in the Koran': What Is Modern about Modern Chinese Poetry," in Christopher Lupke, ed. *New Perspectives on Contemporary Chinese Poetry.* New York: Palgrave Macmillan, 2008. Pp. 9–26.

Yeh, Michelle, and N. G. D. Malmqvist, eds. *Frontier Taiwan: An Anthology of Modern Chinese Poetry.* New York: Columbia University Press, 2001.

Yeh, Wen-hsin, ed. *Becoming Chinese: Passages to Modernity and Beyond.* Berkeley, CA: University of California Press, 2000.

Yi Cheha. *Kwanghwasa.* Seoul: Munhak Sasangsa, 1986.

Yi Hanbyŏn. "*Sŏyu kyŏnmun* e pat-adŭlyŏjin Ilbon ŭi hanjaŏ e taehayŏ." *Ilbon-hak* 6 (February 1987), pp. 85–107.

Yi Hanch'ang [Lee Han-chang]. "Haebang chŏn chaeil Chosŏn-in sahoe-juŭijadŭl ŭi munhak hwaldong: 1920 nyŏndae Ilbon p'ŭro munhak chapji e palp'yo doen chakp'um ŭl chungsim ŭ ro." *Il-ŏ Ilmunhak yŏn-gu* 49:2 (May 2004), pp. 349–73.

Yi Hansŏp (I Hansoppu). "*Seiyū kenmon* [*Sŏyu kyŏnmun*] no kanjigo ni tsuite: Nihon kara haitta go o chūshin ni." *Kokugogaku* 141 (June 1985), pp. 39–50.

Yi Kwangsu. "Ai ka," in Kurokawa Sō, ed. "*Gaichi*" *no Nihon bungaku sen 3*. Tokyo: Shinjuku Shobō, 1996. Pp. 21–26.

——. *Ilgi*, in *Yi Kwangsu chŏnjip* 19. Seoul: Samjungdang, 1963.

——. "Kim Kyŏng," in *Yi Kwangsu chŏnjip* 1. Seoul: Usinsa, 1979. Pp. 568–73.

Yi Myŏnghŭi. "Ilmunhak pŏn-yŏksŏ ŭi pyŏnch'ŏn kwajŏng e kwanhan yŏn-gu: 1895–1995 nyŏn ŭi 100 nyŏn-gan ŭi Ilmunhak pŏn-yŏksŏ e kwanhayŏ." *Kyŏnghŭi Taehakkyo Taehakwŏn Il-ŏ Ilmunhakgwa* 7 (July 1997), pp. 70–87.

Yi Pyŏngdo. "Kyubang munhak." *Hakjigwang* 12 (April 1917), pp. 41–45.

Yi Sang. "Donggyŏng," in *Yi Sang munhak chŏnjip* 3. Seoul: Munhak Sasangsa, 1995. Pp. 95–100.

——. "Nalgae," in *Yi Sang, Chakgaron ch'ongsŏ* 10. Seoul: Munhak kwa Chisŏngsa, 1977. Pp. 149–76.

Yi Sikmi (Lee Jik Mi). "Kim Ujin hŭigok ŭi pigyo munhakjŏk yŏn-gu: Yudo Murang [Arishima Takeo] wa ŭi pigyo rŭl chungsim ŭ ro." Master's thesis, Yonsei University, 1984.

Yi Sŏkho (Lee Sukho). "Chungguk munhak chŏnsinja ro sŏ ŭi Yang Paekhwa: t'ŭkhi Chungguk kŭkgok ŭi sogae pŏn-yŏk ŭl chungsim ŭ ro." *Yŏnse non-ch'ong* 13 (1976), pp. 117–31.

Yi Sŏn-ok. "Ilje kangjŏmgi chŏnhu Ilbon munhak e nat'a-nan Hanguksang." Ph.D. dissertation, Tanguk University, 2004.

Yi Sugyŏng (Yi Soo-kyung). "Shokuminchiki no Kin Kichin [Kim Kijin] oyobi kanren chishikijin kenkyū." Ph.D. dissertation, Ritsumeikan University, 2000.

Yi Yu-hwan. *Zainichi Kankokujin gojūnenshi: hasseiin ni okeru rekishiteki haikei to kaihōgo ni okeru dōkō*. Tokyo: Shinju Bussan Shuppanbu, 1960.

Yim Kyung Taek et al. "Roundtable: What Is an East Asia Publishing Network?" http://www.eapub.net/roundtable.html [URL defunct]. Accessed February 21, 2006.

Yin Yunzhen. "Zhongguo xinwenxue de dongjin xuqu (1917–1929): Zhongguo xin wenxue dui Chaoxian wenxue de yingxiang." *Zhongguo bijiao wenxue* 17:2 (1993), pp. 110–22.

Yokomitsu Riichi. "Hae," in *Yokomitsu Riichi zenshū* 1. Tokyo: Kawade Shobō, 1955. Pp. 191–95.

——. "Jikan," in *Yokomitsu Riichi zenshū* 4. Tokyo: Kawade Shobō, 1955. Pp. 178–92.

——. "Mu Shiying shi no shi," *Bungakukai* (September 1940), pp. 174–75.

——. *Shanhai*, in *Yokomitsu Riichi zenshū* 2. Tokyo: Kawade Shobō, 1955. Pp. 3–141.

———. "Tori," in *Yokomitsu Riichi zenshū* 3. Tokyo: Kawade Shobō, 1955. Pp. 344–56.

Yokota-Murakami, Takayuki. *Don Juan East/West: On the Problematics of Comparative Literature.* Albany, NY: State University of New York Press, 1998.

Yokoyama Hiroaki. *Nagasaki ga deatta kindai Chūgoku.* Fukuoka: Kaichōsha, 2006.

Yokoyama Keiko. "Chu Yohan ŭi Il-ŏ si chakp'um e kwanhan yŏn-gu." Ph.D. dissertation, Kyŏngbuk University, 1989.

Yŏm Sangsŏp. "Munhak so-nyŏn sidae ŭi hoesang," in *Yŏm Sangsŏp chŏnjip* 12. Seoul: Minŭmsa, 1994. Pp. 212–17.

———. "Na wa P'yeho sidae," in *Yŏm Sangsŏp chŏnjip* 12. Seoul: Minŭmsa, 1994. Pp. 206–11.

———. *Samdae*, in *Yŏm Sangsŏp chŏnjip* 4. Seoul: Minŭmsa, 1994. Pp. 11–418.

"Yŏn-yegye: Ssang-oknu." *Maeil sinbo* (July 17, 1912), p. 3.

Yoo, Theodore Jun. *The Politics of Gender in Colonial Korea: Education, Labor, and Health, 1910–1945.* Berkeley, CA: University of California Press, 2008.

Yŏp Kŏn-gon. *Yang Kyech'o [Liang Qichao] wa ku Hanmal munhak.* Seoul: Pŏpjŏn Ch'ulp'ansa, 1980.

———. "Yang Kyech'o [Liang Qichao] wa ku Hanmal munhak." Ph.D. dissertation, Korea University, 1979.

Yoshida Hiroji. *Ro Jin [Lu Xun] no tomo: Uchiyama Kanzō no shōzō – Shanhai Uchiyama shoten no rōpei.* Tokyo: Shinkyō Shuppansha, 1994.

Yoshida Seiichi. *Kindai bungei hyōronshi.* Tokyo: Shibundō, 1980.

Yoshida, Takashi. *The Making of the "Rape of Nanking": History and Memory in Japan, China, and the United States.* New York: Oxford University Press, 2006.

Yoshikawa Nagi. *Chōsen saisho no modanisuto Chon Jiyon [Chŏng Chiyong].* Tokyo: Doyō Bijutsusha Shuppan Hanbai, 2007.

"Young Women Spearhead Japanese Literary Wave." http://english.chosun.com/w21data/html/news/200511/200511060006.html. November 6, 2005. Accessed April 23, 2006.

Yu Dafu. "Chenlun," in *Xiandai xiaoshuo yidai zongshi: Yu Dafu xiaoshuo quanji.* Beijing: Zhongguo Wenlian Chuban Gongsi, 1996. Pp. 1–35.

———. "Chiguihua," in *Xiandai xiaoshuo yidai zongshi: Yu Dafu xiaoshuo quanji.* Beijing: Zhongguo Wenlian Chuban Gongsi, 1996. Pp. 697–727.

———. "Chunfeng chenzui de wanshang," in *Xiandai xiaoshuo yidai zongshi: Yu Dafu xiaoshuo quanji.* Beijing: Zhongguo Wenlian Chuban Gongsi, 1996. Pp. 260–73.

———. "Wuliunian lai chuangzao shenghuo de huigu," in *Yu Dafu wenji* 7. Guangzhou: Huacheng Chubanshe, 1984. Pp. 178–81.

———. *Yu Dafu quanji.* Hangzhou: Zhejiang Wenyi Chubanshe, 1992.

Yu Kilchun. *Sŏyu kyŏnmun*, in *Yu Kilchun chŏnsŏl* 1. Seoul: Il Cho Gak, 1982.

———. "Sŏyu kyŏnmun sŏ," in *Yu Kilchun chŏnsŏ* 1. Seoul: Il Cho Gak, 1982. Pp. 3–8.

Yu Qiuhong. "Lin Shu fanyi zuopi kaoshuo," in *Lin Shu yanjiu ziliao.* Fuzhou: Fujian Renmin Chubanshe, 1983.

Yu Yaoming. *Shū Sakujin* [Zhou Zuoren] *to Nihon kindai bungaku*. Tokyo: Kanrin Shobō, 2001.

Yu Yŏ-a. *Hanguk kwa Chungguk hyŏndae sosŏl ŭi pigyo yŏn-gu*. Seoul: Kukhak Charyowŏn, 1995.

Yu Yue, ed. *Dongying shixuan*. No publisher, place of publication, or page numbers recorded, 1883.

Yun Ch'iho. *Yun Ch'iho ilgi* 3. Seoul: Kuksa P'yonch'an Wiwŏnhoe, 1973.

Yun Ilsu (Yoon Il-Soo). "Chunggukŭk ŭi Hanguk suyong yangsang e kwanhan yŏn-gu." Ph.D. dissertation, Yŏngnam University, 2001.

Yun Yunjin. "Chung-Han hyŏndae munhak kyoryu kwan-gye e taehan yakganhan koch'al," in Kanhaeng Wiwŏnhoe, ed. *Han-Chung munhak pigyo yŏn-gu: Hŏ Hoil kyosu chŏngnyŏn t'oeim ki-nyŏm nonmunjip*. Seoul: Gukhak Charyowŏn, 1997. Pp. 363–82.

———. *Han-Chung munhak pigyo yŏn-gu*. Seoul: Sŏuŏl Ch'ulp'ansa, 2006.

Zabus, Chantal. *Tempests after Shakespeare*. New York: Palgrave, 2002.

Zarrow, Peter. *China in War and Revolution, 1895–1949*. New York: Routledge, 2005.

Zeng Guangcan and Wu Huaibin, eds. *Lao She yanjiu ziliao* 2. Beijing: Beijing Shiyue Wenyi Chubanshe, 1985.

Zeng Xianzhang. *Zhang Weixian*. Taipei: Guoli Taipei Yishu Daxue, 2003.

Zhang Fugui and Jin Conglin. *Zhong-Ri jinxiandai wenxue guanxi bijiao yanjiu*. Changchun: Jilin Daxue Chubanshe, 1999.

Zhang Guangzheng. "Zhang Wojun yu Zhong-Ri wenhua jiaoliu," in Peng Hsiao-yen, ed. *Piaobo yu xiangtu: Zhang Wojun shishi sishi zhounian jinian lunwenji*. Taipei: Xingzhengyuan Wenhua Jianshi Weiyuanhui, 1996. Pp. 83–101.

Zhang Lei. *Akutagawa Ryūnosuke to Chūgoku: juyō to hen'yō no kiseki*. Tokyo: Kokusho Kankōkai, 2007.

Zhang Shaochang. "Women weishenme yao yanjiu Riben." *Riben yanjiu* 1:1 (September 1943), pp. 2–3.

Zhang Shenqie. "Dui Taiwan xinwenxue luxian de yi ti'an." *Taiwan bungei* 2:2 (February 1935), pp. 78–86.

———. *Tan Riben, shuo Zhongguo, Zhang Shenqie quanji* 6. Taipei: Wenjing Chubanshe, 1998.

Zhang Shifang. *Zhanshi Riben wentan*. Qianjin: Qianjin Xinwenshe, 1942.

Zhang Tianyi. "Chouhen," in *Zhang Tianyi xiaoshuo xuanji*. Beijing: Renmin Wenxue Chubanshe, 1979. Pp. 74–95.

———. "Yijian xiaoshi," in *Zhang Tianyi wenji* 3. Shanghai: Shanghai Wenyi Chubanshe, 1985. Pp. 297–320.

Zhang Wojun. "*Aiyu* [Aiyoku] yizhe yinyan," in *Zhang Wojun quanji*. Taipei: Renjian Chubanshe, 2003. Pp. 357–58.

———. "Guanyu Daoqi Tengcun [Shimazaki Tōson]," in *Zhang Wojun quanji*. Taipei: Renjian Chubanshe, 2003. Pp. 164–69.

———. "*Liming zhi qian* [Yoake mae] shang zai liming zhi qian," in *Zhang Wojun quanji*. Taipei: Renjian Chubanshe, 2003. Pp. 170–76.

———. "Ping Juchi Kuan [Kikuchi Kan] jin zhu *Riben wenxue annei* [Nihon bungaku annai], in *Zhang Wojun quanji*. Taipei: Renjian Chubanshe, 2003. Pp. 161–62.

———. "Riben wenhua de zai renshi," in *Zhang Wojun quanji*. Taipei: Renjian Chubanshe, 2003. Pp. 196–205.

———. "Riben wenxue jieshao yu fanyi (yanliang)," in *Zhang Wojun quanji*. Taipei: Renjian Chubanshe, 2003. Pp. 449–53.

Zhang Xiangshan. "Bungaku ni akekureta hibi," in Jinmin Chūgoku Zasshisha, ed. *Waga seishun no Nihon: Chūgoku chishikijin no Nihon kaisō*. Tokyo: Tōhō Shoten, 1982. Pp. 152–63.

Zhang Xingjian. "Hon'yaku bungaku ni tsuite." *Taiwan bungaku* 2:1 (February 1942), pp. 7–9.

Zhang, Yingjin. *The City in Modern Chinese Literature and Film: Configurations of Space, Time, and Gender*. Stanford, CA: Stanford University Press, 1996.

Zhang Zhang. "Zhang Tianyi yu waiguo wenxue." *Zhongguo bijiao wenxue* 4 (March 1987), pp. 195–202.

Zhang Zhen. *An Amorous History of the Silver Screen: Shanghai Cinema, 1896–1937*. Chicago, IL: University of Chicago Press, 2005.

Zhang Zhongliang. *Wusi shiqi de fanyi wenxue*. Taipei: Xiuwei Zixun Keji Gufen Youxian Gongsi, 2005.

Zhao Binghuan. "Han-Zhong xinwenhua yundong zhi fayuandi: 20 shejichu Han-Zhong xinwenhua qikan bijiao yanjiu." *Zhongguo bijiao wenxue* 42 (2001), pp. 64–73.

Zhao Changyou (Jō Chan'ū). "Ha Kin [Ba Jin] no Nihonkan oyobi Nihonjinzō: sanjū nendai no Tokyo taizai o chūshin ni." *Ajia yūgaku* 13 (February 2000), pp. 86–98.

Zhao Mengyun. *Shanhai bungaku zanzō: Nihonjin sakka no hikari to kage*. Tokyo: Tabata Shoten, 2000.

Zheng Zhengqiu. *Xinju kaozheng baichu*. Zhonghua Tushu Jicheng Chuban Gongsi, 1919.

Zhong Lihe. *Zhong Lihe shujian*, in *Zhong Lihe quanji* 7. Taipei: Yuanxing Chubanshe, 1976.

Zhong Ruifang, ed. *Lü Heruo riji, 1942–1944*. Tainan: Guojia Taiwan Wenxueguan, 2004.

Zhong-Han Wenhua Jijinhui, ed. *Di wu jie Zhonghan xuezhe huiyi lunwenji*. Taipei: Zhonghan Wenhua Jijinhui, 1983.

Zhou Yichuan. "Minguo qianqi liuri xueshengzhong de nuxing," in Zuoteng Bao [Satō Tamotsu] Xiansheng Guxi Jinian Lunwenji Bianji Weiyuanhui, ed. *Zhong-Ri wenshi jiaoliu lunji*. Shanghai: Shanghai Cishu Chubanshe, 2005. Pp. 193–216.

Zhou Zuoren. "A Q zhengzhuan," in Deng Keyun, ed. *Lu Xun shouce*. Shanghai: Bolan Shuju, 1946. Pp. 225–28.

———. "Cangying," in *Zhou Zuorenji* 1. Guangzhou: Huacheng Chubanshe, 2003. Pp. 99–101.

———. "Cangying," in *Zhou Zuoren zibian wenji* 9. Shijiazhuang: Hebei Jiaoyu Chubanshe, 2002. P. 24.

――. "Daoqi Tengcun [Shimazaki Tōson] xiansheng." *Fengyu tan* 7 (November 1943).

――. *Lu Xun de gujia*, in *Zhou Zuoren zibian wenji* 16. Shijiazhuang: Hebei Jiaoyu Chubanshe, 2001.

――. "Riben jin sanshinian xiaoshuo zhi fada." *Xin qingnian* 5:1 (July 1918), pp. 27–42.

――. "Ruce dushu," in *Zhou Zuoren ji* 1. Guangzhou: Huacheng Chubanshe, 2004. Pp. 509–12.

――. "Sifa," in *Zhou Zuoren ji* 1. Guangzhou: Huacheng Chubanshe, 2004. Pp. 159–62.

――. "Xu," in *Xiandai Riben xiaoshuoji*. Shanghai: Shangwu Yinshuguan, 1930. Pp. 1–2.

Zhu Tianxin. *Gudu*, in *Gudu*. Taipei: Maitian Chuban Gufen Youxian Gongsi, 1997. Pp. 151–233.

Zhuan Yuean. *Duyutou de jiushudian ditu*. Taipei: Yuanliu, 2003.

Ziolkowski, Theodore. *Varieties of Literary Thematics*. Princeton, NJ: Princeton University Press, 1983.

Zola, Émile. *Germinal*. Paris: Fasquelle, 1978.

Zuoteng Bao [Satō Tamotsu] Xiansheng Guxi Jinian Lunwenji Bianji Weiyuanhui, ed. *Zhong-Ri wenshi jiaoliu lunji*. Shanghai: Shanghai Cishu Chubanshe, 2005.

Zwicker, Jonathan. *Practices of the Sentimental Imagination: Melodrama, the Novel, and the Social Imaginary in Nineteenth-Century Japan*. Cambridge, MA: Harvard University Asia Center, 2006.

Index

Wencong (Literary Collective, 1939), 75, 410n57

Wenhuahui (Culture Association, 1937), 75

Wenxuan (Literary Selections, 1939), 75

"Wenxue shenghuo wushi nian," *see* Ba Jin

Wenxue Yanjiuhui (Literary Research Society), 72

Western imperialism, 229-36, 392–93n27; in Asia, 3, 7, 8, 16, 34, 39, 40, 97, 140, 150, 152, 156, 320; *see also* empire

Western literatures, in China, 10–11, 19, 43, 116, 124, 131, 137; in Japan, 10, 19, 33, 35, 43, 45, 68, 96–97, 99–100, 116–17, 124, 131, 142–44, 221; in Korea, 10, 19, 43, 116, 124, 131, 137, 145, 191; in Taiwan, 10, 19, 43, 103, 116, 123–24, 131, 172; Japanese literature as providing access to, 10–11, 18, 81, 87, 106, 113, 207, 210; transculturated in East Asia, 3, 17, 24, 26, 211, 216, 238, 385; *see also* Chinese transculturation, individual writers, Japanese transculturation, Korean transculturation, Taiwanese transculturation

Wheat and Soldiers, see Hino Ashihei

When the Purple Mountain Burns, see Qi Shouhua

When We Were Orphans, see Ishiguro Kazuo

"Whereabouts of Chinese Resistance Writers" ("China hangjŏn chakga ŭi haengbang," 1940), 95

White, Gilbert (1720–93), *Natural History and Antiquities of Selborne* (1789), 303

White Birch Society (Shirakabaha, 1910), discussed by Taiwanese writers, 30; friends with Chinese, 57–58; friends with Koreans, 312; in Chinese intertextualization, 97, 242, 314–17, 446n117; in Chinese

translation, 58, 180, 430n21; in Korean intertextualization, 242; read by Chinese writers, 97; read by Korean writers, 312; read by Taiwanese writers, 30, 69; *see also* individual writers

White Countess, see Ishiguro Kazuo

Wild Grass, see Lu Xun

Wilde, Oscar (1854–1900), *Picture of Dorian Gray* (1890), 454n65

Wind-Up Bird Chronicle, see Murakami Haruki

"Wings," *see* Yi Sang

"Wings (II)," *see* Kim Yongho

"Wo zai Riben canjia zuoyi shige yundong de rizi," *see* Lei Shiyu

Woman in the Dunes, see Abe Kōbō

"Woman Trouble," *see* Kunikida Doppo

Woman Who Took Poison, see Iwano Hōmei

"Woman Who Took Poison," *see* Chŏn Yŏngt'aek

women, Chinese women in Japan, 29, 42–43, 393n28–29, 404n56; feminism, 16, 41, 135–36, 169, 171, 228, 248; ideals of, 228, 425n61, 448n134; Japanese women abroad, 149, 198; Korean women in Japan, 29, 42–43, 393n30; subjugation of, 153, 228–31, 249, 251, 443n82; Taiwanese women in Japan, 29, 42–43, 394n30, 405n56; violence against, 14, 189, 201-7, 278–79, 288–89, 337–42, 377, 436n96, 455n79; writers, 48, 132, 182, 223–24, 228, 248, 311, 423n47, 440n43, 441n64, 466n171; *see also* modern girl, individual themes, individual writers

Wordsworth, William (1770–1850), 30, 243

world literature, 23, 65, 112, 214, 237, 445n106

Harvard-Yenching Institute Monograph Series
(titles now in print)

LaVergne, TN USA
04 October 2009
159791LV00001B/1/P